---- ★ ----

The bodies lay lined up behind two couches and a long chest with its lid open and what looked to be jumbled rolls of paper inside. Art Sleem lay along the chest. He was hidden from the windows, but if she'd been looking in the other direction instead of at the posters of Evan Black's films on the rear wall on her way to the phone, he would have been visible to her. The other two had the privacy of the couches to be dead behind.

It was hot and still, with all the pavement and decorative rock and white stucco reflecting back the sun. And a long way to the guardhouse.

She could still smell the bitter scent of gunfire she'd curiously overlooked until she saw all the dead. But it had been the crack of an upstairs floorboard that sent Charlie Greene out that kitchen door on the run.

---- ★ ----

NOBODY DIES IN A
casino

Marlys Millhiser

W🌐RLDWIDE.

TORONTO • NEW YORK • LONDON
AMSTERDAM • PARIS • SYDNEY • HAMBURG
STOCKHOLM • ATHENS • TOKYO • MILAN
MADRID • WARSAW • BUDAPEST • AUCKLAND

*For my sister members of Femmes Fatales,
with whom I share a newsletter,
a Web site (http://members.aol.com/femmesweb)
And a very special bond.*

NOBODY DIES IN A CASINO

A Worldwide Mystery/January 2001

First published by St. Martin's Press, Incorporated.

ISBN 0-373-26372-4

Printed in U.S.A.

NOBODY
DIES IN A
CASINO

Charlie Greene and her author would like to acknowledge the help of Tony Fennelly on astrology, Gail Larson on blackjack, Jay Millhiser on Vegas and aircraft, Lloyd Boothby of the Hilton in the title and editor Kelly Ragland for a patience that surpasses all understanding. And to Caryl, Pat, Terry, and Barry and Terry in Dallas—they know who they are.

ONE

CHARLIE GREENE decided it was a sign of the times.

Just off a jet, she walked along a concourse at McCarran International Airport beside her boss and between rows of bleeping, blinking, whistling slots. Her notebook computer in her briefcase so she could send and receive office E-mail, one man passing her talking on his cellular and another approaching her doing the same.

She didn't know about the guys on the cellulars, but Charlie was on vacation.

Sure didn't feel like it.

The men on the phones wore shorts. The one coming at her looked into her eyes without seeing her, his vision directed to his conversation. He was a hunk. The one passing her said, "No, Benny, I keep telling you—in Vegas, it's gaming, not gambling." This man was not a hunk. But he did have an air of prosperity.

"Merlin's Ridge?" The hunk's face suffused with an anger that would have made anyone else ugly. "Never heard of it."

"Babe," her employer burst into her thoughts. "Baggage claim's this way. Pay attention. What am I always telling ya?"

Charlie turned to follow him just as the hunk said, "What I do in your plane is your business. I wasn't flying Yucca on your time. You fire me and I'll open up—"

"Hello?" Richard Morse, head of Congdon and Morse Representation, Inc., stood nose-to-nose with Charlie. Congdon and Morse was a talent agency in Beverly Hills, Charlie its lone literary agent. "Anybody home there?"

"Did you hear what he'd open up?"

"Did I hear what who would open up?"

"The hunk on the phone." Charlie pointed to where the guy, his cellular, and Mr. Prosperous had been replaced by a whole new crowd.

I knew I needed a vacation, but eavesdropping on strangers and then getting worked up over it?

"Knew you needed a vacation, but jeez," Richard all but repeated her thoughts—which was even scarier. "No hunks for you tonight. Room service and sleep. Boss's orders."

CHARLEMAGNE CATHERINE Greene checked into the Las Vegas Hilton, unpacked, and stared out the wall of window at the blinking, sparkling, blatant Vegas night. A blimp in the sky sported garish advertising that zipped in flashing lights across its side. An acquaintance had once remarked that Vegas took tacky to an art form. Too true.

She slipped into a long knit dress with a slit up the side, matching jacket, and sandals and headed for the lobby shuttle that would take her the few blocks away to the Strip.

Charlie, probably a little over half Richard Morse's age, knew vacation for her didn't mean sleep. She'd have her room service in bed for breakfast. At about noon.

If everything in one's life had some meaning, which Charlie highly doubted, Richard must function to reinforce her resolution to remain a single mom who seeks fulfillment in her career.

Winning at both the slots and the blackjack table at Bally's, she paused at the Flamingo Hilton's snack bar for dinner and played video poker at the booze bar over a free margarita—postponing losing all her winnings in the next round, people watching.

Funny, how you could enjoy being alone in a crowd.

"This your lucky night?" a suggestive voice suggested behind her. An arm slid around her waist.

Charlie removed it and drained her margarita. "Apparently not."

Well, you're the one who had to wear a slit in your skirt that opens up a whole new side of you. Damn near to your navel.

It does not come to my navel.

Your underwear then.

Charlie slid off the stool, no longer deliciously alone, and came down hard on the foot belonging to the suggestive arm.

"I suppose I can be thankful you're not wearing those damn high heels."

"Evan." Wonderful. Charlie had just snubbed a client. "God, I'm sorry. I wasn't expecting to see you until, what, Tuesday?"

"Apparently not," he mimicked. Evan Black, with his sleek ponytail, a black ninjalike outfit, dark eyes in an olive-tanned face, a boyish smile, and round tinted eyeglasses. "Just out looking for trouble and spotted you the minute I walked in."

"I thought some creep was trying to pick me up."

"I am. I mean, he is." He nodded to the bartender to bring her another margarita, ordered a beer for himself.

Evan had a home here and one in Beverly Hills. The umbilical cord linking L.A. to Vegas was charged by proximity, smog, jet contrails, cash, the flight from taxation, cash, lack of snow you couldn't sniff, entertainment talent and its money.

Evan—screenwriter, director, and producer of low-budget specialized features—had cleaned up at the film festivals and often on the megabuck-proven story formulas at the box office, as well. So the studios making them had begun to court him and he'd sought out Congdon and Morse to represent him. Maybe because in the world of rapacious entertainment conglomerates, Charlie's agency was relatively small potatoes too.

Evan could bomb in the hundreds of thousands instead of hundreds of millions. But when he hit, it was mostly profit. He could attract star talent for peanuts because he offered memorable scripts that taxed and excited them.

A brand-new client worth the earth. And she'd stomped on his foot.

"So, how much have you lost?" He kissed her neck, forgiving her.

"I've been winning, smart cheeks, and I've got the rest of the night to lose it. Wanna help?"

In the spirit of Robin Hood, they decided to hit the Barbary Coast and Loopy Louie's because she'd earned her winnings in the posher casinos.

They were at the craps table at the Barbary, losing, and she'd paused to watch the rippling lights on a keno board ripple across the lenses of Evan's glasses when, over his shoulder, she saw the hunk from the airport. He was in earnest conversation with a blonde in black leggings, high-heeled boots, and a vest that almost hid her nipples.

Evan turned to follow her stare. "That's Caryl. She's my pilot. Cute, right?"

"I was looking at the guy. He's a pilot too. She looks more like a bar girl." With the empty tray wedged against her hip, she looked exactly like one.

"Young pilots don't make much money. Too many people wanting the fun, glamorous jobs, so the pay sucks until they get mucho hours. Unless lightning strikes, they need a day job. In Caryl's case, a night job."

Charlie lost interest in the pilots when Evan's luck changed and the dealer began shoving chips his way. But when his winnings had piled into neat rows of some height, Charlie's client decided he would cash them in.

"You can't do that—you're on a streak, you idiot," she let loose before she could talk sense to herself. She'd become so involved in his winning, she felt like a participant instead of a bystander.

"She's my agent," Evan explained to the fragile woman next to him. Her head shook with palsy in sync with her diamonds strobing back the flashing lights that careened around a DOLLAR DELUXE sign above a bank of slots.

She squinted up at Charlie and patted Evan's hand with jeweled fingers. "You should look into a manager, honey."

"Hey, in the spirit of fairness, Charlie," he said on the way out, "I have to lose my winnings from the Barbary at Loopy's."

They'd reached the delightfully tawdry entrance to Loopy Louie's—it resembled the entrance to a harem in Cecil B. De Mille's seriously senior-citizen dreams—when she saw her pilot hunk again. He was exiting the harem's blue-pink-and-gold doors—tastefully rendered in neon and mirrors—with a somber muscleman on each side. Shoulder-to-shoulder on each side. Without them, the pilot in the middle might be staggering. These guys weren't eunuch harem guards. One had a shaved head, the other shoulder-length curls. The pilot looked bewildered, half-aware, in the process of swelling up around the eyes and neck, but the swelling had not yet discolored.

Mind your own business, Charlie. "Evan, did you see that? The pilot who was arguing with your Caryl, and those goons muscling him out the door?"

"No. Maybe he was counting cards. Come on, agent mine, you have a duty to help me lose money."

Charlie, mind your own business.

"Evan, they've hurt him." But she'd no more than said that than she lost sight of the three too.

The sidewalk was very nearly a solid mass of people, like the sidewalks of Manhattan at morning rush hour, but without the rush. These people sort of slushed instead, slowly pushed for a better view of the "volcano" erupting at the Mirage. It sounded more like a hot-air balloon than an eruption, more of a whooshing noise than an exploding one.

Fire, rising on rather obvious natural-gas jets, but no rocks, spurted thirty to forty feet into the night from a mound in a pond. It erupted on waves of canned music and creative lighting that reflected off upturned faces even here across the street.

She found the three men again because they stood at the curb and took no notice, even when colored lights on cascading water pretended to be flowing lava and steam hissed up out of the pond. The air filled with the scent of stage smoke and raw natural gas, of car exhaust and beer-laden human breath.

The mysterious beacon of the Luxor's pyramid sliced into the heavens, where countless jets, wingtips flashing, circled the landing pattern at McCarran or soared off to find reality. A Steven Spielberg brainstorm run amuck.

And down at Charlie's level, an ambulance tried silently to thread traffic too packed to get out of its way. Traffic moved, but in a slow, solid mass, as if welded by headlights and taillights and blaring horns, side-road and pedestrian traffic ignored until the eruption ended. Interest in this extravaganza that played every fifteen minutes after sunset and alternated with the pyrotechnics of exploding pirate ships next door at the Treasure Island Casino attested to the turnover of tourists and money on the Strip.

The three men at the curb stood so close, their shirts could have been sewn together at the shoulder seams. "What do you bet they're going to try to force him into a car?"

But her client had gone on through the harem doors without her.

Charlie was pushing her way to the curb, her eyes on the three heads not turned toward the volcano at the Mirage.

When the head in the middle disappeared.

The other two moved in opposite directions. If she could get the license plate of the car they'd jammed him into, she could report an abduction to the police.

But they hadn't jammed the hunk into a car. They'd pushed him *in front* of one.

Charlie lost her margaritas in the gutter next to the part of him not still under traffic.

TWO

CHARLIE'S SKIN still tingled from a hot shower when room service arrived with poached eggs on a bed of corned-beef hash, little bottles of catsup and jam, thick slices of toast, a huge glass of fresh orange juice, and a big pot of coffee.

She settled back into the king-sized bed, an abundance of pillows bunched behind her and the tray on her lap. Life and all its little upgrades seemed incredibly precious this morning.

It wasn't noon, as Charlie had planned, more like 8:30. But, for a vacation night, she'd gone to bed early. And not only had she slept, she was hungry.

It had taken forever to get the ambulance through the traffic last night to pick up the body. Somebody from Loopy's came out to cover it with a gaming-table cover. The cops gave up and threaded the crowd on foot. One of them managed to get through on a bike.

Charlie broke both yolks and let them run over half the corned-beef hash, refusing to associate her food with any images of the grisly gutter, even when she topped the mess on her plate with the red catsup.

You made a mistake getting involved to begin with. Stay out of the whole thing.

I thought you were my conscience.

I'm your good sense. This is Rambo's world, not the Good Witch of the West's.

She ate slowly. Hell, she had all morning to fight with her demons and seriously sluggish conscience. Besides, she hadn't kept much down for the last ten hours. It takes strength to face reality.

She really had irritated Congdon and Morse's hot new client this time by insisting on explaining what she'd seen in some detail to the skeptical bicycle cop, the only one who even consented to listen to her. Evan Black, who had come back out when he realized that she hadn't followed him, nudged with his elbow, pleaded with his eyes, and finally told the policeman, "We have to go now, Officer."

The officer had simply nodded with relief. Charlie ate half the hash mess while puzzling Evan's reaction. She finished off the juice, splurged on a piece of toast with the first cup of coffee, and made the mistake of reaching for the remote.

Just in time for the news.

After informing the population of the wonderful weather and not-too-terrible smog, the morning anchor turned to his lovely partner and said, "I understand there was another pedestrian error on the Strip last night."

"Error? He was pushed."

The local newswoman ignored Charlie's outburst and went into a patient but lengthy recounting of the numerous accidents resulting in death on the heavily traveled Strip when pedestrians jaywalked instead of waiting for traffic lights at the corners.

"He wasn't jaywalking. He could hardly stand up."

The guy anchor also ignored Charlie and explained the efforts of the mayor's office to educate tourists on the dangers. "You know, Terry, visitors get so caught up in all the fun and excitement here—they don't mean to break the law. It's such a shame."

"He wasn't a visitor, he was a pilot, dickhead." Charlie spilled coffee down her front.

You know he was a pilot. You do not know he lived here. And we do not say dickhead, even when alone.

"Oh, shut up, all of you." Charlie squirmed herself and the breakfast tray across the expanse of the kingsize.

"Right, Barry, a tragic shame, and the pedestrian error last night is no exception."

"It was murder, you—" At this rate, she'd need another shower before getting dressed.

Remember, we have an ulcer and a daughter to raise.

Libby is raising herself in spite of us...ohmygod, now it's we, us. "I'm too young for Prozac."

Charlie was talking to herself in the mirror, the front of her scanty robe dripping with coffee. Terry was talking on the television about how the poor victim had yet to be identified.

"Shit, I can identify the murderers. What more do you need?"

When the phone rang, Charlie watched it instead of the TV. If it was her boss next door or teenaged daughter back in Long Beach, Charlie would lose her corned beef for sure. If she didn't keep something down, she'd be too sick to care if some poor unidentified pilot's murderers got away with pedestrian error or not.

She finally picked it up, relieved when it was Evan, the client, producer, director, writer.

"Charlie, I hate to do this to you, but Caryl won't listen to reason. She's determined to talk to you."

"Caryl."

"Caryl Thompson, my pilot? The bar girl at the Barbary Coast? We're downstairs. Charlie, it was her brother who died last night. I don't think she's going to take no for an answer."

Charlie slipped into shorts and a shirt while Terry and Barry turned their attention to Yucca Mountain, where the nuclear industry and the military hoped to conceal and ignore the deadly residue of their trades. Hadn't the dead pilot mentioned Yucca Mountain in his phone conversation at the airport? And a ridge she couldn't remember the name of.

The news team went on to relate apparent security breaches—mainly tourists trying to get too close—not only at Yucca but also at Area 51, or Groom Lake, some ninety miles out of Vegas. Here, the air force did not disclose it had a top secret installation to test new aircraft, and so popular myth accused it of concealing everything from the latest time machine to alien body parts. The world was such a loony place the way it was, Charlie couldn't figure why anyone would worry about woo-woo stuff like that. *They* were everywhere. Not the aliens, but people who seemed to have an inexplicable craving for woo-woo.

She'd once had a close encounter of the carnal kind with one of the more famous of these people and could personally attest to the strength of their beliefs. Fortunately, this particular guy had a few other strengths, not the least of them a fantastic back.

Barry and Terry didn't pretend Area 51 was nonexistent, and

they warned that security forces in restricted areas, "armed response personnel," were highly professional, heavily armed, and authorized to use deadly force.

Evan Black arrived disheveled and sweating, and Caryl Thompson was crying. How could anybody's pilot be that young? Obviously, Evan didn't share Charlie's fear of flying.

Charlie fought guilt. He was wearing what he'd worn the night before, along with a morning beard, uneven in length and patchy. He had not slept well like she had. He bent to pick up a flyer somebody had slipped under her door.

A sky blue flyer with a golden cross and an unlikely cloud formation in the background that spelled out "REPENT!"

"...should not be allowed to advertise brothel services in the city," Barry said.

"You've got to tell me everything," Caryl said.

"I already told you," Evan said.

"I want to hear it from her."

"FOR THE TIME IS AT HAND," the inside flap of the flyer said.

Caryl hadn't changed her clothes either. Charlie got them seated on the couch under the window, where the sky backdrop was blue but the few clouds weren't spelling out anything.

She tossed the tumbled bedclothes toward the headboard to cover the suspicious stains spilled coffee had left and ordered up juice, coffee, and bagels. Just as she reached for the remote to get rid of Barry and Terry, Terry said, "Yes, and although the crime rate is high in Las Vegas and gaming is often blamed for it, did you know there has never been a murder in a casino?"

"Hell no, they just walk them outside and push them into traffic while everybody's watching a frigging volcano," Charlie answered her.

Caryl's face crumbled into Evan's shoulder and he sent Charlie a beseeching look.

"Well, folks, now that you know where the safest places in Vegas are," Barry reassured them, "go out and have some fun."

Caryl Thompson made no effort to keep the vest in place and her nipples played peekaboo with the atmosphere. She and her brother had been born in Vegas. Their parents divorced and moved to opposite coasts. "But Pat and I both had work flying the ditch and were building hours, so we stayed. And now, now I don't have anybody."

"The ditch?"

"Grand Canyon."

Charlie described the three men on the sidewalk and her suspicions to Evan and a calmer Caryl. Their breakfasts came and both claimed a lack of appetite, then proceeded to pack most of it away.

"You'll just have to go to the police and tell them who the victim was and that he'd lived and worked here all his life. They're convinced he was a tourist, too excited about the wonders of Vegas to watch where he was going," Charlie finished.

"I know, pedestrian error. There is a lot of that going around."

"Caryl, it was wall-to-wall traffic. If you'd wanted to jaywalk, you'd have had to hop from one car hood to the next. They must have waited for the light to change and cars to begin creeping again and timed a shove to get him to street level at all. He was definitely not himself."

"I can't go to the cops."

"Caryl—" Evan warned.

"You have to. Your brother was murdered."

Charlie, stay out of this. It is not your business. And you don't *know* the dead guy was her brother. And Evan's looking funny. Vegas may be a great place to have fun, but it's a bad place to get involved.

"You're right," Charlie told her common sense.

"She is?" Evan looked from Charlie to Caryl and back again. "I am?"

"Absolutely. I've told you all I know about your brother's death. And the police too. It's up to you now. Would you believe I came here for a vacation?" Charlie stacked their dishes back on the tray, pointedly opened the door to the hall. To hell with her conscience.

"You mean you're not going to do anything?" Caryl was youthfully plump in only the right places. It gave her a healthy innocence, hard to square with the vest.

"Hey, he wasn't *my* brother."

Evan Black and his lovely pilot left, obviously disappointed in her. What did they expect?

They were trying to use her.

Charlie applied a trace of eye shadow, tried to improve on her hair, and grabbed her purse. This time, she would listen to common sense and leave well enough alone. If poor Pat the pilot's sister couldn't talk to the police, Charlie sure as hell wasn't going to. Evan Black wasn't telling all either.

"I'm on vacation." Charlie yanked the door open to a blonde who stopped just short of knocking on Charlie's forehead.

"I am too." The blonde withdrew her knuckles, tightened her tit and ass lines, and walked into the room as if it were hers. "How'd you know? I mean, that I was outside the door before I could even knock?"

"I was on my way out."

Charlie's visitor looked around the room, checked the bathroom. "Are there two of you?"

Actually, sometimes there are, me and my common sense. "Not at the moment."

"I'm Tami." Tami reached into a back pocket of her jeans and withdrew a tightly folded note. "Are you Congdon and Morse, Inc.?"

"Uh…I'm part of it."

"I understood this was going to be a guy gig, but I'm flexible." Tami stretched a well-muscled body to prove her point. Her eyes were an even deeper blue than Caryl's.

"He didn't tell me you were coming."

"Hey, got it. You're a couple who want to go home with fantasies to keep things hot for months, right? Well, I'm your girl."

"Poor Richard."

"I can take care of poor Richard anytime." Tami dropped herself to her knees, and her halter to her waist. "And you too."

Tami reached for the snap on her jeans and for Charlie's crotch.

THREE

IT WAS STILL EARLY. There was only one blackjack table operating in the Hilton's casino downstairs, where acres of crystal hung from the ceiling, at odds with the arcade decor below it.

Charlie made a third player at the table and accepted a free Bloody Mary from the breakfast cocktail server. This was party-twenty-four-hours-a-day town. Right?

Besides, Charlie'd earned it, rescuing herself just in the nick from a fate worse than death. She'd convinced Tami the body-builder to hurry next door and relieve Richard Morse of his anxieties and no doubt a good portion of his cash. The agency didn't cover Tamis as an expense, surely. Did Tamis take Visa?

Charlie might be on vacation, but she had an early dinner date with a local book author at an outdoor restaurant at the Flamingo around six and she was determined to enjoy the rest of the day before that, no matter how many people were struck dead around her. One always dined with Georgette early because the author was in bed by 8:30. Charlie had the feeling Georgette Millrose was not going to be a happy date.

There were six decks in the shoe—a clear plastic box with a ramp on its face that delivered one card at a time—all mixed up together. Dealers rarely played the shoe down much over half-way. Treasure Island had the reputation for dealing down the farthest. With three players at the table and ten burn cards shoved into the discard box, she couldn't know how many face cards and aces had already turned up.

An intense guy on one side of Charlie played a roll of hundred-dollar bills, three at a time, instead of chips. The woman to her left sat whimsically relaxed, seemingly daydreaming, checking her watch as if passing time until a companion arrived to take her to breakfast. But blackjack is a fast-moving game, and her signals to the dealer were on time and to the point.

The dealer was of the silent, stoic variety Charlie preferred. She found the chummy, garrulous types a distraction.

Lights flashed, zipped, and careened around the room, glinting off crystal facets. Metal tokens clanked into slot trays, and a few levers ratcheted. Whistles, calliope bleeps. Vacuum cleaners buzzed before the true crowds descended again. And this was one of the more staid of Vegas's casinos. No wonder nobody died in these places. No quiet place to do it.

Charlie's overly acute hearing, the result of her inability to indulge in loud music as a teen due to tone deafness, could be both a boon and a vexation.

Her aging, horny boss, her close call with his lusty entertainer, even what they could possibly be doing at this moment, the body in the gutter last night, Evan Black the important. Had he insisted Charlie talk to the police again, she would have. But he'd acted disappointed that she wouldn't and reluctant to have her do it. Granted, by the time Evan saw the pilot, he was not readily identifiable. And Caryl with the peekaboo nipples—they all faded as the game took hold. Mercifully, the background noises blended, then receded.

And yet Charlie registered the pit boss's belt buckle, silver and turquoise, with a finger ring to match, the hair on the back of his hands as he turned to keep watch on the dealers at various games around him. The way those hands flexed at his side as if surreptitiously exercising, the crooked seam in one pant leg.

The low cards were playing out. And the kings.

The eye in the sky, circled with crystal lashes, kept watch on the pit boss and the placing of chips at the tables. Charlie did not have the memory to be a card-counter, but with a six-deck shoe that would probably only be played down four decks anyway, she didn't know how anybody could tell how many face cards might be left.

The black globes pocking the crystal and two-way mirrored ceiling offered a decorative contrast, reminding Charlie of alien bug eyes. They held camera eyes instead, taping people and activities in the crystal cavern. No wonder there weren't any murders in the casinos—they'd be documented in the process.

The best places for blackjack were downtown on Fremont, the original Glitter Gulch, where there were casinos that advertised single and double decks. That's where the dedicated locals played.

The reason Charlie and Richard and everybody at Congdon and Morse used to prefer to stay at the Vegas Hilton was the relative absence of children. Now, with the new Star Trek Experience wing, there were more families evident. But here in the old casino, one rarely noticed them. And Richard had some kind of deal on rooms at this hotel. Even if she lost money gaming, it was a cheap vacation.

Charlie was aware on some level of the odors of stale tobacco, spilled beer, dead perfume, sweat, and the chemical deodorizers out to kill them all.

The guy next to her ran out of hundreds and left the table, muttering something about this "filthy town" and the "blasted world." Charlie couldn't tell if he was a Kiwi or an Aussie. She'd never doubted she could lose at gambling. But she also thought she could win. Gamblers are optimists. The shoe was emptied and refilled with brand-new decks, the pit boss peeling the cellophane wrappers off himself.

After the next deal, Charlie, with an ace and a five, scratched for a hit and so did the woman on her left, but by pointing at the table in front of her. She wore her bangs heavy to cover the wrinkles on her forehead, had her hair colored that sandy brown so popular these days, and sported a bemused smile that only toyed with her lips but fairly sparkled in her eyes. She dressed in loose-fitting cream slacks and jacket over a cream silk shell, gold chain necklace, and earrings. The only contrast, the deep tan of her skin and the blue shading on her eyelids.

The woman in cream and gold began to win and she began to play with two and then three black chips at a time and then stacks of the hundred-dollar tokens. The bemused smile turned to silent laughter. She straightened in her chair.

The dealer grew more tense than formal now. The pit boss settled behind him and stayed.

Everybody's guilty until proven innocent in Vegas.

Charlie figured most of the cameras behind the bug eyes overhead were zooming in on this table too, to make sure nobody on either side of the table cheated the house.

This was a hot shoe. There was a streak going here.

Even the security rooms and halls in "that other casino" have cameras taping everything that goes on. Charlie knew, because a few years ago two cops were taped beating a purse snatcher caught in a casino. They were taped beating and threatening to sodomize him with nightsticks. God, you couldn't even die in that mysterious security area all casinos have without being documented.

In fact, Charlie had never heard of anyone just dying in a casino, simply dropping dead of something. Older, and often hugely overweight, people were common in these places.

Charlie's other mind was making money. But nothing like the cream-and-gold woman, who laughed, never making a sound.

"IT WAS AWESOME," Charlie told her boss as they lay side by side on webbed deck chairs by the pool. This recreation deck on the third floor was also awesome. All eight acres of it.

"She counting?" Richard sprawled on his back, trying to hide the bruises forming there.

Charlie would save Tami for later ammunition. Tami had apparently not mentioned Charlie. "I don't think so. It's like when the shoe changed, she knew it would be hot. Like she waited for it to get dealt down less than maybe a fourth of one deck and got interested. She kept checking her watch though. Wonder if that means anything."

"Sounds like you made your move then too. You're supposed to be the psychic—maybe she was watching your reactions."

"No, she started it. I just went with the flow." Charlie'd come out about thirty thousand dollars richer, thanks to the woman of the silent laughter, who must have made more like several hundred thousand. The dealer, pit boss, and hard-faced suits that gravitated toward the pit weren't laughing. "And if I were psychic, Richard, I'd be rich by now. It's not like this is my first trip to Vegas."

"Just don't spend it all in one place." Richard the Lionhearted, as he was known around the office, had a hickey.

"It's all going to the college fund."

Richard raised to an elbow to wipe the steam off his sunglasses with his towel. He had protruding eyeballs that gave him a certain air of authority for no good reason. "What, she's changed her mind again?"

"That, she's good at."

Libby Greene, seventeen, had been waffling about college for the last three years. One time, she wanted to be an astronaut, another an archaeologist, then a stripper, then a doctor in sports medicine, your regular model, movie star, even housewife. She'd been through many careers in her mind, for most of which, neither she nor her grades qualified. Actually, Libby Abigail Greene's qualifications for model and movie star grew more apparent by the month.

Charlie would rather the kid find some rewarding skill to keep her satisfied, fed, happy, and as independent financially as she was temperamentally. Charlie had a life. She hoped the same for her daughter. "She gets her braces off next month."

"Oh, Jesus. Don't waste your money on the college fund."

"Think I'll get it wet."

The water was just cool enough to refresh at the weeny end, cooled enough at the deeper end to be invigorating without being uncomfortable. I won thirty thousand dollars this morning. Saw a murder happen last night. And don't remember when I've enjoyed life more than I do this day. Something's wrong with the script here.

"You look better when you're all wet, know that?" Richard Morse told her when she returned to the lounge chairs. "Now don't get huffy on me, babe. Because I been thinking about your problem."

"Which problem?" Charlie gathered her things, her "all wet" chilling in the dry October breeze up here, and headed for the concrete Grecian Jacuzzi, Richard trotting along behind her. Built to fit twenty-four, according to the sign—you could have crowded in another ten easy. Formed and rounded in mysterious ways to accommodate couples, the molded underwater bench rimming the tub suggested the sign meant twelve couples.

There was only one man in the Jacuzzi when they arrived, bubbles foaming almost to his chin.

She and Richard crawled down into the couple niche farthest from the man in the circle, as people do when they have all the room in the world.

"The thirty thousand problem—wait, is this before or after taxes?"

After—and I don't believe it either. "Before."

"Oh, well…still, Charlie, you know what you should do with it?"

"Gamble it away?"

"Stock market." The wise man with the Tami hickey nodded sagely and slid down into the frothing hot water up to his chin too.

"Same thing, right?"

"Not at your age, babe. You think you're independent because you have a job and a mortgage. Take those away and you're on the street, and your kid too. Time you began to think about compounding."

Richard Morse, the second bane of Charlie's life, her mother being the first, was nothing if not mysterious. Her daughter was just young, and there was always some hope for improvement in that quarter. "Compounding what?"

"Dividends. DRIP. Face it, babe, we're in a risky business here."

"Who isn't?" Take your hunk pilots, for instance.

"Yeah, but we know it. We need to plan for the future. Charlie, you listening to me? What's wrong with you?"

Charlie belatedly figured out what was wrong. That other guy in the Jacuzzi with them? He was one of the two heads who'd walked away from a murder on the Strip last night.

FOUR

"GEORGETTE, how wonderful to see you again."

The outdoor café at the Flamingo Hilton had real flamingos in a garden-pool-courtyard paradise and other exotic feathered and leafy things. It also had paths and nature signs for the educationally inclined and trash music that drowned out miniature waterfalls and surviving birdsong. They sat at a table shaded by the monstrous backdrop of the Flamingo, an umbrella, and a wilting palm imported from California.

Georgette was Georgette as always, bones and skin, with occasional lumps that identified her gender and osteoporosis. Bright red hair and a face that had given up on its lifts, leaving the boldly capped teeth to go where her expression could no longer follow.

"So? I understand you put this kid's manuscript up for auction," she said around the prominent caps. "Reynelda somebody? She was nobody—she's from Colorado, for godsake. And boom, now she's rich and famous." Georgette raised her martini and the rocks in her rings sent facet flashes jumping all over the underside of the umbrella. "Never in all these years has an agent, including you, put a novel of mine up for auction."

If seeing the thug in the giant Jacuzzi spa hadn't wrecked her mood, Charlie knew she could count on Georgette. Last time, it had been that her publisher was not accurately reporting her sales and was stealing her blind and it was all Charlie's fault.

"It might be Reynelda Goff's first novel, but the woman's in her mid-fifties, Georgette. She just got lucky." And, believe me, there wasn't anybody more surprised than I was. "How did you know about the auction?"

"Lucky because you put her novel up for auction. And I knew about it because I read *Publishers Weekly,* young lady. Don't think I live in Vegas because I'm dumb enough to gamble."

How did Georgette afford her lifestyle? And goddamn *Publishers Weekly* anyway. Authors should not be allowed near it.

The thug in the pool had stared at Charlie and finally left the spa. He was the one with curly hair. His presence had to have been a coincidence. But Charlie hadn't stopped looking over her shoulder ever since. She'd wanted to tell her boss about the pilot's death and the man who had left them alone in the spa, but Richard was too busy waxing poetic about dividend reinvestment and compounding.

"She was lucky that certain newsworthy events made her manuscript suddenly marketable. It was like winning the lotto. I mean—I thought you were loyal to Bland and Ripstop after all the years they've published you." Bland had sent a sheaf of detailed material on the status of Georgette's sales at Charlie's request, all pretty much indecipherable, but most publishers wouldn't have bothered. Although her sales were brisk, they were mostly "special sales" to chain stores that discounted books heavily because they could get high-volume deals, which pretty much dried up the author's trickle.

"I'll remind you that three of my novels have been optioned repeatedly by Hollywood production companies. Why are my books never put up for auction?"

Because Hollywood's dumber than New York even. They'll option half of anything that makes it to bound galleys. To date, all but one of Charlie's book authors had at least one option—mostly for cable TV—but still...

Only one of her book authors had ever made it to actual produced feature film, and that author had been long dead when she hit. Her heirs were making out splendidly, however.

Charlie dearly loved being a literary agent. She used to be a New York literary agent, but now she was Hollywood. She'd just as soon dump her book authors and concentrate on screenwriters, but things never quite worked out that way. For one thing, most of her book authors wanted to write screenplays so they could quit their day jobs or get a divorce or whatever. Most of her screenwriters wasted too much time writing novels nobody could sell.

"Georgette, lightning could still strike you like it did Reynelda Goff, but I can't put you or any of my authors up for auction until I know more than one house would be interested. She was an unknown commodity and things just clicked.''

''And I'm just a shopworn old frump—is that right?''

No, you're just a midlist author. Among book authors, there are four kinds—self-published, prepublished, no longer published, and published. Among the last, there are two—star authors and the vast majority, midlist authors. There is no low-list author. ''Of course not, you have published, what—twenty novels in hardcover?''

''All but one of which is out of print. I'm not even selling paperback rights anymore.''

''The paperback market has really constricted. I can't control the marketplace. I mean, it's not like you're starving.''

''No thanks to my agent. It so happens, miss, that I invested large portions of both my late husbands' estates in the stock market. The marketplace works very well for me except with my writing. I want to know why.'' Enlarged knuckles pounded on the menus their waitperson had left and which neither had bothered to open.

''Okay, send me a proposal on the next book and I'll hand it around to see if I can stir up enough interest for an auction. But I'm warning you—there's nothing more embarrassing than throwing a party and nobody comes. And Bland and Ripstop is not going to be happy about this. We're risking a lot here.''

''No, my dear. *We* are risking nothing. Because *you* are fired.''

CHARLE SAT staring at Georgette's empty chair and martini glass, so stunned she ordered a hamburger with fries and a glass of merlot from the waitperson and didn't realize she'd been forgetting to look over her shoulder until someone startled her from behind.

''Well, for heaven's sakes. It's my partner in crime. May I join you?''

Charlie hadn't heard anyone say ''for heaven's sakes'' since *Father Knows Best* on Nick. She'd have minded, but it was the woman in cream and gold. This was the first time Charlie had heard her speak.

''I'm Bradone and I feel like I've known you forever.'' Her

voice fit her perfectly—moderately low, pleasant, mellow, personal.

"I'm Charlie and I—" And I don't know what to say—"Charlie Greene, and yes, please sit down." Charlie'd never been fired before. She'd parted with clients, but never like this.

"Know what?" Bradone put down the menu. That laughter Charlie sensed, barely below the surface. "I'm going to be deliciously naughty and have a hamburger and fries too and a beer."

"Why are we partners in crime and how did you know what I'd ordered?"

"Our crime was all that money we won at the other Hilton this morning. I was seated at the table behind you here and overheard your order. And wasn't that Georgette Millrose who left in such an unseemly huff?" This Bradone—she pronounced it *Brad-own*—was striking—in her way, almost beautiful. "And I know that because I've seen her photos and read several of her books. So there."

"She just fired me," Charlie blurted, knowing better. Then, of course, she had to explain in what capacity she'd been fired and admit to her occupation, which she never did to strangers.

Charlie tried to cut off her urge to confide.

Bradone was Bradone McKinley, and when Charlie asked what she did for a living, Bradone McKinley swirled the end of a naughty french fry into a puddle of naughty catsup and laughed out loud before taking a bite. It must be wonderful to be so happy all the time.

"I play blackjack and sometimes baccarat. I travel the world. I read the stars."

"Are you a card-counter?"

"I'm an astrologer."

"Did you know it was going to be a hot shoe?"

"Not really."

The music had mercifully paused for a while and imprisoned nature was quacking and squawking and cawing and squeaking. The birds must have had their wings clipped, because nobody took wing but sparrows looking for french fry bits.

"Do you always play blackjack so early in the morning?"

"Only when the timing is right and Venus is making good aspects." They both managed to put away about half of their burgers and a fourth of their fries. Bradone ordered wine and coffee for herself and Charlie too. Much as she wanted to get on with her life, Charlie found the woman mesmerizing.

"Works wonderfully, but not always, and it's fun. Works well enough though, that I have to be careful to lose money about a third of the time."

"I don't believe you." Charlie realized she was grinning. In the last twenty-four hours, she'd witnessed a murder, sat in a Jacuzzi with one of the killers, and been fired by a client for the first time—and she was grinning.

Be careful. She's probably setting you up to look at a book proposal for astrologers who want to gamble.

Evening had softened the sun and the breeze was dry and cool, sweet with tropical plants blackmailed somehow into living here. Children splashed and chattered in a swimming pool on the other side of a hillock.

"I know you don't believe me, Charlie. Nobody does. That's the beauty of it. I've been doing this for years. It's a fabulous life. Monte Carlo, Malaysia, Macao, Alaska, cruise ships, Latin America—the world is very literally my oyster."

"Do you have a home base?"

Bradone Mckinley had a home in Santa Barbara, where she retreated when the stars were not propitious for gambling. "And to rest and to study. Astrology takes a lot of study."

She salted away a third of her earnings after taxes, made a point of losing a third—usually at baccarat, because it was faster—and spent the rest for living and traveling expenses. "I love travel, astrology, blackjack, my home in Santa Barbara. I couldn't be happier."

"Any family?"

"Just my cats and a houseboy."

"You should write a book," Charlie said, testing her.

"That's too much work. I already have plenty of money." As if to prove it, Bradone insisted upon paying the tab for both of them. "Notoriety, I don't need. I like my life the way it is. And I so enjoyed watching you winning this morning. You're great company when you're not too intense."

Charlie had enjoyed it too, and the dinner, and the company. She felt a little lonesome when they parted ways on the street outside.

She should head back to her room and check her E-mail. Call Libby. But she turned up the street toward the Treasure Island Casino instead, crossing Las Vegas Boulevard so she wouldn't have to pass the place where the hunk pilot had died. She passed the statues of a triumphant Caesar, out to sack your bank account instead of Gaul, and winged angels lauding the idea by blowing silent trumpets from their pedestals along the drive of Caesar's Palace.

The courtyard of the Treasure Island was red with stage smoke as a pirate ship defied a brig of Her Majesty's Navy with phony cannon shot and firecrackers over the heads of the assembled tourists crowding an enormous wooden gangway entrance to the casino. The brave Brits fired back and many a stuntman on either side met his demise in the broiling waters of battle.

Yes, it was silly, but it made Charlie happy again. If Hollywood was the reality you were trying to get away from, it took something as bizarre as Las Vegas to do it.

She battled her way through the throng—let Mr. Thug try to follow her now, har, har—to get inside to the blackjack tables, where she happily lost and won and lost again thirty dollars that would never compound or DRIP or whatever.

By the time she made it back to the Las Vegas Hilton, her stomach remembered to turn sour over her fat-drenched dinner and the wine. So she stopped by the twenty-four-hour café for milk and dry toast.

Her stomach might feel bad—it was a grouchy stomach anyway—but she felt pretty good.

Until she glanced at the headlines of the *Las Vegas Sun* left on the seat next to her.

A cop on the Strip had been found murdered. No question of pedestrian error here. This was an obvious hit-and-run. His name was Timothy Graden. Timothy Graden left behind a wife and two young children.

There was a picture. He was the bicycle cop who wouldn't believe her at the scene of another murder last night.

FIVE

CHARLIE WOKE UP the next morning much as she had the one before—early, rested, hungry, guilty. She was on a roll here.

Nothing like murder and being away from home to get some quality sleep. She ordered a bagel, coffee, and milk in deference to her type D stomach. A proud and efficient type A personality, Charlie had been saddled with an underachieving digestive track.

I was too sick and tired to do anything about the bicycle cop last night, she told her other self. I mean, what good does it do to kill myself when it wouldn't make the cop, or Pat the pilot, rise from the dead? I am not God.

You are a woman of elastic morals.

I am a survivor in a totally fascinating but corrupt world.

So was Attila the Hun.

Charlie crawled into bed with her diminished breakfast, drank all of the milk first, then turned on the news. Good old Barry and Terry filled her in on a few details of the bicycle cop's demise but didn't report if it had happened on the Strip like Patrick Thompson's. Terry mentioned briefly that investigators were looking for a black limousine, license number unknown, and went on to workers at the Yucca Mountain site who were claiming a cover-up in the investigations into their charges that grains of radioactive sand had been discovered in their baloney sandwiches.

"The DOE's Yucca Mountain Project Office," Barry assured Terry and Charlie, "has pointed out once again that, though the mountain is being prepared to store radioactive waste, no significant amount has been delivered as yet and also that the workers' sandwiches were assembled elsewhere. Workers maintain that large quantities of various forms of hot waste material is even now being tested inside the mountain to determine the facility's usefulness as a safe storage area for the literally infinitely hazardous stuff."

"Meanwhile, that other area is in the news again today too," Terry added, unaware of the bright smear of lipstick on a front tooth. "The apparently unlimited curiosity of tourists in the supersecret government base shown on the maps only as Area Fifty-one caused trouble again yesterday both at tiny Rachel, the closest town, and on an unmarked dirt road that leads off across the vast uninhabited desert. Two hunters from Michigan claim they were forced to turn back by armed men in aviator sunglasses and dark leather jackets."

Terry had gotten the news of her unsightly tooth, probably from the little receiver behind her ear, about halfway through the first sentence. It dimmed her smile drastically. Charlie could see her relief just as the taped interview with the two hunters from Michigan replaced her on the screen.

Officer Graden probably died because of you. He probably made forbidden inquiries about Pat the pilot because you insisted Pat was murdered. So, how safe are you—the star witness?

So, what are you saying? I should have ignored Pat's murder, let it pass for pedestrian error?

Why had Pat been flying over Yucca Mountain? If it was being dug to form storerooms for the bad stuff, what would anybody be able to see from the air?

The hunters from Michigan drove a snazzy Ford Expedition, shown hanging from the end of a tow chain. They were particularly angered that, on the way back toward Rachel on the dirt road, all of their heavy-duty tires had been slashed.

Charlie ate the bagel dry and wondered how "tiny Rachel" could support a towing service. Maybe by putting sharp things in the road after a tourist vehicle had set out for Groom Lake. And she'd read somewhere that the mysterious guards of Area 51's borders wore camouflage uniforms.

She turned off the TV, poured her coffee, and, for penance, took her Toshiba notebook out of the safe in the closet to check her E-mail.

Type A types may sleep better away from home, but they do not vacation like other people.

There was a message from Larry Mann, her assistant, one from Ruby Dillon, Richard's office manager and right-hand woman, one from Mitch Hilsten, superstar. Nothing from Libby—both a comfort and a worry.

Libby Greene had an old car, a new computer, a new boyfriend, and a new part-time job. Charlie didn't know where to expect trouble next—she just knew to expect it.

Libby has made it to seventeen without screwing up major. That's more than you can say.

Ruby wanted to know why the hell Richard wasn't answering his E-mail or her phone calls. Richard, determined he and his subordinate would get away from the office, had refused to bring his pager or cell phone and insisted Charlie do likewise.

Larry hoped she was having a good time and getting some rest. Reynelda Goff was giving her publisher trouble over revisions to *Bewitched and Bedeviled in Boulder,* which, if you knew Boulder, sounded more like a nonfiction book than a historical novel. (Reynelda was of the age to say "an" historical novel.) The title had almost nothing to do with the story. But it did relate to last year's news event in Boulder, which related to why Pitman's Publishing paid such a ridiculous price for it. Reynelda had turned artistic on them—not an unusual happening when big money makes one suddenly famous. But the news event and the fame had faded by now and the book still hadn't made it to the printer.

There was an analogy between publishing and Las Vegas here that Charlie Greene didn't want to think about.

Larry had a few more office details to relate, one a promising query on Sheldon Maypo for a possible writing job at an ad agency. Pitch a treatment for a feature film and get a job writing commercials. Hey, anything's better than nothing, and Shelly wasn't getting any younger.

Charlie finished off the coffee while responding to Larry's questions and warned him of the problem with Georgette Millrose. She was tempted to answer Ruby Dillon's post with Tami the bodybuilder, but Charlie liked her job. She did not mention the two murdered men and her growing concern that the two thugs were responsible for both and that at least one knew she was staying here.

Mitch Hilsten wanted to know why she didn't return his calls, why he'd had to go on-line to get in touch with her. Charlie just didn't know, so she didn't answer his E-mail either.

She locked the computer back in the safe, showered, dressed, and sat on the bed. She had to tell someone of her suspicions about Officer Graden's death. For someone with elastic morals, she was great at guilt.

She checked her electronic Day-Timer. It was Tuesday.

She knew that.

She had a luncheon appointment with Evan Black.

She knew that too. Somehow, she didn't figure he'd show. But she'd be there in case. She had about two hours to kill at blackjack, or finding out which police station housed the bicycle cops, or wandering around openly to see if the goon in the Jacuzzi was following her, or she could just do nothing.

Charlie had lost the skill to just do nothing years ago, when she realized she was a kid with a kid to raise. But Richard Morse saved her the need to make a decision.

"Charlie, I'm in love," he breathed over the house phone. "I need your help."

"Whoa, I don't think I can help you there." I barely fought off Tami myself. "I've been around, but not that far."

"But you're a woman."

"That's not the answer to all problems, Richard. I mean, it's not like compounding or anything." But she agreed to meet him down by the gleaming black Dodge Stealth in the lobby.

"So where's"—she almost slipped and said Tami—"this wonderful new love?" Surely, Tami wouldn't accost Charlie in all this public.

But Richard led her around the Stealth, a prize for some contest that offered yet another opportunity to part with your money, and through the rows of bleeping, blinking slots to the blackjack tables. He pointed to Bradone McKinley.

She played at the same table as yesterday, the same pit boss keeping watch, the one with the clenching fist. Suddenly, he was watching Charlie too.

"Is that class or what? I took one look at her, Charlie, and knew. I just knew. Like in them dumb romance novels. Me, Richard Morse, can you believe it?"

Richard, who'd never read a novel, let alone a romance novel, often talked like a truck driver, but he always dressed well, everything tailor-made just for him, and not in Hong Kong either. Most agents dressed like used-car salesmen. Today, he was suitably dressed down in a tan blazer and shirt open at the neck. Charlie had seen this outfit before, but she'd never seen his face so radiant.

"Richard, that's the woman who turned a hot shoe into a fortune yesterday morning. Remember, I told you at the pool?"

"Can't be—she's losing like a just cause. But look at her—serene and happy as a lobster anyway. That's—"

"Class. I know." Losing is what she's supposed to be doing now. Or lose her livelihood. But Charlie had to admit Bradone McKinley was a whole flight of stairs up from Tami. Richard's dapper outfit included a silk scarf like film directors used to wear in black-and-white movies. It mercifully concealed his Tami hickey. "Richard, you've been divorced three times." And survived our bodybuilder. "What do you need me for?"

"This is different. I wanted you to get to know her. Find out if she is married, involved, you know."

"I had dinner with her last night. She's not married. She has a houseboy. I don't know if she's involved." And she's no kid. Probably no more than fifteen years younger than you, which is not your style, boss. "I do know she travels a lot and is very independent. She's a practicing astrologer."

"I don't care if she's an astronaut. And as long as you know her, you can introduce us."

"Let's wait until she's done losing, okay? She's also very serious about blackjack."

They didn't have long to wait. Bradone was one of two at the table, the other player—an Asian gentleman. The house cleaned up. Bradone rose and bowed slightly to the dealer and her partner in loss, an almost-smile on her lips.

"Just look at that," Richard the smitten effused. "That's elegance. That's Greta Garbo meets Julia Roberts, right?"

Bradone, in powder blue with navy accents today, walked toward them, the grin turning unmistakable, the eyes in full sat-

isfied hilarity. To Charlie, she resembled more Faye Dunaway
meets Agent Scully.

"Charlie, how nice to see you again." The mesmerizing voice
took hold of Charlie as before and Bradone took her arm, over-
looking Richard Morse completely. "You know, I realized after
we parted last night where I remembered seeing you. You're a
very close friend of Mitch Hilsten, right? You lucky girl. And
you didn't even mention it. I told you all about me."

"She doesn't love him anymore," Richard said, taking Charlie's other elbow and squeezing hard. "Hi, I'm Richard Morse.
Of Congdon and Morse? Charlie works for me."

"I never loved him. I still like him as much as I ever did."
I just don't know what to say to him.

"Bradone McKinley." She reached across Charlie to shake
his hand, and he had to let go of Charlie's elbow to take it.
"Have you two had breakfast?"

"Yes," Charlie said.

"No," Richard said, and actually bowed. "But allow me the
pleasure."

"Allow me the pleasure?" Charlie stared at him, but he ignored her.

So did Bradone. "No, I insist. You must come up to the
penthouse."

THE PENTHOUSE put Richard's pseudo-Tudor mansion in Beverly Hills to shame. Marble columns, a butler and a cook.

"I'd heard about these," Richard whispered. Poor Richard,
he only had a suite. And they'd come up on a totally different
elevator. "These are only for the mega-high rollers. What's she
doing playing down in the casino with the riffraff? And blackjack to boot?"

The butler, Reed, poured them coffee. The cook, Brent, was
off in the less formal regions, preparing something Bradone
claimed would amaze them. They were already amazed. And
they were from Hollywood. Bradone was off either making or
taking a telephone call.

"You mean there's more than one of these penthouses?"

"Oh yeah, three anyway." Richard sat, visibly deflated, on

the edge of a billowy couch like he was afraid it would consume him if he relaxed. "You got—what?—eight acres of pool and tennis and putting range deck down there, there's gotta be a lotta here up here." This was the same man who'd said, "Allow me the pleasure"?

Charlie should have enjoyed his discomfort. Instead, she felt sorry for him.

Why? He puts *you* down every chance he gets.

"Richard? I have a problem. I need help."

"*You* have a problem?" He snorted and gestured to the walls of window that looked out on Vegas and beyond. "Look at this. What chance I got with this woman?"

"Richard, Georgette Millrose fired me yesterday. And I witnessed a murder the night before. And I'm fairly sure it had something to do with a cop dying in a hit-and-run later that night. I'm worried the killers might think I have the same information the cop did. All I know is what the guys who committed the first murder—which the cops still think was an accident—look like. And I saw one of them here at the hotel."

"Well, it probably was an accident. Charlie, you don't want to get involved in murder in this town. And has Millrose ever made the *New York Times* best-seller list? After all these years? You're better off without her, and so is Congdon and Morse. Just help me figure out what to do about *my* problem." He gestured around the room again.

"Evan Black was involved with the first murder victim and he's acting very funny about the whole deal."

"Charlie, babe, I'll back you on the Millrose thing to the hilt. But we both know Black is bucks. You know? What have I taught you?"

"Back off Black?"

"Good girl." He patted her knee and sat up straight as their hostess entered with Reed, the butler, and the amazing breakfast.

SIX

CHARLIE GREENE took a cab to Yolie's to take Evan Black to lunch, certain he wouldn't be there. She was determined to enjoy her lunch anyway, to put off going to the police—she never had much luck with them somehow—and to get the taste of the amazing breakfast out of her mouth. It had come in a glass with a long spoon and looked, smelled, and tasted like yak curds. Not that Charlie had ever tasted yak curds, but she knew.

Yolie's smelled of mesquite, cilantro, garlic, and grilling flesh.

To her confusion, Evan Black rose from a table to greet her. He was having a martini. Up. Like Georgette Millrose had last night. Uh-oh.

Evan was shaved. His ponytail gleamed, his black silky outfit brightened with some kind of white flower at the throat where other people might wear a tie. She wouldn't ask.

Knowing better, she ordered a Dos Equis. It would take something special to scrape the yak curd crud from her tongue.

Tongue, shmung. You know beer will go straight to your thighs.

"Oh, shut up."

"All I said was hello."

"Evan, I'm sorry. Myself was reminding me that beer goes directly to my thighs. When I get rattled, I talk to myself aloud. It's so embarrassing."

"Everybody who knows you, Charlie, knows that about you. It's one of your endearing qualities." Behind him, a window across the back wall revealed the biggest indoor barbecue she'd ever seen.

"What, talking to myself out loud?" That's what elderly people do. "Or getting rattled?"

"You pretend to be invulnerable and then blow it every chance you get."

"I do?" I do not.

"It's what makes you so special." Rubber belts drove pulleys that drove something enclosed in stationary horizontal tubes at least twelve feet long. That something rotated three-foot skewers over an open flame. "You try to be tougher than the guys. But you don't have to. You've got the guys in the palm of your hand from the beginning."

"This is some kind of macho stuff." Make her weakness sound like strength so she'll be happy and do what she's told. Been there.

"Such a cynic. Is there no romance in you, Charlie?"

"None." Getting knocked up at sixteen sheds a whole different light on things, trust me.

They spooned an excellent tomato and cilantro-type salsa onto thin, crispy flat bread.

Evan ordered a sampler plate for both of them. She hated when men did that. On the other hand, she did like not having to make the decision right now. When was she supposed to notice this was a vacation?

"So, how's your pilot holding up after the murder of her brother?"

"She's bitter. As she has a right to be."

"Did you know he was flying over Yucca?"

Evan Black had saved the olive in his drink until last. He sucked it off the little plastic sword and said around it, "Now, how would you know that?"

"I told you I'd seen him at McCarran when Richard and I were heading for baggage claim. He was telling somebody about it on his cellular."

"Did he say anything else?" Her client had gone very still behind those tinted lenses.

"Something about some ridge. He was furious."

The waiter brought lumps of flesh on sizzling skewers, hacked slices off onto her plate. Lamb, chicken, beef, pork—this was after he'd filled the table with salad, potatoes, polenta, rice, vegetables, and more salsa. No yak.

"Brazilian cooking," Evan Black explained. "Everything's marinated for days in wine or beer and garlic and spices."

If this was lunch in Brazil, Charlie couldn't imagine dinner.

Whatever it was, it tasted as good as it smelled. But she couldn't get through an eighth of it. This was her third meal of the day and it wasn't even 3:00 p.m.

"I didn't want to get involved in Pat Thompson's murder. It was his sister's duty to go to the police." Charlie tried to see through the dark lenses of his eyewear and into his thoughts, but there was too much light behind him. "She didn't go, did she?"

"No." From a fake banana tree at Evan's shoulder, a dead toucan inspected Charlie.

"And you honestly didn't see Pat come out of Loopy's with those men?" The banana tree was a poorly disguised support column that helped hold the roof out of their food.

"I honestly didn't. We were having fun, Charlie. I didn't really pay that much attention." Brown cloth covered the column/trunk and was embellished with green silk leaves, in need of a dusting, and banana bunches.

"If you knew who he was, why didn't you tell the police after he was killed?"

"Because I had to talk to Caryl first. I didn't know they were brother and sister. I thought they were lovers. But either way, I didn't want her finding out from some cop. I had to take your word that's who he was. And I honestly thought it was an accident, whoever the guy might be. Maybe I still do."

Charlie imagined the dead toucan winked a glass eye at her. "That bicycle cop who at least listened to me for a while?" And you did everything you could to dissuade him. "Have you heard that he's dead?"

"Graden, yeah. Look, Charlie, it's terrible what happened to him, and Pat too. But don't you see what you're doing? You're seeing a conspiracy here. Just because you noticed two guys who turned up dead doesn't mean it has anything to do with you or them with each other."

"In the same night? In a strange town?"

"I saw them both that night, and I don't feel responsible for their deaths."

"Look, I may have elastic morals, and I wasn't there when Officer Graden got hit by that car, but I do know Pat Thompson was cold-bloodedly murdered. And Evan? Yesterday, I saw one of the goons who did it—he was in the Jacuzzi with me and Richard at the Vegas Hilton.''

'''Elastic morals'?'' His teeth didn't glint like Mitch Hilsten's but they showed off nicely against the olive skin and the dark clothing. The sight reminded Charlie that Libby's braces came off next month. ''Charlie, who told you that? You are a very moral person. You're one of the straightest people I know.''

That says something about where you come from, guy.

''Which is why I need to ask you a favor.'' He leaned toward her so earnestly, the flower at his throat nearly brushed his dirty plate.

''Because I'm morally straight, or because I'm seeing a conspiracy here, or because I'm your agent?'' Actually, it took the whole agency to handle Evan Black. But Charlie got to take him out to lunch because he seemed to ''interface'' with her best. More bluntly, in his short association with Congdon and Morse, Charlie seemed able to talk Evan into or out of things Richard wanted him into or out of. ''And what do I get in return?''

''Now you're talking.'' He actually rubbed his hands together. ''I'm going to offer you some totally free information.''

''Yeah, right.'' Charlie slipped the agency's credit card to the waiter, who seemed disappointed he couldn't skewer them further.

''Charlie, I'm the one Patrick Thompson was flying over Yucca Mountain.''

''You?''

''Well, me and Mel, my main man on the camera, and Toby, my second-unit gofer.''

''And in return for this stunning piece of information, I am to...''

''Take a ride with me and Caryl? And Mel? There's something I want to show you.''

''In your plane.''

''Right.''

''No deal. I hate flying.''

''You're on a plane to New York every other time I call the agency.''

"That's because I have to for my job. I love my job. This, I don't. So, no thanks."

When they were out in his car, he tried again, "I didn't think you were afraid of anything—fear of flying? Shit, this is even better."

"I'll take a cab back to the Hilton."

But his Land Rover pulled out into traffic. "Charlie, aren't you wondering what this is all about?"

"Well, let's see—two murders, a totally nasty type in the Jacuzzi with me"—not to mention an almost sexual attack by a Tami bodybuilder, and getting fired by a midlist author—"and I've been here what, three days?"

"No, not that—what I'm all about? What am I always all about. Really?"

Charlie had to stop and think. "Your work."

"Hey, same as you. Right?"

"So Yucca Mountain, conspiracy, and all this is...the next film?" You didn't use the word *movie* with this type.

"Charlie, come with us. It's not nearly as dangerous as driving the Four-oh-five to work every day. Besides, you love to gamble."

"Not with my life, I don't. Why can't we drive?"

"Take too long."

"I'm on vacation. I have time."

"The roads are restricted."

"Evan, tell me this doesn't have anything to do with the tiny town of Rachel and Area Fifty-one. Please?"

He grinned and pulled onto Maryland Parkway.

"You're kidding. Not you. That's been parodied on every TV network and cable too. It's so old, it's panned in commercials. There are people on the Internet bragging about taking photographs of each other peeing on the black mailbox. That story is a dead story."

Reaching across her, he pulled out a thick envelope from the glove compartment and began sorting through colored photographs as he drove.

Barry and Terry smiled at her from a mammoth billboard sporting the moral ALL THE NEWS YOU NEED, WHEN

YOU NEED IT. Terry's teeth were brilliantly clean, but somebody had been taking drive-by potshots at Barry that had pretty much torn away one cheek and drooped his smile like the Phantom of the Opera's.

Evan handed her one of the photos. It showed a lean guy in Dockers pants and backpack clearly urinating against a post, grinning over his shoulder at the camera. You could just make out the tip of his penis at the end of his cupped hand and the lack of graffiti on the white mailbox atop the post.

"So?"

"So, I'm not as out of the traffic pattern as you think. So, I have a very good reason to want to involve you in this new project outside your wonderful agenting skills—two reasons, actually. And so"—he turned a quick grin to her before returning it to the traffic—"if you knew about the brouhaha on the Internet about the desecrating of the sacred black mailbox, you had to have been interested enough to go looking for it there, right?"

"But you'll be the laughingstock of the industry. Why would you do that to yourself? And this is a white mailbox. I know you, Evan, and your work. You are not into alien abduction and that kind of stuff." The black mailbox belonging to a rancher was the only sign on a least-traveled road that told the woo-woo nuts where to turn off to the undisclosed Groom Lake air base, and peeing on it had become a sort of in-joke.

"Forget the fucking mailbox. It's probably been painted orange with blue daisies by now. What is the one constancy in my diverse works?"

"The critics seem to think you have different themes...all presented with dark humor." Charlie had to be very careful when it came to talking "English lit." That was her major in college, and everything she'd learned had been turned inside out once she'd hit live publishing in New York, where she'd worked until a little over three years ago. She could still spout the jargon, but without much conviction. "At least you have themes."

"Exactly. And my theme in this project is conspiracy."

"That's a theme?"

"People's use of and need for it is. You are obviously a subject to explore, since you hold to the conspiracy theory on

Pat's and Officer Graden's deaths. You are determined that you are a connection and somehow partly responsible. And you checked out Rachel and Groom Lake on the World Wide Web.''

"Didn't Mel Gibson do this a couple of years ago?''

"We'll use a different title. And I have still another request to ask of you.''

"I haven't granted your first request yet.''

"We are making progress though—I've got you up to 'yet.' Charlie, I want to approach Mitch Hilsten about this project. What do you think?''

"You know damn well there isn't an actor in Hollywood who wouldn't give his swimming pool to work with you and get to go to Cannes and Telluride and all. I would assume it would depend on his schedule. But Evan, you don't want him.''

"Of course I do. Who wouldn't?''

"He believes in this stuff. Really believes. Do you hear what I'm saying?''

"Yes, darling. That's why I want him.'' And the Land Rover swirled into the Las Vegas Hilton's multilaned and curving "landing strip.''

"Well then, ask his agent.''

"I prefer to approach his girlfriend.''

A gorgeous uniformed kid opened her door. "I am not his girlfriend, Evan Black. He's a friend is all. I thought you were too. But tell you what—I'll go flying with you and Mel and Caryl if you and Caryl will go to the police station with me.''

SEVEN

STARTLED AT HOW smoothly she'd been maneuvered into this, Charlie watched the wind sock whip and the minuscule aircraft taxi from its parking space toward her.

Evan kept his plane at the small airport in North Vegas. And Caryl was his flight instructor as well as his pilot.

Caryl had not gone to the police station with them, but then, Charlie had no intention of approaching Mitch Hilsten about this conspiracy project either.

Charlie hadn't set foot in the Hilton, because Evan took her up on her offer immediately, calling Caryl and Mel on his cellular and telling them to meet him at the North Vegas airport. Caryl had been officially notified of her brother's accidental death and had identified his remains. Charlie swallowed hard at the thought and would never ask how.

At the police station, Charlie repeated her certainty that Pat Thompson had been murdered by the two men who'd walked him out of Loopy Louie's and her suspicion that Officer Graden's death was connected. And that she might be in danger from the same people. "They looked and acted like bouncers."

A pleasant-faced woman took Charlie's statement, keying it in as Charlie gave it, printing it out for Charlie to check over and sign. The officer couldn't be very high up in police hierarchy, because she typed too fast and was able to see them right away. "Maybe Officer Graden believed what I told him that night enough to look into it on his own. Maybe he left some notes in his desk or mentioned it to another officer. I really think you should investigate the possibility."

"Every effort is being made to find the person or persons responsible for Officer Graden's death. Thank you for your help. We'll be in touch." And with a half-smile like Bradone's, the policewoman added, "Enjoy your visit. I'm fairly sure you're in no danger, Ms. Greene."

"That was too easy," Charlie grumbled when Evan whisked her off to North Las Vegas. "And you weren't any help."

"That one is your conspiracy. Remember?"

"Isn't it a little late to be taking off now? Can't this wait till morning?"

"My aircraft may not be big and luxurious, Charlie, but it will actually fly at night."

It certainly wasn't big and luxurious. Charlie always took the aisle seat when flying commercially, so she wouldn't see how far away the ground was. There were four seats in this plane, and they were all window seats.

She absolutely would not encourage Mitch Hilsten to take part in Evan Black's conspiracy project.

At least Evan didn't offer to fly the plane himself. Caryl Thompson, her nice nipples well clothed like any pilot's should be, might be younger than Evan but at least she was an instructor and not a student.

Charlie, however, took no comfort in the woman's swollen eyes and faraway expression. Could grief overcome her pilot training and endanger them all? And Charlie still could not fathom why her own presence should be important on this trip.

This was one of those planes where you had to climb up on the wing and then into your seat by bending your body in ways bodies don't bend. Those in back had to get in first. Charlie was the first to board and the gyrations she had to perform to get into the fourth seat made it pretty clear that the only way she could get out was by plane crash.

Charlie would handle this situation by fantasizing she was somewhere else.

Mel Goodall, the main-man cameraman, crawled in back beside Charlie, took one look at her, and broke up—his long face scrunching into a short one. "It's okay, sweetheart. Old Mel will see nothing bad happens to you."

Old Mel was the angular guy with the penis tip and the backpack in the photograph Evan had shown her. He wore tan Dockers today too and looked more like an engineer than a cameraman. He was probably in his late forties—old enough to know better than to be on this rattletrap.

The pilot crawled in (literally) next and Evan last. Over the sound of the revving engine, hysterical propeller, and violently vibrating fuselage, the producer/director/writer bellowed back to Charlie, "You know my secret, Charlie? The rest have concept—I've got theme."

Jesus, God, Allah, and Buddha save us from the artistes of this world and me from this one in particular.

The artiste put on a headset to match the pilot's and tossed two more over to Mel, who stuck one on Charlie.

Buffeted by gale-force crosswinds, the tiny aircraft hurtled down a too-short runway and made it into the air despite rolling balls of attacking tumbleweed. Charlie's client let out a triumphant whoop, sort of a cross between Tarzan and a football fan.

Charlie Greene closed her eyes.

THERE WAS NO WIND, only warm sun bathing the recreation deck of the Las Vegas Hilton, no nerve-jangling music, no screaming children to splash water and wash out her contacts. Just peaceful adults swimming laps or talking quietly on white lounge chairs. Charlie slipped out of her sandals and net swimsuit cover and stepped to the side of the pool. Her—

"Charlie, open your eyes. That's Yucca Mountain down there," Evan Black shouted in her earphone, then began ordering pilot Caryl to turn and dive.

The midget plane was suddenly on its side, circling like a vulture, Mel manipulating a handheld mini through his window, which was a lot clearer and less scratched than hers. Up front, Evan manipulated outside cameras and watched the result on a monitor.

A flurry of clipped indecipherable messages in a male voice came from the headset.

"Radio contact," Caryl said softly. "Next stop, Dreamland."

"Dive," their leader commanded.

Jesus, instead of slipping into a heated swimming pool, Charlie was about to get shot out of the air by her own government. She hadn't wanted to be here. She'd have taken off the headset, except the rickety plane's noise was more frightening than the cockpit communications.

She'd always been astonished when the flight attendant on an airliner announced passengers could listen to the cockpit communications on channel whatever through the headphones at their seat. It was terrifying enough *not* knowing.

"Charlie," Evan said, "note that we are going in a straight line from Yucca Mountain to Groom Lake."

You are going in a straight line. I are going to lose my Brazilian lunch and yak crud.

"Open your eyes," Mel yelled, and shook her shoulder. "Or you'll get sick."

Tell me about it.

But she opened her eyes. They couldn't be more than twenty feet off the ground. Which was fine if the ground stayed flat. The ground did not stay flat. Charlie lost it. Not the lunch, but her control. "What are you guys, fucking nuts? Flying this low—don't tell me about going under radar. They can pick us off with a BB gun from here."

Then she lost her lunch. Mercifully into a plastic bag Mel held under her mouth and closed quickly afterward. The cockpit still smelled awful.

"Reminds me of flying Vomit Airlines over the ditch." Caryl sounded almost nostalgic.

Here was Charlie Greene, scudding along the uneven ground with a bunch of loons.

"Everybody keep watch for roads, installations, stray vehicles, and buildings to avoid," their pilot instructed, taking over the command. "I've got all I can do to keep an eye on the landscape and the wind. This could get serious here."

Charlie could see the plane's shadow whipping over gullies and sagebrush and scratchy-looking bushes. Charlie was not fond of deserts in general, but southern Nevada was the meanest, ugliest of them all. The sand looked more abrasive, the rock more scoured. Even the mountains were deserts.

They almost crawled up the side of a low, sullen mountain range and dove down the other side, along a valley, and then up and out and over again.

Charlie closed her eyes. Had Pat Thompson been murdered for doing just what she was doing now?

"Almost there," Caryl said.

Charlie opened her eyes without meaning to.

"How much time can you give us?" Evan asked the pilot, and swung back to his monitor.

"Not much."

"We don't need much, got good stuff last time. Ready, Mel?"

"Loaded and ready."

"Start your cameras, boys." Caryl took them over a rise, barely, and Charlie caught a glimpse of runways wider and longer than anything she'd seen at Denver International, and immense shedlike buildings.

Then an orange light flooded the cabin. It didn't seem to bother the others. Charlie couldn't figure out why.

"CHARLIE, open your eyes. This is stupid."

"You sure she isn't dead?"

"She's not dead. She's warm. Feel her."

"We're all warm, with that fire. Doesn't mean she's not dead."

"First piece of civilization we meet, we get some food in her. She lost all her Yolie's. At least it didn't go to her thighs."

Charlie lay flat out on the hard sand, except for her head, which rested on Evan's lap. A scratchy bush next to them waved its branches in the wind stirred up by the burning plane. Mel gathered tumbleweed and threw it into the flames. The smoke went straight up, leaving most of the sky dazzling with stars—a few of them shooting. Burning plane? "Did we crash? Am I hurt?"

"I don't think so. Try to sit up. No, we didn't crash." Evan sounded high, hyperexcited.

Charlie made it to her hands and knees. "Did we all make it out?"

But he had left her to help Mel throw tumbleweeds on the blaze. Its warmth felt good in front. Her behind felt frigid. Nothing felt injured. She made it to a wobbly standing position. "Where's Caryl?"

"Right here." The pilot walked past with armloads of dried tumbleweed. "Thanks for caring, Charlie."

Charlie stumbled closer to the fire's warmth. "If we didn't crash, why is the plane burning? Are you trying to make a beacon so search parties can find us?"

"No, we're destroying evidence," Mel explained with glee.

This guy needed help.

"And here's our second-unit gofer with the van now," Evan said, just as happy.

Distant headlights bobbed toward them.

"God, let's pray that's Toby." Caryl sketched a sign of the cross between her nipples.

"Women are so damned negative," Evan told Mel. "Why is that?"

"Damned if I know. But here's the cameras and Charlie's purse. Better get them and our asses out of here. Our trackers have to have seen this fire by now."

"What if everything doesn't burn?" Caryl insisted as the men rushed her and Charlie toward the approaching lights.

"Too late to worry it now. Life's a gamble, right?" Evan did his victory whoop again.

Charlie was glad to be alive. But she could do without that whoop.

"SEE HOW EASY conspiracy is to manufacture, Charlie?" Evan bit into his Big Mac while she stuffed a bite of Ronald's Filet-o-fish into her mouth. The van sat in a far corner of a McDonald's parking lot.

The ride had seemed forever. The driver, Toby, remained cheerful even though Mel and Evan teased him endlessly about his lowly gofer status and about all his uncles. He'd dowsed the headlights, but the farther they got from the burning plane, the more the starry night illuminated the landscape around them. And probably them to anyone looking for them.

"How did you manufacture the orange light?" Charlie asked. That had impressed her.

"What orange light? Anybody else see an orange light?"

"Stop making fun of me, Evan."

"I don't know about any orange light. I do think you got a little overexcited."

"Overexcited, hell—she blacked out on us," Mel said.

"I saw an orange light," Charlie insisted.

"She's remembering the plane burning."

"That didn't look orange to me."

"Don't let these jerks get to you." Toby had a lopsided grin and dark curly hair cut short in back and on the sides, but curls tumbled down over his forehead. He sucked the last of his cola through the straw and started up the van.

"Hey, Tobias," Mel said, "what's your uncle Louie going to say about tonight?"

"Why should he even know? He doesn't have anything to do with this."

"You tell him everything, don't you?" Evan did his boisterous guy laugh.

"Is he in for a surprise tonight." Mel joined his boss in the hilarity. "Isn't that right, Charlie?"

"Planes can't just disappear." Charlie didn't know what was going on, but she didn't find the whole thing a bit funny. "They'll have search planes out looking for it when it doesn't come back."

"All records have mysteriously disappeared, right, Toby? And all records of my ownership too. Damnedest thing."

Toby apparently had this friend who worked at the little airstrip in North Vegas.

"Yeah, our gofer here's got friends in high places and too many uncles."

"What I got, Goodall, is contacts. You're just envious."

"Clear as the skies were out there, some airliner will spot that fire and radio it in," Charlie persisted. She'd gotten involved in real trouble here. "You can't walk off and leave a whole plane. They'll find some identifying thing in the ashes, some metal gadget that won't burn. And they'll come after you, Evan. Why burn your own plane? Why not just fly off with it?"

"Because then they'd have had time to scramble and blow us out of the air. This way, they know where the plane is and all trace of any of us better be burned off what's left of it."

"Why are you so hot to involve me in this?"

"I wanted your take, as a conspiracy freak, on Groom Lake.

And I wanted you to be able to tell Mitch Hilsten what you saw firsthand. Simple, right?''

"Wrong, Evan. Serial numbers and things like that don't burn. The original owner at least has got to be on file somewhere."

"What can I say? Life's a gamble, Charlie." But everyone had grown suddenly somber. "All we really need is a little time and some magic will happen—won't it, Toby? And everything, including you, will be safe as grass, Charlie."

The van turned onto a heavily lighted parkway, and for a second a teardrop glinted in a free fall from Caryl's face before it was lost in her dark clothing. She hadn't joined in the teasing and laughter. More tears formed on her lashes, but her voice came more vengeful than sad. "The plane was listed originally in my brother's name. Nobody can go after Pat now."

EIGHT

CHARLE STLL FELT strange as she stepped up to the Hilton's glittering entrance. For once, it wasn't her stomach. The McFood seemed to have settled peacefully. More her head—not an ache exactly. Maybe it was just her anger at how Evan Black thought he could use her. It would take more than magic to get them out of this.

"Holy shit," a man said behind Charlie, and she turned at the door, to see him stepping out of a cab. The inside light and the cab's headlights sat in a sea of night under the immense marquee. All the lights and the razzamatazz at the fountain and the rows of lights under the marquee had gone out.

A bell captain passed her on his way to the luggage the cabbie was unloading. "Talk about blinding night, huh?"

It was spectacular. Charlie had an errant thought: If all the lights went out in Vegas, would it still exist? Like, if a tree falls in the forest and nobody sees it...

Get thee to bed, Charlie G, you're all done.

For once, we agree.

The elevator quit on her a floor below hers, but at least the door had already opened to let her out. None of the elevators seemed to be working up or down, so she took the stairs one flight to her room, flicked on the lights, flicked off her clothes, and stepped into the shower just as the lights went out. She showered by feel and managed to find her nightshirt and the bed by the light of the Vegas night outside the window.

But then she couldn't sleep. It had been one hell of an un-vacation day. And the room was stuffy without the ventilation fan blowing canned air into it.

Finally, Charlie took her frustration to the wall of window and, kneeling on the couch to face it, reassured herself that life was indeed still normal, fully aware of the irony in that. She had no idea which direction Yucca Mountain and Area 51 and the smoldering ruins of a claustrophobic little airplane might be—but she was alive, warm, fed, and well. And she decided she must have imagined the orange light, a vestigial smear of which she imagined still lurked somewhere at the back of her eyeballs. Which didn't mean the United States government was collecting her DNA from a portion of the plane that hadn't burned.

The electricity might be out in her room and parts of the hotel, but the lights of the Strip drowned out the star show that played over Area 51. Closer in, the immense Hilton sign still had juice. It flashed alternate messages across the night—WELCOME AMA and MOST CASH BACK and TWENTY-FOURTH CENTURY IS NOW.

Across the street, BOYZ R US. A block up the street, the spindle of the Stratosphere's Tower was lighted from below and above, the restaurant on top looking like a spaceship with the crazy roller-coaster lights crawling around its top. Below, a string of Metro Police cars, lights flashing, sirens ominously stilled, pulled into the winding drive of the Hilton. You rarely heard emergency sirens here, peculiar for a city this large and busy. Maybe warning sirens would nullify the party ambiance. Had they come for Charlie already?

She waited as long as she could and then crawled back into bed and slept through to noon, like someone on vacation should, the ventilation fan and all the lights on when she woke. And no authority at the door to arrest her. She dressed in front of the TV and Barry and Terry on *Live at Noon*.

Nothing new on the hit-and-run murder of Officer Graden. The man guilty of trying to jaywalk Las Vegas Boulevard had been identified as Patrick Thompson, a local pilot employed by a small "undisclosed local airline." No apology for their having blamed his rash decision to cross a gridlocked street during volcano rush hour on his status as a stupid tourist.

And a mysterious power outage at the Las Vegas Hilton.

"So far, Nevada Power has not identified the cause," Barry told Charlie. "But it affected only certain areas in the hotel and casino—not the entire building."

"Yes, Barry, but people were trapped in elevators, some up to ten minutes. Bets on the casino floor had to be put on hold until emergency generators kicked in, and the probable cause was an apparently successful robbery.

"With the lights out and surveillance cameras temporarily out of commission, clever robbers either took advantage of the outage or planned it to rob the cage at the Las Vegas Hilton's casino. The Hilton has not disclosed how much was taken, but the thieves were gone by the time police arrived. Hotel security is still checking for possible clues, but all guests are assured the building is safe and the casino remains open.

"Sources hint that this was unlike the recent rash of casino-cage robberies by Los Angeles gang members. It appears to have been a far more sophisticated bunch of thieves. Only slight injuries were reported.

"Never fear though—Captain Kirk and Mr. Spock were not affected by the outage."

"Right, they don't operate on electricity. They operate on warp drive or something."

Charlie decided against room service. She wanted to get downstairs, where there would be people. She was in the bathroom doing her face and hair when the TV couple went on to the next story.

This one about a downed aircraft located on the perimeters of the undisclosed Area 51.

"There were no survivors," Terry announced sadly, as well she might.

"Yes, Terry, the plane was incinerated in the crash. Officials are searching local and area-wide airports for clues to the aircraft's point of origin, and they ask anyone missing relatives or friends who might have been flying a Mooney 201 aircraft yesterday to contact local police or the Clark or Lincoln County Sheriff's Department."

"The air force has no comment," Terry added unnecessarily. "And for you UFO buffs, the word from Rachel is that there were no disturbing incidents in the night sky out that way last night."

"Terry, this only goes to reinforce the warnings this station, editorials in the *Las Vegas Sun,* and law-enforcement officials in Lincoln and Clark counties have been repeating for some months now—the ridiculous interest in the vast restricted areas and wastelands in this state can be dangerous, unfruitful, and deadly.''

"Right, if you want to have fun, come to Vegas instead.''

Charlie had no more than switched off the set than came a pounding at her door.

Jesus.

"Housekeeping?'' a frightened voice queried from the hall.

The peephole revealed an Asian woman. Charlie was somehow not surprised when two robust gentlemen in suits entered the room with the housekeeper. Hell, she'd opened that same door to Super Tami, hadn't she?

Totally polite and humorless, one, in the interests of the protection of all hotel guests, asked permission and explained the need for a search of her room—possibility of robbers in the hotel. He went on to question her activities the night before. She lied. Instead of fleeing a burning Mooney 201 somewhere near an undisclosed Area 51, she'd been playing blackjack at every casino on the Strip.

Meanwhile, the other totally polite and humorless suit—public security folks here wore dark blue policelike uniforms—looked for robbers in her drawers, empty luggage, behind the couch, in the shower, in the closet, and had absolutely no trouble with the combination of the small safe where she kept her notebook computer.

Having determined that neither robbers nor their proceeds lurked in Charlie's room, they solemnly rechecked her identification and went off to secure other areas. She left the Asian housekeeper to do her job and sought sustenance downstairs.

The coffee shop, awash in dangerously aging waitresses, fake red flowers on fake vines hanging from fake-wood rafters, fake trees planted in fake stucco Southwestern adobe-theme planters, was uncrowded for this time of day, and Charlie sat facing the room. Having been here often enough to know the food wasn't even pseudo-Santa Fe, she ordered an omelette and studied those souls on her side of the fake stucco planters who would brave a hotel with electric and robber problems.

No thugs in sight, no commando types from her government—just Bradone McKinley and Richard Morse across the room, in a booth for two, facing each other over the table, coffee cups to lips and postures suggesting her boss had scored.

No way. Charlie was imagining again, like the orange light she and apparently the denizens of Rachel, Nevada, hadn't seen.

Charlie gulped at her own coffee and tried to blink smears from her contact lenses. She'd have thought Richard would have lost interest after the yak crud, and why would Bradone dine here, with her own cook and butler upstairs?

You haven't checked for messages at the desk or E-mail from Libby or the office.

"Well, I have to eat, you know."

"I know, sweetie, and here's your omelette." Her server was considerably older than Edwina, Charlie's mother.

"Thanks, uh…this looks wonderful." Charlie determined to open a retirement account the minute she got home, and added sheepishly, "I talk to myself."

"Don't we all, sweetie?" The elderly server walked off on ankles swollen to the knee. Her name badge identified her as Ardith.

Ardith shouldn't have to be working now.

Yeah, she could be starving instead.

Big tip, right?

The omelette wasn't anything you'd order wine with, but it was smooth and bland and comforting.

"You eat too many eggs, kid." Richard stood over her, Bradone, with that sort of smile, behind him.

"I know." And I had McDonald's last night. What could this impressive woman see in Charlie's boss? "Did you hear about the robbery?"

"Yeah, we missed all the excitement, didn't even notice the lights went out. So how did the lunch with our boy Evan go yesterday?"

A lot better than a little airplane ride later. So, they *had been* together last night. Life was becoming one big mystery. "We need to discuss Evan Black, Richard, and his new project. He's getting himself and me into some trouble."

"We'll be on the pool deck. Check the office messages and come on out when you're done."

CHARLIE'S E-MAIL had some personal messages as well as news from the office. And the message light on her telephone was blinking. Would there never be time for blackjack on this trip?

The voice mail was from her mother. Funny, Edwina Greene had a computer, but she never E-mailed Charlie. The last thing Charlie wanted was to answer it, but the last time she'd ignored her mother's needs, she hadn't discovered the woman had cancer until Edwina'd gone into the hospital and a neighbor called to inform Charlie of the pending mastectomy.

All in all, Charlie thought she carried her burden of guilt pretty well for the unwed mother of a terrifying teen. She didn't ever expect to get hardened to it, mind you, but she'd managed to make a place for herself and her daughter in this world. Talking to her mother, however, always diminished any pride she might have built up in her triumphs.

Stop whining and call your mother.

Charlie's mom lived in Boulder, where she worked as a professor of biology—rats and bats—at the University of Colorado. Where Charlie was born and her daughter conceived on the wrong side of a tombstone. Charlie's greatest nightmare was that Edwina would move to Long Beach and the world would ask three generations of totally incompatible women to live in the same state.

Charlie loved her mother—she just couldn't stand her.

"Well, it took you long enough." It was as if Edwina had been sitting on top of the phone.

I've been busy, like, you know, dead people, crazy clients, midlist authors on a toot. "So what's the problem now?"

"'So what's the problem now?'" her mother mimicked, and Charlie took a pillow off the bed to kick. "I'm the problem in this family, right?"

"Edwina? I'm listening. But only through the next three words."

Whoa, is that power talk?

Charlie couldn't believe she'd said it either.

"Three words. Never..." and Charlie's mother hung up.

I'm going to kill that woman.

You are not, she merely followed your orders. You do not order your mother.

Charlie punched her mother's number, determined not to begin the conversation with an apology. "I'm sorry. What's wrong?"

"I don't know. How many words do I get?"

NINE

"LARRY SAYS Pitman's has given Reynelda another deadline extension, but this is it, and the book clubs are pissed because their schedules are shot to hell too," Charlie told Richard Morse, who was splayed contentedly on the lounge chair next to that of the lovely Bradone. Bradone, a tad thick in the thigh, could be hiding some corrective-surgery scars under her one-piece, but the woman was firm and shapely for any age. Her houseboy probably doubled as a personal trainer.

Richard sagged some about a middle that had been lipoed at least once that Charlie knew, thanks to documented office gossip. But he looked pretty good compared to gray chest hair nearby. Didn't even bother to hide his hickey.

Richard roused himself enough to ask Charlie, "What's your mother say? She knows this Goff woman better than anybody."

Charlie's mother had claimed on the phone to be on the verge of suicide because of hot flashes now that she couldn't have hormone-replacement therapy. Charlie had told her to sit in front of a fan in her office and to air-condition the house.

Edwina had hung up again. Charlie dialed again. Apologized again. Jeesh—you'd think hot flashes were fatal.

"My mother says Reynelda Goff is suffering from menopausal symptoms and has these panic attacks that—"

"Jesus Christ in a chorus line, is nothing safe from old women in menopause?" Richard sat up and whipped off his sunglasses. "Well, I mean, most broads don't make such a big deal of all that shit," he added weakly when he noticed Bradone had whipped off her sunglasses too.

"'Broads'? I haven't heard that anachronism in years. You do mean shit like breast cancer," Bradone McKinley said, far too politely. "If she can't take hormones—"

"No, it's my mom who had the breast cancer and can't take

hormones," Charlie said, coming to her boss's defense. She *must* love her job. "Reynelda's a neighbor of Edwina's who—"

"Who wrote a book and got menopause," Richard chimed in, but then he added disastrously, "Why can't beautiful, young, sane women write books?"

"I expect they do." There was something reassuring in Bradone's smirk and the possibility that the planets had not stood still for her because Richard Morse scored.

Poor Richard, so insulated by his power status in the positioning of the genders in the Hollywood universe, didn't hear what he really said. He'd even get torqued when Charlie refused to appreciate insulting jokes. And yet he could be so savvy in other ways. Didn't add up.

You're the one who told her mother to sit in front of a fan.

"Ruby is about to implode if you or I don't answer her messages, Richard. And I don't know how to answer them."

Richard decided Charlie could tell him what Ruby Dillon wanted and he could give Charlie the answer and she could tell his office manager. All because Charlie knew how to E-mail.

"I'm not your secretary." But she jotted down a few notes to pass on to Ruby as he tried to impress his new girlfriend with sage answers to mundane office matters.

That was another thing. If you didn't learn the new technology, you'd fall behind at Congdon and Morse. If you did, someone above you in the food chain would use you and these skills to make his more important work easier. Charlie had other serious misgivings with these timesaving electronic devices that ate up all your time to learn and, when you finally did, forced you to upgrade to something new and the "learning" started all over. Libby'd had to help her out more than once. But Libby learned computer-ease at school, far earlier in life than Charlie. Larry, Charlie's assistant, treated it with contempt and deigned only to use E-mail, the word processor, and a spreadsheet to log Charlie's schedule, phone calls, and the script submissions that crowded his cubicle.

No message from Libby today. Libby hadn't contacted Edwina either. Charlie could only hope and swallow a lot. She hoped Libby would contact their neighbor Maggie Stutzman if anything earthshaking occurred. Both Maggie and Libby had instructed Charlie to take a vacation and not call them. They'd call her.

"What about our boy in Folsom?" Richard asked importantly and informed Bradone, "Keegan Monroe, screenwriter, inked *Phantom of the Alpine Tunnel, Shadowscapes,* and *Zoo Keepers.*"

Edwina was threatening to go off tamoxifen—a drug prescribed to block natural estrogen production in her body—because the unnatural estrogen prescribed to head off hot flashes, panic attacks, heart disease, osteoporosis, and old age had given her breast cancer.

Everything Charlie'd read said that synthetic estrogen did not cause breast cancer.

"Actually, Keegan's on chapter ten of his novel," Charlie answered. Which is further than he'd ever gotten before.

"Christ, with all the time he's got on his hands, he could of written three *Moby Dicks.* Tell him to finish the damn book and get back to screenplays that make money."

Edwina, who smoked, had said, "Well, tobacco companies used to say cigarettes don't cause cancer too." She'd sent Charlie a folded insert that had come in the box containing an old Premarin bottle. It listed, in minuscule print, breast cancer as a possible side effect.

Now Edwina had found a new wonder drug on her own. Something she called "snake oil."

"Snakes don't make oil, right?" Charlie asked, interrupting whatever it was Richard was saying.

"No, dinosaurs do." He hated being interrupted. "Snake oil—where the hell did that come from?"

"Edwina called. She wants to go off the tamoxifen and rub this stuff on her skin instead."

"Rub snake oil on—your mother's always been a few bricks short of a bale, but—"

"*Snake oil* is a term used historically to mean a magic elixir, a medicine or concoction that can cure all your ailments at once," Bradone explained. "Hucksters used to sell it at fairs and outdoor markets. They probably still do, but by mail-order catalog. It often contained a good dose of alcohol or a potent drug like cocaine.''

''Not even somebody with menopause should rub good hooch on their outsides,'' the president of Congdon and Morse said with weary disgust.

''She mentioned something about yams too.''

''She's going to rub herself with sweet potatoes?'' Richard was on his feet. ''I'm going to the gents.''

''Where did he learn to speak like that? Old movies?'' The astrologer watched Charlie's boss strut off and almost laughed.

''Thanks for not jumping on the 'few bricks short of a bale' thing. That was a trap. He mixes metaphor, analogy, and worn-out sayings on purpose. But when he wants to, he can be sort of intelligent.''

The astrologer turned her amused attention to Charlie. ''I expect your mother was talking about wild-yam cream. The wild Mexican yam root contains natural progesterone and helps to adjust hormone levels at all ages and for both sexes, but I've known women who have been on it for months with no results. It depends on who's making it and how reliably it's standardized.''

Because of the aging of the baby boomers, this was the latest snake oil, according to Bradone, and everybody wanted in on the profits.

''Why can't the drug companies make and standardize the cream in their labs? The FDA could test it.''

''Because drug companies can't patent natural products. It wouldn't pay them to make and test a drug anybody who wanted to could make. Charlie, I think your mother should think long and hard before disobeying her oncologist. Cancer's not to be toyed with. We don't know that natural hormones react that much differently from synthetic hormones.''

Forget the IRA and the DRIP and the compounding. Charlie decided to die before ever reaching the age of the dreaded menopause. She wouldn't want people like Richard talking about her that way.

''Are we done with the sweet potatoes, ladies?'' Richard asked with severe condescension upon his return. ''Any more agency business I should take care of?" He picked up his towel and glasses case. A signal for Charlie to say there was no more business for today.

Actually, the sweet potatoes thing wasn't the worst. Mitch Hilsten threatened to come to Vegas if she didn't answer his E-mail. "Evan Black and his project, remember? I'm in trouble, and so is he."

"Oh, you're always in trouble. Relax, kid. Catch me later. Got to go now." He reached a proprietary hand down to Bradone, who took it to rise from her lounge chair.

"I'll see you later too, Charlie. I have this delicious secret to share with you." When he'd turned away to the Grecian Spa, she mouthed, "About Richard."

Charlie looked at the pool, where two kids had cleared out the adults with power cannonball dives. Thanks a lot, Captain Kirk. Where were these security types when you needed them?

She hurried to her room and changed into comfortable clothes instead of answering the office business or checking for more E-mail. To hell with Richard, and Evan Black too. Life was short and unpredictable and she'd never felt more aware of that. She wanted to be like Bradone, who knew how to live life to the hilt.

Charlie, catching herself grimacing at the mirrored elevator on her way down, forced her mouth to grin, and took a shuttle to the blackjack tables on Fremont Street. She had thirty grand to lose, since she wouldn't live to see menopause and Libby wouldn't make it to college with her braces off.

COMPARED TO the ever-raging extravagance of the Strip, Fremont Street had gone seedy and become a refuge for locals. Like organized crime of old, organized corporate America had a finger in most pots, and entertainment in all forms was particularly vulnerable to its ready cash. Gambling was a uniquely profitable form of entertainment, and someone up there had looked down on Fremont and seen a bargain.

The street was now a covered mall, hostile to panhandlers and overt lewdity, its dome a state-of-the-art laser show at night, with enough music and panoramic extravaganza to make your neck ache. The spectacle emptied casinos and shops so locals and jaded people like Charlie could slip in and find single-deck blackjack with few other players and not too many nasty rules. But it was daylight and the casinos were crowded.

Mitch Hilsten threatening to come to town. No word on what Libby and her new boyfriend were up to. Whatever they did, they probably couldn't do it in the house. Tuxedo didn't like him. For once, that damned cat showed some sense.

Determined to lose money, probably the easiest thing to do in Vegas, Charlie couldn't.

Blackjack was the one game where you could supposedly beat the house advantage by paying strict attention. She couldn't remember lunch, never mind the cards.

Dumb Richard having his way with savvy Bradone. Wild sweet potatoes, for godsake. Probably the CIA and the FBI and the IRS, and the armed response boys—they all had to be in cahoots—were looking for Charlie because she flew over Area 51. With all this, nobody could have concentrated. And still she won.

"Lady, you need a drink or a massage, know that? Here you are winning and yet you are not happy," said a man beside her. "What'll it be?"

What would Bradone do in this situation? Lighten up, she could almost hear her new friend say, go with the flow.

"Red zin," Charlie answered the man, and watched the dealer push more chips her way. The only thing Charlie hadn't been worrying about was the Thug.

This occurred to her suddenly because the man beside her, at the moment explaining very meaningfully to the cocktail hostess that yes, there was too such a thing as red zinfandel and she'd best get a glass of it here in a hurry, was the Thug.

TEN

WHEN IT CAME, the red zin tasted exactly like the ubiquitous house burgundy, sort of like your well wine. Charlie didn't mention the wine problem to the man who'd nudged poor Patrick Thompson under the wheels of a car. Charlie wondered if that car was a black limo like the one that took out Officer Timothy Graden. Or maybe the same one. How many cars had run over the hunk pilot before Charlie made it to the curb to view the result? How could the people in that first car have missed seeing the act in progress? Or were they looking over their shoulders at the volcano?

No, Charlie didn't think she'd complain about the wine.

Still, she kept winning. Maybe it's better not to concentrate—which she certainly wasn't. And every time she looked up, some people at the bar waved in her direction. Charlie wanted to cash in and get out of the Golden Nugget. She'd have been happy to give it all back to be able to leave for free.

The Golden Nugget, unlike most casinos, did not rely heavily on the color red. Colors here were a soothing plantation white—read cream—with gold trim. Latticework and mirrors. Taupe upholstery. If not for the presence of the Thug, Charlie would have felt comfortable here, would have calmed down, enjoyed herself. And if not for the strange people over at Claude's Bar who continued their unnatural interest in her. An overweight man and two women of girth.

"What you've got to understand, Mrs. Greene," the Thug said kindly, "is that the odds are against us all."

Mrs. Greene. Did that mean he knew about Libby? After the battering motherhood had taken—people still thought of mothers as "Mrs." Charlie took a slug of the official wine of the non-astute. Now it tasted like ashes.

The expanse of his shoulders would make more than two of Charlie's. His suit was gray, his manner overpolite. His dark hair, streaked with gray, hung in curls to those shoulders. Something mesmerizing about the thick lips and uneven teeth. Charlie wondered what Evan Black would think of her conspiracy theory now.

"But here you are, Mrs. Greene, beating the odds. And not enjoying a minute of it. It's obvious, right?" he asked the dealer, who remained noncommittal and nodded at the two cards dealt Charlie. The dealer showed ten.

Charlie waved away a hit without bothering to look at what she had. The three other players scratched for a hit.

All went bust.

Mr. Thug took Charlie's cards and laid them out. The ace and the jack of spades. Charlie smelled a setup.

She would have to talk to Bradone about how to lose. If she lived long enough to make that necessary.

"Excuse me, ma'am?" The overweight gentleman waver appeared suddenly at her side. He wore Bermuda shorts. Yes, they were plaid. Yes, he wore bifocals and a baseball hat and a grin to tear a face apart. "I hope you're not offended, but we"—and he motioned to the two well-stocked women grinning at her from stools at the bar—"wondered if you're that girlfriend of Mitch Hilsten or just a look-alike? I mean, we already seen four Elvises in two days."

Charlie tried to decide whether the setup was Bermuda Shorts or the Thug. Or the dealer dealing her such treasure. Somehow, Bermuda Shorts didn't seem a likely tie to the other two.

"It don't matter. I'm Ben Hanley, and they're my wife and her sister. We'd like to buy you a drink anyway. When you finish your game. We been watching you and wondering. And finally Betty figured out where we seen you before. On television. You know, when you and him fell off that cliff? Mitch Hilsten, I mean."

"How nice. I'd love to join you and the ladies," Charlie gushed, and turned, to find the curly-haired thug no longer at her side.

THE BEN HANLEYS and her sister not only bought Charlie a drink but accompanied her to Binions and the Las Vegas Club, helping her lose some of her winnings from the Nugget. She didn't see Mr. Thug again that afternoon, but he could have set a stranger on her tail. And there were still all those government types getting ready to pounce.

The type of people Charlie would usually avoid, Ben, Martha, and Betty, the sister, were reasonably good company for shields. They may have saved her life or her kneecaps, and she hoped she wasn't putting theirs in danger.

She took them back to the Hilton and treated them to dinner at the Baronshire. Betty and Martha, motherly types, soon had Charlie talking about her life and her relationship with Mitch Hilsten.

Charlie didn't want to be alone—even in the crowd that was Las Vegas. These people, unintimidated by the dark room and the formality suggested by the decor, were flying back to Wisconsin tomorrow and she'd never see them again.

"Mitch and I are just friends. We don't travel in the same circles—I mean, he's a superstar and I'm a literary agent," Charlie explained.

"That sure wasn't what it looked like on the TV," Betty said, emboldened by martinis. Everybody seemed to be drinking martinis these days. Both sisters did, but Ben stuck with beer. He ate as if there were no tomorrow and all the alcohol had made him quiet and flushed. He looked like a heart attack waiting to happen.

Both sisters wore round trifocals that covered half their faces and made their eyes appear larger than their noses. If Betty's hair hadn't been died flat black and Martha's allowed to stay almost white, they could have been hard to tell apart at a distance.

"Well, okay, we spent one night together in a seedy motel"—Charlie's unwanted fifteen minutes of fame—"but it was—"

"Just one of those things?" Martha lifted a dripping blood-drenched bite of prime rib to her mouth and chewed it a little so she could talk around it. "On TV, he looked exhausted, as I remember."

Charlie had met Mitch Hilsten in the Canyonlands of Utah at the wrong time of the month. Poor guy had been a teenage fantasy of hers and didn't stand a chance. But he took their encounter seriously, couldn't seem to understand Charlie's hormonal cycles—which her biologist mother inelegantly termed "estrus."

"Well yeah, they both did." Ben Hanley came to Charlie's defense. "Hell, they'd just been rescued from death on a cliff."

It had been over a year ago. Charlie's writers would have killed for that kind of exposure. Hell, she could have been on *Oprah.* Charlie just wanted to live it down.

She respected and admired the superstar, but, accustomed to years of celibacy at a time, she frankly preferred that blessed state. Life held enough complication. Every now and then, those one or two dangerous days of the month would come along in conjunction with opportunity and a man of easy virtue.

Raising a daughter had always been her excuse to avoid entanglements. What would she do when Libby left home? Much as Charlie longed for that day and some peace at last, she feared it.

She'd even started tracking those one or two days a month on the calendar and, when possible, arranging her schedule so they wouldn't interfere with her emotional independence. If she believed in astrology, she'd have asked Bradone which of the planets to consult.

But she couldn't begin to explain all this to three grandparents from Wisconsin. So she studied the pictures of grandchildren, complete with dogs and ponies and flaxen hair. She exclaimed over their beauty, hoping Libby wasn't out this night making Charlie a grandmother at thirty-three.

These people were so comfortable and safe, she let them a short way into her family. Even admitted to her unmarried state and seventeen-year-old daughter. They clucked and sympathized. "But look what a success you've made of your predicament," Betty said.

Charlie wondered how they would regard her when they got home and the bloody prime rib and buttery lobster, the martinis and the wine, and the sinful glitter of Las Vegas had worn off.

She even blurted out her problems with Edwina and the

dreaded hot flashes. Probably because Charlie's response about the fan kept her guilt close to the front of her thoughts.

"Well, stop right there," Martha said. "Because my sister's got the cure for that. Show her, Betty."

Both women carried purses the size of carry-on luggage. Betty proceeded to fish around in hers and bring out a small white jar. Charlie, who'd imbibed more than enough fat and alcohol herself, was about to make a smart remark about sweet potatoes when a smeared contact lens cleared enough for her to make out the words *wild yam* on the label.

Seems the widowed Betty supplemented her Social Security and what remained of her husband's pension by selling the snake oil to hormonally challenged folks in a three-county area.

"She's everyone's dealer," Martha said proudly. "Everyone I know."

"Supplier," Betty corrected, and went on to assure Charlie that the Mexican wild-yam root also cured migraines and PMS, as well as high blood pressure and depression, memory loss, bloating, lack of interest in sex, and weight gain, because all were caused by hormonal imbalance.

When Charlie finally bid them good-bye at the ticket booth for the Hilton's stage show, she felt coddled and mellow, sort of removed from that persistent threat that Mr. Thug or armed guys from Groom Lake lurked around every corner. She decided to laze in the kingsize with TV until she fell asleep.

But when she opened her door, the message light blinked on the telephone. She was tempted to ignore it. But what if Libby needed her?

An urgent message from Richard. She fought the temptation to ignore that too and punched his room number.

"Jesus, been trying to reach you all afternoon. Big party at Evan Black's. Impromptu screening. He wants you should wear some skirt with a slit up the side. Said you'd know which one. Bradone's invited too. You got ten minutes to get beautiful, babe. Gonna be footage of undisclosed areas to knock your eyes out."

ELEVEN

EVAN'S HOME was your regular Southern California expatriate stucco and marble—vast in design, limited in imagination. Brand-new, with peeling paint and expensive tile applied with south-of-the border labor, slipping and chipping. Even in home building for the rich, Las Vegas knew how to take the customer.

Half the full-grown desert palms were dead or dying, propped up with two-by-fours. All had come from California tree farms. They were often planted by helicopter.

Charlie had one in Long Beach that would put any of the live ones on Evan's property to shame. But then, the whole first floor of her condo would fit nicely into his foyer.

Bradone wore a long, low-cut cream-colored creation set off by an allover tan, gold chains, and amused blue eyes with color-matching shadow. Richard glowed in proud accompaniment.

Evan Black, obviously taken by her too, tore himself away to tug Charlie into a pantry with a dumbwaiter and announce, "Hilsten's interested in the project. Thank you, thank you."

The producer/writer/director picked up Charlie and her split skirt, whirling around with them at arm's length like a postal employee with an assault rifle, and managed to tip over a tray of crystal too leaded to break. The sound was impressive though.

"Anything you want, just tell me, Charlie love. It's yours." He was actually wearing a suit, black, of course, and without collar or lapels, but the closest to one she'd ever seen him in. The purple shirt sort of demolished the effect.

"You talked to Mitch?" How was it, when Charlie *did* do something, nobody noticed?

"To his agent and his agent talked to him."

"Evan, put me down. Now."

"Charlie, with Hilsten on board, we've got Ursa Major tied up. I just know it."

"Then why are you thanking me?" But she knew the superstar. "You used my name."

"All I said to his agent was that you were *my* agent. Anything wrong with that?" Evan Black had stopped whirling Charlie, now he hugged her. He had a black belt in something or other and a lot more strength than necessary. "Oh Charlie, the sky's the limit. I owe you one, doll. When you decide what it is, just ask."

"I'm asking—I don't want you getting me in any more trouble like that flight yesterday and Mitch Hilsten in none."

"Babe"—he chucked her under the chin—"you're not in any trouble. Dr. Evan's magic is going to fix everything."

Dr. Evan swept back to his guests, leaving her to face the not-so-dumb waiter who had to pick up all the crystal.

THE SCREENING ROOM had couches and love seats, and recliners that vibrated, instead of theater seats. It had floor cushions, a small screen and a huge screen and a medium-sized one, all movable like stage props. It had two bartenders and small movable tables with round marble tops to hold food and beverages.

The screens moved on wheeled mechanisms—a few of which needed oiling. No buffet hors d'oeuvres here. Caterers in faux tuxes—ultrashiny and ill-fitting—maneuvered among the seated and the sprawled with trays of delights that made Charlie's overworked system shudder. She grabbed a recliner so she could be alone and accepted a glass of lemon springwater and two crackers to nibble slowly so the wandering servers would leave her alone.

Soon surrounded by people on floor cushions, she felt like a fat Cleopatra on a barge only slightly above the plebeian waves.

"So, uh, you want this thing to vibrate?" A large hand with manicured nails rested on the left arm of her recliner, the index finger poised above one of the buttons on its tiny console. Charlie didn't want to contemplate what else this chair could do.

"No," and she grabbed the hand with the impending first finger, only to have it flip over to hold hers. Charlie looked into the patient eyes of Mr. Thug.

He used his other hand to press the button and the chair began to gently quake.

"Why are you following me?" You think I saw you help shove Patrick Thompson under a car. You know I described you and your bald buddy to Officer Graden, the bicycle cop. Now that he's dead, I'm to be next, huh?

"You see too many movies." He gave her hand a forceful squeeze and let go of it to lean against the recliner and watch as their host stepped to the front of the room.

Evan grinned, rolled his shoulders up and back repeatedly as if warming up for a workout, his swarthy skin so smooth, it looked greased, his voice pure Teflon. "You"—and his gesture swept them all in—"I am so amazed you could come on such short notice, and so grateful. Me"—and he hugged his shoulders—"I'm so excited about my new project, I couldn't wait to let a few of my closest friends in on it. I'm like a damn kid at Christmas. You know?"

Charlie hadn't noticed any talent in the room, but there must be money. This warm-up act smelled of sales pitch.

"What you are about to see is uncut, unedited, raw. It's the germ of my next creation. It's not even thought out yet. Right now, it is without sound, music, concept. All I've got, my friends, is theme. And a damn good agent."

Whereupon he gestured directly, unmistakably at Charlie. Whereupon everyone swiveled to stare at her as she tried to sink out of sight in her quaking recliner. All agents want to be famous—off-camera, offscreen, off-line. In *Variety,* in *Publishers Weekly.* But not in person.

"Mitch Hilsten is even now on his way here to see what you are about to see first. I think he'll like it. And if he does, he will have the lead in what will come of this germ. I ask you to keep in mind one thing only, a word. That word is"—and he paused as the lights dimmed and sky and cloud filled the midsized screen—*"conspiracy."*

"You never told me Hilsten was coming here," her boss rasped in an attempt at a whisper. Yucca Mountain from God's viewpoint appeared at an angle on the screen. A clearly defined, ragged shadow ditch Charlie didn't remember seeing when she flew over it emanated from either side and extended to the horizons. But she'd had her eyes closed a lot.

"Phony fault line," the man at her side complained. "There's no quake activity out there. Damned enviros screw everything around to suit their prejudices."

After several dead frames, the shadow of a small aircraft scudded over rocks and gullies and sagebrush and scratchy-looking bushes, mean sand, and scoured rock.

Richard had crawled through the bodies to her barge. He snarled back at the shushes rising around him, not that there was any sound from the film to be masked. "You gotta stop pissing me off, kid."

"I didn't know, Richard. Remember, you didn't have time to discuss Evan and his project this afternoon at the pool." And somebody with more clout than Charlie Greene should have advised Congdon and Morse's hot new client that this kind of advance, "not even thought out yet" screening was a big mistake. Like her writers killing a story by talking it to death before writing it. But that wasn't what was important right now. "I told you there was trouble."

She stressed the last word of that sentence and tried to gesture with her eyes toward the gray-tinged curls beside her chair.

Either Richard Morse, a man with incessant nervous tics, trembled with anger or her quaking chair caused her to move, which made it seem as if *he* moved. "I got news for you, Greene—"

Charlie never heard the news, because she looked past him to the screen to see a live Patrick Thompson in the pilot's seat of a small, cramped aircraft. The cameraperson sat in a rear seat and the hunk turned with a gorgeous smile, his eyes electric with excitement. She hadn't seen how truly hunky he was when he had exchanged threats with someone at McCarran International on his cell phone. He hadn't been happy and excited then. He hadn't when walking, dazed, out of Loopy Louie's either. Charlie hugged herself so hard, it hurt her elbows, trying to not remember the thing he had become in the gutter.

The next shot showed Charlie in a rear seat, throwing up her Yolie's lunch into a plastic bag.

Richard still whispered from the floor in front of her, but the low voice to the side of her chair cut through her haze of fear, revulsion, and indigestion.

"There any trouble in this town you don't have a piece of, lady?" The Thug rubbed the deep cleft in his chin with his left hand. He wore a turquoise ring similar to that of the floorman at the Hilton.

Why would Evan invite you here? "I came here for a vacation. I just want to play blackjack."

The plane's shadow crawled up and over a low sullen mountain range and dove down the other side.

"And Lazarus keeps hinting you're going to jump ship for ICM. I'll sue your socks off, Greene," her boss threatened, unaware she hadn't been listening. Lazarus Trillion was Mitch Hilsten's agent. "He's also worried Hilsten will switch to you if you do. Then I'll sue more than socks."

"Richard, I don't know what you're talking about—but this guy right here is the one who—" Now, wouldn't you know, her boss wasn't listening to her. He'd turned when everybody else gasped and "whoa"ed and someone even swore at the sight of runways many times wider and longer than those at Denver International Airport. At immense shedlike buildings and a row of unmarked 737s parked at the edge of a runway near huge hangars. A series of rapid-play still shots showed full-sized buses with blackened windows moving in odd jerking paths toward the jets, some already unloading passengers, others driving off presumably empty. All seen through a faint orange haze.

Amid a few jeers of "Area Fifty-one" and "Dreamland," delivered with a mixture of amusement and discomfort from the assembled, Richard said, "Listen, I want to know the minute Hilsten hits town. I mean it. And I'm through with this. Call a taxi, we gotta leave early."

"Where are you going? You can't leave me here."

"Bradone's got a date with the high rollers. Baccarat. I want to watch—what's your problem?"

"Richard, this man wants to kill me—you've got to listen."

"What man?"

Charlie, still seeing orange, could see through it well enough to determine that the floor beside her chair was empty of thugs.

TWELVE

RICHARD MORSE, Bradone McKinley, and Charlie's murderous thug missed the highlight of Evan Black's screening—the casino robbery at the Las Vegas Hilton.

"And now, ladies and gentlemen, for your eyes only, the proof of the pudding," he said, introducing it with relish.

If the audience had been disturbed but dubious earlier, it turned downright hostile now. Yet no one got up and left. No outright jeering, but you could feel the exasperation in the air, hear the grunts of disgust as an infrared camera showed the Hilton's casino in varying shades of sickly luminescent green. It quite clearly caught three figures in identical dark clothing, gloves, and full head masks threading their way through the confusion of people caught in a crowd in total darkness.

These figures wore goggles and could obviously see where no one else could. One mugged for the camera by blowing out a cigarette lighter every time a guy in a Stetson tried to light it. He gestured with what appeared to be a stick, maybe a yard long, but didn't offer to hit anyone with it, more as if to make a point of the thing for the camera.

There had to be four people in the gang. One on the camera, which bobbed between the two making their way into the cage, and the guy snuffing out matches and lighters close by. When a guard with a flashlight searching out possible trouble in front of him began to turn his light back toward the cage, the light-snuffer shoved a disoriented tourist into him. She probably weighed in at over three hundred pounds. She and the guard went down while the light-snuffer took advantage of the guard's guard going down as well to grab the flashlight.

There were other flashlights approaching by now, but the two robbers raced out of the cage with bulging bags and leapt over the downed guard and his heavy oppressor. Charlie knew the casino at the Hilton well enough to detect the fact that the four fleeing robbers did not head toward the hotel's front door. They raced back toward the sport's book area and a back door she'd used today to catch a shuttle to Fremont Street.

This whole robbery and even the clowning for the camera had taken place faster than the time it would take to describe it. The cameraman turned for a shot of security guards armed with flashlights spilling out of a side door Charlie recognized as leading to the restricted area with its warren of security rooms.

It was then that the light-snuffer revealed the purpose of the mysterious stick. With the camera, and presumably the cage robbers behind him, he waved it like a wand across the phalanx of uniformed guards. They stopped. In midstride.

"Oh, come on, Black, not even the government's got that kind of weapon."

"Yeah, man, you faked those shots. We know you."

"Fancy laser, must be a phaser," added someone who felt good enough to joke. "Beam me up, Scotty."

This was a strange crowd for a money party. It had to be three-quarters male. Very few trophy blondes. And half the guys talked like her boss. Even stranger, the less delighted these people seemed with Evan's offering, the more delighted he appeared to be with them.

The wand and the camera panned around to the casino, where the guy in the Stetson stood with his cigarette lighter raised and eyes unblinking. The only moving thing in that confused crowd was the heavy woman who'd landed on the first casino guard. She moved, but as if she was clawing her way through Jell-O.

"Payoff time, cash only," Evan said mysteriously from the back of the screening room when the film suddenly cut to the desert, a burning Mooney 201, and color. Charlie lay spread out on the abrasive sand, shadows of the leaping flames dancing on and around her. A scratchy bush that sat above her head like a tombstone whipped in the wind.

Even to Charlie, she looked dead.

"VULNERABLE, not dead," Evan Black insisted after everyone had left. His eyes burned with triumph. He must be on something. This whole screening did not make sense and certainly wasn't a triumph. He hadn't proved he could make a successful project from what he'd shown. He'd proved that he could break the law and fly over restricted government property and that he could rob the Hilton. Why would he reveal the burning Mooney if he'd burned it to get rid of evidence?

"The footage of you is to further entice Mitch Hilsten."

"When's he getting here?"

"Saturday, I hope. His plane from Nairobi was delayed due to nascent rebellion among the downtrodden with access to explosives."

"Mitch is in Nairobi?"

"You didn't even know where he was? He knew you were here." Evan was down to his purple shirt now, sitting on the floor, where servers and barmen picked up plates and glasses while pretending he and Charlie weren't there. He and Charlie pretended the same back.

"I got an E-mail yesterday. Guess I didn't check all the address and routing crap ahead and after it." Damn stuff took up more room on the screen than the message.

Her client's barely contained elation had to mean he was under the mistaken impression his had been a successful screening. Talent is hard to fathom. The more successful, the more deluded they can become, denying the haunting fear they can't do it again. This time, someone will figure out they're faking. They're not sure how they accomplished the success they've become addicted to and fear losing it.

Personally, Charlie was convinced success in the entertainment business had mostly to do with being at the right place at the right time with the right idea. Plus business acumen. Plus a lot of sheer dumb luck. Talent is not that uncommon and few are chosen. When it happens, though, you really need a damn good agent.

This agent thought Congdon and Morse's hot new client was losing it. Or was it just that she was too tired, hadn't really gotten a start on her vacation yet?

"Some of the footage came from satellite, some we swiped off the Net, and a lot of it we'd taken on previous trips. You haven't even seen most of it—the ground stuff. You haven't seen the best yet."

"Why wouldn't you show the best to backers?"

"Backers...oh, yeah." He slipped out of his shoes and socks, reached for his toes and lifted them and what followed toward the ceiling, and held the balancing act on his tailbone. "You know the best part about this backing, Charlie? No interest, no taxes, no payback."

"There's no such thing as free money."

"Charlie love, trust me."

"Trust you? This screening involved you, and me by association, in a casino robbery and an illegal flight over Groom Lake. Evan, I have a kid, I don't appreciate your exposing me that way. The mob may not run Vegas anymore, but the corporate-military complex is an incredibly lethal instrument."

"'Corporate-military complex.' You are such a living, breathing example of my conspiracy theme, you're wonderful." He lowered his legs to pretzel them into a lotus position and did some more deep breathing.

Charlie'd tried that lotus thing once and gotten a cramp in her leg. Her daughter and best friend, Maggie, practically had to sedate her to straighten her out. They were almost crippled themselves with laughter.

By the time he was standing on his head, she bent over almost to the floor to assure Evan Black, "I'm not leaving until you tell me about Mr. Thug. And I don't want to hear any magic shit either."

CHARLIE RODE BACK to the Hilton with Toby, the second-unit gofer, fuming about Evan's denial of any knowledge of the curly-haired goon. "We didn't check names at the door," he'd said. "Anybody could have come in. People brought friends, you know. It was a party."

When she'd insisted the man was one of the two who had walked his pilot, Pat, to the curb and shoved him under traffic on Las Vegas Boulevard, her client insisted that since he hadn't seen any of it happen, he wouldn't have recognized him tonight.

They were on the Maryland Parkway and Charlie looked up

at the lighted billboard with Barry and Terry through that orange smear again. This was the time of night you decide such manifestations mean you've got a brain tumor—she'd probably picked it up by being irradiated over Area 51. Barry's face had been repaired and the restored side looked more like one too many lifts than the other side even. The orange sheen overlay made Terry's bright red Realtor's jacket look anemic.

"So, I suppose you were in on the great Hilton heist," Charlie fished.

Toby wasn't biting. "Like to get my hands on one of those magic phasers. I do magic sometimes, you know."

"What's this magic thing Evan keeps promising is going to make everything just fine?"

"If it works, it's going to be awesome. And funny as hell."

"If it works—"

"Magic's like that." An unusual young man with black floppy curls and a wiry energy, Toby seemed eternally happy, but then the expression in his wide-set eyes would turn abruptly sharp and serious. Maybe it was the magician in him.

Charlie blinked. "Why did I start seeing orange light again with the Groom Lake shots? I'm still getting fragments of it. And that's just from the film."

"Evan's always said you got a great imagination for an agent."

Her only comeback, the soap-opera cliché, "What's that supposed to mean?"

"Hey, nobody else sees this orange."

"So where was Caryl Thompson tonight?" And her tits.

"Her folks are in town for the funeral. To hear her tell it, the two of them together are worse than a dead brother."

"Do you know the big man sitting beside my chair tonight?"

They swirled into the palm-lined drive of the Las Vegas Hilton and pulled to a stop under the lights of the huge marquee and he surprised her with an answer for once. "Yeah. Name's Art Sleem."

"There was money in that room tonight, but Sleem's boss, Loopy Louie, wasn't there?"

"Sleem works for a lot of people." Toby's expression had

gone serious on her. "He the man who shoved Pat under traffic?"

"Yeah. Does that mean Loopy Louie ordered the execution?"

"Means Art Sleem works for too many people." Toby nodded at some inner thought and stopped grinning. "Only in Vegas."

"But the party was about money."

"That's what everything's about. That and magic."

"So what was Art Sleem doing at the party uninvited?"

"Looked to me like he was trying to put the make on you."

TOO TIRED for blackjack but too wired to sleep, Charlie stopped
at a bank of slots near the Dodge Stealth in the lobby before
going upstairs. *Starlight Express* was just letting out and lines
of people paraded toward the front entryway or wandered into
the casino, drawn by strategically located slots suddenly heaving
up heavy metal into their made-to-be-noisy trays.

Unfortunately, Charlie's was not one of them. The squeals of
delight, sound effects, and flashing red lights were random, but
not on her row. The Hanleys and Betty showed up at a rigged
triumph nearby and Charlie called out to them. Illogically happy
to see them one more time, she almost wished they weren't
getting on a morning plane for Wisconsin.

"Oh Charlie, that was a great show. Can't believe people can
dance like that on roller skates." Betty gave Charlie a hug.
"You should be in bed. You're too young to look that tired."

Martha Hanley snagged a passing cart and bought a round of
dollar tokens for everybody. "Hell, *we* should be in bed. But I
still have a little change to lose, and I can sleep in Kenosha."

She plugged a slot two down from Charlie, Ben the one next
to Charlie, and Betty sat on the other side of her—ordering
Bloody Marys all around from a passing waitress.

God, these people were refreshingly real. Charlie felt so
threatened by Art Sleem and even Evan Black, she had half a
mind to take a morning plane out tomorrow herself. Leave all
the shit to pompous Richard Morse. That way, she could also
avoid Mitch Hilsten. What a deal.

Charlie'd never had a slot go off on her. She didn't play them that often, but she'd sat next to a jackpot once. So when the clanking racket began in the tray in front of her and the red light energized on top of her machine, she sat in dumb surprise. This is what's supposed to happen. This is why I came to Vegas. She still didn't believe it.

But Betty was on her feet, screaming, literally lifting Charlie off her stool, when they both went down. Because Ben Hanley's battle with his own body knocked them down.

Everybody but Ben Hanley got up eventually. He couldn't, because he was dead.

THIRTEEN

"THEY" TRIED to tell Charlie that Ben Hanley had had a heart attack. Even she'd dubbed him one waiting to happen.

She had also noticed him drinking her Bloody Mary. He'd downed his and absently picked up hers the next time he reached, his mind more on the arrangement of the fruit lining up in front of him.

She hadn't thought much about it and couldn't have touched even a glass of water by this time in her unvacation. Besides, these free drinks weren't called "well drinks" for nothing. They were pretty well watered. You were supposed to get loose, not comatose.

Amazing how quickly and smoothly she and the Hanleys and Betty had ended up behind that forbidden door. That very door the guards had rushed blindly out of with their blazing flashlights on Evan's film.

Ben Hanley wasn't pronounced dead until a good half hour after that door closed Charlie and his family in with him. But Charlie Greene, who had been running into a lot of this lately, knew he was dead before she and Betty managed to get out from under his inert form on the casino floor.

She'd glimpsed banks of TV monitors lining the walls of a room off the hall as they passed to this office. Charlie sat on a couch between Betty and Martha, unable to believe she'd met these people only this afternoon, while a couple of uniformed guards and then a battalion of EMTs tried to resuscitate Ben Hanley.

When they heard the distinct sound of a bone cracking in Ben's chest, the three women grabbed one another's hands in an involuntary motion.

"Why do they keep doing that?" Martha whispered, her glasses steaming over at the top, her hand hot and sweaty. "My Benny's dead."

"Remember when they resuscitated Pop?" Betty's hand felt cold and sweaty. "Lived—what?—ten, eleven years in a lot of pain from a cracked sternum. Never did heal."

"Had to put him in a nursing home." Martha blinked enormous eyes behind enormous glasses. "Betty and me weren't about to quit our jobs, neglect our children and husbands to change diapers on somebody bigger than we were. They had to catheterize him every six hours."

"Cost thousands of dollars a month. He didn't know who he was, didn't know who we were either."

"That's when Martha and I made a pact," Betty confided. The sisters promised each other that the first to go would not be forced to linger. But they hadn't made a pact with Ben Hanley. They also hadn't noticed many resuscitated people over a certain age being successfully rehabilitated.

"Ben carried on like a baby when his sisters wouldn't give up their livelihoods to take his mother in when she got Alzheimer's. And I wouldn't either."

"You didn't give in then, Martha."

"I'm not giving in now." Martha squeezed Charlie's hand and leaned across her to look into Betty's glasses. "Benny went like he'd want to—enjoying himself on vacation."

"Yeah. In his favorite place, Las Vegas."

"Favorite place after Kenosha, Wisconsin, you mean."

"Right. And doing what he loved best…after fishing. Playing the slots."

"What do you think we should do, Charlie?"

This was so far out of Charlie's league, she could only shrug helplessly, but she stood as both women rose to their feet and, lifting their hands in the air—hers too—called for a stop to the degradation of Ben Hanley's poor carcass.

CHARLIE DIDN'T LINGER over breakfast in bed, but grabbed a quick shower, read her E-mail, and hurried down to the coffee shop. She didn't want to be alone in her room this morning either.

People can too die in a casino, and they can be murdered too. She ordered one egg poached soft, a piece of dry toast, and a cup of hot milk from Ardith, the elderly waitress with the thick ankles who'd served her yesterday.

"You going to do with it what I think you are, sweetie? Because if you are, there's better remedies for hangovers." When Charlie didn't answer she added, "Not even coffee?"

"I'll eat my breakfast first and then see if my stomach wants coffee, okay?" Everybody's a doctor. "Please hurry it."

If someone wanted to murder you, they could have gotten in your room while you slept. Maybe Ben Hanley really did die of a heart attack.

Betty and Martha were sure that's what it was. "Doctor's been warning him to stay away from his favorite foods, but he figured life wasn't worth living if he couldn't eat what he wanted. Only time he drank was on vacation or with his cheese balls during a Packers game."

They wouldn't let her stay with them. "We got each other. And, honey, he was so lucky to go that way and that fast. We'll miss him, but you don't know how awful it can be growing too old. You're exhausted. We'll write to you from Kenosha."

And that had been it. These people who'd been in her life for one day, one of them dead because of her, the other two already making plans to combine households.

I'm beginning to feel not only threatened but dangerous to others. Three dead in four days. And four more days to go.

It's possible Evan's right about your tendency to believe in conspiracies. You could have nothing to do with these deaths. You could be having panic attacks like Reynelda Goff.

I should leave today. Three dead in four days is a little much for coincidence, or panic attacks, either.

But Charlie and her good sense agreed to have a calm, soothing breakfast before making any plans.

"Good idea," Ardith told her. "You and yourself done talking?" And with a flourish, she presented Charlie the poached egg already on top of the toast, served in a soup bowl, and a small pitcher of milk. "See, milk's still steaming. Bone appetite. There're pills now you can take for ulcers. Know that?"

Charlie did know, but they were for the bacterial kind. Hers was more of the raising a kid half her own age and three people dying around her in four days kind.

Charlie poured the steaming milk over the poached egg on toast and added salt and pepper. She ate slowly, testing her system. It was an inexplicably calming meal that turned other people green to see her eat, but it worked for her. Maybe she'd die early like Ben because she ate what worked at the moment.

Just because Patrick Thompson and Officer Timothy Graden were murdered didn't mean somebody like Ben couldn't die mercifully quickly and easily next to her slot machine. Even in a casino.

Nothing like poached egg on milk toast with salt and pepper to bring things into perspective. She used the soup spoon Ardith had brought to finish the last of the milk and looked up to find the older woman standing above her with the coffeepot.

Charlie nodded and her server shook her head as if she'd seen everything. But she poured Charlie a cup of the empowering brew before removing all evidence of the disgusting meal.

Thus fortified, her universe in at least partial balance, Charlie finally confronted the thought of the morning's E-mail, which she'd answered before heading to breakfast. Libby, Mitch, Larry.

Libby's car and Eric, the boyfriend, were apparently still alive, because she didn't mention them. The problem was Perry Mosher. Libby'd been through a series of part-time jobs, usually quitting them in a few months. Charlie had the feeling it was her daughter's looks that overcame her lousy work record and explained her ability to get another job.

But this was the problem Charlie had dreaded. The boss couldn't keep his hands off the kid's butt. What should she do?

When Libby asked her mother for advice, Charlie knew no answer would suffice. It was a trap. The best answer would be for Libby to keep her mouth shut and quit. Warn her friends to stay away from the creep.

Libby, however, had not been raised to give up without a fight. She worked at a pet supply and grooming store, Critter Spa and Deli, in a small shopping center in a not-too-scary neighborhood.

Charlie had sent back the message, ''Tell Perry Mosher to knock it off, and if he doesn't, look for another job.''

But she knew that was too easy. That kind of harassment can be subtle and excused as a joke, any protest treated like an exaggeration and turned around to belittle and embarrass the protester. Perry didn't seem dangerous, but he was icky, the thought of him touching Libby disgusting.

Mitch's message that he had finally taken off from Nairobi—how could you E-mail from Nairobi if the downtrodden were blowing up stuff? What the hell was he doing in Nairobi? She'd checked all the routing information and, sure enough, he was there or had been. Anyway, he expected to be in Vegas by Friday night, Saturday at the latest, and couldn't thank Charlie enough for suggesting him to Evan Black, whose work he admired to the nth.

Shit, he's going to decide he owes me again.

Then there was Larry Mann, her assistant—whose butt she wasn't even allowed to think about touching—with the weirdest message of all. Jethro Larue at the Fleet Agency in New York had asked for Charlie to turn over all files on Georgette Millrose, as he would be her new agent. He'd had the gall to offer terms, which were spitting insults, on possible future subrights income on properties Charlie had sold for Georgette.

Georgette had moved fast. Granted, Charlie hadn't read her recent books because the speedily displaced editors at Bland and Ripstop had offered to take each opus as it came. Georgette's historicals were thinly veiled romances without the raw sex.

But the real shocker was that Jethro Larue wanted to represent Georgette Millrose. Charlie's life was so unexpected, even when she wasn't dealing with murder.

An incredibly thick wad of bills landed on the table where her poached egg on milk toast had sat a short while before and Art Sleem said, ''You won the jackpot last night.''

FOURTEEN

"THOUGHT YOU worked for Louie…at Loopy's," Charlie heard her confusion say.

"I get around. Not nearly as good as you." His curls were not really shoulder-length. They were collar-length, and then only in back. It's just that he didn't have a neck. "Me, I'm not lucky like you." His lips were full and sensuous, a small spacing between his two front teeth, a Roman—no, an Arab hook to the nose. "But you? You been very lucky lately." A wry, intelligent, aware smile. "Very lucky."

Red alert. What time of the month is this?

Don't be silly. Not even you can forget he kills people.

"It's like wherever you go, people die."

"Wherever *I* go?" Charlie took a slug of coffee and sucked air. The cup was empty.

"Let me get you some serious coffee." Art the thug took a hundred-dollar bill off the top of the roll and handed it to Ardith. "Keep the change."

There was a serious coffee bar out in the lobby by the sleek black Dodge Stealth. Art Sleem ordered them each a skinny latte. He selected a shaker off the counter. "Nutmeg, right?"

"How did you know?"

"Simple, you look like a nutmeg type." He sprinkled it on the foamy milk atop her drink. "What about me?"

"Sugar."

"Right." And he dumped in enough to kill the foam. "Told you it was simple." He led her down a couple of carpeted stairs to the very bank of slots where Ben Hanley died the night before. "Sometimes things are simple. Sometimes they're sheer dumb luck."

He sounded like an agent. "So you're not just a bouncer at Loopy Louie's?"

"Like you, I wear many hats."

"What's that supposed to mean?" There I am doing it again. Next thing, I'll be asking him how he feels.

"Well, look at you. Young, beautiful, apparently gifted, a Hollywood agent, girlfriend to superstars. An adventuress who thinks nothing of flying over restricted areas."

Ben Hanley's eyes had glassed over by the time she and Betty looked down at him. His mouth open and tongue distended as if he'd choked.

"A woman who plays the dollar slots after winning big at blackjack at two casinos in just two days, instead of the five-dollar slots. We don't have a profile on your type. We need a profile on your type."

"Who's we? And what's my type?"

"A woman so above money, she forgets a jackpot."

Charlie had seen death before, and when large men had appeared almost instantly to pick up Ben and escort the rest of his little group away from curious eyes, she'd noticed the wet spot on that carpet. And on Ben's plaid shorts. He had died in a casino. She should have made known her concern last night that the lethal drink had been meant for her, but she hadn't wanted to spoil the man's death for his widow and sister-in-law. They were so pleased at how clean and fast it was. Do people as needy as their parents really linger that long?

"A woman who hobnobs with the high rollers and the hicks of this world, as if they were no different. A woman of great tolerance."

Charlie repressed the brief memory of her distaste at having to care for her own mother after a mastectomy. If the gods expected Charlie to give up her only life and her sanity to nurse Edwina if she got old and "lingered," the gods were in for a shock.

"You surprise me, know that?" Art Sleem said. "Why'd you go off and leave your jackpot?"

"We had a little emergency. Somebody died, remember? Right about here." You must have been here too, to know I'd won and to collect the money. And to maybe lace my drink with a lethal dose of something.

"Nobody dies in a casino."

"What is it you want, Mr. Sleem?" Another great line.

"I want to help you."

"Translation, you want to warn me."

"No, I want to help you *understand* things."

"Things like nobody dies in a casino."

"And things like, nobody's luck holds forever. Stay away from dangerous places." They were sitting on stools and he pushed at the carpet with the toe of a hand-polished shoe. "Things like always watch your back, if you don't. Things like, we don't like counters here."

"I'm not a counter. I can't remember lunch."

"Things like friends in high places can't be counted on to save your ass. Like, you and your friends are not free to go wherever you want."

"Who do you work for anyway?"

"I'm freelance."

"Freelance killer?"

"Educator. Casinos are private property. You aren't free to do whatever you want in one."

"I can't count cards. I didn't expect to win all this money. I came here for a vacation and to play blackjack."

"Restricted areas are off-limits too. You aren't free to ignore the rules."

"Know what? I think you're the one with a problem. I think you're trying to make me the answer to a question only you know." If there's anything to be learned from modern communication techniques, it's, when in doubt—babble. "Lousy problem solving, Art. You need an educator yourself. And another thing—"

"How is it you know my name?"

"Your reputation precedes you."

Whoa, that's your third cliché in the last two minutes.

Oh, knock it off.

"Well, you tell your high-roller friend she better be careful." Art Sleem was about to say more, but the pit boss with all the turquoise jewelry and the excess hair on the back of his hands came to stand over them. "Hey, Eddie, how's it going?"

"Just great, Art. This woman bothering you?"

"Nah, just good friends. Good seeing you again, Charlie."

Charlie was trying to digest this strange interchange when Sleem headed for the revolving door to the real world.

"You're good friends with Art Sleem?" Eddie was still standing and Charlie still sitting on her stool. She watched his hand flexing.

"No, I don't know anything about him, but he seems to know everything about me. Does he work here?" Charlie explained how he had delivered her lost jackpot winnings to her table in the coffee shop. "And I saw him in the spa by the pool the other day."

"You're a guest here? You lost a jackpot...oh yeah, the guy who got sick in the casino last night. I heard about that—not my shift."

Actually, Eddie, he checked out, rolled his last dice, threw in the towel, gave up the ghost, and drank his last drink—the one meant for me.

Charlie thought she was talking to herself until he said, "Nobody dies in a casino."

"Oh. Right. So if he doesn't work here, how did he get my jackpot? Sleem, I mean."

"I'll look into it." Eddie headed straight for that door to this casino's secure area that Charlie had been shepherded into with the corpse from Kenosha.

She had never seen Eddie out on the floor here except when Charlie's high-roller friend had been playing blackjack.

You haven't been looking for him either.

That's true. But I will be now.

Does that mean we're staying in Vegas?

For a little longer. I mean, if Art and his buddies want to kill me, they can certainly find me in Long Beach. Don't you want to know how much money I've got in my purse?

Charlie's purse was too small to carry that much money comfortably, but before she could count it, Eddie was back. "Charlie Greene, comped to room twenty-one fifteen, Congdon and Morse Representation, Inc." He read off a sheet of paper, "Residence, Long Beach, California."

Eddie had another man with him. This one didn't carry the beef most of these guys did. Tall, skinny, stooped.

"Comped? Richard got these rooms comped? How did he do that?" And here she'd thought he was being generous for a change.

Eddie shrugged. "Not my department. This is Mr. Tooney. He'd like to have a word with you."

Mr. Tooney was with the IRS. Charlie had heard tell there were more IRS agents in Las Vegas than any other city in the country. Made sense.

She asked for identification, he showed her a card. She had no idea if it was real or faked. "I hope you are who you say you are, Mr. Tooney, because I have a problem."

"Yes, you do, Mrs. Greene," he said quietly. He led her down a wide hallway that led to the auditorium where Ben and family had enjoyed *Starlight Express* last night, then to a quiet corner of a bar not open until evening.

"What did you mean, 'Yes you do'?"

"You first." He brought out a notebook and pencil instead of an electronic notepad.

Charlie told him how and why Ben Hanley had been murdered, told of witnessing Patrick Thompson's murder and trying to convince Officer Timothy Graden. "Art Sleem probably killed him too. I can prove he did Ben though, Mr. Tooney," she said when he stopped writing and started doodling, "because if he hadn't been here, how could he have known about the jackpot?"

She put the pile of bills on the table in front of him as evidence. She hadn't even had time to count them, but the bills she'd seen were all hundreds.

Mr. Tooney, Matt Tooney, according to the card he'd showed her, counted it swiftly. "Your story is very inventive," he said. "You should take up writing. But murder is really not my specialty, Mrs. Greene."

"Miss Greene. Well, what do we do? That man is dangerous."

"My bailiwick is money. And we have here just short of two hundred thousand dollars."

"Art Sleem took back a bill to pay the waitress for my breakfast and told her to keep the change." But then it hit her. "I won two hundred thousand dollars playing the dollar slots? Come on. They don't pay a jackpot like that with cash anyway." They present you with a check and an IRS form.

"Actually"—and he brought a check out of his wallet and handed it to her—"you won ten thousand. And here it is, and here's your tax form."

"So what's all this?" She gestured to the piles of bills he'd lined up carefully, with Ben Franklin's picture facing up and toward him.

"That's exactly what I and the management of the Las Vegas Hilton's casino would like to know. Apparently, Mr. Sleem was paying you for something else."

"Listen, Matt Tooney, that jerk is trying to kill me. He followed me to the pool. He followed me to Fremont Street and to a screening last night. He never stopped threatening me."

"Screening?"

"At Evan Black's house. He makes movies, you know." Charlie didn't mention the content of the film. Somehow, invading secret government airspace and watching a successful robbery of this very casino didn't seem like the thing to bring up. Like they say, when dealing with the bureaucracy, don't offer more than is asked, and she'd already broken that rule. "Maybe Sleem figured once I was dead, he could get his money back. But if you're going to kill somebody, why give them money? This whole thing doesn't make sense."

"Exactly," said the man from the IRS.

FIFTEEN

MATT TOONEY suggested that Charlie go to the police with her story and refused to take the $200,000 off her hands.

Charlie explained she'd been to the police and hadn't heard back and that she didn't want the money.

"Everybody wants money," said the tax man. He ought to know.

"Yeah, right, and nobody dies in a casino. Don't you care that this poor guy was murdered? That his death was a mistake? That I was supposed to die? That I could be next? I mean, I know you're specialized, but jeez. And the police can't do anything until after I'm dead. Probably write it off as pedestrian error or 'Stupid tourist takes dive off the Stratosphere Tower, sources say she was depressed.'"

"This screening. What was its purpose?"

"It wasn't a screening so much as a sales pitch for money, far as I could tell. Project was still an idea waiting funding."

"Money, funding." Mr. IRS looked at the cash on the table.

"You think Sleem was giving me money for Evan Black's next project? But why wouldn't he say so? Why all the threats? Why not just give it to Evan?"

"You're his agent."

"I just handle his writing contracts and his dealings with other writers for the agency. I mean, I don't do finance stuff. In fact, I don't do most of his stuff." Truth be known, most of the contract work is done by the lawyers anyway.

CHARLIE DIDN'T KNOW where to start, but, fed up with a helpless situation and fortified by anger, a poached egg on milk toast, and a skinny latte with nutmeg, start she would.

But first she ran upstairs to change into shorts and sandals and check out the voice mail message from the office. Ursa

Major was dropping the option on *Letters to Morticia.* Another disappointment. She called Larry to discuss how he would break the news to the author—gently. "Poor guy was counting on that money."

Her little purse stuffed with enough money to pay off her mortgage twice, she had the doorman hail her a cab for Evan Black's house. Charlie was so charged by the time she got there, she sent the cab on its way before she realized no one was home. This was a gated community, with a live guard at the gate, but Charlie was on the list of people to be admitted, and the guard must not have noticed Evan leaving.

She stood next to a propped-up dead palm tree and saw something she hadn't last night in the dark. Evan's house was on a lake. A lake in the desert.

Unable to raise anybody by pushing the buzzer on the gate to the courtyard, she walked around the high pretend-adobe wall until she came to the lake and stepped easily around the wall's end. A sleek cabin cruiser sat almost completely still on the glassy dun-colored water. Evan's backyard consisted largely of pool and fancy tiles. The clear blue of the water in the pool dazzled.

The front might be gated at the road into the development and at Evan's courtyard, but the back of the house, mostly window, was wide open. Charlie could see many houses similar to this along the lakefront—stucco, tile roofs, impossibly stilled boats tethered at most of them.

Traffic was not that far away, yet it was quiet here. The unrippled water made no sound, even the incessant air traffic from McCarran seemed muted. Eerie, like walking around in a void. Only the sound of Charlie's shoes as she crossed the gorgeous blue-and-white figured tiles that cracked and buckled and just plain came loose at irregular intervals.

Charlie had little patience with female-in-jeopardy novels. But every now and again, that primordial fear men needed women to feel, so it was worth their valor to go out and kill mastodons, overtook even Charlemagne Catherine Greene.

Losing some of her determination, she decided to see if she could get into the house to use a phone to call another cab. If not, she'd hike back to the gatehouse and ask the guard there to call her one.

All these houses, set close together along the lakefront, were two and three stories high but long and narrow—allowing access to both street and lake for the maximum number.

She walked along the windows, one panel of them after another. Here is where the living took place in this house. The whole first floor was one great room with kitchen, dining room, lounge, and office space sharing the sunlight and lake view. Comfortable, beautifully thought out and coordinated, this was a different house from the one she'd seen last night. There were two sides to this house, as there appeared to be to Evan Black.

Among the panels of windows were doors with glass panels of their own and doorknobs. She tried one, expecting it to be locked. It was. But at the other end of the length of windows between pool tile and house, a door stood ajar on the kitchen end, where she'd started. Why hadn't she noticed it?

Because in this direction you can see it better and you were too busy ogling somebody else's private space. That's where you began snooping and your concentration was off.

I'm not snooping. And it could have been opened just slightly behind my back while I walked this way. To lure me in.

But a barely visible wire along the bottom of the window line, which was about knee level on Charlie, made her retrace her steps to the suspicious door. Even less perceptible were tiny round sensors attached to the framework between windows.

A fairly quaint alarm system. I could deactivate that with scissors.

It must be deactivated already if the opened door didn't set it off.

It could signal the guardhouse at the main entrance instead of making lots of noise here.

What do you really know about these things?

Nothing but what I read in scripts and manuscripts. You can pick up a lot that way. Like recognizing that somebody else already deactivated it—it's cut right here.

Two ends of the wire drooped in defeat at one edge of a window frame.

That's stupid. Cutting it should send that signal to police or the guardhouse.

Not until she was inside did Charlie realize the front of this great room was open to three stories. A balcony with a staircase at each end connected the second story to this one. A second balcony extended out over the first. All three floors sharing the sun and view. Blank digital clocks on oven and microwave told her the electricity had been cut before the alarm system.

A cordless phone sat upended on a cluttered desk on the back wall under the balconies. A photograph of an enormous building, literally dwarfing the cars and trucks parked around it, caught her attention as she picked up the cordless. And found it dead.

It needs electricity too, stupid. Maybe we should sort of ooze on out of here?

This is the scene in amateurish mystery novels where the female sleuth, instead of listening to her good sense, climbs the stairs and finds a body. Knowing better, Charlie Greene headed straight for the door she'd entered.

And found three.

CHARLIE'S HEAD pounded in rhythm with her shoes pounding the pavement back to the gatehouse. She'd tried ringing bells at the locked gates of several courtyards along the way but was answered only by barking dogs who fell silent the minute she retreated.

"This fries it. I've had it. I'm out of here." She knew she was talking out loud and didn't care. "Six bodies in five days. Gotta be a message there somewhere."

Walking in this direction, she could see that, though Evan was on a lake, most of the homes backed on canals where they could run their boats out to the lake.

One thing for sure, Art Sleem would never demand his two hundred grand back. He hadn't been dead long, but dead he was. Charlie hadn't needed to check to see if he'd wet his pants to know that.

She'd wandered farther into her mysterious client's home than she'd realized to pick up the phone, absently snooping along the way.

When she turned back toward the getaway door, the bodies lay lined up behind two couches and a long chest with its lid open and what looked to be jumbled rolls of paper inside. Art Sleem lay along the chest. He was hidden from the windows, but if she'd been looking in the other direction instead of at the posters of Evan Black's films on the rear wall on her way to the phone, he would have been visible to her. The other two had the privacy of the couches to be dead behind.

It was hot and still with all the pavement and decorative rock and white stucco reflecting back the sun. And a long way to the guardhouse.

She could still smell the bitter scent of gunfire she'd curiously overlooked until she saw all the dead.

But it had been the crack of an upstairs floorboard that sent Charlie Greene out that kitchen door on the run.

SIXTEEN

CHARLIE RETURNED to the murder scene in a squad car with Officer Leach. The guard at the gatehouse swore he'd let only one unauthorized man into the subdivision and that because the man had official government identification. That would have been Tooney flashing his IRS card for the last time.

"How'd the other two get in here?" she asked the officer when she'd demonstrated how she gained entrance and explained the squeaky floorboard upstairs.

"Probably rented a boat. Tied it up behind some other house. Takes more than a little water and a gate to keep out the bad guys."

After determining the bodies were all indeed dead ones, Officer Leach ordered her out of the house and around the wall, drew his sidearm, and crept up the stairs before she'd even reached the pool. He didn't look old enough to be a cop. She was back in the kitchen the minute he disappeared.

Art Sleem wasn't wearing his turquoise ring. And the other man who wasn't Matt Tooney had an indentation on his ring finger.

Officer Leach was up there for what seemed an inordinately long time. Charlie grew more curious about up there and less enthused about down here with the dead men.

Careful not to touch the banister, she climbed the stairs, knowing she was still shedding skin scales and hair dust or something to confuse the crime scene. But Charlie figured she'd already done the damage when discovering the bodies to begin with.

The next floor was the main level from the street side. Here were the foyer and the butler's pantry, where she and Evan had dispersed the crystal last night. A small formal living room and dining room dominated one side of the house, the other taken up by the two-story screening room and elegant his and her bathrooms.

The bedrooms must be off the balcony above. Funny how brave she felt up here now with one cop, young but armed. And there were reinforcements on the way. Floorboards do creak on their own. Houses settle. Probably a lot when at the edge of a lake.

This house seemed to hold its breath as Charlie ascended to the third and final floor.

Two small bedrooms with a connecting bath. A master suite with a huge bath/dressing/exercise room combined. All thoroughly searched and left undone.

The young cop stood next to the Jacuzzi in the master bath, talking to Dispatch on his cellular. He gave Charlie a hard look but went back to his conversation.

"Looks like a burglary as well as murder. Bedrooms torn up. Downstairs put back together, but in a hurry. Up here, it appears the perpetrators had no time to return rooms to normal. May have been surprised by Miss Charlie Greene, Evan Black's agent, or so she says, entering from below. Could have easily made their way out the front from the second story when she entered on the first. Yeah, she's here," and he mouthed to Charlie, "Don't touch a thing."

She nodded and looked around instead.

Despite his reputation for thrift on his projects, Evan lived well. His Malibu home was grander than this. The last she knew, he was planning to build a third home in either Sun Valley or Telluride. And she knew of a condo on Kauai.

Even with the king-sized mattress pulled off the innerspring, there was something about the care with which the bedding had been stripped but not quite removed. It appeared to be placed in folds on the floor, suggesting the searchers had intended to return things to normal.

And the young officer was right about the first floor too. Charlie wouldn't have noticed, but, now that he'd suggested it, she could see how the rolls of paper, maps maybe, had been put back in the chest, but not neatly enough to allow the lid to close.

And she could see the desk down there with the dead cordless and the picture of the improbable building. The normal clutter of a working desktop was strangely organized. Your regular shuffling of overwhelming paperwork, but the stacking was weird.

Odd-shaped piles…wrong somehow…the stacks too even heightwise and too quickly arranged. Photos, drawings, scripts, diagrams, and junk mail stacked more by size than subject, but the stacks still oddly shaped. What was she looking for?

And the photo of the gigantic building, surely some Hollywood prop engineered with photography instead of actual construction, appeared to have toppled from a pile of what looked like household bills mixed with restaurant flyers and prostitute handbills available on the Strip. Organized by haste and stack height rather than by subject—that was it.

Anyone living in the house would know something was wrong immediately. But at first glance, strangers like police and literary agents might not. Charlie looked back at young Officer Leach with respect.

Charlie learned something about her enigmatic client too. It took a bit of looking beyond the search destruction to know what it was though. One, he was tidy. Two, he was not celibate. Interesting objects had been pulled off closet shelves and dresser drawers, the very least damning of which were condoms, K-Y jelly, scented aerosols, and flavored creams. Various cruel-looking mechanisms. A puzzling array of chains, hooks, ropes, and pulleys. Rotating hooks in the ceiling. All suggested an athletic sex life. Not surprising. But again, he was tidy, or maybe realistic—no mirrors.

Which doesn't mean there aren't hidden cameras and snuff videos.

Well no, but Evan *is* tidy. He wouldn't leave three dead men in his great room. And where the hell is he?

EVAN BLACK returned shortly after the reinforcements arrived. He'd been at the funeral of Patrick Thompson and helped to disperse the poor pilot's ashes from an airplane over the landscape of his family's request. Charlie didn't want to know.

She sat in a canvas deck chair pulled up to a glass-topped table on Evan's pool patio. The white tile had blue Aztec-type markings. So did the table's umbrella, unfurled now to shield them from the sun. She, Evan, Detective Jerome Battista, and an undisclosed person of authority, who would have worn an overcoat on the Fox Network even in this weather, lunched on turkey subs, bottled water, and crinkled potato chips from some take-out.

Charlie finished off her water before unwrapping her submarine, and Mr. Undisclosed, in shirtsleeves instead of an overcoat, pulled another out of a bag at his feet. He wasn't wearing a ring on his wedding finger. But had one recently left an indentation? He handed her the water with a purposeful look, presumably to make a lasting impression.

He probably hadn't witnessed six dead bodies in five days. Now, *that* makes an impression.

All the water took care of her headache and she bit into the sub with more interest than she'd expected to. Moist roasted-tasting turkey slices—not the slimy cold-cut type—smeared with mayonnaise and cranberry sauce, topped with onions, black olives, shredded lettuce, and sprouts.

The men watched her, almost fondly. Men did that. She would not think about it.

Evan patted the elbow she'd bent to allow her hand to feed her mouth. "My lovely agent here is a fast-food connoisseur."

"Oh, that reminds me." Charlie grabbed one of the hundreds of napkins that always accompanied these meals to wipe the mayonnaise off her fingers and reached into her purse. She handed him the $200,000 minus the hundred-dollar tip. "Compliments of Art Sleem, body number four."

Boy, did she have everybody's attention.

Evan looked especially astounded, but he'd earned any worry it might cause him. Charlie figured the more open she was in front of the authorities, the less trouble he could get her into.

She answered her client's look with a wink. Don't ask me for sympathy, guy. Too many bodies under the bridge, and half-assed nonexplanations of things you are intent upon involving me in. Just handing you back a little bit of the grief, my friend. Enjoy.

She popped the air out of her bag of crinkled chips, feeling more in control than she had since Art Sleem and company presented her with matching bullet holes in their foreheads. No sign of struggle, as if they'd lined up for execution. All laid out in a row. And all that blood in their eyeballs and spreading into the carpet. Recent kills. Somebody had caught them searching this house. She was lucky that somebody hadn't caught her.

Detective Battista held out a hand still smeared with mayo and wearing a wedding band. Evan handed over the money. But Battista, who looked more like a male model than a cop, asked Charlie the obvious question instead of Evan Black. "One of the dead men gave you this money for Mr. Black? When?"

"Well, that's what Matt Tooney thought the money was for, anyway. He's body number six. As well as IRS." And Charlie described her morning.

Evan waited for the half of her sandwich he knew she wouldn't eat and she gave it to him. The other two stared at her, baffled.

"There's only three bodies in there—not enough for you?" Mr. Undisclosed asked. Baggy eyes and jowls, beer belly, gray hair clipped to within an inch of its life. "Oh yeah, the one in the casino. I'm still missing two bodies."

"She's very imaginative for an agent." Evan hugged her.

Detective Battista cut through the crap. "So, why did you come out here, Miss Greene?"

"To give Evan the money. Even the IRS wouldn't take it off my hands. I don't like wads of unexplained cash and thought I'd dump it and all the trouble it might bring on Evan."

"Don't listen to her," the writer/director/producer said with his beguiling grin. "She loves me. Honest. Best agent I ever had."

"So, the other two bodies," the fed insisted.

"Patrick Thompson—the native Las Vegan and pilot for the nonexistent airline that flies workers in unmarked planes to Groom Lake and who did not die by pedestrian error on the Strip—he's number one, and number two was Officer Timothy Graden."

"You were at the scene of the hit-and-run that killed Tim Graden?" Battista's sleek face tensed, dark eyes focused to a squint.

"No, but I did witness Thompson's murder and explained it to Officer Graden, the only one in authority there who would listen to me. And look where it got him."

"Do I detect a certain leap in reasoning here?" the fed asked. "The bicycle cop was a victim of a hit-and-run because you told him about what you imagined happened to Thompson? And as I'm counting, we suddenly went from not enough bodies to too many. There's still one unexplained."

"I told you, didn't I, that there were two goons who walked Pat Thompson out of Loopy Louie's?"

"Oh yeah, and shoved him under traffic that wasn't moving." The fed—what else could he be?—started in on the guy method of handling problems with those lower in the food chain. His condescending smile directed around the table showed the over-bite of preorthodontist days.

"Same kind of traffic it would be tough to get killed in jay-walking," Charlie countered. "Anyway, the bald corpse, number five, was Sleem's accomplice in this."

Undisclosed went for the gold. "And what would you say, little lady, if I told you that Mr. Arthur Sleem worked for the government of the United States?"

"Then I'd say the government's in a whole lot of trouble."

"Told you—conspiracy. Right?" Evan beamed at the two other men and would have hugged Charlie again if he hadn't caught the look in her eye in the very nick.

SEVENTEEN

"A TRIPLE MURDER at the Las Vegas home of producer-writer, Evan Black, the young genius behind such award-winning films as *All the King's Women,* a fictional exposé of presidential fornication throughout history, and the hilarious docudrama of attempts to hide bungling at the highest levels of corporate America—*The Accountant in the Wardrobe*—starring Mel Gibson and Tom Hanks, has left the Lakes neighborhood and Las Vegas police stunned." This was Barry on the local evening news. He couldn't have gotten through that whole sentence if not for the fact that he spoke even slower than Frank Sinatra used to sing and so could breathe after every three words and you didn't notice.

Did he and Terry work morning, noon, *and* evening broadcasts? Charlie sprawled in an enveloping chair in front of a mammoth TV that lowered from the ceiling on command in Bradone McKinley's really swell accommodations high atop the Vegas Hilton. She accepted a chilled gin martini from Reed the butler. It might be poison, but it had to be a hundred flights up from yak crud. And this had been *one long* afternoon, baby.

Evan Black, "the young genius," spread out on a floor pillow at her feet, using her chair for a headrest. "Hey, what about *Waiter, There's a Government in My Soup?*"

"Never got released." Richard Morse cuddled with their hostess on a couch so puffy, all Charlie could see was his head.

"Still the best film I ever made."

"How come," Charlie asked, "we're the same age, but you're a young genius and I'm not young anymore?"

"Because you're not a genius. Geniuses are supposed to be old, so, if they're not creaky yet, they're young."

Since Evan's house was a crime scene under investigation, they let him pack an overnight bag and told him he'd have to spend the night elsewhere. He was going to spend it in Richard's room since Richard would be up here.

"Last night," Terry took over, "Black reportedly held an advance screening of an as-yet-unmade film, using raw footage of various scenic wonders of our area, including Area Fifty-one and Yucca Mountain, amazing special effects, and even, get this, footage of the robbery at the Vegas Hilton's casino."

"That Black's always out ahead of the crowd, isn't he?"

"Yes, Barry, and it sounds like Vegas will be in the movies once again. Sources say that none other than Mitch Hilsten will star in Black's latest flick."

Except for a helicopter video of the Lakes subdivision, busy with emergency vehicles, and another of Detective Jerome Battista refusing to talk to reporters as he entered a building, the only visuals the broadcast had for this segment were stills. Stills of Evan, Mel, Tom, and Mitch. And then one of Charlie.

"You gotta have a new picture taken," Richard remarked. "Haven't looked like that since Libby caught puberty."

"Black was reportedly attending a friend's funeral today and the bodies of three men, as yet unidentified—"

"I can identify them," Charlie said.

"Shut up," Evan said.

"...discovered by Black's Hollywood agent, Charlie Greene," Barry said.

"If this gets picked up by the networks, you couldn't get better publicity," Bradone the astrologer told Evan the genius and predicted, "People will be throwing money at you to get in on the ground floor."

"They already are," Charlie said.

"Shut up," Evan repeated, and asked Bradone, "How much you in for?"

"Don't listen to him," Charlie's boss warned his new girlfriend. "That's not how funding goes."

"Life's not legal without the middleman, huh, Morse?"

"Georgette Millrose," Terry began, and a pub photo flashed on the screen.

"Talk about needing a new photo." Charlie could hear the

sour grapes in her voice. "She hasn't looked like that since World War Two."

"...local celebrity and author of twenty-some romance-filled thrillers, announced today that she would be signing on with Jethro Larue at the Fleet Agency in New York."

"What, she hired a publicist?" Everybody knew midlist writers were not news, especially in their hometowns. "How'd she get that kind of press release on TV?" Charlie waved away Reed and another martini, as did Bradone. The guys accepted.

"No dead grass under that Jethro Larue," Richard Morse pronounced. "Face it, you were just coasting with her."

"But you're the one who told me not to—"

"Shut up," Richard said.

Charlie and Evan had spent the afternoon answering questions both separately and together and were still on the pool patio when the bodies were carried out. They'd offered up skin cells, hair and blood samples, and mouth swabs. Evan looked patiently through the mess of the upstairs and could find nothing missing, nor in the rest of the house either. Charlie did, but kept her mouth shut.

When Battista and Mr. Undisclosed grew intimidating over what the murdered men might be doing in the house, what the burglars might have been after, and whether he or Charlie thought the dead men might be the ones who'd searched it, Evan refused to say more without his lawyer. Charlie continued to keep her mouth shut.

Over a simple supper of baked potatoes, leafy salad, and hot crusty rolls, whipped up on a moment's notice by Brent the chef, Charlie asked Evan about the picture of the exaggerated building. The simple baked potatoes were topped with a creamy wine sauce creation—thick with hunks of real crabmeat, button mushrooms, pearl onions, raw asparagus tips, and every kind of tasty tiny herby thing. So it took him awhile to answer.

"That's not fake. It's the DAF. Starwars Device Assembly Facility. That was a real picture we took, from very high up. Been building it since Reagan to assemble weapons we don't need anymore. It's over by the little town of Mercury." He turned down Brent's wine choice and ordered another of Reed's martinis. Not to be outdone by the younger man, so did Richard. Bradone McKinley's amusement threatened to make a breakout.

Charlie also turned down the wine. One, it was white. Two, she had enough of a buzz on one martini.

"I read about that building." Bradone allowed a chuckle. "Cost something like a hundred million to build and eight million a year just for maintenance and security."

"It's actually a group of buildings inside a concrete fortress with security sensors, razor wire, and those famous 'armed response personnel,'" Evan told her.

"I've heard of those ARP guys," Richard said. "There's private companies that hire them out to government installations just like commercial security services do to businesses. Only these ARPs are ex-military security instead of ex-cops."

"There's a lot of ex-ARPs on the market now too," Evan added—not to be outdone by the older man. Men compete on everything. "Especially in Vegas, with all the loose cash. There's lots to secure and not enough mob presence to see that it's done quietly and neatly. And they're becoming more political, patriotic. Organizing and going out in groups to take care of people who do antigovernment things. They're like the reverse of the antigovernment militia movement but better armed and trained and with friends in high places. How does that tickle your little conspiracy phobia, Charlie?"

"Seems like you might be asking yourself that question, since you're continually baiting the keepers of the secrets out at Groom Lake. Maybe they'll come after you."

"Maybe they already have."

"A picture of the DAF was on the desk when I found the dead men. But it disappeared before we left."

"Maybe that's what whoever searched the house was looking for." Evan snapped his fingers. "We've got a real detailed plan of that state-of-the-art security system."

"Where'd you get something like that?" Richard wanted to know.

"Off the state-of-the-art Internet."

Charlie actually finished almost all of her baked potato and the men had seconds. They retired to the ploopy couch to argue over how a great project really gets funded and why agents and bankers and brokers are important to the process. Their speech was slurred. They ordered coffee and brandy and didn't seem to notice when Bradone lured Charlie out onto the roof patio.

Charlie wanted to stop and enjoy the amazing light show that was Vegas, the shadow mountains ringing the horizon, and the steam rising off the Jacuzzi next to the pool. But Bradone tugged her through the glass doors of an elegant bedroom and tossed a couple of pieces of cloth at her. "I bought this for my niece, but you can have it." She was already pulling off her own slacks and blouse.

"But I haven't shaved my you-know. I mean—"

"Hell, I don't care. And those guys will be passed out by the time we get wet. Brent and Reed are gay and not easily impressed. Now hurry, dessert is in the Jacuzzi."

Yes, Charlie had a thought or two about whether or not lovely Bradone was bi. And what this dessert might be. But she put on the bikini and ignored the pubics—it had been that bad a day. Now that Sleem and his bald buddy were dead, all she had to worry about were the ARPs from Groom.

"Finally, I have you all to myself." Bradone laughed low. "You've been so busy finding dead bodies and Richard's been so...very attentive."

"I was a little surprised"—*stunned* was more like it, but Charlie too was choosing her words carefully—"at your interest in him."

"Yes, well, he's something of a novelty. I've always liked novelty."

"Nothing stays a novelty for long."

"No, nothing does."

Dessert was a chocolate mint and coffee. And if the guys weren't asleep already, they were certainly quiet in there.

The water bubbled warm against her mostly nakedness. The air blew chill against her face. The rich coffee went down hot. Charlie sighed. "Here I am, a mother, and I can see all these people murdered and feel this good afterwards. Do you suppose Hollywood has hardened me?"

"There's a lot to be said for the survivor syndrome."

"Don't forget good old guilt. I seem to get nourishment from it." Charlie could feel tight muscles relaxing. Even her bones seemed to be readjusting more comfortably in their ligaments and sinews, or whatever kept her together.

"You're not worried that the police think you killed those three men today?" An edge of concern crept into the modulated voice.

"I don't know. But I have had a connection with six murders in five days, and the cops don't think three of them are murders even. Well, maybe the hit-and-run. Driving me nuts."

"Six?" Now Bradone McKinley sounded incredulous but listened without interrupting as Charlie described once again the deaths of Patrick the pilot, Timothy the bicycle cop, and Ben Hanley who drank from Charlie's glass. She went on to describe what little she knew or suspected of Art Sleem, Tooney, and the bald thug, whose murders in Evan Black's great room nobody denied.

"So what's the connection?"

"The only one I can see," Charlie said helplessly, "is me."

"Why not Evan? He would seem to have more of a connection."

"Not with Ben Hanley from Kenosha, Wisconsin, he doesn't. Bradone, would you believe I feel worse about that death than all the others combined?"

SUBDUED LIGHTING aimed downward highlighted curving stone pathways among shrubs in pots, flowering plants, small fountains and statuary, concrete gargoyles, and the bottom of the kidney-shaped swimming pool in the penthouse garden. The hot tub sat on a raised platform, so that even the mostly submerged could view the dazzling display of Las Vegas at night, the city streetlights blazing in lines radiating in all directions, the airliners blinking overhead.

All around, the mountain ranges hunkering on the horizon, forming a circular frame to keep reality at bay.

Steam made Bradone McKinley and the arm she raised toward the heavens appear to waver and warp as she pointed out the constellations either by direction or by distinguishing stars that managed to stab through the light refraction from the gaudiest city in the world.

Charlie had begun to tense up again with all the talk about dead bodies, and the astrologer's soothing, melodic voice calmed her. She caught herself yawning as Bradone carried on about planets and houses and moons rising.

"Charlie, what if even one of those planets has some life-form? What if that life-form is even now on its way here? Or already here?"

"What if that life-form has its own system of astrology? What if it reads some significance in the position of our solar system, Earth even?"

The older woman lowered her arm and her head suddenly to ask Charlie the date and time and place of her birth. Charlie answered the best she could remember from what Edwina had told her and then Bradone grew far too quiet for far too long.

"So what's the prognosis, stargazer? Is the body count over for the week? Am I going to salvage some vacation here or what?"

"We should meet for breakfast," Bradone said instead of answering. "Somewhere away from here and Richard and the police. There are so many things I want to ask you, Charlie. About Mitch Hilsten and Georgette Millrose. About Evan and that strange film we saw at his house last night."

Charlie noticed she didn't mention learning more about Richard Morse. "Bradone?"

"Look, I'm going to run your chart tonight." She steamed all over when she stood and reached for a towel. She didn't look real. "I'll pick you up at your door, call you first, think of a place we could go."

"Bradone, talk to me."

Bradone stood on the tub deck with the towel wrapped around her, head cocked to one side, the edges of her hairdo dripping, honest-to-God shooting stars zipping above her. It was creepy. "You're really very perceptive, aren't you, Charlie Greene?"

"No, I'm really very scared." And I don't even believe in astrology. The gambling blimp's tacky advertising board flashed PLAY KENO! over the stargazer's left shoulder. "Are the murders over with for what's left of the ruins of my vacation or not?''

For the first time since they'd met, Charlie heard uncertainty in the woman's tone. ''Somehow, I don't think so.''

EIGHTEEN

THE NEXT MORNING, a limo drove Charlie and Bradone to a secluded restaurant on the edge of a golf course, far from the glitz of the Strip and Fremont. They sat at an outside table in the sun, grape-arbor decor separating the tables from one another but opening onto the view of bright green greens and distant golfers.

Bradone pulled a cell phone and a paper notebook like Matt Tooney's from her purse. Dressed to kill in a wide-brimmed straw hat and country-club dress, Bradone looked great in black too. But that choice in color didn't make Charlie feel any easier.

"What did the charts and planets and stuff have to say?"

"May I suggest the creamed eggs on croissant?"

"You said if I came here, we'd talk. You're not talking."

"Let's do talk. But not about dead bodies until we've had some coffee and food." Sun drilled through the holes in the straw brim of her hat to pinprick her face and throat. "Have you heard from your mother since last we talked?"

"Well, no, but that's not the problem right now, is it?" And Jesus, why are you in black and hardly any makeup?

Was the shading on her lids charcoal color instead of blue because she'd been up all night running charts about Charlie's future and didn't like what the stars were saying?

Don't forget you don't believe in astrology.

"Charlie, remember when I told you I had a secret about Richard? At the big pool on the recreation deck?"

"Not really, but what were you doing down there anyway when you had your own pool at the penthouse?"

"It was important to Richard. Men need to feel less vulnerable now and then. You know that."

The arrival of coffee and orange juice helped settle Charlie's nervousness. Bradone McKinley's voice was not so soothing and melodic this morning.

"What I found funny about your mention of wild-yam cream and your mother's menopausal problems was this." Bradone drew a small white jar out of her black straw purse. It looked a lot like the one Ben Hanley's sister-in-law, Betty, had shown Charlie at dinner at the Baronshire. "Read the label."

WATER-DEIONIZED, WILD YAM EXTRACT, GLYCERYL STEARATE, PEG-100 STEARATE, ALOE VERA GEL, GLYCERINE, STEARIC ACID, SAFFLOWER OIL, PROGESTERONE, JOJOBA OIL, CHAMOMILE EXTRACT, BURDOCK ROOT EXTRACT, SIBERIAN GINSENG, PROPYLPARABEN.

"Bradone, people are dying like flies all around me. I could be next."

"I swiped this from Richard's shaving kit. Read the directions."

Apply to soft skin regions such as neck, chest, buttocks, inner thighs, inner arms after showering for symptoms of advancing maturity such as incontinence, impotence, memory lapse, stiff joints, and insomnia.

Despite her growing anxiety, Charlie couldn't stop the smile spreading across her face. "You mean my boss rubs sweet potatoes on himself? How come he made so much fun of my mom?"

"Because he'd never read the ingredients on *his* snake oil. Just the name."

The stuff was called Bubba's Youth Enhancer for Men.

"Tell me about Mitch Hilsten," Bradone demanded when a muffin and fruit plate arrived for her, creamed hard-boiled eggs over a croissant with pineapple hunks for Charlie.

"He's divorced with two grown daughters—"

"Everybody knows that. I mean, what's he like in bed?"

"Like, does he snore or what?"

"Richard says you're smitten with your secretary, who's gay."

"How's Richard in bed?"

"Not bad for his age."

"Must be the sweet potatoes."

Bradone tried again. "Is Mitch Hilsten as owly and pouty and reclusive as he appears in interviews?"

"Actually, he's very sensitive and thoughtful and pretty cheerful. He just doesn't like the press."

"That's not smart."

"Seems to be working for him." Mitch's career was sky-rocketing after a scary decline. He'd always been a household word with the public but was too good-looking for Hollywood's recent infatuation with scuzzy everyman heroes.

"Does he have a lot of moles or anything?"

"Not really. His teeth are capped. Did you know his smile was insured through Lloyd's of London when Lloyd's was the place to be insured? One time, I was in the Utah dessert with him and that smile nearly blinded me."

"Charlie, can't you throw me a crumb?"

Charlie pretended to consider the request while enjoying her food instead. "Okay," she relented. "Mitch has the most wonderful—" She caught the waiter's eye and raised her cup. "The most beautiful—"

"What? The most beautiful what?"

Charlie shook more pepper onto her creamed eggs and picked out a big hunk of hard-boiled egg to savor. "Back."

"Back of what?"

"Back of his back."

"You slept with Mitch Hilsten and you looked at his back?"

Once. One night. And I'll never live it down. "Look, he's threatening to be here tomorrow. You can see for yourself."

"His back?"

"It's very nice." Charlie wondered how much Bradone was paying for that limo and driver waiting out front.

"Okay, you win round one." The astrologer put her hands up, palms outward. "How about Georgette Millrose?"

"She fired me and signed on with Jethro Larue. It happens. She got tired of being midlist. I don't know an author who isn't tired of it. Maybe Jethro knows something I don't."

Bradone's phone mewled faintly and she opened her notebook as she picked it up. She listened carefully to somebody named Harry, turning pages in her notebook that were scrawled with diagrams and iconlike sketches. She studied one at the very back that had a plastic-coated table of figures and signs and dates.

"Sell Singer and buy Stryker and double the number of shares we discussed yesterday.... Harry, you know I don't care about your little insider tips. Do what I say, like a good boy." She punched him off and closed the notebook. "My broker. He's not very clever, but I never take his advice."

"You play the stock market too? I thought you just gambled at the tables."

"Charlie, I have to invest my winnings so they'll grow. You have to lose big-time to be allowed in the high-stakes games."

"I'd think just paying to stay in that penthouse would make the Hilton happy enough."

"Those penthouses are comped to a select few who are expected to lose heavily. Trick is to lose a few million one time, win it back, say, the next two times you visit a resort."

"A few million?" Charlie searched for words that weren't there. "I suppose you have DRIPs too."

"Of course. The secret to the stock market is not playing it, but in compounding."

Did everybody know about this but Charlie? "Okay, we're even. You win round two. He whistles."

"Who whistles?"

"Mitch Hilsten. Instead of snoring."

"WERE YOU REALLY flying over Yucca and Area Fifty-one or was that trick photography?" They were in the limo. The driver had been ordered to drive around for a while. "Tell me, Charlie."

"Not till you tell me why you're dressed in black and why you are avoiding talking about the one thing I want to know."

"Black seemed the proper mood for what I wanted to do with you today."

"What, bury me?"

"If I'm to help you, we'll have to do some detecting. But

first, I have to know about Area Fifty-one and that robbery at the Hilton's casino.''

So Charlie, who hated detecting, described her experience with the illegal flyover of undisclosed areas on the vast government reservation of the Nevada desert. ''When I got back to the Hilton after that sickening flight with Evan and his motley crew, the lights went out. I didn't know about the robbery until the next day.''

And why am I trusting you with all this?

''Trust your instincts, Charlie, they're good ones.''

Tell that to Georgette Millrose and Jethro Larue.

Charlie's impulse to trust this woman made her skeptical, but she felt drawn to Bradone as she might a female mentor or even a mother. Charlie, who was adopted, wondered fleetingly if her birth mother was more like Bradone than Edwina Greene. And then felt immediately guilty. But she also felt an unconditional acceptance here she never had with her mother or daughter.

Bradone doesn't know you as well as your mother and daughter.

''This is all so peculiar.'' The stargazer who earned her living gambling and compounding removed the oversized sunglasses to chew on an earpiece. Vertical worry lines formed at the corners of her mouth and between her eyebrows. ''This plane you and Caryl Thompson, Evan, and his cameraman flew in was the burning plane out by Rachel on the news, wasn't it? The Mooney.''

''They torched it themselves. I suppose so they couldn't be traced to it. But then why did Evan show it burning at his little titillating screening? I think he's gotten us all in a lot of trouble.''

''I'm afraid I do too. He's acting like a little boy, thumbing his nose at the authorities.''

''He says it's all going to be fine because of some magic he's intending to pull off. Somehow I don't find that reassuring. You've got to watch out for these geniuses.''

''This morning's paper claims all aboard that plane were incinerated.'' The astrologer's worry lines deepened. ''The story used it as a warning to people trying to invade that air-space, hinting that it was shot down by keepers of the secrets out there. Evan's armed response personnel? They must know you all got away.''

''They could sift through the ashes and notice there are no charred bones, and now, after the screening, they have to know who we are.'' They'd also be able to tell the Mooney landed instead of crashing. Why was the truth being covered up here? Force of habit? Were military authorities playing along with Evan's amateurish stage setting for a reason? Maybe they were getting ready to spring a surprise of their own. What if that wand thing, that fancy laser-phaser in the casino-heist clip—wasn't special effects?

''So the young pilot was murdered because he angered somebody by flying Evan and crew over restricted areas when he himself was a pilot for this airline ferrying workers out to those same areas. And Timothy Graden died because you told him the pilot's death was murder and not jaywalking, and he may or may not have suggested same to someone or left a note or two around the police station declaring such—that one's pretty weak, Charlie.''

''What if he did some investigating of his own?''

''And Ben Hanley from Kenosha, Wisconsin, died because he drank a poisoned drink meant for you. A tiny mention of that in this morning's paper claimed he died of a stroke in his room at the Hilton.''

''They were staying at Circus, Circus.''

''Okay, but that means your life is in danger.''

''Not if Art Sleem poisoned the drink. He's dead.''

''But you think he was working for someone else. That someone isn't dead.''

''Art said he freelanced. He was a bouncer for Loopy Louie's. The government guy investigating the murders at Evan's said Art worked for the government.''

''Sounds like he was for hire by anyone. We need a motive for three easily documented murders. Sleem, Tooney from the IRS, and the other bouncer from Loopy's.''

''I thought astrologers read the stars for answers. You sound more like a cop.'' Much as Charlie hated detecting, she enjoyed this woman. Must be fun to live life as one big adventure.

"We need the deductive methods of the police and have at our disposal added insight. But who could walk up to three grown men and have time to shoot each squarely in the forehead without at least the last one lunging forward and getting shot less than squarely? They were most likely at Evan Black's house for nefarious reasons, but what would two bouncers have in common with an IRS man? And how did Tooney get there before you if you'd just left him at the Hilton?"

"Stolen money? And they might not all have been shot at the same time, but in different parts of the house and moved to the great room. And I changed clothes and made a phone call before I left. Maybe Matt Tooney got a faster cab than I did, surprised Sleem and the bald bouncer searching the place. Maybe they shot him." Or were they looking for the wand-phaser?

"Who shot them?"

Charlie leaned toward her friend's hat brim and whispered, "Can we trust this guy?" She gestured toward the driver and the glass panel between them. There was something about the back of the guy's head under the improbable cap...or was it the neck? "Do we know it's really soundproof back here?"

A touch of the familiar playfulness returned to Bradone's expression as she picked up the speaker phone and rapped on the window. "The Janet Terminal, please."

NINETEEN

CHARLIE AND the stargazer gazed through a chain-link fence at an unmarked building on a far corner of McCarran International Airport. An eight-foot chain link with barbed wire in a Y formation on top, as if intended to keep people in and out at the same time. According to legend, this is where Patrick the hunk and his fellow pilots would have picked up and returned the workers they transported between Groom Lake and Vegas.

Behind them, their smirking driver leaned against the limo, and every time Charlie glanced over her shoulder, he raised thick black eyebrows above small round sunglasses. He wore a dark suit but with a tam-o'-shanter pulled low over his forehead.

Between them and the driver stretched an unnecessarily wide drainage ditch of hardscrabble graded sand/dirt. Charlie had painful pieces of it in her sandals still and dreaded the return trip. It was more like a dry moat that extended around the front of this little corner of the airport, as well.

Across the side road, along which the limo was parked, a concrete block wall formed the back of a row of hangars for the private jets of the elite, according to Bob, the smirking driver. Charlie had an irrational problem believing in men named Bob. The eyebrows alone made him highly suspicious.

"How do we know this is the Janet Terminal?" Bradone asked. "There's no sign on the building."

"If there was, it wouldn't be undisclosed," Bob said.

"But it could be a warehouse, a repair shop. Anything."

A small nondescript concrete building in tiered levels and two-tone gray. Its windows either heavily tinted in bright green or covered with inside shades of that color. No markings, no flags, just a plethora of tall light poles among the cars in the lot and surveillance cameras on the corners of the building. The tails of two white airliners with no insignia were poised over the roof, one on each side.

"So now what?" Charlie asked.

"Let's try another tack"—Bradone lowered her voice and turned away from their driver—"now that we're not in the car. Let's start with murder number one. The pilot was connected with Area Fifty-one through this airline, with Evan through flying him over it, and with Art Sleem, a freelance enforcer who could well have had more than one employer."

"I can't believe Sleem really worked for the government."

"Governments hire temporary help just like everybody else. And a lot of it undercover so they can't be held accountable. No reason why Sleem couldn't be working for Loopy Louie and one small sliver of the government. Maybe himself too. But what, Charlie, if all this was connected to the robbery at the Hilton casino, as well?" A jet screamed low overhead and a whirly little wind tunnel, which may or may not have been caused by it, lifted Bradone's hat high in the air, flipped it a couple of times, and dropped it on the other side of the fence.

"Looks like you blew your cover," Bob said behind them, and guffawed.

THEY DUMPED Bob and the limo back at the Hilton, slipped into their rooms, and, ignoring telephone message lights, donned blue jeans and shirts for the Jane Doe tourist look. Charlie felt pretty silly by the time she met her accomplice outside a corner door by the glass elevator on the outside of the building.

Bradone looked mysterious behind her Jackie Onassis sunglasses. Avoiding all ears, they walked to the Strip. "I have the feeling the police are going to be looking for you with further questions. We'll just keep moving and thinking and sorting this out. You may be safer away from the hotel."

Charlie would rather be playing blackjack. "Art Sleem never seemed to have much of a problem finding me."

"Good thought." Bradone pulled her into an alley behind the old Debbie Reynolds theater and museum, the pictures of the stars—Marilyn Monroe, Gary Cooper, Joan Crawford, John Wayne, Judy Garland—still gracing its front. All beautiful then. All dead now.

They watched for passing foot traffic. There wasn't any. The heat coming off Debbie's white stucco met that of the white-painted concrete block of the Bank of America, where they stood about midalley.

"See, what you have to understand about astrology, Charlie," Bradone started off again, "is that it doesn't give answers. It gives clues. Its study can recommend paths to follow and those not to take. Think of it as more like a road map than a manual."

"Sounds more like new software." Like, not a lotta help. "You must have had some opinion last night when you suddenly went all serious and then stayed up running charts."

"All I really know at this point is that it's not a good time for you to be in the position you're in."

"What position *am* I in?"

"The position of being in great danger."

"There's a good time for that?"

"Charlie, Mars is squaring your sun." Just the way her modulated tone deepened, that hint of breathiness that crept into it, the dread when she made that ridiculous statement—she could have been a doctor informing Charlie her cancer was inoperable.

Charlie couldn't swear that the sinking feeling was her stomach, but something somewhere was sinking. "God, that reminds me—Art Sleem, while loading me down with threats he called 'warnings' yesterday, said to warn my high-roller friend she better watch out."

"You're making that up to get even with me for being so obtuse. He didn't even know me."

"No, honest. Maybe he was working for the Hilton too. Maybe they're onto your scheme. He kept talking about nobody liking counters and casinos are not public property—they're private. Which, I suppose, means they can make their own rules."

"I hate to tell you this, but it's even worse for me to be in a dangerous position about now."

"What are we going to do? We can't just keep walking."

"I can think of three things right off the bat and I'm sure there are more. But we have to make a game plan first. We need to talk to Officer Graden's widow and to that pilot's sister, and I think we should visit Loopy Louie's."

They turned left onto Las Vegas Boulevard.

"But take heart. Venus is on your part of fortune in your first house. Otherwise"—Bradone shook her head as if in disbelief—"I've never seen a chart like yours."

THEY SAT AT the bar at Loopy Louie's, Charlie looking longingly at the blackjack tables across the room.

"Don't even think about it." Bradone studied a small calendarlike chart that fit in her billfold. "This is no day for you to chance anything. I expect you've been on a winning streak the last few of them though."

"I thought it was all a setup having to do with Art Sleem, after the hot shoe I shared with you, that is. But it was really the planets and the houses and moons rising and stuff, huh?"

"You were in Venus trine." Bradone took a long swig of cold beer.

Charlie stuck with a diet Coke. "I don't get you. You serve your guests yak crud and then you drink martinis and beer. What's the deal?"

Bradone peered over her reading glasses and billfold star chart. "Yak crud?"

"Breakfast on Tuesday, remember?"

"Oh, I thought you knew." Her laugh, out loud for once, turned heads for some distance, even considering the noise in the place. Trying to hide with this woman around was fruitless. "You seem so intuitive."

Loopy Louie's was literally indescribable, and this was Charlie's first time here. It had still been under construction on her last trip to Vegas and she'd never made it inside the night Pat Thompson died. "Tasted like chalk ground into goat's milk. Left a coating on your tongue like a hangover gone postal."

"It was a test of Richard Morse. Your opinion of him was obvious. I had to form my own."

He apparently passed.

The bartender was dressed like a eunuch, the dealers like sinister bedouins, and the floormen like even more threatening Arab oil guys—black suits with fezzes (red upside-down flowerpots with tassels). The bar girls were draped like belly dancers in gossamer veils and transparent harem pajamas over G-strings.

Even the noise was different. The calliope bleeps of slots else-where were cymbals, gongs, tambourines, camel calls, and weird pipe music here. The racing, blinking colored lights meant to stir up excitement in other casinos were muted colors seen though gossamer scarves blown about by ceiling fans and re-vealing huge lighted scimitars when they parted.

Charlie wasn't sure whether to be on the lookout for Bogart, Lawrence of Arabia, or the Ayatollah. The more she saw of this place, the more mundane and reassuring Bradone-the-astrologer became.

Charlie plugged a quarter into the video poker monitor em-bedded in the bar top to calm her nerves and get her drink free. And lost four dollars in quarters as fast as she could plug them in. Expensive Coke.

Bradone McKinley drew a computer printout from her bot-tomless purse and grew so agitated over it and her calculations, she ordered another Heineken.

"Maybe you shouldn't have sold the Singer and bought the Stryker," Charlie said with little sympathy. "Do you run your charts on a computer?"

"I've got a notebook in the penthouse loaded with special software. I don't know how we managed without them."

The eunuch leaned over the bar to look at Charlie's monitor. "I never seen anything like that. Must be something wrong with the machine."

"Nah, it's just the stars and the houses and the moons falling. You know, trines and stuff. Don't worry about it."

The clamor of a gong startled Charlie into dropping the quar-ter she was about to play and lose.

Shift change.

Blondes replaced red-haired Arab potentates with freckles and steely eyes. Sweating bedouins in full headgear and robes were replaced by already-sweating new ones. Their eunuch pulled off his rubber baldness to scratch a full head of matted hair as his bald replacement stepped into the bar pit.

And a man, even shorter and older and less impressive than Richard Morse, stepped up to the bar between Bradone and

Charlie. "I am Louie Deloese. And you, I understand," he said, leaning down to pick up Charlie's quarter and handing it to her, "discovered the body of my good friend Arthur Sleem."

TWENTY

LOOPY LOUIE did not look Middle Eastern, Mediterranean, Arabian, French, or even loopy. He looked inconsequential, small graying mustache and piercing blue eyes notwithstanding. His little office looked even less consequential. "I understand my friend Arthur gave you some money."

"Two hundred thousand in cash," Charlie answered. "Did he work for you?"

"Arthur Sleem worked for whoever paid him, Mrs. Greene. As I have learned, to my dismay."

"Even the government?"

Louie shrugged narrow shoulders. He didn't look Las Vegas either, in a tweed jacket over a pale blue shirt and frayed collar.

"Who has more money than the government?"

There had been no real overt threat as yet, but Charlie didn't feel safe. It must have showed.

"Mrs. Greene—"

"Miss."

"Miss Greene, I just want to know what happened to the money and the details of Arthur Sleem's death. You are in no danger—not from me anyway."

"I'm just concerned about my friend," Charlie lied.

"That is no problem." He opened a side door of his desk, clicked some buttons, and the wood paneling on one wall parted to reveal a bank of monitors like those in the security area of the Hilton. One of them showed Bradone still engrossed in her billfold chart and scribbling things in her notebook.

Is that why she wanted to come here? Couldn't she have done that anywhere?

Well, she could have been showing more worry over me.

Why? She can tell what will happen to you by her charts.

"You see? Your friend is fine." But Louie Deloese left the panel open and that monitor on.

"Art Sleem delivered a whole lot of threats, threats that he called 'warnings,' along with the two hundred thousand in cash, Mr. Deloese. One of them was that my friend should be careful. What does she have to do with any of this?"

"Where is the money?" he countered.

"I went over to Evan Black's yesterday to give it to him because I didn't know what to do with it, and I found the three murder victims instead. The last I saw of your money, it was in the hands of Detective Jerome Battista of Metro Police."

He nodded and turned to the monitor, chewed on a fingernail. "Miss McKinley is a well-known high roller. She beats the odds more often than is comfortable, but she does not fit the profile of a counter. Arthur might have been asked to let her know subtly, say through a friend, that she shouldn't push her luck. This is, of course, only conjecture."

"By the gaming commission?"

Louie gave the eye roll and sigh that signified he was dealing with a doofus—which he was. "Someone at the Hilton casino? Or the Mirage? She frequented both. Or Bally's? They see her often." He watched Bradone scribble and drink beer. "Intriguing woman. But high rollers usually pay out better. Now, about Arthur's demise."

Charlie, still feeling honesty would be more likely to get her out of this and still feeling intimidated, described how she found Sleem and the others all lined up behind the furniture in Evan Black's great room, with identical bullet wounds in the center of their foreheads. She wanted to ask him about the third man on the floor of the great room, but she didn't know how to word it. Like, Who was that balding friend of Art's who helped him shove Patrick Thompson under the wheels of a car in front of your casino last Sunday night? Instead, she described how Evan Black's house had been searched.

"Was the two hundred thousand meant for Evan's new project? Why in cash?"

"This, after all, is Las Vegas, Miss Greene."

"A bet? You were paying off a bet? You gave it to Art Sleem to give to me to give to Evan?"

He did the eye roll for doofuses again. "I was honest with

you. Do not pretend you know nothing of Mr. Black's wager of the century, Miss Greene. He has become a very wealthy gentleman."

"Free money for his project. Even Evan Black can't get away with stealing money."

Deloese shrugged, gestured with both palms upward. "The odds that it would be the Vegas Hilton were minuscule—it has the best security in town. Most, including me, thought it *would* be here. It was brilliant. So I am assuming your client would know better than to keep his winnings in his home."

"Stolen money is hardly winnings."

"I'm a little confused as to whose side you are on, Miss Greene. But I assure you the money taken from the Hilton is minuscule compared to those winnings. Everybody in town wanted in on this bizarre wager."

"But why did Sleem say it was the money from a jackpot I'd won at the Hilton casino?"

"In a way, it was. But for the lights going out at the casino, which won Mr. Black and, I assume, those connected to him a true jackpot. I saw to it that my relatively small debt to Mr. Black was paid. And then I think my friend Art Sleem decided to become greedy."

"Why are you telling me all this?" Nobody else will tell me anything.

"Because I think you, as a representative of Mr. Black, are not as confused as you pretend. Because those lights went out at the Hilton as you entered it. And because I can help Mr. Black with another problem. Tell him there is a channel, most secure, by which he can move tangible assets. I know he will have other offers, but I think my charges will undercut them. If he'd like to discuss this, my nephew will set up a meeting."

He stood and reached across the desk to shake her hand in dismissal. "I think I would be very careful if I were you, Miss Greene. There are those who will tie you to the robbery, but even more dangerous are those outraged by the method used so casually to achieve it. And she"—he looked back at the monitor, where Bradone started on yet another Heineken—"she should be careful too, your friend. Arthur was right about one thing. I do not believe the stars will be of much help."

EMILY GRADEN lived in a white stucco duplex with a red-tiled roof. Inside, all was white except for yellow furniture, blinds, and carpet. Charlie felt like she'd walked into a daisy.

Emily Graden was packing boxes of dishes on the kitchen table. Emily and her children would move in with her parents until she could find less expensive rent. They were down to a teacher's salary. The little boys were already with Grandpa, and Grandpa wasn't well. All this, Charlie and Bradone learned from Emily's mother before they reached the kitchen. A collection of framed movie posters lined the entry hall, one of them for *All the King's Women.*

Graden's women looked hollowed out and empty, in shock over the abrupt change their lives had taken.

Charlie'd called ahead to explain she had witnessed the accident Timothy Graden was probably investigating at the time of his murder. What she didn't say was that if she hadn't insisted he look further into the young pilot's death, Emily's husband might still be alive.

Charlie felt awful. She looked to Bradone for guidance. But the astrologer'd had one too many Heinekens or trines in the wrong house—whatever.

Charlie tried to ignore the high chair in the corner, gunk still smeared across the tray and caked on the armrests that held it in place. Libby used to do that. When she wasn't hurling the whole food dish at the wall.

Emily Graden leaned against the counter in front of the sink, hugging her ribs. She would be a pretty woman when her face wasn't bloated with grief. She wore the same kind of faded denim jeans as Bradone and Charlie. So did her mother. The great homogenizer, like aprons and hats were once.

"Did you see your husband after I did? Did he say anything about Pat Thompson's murder or my reporting it?"

"He called. Said he had to look into an accident and might be later than usual, see if I could get Mom to take the kids for a few hours the next morning." He worked nights, she worked days. "Said he was on his way to the Janet Terminal."

Emily Graden's mom made a hissing sound.

Bradone finally came back on-line. "The papers and broadcast-news services gave no details about where the hit-and-run occurred or who found your husband. What happened to his bicycle?"

Grandma banged two skillets and a saucepan into a box and threw in a can opener to enhance the racket. Grandma was about to kick them out. You didn't have to be intuitive to know that. "You don't have no right to come in here and ask questions of a grieving widow. Shouldn't have let you in. But she said to."

"It's okay, Mom. I assume the bike is back at the station. He took his own car to work. He told me he was going to check something out on his own before involving the department."

Grandma opened a drawer, took out a cleaver, and studied it. "But they found him out on the road to the Cherry Patch. Said I shouldn't want everybody to know about that." Emily looked at Bradone as if she might consider trusting her. What secret powers did the stargazer have? Besides a compelling personality and a tankful of Heineken.

"The pedestrian killed on Las Vegas Boulevard that night was a pilot who flew workers out of the Janet Terminal, and for producer Evan Black on his off-hours," Charlie said.

"I know. His sister phoned. Wanted to know if the department had found the vehicle that ran Tim down."

"Have they, Emily?" Charlie just wanted to get this over with and get out of there.

"Apparently it was a limo like the ones used by several services that ferry men out that way. They're looking for the driver."

Brothels were illegal in the city but existed less formally than the legal whorehouses in the county that advertised in the city (even on top of taxicabs). Limo services made a good business transporting vacationing johns out to the flesh and back.

"Was his car damaged?" Bradone insisted. "Was he in it when he was hit?"

''It was in the ditch, out on One Sixty.'' Tears came then, without sobs. Emily reached for the Kleenex box next to her.

''Emily, you got two kids, *and* a daddy with one foot in the grave. What's the matter with you?''

''Tim wasn't going to any whorehouse, Mom. He was dumped out there after he was run over. And these women look like they believe me.''

TWENTY-ONE

CARYL THOMPSON'S CONDO was white stucco on the outside with, a red-tiled roof too. It was attached to three other condos on a street of similar combinations, all with tiny front yards and gated patios at the four corners.

Inside, Caryl's home was largely beige. Beige furniture, carpet, and blinds. Tall dried wheat grass in a floor vase. Three-story, with a drive-in basement garage. Two humongous cats moved over on the sofa to make room for Bradone and Charlie.

At Bradone's insistence, they'd dropped in without calling first this time, giving Caryl less time to fabricate answers to questions she'd expect to be asked. The astrologer reasoned that since Charlie was Evan Black's agent and Caryl worked for him, they'd gain admittance.

Dressed in sweats, sweat, and stringy hair, still gasping after her run, Patrick Thompson's sister sprawled on a recliner. A concrete gargoyle leered from the hearthstone of a gas-log fireplace.

The feline who chose Charlie to torture began kneading her thighs through the denim of her jeans, hard enough to make her squirm.

"Why did you call Timothy Graden's wife?" Charlie wedged an index finger under each of the offending paws to pry the pricking nails loose. "If you didn't think your brother's death was murder?" The fat cat hissed and bit Charlie's thumb before crawling off her and onto as much of Bradone's lap as its obese partner had left vacant. "I mean, you wouldn't go to the police, so you must not have thought it was. Or is it that you are just as involved in whatever Patrick was that you're afraid to?"

"Look, my brother is dead. My parents just left, hallelujah, and I must have run ten miles to get those two disasters out of my system. And now you turn up. I have to shower and get to work." The bones in Caryl's face looked larger without makeup, her eyes smaller. "How did you know I called Emily Graden?"

"We just came from there." Charlie sucked her thumb and tasted blood. "Was your brother run over by a limo too? The kind that takes johns out to the Patch? Did you think it might be the same one?"

"Having them both run over the same night—of course I wondered. And, yes, I'm just as involved as he was." Caryl pulled the stringy hair up off her face and neck and knotted it behind her head. "And now you are too, Charlie Greene," she said, and shrugged. "Involved, I mean. These people don't take prisoners."

That's exactly what Charlie was afraid of. A roomful of people had seen her flying over Groom Lake with Evan and company. It was documented on film. "You mean the government?"

"Might as well be. You're Evan's agent, ask him."

"Where did Pat live?" Bradone asked.

"Here. He had too many girlfriends to move in with one. But a sister—what the hell."

Bradone reached across seventy-five pounds of cat fur to right a picture frame lying facedown on the end table next to the couch. She held it up for Charlie to see and then for Caryl Thompson.

"That's him. Patrick," Charlie said.

Patrick's sister just looked away.

"He was beautiful." Bradone laid the picture frame down as she'd found it. "I'm sorry for your loss. But why would he risk so much for Evan Black? What did he want out of life?"

"His own plane. That's all he ever wanted."

"Evan was going to buy him a plane?" Charlie thought that sounded too generous for a low-budget producer. "Why?"

"Pat would share in the profits and buy a plane. Eventually, he hoped to own a charter service."

"To produce something of this size, Evan will have to go to a studio. There won't be any profits. Not after production costs and wages and once Evan Black and Mitch Hilsten take a percentage. There're never profits."

"Is that really true?" Bradone asked, "or just Hollywood paranoia?"

"Well, if there are, they get absorbed in the grease that's cooking the books." That's why damn good agents demand every cent they can squeeze out of a project up front for their clients and why the guilds make all the salaries so expensive.

"Pat was to be paid up front," Caryl said, as if reading Charlie's thoughts. Then she stood, so they also had to. "And now I will be paid instead."

"Paid for what?"

"For goods delivered." She walked to the door and opened it. "Just one more thing," Charlie pleaded. "That fancy phaser-wand thing one of the robbers waved around in the film—that was special effects? Or some real doohickey from, say, Groom Lake? That and the gizmo that turned off the lights at the Hilton? And what else, Caryl? Was your brother killed for smuggling secret stuff out of Area Fifty-one?" What kind of trouble had Evan gotten Charlie into?

Caryl Thompson ushered them out onto the patio without answering and even opened the gate for them.

"Pat wanted a plane. What do *you* want out of life, Caryl?" Bradone insisted.

"I want to help Evan get even with the people who ordered my brother's death." And she closed the gate and then the door as she went back into the house.

CHARLIE WHISPERED an explanation of the wand-phaser to Bradone in the cab that had waited outside for them and the effect it supposedly had on those caught in the dark at the casino robbery. "I'd bet it was Evan waving it, and I just assumed he was showing off, that maybe it had some connection to the Star Trek Experience at the Hilton. If it was real, it was awesome."

"If only the heavy woman could move, it might mean that the phaser couldn't affect her as much because she had more mass to penetrate."

"That could be faked. There's little Evan can't do with film—although there wasn't time to work up computer animation. But if Patrick persuaded one of the workers to spirit some secret weapons off the Groom Lake base for Evan's conspiracy project..."

"For the price of an airplane of his own," Bradone said thoughtfully. "'Goods delivered.' Wonder what all those goods were?"

"The infrared camera and goggles can be bought on the open market. Could be just copies of important papers or plans that Evan could use in the project."

"Whatever it was, its theft explains why Caryl's brother had to die." Bradone tapped a tooth with her sunglasses, nodding sagely. "The keepers of the secrets out there might have wanted to make an example of him among workers and those who fly them to work. And why Emily Graden's husband was going out to the Janet Terminal."

"The question, Detective McKinley, is Evan Black's role in all this. I'm not sure I'd trust him as far as Caryl Thompson does. And Loopy Louie's offering Evan some kind of way to get, I thought, all his winnings out of the country. Sounds like he's bidding against others for the job. I wonder if it's also to get some secret doohickys out."

"Wish we could talk to Evan while avoiding the police, the murder or murderers, and—"

"Richard Morse?"

"And Richard Morse. Don't underestimate the man's usefulness to you, Charlie. He has great admiration for your abilities. In his way, I think he's very proud of you."

And you're getting tired of him. And I'm tired of small favors Richard's pride lets him drop, "in his way."

THEY LEFT THE CAB on a street corner and walked a few blocks to a deli with outdoor seating in an inner courtyard. Bradone made a discrete phone call to her butler before their salads arrived. She made another after they'd been served and spoke to Evan Black himself, giving directions to their location.

"Someone named Mel will pick us up in about forty-five minutes. So we can relax and enjoy our meal."

"Mel is Evan's cinematographer. What are they up to?"

"Same thing we are, trying to avoid the police. Evan left word with Reed so we could get hold of him. It seems Metro has taken Richard Morse in for questioning.''

''Richard doesn't know anything. He's been so smitten with you, he won't listen to what I've been trying to tell him about all this.'' Charlie put down a fork full of radicchio, sprouts, arugula, and godknows. ''What? That's not all. I'm not being intuitive. You look funny.''

Bradone speared a cucumber slice and took an eternity to chew it. ''Looks like we're going to get our chance to talk to Evan.''

''God, are there more bodies?''

The unreadable expression on the stargazer's face grew even stranger. ''Evan doesn't want to spend time with the police because of an important meeting. And he wants you there too. I guess I get to come along by default.''

''What meeting? Will you stop this?''

''Charlie, Mitch Hilsten is in town.''

TWENTY-TWO

"Do you know parents drive kids to schools two blocks from home in neighborhoods so safe no kid has been molested by anybody but relatives and family friends for decades?" Evan Black, the young genius, swung his legs from side to side over the edge of an upper bunk and gazed down on them all. The hanging light fixture over the table, a gas lantern with a lightbulb in it, swung in rhythm with his legs across his little round glasses. "Kids are safer out on the streets than in the house."

He was making Charlie seasick. She and Bradone sat on the bench on one side of the galley table, Mel Goodall and Mitch Hilsten on the other. Mitch leaned against the bulkhead of the boat Evan had borrowed for the meet, tied up at a marina somewhere on Lake Mead.

"All because the media makes big on false statistics and rare but memorable occurrences in a small portion of the population."

Mitch had one elbow on the table and one on the sink counter. He was in his denim mode—clothes faded to powder blue, like his eyes, like Charlie and Bradone's pants. He faced Evan, hands clasped in front of his mouth, biting one knuckle, watching the writer/producer with skepticism.

Charlie blinked. Skepticism? Mitch Hilsten, who believed in every kooky thing that came down the Ventura Freeway? Maybe he was acting. Hard to tell with this guy.

"And then the rest of the entertainment industry picks up on the latest fear—books, movies, documentaries of odd events make us feel they're common. Somebody figures out how to train police and psychologists and publishing houses on how to handle the fear, discover it, treat it, prosecute it, recognize it. Hell, a whole new industry or three are invented right there, job descriptions and new college studies—not to mention pulp genres. It's beautiful, man."

Mel Goodall pretended sleepiness but watched Charlie through slits.

"People are even afraid of the fucking sun. Kids get fat and turn into listless couch potatoes because nobody wants to smear sunscreen on them every time they want to go out and play. Old people suffer from vitamin D deficiencies because the sun will give them cancer. Hell, life will give you cancer. Everything's gotten out of hand. One baby is swiped out of a nursery in one city and every hospital in the country's got to have surveillance cameras and security checks on the obstetric wards," said the man, responsible for stealing government secrets, joyfully. And he'd already involved Mitch in that theft by announcing his probable participation in the project.

And Charlie, caught in a quandary, watched Evan. Hard to square this boyish, excited, earnest, creative creature with the man who showed no emotion other than impatience with Charlie when she insisted on discussing with Officer Graden his personal pilot's death on the street in front of Loopy Louie's.

The man who promised Patrick's sister he would get even with the people who ordered that death and yet told Charlie he wasn't sure that it hadn't been an accident. Who were the people who hired Sleem and the bald bouncer to walk Patrick into the traffic? How did Loopy Louie fit into all this?

Again, she looked to Bradone for guidance, but the astrologer had zoned out the minute Mitch Hilsten came into view. She squirmed every time he inhaled.

The boat, sort of a motorized sailboat, rocked with the lantern light crisscrossing Evan's glasses, nudging the dock gently. Nobody but Charlie seemed to suffer from indigestion.

"So, what's all this got to do with Groom Lake?" Mitch slid a studied glance at Charlie.

"It's the ultimate in conspiracy. Okay, maybe along with Roswell."

"But what's the purpose? To poke fun at people's beliefs? Eccentricities? What?"

Charlie gave Evan an "I told you so" smirk.

"No, man, to poke fun at their fears. We're talking concept here. Theme. Groom Lake is the epitome, but only symbolic, of the way conspiracy has taken over our lives. We don't trust anybody in a position of authority because the press and entertainment industry, one and the same, blow mistakes and corruption out of all proportion. And you know what, man? They're…we're going to make our fears happen. And that is the theme behind *Conspiracy*. We'll start with the small stuff—like perfectly healthy kids in bad need of exercise being driven to school two blocks away, never allowed outside without sunscreen, women in grocery stores scared to death the food's unsafe in the cleanest country in history—all the way to the billions spent on things that aren't needed, like Star Wars, all because of fear.''

"Is there any script here?" asked Mitch, still skeptical but now showing some interest.

"Script it as we go. You know me, or you've read how I work. But see? The conspiracy is us, Mitch, living our lives out of fear of things that mostly don't happen or don't happen to most. The cause of the fear is not the dangers real or imagined in this world, but the media hyping them out of proportion to their impact in the name of news-entertainment. Fiction that becomes fact because we believe it so strongly. We could be missing the best days of our lives, Mitch, the best days of our country, the best days of our planet.''

There were smears on both of Charlie's contact lenses—she could be missing something too. How do you finance without a script? And why hadn't he pitched this way to the moneymen at the screening? He'd have had them pulling out checkbooks in droves instead of groaning.

Hell, because they were groaning and pulling out cash instead. To pay off the stupid bets that Evan couldn't pull off a casino heist or which casino it would be. Did he really have enough money from that wager to produce the film himself?

Even given her mistrust of him, there was no mistaking this producer's energy and enthusiasm now. Charlie could feel it in the small space.

"What do you think, Mitch? It's okay, tell me.''

"Well…it's kind of murky.''

Charlie took another look at the superstar. Was this a new Mitch Hilsten? She thought he ate murky for breakfast.

"I know this is long for a pitch, but you're a deep mind."

"Where do I fit into this?" the deep mind asked.

People will flock to see you do anything. Even if it's stupid. That's how you fit in.

"You, Mitch, are a pilot for Janet. You know what that is?"

"Call name for a certain airline flying workers out to Groom."

Charlie was not surprised he knew that. Mitch probably knew all about compounding and DRIPs too. Even with smeared lenses, she was seeing all kinds of holes in this theory, but wouldn't think of interrupting a young genius and a superstar. AIDS, for instance. Cigarettes, for another. Or were they not part of the conspiracy theory because they were very real dangers?

"Your wife is the one taking your young children to school, panicking at the fresh-vegetable bins at the local grocery because of a TV newscast reporting one child dying a mysterious death after eating an avocado or something. This is all short background playing behind the front credits."

"Hope my wife isn't Cyndi Seagal. She drives me nuts."

Evan had him and knew it. His smile said it all. As his agent, Charlie should be happy.

"Nah, she's too old. We'll come up with somebody."

Cyndi Seagal, younger than Charlie by several years, was a client of Congdon and Morse Representation, Inc., on Wilshire Boulevard in Beverly Hills. And a favorite of Richard's. She was also a hell of a lot younger than Mitch Hilsten. She and Mitch had starred together in the hit that had rejuvenated his career. Didn't seem to be doing as much for hers.

"But the point here is Groom Lake—Area Fifty-one is the ultimate showcase of what happens when people feel victimized by what they perceive to be a conspiracy. Their fears come true. Their belief in those fears, instigated by a callous media, make them so. And nowhere more than on the vast military-owned desert spaces of Nevada. This is no big Spielberg extravaganza,

Mitch. It's a quiet, low-toned, 'creep up on you and you'll never forget it' film."

"*Psycho* meets *The Player*," Charlie interjected.

"Exactly." Evan's approval was discouraging. She'd thought she was being funny.

"Where are you going to get footage to pull that off, Black? Fake it in a studio? Computer animation?"

"Don't have to," Evan said.

"Already in the can," Mel said. "Right, Charlie?"

"You'd have seen it by now, if I could get in my house. There's a lot of it Charlie hasn't seen either. Most of it, in fact. Some great satellite stuff."

Mitch turned his full attention to Charlie now. "Hear you found the bodies. Rough. I'm sorry. Tell me you're not going to do any investigating."

"I'm not going to do any investigating."

"Charlie?" Bradone came out of her trance.

"I'm just helping Bradone. Tagging along, you know."

"No, I don't know." Mitch turned around to face Charlie and thus Bradone across the table. The astrologer sunk back into her trance. "But Maggie says you're in bad need of a vacation, and this doesn't sound like one."

Oh really? "You talked to Maggie Stutzman?"

"Well, you wouldn't answer my E-mail."

"Everybody's ganging up on me. Jeesh."

"See? Conspiracy." Evan rubbed his hands in obvious glee. "Charlie's indicative of the national mood. Everybody who sees this film is going to relate. And they'll never forget it was Mitch Hilsten who was flying for Janet. How did you know it was called the Janet Terminal, Mitch?"

"The Internet." But Mitch was still glaring at Charlie.

"Well, okay, enough. Maybe we better go topside and let you two have a big fight and then kiss and make up or whatever you kids do." Evan jumped down from the bunk and held an arm out to Bradone. "Come on up and tell me about your investigations, Detective McKinley."

"Wait, how do you know that nameless government guy with Battista hasn't confiscated this footage you're so proud of?"

Charlie called up after him. And all that cash Loopy hoped you weren't keeping at home?

Mel Goodall rose and stretched, chuckling. "Because the can wasn't in the house."

"Was it there yesterday when those three men were murdered?"

"Nope."

"Maybe that's what they were looking for."

But Mel and his long, lean Dockers disappeared above deck, leaving Charlie and Mitch to stare at each other across the table.

"Sounds like you're going to deal."

"Certainly going to think about it, and seriously. Evan Black is becoming an icon in the industry. I keep thinking I should pay you instead of Lazarus. You've done more for my career."

"Mitch, I admire Evan's work as much as you do. But this project is being financed illegally, and I think you should walk away from it. And I didn't do anything to get you this part."

"You suggested me to your client for it."

"He wanted me to ask you because he thinks I'm your girlfriend. He thought he was using me. But I didn't ask you. He merely mentioned my name to your agent, hoping that you'd think I lined this up. I didn't do anything, Mitch. I've been too busy with all the dead men."

"And you didn't get Richard Morse to suggest me for the role in *Phantom of the Alpine Tunnel* when Eric Ashton walked at the last minute, I suppose. The role that turned my sliding career around."

"I've told you a million times, Richard called me to approach you for the part the morning after our one infamous night together in that rat-infested motel in Moab. He thought he was using me too, but I didn't do anything that time either."

"What do you mean, you didn't do anything? Most exhausting night of my life."

"I mean I didn't ask you about the part for Richard. He suggested I sleep with you to get you to play it. The pig."

"But you already had."

"Not to get you to take the part—it was just—"

"Estrus. I know," he said fondly. "Know what?"

"No, what?"

"I've had my astrologer charting this estrus thing."

"What?"

"Guess where the moon is tonight, Charlie? It's in your eighth house."

TWENTY-THREE

"TERRY, DID YOU KNOW that Mitch Hilsten is in town?"

"Yes, Barry, he's shacking up with that Hollywood agent Charlie Greene. She represents Evan Black, the young genius."

"Yeah, well, did you know this Charlie Greene is an unwed mother and that she told her own poor old brokenhearted mom to sit in front of a fan when she complained of hot flashes?"

"Really? She's shacking up with Mitch Hilsten at Loopy Louie's. We better get a camera crew over there right away."

"And Terry, that's not all—this Charlie Greene is responsible for the murder of Ben Hanley from Kenosha, Wisconsin, as well as Officer Timothy Graden, who left two small sons, one still in a high chair, and she's been stealing secret weapons from our government."

But the combination of the words *camera crew* and the fact her eyes burned brought Charlie upright, heart trying to pound its way up her throat. She should have discarded her contact lenses and let her eyes rest overnight, replacing the lenses with fresh ones in the morning.

There was no camera crew and it *was* morning. She didn't have any new lenses with her because she was at Loopy Louie's, just like the news team said.

But the TV screen was black, the set silent. It sat huge and square and out of place in the center of the room on a round table that revolved to face any direction ordered. Instead of exhibiting the ugly bulges of most TVs, the back of this one had a pictured cover depicting a view of sand dunes and desert palms rippling in a wind that blew at the flaps of the tent door framing the scene. Like the old animated beer signs.

Another table surrounded the square TV's rotating table, this one narrow and itself encircled by a continuous round divan. The narrow table contained the remains of a sensuous dinner eaten and drunk in installments, interspersed with business utilizing other sensations.

The round bed had gauzy curtains looped back with menacing curved scimitars. A scimitar hung above the bed too, just below the mirror in the ceiling. Charlie looked away fast. Not the time of day to be looking in a mirror.

With the bed round, the bedside amenities sat along a shelf at the top, and of course the only remote within reach was on the other end of the shelf. Actually, there were four remotes in the room, and one made things rotate, including the bed itself, but Charlie wasn't up to that either.

So she had to reach across the superstar for the one on the shelf. Round beds, even as large as this, force people to sleep pretty much in the center, unless they are curling up in fetal positions.

Mitch stretched out right alongside her, facedown, back bare. Charlie smelled like canned tuna fish.

Mitch was not as tall as he looked in his films, but his back was state-of-the-art. It had heavy muscle and some moles and a patch of fine blond hairs where it tapered toward the buttocks, a scattering of freckles across the shoulder blades. Muscle and bone were well defined, any love handles exercised off.

Mitch was basically a granola, yogurt, pasta, fish, fruit, and vegetable guy unless he felt amorous. Then it was red wine and red meat.

Remote in hand, Charlie paused to measure. The entire length of her arm and hand with remote extended could not reach across the width of his shoulders. In the attempt, she brushed the marvelous flip side and he groaned.

"Guys with smiles insured by Lloyd's of London shouldn't sleep on their faces."

"Protecting myself." He lifted his face off the pillow to shake his head. "Jesus. Gotta up my insurance to cover more parts." He lifted to his elbows and reached above them for the phone. "I need coffee."

"I need eggs."

"What I really need is oysters, raw."

"Do they work?"

"I doubt it. How do you want your eggs?"

"Over easy, toast, orange juice. Coffee." Charlie punched the remote to Barry and Terry. "No potatoes."

"I'll eat your potatoes." He ordered and then added, "Just leave it at the door."

"Raw oysters and camel fries?" Charlie wasn't shocked to find Barry and Terry on the screen—they seemed to live at the station. But she was surprised to find it the noon broadcast.

"You must have a bladder to match your libido," Mitch said when he came out of the bathroom to find her immersed in the noon news. Their clothes were still scattered across the divan.

How come he didn't smell like canned tuna? Wasn't fair. There'd been no time to talk to Evan last night, and Mitch didn't want to discuss business, like why he should turn down this project.

He gathered the congealed and bloody remains of their prime-rib dinner, placed them on the wheeled table on which they'd arrived, and rolled them toward the door.

"Mitch, do not open that door until you put on a robe. There could be a camera crew out there."

"Why would there be a camera crew out there?" He looked down at himself, which was everywhere apparent. He was blond of hair and tan of skin wherever the sun got to him. If only he could see his back, where she had left not one scratch anywhere. A work of art is to be respected.

"I don't know. I just sense that it might be."

Mitch disappeared immediately and reappeared looking like Lawrence of Arabia without the headdress. His powder blues damn near shimmered. Problem was, Mitch Hilsten believed in Charlie's nonexistent powers of being able to "sense" things.

It drove her nuts.

"...last night at Rachel. In other news—"

"Rachel?" Lawrence whirled his robe and all back into the room. "What news about Rachel?"

"I don't know, it's over."

"Four young men are dead and five wounded after the shoot-outs yesterday afternoon in front of Loopy Louie's and a second outside the Golden Nugget. Mayor Jan Jones has requested law enforcement be beefed up on the Strip and on Fremont Street. Authorities believe the incidents are drug-related and have videotape of them in progress at both places."

"Yes, Barry, since the private security guards at the two casinos in question were armed only with nightsticks, they had to wait until the shooting stopped before entering the fray. The killers escaped, but the security guards—and the Metro officers who arrived shortly thereafter—chased fleeing tourists with camcorders instead of armed killers. Witnesses say that the acts, the murderers, and the victims are captured on film from every angle and at every moment because so many vacationers use video cameras."

"Modern technology has certainly changed the world and the way we do things," Barry concurred. "The debate now seems to be—should private security guards at the casinos be armed?"

"And should they be allowed to tackle fleeing tourists with camcorders?"

A taped interview with one of the fleeing tourists followed. The tourist's face and voice were disguised, but his fear was not. "Hey, man, I just filmed it because it would be fun to show family and friends at home, okay? I don't want to be no witness at no murder trial, man, you know? On *Good Cops, Bad Guys,* the cops catch the bad guys. On the real-life channel, the bad guys' friends catch the witnesses, man. You know?"

"But your identity is kept a secret from the bad guy," the interviewer insisted.

"Yeah, man, but not from his lawyer. Makes the witness a sitting pigeon. Lawyer tells his client—moral obligation. Client tells his friends—witness meets unexpected death. Works for everybody but the victim and the witness. Hey, man, don't start in on witness-protection stuff. All depends on who is greasing whose what. You know?"

After commercials for Coca-Cola, Chrysler, IBM, Sustacal, and Depends, Terry came back on a sad note. "Services were held this morning for Officer Timothy Graden of the Metro Police, the young father of two small sons."

Emily Graden and one small son walked between rows of somber police officers standing at attention. Her husband's casket carried before her, Grandma carrying the other small son behind her. Emily wore the expression of the widow—anger and helplessness seeping through shock. "Authorities are still tight-lipped about their investigations into the hit-and-run that led to the officer's death and the motive behind it."

Charlie looked away.

After commercials by Coca-Cola, Chrysler, IBM, Sustacal, and Depends that played through twice this time, Barry came on with the news of another upheaval on yesterday's stock market, which had sent food stocks broadly higher and technology stocks plummeting.

"Mitch, do you know what a DRIP is?"

"Guy who doesn't eat raw oysters."

"JEEZE, BABE, you look great." Charlie's boss stuck his nose in her face. "Nice to know somebody's getting a rest out of this vacation." He nodded spastically and lowered an eyelid halfway, somehow making it stay that way.

"Richard, why did the police call you in for questioning? You don't know anything."

"I mean, your skin glows, dewylike. And your cheeks are rosy. Your eyes aren't even red."

"That's because I'm not wearing any contacts and I can't see across the room. Now—"

"And your voice is softer and those anger lines between your eyebrows are gone. Your color's terrific. I should make you take a vacation more often, kid. You win a pile of money, get laid, or what?"

Bradone was cracking up. She was the lump rolling on the couch next to Mel Goodall, whom Charlie identified by his length.

They were in Evan's great room. In the kitchen part of this room, he busied himself cooking pasta-something. It did smell good, but Charlie was so ravenous, she could eat the pan.

"So," her boss said, "when is Hilsten getting into town?"

Evan howled. Mel hooted. Bradone's laughter broke into choking sounds.

"What the hell's the matter with you guys?" Richard Morse finally tuned in. "Charlie, what's going on?"

"Mitch'll be here in time for dinner, Morse," their host intervened. "Pour everybody some more wine, will you? Especially Charlie."

"Richard, what did they question you about?"

"About you, Charlie."

TWENTY-FOUR

INTERESTING THAT they all ate Evan's marvelous pasta-something by candlelight in a room where three men had died and it didn't smell of death. It smelled of garlic and onion and basil.

And Charlie.

She'd showered before leaving Loopy's but wore the same clothes she had the day before. It was embarrassing. Everyone else in the room pretended not to notice.

Everything so softened by candlelight and myopia and wine. Everyone blissful, tired, content. Three men lay dead the day before yesterday on the other side of that furniture there.

The only sounds—the chomping of mixed lettuces, the slurping of fine Chianti, the crunch of crusty bread, an occasional soft sigh.

Mitch sat across from Charlie and next to Bradone, who was struck dumb again by his august presence. She should have seen him eating raw oysters and camel fries for brunch.

The superstar had dropped Charlie off here and then sneaked into her room at the Hilton to get her some fresh contacts. Hard to imagine Mitch sneaking anywhere, but he'd worn sunglasses to hide the powder blues and promised he wouldn't smile and expose the famous flashing teeth.

He waited until they'd settled over dark roasted coffee, French-pressed, and sliced pears with cheese and chocolate truffles to explain what had taken him so long.

"Charlie's room at the Hilton's been tossed. Hard," he announced virilely. "Found her box of contact lenses under the bed. What the fuck's been going on around here, Black?"

"I've been trying to tell you, but you won't listen," Charlie snapped. Evan had put off her questions too. When she'd told him about Loopy Louie's strange offer, he'd said that Toby'd already mentioned it.

Now, Evan belched with pleasure. "Bring your coffee. Somebody grab the wine and the dessert trays. Come on up to the screening room. And we'll show you, Hilsten." He laughed and swung his ponytail back over his shoulder. Right now, he reminded Charlie of a pirate, but then, she wasn't seeing clearly. "Charlie, you put your eyes in. I want you to see this too. Maybe it'll answer some of your questions."

"Tell me they didn't take my laptop," Charlie whispered to Mitch when they stretched out on floor cushions in the screening room.

"I didn't see one, but the place is a mess. I reported it to hotel security and promised to bring you back there tonight to see if anything had been taken. Where'd you keep your computer?"

"In the safe in the closet. Though I don't think that safe's very safe. I saw a security man operate the combination from memory." Charlie took a sip of coffee and a slug of wine.

Why me, Lord? It's like I'm marked.

"Does what happened to your room have anything to do with those concerns over the conspiracy project you keep going on about?"

"The financing is not legal."

"Wouldn't be the first time. They searching your room for money?"

"I suspect for what turned the lights out at the Hilton."

"Anyway, it's going to be okay, Charlie." He gave her shoulders a proprietary squeeze. "I'll help you clean up the mess at the Hilton."

"Yeah, right. And we'll spend tonight in my room, I suppose."

"Well, I'm not leaving you there alone. Besides, my astrologer's calculations say you're not done yet." The bastard chortled. "And that this should be your best month of the year. Venus is transiting your sign."

"You want to know why I'll never really get in a relationship? I hate the smell of tuna."

"You do not smell like canned tuna. I told you."

"What do you know? Men have no sense of smell." And Charlie crawled over to Bradone's cushion.

"Quiet on the set," their host joked. "Roll it, Mel. And somebody pour Charlie some more wine."

This time, the footage started with security guards wrestling a camcorder away from Evan Black while their cohort bopped Evan with a nightstick.

"That's right, Black. I forgot you always do a cameo in your films." Mitch sounded appreciative.

"Is that guy really hitting you, Evan?" Bradone sat up.

"Put it on pause, Mel." Evan rose to stand in front of the stilled frame of himself being beaten and pulled his shirt down at the neck like a teasing stripper to reveal a black-and-blue shoulder, turned around to lift the shirt from the waist to reveal a bruised back.

"Don't look, Charlie," Mitch advised.

"I hate you."

"I know."

"How'd you know when to be there?" Richard raised up on one elbow to stare at the stilled screen with his bug eyes. "You didn't set this up, I hope."

"Nah, Mel and I were out in the van, had the radio on. We got there just in time to get attacked by the law. It was beautiful. Never say I don't do my own research." A self-satisfied Evan walked away from the screen. "Okay, Mel."

The cameraman shooting Evan's beating, probably Mel, turned away from the scene, camera still running. He was running himself, as were all kinds of people with him. Their race down the Strip was a study in control, the man behind the camera holding it in front of him, the world leaping and jostling around him in a frantic but oddly rhythmic step. Like the rescued film of a dead reporter caught in war-torn wherever.

"Holy moly, Superman," Richard Morse said.

"That's Batman, I think." Gullible Mitch fell for it.

But even then Bradone sighed and turned her head to Charlie. "If you don't get back over there, I will."

"Be my guest." Charlie took a slug of Chianti.

"You want to cuddle up to Richard?"

Charlie took another slug and thought it over. She crawled back to the cushion next to Mitch but asked Richard, "What did Metro want to know about me? You never said."

"Just a background check. I'm your employer, remember? Wanted to know how long you'd been with the agency, what you do there."

The next scene showed the same security guards jumping over wounded and dead victims of the shoot-outs, probably borrowed from someone else's camera. A shot obviously out of sequence in real time, but Evan often used that technique to startle audiences. Critics called it a "conceit," disciples, a "trademark." Charlie had always liked Evan's films in spite of herself and had to admit that with careful editing, it worked.

"They especially wanted to know what you do for Evan, here. If you're sexually involved—"

"Richard—"

"They're cops, Charlie, they're supposed to ask things like that."

And then came the footage of Charlie laid out in the desert night with shadow flames for lighting and that gross bush at her head like a tombstone.

Mitch tensed beside her, put an arm around her, drew her into his warmth.

That made Charlie tense. She loathed heroes.

"Besides, I told them you were not sexually involved with Evan and that it's a damn shame. You could use a little."

Mitch put a hand over Charlie's mouth and held her down until she calmed. But Bradone and Evan howled in unison.

Which made for a seriously strange sound.

The next sequence brought them all back to the matter at hand. Charlie and Mitch sat up. Richard raised himself on an elbow again to see better. Evan gave a satisfied sigh.

It was the "ground stuff" he'd kept baiting Charlie with.

This was all shot without sound, which made it spooky. Knowing Evan, who loved to play in the Foley studio, there would be lots of silence in the finished product and real or natural sounds mixed with the score, or sounds from another film even. Charlie could imagine him mixing war sounds with the shoot-out in front of Loopy's. Instead of police sirens, there might be air-raid sirens from the bombing of London during World War II. Just enough to throw you off.

Sometimes he'd begin a scene with sounds from the last sequence. He liked to call this technique "transition." Again, it would be labeled conceit—distracting and unnecessary—by some, brilliance by admirers. You either liked or hated an Evan Black film. They were as controversial as their maker. And more than once he'd been termed *mad*—as in nuts. Charlie had always wondered how, in Hollywood, you could tell.

But when his projects worked—and probably three-fourths did—they grossed bucks, big bucks on the cheap. Because he did so much of it himself. No second unit on his films, despite Toby's title. No power struggles between egos on the set that drove costs up on most projects. Talent or production crew, they were free to walk, because he wasn't paying squat anyway and there were people lined up to take their places. People worked on a Black film as a way to become better known in their specialty, not for guild or union scales. Studio brass got intimidating, interfering, Evan would walk the project to another studio, never shooting anything in L.A. While endless lawsuits were being filed, threatened, some scheduled in court, he was garnering awards. If this guy was nuts, he was like the Einstein of nuts.

The question was, Was he capable of murder? And treason?

THE RAW OYSTERS and camel fries seemed to have worked, but Mitch ordered up a deluxe hamburger and french fries sometime in the wee hours. And a bottle of red.

Charlie'd had enough of everything but sex. Well, she did eat one fry. Okay, five, but that was it.

Between bouts of lust that had little to do with the lustee—he could have been anybody that night—in her savaged room at the Hilton, which she and the lustee had no time to put right or to inform security of what might be missing from the obvious search, Charlie dreamed. And when awake, she relived that ground stuff.

It was awesome. In her head, she mixed the sound herself.

Groom Lake even in wide angle from a nearby mountaintop stood well disclosed, impossible to hide on open desert. The massive runways looked able to launch a fleet of ocean liners, or aircraft carriers three at a time—side by side. What could possibly require such spaciousness? No stealth bomber needed anywhere near that width or length. And those runways were in excellent condition, not patched up like at most airports.

The vast hangarlike buildings and sheds sprawled low, flat, and again were impossible to hide. Perhaps the only option *was* to deny their existence. Stranger things have happened. The fleet of white 737s, unmarked but for a wide red stripe along the side pocked by the windows, showing white here, lined up as she remembered them from her brief flight over that ridge with Caryl Thompson, Evan, and Mel. Just before the orange light knocked her out.

That orange light, really more of a thing, had more substance than normal light does. Yet Charlie couldn't be sure it was an object. Round, huge, and spinning, it reminded her fleetingly of a sun before it vanished. It didn't go away or dissolve or spin past the little Mooney. It couldn't. It filled the sky. And then it just simply wasn't. Like it had never existed. This was not on the footage in Evan's film—it was in Charlie's head, at the back of her eyeballs, leaving the orange smear that still returned now and then.

Or it was in her dream. Her imagination. Probably induced by the french fries. And a sex and Chianti hangover.

No, on the screen in Evan's screening room, the Groom Lake, or Area 51, sequence had continued with the wide-angle lens turning in a slow circle, panning empty desert and low mountains until it faced an enormous eye. It seemed to be some sort of surveillance or sensor thing on a tripod. The wide angle moved on to people in denim and straw hats sitting on rocks, raising sandwiches and beer cans to the camera, bloated distortions, too large because they were too close to the lens. It continued its circle to come to a stop on what appeared to be barren desert scenery.

Until you noticed the dirt road snaking off to the horizon, the white Jeep parked to the side, and two or three figures bent over the road next to it. About all you could see was their movement, not its purpose. Spreading tacks? And in the distance where the road dropped over into a gully, was that a tow truck?

"I still don't see what all this, as impressive as it is, has to do with Charlie's room being tossed," Mitch had said either at the end of the screening or in her dream, or both.

"They're looking for clues as to how she did it. There are bets still out there." Was it Evan who said that? For real or dream?

"Do you know who searched my room? Was it those good old boy reverse militia guys? Retired ARPs?"

"Wouldn't be a bit surprised, but not to worry, Charlie. A magical event is about to occur that will make them all look so silly, they won't dare get smart with us."

But before Charlie could ask the young genius what this magic was, she was sucked into a giant orange and taken advantage of. Was it a dream, Mitch Hilsten, or an omen?

TWENTY-FIVE

CHARLIE SHOWERED and dressed before Mitch Hilsten stirred an eyelash, studied herself in the mirror in the bathroom to see if she really did look different, younger, less stressed, dewy—like her boss had said.

She didn't look bad. She felt great. Her room was still a mess, the search a thorough one, but her computer was safe. Surely "they" had found what they were looking for. She downloaded her E-mail and hurried downstairs to the serious coffee bar in the lobby next to the black Stealth. And next to the bank of slots where she'd won a jackpot and Art Sleem had dumped cash and warnings on her in the morning, before getting himself murdered in the afternoon.

She took her skinny latte with nutmeg to the café and looked for Ardith. There was something reassuring about Ardith and her attempts to mother Charlie's eating habits.

But it was a harried Bobby Sue—the name badges gave only first names—who stopped by Charlie's table with the menu, masticating gum as if holding her face together depended on it. "First time in fifty years Ardith Miller's missed work, except once when the union struck and another time she got the flu. I'm working her section too."

"Fifty years?" Charlie reconsidered her retirement options.

"Something's happened. I just know it." Maybe not fifty years, but Bobby Sue had been around awhile herself. Her ponytail was snow white and thinning. "Something bad."

Charlie, who'd eaten only five french fries—okay, maybe seven—last night while the granola-boy lustee consumed a huge hamburger, decided it was time for two eggs. Over easy so she could cut up and scramble them on her plate, making the whites all yokey, and then dip her toast in the yoke that remained. Well? This was a rough vacation.

She sipped her latte, felt the caffeine booting her up in that marvelous way it did only first thing in the day, booted up the Toshiba notebook on its battery power, and read her E-mail while breakfast cooked.

The news from Larry—three out of five really important deals she had going were toast. The industry was like that—string you along with awesome fantasizing material for months and then kick you in the stomach with rejection in one afternoon. The worst part—Charlie got to break the news to the writers, and she'd better do it before they read it in the trades.

Nebula had decided not to renew the option on Parnell Davidson's legal thriller. Universal had rejected Jerry and Leo's final script revisions for *Thelma & Louise: The Early Years,* and Mega Studios had scrapped the *Trojan Hearse* project. Charlie represented three of the writers on that baby.

The new office witch, Ruby Dillon, threatened to quit if Richard didn't call her immediately, which was yesterday. Lovely Libby had decided she was going to college to learn to become a veterinarian and Tuxedo the Dreaded had gained forbidden access to Charlie's closet and peed on all her shoes.

"It really stinks in there," the kid reassured Charlie. No word about the groping boss, the retarded boyfriend, or the second-hand car that defied all emission standards known but which Libby managed to get passed anyway. All together, a worrisome communication.

But even more worrisome—a message from an address she'd never seen before and unsigned, the server something obscure she'd never heard of. "Good thing I know where you live. Too bad you don't know where I do. Will they call it murder or suicide, do you think?"

She'd already consumed her meal before it occurred to her that just because Art Sleem was dead didn't mean "they" had given up trying to poison her.

Charlie hoped the unidentified message was just one more threat from Sleem, powerless now that he was dead, and not some "they" who took no prisoners. Could somebody be threatening Libby, still back in Long Beach, where Charlie lived? She got on a pay phone in the lobby to leave messages with her neighbors Maggie Stutzman and Jeremy Fiedler to keep an eye out for Libby and any strangers hanging around the compound, explaining the E-mail letter.

Then more calls to commiserate with six writers. They'd every last one already heard the bad news. Trying not to, they blamed Charlie. She was the middleman-woman. The shield and the target for both sides.

CHARLIE PEELED a couple of hundreds off her roll and threw them on the blackjack table. One thing, the tossing of her room hadn't been your ordinary robbery, not that she'd ever suspected it was. Her cash winnings were still in the safe with her computer.

Please tell me we're not going to investigate.

Why, you think I'm not up to it?

Charlie, we are staggering under a load of problems now. We can't take on any more.

We are being threatened by E-mail, stumbling over dead bodies by the truckload, involved in scary, maybe antigovernment, stuff, and I am worried about Ardith Miller.

Ardith Miller—the waitress we barely know—

Did not show up for work today after fifty years, minus a union strike and sick leave from the flu. And she knew me.

Lots of people know you.

Doesn't keep them from going to work.

Your problem is not conspiracy. It's guilt. You take on responsibility for a waitperson not showing up for work when you've seen her maybe two, three times.

What are you today, my conscience or my good sense? Charlie did wave away the cocktail person. No more drinks in this casino.

I'm the you you don't want to listen to. Call me what you want.

So now what do we do?

"Decide whether to stand or hit would be nice." This dealer was a woman and as unfeeling, unemotional, and unimpressed a robot as you could imagine.

Until Charlie scratched for a hit and asked, "Do you know Ardith Miller?"

The dealer squeezed the card she'd slipped from the shoe. It hit Charlie in the face.

Eddie, the pit boss with the hairy, flinching hands and turquoise jewelry, appeared from nowhere. "You gonna make it, Zelda?"

Zelda nodded, blinked a lot, took in a raspy breath, and retrieved the errant card. It mated with Charlie's hand to produce twenty-one.

There might be something to this idea of not concentrating on what you're doing while playing blackjack. Made more sense to Charlie than moons, planets, stars, houses, and trines.

"It's you again," Eddie said from behind the stoic Zelda.

"She knows." With what looked like a rapid waving of her hand, Zelda clicked cards from the shoe to begin a new game.

"You know?" Eddie watched every move at the table and Charlie at the same time.

"I know," Charlie said, and she did. "Ardith Miller is dead for no good reason." She beat the house on the next hand too.

What she didn't bring up was the fact she hadn't a clue why or how. Hell, at her age, Ardith could have dropped dead of a heart attack. Charlie didn't like knowing things. It was depressing. I am *not* psychic.

The game played out, Charlie doing well, if not as well as the house. The two men at her table were losing heavily, keeping a balance to this game of chance. A new dealer appeared to replace Zelda, who apparently was not stoic enough, and Eddie escorted Charlie to the very room in which a zealous staff had broken Ben Hanley's sternum while he was dead.

The world was a fun, exciting, dangerous place. And totally screwy.

"I just meet somebody and they die," Charlie explained to Eddie and a couple of suits in the secure area. "When I heard Ardith hadn't shown up for work today after fifty years, I just figured it had happened to her too."

"After fifty years of what?" The suit with reams of paper on his lap and a ballpoint pen poised above the top page looked up at her. He had to be a lawyer or a super-number-cruncher. Charlie met this type all the time in showbiz. They financed things or worked for those who did. They were seriously powerful dudes, whether they worked for banking interests or Pepsi or gaming.

"Being on time to work."

"Do you always become so involved with resort staff when you travel?" He lifted eyebrows carefully trimmed. Older guys often make money but no sense—they go bald and then grow long hair in their noses and eyebrows.

"You don't look very sad." The other suit leaned forward—no paper or pens on his lap. He must be even higher on the honcho ladder. "About the waitperson's death."

She noticed these suits didn't feel the need to introduce themselves. Like the shorthaired fed with Detective Battista.

"I'm just numb. She's what, number seven in a week?"

Both suits wore shiny gray and sported tailored gray hair and spa suntans. And very expensive eyeglasses. This was obviously big money sitting here. Why? For the death of a waitperson? Charlie didn't think so. Both wore plain silver bands on their wedding fingers.

"Seven what in a week?" Eddie was trying to keep things rational for his bosses.

"Seven murders. Might not be that big a deal in Vegas, with all the loose change around, but that's one for every day of my vacation, if you can call it that."

"You've been involved in seven murders in a week?" This was the guy with no paper on his lap.

"I've just been involved with the victims, which does not make me feel comfortable. My Las Vegas experience has been ruined by death, violence, and destruction."

The lawyer/accountant type leaned over the paper on his lap and raised his chin to study Charlie without sympathy through the magnification at the lower end of his eyewear.

"Why do you suppose your room here at the Hilton was so methodically searched? And have you found anything missing?"

Charlie remembered her dream. "They,"—the ones who probably work for you—"wanted to know how I did it."

"How you did what?" one suit asked, but all the men wore identical expectant expressions.

"Someone thinks I had something to do with the power outage the night the casino was robbed. Maybe that I had some kind of device that could make it happen. I think they were looking for it. They didn't touch my cash or a valuable computer. If they took anything, I haven't missed it yet."

But Evan Black knew what they were looking for. Charlie was sure these men were not to be tarried with, even by Evan Black. Why would he risk such a thing? And involve Charlie too? And now old gullible Mitch?

Charlie needed to talk to Bradone. But when finally released from the inner sanctum, she found that Bradone McKinley had checked out of the hotel.

TWENTY-SIX

"WHY WOULD SHE check out and not say good-bye? What if she's number eight?" Charlie asked Mitch, who was back to coffee and granola—granola he glopped up with yogurt instead of milk. Tickled Charlie's gag reflex just to look at it.

"Number eight what?" He sat on the foot of the bed with the room-service table on wheels in front of him. He didn't even have the TV on. "God, how do you do it?"

"Eighth dead body in seven days. Good thing I'm leaving tomorrow." She began tossing the stuff strewn on the floor into drawers. "And you're the one who had to have a deluxe hamburger, fries, and a bottle of red zin at two in the morning."

"Who's the seventh dead body?" He did look some worse for wear. "And you ate half the fries."

"I only had seven—okay, maybe nine. There must have been fifty on that plate anyway. Ardith Miller, a waitperson down at the café, didn't show for work this morning after fifty years."

"You know, Charlie? We sound married. Here we are talking away, making no sense at all. And we understand each other."

"Now don't start on that." Charlie found another pair of panties under a pile of sofa cushions, and couldn't believe how many she'd brought along. What could the people who searched this room think Charlie possessed that turned out the lights in the casino and a good part of the hotel?

"Haven't you ever wondered what it would be like to be—"

"To a man who eats raw oysters with camel fries? I don't think so."

"See, there we did it again. We're a natural."

"Mitch—"

"Okay, so what happened to Ardith Miller?"

"I don't know. I just know she's dead."

"What's that got to do with you? It's not like you don't have an alibi for last night. Boy, do you have an alibi."

"I just know that if I hadn't come to Vegas, she'd still be alive. Because people I've been meeting are dropping like flies." She was really tossing stuff now, just to get it out of sight and out of mind. The fact someone she didn't know had touched it was almost worse than Tuxedo peeing on her shoes. "She was murdered like the rest of them, I'm sure of it. You just might start looking over your shoulder yourself, guy."

"Know something else? We've had two very full nights together and you're not even talking guilt. We're making progress. Our relationship."

"It's just Vegas. Even *I* can't feel guilty in Vegas."

"When you say you're sure of these things, do you mean your special sensing ability has kicked in?"

"Besides, dead bodies are distracting. And I do not have a *special* sensing ability. But I can see with my *commonsense* ability. Mitch, if in one week you came in contact with seven— and I hope to God Bradone won't make an eighth here—people who later turned up dead, you would see a pattern too. And if I were psychic, maybe I'd know the reason."

"But they don't have anything in common, at least most of them don't."

"Yes they do. One thing. Me."

"What about Vegas itself? What about Evan Black?"

"He didn't know Ben Hanley or Ardith Miller. But he sure had connections to the rest. Mitch, we've got to talk about Evan—"

"I really think you're making something out of this that isn't there. You're always blaming yourself for stuff that isn't your fault."

"Good, fine. You believe what you want. That's your right. Just listen to me about—"

"Wanna see my back?" He had the nerve to look smug.

She reached for a table lamp to lob at him, and the only thing that saved the superstar was the phone. Charlie always threw a fit when her writers used that ploy.

Bradone McKinley's relief that Charlie and not Mitch picked up came in an exhaled grunt. "Don't say my name. Act normal. I'm on a cellular in a rental car outside the Hilton. Come down as fast as you can. Don't tell anyone where you're going and don't use the lobby door. The paparazzi and TV crews are setting up shop. They probably discovered that you and Mitch are a hot item upstairs. Remember the side door we used the other day, by the glass elevator? See if you can get there unnoticed. And Charlie, put on some jeans and walking shoes. Bring a jacket. We got work to do.''

CHARLIE ALMOST walked around the white Jeep Cherokee with heavily tinted windows standing directly in her path, until it beeped at her.

"What are you doing in this? And why all the clothes? It's hot out here."

The astrologer was in a safari outfit—Banana Republic right down to the weird khaki hat. What role was she playing today? Much as she was drawn to this woman, Charlie had her doubts.

The Cherokee blasted out onto Paradise. Bradone switched on the air-conditioning and headed south. "Check to see if we're being followed."

"I thought you'd left without saying good-bye." Charlie checked, to see them being followed by your normal three lanes full of cars.

"I was comped in the penthouse longer than most people. I've just moved to another hotel. I would have gone home, but I feel I must stay and help you."

"Why were you comped longer than most?" They took Flamingo east to the 515 and headed north.

"Because I was smart enough not to lose my shirt fast enough. When are you leaving Vegas?"

"Tomorrow. Bradone, what is going on—where are we headed?" They were headed out of town.

"Charlie, you can't leave tomorrow," Bradone said fifty miles or so later. "You can move in with me. We have to get to the bottom of all this."

"All this what?" They'd picked up I-15 until they came to State 93 and turned north. No one was following. The landscape looked like it always did when you left Vegas in any direction— bleak.

"All this murder. Don't doubt me now. You need me."

Charlie told Bradone about Ardith Miller and the unknown threatener on her E-mail and about getting called into the security room at the Hilton. "Zelda, the dealer, told Eddie, the floorman, that I knew—I'm assuming about Ardith. And that was it. I was behind closed doors with threatening suits. I know she's dead."

"Charlie, I realize it sounds unlikely, but it is possible that all these deaths are not connected. Most of them surely, but not all. Was Ardith's death what they questioned you about? These threatening suits?"

"They seemed even more interested in what might have been missing from my room after the search."

"And was there? Anything—"

"Not that I could see. My computer and cash were still there." Not to mention two zillion pairs of panties. Better I should have packed all my shoes so the cat couldn't have fixed them. "I figure someone was looking for a device of some kind I could have used to turn off the lights at the Hilton that night, so somebody could rob the casino."

"Anybody could cut wires or pull switches, couldn't they?"

"Not that selectively, I wouldn't think. Given that the lobby and casino clear through the sports-book area are on one electrical system, that outage followed me that night. From the marquee outside right up to my room. Most of the building and attached convention center weren't affected at all."

"The penthouse wasn't and the Star Trek addition—that's true. But Charlie, the Hilton has made no statement as to the amount of money stolen. Metro does not appear to be searching for the robbers. It's all being quietly ignored. Why isn't the press hounding them about it?"

"Yeah, why isn't the Hilton heist page-one news?"

"Precisely. There's something going on here far stranger than your happening to pick this week to come here on vacation. It's bigger than you. And it's not your fault. But you are liable to be swept up in it anyway."

Like, I already am. "What's going on?"

"I'm hoping you can tell me, Charlie. That's why we're heading for Area Fifty-two—"

"Fifty-one."

"Oh, right. Groom Lake, whatever." The floppy hat and huge sunglasses hid too much of Bradone's face.

Not only was there nobody following, they didn't meet anybody. "How is it you know the way so well? Bradone, have you been here before?"

"Actually, I have—but I wasn't driving. You're going to have to help me watch for a town named Alamo."

"On this road, you could miss a town named anything."

"There's some bottled water in that grocery bag in the backseat and some fruit and sandwiches, when you're ready. I'll have an apple and water, please."

There were pillows and blankets on the backseat too. "That's why the jackets and comfortable shoes. You're planning to spend the night up there."

"Probably safer for you there than in Vegas."

"Bradone, I really do have to get home and back to work. I appreciate your wanting to help me, but I can't spare the time. I might not be safe in Vegas, but I know I'd be safer in Long Beach than at Groom Lake."

The astrologer leaned into the wheel, as if eager for adventure. "What if that threatening E-mail letter was written on *your* computer by whoever searched your room?"

Any other day, an adventure with Bradone McKinley would be a blast. But not today. Not after seven dead bodies—assuming Ardith *was* dead. Not after watching Emily Graden, holding the small hand of one of her sons, walk in the funeral procession behind her husband's casket. "With my software, there's no way to write a letter to yourself, to the in box. Anything you write on it goes in the out box."

"I imagine some hacker could figure out a way quite quickly, but, disregarding that, someone could bring in another computer and E-mail you."

"I don't see that as a reason for our having to come up here and spend the night."

"If they were looking for something in your room that would

turn out the lights at the casino, they must have been looking for some kind of high-tech device. Charlie, you said Evan was one of those masked burglars we saw on his film.''

"With Mel shooting it. And probably Caryl and Toby too. Evan had to be the one snuffing out the guy's lighter. Toby picked us up when we left the burning plane on the desert.''

"And they dropped you off at the Hilton lobby and the lights went out as you moved through the building.''

"It was more like just behind me. But I don't have a device. Maybe they found it.''

"Maybe they slipped something in your purse or clothes that shut down the electricity selectively.''

Charlie turned out her purse in her lap and fingered everything before putting it back in. "Another of Pat Thompson's goods delivered. Everything seems to come back to him.''

Detective Bradone laughed, took a crispy bite of apple, and gunned the Cherokee toward Alamo. "This case is beginning to come together, Charlie.''

Charlie had the uneasy thought that no one but the astrologer knew where she was at this moment. Or where she was going.

TWENTY-SEVEN

THERE WASN'T MUCH to Alamo, where they stopped for gas and directions, the latter not adding measurably to Charlie's confidence in this trip. A few miles up the road, they turned off at Ash Springs—a few house trailers. A Texaco station—closed. Not a car or a soul in sight.

"What do people do out here to keep from going nuts?"

"Maybe they eat. Way past time for those sandwiches. Let's have the chicken now and save the roast beef for dinner."

"Bradone, I have to catch that plane tomorrow." But Charlie pulled the bag over into the front seat. Sliced baked chicken breast with some kind of Yuppie sauce instead of mayo, with nut slivers and sprouts, shrooms and black olives. It was delicious, but having anything to eat out in this wasteland would have seemed a luxury.

Scraggly, stunted Joshua trees flew past the Cherokee and sickly cactus topped with bunches of long spikes gathered at the bottom and splayed outward like a bouquet of swords.

"So, Evan and company somehow managed to put something in my purse or on me when I blacked out, and it shut off the lights so they could film themselves robbing the casino, and it came from Groom Lake. Smuggled out by Patrick Thompson." Charlie hadn't found anything in her purse. "Bradone, we can't get anywhere near the place and wouldn't know what to look for if we did. We are not detectives. This trip is just going to involve us further in what you yourself termed 'something bigger than we are.' We're totally out of our league and should leave it to the professionals."

"Which professionals? The ones who ordered Patrick's murder? Or the police, who were so sure he was a silly tourist who jaywalked under that car? The casino suits, who seem more interested in how the lights went out than what happened to the money? This trip gets you out of Vegas."

High-voltage power lines and desolation lined the road. Far away, bumpy rock mountains surrounded them.

"So will that plane tomorrow." A desert's lack of trees was stunningly apparent here. So boring, Charlie wanted to fall asleep.

"When does it leave?"

"Five something."

"No problem. We'll have you back by then."

"Bradone, when were you here before, why, and who with?"

"How do you know I was with someone?"

"You said you weren't driving, and you had to ask directions in Alamo."

"See, you are a detective. I was here with a group of astrologers on a field trip. Aren't these sandwiches good? This is an onion-dill bread that's so hard to find anymore. There's this wonderful deli—"

"We're beginning to sound married." Every mile closer to the dreaded secret installation made Charlie's mouth drier.

"Have some water. You may be dehydrating."

A smoggy haze at the base of the bumpy rock mountains cut them off from the desert floor, appearing to levitate them. There could be a big power plant nearby...or something even more suspicious.

Charlie decapped a bottle of lukewarm liquid—springwater, of course. Amazing how many springs had cropped up since bottled water became the rage. "Why do we have to stay all night?"

"Because night's when you can see things in the dark. The lights and everything. And I want you to get close enough to maybe see what made you black out. Like the lights did at the Hilton."

"It wasn't really black."

"It was orange, wasn't it?"

"Did I tell you that?"

Ugly landscape. Worn-down mountains. That ground layer of haze couldn't be moisture. So many dust devils. Maybe it seemed like so many because she could see forever. Charlie didn't feel comfortable in wide-open spaces.

"You didn't have to." Bradone laughed for no reason. This crazy woman could enjoy herself anywhere. "I've been here before, remember."

"It happened to you? You saw the orange light? But I was in a plane."

The vegetation grew relatively lush as they approached the summit of the first mountain range. But the valley on the other side was back to dust devils and hardscrabble.

Their paved road stretched across the valley ahead in a straight line. They met one car leaving the valley as they entered it.

The sides of the road were strangely free of broken beer bottles and trash. But a sign with a litter barrel, signaling there was one coming up, stood riddled with bullets.

More frequent were the yellow signs warning OPEN RANGE and featuring the profile of a feisty black bull, reared back as if he was cocked and ready to go. They came across one huge red bull for real. He gave them a grouchy stare.

Charlie didn't know she'd dozed off until a roaring sound jolted her awake. The car swerved all over the road. "Did we hit a bull?"

"No, but we're lucky we didn't crash into something. I went to sleep at the wheel."

"But that sound—"

Bradone pointed ahead where something rose into the air on a plume of smoke while she fought the Cherokee to a safe landing on the shoulder. "God, I'm sorry. You were having such a good nap, I didn't realize I was too. Whatever that thing was, it may have saved our lives."

"Let me drive for a while and you can sleep," Charlie offered. Let me get behind the wheel and turn this baby back to Vegas.

"Thanks, but I'm fine." Bradone's smile seemed to know that's what Charlie would do. "Rachel's not far, and after that encounter, adrenaline alone will keep me up and running for hours."

"That was no flying saucer. I don't think they smoke."

"Some military aircraft, more likely. He sure came in low. Lucky for us he did." They scanned the skies for others.

But the only things on this road were dust devils and scattered cows watching them with suspicion. Then a gravel road stretched across the valley in a straight line to the next low heap of mountains. A dust plume followed a vehicle many miles off.

"I don't see how you could hide anything out here. Can't even find a private place to pee."

"Hang on, Rachel's just ahead." The Cherokee passed up the graveled road and stuck to the blacktop.

"I can see for a hundred miles and there's no town." Charlie was only partly wrong.

THEY SAT STARING through the Cherokee's tinted windows at the Area 51 Research Center across the road. The Area 51 Research Center was a permanent mobile home house trailer with a pickup parked at its contrived wooden porch. Two tall antennas, a satellite dish, three wandering cows, and twisted metal wreckage served as lawn ornaments.

"Oh, come on, Charlie, you're too young to turn off interesting experiences. This whole place is a hoot."

This whole place was a few dusty mobile homes with a couple of clapboard buildings thrown in for good measure, most of them acres apart.

"This is a long way to come for a hoot. Bradone, I don't want to meet up with that orange thing again, okay?"

But Bradone slammed the Cherokee's door and crossed the road, taking the keys with her.

Charlie raised dust when she hit the dirt.

Why do I get involved with people like this? I was sure she was an unusual and interesting woman. Instead, she turns out to be a nut, and here I am at the end of the earth with her.

I want to go home. I don't like this.

Well swell, when you figure out how, be sure and let me know.

By now, Charlie too had crossed the road. The trailer home next to the nut institute advertised alien T-shirts by hanging them outside as lures. A cow ambled over to take a lick at one.

Five cows, Bradone, waiting for her on the research center's wooden porch, and Charlie the gullible were the only living things moving in all of Rachel, Nevada.

Whenever Charlie left the fiction that was Hollywood to reassure herself in the real world, she found the real world stranger than fiction.

Inside the Area 51 Research Center trailer, a little guy dressed like a truck driver sat glued to a computer screen, a phone receiver tucked between a shoulder and an ear. "Be with you in a minute," he mouthed, then said to someone on the phone, "Yes, sir, there's close-ups of the base, aerial and satellite pictures, and topo maps. Yes, sir, Visa and MasterCard."

All the while, his fingers flew over the keyboard doing something else because he had to switch files to key in the guy's order, address, and credit card number.

Maps and photos clung to the ceiling and the walls above bookcases. A table in the middle of the room offered books, pamphlets, and UFO newsletters—stacks of them. No pictures of big orange things.

A normal-appearing woman in a midcalf dress and tennis shoes stepped out of a back room with still more stacks of stuff, and something brushed against Charlie's leg and stepped on her foot.

At her gasp, the truck driver stood to look over his desk to the floor at her feet. "Name's Underfoot 'cause that's where he lives. He's from Mars, isn't he?"

The woman stacking stuff under the table paused to think, then shook her head. "Venus, I'm sure. He's a she."

Meanwhile, Underfoot had fallen madly in love with Charlie's socks. Bradone picked up the black-and-white cat and it fell madly in love with the stargazer's throat.

She bought a booklet and several maps from the guy who dressed like a truck diver. He swiveled in his chair to look out the front windows at the white Jeep Cherokee across the frontage road. "Sure hope you nice ladies aren't planning to take that 'over there.'" He nodded in some vague direction. "Because 'over there,' they know their own."

TWENTY-EIGHT

CHARLIE SAT in the Cherokee, watching Bradone fight the wind for her floppy safari hat as she leaned against a wooden telephone pole and talked into a pay phone in a black box attached to it. Probably one of the more ridiculous sights in a given lifetime. Indiana Jones's mother meets V. I. Warshawski.

Bradone didn't trust the cellular to work out here and worried that the mysterious technology at Groom Lake would find a conversation on the airwaves easier to pick up than one on wires anyway.

The wind grew chilly as the afternoon wore on and Charlie punched the windows up. A turpentine smell permeated the enclosed space.

Besides the Cherokee, two pickups and a motorcycle parked in front of the Little A'Le'Inn Motel/Restaurant/Bar/RV Hook-ups. The sign on the side of the shedlike building, and another out at the roadside, pictured an oval bald head with those giant black almond-shaped eyes, sloped upward at the outer edges, so popular in extraterrestrials these days. It assured Charlie EARTHLINGS WELCOME.

A grand, if scruffy, tourist trap with tongue in cheek, out in the middle of nothing. The Little A'Le'Inn, a gas station, the T-shirt trailer, and the Research Center comprised Rachel's commercial district—all located along the frontage road and separated by weed acres. What else did the people around here have to do? It looked like welfare-check city.

Well, this earthling has to pee.

Inside the A'Le'Inn, an older couple with drinks in hand played at the one tiny bank of slots. Four guys in baseball caps, plaid shirts, tight jeans, and cowboy boots leaned on pool cues to watch her. Along one side of the room stretched a saloon bar with bottled libations on the wall behind it and diner stools in front of it. Eight or ten dinette sets, mostly fifties chrome and tape-patched red plastic, helped the pool table fill up the room.

Charlie was about to ask directions when one of the guys pointed a cue at a door opposite the bar. A vertical poster covered it:

WARNING, THIS IS A RESTRICTED AREA. DO NOT ENTER. IT IS UNLAWFUL TO MAKE ANY FILM, PHOTOGRAPH, MAP, SKETCH, PICTURE, DRAWING OF THIS INSTALLATION. TRESPASSERS ARE SUBJECT TO IMMEDIATE ARREST AND CONFISCATION OF ALL PERSONAL ITEMS. USE OF DEADLY FORCE AUTHORIZED. 18, U.S. CODE 795/797 AND EXECUTIVE ORDER 10104.

Having taken time to read the door, Charlie nearly didn't make it on time into a one-commode bathroom with a window that opened to a world of jumbled house trailers. They had to be the motel part of this joint. The only warning inside the room was to please not flush sanitary pads et cetera because of the primitive plumbing and Rachel's earthbound sewage system.

When Charlie stepped out, Bradone, obviously still enjoying an adventure, raised a Coors to her from one of the chrome dinette sets. Two more men sat at the diner bar. A florid guy stood behind it and watched Bradone.

"I've ordered us alien burgers and fries for dinner. We can save the dinner subs for breakfast."

"Bradone—"

"And I've ordered you a glass of red."

"Bradone—"

"I didn't ask. Probably dago, but we'll need—"

"We just had lunch and I am *not*—"

"Here's your dago." A cheerful woman in comforting stone-washed jeans and Reeboks set a glass in front of Charlie. "Actually, it's a not-too-bad merlot."

"You have merlot?"

"See, this seriously finicky extraterrestrial left it behind. I don't figure he's coming back. Probably got shot out of the sky by the government or Steven Spielberg.'' She set another Coors in front of Bradone and winked at Charlie. ''Be back with your aliens minus the secretions in a sec.''

''Secretions—''

''Cheese.'' Bradone drained the first Coors and reached for the next. ''I didn't think we needed the extra fat.''

The alien burgers differed from earthly burgers in that they came in oblong sesame-seed buns instead of round. Charlie ate half the burger and a fourth of the fries but, unfortunately, drank all of the wine.

Bradone insisted on a doggy box for the rest of their dinner and retrieved two large thermoses from the Jeep to have filled with hot coffee.

''Now you ladies be good girls and drive straight back to Vegas, hear?'' the proprietor cautioned with a wink when he took their money.

''Just don't do it too fast,'' his wife added.

The boys around the pool table leered.

Knowing it was the wine talking, Charlie pointed out two things that should have been of interest as they drove out of town. The first was that she had no intention of sleeping, let alone breakfasting, near some forbidden military installation and, second, the proprietress of the A'Le'Inn had warned Charlie, when Bradone visited the restricted potty, about the real danger in this ''neck of the woods.''

''What we really need to worry about is cattle mutilation.''

''Oh well, that's a relief.'' Bradone made a shooing motion with one hand. ''Tell you what, you worry about it for me. I've got a lot on my mind right now.''

Then why did you drink three bottles of Coors? ''No, listen to me, the cattle mutilate us. That's why she didn't want us to drive too fast.''

''Right, they crawl in the Jeep and cut us up with their horns. No more wine for you, my dear.''

''No, they wander onto the road in front of us and we and the Jeep get mutilated. I suppose they do to, but we wouldn't know by then. Just slow down, will you?''

The intrepid adventuress was already slowing down, not because of road cattle, but to turn the Cherokee onto a side road where a large white graffiti-riddled mailbox stood out like a lone sentinel. A wooden sign tacked to its base read STEVE MEDLIN HCR80.

"Is that—"

"The black mailbox." Bradone let the low melodious laugh loose. It was a lot like her voice. "Charlie, cheer up. This is going to be so much fun. Aren't you even a bit curious about Groom Lake?"

"No." Actually, she was a bit, but knew there was no way Bradone McKinley was going to get them into the base or would know what to do next if she did.

Charlie argued all the way to the warning signs. Her astrologer had gone over the edge. They'd left a plume of dust along the washboard gravel, marking a trail that had to be traceable by satellite.

It was nearly dark when they pulled up behind three other vehicles, one a pickup camper. Charlie planned to ask someone in them for a ride back to Vegas. But they were all empty. Her panicky feelings began to interfere with her breathing. She knew Ardith Miller was dead and she *knew* she didn't want to be even this close to that orange light again.

"Were we supposed to meet somebody here?"

"Let's get out and stretch a little. Be noticed."

"By who?"

"Whom." Bradone pointed to tripods on rock inclines on each side of the road. Spikes on top of them sported what appeared to be white-painted coffee cans on their sides and small antennas pointing northwest. "They look fake, don't they? Might well be."

Signs similar to the one on the Little A'Le'Inn's potty door peppered the low hills, as well. USE OF DEADLY FORCE AUTHORIZED seeming to stand out in the decreasing light down here. Up there, the sky began to glitter.

Bradone crawled up a forbidden incline and sat next to an orangish post. "Don't worry, Charlie, I'm not trespassing until I step around this stake. Enjoy the night sky."

"So, what are we waiting for? I demand we get back to Vegas tonight. I'm not kidding."

"This is what we're waiting for."

"This" was the thrashing blades of a helicopter.

Which weren't nearly as noisy as the squealing, swearing, laughing figures who came charging over the incline and past Bradone, shoving Charlie aside. Two women and five men and everyone of them sporting video cameras on straps around their necks.

"Out of here," a guy roared in her ear, and before Charlie could control her surprise, the helicopter blades above threw grit in her contact lenses. Three vehicles almost ran her down in their haste to turn around and head "out of here." The nutty astrologer pushed her back into the white Cherokee.

"Show time," Bradone yelled, and gunned the Jeep to follow the other trespassers.

Charlie, busy trying to find eyedrops in her purse, didn't realize they were not staying on the gravel road that eventually met the paved highway like the vehicles ahead of them until the Cherokee bucked like a tortured rodeo bull and she and her purse and her eyedrops landed on the floor under the dash.

She yelled, pleaded, and swore before Bradone hit the brakes and the bucking stopped. "Get back in your seat," she said patiently, "and this time, put on your seat belt."

Before Charlie could regain her seat and composure, she found herself deserted. The dash and headlights were out. Only a small button stayed lighted on the dash. Suddenly, it went out too. No helicopter hovered above. They were obviously off the road and the keys were not in the ignition.

When Detective McKinley jumped back into the driver's seat, she deposited heavy-duty wire cutters on Charlie's lap. Off they started with neither lights nor logic. Charlie hefted the wire cutters experimentally.

"Don't even think about it," the older woman warned, but with a grin. "Just be a good sport a little longer."

They stopped again when that small light blinked on the dash again. Bradone took the wire cutters with her and came back soon after the small light died. They started off across country for a short but jouncing distance and parked up against a rock outcropping.

"Okay, Charlie, we've got to cover this thing." She pulled a dark tarp out of the back of the Jeep and they spread it over the vehicle and themselves, Charlie still complaining but too afraid of what she didn't know about all this to refuse to hide. The tarp smelled like turpentine.

"What, you think we look like a rock here? You think they don't know exactly where we are? They've been tracking our dust for miles."

Bradone peered out of a crack in the tarp edges and a faint light shown on a face that appeared surprisingly older. The sound of the helicopter drew closer. "Then why are they circling over there, Charlie, and not here?"

Charlie looked out, to see the helicopter hover over tossing Joshua trees, raise spectral dirt clouds in the searchlight that shone down from it. It wasn't nearly as close as it sounded.

Bradone shoved a water bottle in Charlie's face. "Drink as much as you can now. We can only carry so much once we leave the Cherokee behind."

"I am not leaving the Cherokee behind." But Charlie took a swig or two or five, mostly because fear and wine had dried out her mouth. "I'm going to give myself up before we get inside the restricted area and come face-to-face with that authorized deadly force. And I strongly suggest you do too."

"Charlie, I think there's something you should know first."

"I'm not listening to you anymore. You're crazy."

Charlie threw back a corner of the tarp, but before she could rush out and flag down the authorities, Bradone said, "We're already inside the restricted area."

TWENTY-NINE

THE MINUTE the helicopter disappeared, they took off in the Cherokee again. "We won't be going far this time. Hang on."

"Did you ask the stars about this?" Charlie could not believe they were out from under the tarp, moving across country, with no headlights. Behind enemy lines. The enemy was armed and they weren't. "They'll follow our tracks."

"Charlie, will you stop whining? The helicopter stirs up so much dirt, it destroys the tracks."

"What if the white Cherokees come after us?"

"There aren't any motion detectors on this side of the boundary. At least there didn't used to be. They can't mine the whole damn place with them. This restricted area is humongous."

"You mean there were motion detectors on the outside of the boundary?"

"That's why the wire cutters. That's what the helicopter was investigating. It must have triggered a signal to somebody that they'd been disabled. Least we know they work. I always wondered if they were just there to intimidate curious tourists."

"I thought Evan was bad about getting me into trouble."

"I have to tell you about the last time I was here." The outrageous woman laughed again.

"Stop that. They can hear your laugh clear back to the Pentagon."

"The last time I was here, we almost stumbled over a bunch of ground troops slithering around on their bellies, loaded down with fantastic equipment. Oh Charlie, it was so funny—wait a minute, I think this is it."

"What? The edge of a cliff? How can you see anything?"

"I almost can't." She stopped and studied a sketch with a penlight. Looked up at the sky and back at the terrain around them. "Pretty sure this is it. Be back in a minute."

"Don't leave me here alone." Charlie'd gone from half-considering knocking the woman out with the wire cutters in order to get control of the Jeep to wanting to cling to her for safety.

But Bradone returned as suddenly as she'd disappeared to drive the Jeep Cherokee into the deeper darkness of a cave.

"What if they have land mines around here?"

"Then we're in big trouble." Bradone turned on the dome light to parcel out food and water between two backpacks—even the cold, greasy leftovers from the Little A'Le'Inn. "We can snack on these tonight. It'll be like a slumber party."

"Why can't we stay here in the cave?"

"Because we can't see anything in here, silly. And this isn't really a cave. It's a mine tunnel, long abandoned. Probably full of bears and lions farther in, so you better stay with me."

Charlie followed her over hill and dale and across rocks and rubble, carrying rolled-up blankets and pillows tied across the top of the pack. Not because she thought there were bears and lions in the mine shaft, but because right now getting into terrible trouble with the air force and the armed response personnel didn't seem as terrifying as being left alone out here at night with no idea how to get back out.

The crunch of their shoes, the brushing sound of scurrying night creatures when Charlie stopped whining and Bradone stopped to get direction from the stars. Was she looking at the position of the constellations to chart their course? Or searching for UFOs?

There are no such things as UFOs.

Without a trail, the going was risky. Sometimes a shadowed rock looked like a depression. And vice versa. Charlie followed as precisely in Bradone's footsteps as possible in the surreal lighting, hoping for a warning of cliff drop-off or rattlesnake or alien presence. Or more likely armed response personnel guys with big rifles. It was just her imagination that the smell of oranges was in the air. That's all it was.

Her guide and tormentor went on and on about her last visit here and the ground troops. Charlie was sure pursuers could hear the chatter, but the woman would not lower her voice.

"We could see them. They couldn't see us. They wore goggles like you say were in Evan's film, but we could see without flashlights because of the starlight, like we can now. They couldn't see anything. They were crawling around and into each other with these imposing guns—more boy toys, swearing and sweating. And it was chilly.''

"Why were they crawling around on the ground? This is air force, isn't it?"

"Oh, who knows? Some silly war game, but these goggles didn't work as well as the ones on the robbers in the now-famous Hilton heist. The packs on their backs, Charlie, they were computers, and these guys could not only not see, their computers were taking forever to boot up and were so heavy the men under them could barely get to their feet.''

"You're making this up."

"No. They were testing this new technology and the computer was supposed to tell this sweating kid where the enemy was and everything. You should have heard them. It was also telling them the weather, which was inaccurate."

"Boy-toy stuff like Pat the pilot smuggled out of Groom Lake for Evan. Bradone, we didn't have to come out here to figure that out. We already had, and we're both too old for slumber parties. Wait, that light on the dash that told you where the ground sensors were. Where did you get that?''

"Same place I got the Cherokee—from Merlin. That's nothing extraordinary. But maybe that wand-phaser thing—think of it—small enough to hold in your hand, but it can freeze an entire crowd in their tracks without harming them. Can you imagine what a weapon that could be? All kinds of things are tested out here.''

"Merlin who? And that's all the more reason why we shouldn't be out here."

Bradone turned unexpectedly. Charlie bumped into her, lost her balance, and she and the pack and the bedding came down on her tailbone. This place made the surface of the moon seem cushy. And it smelled like orange juice. No, it didn't.

The astrologer stood above her with arms crossed and stars shooting every which way over her stupid hat. Her face in shadow. "Charlie, Richard says you don't like to admit to your psychic powers, so—"

"I don't have psychic powers. But you get labeled with that condition just once and every time your plain old garden-variety common sense comes up with a logical explanation for anything, it's hailed as psychic phenomenon. Total pain in the keister."

"But you know Ardith Miller is dead." She reached a hand down to help Charlie up. The starlight was so bright, it made shadows.

"I don't *know* know it—but she hasn't missed work in fifty years—"

"She could be too ill to call in sick."

"That wouldn't account for the horrified look on Zelda the dealer's face this morning." Charlie dusted grit off the seat of her pants and whined, "What does that have to do with anything? So we're out here because we have to see some lights in the dark, find out why I blacked out on the Mooney, have an adventure, and a lot of fun, and—"

"Get you out of Vegas, where I don't think you are safe—"

"I'm 'safe' on a forbidden and undisclosed military installation where probably even the cleaning ladies have permission to shoot me on sight? If the snakes don't get me first."

"But mostly, we're out here to give your exceptional garden-variety common sense a chance to study some uncommon phenomena and hopefully come up with some logical explanations."

"Is that all? Why didn't you just say so?"

TUCKED IN THEIR blankets and munching cold fries, they watched the amazing heavens. Charlie raised up on an elbow occasionally to look down on a supersecret air base that didn't exist. It looked more like an oversized, well-lighted factory complex with runways.

Charlie, convinced her companion was suicidal and intent upon taking Libby Abigail Greene's mother with her, consoled herself that at least Libby was seventeen. She'd inherit Charlie's winnings in Vegas and the equity in the Long Beach condo and the college fund. And a trust would dole it out until the kid was twenty-one, in case a jerk boyfriend decided he should spend it for her.

She had her grandmother. And Maggie Stutzman, Jeremy Fiedler, and Betty Beesom, who all lived in their little gated compound. Larry Mann would keep an eye out for Libby too. And someday Libby would get her grandmother's money as well, not that there was much of that. The kid would not be without resources just because she would be without Charlie.

But who would take on Edwina Greene and her hot flashes?

The stars so very clear, the heavens so full. "This is probably the last night sky I'll ever see."

Bradone laughed aloud again. Why couldn't she go back to that safe silent laughter? "You are so melodramatic and droll. I thought you'd be happy to solve some of the mysteries that surely lie out here where Patrick Thompson flew workers who come and go from the Janet Terminal, where the bicycle cop felt he had to go before alerting the whole department, and got himself killed. It's not Patrick we keep coming back to in our investigations, Charlie, it's here. I maintain that Ben Hanley was a natural death. So we've taken care of almost half the dead bodies already, and we just got here."

"We don't know who ordered any of the murders, Bradone, and we only know who performed the first one. But not to worry, I'm peaceful, composed. My stomach isn't even hurting." Charlie stuffed another cold, greasy A'Le'Inn fry in her mouth. "I'm resigned to my own death."

"No dear, the stars are with us tonight, trust me. That is, if you were accurate about the date and time of your birth. Were you, Charlie? Many people don't know."

"Well, I am one of them. I'm adopted. Edwina has that information somewhere."

Bradone was silent for so long, you could almost hear her holding her breath. But when she spoke, the melody was gone. "You fool. You crashing imbecile. You fucking cretin. You slathering cunt. You—"

"Well, the day is right, and the place. But the time—I think I was remembering Libby's birth." It felt kind of nice to be upsetting Bradone the detective for a change. "I mean, what's the big deal?"

"*What's the big deal?*" The woman's invective continued and grew even coarser. That generation really knew how to swear. But it was interesting that after all Charlie's pleading before, *now* Bradone whispered.

She ranted on until even her whisper grew hoarse, then sat up, letting the covers puddle around her waist. Her arms flung gestures at the sky and Charlie and the creepy earth around them.

"Do you realize what you've done, Charlie Greene? You've added two more bodies to your death count. Ours."

THIRTY

THE A'LE'INN FRIES felt better to Charlie's ulcer than the ground did to her butt. "Okay, so now what?"

"Shut up."

Charlie lay back in her bedding, awaiting death by murder. "You sound like my mother."

"Then I'm elated that I never had children. Charlie, why do you hate me so?"

"Because your presentation sucks. You come on like a spy novel. 'Trust me, Charlie. Follow me behind enemy lines. With full unquestioning cooperation. Because I am your friend. I know all and you are stupid.' And then it's, 'Oh my, it's your fault, Charlie. You've put us in dire and deadly danger.' Hell, I'm the one with a kid and a crazy mother—all you're responsible for is a fun life, two cats, and a houseboy."

"You're right. I've been stupid."

"No, babe, you've been manipulative. I've been stupid to let you get me this far. And you know what we're going to do about it? You are going to tell me in plain language your full agenda here."

"Or you will do what?"

"I will walk down to that nonexistent base and turn myself, my blankets, my pillow, and my backpack in to the authorities. And I'll turn you in too. Your story better be good. You got yourself ten minutes, max."

"How do you know they won't shoot first? Before you can say a word? Deadly force is authorized, don't forget."

Charlie sat up and began rolling her blankets.

"Okay, but you're such a skeptic, I didn't think you'd understand." Bradone's phone call from the naked telephone pole in Rachel had been to the guru astrologer who led her field trip here just a month ago. He had confirmed her reading of the charts by doing his own and helped her remember how to get to the mine tunnel. "His name is Merlin."

"The guy who rented you the Cherokee and told you to cut the wires on the ground sensors." Charlie rolled up the other blanket. It was cold out here. "Cut to the chase, McKinley."

"He's Merlin Johnson."

"You are so squirrelly, I don't know how I could have thought you fascinating."

"Keep your voice down." Bradone pulled the puddled blanket up over her shoulders.

"Why? We're dead anyway."

"Not necessarily, but our chances of being in that condition are better than they'll probably ever be in our lives."

Oh yeah? You never hung from a cliff in the Canyonlands of Utah with Mitch Hilsten. But Charlie sat on one blanket and wrapped the other around her shoulders for warmth. This place was weird. The air even smelled sweet.

Bradone, Merlin, and the rest of the group had come here to study the stars. The constellations were so snapping clear behind the astrologer now that it was really dark, Charlie could see why. But there had to be other remote areas away from city lights where they could have done that at less risk. For sure Charlie and her stargazer would have to spend the night if they weren't captured. They'd never be able to find their way back to the mine tunnel in the deep of this night.

"Your coming here before to study stars does not explain why you dragged me out here tonight. Nor what you plan for us now. Bradone, I really liked you. If you'd just been up front with me."

"There's something about this place, Charlie, that clears the mind. Something in the air like no place else. And this place could be related to all of the deaths but Hanley from Kenosha and I don't know about Ardith Miller. The three men who invaded Evan's house and died for it could have been looking for those boy toys and the films of Area Fifty-one Evan showed at his screening, right? And I think either Evan or someone working for him killed them."

"You couldn't have figured that out in Vegas? Tell me something new or I turn us in. I'm not kidding, Bradone."

"You saw the two bouncers kill the pilot. They probably killed the bicycle cop because he went to the Janet Terminal to look into things he wasn't supposed to know about. So we've solved five murders and they're all related to this place. And when we came out here before, we got more than we bargained for."

"Those ground soldiers got their computers together and were out to kick butt."

"No, we saw more than stars and airplanes. And Charlie, one of our members swears he was seeing everything through an orange haze for a week. He'd gone off on his own and disappeared for over an hour, and he too is psychic."

"Give me a break—"

"He'd been abducted, Charlie. You may have been too."

This woman was logical and deductive one moment and totally off-the-wall the next. "Look, give it up. Evan Black may be able to beat a dead horse and make it live again, which I doubt, but you don't stand a chance. Conspiracy theories are dying in video stores even, but alien abduction is out, babe. What's that noise?" But Charlie knew.

"Quick, cover yourself completely with both blankets and curl up around your pack and the pillow. Breathe shallow and don't move a muscle."

"What, they're going to think we're rocks again?" But Charlie did as she was told.

"The blanket ends mustn't flutter in the wind. Try to keep them battened down all around. And keep your smart mouth shut."

This helicopter was but a whisper of the one trying to flush them from the boundary line. This one whished, where the other slashed the air. Charlie was torn between wanting to hold the blanket down and throwing it aside to see this stealthy machine. This might be a more controlled chopper, but the air it heaved around tugged at her hiding place. The earth under her vibrated.

Fine, so the military was developing new weapons with which to defend Charlie and her livelihood. It made sense to do it in secret. She had no business being here. This was not a conspiracy. It was not an other-world experience. It was a senseless intrusion on her country's vital secrets, which she had no need to know and wouldn't have understood if she did.

Maybe they'd give Charlie a chance to say that and not just shoot her first. Maybe she could promise to never talk about being here. Maybe they'd put her behind bars so Libby would not only have an "UM"—her label for unwed mother—but a jailbird for a mom.

Charlie burped Little A'Le'Inn merlot; her stomach had the good sense to start the familiar burn. She loved her country—well, most of it. She wanted to live to see Libby graduate from high school and college. And Charlie wanted Edwina beside her so she could say, "See, I can be successful at motherhood."

"Charlie? You can come out now." Bradone pulled the covers off Charlie's head and appeared as a shadowed silhouette against the star dazzle. "Sounded like you were crying. Human, after all, are we?"

"Go to hell." Charlie pulled the blankets back over her face.

"Okay, but you're missing the best part of the show. It's even better than—oh no. God, Charlie, don't—"

Charlie was trying to pull her cover aside to see what brought on the sudden panic. But the covers fought back. Damn near smothered her. "Let me out. I have to throw up."

By the time she'd heaved up everything she'd eaten for the last year, Charlie was tasting blood. But she was seeing orange.

"You do a lot of that, don't you? Keep your eyes closed." Bradone sounded mesmerized instead of mesmerizing. She sat on her blankets in a lotus position, legs pretzeled, forearms resting on knees, hands cupped with thumbs and forefingers pressed together. The stars either gone or diluted in the brightness of the light around them.

"Ulcer. Why should I keep my eyes closed?" Charlie moved her bedding away from the stench of vomit and sat on the other side of her companion. No point trying to hide in this brightness anyway.

A yellow-orange globe thing rose slowly into the sky. When it stopped, it hung over the base like an artificial moon. It was not the orange thing that made her pass out the night the Mooney burned, the thing that Charlie dreaded from somewhere deep and hidden.

"There's medication for ulcers." Bradone had her eyes closed, like she was in a trance. "If you look at it, it will get you."

"That's for the bacterial kind." The scene reminded Charlie of sitting on the edge of a volcano. At least the lighting did, not the temperature. Or the smell. It was a heavy citrus now. "My ulcer is caused by stress."

Every building on the base was lighted. The runway lights streaked along in front of the buildings and out until they were hidden behind a peak on another ridge. A higher set of ridges behind the base stopped the stars from reaching the ground. The lights of the giant complex twinkled back at the stars as the orange cleared from her vision.

"They can be cauterized now, you know," Dr. McKinley proclaimed. Why did older people think they knew everything?

"Been there, done that. My ulcer is 'persistent' as well as nonbacterial."

The blinking lights of a plane approached, circled, and landed—tiny on the vast runway.

"I am sorry, Charlie. I should never have brought you out here." Her hat gone, her hair tousled, bathed in the odd light, Bradone made Charlie think of a high priestess in an old Stewart Granger movie.

"Exactly what I've been saying all day and half the night." They were not on the first ridge next to the nonexistent base, but on the second one back. It was higher and angled differently. She couldn't see the entire base, but a good deal of it.

"Be sure and keep your eyes closed, Charlie. Concentrate on keeping your mind your own."

"Right." Like, you drag me all the way here to see something and then I shouldn't look at it.

The helicopter hovered out over the base now and Charlie couldn't hear it at all. It began to bob up and down before the orange globe as if inviting it to dance. This orange globe was solid.

Nothing more than a black shadow in front of the lighted globe, the helicopter had a triangular shape, no tail or tail propeller. The only propeller sat atop the point of the triangle and rotated so fast, it looked solid. The machine under it reminded Charlie of a flying pyramid with four stubby legs, one at each corner of its base.

A flat, elongated triangular craft flew circles around both the globe and the bobbing pyramid. It flew on its side at dizzying speed.

"As soon as we can open our eyes, Charlie, I'll get you some bread for your stomach from one of the breakfast subs and some water. Hang on."

Another more conventional helicopter joined in the dance. It hovered and zigged and zagged instead of bobbing. The three smaller craft looked like dancing shadow moons around a planet.

"Doesn't your doctor offer dietary advice?"

"Last time, it was 'Stay away from raw vegetables and stress.' Changes every time he reads about a new study in the health section of the *L.A. Times.* Hey, if I carried some doohickey into the Hilton that shut off power, why did it *stop* shutting off the power?"

Something, somewhere, throbbed. More an air-pressure thing than a sound.

"It could be remote-controlled, or like the little bug that warned us of the ground sensors—only built to last for a short time after being activated," Bradone said, actually making a little sense. Maybe there was something in the air here.

The one thing they couldn't have found when searching her room was her purse, because she'd had it with her. Now she pulled it from her pack and felt the linings inside the compartments. Nothing. She felt along the strap and the metal things that connected it to the purse. But when she felt along the bottom of the outside, one side had two studs and the other three. And that third was about twice as big as the rest.

"Maybe you could marry Mitch and not have to work. Yours is a stressful job."

"My work is the one part of my stress I enjoy." Unlike dead bodies, menopausal mothers, hormonally overdosed daughters, and the prospect of dying right here. Or going to jail because I am right here. Could Charlie offer the stud to the armed response personnel?

At least her government appeared to have a handle on cool new technology. That yellow-orange globe wasn't suspended from anything visible, sitting on anything, moving in any way, not even floating. That ought to keep aggressors restrained until they could be tranquilized with McDonald's, Coca-Cola, Pizza Hut, theme parks, and shock/schlock movies.

The stationary sphere seemed too far away to be responsible for the glow from below their ridge that had reminded her of sitting on the edge of an active volcano.

Charlie was sure of that when the thing that had made her see orange the night the Mooney burned, the thing she'd dreaded asleep and awake since, the thing that *was* responsible for tonight's volcano glow, rose up out of the valley between their ridge and the one bordering Groom Lake on the throbbing pressure in the air.

The throbbing filled Charlie's head. The orange thing filled the world.

THIRTY-ONE

BRADONE STOOD ON the edge of the ridge, perilously close to the sickly orange mist. She screamed with her hands over her ears, as if she didn't want to hear herself either.

Charlie would never say so if captured, but she thought her government was beginning to overdo this. Sure the woman was about to topple into the mist, Charlie squirmed across jagged earth on a sore belly to grab her by the ankles and yank her feet out from under her.

Bradone fell forward and would have gone over the precipice if Charlie hadn't hung on and dug the toes of her shoes into the jagged earth.

Duh—why *wouldn't* she fall forward? You pulled her feet out from under her.

Look, it's easy for you to show up whenever you feel like it to be critical, but I live in this body, okay?

Yeah, well, heads up, this body is trying to slide over a cliff again.

The problem was not only Bradone. The problem was also the shoes Charlie had dug in the toes of to stop their slide into oblivion. Keds don't have tough toes. It's not like they were rushing to their doom, more like a slow, inexorable slippage. Bradone, inert and silent, as if she'd been knocked out or killed in her fall, hung about halfway over the side. All Charlie could see was her rump.

Any more of Bradone McKinley over the edge and the weight would increase the speed of their slide toward death. Didn't take a rocket scientist to figure that out.

More of Bradone went over the side. Charlie couldn't see much through the orange fog by now but knew this because her sore belly was scraped of clothing as she followed Bradone.

Any common sense worth its salt would have commanded Charlie to let go of the dead weight of the astrologer, but there wasn't time anyway. She had only two thoughts before death. The first was anger. Charlie was too young to die.

The second was, Oh please, world, give Libby a chance. No time for thoughts of Edwina and Maggie and Larry and Mitch and all the others.

Charlie's hands were still locked around Bradone's ankles as they followed her over. She tried to open them at the last minute, but they'd frozen.

The hair on the back of Charlie's neck did not rise when it too went over. But the entire skin under it did when something grabbed her own ankles.

Sort of a patriotic tingle. The government. Charlie's government. Some ground trooper or foot soldier or some armed response person from a white Cherokee must have seen their plight. Right?

Amazing that her front wasn't scraped off down to the ulcer as she, still locked onto Bradone, was hauled back to level ground. Poor Bradone bumped up over the edge to safety in hideous notches. When only the stargazer's hands and wrists remained hidden in the orange fog, Charlie dared to steal a glance over her shoulder at their rescuer. She even gave half a thought to what she'd do if it were a little bald alien with huge black almond-shaped eyes that slanted up at the outer corners.

She'd hoped for a big strong John Wayne marine type in a camouflage outfit who'd be sternly disapproving—"Listen, little lady"—but would listen to her before shooting.

The caboose on the end of their short train to disaster was not her government. Instead, Toby, Evan Black's second-unit gofer, with the lopsided grin, lay sprawled on his stomach, the toes of his sensible hiking boots dug into the hard dirt. Beside him a pair of upright, long, lean Dockers.

Head and shoulders enshrouded by clouds of orange, Mel Goodall clasped a camera to his chest.

"So, NOBODY but me saw orange." Charlie accosted Toby as they tried to revive the prostrate astrologer.

"I never saw that before."

There appeared to be something solid in the orange mist that obliterated the air base, the giant globe with the black aircraft bobbing or zipping around it, the next mountain range, and that side of the sky from horizon to horizon. And still it continued to rise up out of the valley next to them.

"Shouldn't you be shooting that?" Toby asked the main-man cinematographer. Whatever was inside the roiling mist was more unidentifiable than invisible.

"Can you believe that mother?" Mel said. "I'll never eat another orange as long as I live."

The odor did still suggest the fruit but smelled too concentrated now, too…chemical-like—like something you'd use to cover an even worse odor. Charlie had finally met up with what she'd feared.

"Do you think it's giving off deadly fumes? Chemical warfare? Why does it have to be that big? Talk about overkill. Like the hydrogen bomb. No wonder our taxes are so high," Charlie babbled and tried rubbing the back of Bradone's hand. It felt warm still. She didn't have the heart to feel for a pulse. Bradone had been the closest to the thing.

"What's that supposed to do?" Toby started on the other hand.

"I don't know—I saw it in a movie. Is Evan here?"

"Too risky. Lose him, we're all out of a job. Which reminds me," Mel said, sliding the camera into a cloth bag, "I gotta get this contraband out of here. Tobias, ol' boy—"

"I know. Come visit us in prison."

But Mel was off across the Mars-like terrain with strides so long, shadows swallowed him in seconds.

"What do you mean, visit us in prison?"

"We're parked right behind you. Minute ol' Mel takes off out of there, those security boys'll be all over that mine tunnel. Looks like I'll have to carry her. You grab the blankets and packs. I'm for taking my chances with security types—might get shot, but this thing is unhealthy in a way I don't know."

"If we're going to die from orange gas, we've already been infected. How did you know where to find us?"

"We didn't even know you were here. Vegas news is reporting you and Hilsten have eloped or something. He come with you?''

"He doesn't know anything about this little side trip. How did you find the mine tunnel?"

"Guy named Merlin—"

"Now stop that—"

But the megalithic orange thing with all its gases finally cleared the ridge and the pulsating air grew horrendous—palpitating Charlie's eardrums, forcing air into her nose and mouth one second, trying to suck it out the next. Loose dirt spurted in all directions and Charlie closed her eyes to protect her lenses. Imprinted on the back of her eyelids was a silhouette of Toby's shadow standing up against the orange light with the lump of Bradone McKinley hanging over one shoulder.

When Charlie opened her eyes, she was alone.

THIRTY-TWO

LIGHTNING AND thunder filled the world. Charlie could see the giant air force base now and the self-suspended yellow-orange globe with even more satellite aircraft around it.

Above and behind her, stars once again littered the heavens.

The orange thing might be gone, but everything had an orange hue now—even the darkness. "Toby?"

The bastard had gone off and left her.

CHARLIE SAT ON a pillow and chewed soggy mayo and mustard-flavored bread. She sipped bottled water just as cautiously. And jumped every time lightning streaked from the cloudless sky.

If Libby heard Charlie had eloped with Mitch, she'd probably run right out and get pregnant. Libby hated Mitch.

Charlie put all the food and water in one pack, tucked one rolled blanket through the straps meant for a sleeping bag, and waited for dawn.

She didn't like being alone with wilderness and discomfort. What if the orange thing came back? What if it wasn't really gone?

Oh hell. She opened a thermos of Little A'Le'Inn coffee and poured a cup in its lid. Just the smell made her feel better. Well, two years ago it had been "Stay away from caffeine, booze, and soda" with that doctor. This year, it was fresh vegetables and stress. The coffee made her happy—thus alleviating stress, right?

Charlie would simply walk down into the valley in front of her and up over the next mountain range and turn herself in to her outrageously extravagant government. If they shot her, they shot her. No good trying to find that mine tunnel. Toby and Bradone and the Cherokee would probably be long gone already arrested by armed response personnel.

We aren't feeling a tad sorry for ourself, are we?

If you aren't going to be any help, leave me alone.

Do you really think even your extravagant government can make lightning in a cloudless sky?

"Oh." Charlie drained the thermos cup and poured another.

That would take Mother Nature or God or—

Little orange aliens?

Both Charlie and her inner voice knew that simply because something appeared to have no rational explanation did not mean it didn't. But she decided she was too out in the open for all this lightning, no matter who or what was responsible for it.

Maybe it would be safer down there with the government. Charlie didn't have a better idea, so she crawled over to take a peek at the drop. The grade wasn't real steep as far down as she could see, which wasn't very. But, with all the lightning around, her position on this promontory didn't seem like a good plan either.

Well, don't stay here and be a lightning rod.

Maybe go back the way I came and look for the mine tunnel. Maybe find a ground sensor and set it off and the government will come for me.

"Charlie?" Bradone McKinley stood swaying not six feet away, unaware she'd nearly startled a nervous literary agent over the edge of a cliff.

"Where's Toby?"

"Who's Toby?"

"One of Evan Black's entourage. I told you about him."

"After what happened to me, I can't be expected to remember much." The astrologer looked like a tousled, battered doll in the half-light. The impression of command had mutated to defeat.

"Nothing happened to you." Charlie didn't have to be psychic to know where this was heading. "Last I saw Toby, he was walking out of here, leaving me to my fate and carrying your unconscious body over one shoulder."

"Oh, the man laid out half-dead at the entrance to the mine tunnel.... I think he may have tripped over a rock. But how did he get here, and why was he carrying me over his shoulder? Charlie, I can't find the words to tell you how disturbing this whole thing has been. Did this Toby rescue me from them?"

"Them who?"

"The aliens. On the huge orange ship. The voices in my head." Bradone grabbed her temples.

"Nobody did anything to you, Bradone. Nothing happened. Got that?"

"Charlie, I was raped."

"I had a solid hold on your ankles and a great view of your crotch the whole time you were hanging over the edge, damn it. You didn't go anywhere. You were not abducted."

The orange globe out over the air base had disappeared while they talked, and all its satellites too. Except for the elongated triangular aircraft. It swooped up the valley toward them now with no warning and very little noise.

They were too buzzed already to hide.

"Must be a smaller craft from the spaceship," Bradone said.

"It's a new test plane you'll be glad to have when Saddam and Muslim fanatics unite to spread nerve gas across the country or poison our water supply."

"Charlie, no aircraft could intercept nerve gas. Some suicidal stooge could bring it in on a United Airlines flight. And our water's already poisoned."

"Yeah, well, there's no spaceship here either and nobody could rape you while I was holding on to your ankles."

Planes lined up behind one another to land on the humongous runways, their lights emerging from the sky full of fading stars and brightening as they approached.

"More spaceships," Bradone said through shallow breathing.

"737s from the Janet Terminal delivering a shift of workers."

"You can't know that."

"I think we should see if Toby has left us the Jeep. Could you find your way back to the mine tunnel before it gets any lighter?"

"The stars are disappearing fast." But Bradone staggered off with considerable confidence for a woman who had just been raped by orange aliens.

Was it possible they could actually get out of here without being arrested or shot by security forces who worked for an installation that didn't exist? Armed response personnel whose nonexistence put them above the law because deadly force was authorized?

Charlie and her common sense didn't even have to discuss that one. Not a chance. But they followed Bradone in better light than they'd had the night before.

"Maybe you were raped too while holding on to my ankles."

"Bradone, let it rest. Toby was holding on to my ankles, or we'd have both gone over the side. Nobody was raped. Not even Toby, because Mel Goodall was standing behind him."

"I know what I saw and what I felt."

"Please don't write a book about it."

"How DID YOU and Mel know about our ridge?" Bradone demanded of a dazed Toby they'd found sitting up in the tunnel.

"Guy named Merlin advertised it on the Internet."

"Damn him. He sold out," the stargazer-turned-detective said, and made a gurgling sound, as if she were choking on the thought.

"You get this Cherokee at Merlin's on I-Fifteen?" Toby was in worse shape than Bradone—a purpling knot on his forehead, dried blood on his cheek and down his neck, one eye swollen nearly shut. And he kept trying to chew on a loosened tooth. He'd wrapped his muscle shirt around his head and his jacket opened on a scraped chest.

"The car rental was named Merlin's, and you are surprised he sold out?" Charlie asked Bradone. Charlie was driving, since she was the least injured.

"I thought it a coincidence."

"How many Merlins do you know?"

"The sign didn't say Merlin Johnson."

Charlie didn't care what the advertising claimed, these Cherokees were not off-road vehicles. Bad-road vehicles, maybe. The damn thing managed to hold its doors on as they bucked over assorted rocks and gullies and rocks *in* gullies. Tanks might be off-road vehicles.

"No kidding? Merlin's last name is Johnson? Cool. So is mine. But there's a lot of us around." Toby leaned forward from the backseat between the two bucket seats in front, trying to help

Bradone with directions. He was about all Charlie could see in the rearview mirror. "There, those tracks? We're on course—those are Mel's."

"What was he driving?" Charlie bit her tongue as the front tire on the driver's side ka-chunked down off a boulder.

"One of these from Merlin's. Weren't about to fuck up our own stuff or Evan's. Besides, these babies got special reversible license plates. Little lever there under the dash by your right knee does the front. First helicopter we see, I jump over the seat and switch the one on the rear too."

Bradone turned to Toby. "I've been raped. Have you?"

The second-unit gofer was pretty perky, considering blood matted his black curls to his forehead. But that question stopped him for a while. "Nnnn-ot in this lifetime, I don't believe, no."

There would be gas in Rachel if they ever got out of this rock and cactus warren without killing Merlin's Jeep. Without being shot dead from a dark helicopter above or the government's white Jeep Cherokees down here. But Charlie would try to make it to Alamo for gas and bandages. She didn't want to backtrack. Was it possible she was escaping the orange thing?

"Hey, turn left here. There're the tracks to a real road." Toby gave a lesser second-unit Evan Black victory whoop. "Oh baby." He patted Charlie's shoulder. "You *are* the best agent in the biz."

"So Merlin Johnson gave you a map with the rental." The alien rapee did not sound so pleased at their possibly imminent survival.

"Yeah, to Merlin's Cave and Merlin's Ridge. We paid extra because he had a scout out here cutting the wires on the ground sensors." Toby laughed for no reason. "Said it'd be a breeze."

"Why did you contact him last night? I mean, that is a suspicious coincidence," Charlie said.

"Merlin's Cave and Merlin's Ridge?" Bradone was coming alive again. "That imposter, that motherfucking bastard, that—"

"Man, that generation knows how to swear, huh?" Toby managed to choke off the unwarranted hilarity. "Evan had a deal with Merlin to contact him when the time was right to go out to Mer—uh, the ridge and get footage. How'd you get out here?''

"We followed the stars," Charlie answered dryly, "and cut the wires on the ground sensors for you. And solved five murders in the clear air."

"You solved five murders?" Toby feigned astonishment for the rearview mirror.

Charlie explained their deduction, which didn't seem as logical as it had last night in the orange glow.

"You think Evan killed those guys in his house? He wouldn't kill anybody."

He might ask you or Mel to. Which would be the same thing. Then she remembered where she'd heard of Merlin's Ridge, at McCarran, where she'd first seen the first-to-be body. Patrick the hunk had mentioned it to someone over his cellular. Probably someone at the Janet Terminal.

Charlie barely missed a sickly Joshua tree and did kill the engine as they rounded a hill and saw two dark helicopters above an advancing contingent of white Cherokees sending up dust for the choppers to chop into clouds.

Libby Abigail Greene was about to become an orphan, or worse—the daughter of a jailbird.

THIRTY-THREE

"Man, most of that stuff coming at us is Merlin's Cherokees," Toby Johnson said. "Start your engine, damn it."

"How can you tell?" Through holes in the mushrooming dust, Charlie noticed a pickup camper about third in line and then more of them interspersed among the white Jeeps farther back.

"We have a chance," Bradone said low and more vengeful than melodious, her tone reminding Charlie of Caryl Thompson. "Don't flood the goddamned motor."

"Chance for what? There're two helicopters this time."

"Yeah, but they got all Merlin's friends to baby-sit here." The second-unit gofer grinned around his loosened tooth. It was not a pretty sight. "Go for it big time, agent lady."

Charlie saw one of those motion sensors Bradone had cut, unwittingly abetting Merlin Johnson, before she ran over it to avoid the barrage of pickup campers and Cherokees coming at them. It resembled a big rusty can connected to an oblong box by wires, something like an amateur bomb might look. The helicopters appeared to have help in their attempt to round up the herd of curiosity seekers and nuts from two official white Cherokees with light bars on top.

Charlie almost overshot the gravel road when they came to it because of the dust still in the air. One of the helicopters peeled off to head their way. She gunned her unofficial Jeep onto the road, throwing up a plume of white-gray rock dust herself. That plume couldn't be missed from the sky, probably couldn't be missed from outer space. She'd get them as far as she could.

"Just pray there aren't any cattle on the road this morning." Charlie floored it. "Just get us to Alamo, baby."

Car chases were one of Charlie's least favorite kinds of scene in action movies, ranked right up there with vivisection. Now she knew why.

"Wait, stop a minute," Toby ordered after a few miles. The windows were so covered with dust, he had to step out of the car to use the binoculars commandeered from Bradone's endless supply of expedition provisions.

"Hurry up," Charlie warned, "or I'll leave without you." She'd thought he needed to relieve his bladder. They were off again before he could get the door closed.

"That chopper isn't following us. He's parked behind Merlin's caravan and the other one's in front. God, I wish we could have got some footage of that." His eye was swollen in a permanent wink now. "Maybe somebody back there's getting it on video and can smuggle it out in camper bedding or something."

They didn't turn off the way they'd come on the road to the black mailbox, now white, connected to the paved highway leading into Rachel. Instead, they headed straight on the gravel road until it reached the pavement on its own, putting them much closer to the road to Alamo. Charlie's inner ears tickled unbearably from the vibration of their washboard journey.

"What makes you think we're going to get away with this?" Charlie asked Toby.

"All we got to watch for now is the Lincoln County Sheriff's Department, which Merlin says is getting fed up with having to use manpower to back up a government installation that's not there. That Merlin, he's really something, I tell you."

"Wouldn't it be simply lovely," Bradone said, "if that Merlin were in the captured caravan back there?"

"He's got to be nuts if he thinks they're going to let him continue to run a scam like this. How could he invest in all these Cherokees knowing they'd be half-ruined by going off the road and he'd be closed down in a week or less anyway?"

"Seeing as he's so smart, Mel and me figure he leases the Cherokees from other dealers." Something in the gofer's expression in the mirror reminded Charlie of someone else, but the memory byte was gone before she could nail it. "I mean, hell, he's renting these out of a tent, probably never planned on being around long."

"For what purpose?" Bradone tried to turn around in her seat to look at Toby and groaned. Her ribs had to be bruised from hanging over ledges and Toby's shoulder.

"Who knows? Very mysterious, that Merlin. Did I tell you he's a magician too? Maybe he's just trying to annoy the nice people at Area Fifty-one. Maybe it's a scam we haven't figured out yet."

"That's a lot of effort and money just to annoy someone. How long has he been in business?"

"Couple days. I'd be willing to bet, we get back to Merlin's, there's no Merlin. Checks cashed to a drop somewhere, he and the cash disappeared already. I just hope we won't be turning this sucker in to the police."

"How is it you know so much about Merlin?" Bradone asked.

If Bradone ever caught up with her mentor, Charlie figured he'd be left holding a whole bunch of regret.

"Me and Mel checked him out for Evan." Toby opened the back windows, that almost goofy delight with life everywhere on his battered face, except for the deadly serious look in the one eye remaining open. "He was into astrology, voodoo, and this deal where you could get credit cards good all over the world, no matter your credit rating."

"Why would Evan check out Merlin? Bradone, when you were here before, did you come in white Cherokees?"

"Two of them. I never questioned where Merlin got them."

"Hell, he's probably into all kinds of other stuff too. Reminds me of Mel and Evan, and damn near all of Hollywood, for that matter."

"If you knew this about him, why did you rent from him?"

"Hey, we do fiction, you know? It's all grist, babe."

Bradone seemed to have forgotten her exceptionally personal close encounter of the orange kind. She leaned toward Charlie to watch Toby in the rearview mirror. "Have we met before?"

"Saw you at Evan's the night of the screening. We weren't introduced. I'm just a gofer—Jesus, what's that?"

Charlie, still flooring the poor machine down the road, pumped the brake and the windshield washer to see whatever it was, praying it was not a great huge stupid bull standing on the center line. She just wasn't up to cattle mutilation.

A machine of some kind, an aircraft, flying lower than a crop duster, streaked down the center line toward them. It tipped a nose with a hummingbird proboscis straight into the air at the absolute final moment, soaring over them with a sucking sound instead of a roar.

Charlie and the Cherokee fought each other and her heartbeat all over the road and off it and back onto it and then off it again before coming to a phenomenally abrupt halt.

"Get us out of here," Bradone shouted. The second unit gofer, who had not been belted in, grunted in the backseat and Charlie sat there, stunned to find the engine still running.

Her contacts were dry and gritty, there was grit between her teeth. Buzzy from lack of enough sleep, coffee, water, eggs, and vacation, Charlie wanted a hot shower to quell the itches in the most private of her parts. She wanted to tell the whole world to go to hell, beginning with the inhabitants of this car.

But Charlemagne Catherine sat tall and pulled back onto the two-lane highway that was in good repair but seemed to have more cattle and airplanes on it than it did cars.

She mashed the pedal. At least she wasn't falling asleep like she had on the way in. "We are going to make it to Alamo."

It couldn't have been ten minutes before her passengers were screaming at her again and Charlie mashed the brake instead. The Cherokee screeched and zagged all over the pavement and shoulders on both sides. This time, they came to a stop up against a poor Joshua tree with a rock behind it.

The rock won.

The lumbering animal that had caused this event stopped lumbering and began to trot toward them, testicles and such swinging in the wind.

"God, that's a lot of beefsteak," Toby murmured.

Merlin's white Jeep Cherokee eeeeked, sputtered, and died.

"Toby, find the eyedrops in my purse. My contacts are killing me." Charlie turned back to her task of restarting the engine, to find eyes much larger than hers and just as bloodshot staring in her open window. The beefsteak snorted, lowered his head, and farted.

"Punch your window up." The stargazer coughed.

The big red bull with the big curved horns pawed the desert floor, lifted his head and then his tail, and, before Charlie could get her wits and the window under control, squirted out two days' graze.

"What purse?" Now the gofer was coughing.

"Mine's up here." Bradone pointed to the floor at her feet with the hand not covering her nose.

The engine eeeked, growled, and purred into being.

"It was in my backpack."

The bull, apparently satisfied with his statement, lumbered off to the middle of the road, where he seemed more at home.

Charlie backed the bruised Cherokee in the same direction, her eyes watering from that portion of the bull's statement that had joined them. Tears floated her artificial lenses. She opened all the windows from her center console to clear the air.

"I got no pack, no purse. I got a big canvas thing. I got a grocery bag with one apple—"

"What do you mean, no pack? There were two." Charlie drove more sedately now. "Keep looking."

"Oh, Charlie." Bradone had tears in her voice, if not in her eyes. "We left the packs and your purse with your identification back at—"

"Merlin's Ridge," Toby finished for her, sounding like doom incarnate.

THIRTY-FOUR

CHARLIE AND her companions made it to Alamo, with a sheriff's car in not very hot pursuit. They bought gas and snacks and water and a pint of whole milk for Charlie's ulcer. The sheriff's car roared past as if the deputy didn't see them. Toby cleaned up his wounds in the men's room.

"My purse had my identification, lots of cash, and an extra metal stud on the bottom, which probably turned the lights out at the Hilton. Not too incriminating."

Bradone had left her purse, too large to fit in the pack, in the Jeep in the mine tunnel. Charlie certainly wished she had. "When Toby abandoned me, I put what I thought I needed to walk to the base in one pack. I'm sure not going back for it."

Toby came out of the little convenience store all smiles, hair dripping where he'd washed the blood out. They remembered to turn the license plates but never saw the representative of the Lincoln County Sheriff's Department again.

Merlin's tent office on I-15, just outside of Vegas, resembled a fireworks stand, striped with red, white, and blue. They turned the Cherokee in to a kid, maybe Libby's age, who kept glancing at Toby with suspicion but would give out no information on Merlin. He didn't even charge Bradone for the dents and scrapes that driving off the road in Area 51 had put on the Jeep.

Charlie should have suspected something right then, but she just wanted a shower.

They called a cab to get back to town, then looked at one another, undecided, when the driver wanted to know, "Where to?"

"Well, don't look at me." Charlie had no plan, no money, no credit cards, no plane ticket, no clean clothes, no ID to retrieve her belongings, which had probably been removed from her room at the Hilton. She might well lose her job and her freedom when that stud was found on her purse. And her eyesight. Her contacts were scratching again.

And her government, which she stoutly supported, could even now be tracing her life's history on the Internet using the information on credit cards, phone numbers, and the driver's license in her billfold. She wouldn't be hard to find. She'd have to rat on Evan to explain the stud.

Bradone suggested they try to retrieve Charlie's luggage anyway. "I expect the paparazzi have followed your Mitch Hilsten elsewhere."

But she sent Toby into the Hilton to use a house phone to see if Charlie still had a room and to do the same with Richard Morse. "I've got a card key to Richard's room. We'll see if we can't jimmy the connecting door."

Toby returned to say Charlie and her boss, still registered, did not answer their phones.

"Maybe we can move your luggage to Loopy Louie's until we think of something better. I'm not registered under my own name."

"Louie Deloese knows who you are by sight," Charlie pointed out, "and why wouldn't your paparazzi have followed Mitch to Loopy's? That's where he was staying."

"We'll go in the back way both places."

They rode up the Hilton's glass elevator on the outside of the building to avoid the lobby, Charlie wondering why the stargazer trusted the gofer, since she was so paranoid.

Charlie studied the interplay between Toby and Bradone. She kept slicing glances his way. He kept pretending he didn't notice. Charlie kept trying to remember who he resembled.

But they were all startled at the ease with which Toby triggered the dead bolt of the connecting door to Charlie's room. He looked at them and shrugged. "What can I say? I'm a magician."

Richard's room was a suite with a separate bedroom and a dressing room. Charlie's room was the extra bedroom to the suite. She checked the closet and found Richard's clothes still hanging there. In her own closet, the safe still held Charlie's computer, the wardrobe drawers all her panties. Her companions helped her cram everything into her luggage.

SHOWERED, SHAMPOOED, shaved, deodorized, teeth brushed, contacts soaking, and wearing her glasses, which she never let anyone see her in but Libby and her neighbors in the condo complex. Clean jeans and soft gauze bandages, purchased in Alamo, under her shirt. And not arrested yet. Charlie savored the moment.

Nothing rotated here in Bradone's room at Loopy Louie's. No scimitars. The bed square, the TV on a corner table. This room was not as exotic as Mitch's, but the wallpaper featured endless lines of camels parading between endless palm-filled oases and rolling sand dunes.

Toby, showered and wearing one of Charlie's sleeping shirts and a pair of Bradone's shorts, opened the door to the room-service bedouin. Charlie could smell the coffee.

Bradone, dressed in two skimpy towels, one on her hair and the other wrapped around her body, barely, signed the tab, paraded to her purse and pulled out a bill that pleased the bedouin as much as her attire. "I know you aren't housekeeping, but could you see that we get more bath towels, soap, glasses, and whatever? And the evening newspaper? There's another one of these for you if they are all here in under ten minutes."

Everything was there before Charlie got her second sip of coffee. Rich people know how to get things done. Must have something to do with compounding.

Charlie had a creamy Allah omelette without camel fries. She and her stomach had begun to settle in when Bradone passed her a section of the newspaper and pointed out a small article at the bottom of a page.

LONGTIME LAS VEGAS RESIDENT
KILLED IN ROBBERY.
Hilton Hotel food server, Ardith Miller, shot at bus stop, apparently for her tip money, authorities say.

"I told you so."

"Now listen to me, girl." Bradone shook a disciplinary finger at Charlie. "You had nothing to do with that death. People are robbed all the time, and sometimes it gets violent. She waited on thousands of people, who have no more reason to feel responsible for it than you do."

"Probably got killed for that hundred-dollar bill Art Sleem tipped her for my breakfast."

"You know how many hundred-dollar bills there are floating around this town? Tips all go in a pool and are divided up at the end of a shift anyway. The busers share in them, and the tax man too." Bradone's distress over her extraterrestrial rape had been replaced by an angry control.

"Shut up. Listen to this," Toby shouted, pointing at the TV.

"Metro spokeswoman, Camilla Hardy, has finally released some information on the triple murders at the home of filmmaker Evan Black." Different news team, different channel. Two guys this time, but they followed two identical replays of the Depends commercial, seen on Barry and Terry's channel.

"Police are now disclosing that the three victims, Matthew Tooney, Arthur Sleem, and Joseph Boyles were all murdered at different places in the house and then moved to one location in the family room."

"They have confirmed that not all three were killed with the same weapon," the other guy added. Both late forties, one in a blue blazer, one in a tan. "Sources say two were killed by the same gun and one, rumored to be Tooney, by a different-caliber weapon. Matthew Tooney has been identified as an investigator for the insurance company covering the casino at the Las Vegas Hilton." This was the tan blazer with the homey smile. So Tooney wasn't IRS. Maybe that's why he let Charlie keep the money.

The blue blazer had a squint that gave him a more serious demeanor. "The other two victims of last Thursday's shooting spree, Boyles and Sleem, had been employed as security for several casinos on the Strip, most recently, Loopy Louie's."

"Also, sources close to the Metro Police Department say that only a few thousand dollars of the money, stolen in the daring raid on the Las Vegas Hilton's cage in the wee hours of Wednesday morning, was missing.''

"The money from the casino robbery, found near the door of the separate security building behind the hotel yesterday morning, had been stuffed into black plastic garbage bags.''

"That's why all the reporters and TV trucks pulling up to the Hilton when I came to get you, Charlie. I thought it was you and Mitch that attracted them.''

"There's Ardith, the waitperson.'' Charlie pointed at the stilled frame of black plastic bags lying up against a metal grate and several people walking away. One bag had bills spilling out of a tear in its side. "The one with the thick ankles. She'd come to work after all, but left with a stash.'' Poor Ardith. If Charlie had been her age in her job, she'd have grabbed extra cash too.

"Now you know it's not your fault,'' Bradone told Charlie.

"The real mystery to all this is why steal money and then return it?'' The blue blazer tightened his squint on this one.

But Charlie knew. "Because Evan and crew made more money for the conspiracy project by collecting on a bet that you couldn't pull off the robbery than if you'd kept the money, huh, Toby? You guys never planned to keep it, did you?''

The second-unit gofer gave her a bland smile and raised his eyebrows in a way that reminded Charlie of Bob, the limo driver.

"That's why that phony screening before Mitch got here. All those people were in on the bet or represented others who were, right? That's why the cash, only—Evan's going to fund the conspiracy project with bet money, he won't have to pay back from profits—it's free money, not a loan. It's probably all under the table, so no taxes either.''

"They don't call the guy a genius for nothing. Nobody thought he could pull it off without hurting anybody. The odds were something else.'' He shook his curls. "It was beautiful. Even I was impressed.''

"Is that why it hardly made the headlines?'' Bradone asked.

"Word was out on the street for anybody tuned in. But nobody thought it would be the Hilton. It's got the tightest security. Most of the betting favored Loopy's or one of the casinos on Fremont. I didn't know until the last minute. They didn't let me in on anything much because of my uncle Louie. I figured they had you pegged to douse the lights for them, Charlie. Maybe they picked the Hilton because you had a room there. Only in Vegas, man.''

"...no new leads in the disappearance of heartthrob Mitch Hilsten and girlfriend, Hollywood agent Charlie Greene, who have been missing for over twenty-four hours.

"Friends say the two have been estranged recently and may simply be off making up in private.''

"What friends? If Libby sees this, I'm dead. If Edwina's been saying that, she's dead.''

"And now here's Greg Torpor with sports. Hey, Greg, how about those Atlantic No Doz, huh?''

"Yeah, Don,'' Greg wore a sports shirt, with hair trying to grow out of the open collar, "it was a great weekend for football and the No Doz too. You know?''

Just as the music and all these huge black guys in helmets revved up, Bradone hit the mute.

"What is it with women?'' Toby Johnson complained, and went back to his lamb curry something.

There'd been no news of Merlin's Caravan on the local newscast, but there certainly was on the national.

"Yes!'' Toby raised his fork at the screen when their hostess unmuted the set. "Way to go, Merlin.''

This segment made much of the fact that the supersecret air base was simply not acknowledged by the United States government and then showed the signs forbidding photography of this or any part of "this installation.''

From then on, Area 51, or Groom Lake, was referred to as "this installation'' and stills and videos of it appeared distant but from every angle imaginable. Many looked to Charlie as if they'd been taken from Merlin's Ridge.

The best shots of all were from the inside of some of the vehicles in the caravan and of the two Cherokees with light bars coming close to cameras, the men with threatening sunglasses motioning drivers to stop and then cursing when someone else in the line ahead broke loose.

"Told you they'd pack some of that stuff out in their sleeping bags," Toby purred.

Shots of the dark helicopters on the ground in front and back and of people, some of them kids, pulled from their vehicles and the vehicles searched. There did not appear to be enough searchers, several of whom were shown being bitten by family dogs.

A chuckling anchor, sitting in for Tom Brokaw, said, "Wait, this gets better."

More laughter from those working in the studio with him.

"Seems just as all forces were mobilized on one front and military Humvees of the plain old camouflage color came bouncing across the terrain to help out beleaguered security personnel, word came that another section of the perimeter had been breached the night before. And another caravan was now leaving from a different direction."

Somebody on the ground had videotaped a long line of four-wheel-drive enthusiasts heading through Rachel from a side road onto the paved highway. Studio jokesters added the triumphant score from *Star Wars* to accompany the sequence.

"They must have come out behind us." Bradone sat on the bed, holding her plate on her lap. "I wonder who cut ground censor wires for them? Could we have just been a decoy?"

Toby Johnson sat on the floor, eating off dishes perched on a corner of the coffee table in front of Charlie. He turned around on his tailbone to face their hostess, reminding Charlie of Evan Black exercising after the big screening.

"Merlin thinks of everything." He rotated his coccyx back to his dinner, Charlie hurting for him, and raised those eyebrows again. "But he tries to never be there when 'everything' happens."

"You know Merlin?" Charlie asked. "He's really Evan, right?"

"I've met Evan," Bradone insisted. She'd dressed in black again, pants and comfortable shoes. Black jacket and a black scarf around her hair. She looked like a cat burglar. "He's not Merlin."

"Toby, why did you go off and leave me on Merlin's Ridge?" Charlie asked.

"You disappeared over the side. I couldn't see you in all that orange. I was going to lug our unconscious hostess back to the tunnel and come look for you, but I tripped while still lugging."

"I never went over the side." If Charlie wasn't responsible for half the grief that was happening around her this week, Evan "Genius" Black had to be. There was simply no one else.

Though Bradone comes up in your doubts more often than you want to admit.

What could be her motive? Misled as she is, she's always trying to help.

Right now, she was staring murder at the back of Toby Johnson's head.

What motive could Evan have?

For that Merlin caravan thing, he could have a lot. Like Toby said, he could buy video and stills off amateurs—which some filmmakers wouldn't touch but which Evan could turn into gold. This guy had motive.

"Toby, did Evan Black set up this Merlin guy and his scam to entice all the UFO and conspiracy nuts out to Groom Lake? As a cover for something he wanted to do or to draw attention to its obvious existence?"

Toby batted those eyebrows this time. "Pure magic, right?"

"Oh no, is this the magic event Evan's been promising would get us all out of this mess?" It would make Charlie's government look silly if they went after him now for successfully invading and filming and making a motion picture about an "installation" that didn't exist.

Charlie looked at Toby Johnson and saw Bob the limo driver again. Add the fake eyebrows, the little round sunglasses, and cover the dark curls with a tam-o'-shanter...

Toby returned her look. "Got us a flashbulb here, do I see?"

What he didn't see was Bradone on the bed behind him pull a small gray pistol from under her pillow.

THIRTY-FIVE

"BRADONE, HE GOT US out of Area Fifty-one alive."

Standing on the bed, the astrologer was doing that asinine stance you see on TV, legs spread, knees bent, both arms extended to steady the nasty little thing in her hands.

"Charlie, he's Merlin." Her lips drew back from her teeth.

"And our murderer."

"Don't forget," Toby said, the little gun rising with him as he got to his feet and began to raise his hands in the air, "Merlin is also a magician." And before he'd fully straightened, he leapt with the ease of a gymnast, lifting and spreading his legs so his toes met his outflung hands. Bradone's shot merely creased the cloth of the saggy butt of her shorts, which he was wearing. When he came down, it was on Bradone, forcing her back on the bed, the little gray pistol his in an instant.

There was a frantic banging at the door to the hall. Charlie raced to open it, knowing it could be her government come to arrest her, but Toby looked like he might be considering using Bradone's gun. He yelled for her to stop, but by then the door was open.

Jerome Battista, two uniforms, and Mr. Undisclosed pushed past Charlie into the room and Toby threw Bradone's little pistol to the floor.

You could hear shouts and pounding now all up and down the hall, the strident official voices of police and the confused voices of hotel guests. Loopy Louie's was being raided.

"WE KNOW YOU WERE collecting great sums of cash for Evan Black. We know you helped him with the holdup at the Hilton casino by shutting down the electricity." Mr. Undisclosed drove out of the parking lot behind Loopy Louie's. A sea of light bars on cop cars strobed the night and, above it all, a harem girl and a camel jitterbugged in neon atop the hotel.

Who's we? Who, exactly, are you?

"We know that on at least two occasions you trespassed on high-security areas. That you stole top secret weapons. The charges against you are astronomical, Ms. Greene. And growing by the hour."

Why was she alone with him? Funny how dark it was once you'd left the Strip.

"We know that you were involved in the murder of Joseph Boyles, Arthur Sleem, and Matthew Tooney. What do you say for yourself?"

"Nothing until I see a lawyer."

"In my business, Charlie"—his voiced oozed condescension, made her want to hit somebody. She wished she had the nerve to make it him—"lawyers are not an option."

"If you're not with Metro or the federal government—"

"There are higher sources of power. Believe me."

"You work for God?"

The car braked, whirled into an Amoco station, and stopped just short of a parked eighteen-wheeler. Charlie was tempted to make a break for it, but he switched on the overhead light and grabbed her wrist, squeezing it so tightly, her hand went numb and floppy.

"You are in terrible trouble, lady." His expression was swearing even if his mouth wasn't. His teeth looked even more jumbled when he grimaced. "And you are not alone in it."

He released her and handed her an envelope. In it were four colored photographs. One of Libby Abigail Greene caught stepping out of her heap of a car to slap the obelisk in front of the gate to their condo complex. Even the still had captured the child-woman's fluid beauty. The obelisk was supposed to open the gate only to those with cards but often took extra persuasion. Damned thing seemed always to be on the blink.

Then a photo of Edwina Greene, who said things like "on the blink," which Charlie picked up through osmosis. Her mother was walking past Colombia Cemetery, where Libby'd been conceived. Edwina, her briefcase in hand, wore a stunning pantsuit and either wore a wig or had found a better hairstylist since Charlie last saw her. She was obviously on her way to her office and students at the University of Colorado in Boulder.

Edwina had turned into an angry but stylish late-late bloomer after her mastectomy. She'd never be good-looking, but she'd certainly experienced a transformation.

Then a photo of Larry Mann driving out of the underground parking garage at First Federal United Central Wilshire Bank of the Pacific in Beverly Hills, where Congdon and Morse Representation, Inc., had its offices. They'd caught Larry, gorgeous and fully aware of it, at the required stop onto Wilshire.

They had sent out intimidation photographers to the exact nerve centers of Charlie's life. They certainly did know where she lived. Whoever "they" were.

The fourth picture was of a man Charlie didn't know, but figured it was meant for Bradone's threatening envelope—he was young, dark-haired, well built—lounging in red swim trunks on a redwood deck, with two cats on his lap.

"So, do we deal?" the grizzle-haired man asked, and took the photos from her.

"Doesn't sound like I have anything to deal with. Even if you're with the CIA or the FBI, you have to let me have a lawyer, don't you?"

"Let's start with what you used to turn the lights out at the Hilton."

"It's attached to the bottom of my purse, which is not with me because I left it out at Merlin's Ridge."

"That's another strike against you, lady. You and your friends making a laughingstock of patriots. You don't deserve to inhabit the same planet with those intent on keeping sensitive information and weapons out of the hands of our enemies and keeping our country safe."

Even with the thudding of her pulse in her ears, the car was quiet after the sirens and panic and shouting and screaming at Loopy Louie's. What could have forced the Las Vegas police to go public on a gambling night on the Strip? "Why are you and Battista raiding Loopy's?"

"Battista's looking for that illegal gambling money you

helped Black accumulate. My friends and I were looking for you and your coconspirators. You and Louie Deloese helped Black set up this Merlin business to make security at Groom and the objectives of the base itself a laughingstock. Now I'm going to let you out of this with your life on one condition—you're going to tell the truth to the press."

"I don't know what the truth is."

"You will."

"That's a very interesting ring. Is it real turquoise?" You weren't wearing it when I saw you last, but Battista was wearing his plain wedding band. Arthur Sleem wore one like yours, as did Eddie, the floorman, and, she'd be willing to bet, Joseph Boyles. Whoever murdered Sleem and Boyles took those rings. "Is it a wedding band?"

Charlie received no answer as they whizzed by the open gate to the Lakes subdivision, where Evan Black lived.

CHARLIE SAT between Richard and Mitch on floor cushions, Evan's screening room pitch-dark. Mitch snorted like the red bull on the highway this afternoon. "Where the hell were you? I was worried sick."

"Out at Groom Lake with Bradone."

"Oh great, helping her detect, I suppose. Will you never learn? Oh honey, I'm sorry. I didn't mean to make you cry."

"I'm not crying. And I'm not honey."

"Don't these guys know it's against the law to kidnap people? I don't believe this." Richard and Mitch had teamed up to find Charlie and were in Mitch's room when the raid hit. "They hauled us out here without official or nonofficial explanations. Christ, Charlie, we were in a paddy wagon and the driver says he's neither police nor government, they just cooperate with each other sometimes. He says, 'I'm private, so your butt's mud, man. You don't have any rights.'"

"I think these are the ex-ARP reverse militia nuts Evan told us about."

"Quiet on the set," Mr. Grizzlehead said.

Only a select few of those rounded up at Loopy's had been brought here, led into the room in the dark.

"Ladies and gentlemen—"

Lights came on screen. Charlie and Bradone stood in the orange glare on Merlin's Ridge, hair waving in odd jags, as if electrified instead of windblown. Bradone covered her ears with the heels of her hands, her mouth open in a scream. As usual, there was no sound in Evan's screening room. Mel and Toby must have been behind them on the ridge longer than Charlie realized.

The camera couldn't begin to encompass the thing rising up out of the valley as a backdrop to Charlie and the stargazer or even to suggest its size. All the frames showed was a tiny portion, and that it was moving up.

The camera distorted the reality by making it look as if she and Bradone were actresses working in front of orange stage smoke. Charlie hit the dirt and grabbed her friend's ankles. The astrologer fell forward and both began their slide over the edge.

Mitch snorted again. Charlie had visions of him and his parts trotting down the highway to Rachel.

Before Bradone's rump tilted over the edge, the camera tilted up and the view was of what was inside the orange mist.

Spielberg figures, scrawny and long-limbed, walked in and out of view. One came up close and its benevolent oval-shaped head without hair or ears or nose came into focus. One of the almond-shaped eyes that turned up at the outer corners winked.

To Charlie, the message here was that everything was safe, all explained, under control, no threat the government couldn't handle. This is the version she was to tell if they were to let her leave. She figured she was a spokesperson because of the unwanted and inaccurate publicity about her being Mitch Hilsten's girlfriend.

Worked for Charlie.

She relaxed, began thinking of real life again. Libby and her damn Eric and car and employer. Keegan Monroe and his damn novel in Folsom prison, even Edwina and her hot flashes. And all the stuff coming down at the office. Ulcer thoughts. Oddly comforting.

But then memory images of what she'd really seen in that orange cloud intruded. The shapes barely visible inside the billowing orange gases had been vague rectangles and squares and a few triangles. Charlie's first thought was of an endless rotating array of office cubicles as seen from overhead, with small moving shapes inside each.

But hey, if it meant she could return to her life with all its demands and drawbacks and rights, Charlie could believe in little bald aliens with no eyelids who could wink anyway. Cool by her. Noooo problem.

Well, aren't we Little Miss Spineless? Where's your sense of integrity? Justice?

Got lost in the deep mud.

"Is that what you saw on Merlin's Ridge, Bradone McKinley?"

"No," Bradone's sense of integrity answered clearly off to the right of Charlie's little grouping.

"And you, Charlemagne Catherine Greene?"

"Yes." You betcha.

"Charlie?" Bradone sounded hurt and surprised.

"Was it really, Charlie?" Mitch sounded incredulous. But then, like Bradone, he too was an abductee.

Charlie's world was drowning in flakes. Who needed aliens? Different shots of the base, with the buildings cleverly cropped or clipped or somehow "disappeared" from the frames and the runways looking like geological anomalies, or riverbeds maybe.

But someone whose voice Charlie didn't recognize had the temerity to ask, "You the guys denying access to any new Groom Lake photos on the Internet? Blaming it on the provider?"

A light scuffle and the speaker was silenced. Could it have been Toby?

The next question sounded after frames of a plane aloft, dropping orange flares near the black mailbox (now white under its graffiti) for the Medlin Ranch.

"Is that the other orange thing you saw, Charlie Greene?"

"Absolutely." Charlie was a convert. Her government needed to do this stuff. In private. And it had some serious muscle in this room, official or not.

Next came a big orange balloon, which was not the fascinating thing she saw suspended over the forbidden air base, rising on air and not sitting still.

"I saw that too," she offered before Mr. Undisclosed could even ask. She'd confess to anything orange.

The show went on for maybe another half hour, very boring and inaccurate, but Charlie Greene confessed enthusiastically to the authenticity of every scam deployed. Bradone's sense of integrity had stopped complaining altogether, but Charlie'd heard no more scuffling and hoped her misguided friend had seen the light. Took more than a stock market to keep you afloat in this world.

The medium-sized screen was left lighted from behind, a tall, round dunce's stool placed before it. The screen light went out, and when it came back on, the shadow shape of a stocky man sat there, one leg extended so the foot could reach the floor, the other knee bent, its foot resting on a lower stool rung. Sitting straight, he had his hands placed somewhere in the darkness of his front.

But the slight repetitious movement of one arm identified him. The flexing of the hand—carpal tunnel syndrome? Some urge to strike out? Insane-behavior control?

"Name?"

"Edward G. Hackburger," Eddie, the floorman at the Las Vegas Hilton, answered.

"And your connection to the place shown on the piece of movie just played?" The questioner was not up on film lingo.

"I worked ARP on Nellis for twenty years before becoming head of Hilton security. The two ladies in the stage smoke were guests of the Hilton. And after watching *Starlight Express* two hundred times, I know stage smoke."

"And why are you here?"

"I'm investigating the robbery of our casino last week."

"Did you know Arthur Sleem, Joseph Boyles, and Matthew Tooney?"

"Yes, sir. Sleem and Boyles used to work ARP on Nellis with me. Matt worked for the company insuring the casino at the Hilton."

"Have you ever been employed directly by the United States government?"

"Not since the marines thirty years ago, sir. ARP service is provided by independent security companies."

Mitch was next. Even in shadow, he came over gorgeous, confused, and rumpled. He'd come to Vegas to discuss a film project with Evan Black and to see his friend Charlie Greene.

His friend Charlie Greene gnashed her teeth and her boss squirmed next to her. "Stop that, jeeze."

"Have you ever been to the place pictured on the screen just now?"

"Groom Lake? Just over the Internet, but once I—"

"That was not the question, Mr. Hilsten."

The question was repeated until the answer made no mention of Groom Lake, only "the place."

Made sense if Groom Lake did not exist. One up for Charlie's government and Mr. Undisclosed, who didn't work for it, just cooperated with it when it was advantageous.

Richard came to Vegas for a vacation and didn't give a fuck about "the place." He had an important business to run and had to get back to L.A.

Bradone came to Vegas for a vacation and went out to "the place" to look at the stars. She was a student of astrology.

"Did you have anything at all to do with the robbery of the Hilton casino?"

"I didn't know about it until the next day."

"You had other things on your mind that night," the questioner led. He might as well have said, "Ve haff veys…"

"I have other things on my mind every night." All in black, legs crossed, one heel hooked over the middle rung, voice dripping controlled rage, Bradone McKinley made the most impressive backlighted shadow yet.

Caryl Thompson was next. No amount of screwy lighting could hide her identity. The shape, the breath within the diction, the tragic yet lovely droop to the shoulders…

Give it a rest, Charlie. She'll get old too.

But the questioner's voice softened some. "Were you ever at the place shown on this film?"

"No," the well-stacked pilot answered.

Caryl Thompson wasn't asked about her brother's death or her flights over restricted areas for Evan Black. When asked what she did for a living, she said she worked as a beverage server at the Barbary Coast. Which was true, according to Evan, her day job was what paid the rent. Where *was* Evan Black?

Conspiracy may be maniacal, but truth could be slippery too.

By the time the lights went out on Caryl, Charlie was all too aware that neither Richard nor Mitch had returned to her side.

And figures too dark to see lifted Charlie by the arms, propelling her to the front of the room.

THIRTY-SIX

CHARLIE HAD COME to Las Vegas on vacation, to play blackjack and to meet with clients Georgette Millrose and Evan Black. She had gone out to the place to see the stars with Bradone McKinley, whom she had met playing blackjack.

"And what did you see there?" Mr. Undisclosed was invisible from here too, but she directed her answers to a pinpoint of light at the back of the room.

"Lots of stars and orange stage smoke?"

"And the night of the robbery at the Las Vegas Hilton, where were you?"

Charlie'd so hoped he wouldn't ask this one. Actually, there were a number of things she hoped he wouldn't ask. And why hadn't he asked the well-stacked pilot/beverage server, Caryl Thompson, that question in the same way?

"I was returning from a burning airplane, in a van driven by—"

"Back to where?"

Shouldn't the question have been *from* where? "To the Hilton, I—"

"And what happened when you left this van?"

Charlie described the lights going out behind her and then the elevator stopping on the way to her room and then the lights in her room going out when she was in the shower. Funny how total intimidation can make you so eager to please.

The lights went out in this room and she was lifted back to her floor cushion. Still no sign of Richard and Mitch.

Toby Johnson took the stool next and now Detective Battista asked the questions. Even in shadow, Toby's jauntiness was gone. He leaned to one side, swaying slightly, spoke through a swollen mouth. His injuries had been added to.

He lived in Vegas and worked for producer Evan Black.

"Who else do you work for, Toby?"

"Sometimes I drive a limo for my uncle Elmo."

"Who else, Toby?"

"Sometimes I do magic."

"Who do you do magic for, Toby?"

Long pause here. An arm came out of the dark to prop him up on one side, another from the other to keep him from falling off the stool on that side, neither very gently. "I want a lawyer."

"Who do you do magic for, Toby?"

"My uncle Merlin."

"He *is* Merlin." Bradone's voice cut from behind Charlie. Charlie listened for a scuffle again or, worse yet, a scream. She couldn't detect anything.

"What do you do for your uncle Louie, Toby?"

Toby Johnson didn't answer, even with more jostling.

"When Metro's Officer Timothy Graden tried to visit Evan Black to investigate the death of Black's personal pilot, you intercepted him with your uncle Elmo's limousine. And dumped the body on Highway One sixty, where your uncle Elmo's limo regularly delivers johns to the establishments out that way."

"Art Sleem stole the limo to kill Graden and cover his taking out Pat. He wanted me to get the blame."

"So you took out Sleem and Boyles."

"I want a lawyer" was all Toby would say.

"You're not in court. Elmo Johnson's limo service is licensed under the name of Tobias Johnson."

"I lent him the money is all."

"On a gofer's salary? And you don't have an uncle Merlin. You are Merlin, like the lady said. And every lease and rental place for hundreds of miles is out of white Cherokees."

"We got you on fraud and murder, got you locked tight. Want to deal and squeal? We want the guys you took your orders from, pimp." This was Mr. Undisclosed again, who cooperated with the government. Maybe he was a temp.

Charlie figured Toby got some of his orders from his "uncle" Evan. And did that same limo run over Patrick Thompson? Was Toby driving then? Sleem wasn't. But Vegas was full of limos. Toby had access to Evan's house, could have killed Art Sleem and Boyles. Because they tried to pin Officer Graden's murder on him. Or because Evan told him to. Or his uncle Louie did.

Before Toby could say whether or not he wanted to deal, Mel Goodall replaced him. Charlie couldn't tell if Mel had been roughed up or not.

Somewhere at the back of her exhaustion—this looked to be her second full night without sleep—Charlie wondered what Evan Black's role could be in this staged performance. It seemed too pedestrian for him. Maybe with Mel up there, she'd find out.

Mel lived in Vegas in this house and worked for Evan Black. He'd been to "the place" quite a few times. He had shot that footage from Merlin's Ridge even though he knew it was against Section 18 of U.S. CODE 795/797 and Executive Order 10104, which made it illegal to photograph the installation. And he'd done so for producer Evan Black.

Matthew Tooney had come to the house looking for proof that Evan was behind the Hilton casino heist after he'd seen the money that Charlie tried to give him. He figured Art Sleem was paying off Evan Black for the heist through his agent.

"It was paying off a wager, wasn't it? A wager that Evan Black could not pull off the casino robbery, and there were even odds on which casino the attempt would be made on."

"Yeah."

"What happened to the casino money?"

"Left it in black garbage bags at the back of the hotel."

Was all this being displayed for someone other than Charlie? Were there others who were supposed to tell the "truth" to the press?

Mel and Toby came home after the weird funeral service for Patrick Thompson while Caryl, Evan, and Patrick's parents distributed his ashes over Nellis, to find Tooney dead on the floor of the great room and Sleem and Boyles ransacking the house.

"And what were *they* looking for?"

"The real money."

"The money coming in from high rollers all over town who bet that Black couldn't pull off the heist. The money that would have paid for his next project."

"Yeah."

"So who shot Sleem and Boyles?" Charlie spoke up and then slapped a hand over her mouth. Dumb, that was dumb, Charlie.

"I don't know."

"I think you do, Mr. Goodall. And I think you know who paid them to find that money too. It wasn't Toby Johnson, was it? Where is Evan Black?"

"You don't know?" Genuine surprise on Mel's part.

"He's taken the 'real' money and left you holding the bag, hasn't he?"

"Evan wouldn't do that." Uncertainty, just a hint, but it was there, somewhere in the inflection.

"Where is he, Mel?"

"I don't believe he's gone. You're lying." Mel was apparently not as intimidated as Charlie.

"And he shot Sleem and Boyles, didn't he?"

"He never killed anybody in his life." Disdain now, and the hint of triumph this time. Mel knew his questioners didn't have all the right answers. He'd probably watched Toby kill Sleem and Boyles.

But instead of pressing the point to get at the real truth, they turned out the lights and Louie Deloese sat next on the stool.

Charlie decided that they already knew the truth, or that they didn't want to know the truth, or that they wanted to conceal the truth.

Loopy Louie wanted a lawyer too and he was about as loopy as a brain surgeon. His little body exuded fury. He would say nothing.

"Your nephew has confessed, Louie. Give it up."

"THEY'RE NOT CONVINCED," Battista said, standing directly behind Charlie. "I'm not sure I am either."

"Then let's convince them," the mysterious Mr. Undisclosed said. "And convince you too."

THIRTY-SEVEN

"BOY, DO THEY do their homework, or what?" Charlie had described the photos old Grizzlehead showed her. She and Bradone were now locked in a closet. "Was that dark-haired guy in a bathing suit—the one with the pecs—your houseboy?"

"Charlie, how could you lie like that about what happened at Merlin's Ridge?" Now Bradone was the one doing the whining. "About the orange spaceship?"

"I was hoping to get out of here with my skin. Don't you see? Those stills were meant to warn us that people close to us would be in danger if we don't cooperate and believe what they want us to. I'm supposed to reveal to the press what they want me to."

Funny, they hadn't shown a picture of Mitch, whom the press kept insisting was her boyfriend. Was that because he was here? Or because they knew her innermost thoughts? If Charlie lived, she'd never cheat on her taxes again.

"What do you think they're going to do with us?" Did they have everybody secluded off in closets? How many closets could this place have? "Maybe they're going to set the house afire and burn all evidence of what went on here. Mainly us."

"Just what was it that went on here?"

"Some fairly high-level secrets were either revealed or concealed here tonight." Grizzlehead might be private security with a tacit license to get done what needs to be done, but Battista was an officer of the law in this city. Charlie couldn't believe he'd stick his neck out that far.

They bumped into and away from each other, trying to slip past the shelves of thick towels at their backs, feeling over the doors in front of them.

"Now you sound like Evan Black. This is bigger than a conspiracy, Charlie."

"Where is Evan?" What's bigger than a conspiracy—other than World War Three or *E coli* from Mars?

"Off to Brazil or somewhere he can't be extradited. And carrying off with him the cash prize of a lifetime."

"I don't pretend to understand Evan Black, Bradone, but I can't imagine him leaving his work. I can see him blowing up the World Trade Center to get footage, but not cutting himself off from the industry. His identity is his work. Money just rewards it, shows him he's good."

"This is a linen closet," Bradone said suddenly.

"I know."

"Who has locks on a linen closet?"

"Oh." Charlie, instead of feeling for hinges or bolts she could pull out, pushed at the center of the doors instead, and it moved outward like those she had at home in Long Beach would if she'd ever thought to shut herself in her own closet.

"We are not dealing with great minds here." Bradone grunted, pushing her side open too. There was a little light out in the hall. Enough to see that the doors had not moved far. Something was stacked up in front of them.

Bodies. Still warm.

Charlie ran her hands over the wall, searching for a light switch. "Though I don't think they are either—working with great minds, I mean." She and Bradone hadn't even tried the doors, they'd been so intimidated. And exhausted. Charlie's ears rang with it.

"It's Richard…and Mitch. They're breathing but zonked. What are you doing?"

"Looking for a light switch."

"Charlie, there's all this starlight."

Charlie'd had it with Bradone and her stars. But when she reached the wall switches, they didn't work. The juice had been cut off to the house. She whirled to explain to the stargazer exactly where she could stick her stars, to see they were on the top balcony and the ghostly light of night shone on the lake outside through the window wall on the back of the house.

"You smelling what I'm smelling?" Bradone asked.

It was faint. But it was there. Smoke. "That's not cigarettes."

They tried to revive the men, with no success. So they dragged them down the stairs to the next-level balcony, which had egress to the outside by way of the front door on the street side. The deadweights nearly knocked them over backward.

When they reached the second balcony, Charlie dropped Mitch's armpits and raced back up.

"What are you doing, you total idiot?"

"Looking for others left lying about—Evan, for one."

"But he's run off with the bet money, I tell you."

With so little light, Charlie had to feel for doorways and closets and then determine by feel which were clothes and which had people in them. And try to remember the layout on this floor. Shoes with feet helped out a lot. Head hair was good. She didn't have time to discern dead from alive or identity or friend or foe. Which by now was a blur of the first order anyway.

Shit. Not only had she lost her mind, she'd lost her eyeglasses. She was so used to wearing contacts, had been kept in the dark so much, *now* she noticed.

But she'd found six bodies alive or dead and had dragged them to the top of the stairs before the density of the smoke panicked her. She screamed down for Bradone to come and help.

There was no answer.

THIRTY-EIGHT

WHEN SHE GOT the first body down to the second balcony, Charlie knew why Bradone hadn't answered her call for help. The smoke was so thick, nobody could breathe.

Literally without thinking, she raced back upstairs, found the master bath by feel and panic, grabbed a towel from the rim of the Jacuzzi tub, soaked it in the stool, and wrapped it around her head. She felt her way out into the top hall, tripped over one of the bodies she'd left, and tumbled down with it to the really bad air on the floor below.

Charlie bounded back up for another, and this time just shoved it downstairs, knowing she had so little time herself. And then three more, hoping they'd land on one another for cushioning. Then the last, and she tumbled down after it, hoping she hadn't lost count or left somebody still up there.

She crawled over all the bodies on the second balcony to slide down to the first floor. The smoke was much less here and she opted for trying to push everybody down here and then pull them out onto the pool deck, because the way to the front door appeared to be what was on fire.

She envisioned countless dead and broken necks as she shoved every body she could find on the second balcony down the stairs to the great room.

And then she dragged them one at a time outside to air, telling them to breathe, please, grabbing a breath herself and holding it before racing in for the next body.

Some body was stirring on one of her trips out. She'd become an automaton by now, hero or dupe. The last time in, she couldn't find another body but thought she could see flame.

No contacts, no glasses, no sleep, no mind—who knew what she saw? But she struggled back outside, and one of the bodies sat up.

"Charlie?"

Charlie would have sighed if she'd had breath. She'd saved Mitch Hilsten again and gotten caught in the act.

But he could see, so she convinced him to help her drag all the bodies on the patio to the boat.

He seemed to be coming to. She seemed to be going out. Next thing she knew, she was gone.

CHARLIE WOKE HERSELF, coughing up the smoke in her burning lungs.

"You think you guys could keep it down?" Evan said from above her, and she realized she wasn't the only one coughing. He turned from the wheel of the small cabin cruiser to look at her and the mass of huddled bodies at his feet. "Thanks, Charlie. Already owed you one, remember? I was meant to go up in flames with my house. So now I owe you two."

Since one of the tinted lenses was gone from his eyewear and since Charlie was in her groggy state, plus had no eyewear at all, Evan Black appeared to wear two expressions at once—the tinted side obscure and blank, the naked one animated with mischief. No one else seemed to notice the ambiguity here.

"God, I hate heroes."

Mitch put a flask in her hand. "It's just water."

Even with her foggy vision, Charlie could see the others, sort of, because of the light. A little of it was dawn. A lot of it was flames in the sky.

"Oh, Evan, your beautiful house."

"That's okay—we got the can." Mel grinned at his boss. "Drink some of that, will ya? Then hand it to me."

Mitch, Evan, Bradone, Caryl, Mel—Charlie counted. "Not everybody made it, huh? I broke somebody's neck shoving you all downstairs, didn't I? I didn't know what else to do."

"Oh God, there she goes with the guilt again." Bradone grabbed the flask from Mel.

"Where's Toby, and Louie Deloese? Was there someone else?" Charlie had no idea how many people were in that house sending orange-red flares up into a dawning sky.

"Last I saw of Loopy Louie, he was dragging Toby 'Merlin' Johnson out around the wall to the next yard," Mitch told her.

"I was so busy dragging people to the boat, I didn't have time to go after him. But they were on the pile of us you left out on Evan's pool deck."

"Don't worry, my men will get them." Detective Jerome Battista rolled over to face her.

"You? I thought *you* were with *them*," Charlie said.

"Them. You. You sure you know the difference?"

Actually, she wasn't. She'd sort of hoped he knew.

All that questioning and public confession in the screening room was meant to show the whole story. There should be no need for inquiring minds, like Charlie's and Bradone's, for instance, to continue inquiring. If that didn't do it, the still pictures of loved ones should have made the point. And Battista had been in on it up to that point.

Everyone had been left with a terrible thirst and, except for Charlie and Bradone, with varying degrees of lost time.

"Could it have been that wand you used on the casino patrons at the Hilton?" Charlie asked Evan.

"It's possible they found it, turned the power up to black people out that long. What do you say, Detective, were we zapped with a fancy handheld laser developed at Area Fifty-one or stolen from aliens who landed out there in a giant orange?" The writer/producer turned his dual expressions on Jerome Battista.

Battista returned the look as calmly as he could with eyes still watering from smoke and coughing. "You all saw the film—there is no air base at Groom Lake, or Area Fifty-one, and that orange mist was stage smoke—thus there's no fancy laser either."

"They left me and Bradone conscious in a closet that didn't lock, with Richard and Mitch outside in the hall, in need of rescuing, tucked the rest of you and Louie Deloese and Toby away unconscious in closets to burn to death. Bradone and I would be so busy dragging Mitch and Richard to safety, we wouldn't have time to look for you."

"Give ya twenty to one ol' Loopy and his nephew land on their feet, somewhere out of the country," Evan said.

"You're on," Battista snapped back. "We got witnesses."

Charlie would never understand men. "What happened to old Grizzlehead, your undisclosed flabby sidekick? What about Eddie Hackburger? I mean, why did I get the feeling that the three of you were running that show? And Bradone and I had been given all this unsolicited information so we could be witness to the facts as they wanted them presented. What made them think we'd be chucking up all that misinformation to the press right now in Evan's backyard while the rest of you were burning with the house? I don't get the logic."

Evan and Battista took turns explaining that the retired ARPs expected to be believed no matter what, because their say-so should be enough.

"They are strangely out of the loop and can't handle people flaunting strict orders, questioning authority that has permission to use deadly force. Hey, they watch *Good Cops, Bad Guys* instead of *The X-Files*." Jerome Battista added, "This is off the record you, understand. I'll deny any of it."

"Even with all these witnesses?"

"Yes, ma'am."

"All of which makes them wonderful tools for private and public security forces at all levels." Evan cut the engine and they drifted into a dock somewhere across the small lake from the burning house. The sirens and the helicopters did not sound that far away. "Even for police departments, casinos, and other corporations. And your government."

"They have an intimidating air of authority and can get things done faster than public institutions, which get so much press coverage." Detective Jerome Battista grimaced but met the eyes of a hushed and somber group of survivors. "The system could not function without them. There are so many limitations imposed on law enforcement."

Charlie couldn't see well enough to be sure that all the expressions on the boat mirrored the haunted one she knew she wore. But she couldn't see why they wouldn't.

"They do tend to meet untimely ends, if that's any consolation," he tried to reassure them.

"But they turned on you too."

"We've worked with these same freelancers before, to our

advantage. Problem is, you never can be sure who else they are working for at the same time. In this case, they had their own agenda, and I should have seen it coming. They are highly patriotic and totally lacking in humor. Evan's project and everything about it would be a slap in the face to that crowd. I was not let in on the very last play in this particular game.'' Battista sat up straighter and clutched his ribs. ''Which reminds me, Mr. Black—about the money from that illegal wager I've been hearing so much about—''

''All burned up,'' Evan said sadly, and he and Mel began handing Richard and Bradone onto the dock. ''Charlie saved you but not the loot.''

''It's still illegal—the wager itself.''

Mitch reached down to help the homicide detective out of the boat next. And then reached for Charlie's hand, but all movement between dock and deck stopped when what was left of Evan's house exploded. Sudden bolts of lightning flashed from a cloudless sky.

''Jesus, what could have done that?'' Richard grabbed Bradone as if to save her. She pushed him away.

''Must have been the water heater, huh, Battista?'' Evan watched the smoke roil and billow—turn orangy like a volcano or— ''Couldn't have been anything from an air base that doesn't exist, huh?''

''Talk about your conspiracy theory,'' Charlie told Evan as she left the boat. ''You can't claim it was just our paranoia that created this whole last week.''

''In a way, it was, Charlie. Somebody's paranoia.''

THIRTY-NINE

"CHARLIE, ALL I can say is how sorry I am for doubting you."
Bradone stood on the curb with the luggage she'd reclaimed
from the lobby of an empty Loopy Louie's. Hotel guests had
either taken planes out or relocated to other hotels after the raid.
"I forgot in all the mayhem that you were a sensitive."

"Sensitive about what?"

"About lying in front of those people, about the orange spaceship and what we really saw on Merlin's Ridge. I should have
known you knew the truth all along. And you saved all our
lives."

"I didn't know any truth."

"But I wanted to simply get Richard and Mitch and us out
of the house to safety when we smelled smoke, like the elderly
ex-ARPs wanted us to. You ran back upstairs, looking for the
others. You must have known something I didn't."

"No, I just figured that's what I'd do if I wanted to get rid
of some of the people left unconscious in the house and use
others who had been convinced to cooperate, by threatening their
loved ones, to explain what happened afterward. That's why the
silly confession staging to explain all the dead bodies ruining
my vacation and why and how nothing of importance really
happened out at Area Fifty-one. I was surprised they wanted to
get rid of Detective Battista though." And Evan Black had to
know more than he admitted. What really happened to the real
money?

"And burning down the house might also get rid of the true
film shot by Mel on Merlin's Ridge."

"And any other secret goodies spirited out of Groom Lake
by Patrick Thompson." Like lightning out of a cloudless sky.
"Can't find what you want—burn the place down so nobody
else can find it either."

"Mel's film in its real state might prove my abduction, and maybe yours too."

"Nobody was abducted, Bradone. I'm a sensitive and I know these things." Jeesh.

But they hugged good-bye as the stargazer's limo drew up to take her to the airport. It stopped right where the hunk pilot Patrick Thompson died. Charlie wanted to go home too. Richard was finding them tickets.

Back in the lobby, some guests still sorted through piled luggage. Others looked for someone to complain to because they couldn't find theirs. The news sources reported the raid as a massive drug bust and excused the closing and search of the casino on evidence that Louie Deloese was a drug lord.

Charlie figured it was Evan's bet money the authorities were looking for here too, especially if he'd taken Louie up on his offer to provide a conduit to get it out of the country. It would have been embarrassing to reveal Evan Black's successful stunt of the decade. Charlie wondered if Loopy Louie'd been had by the authorities, both official and non. If Evan was about to make his first-ever big-budget picture. Louie might appear small and inconsequential, but Charlie wouldn't want him for an enemy.

Was the undisclosed motive behind everything ultimately to ensure Groom Lake remained undisclosed?

"Well, guess this is it till next year, huh?" Mitch Hilsten, superstar, said behind her.

"Next year?" Charlie turned with resignation. I should be so lucky.

Fans still blew the gauzy veils around on the ceiling. The one above Mitch hid and then revealed a nasty-looking scimitar with regular and sad monotony. Loopy Louie's had been gloriously, unabashedly silly in a seriously silly town.

"My astrologer says your cycles are winding down as you get older and—"

"As *I* get older? You're the one who has to eat raw oysters and insure all your parts. Not to mention that you have well over ten years on me."

He put a finger to her lips and drew her close as cameras

buzzed and clicked and whirred around them and mikes on
booms lowered overhead.

"Yeah, but I'm a famous superstar." He had to whisper in
her ear so she could hear over the rude chorus of rude questions.

"Jesus, wait till Libby sees this."

"I think it's about time Libby gets a life." And then the jerk
kissed her for the benefit of the rude intruders. "Charlie, would
you consider becoming my—"

"No."

"Agent?"

"No."

"Why not? I get more work and publicity through you than
I do Lazarus."

"Tell me you and Evan aren't going through with the conspiracy project. Mel Gibson and *60 Minutes* and Oprah and everybody already has. It's going to take more than free money."
They stood close, spoke low. Charlie hoped all the noise the
reporters were making would cover their conversation.

Evan Black had waited until the rest were on the dock before
he took off with Mel and Caryl and presumably "the can,"
leaving Battista shouting threats after the disappearing boat. The
detective had been duped by the freelance ex-ARPs and now by
a real professional—a Hollywood producer.

"You bring charges against my client," Richard Morse
warned, "you're going to open up a can of crocodiles. There
are too many witnesses to Groom Lake and to your interrogation
methods."

Mitch said now, "I wouldn't miss this one for anything. Not
only do I get to work for the young genius but we got stuff in
the can, Charlie, that will make Spielberg jealous. Trust me."
And he was gone, half the cameras following and, damn him,
the other half attacking Charlie.

She took a lesson from Loopy Louie and said nothing. Just
lowered her head and pushed through the swirl around her, having not a clue where to go. She looked up once and thought she
saw a familiar face behind one of the booms. When one of the
eyes on that face winked, she recognized Toby "Merlin" Johnson, the dark curls disguised by a eunuch wig, the face still

bruised, but both eyes open. She would have liked to thank him for saving her at Merlin's Ridge but didn't dare expose him. She'd saved his life too now, she supposed.

She walked on with her half of the pushy, increasingly insulting entourage, most demanding to know where she and Mitch had been hiding and if they'd secretly wed, until an arm pulled her through a concealed door into a Loopy Louie's security area, all its monitor screens black now. Mr. Undisclosed, with the close-cropped hair and crooked teeth, held out her purse. The freelance ex-ARP who evidently did not die in the fire that destroyed the house and its secrets.

He was so quiet after the paparazzi, she could barely hear him. "Since you've been cooperative, I'm going to make you a deal."

Just your small black unassuming strap bag with too many pockets.

"Your driver's license, Social Security card, business cards, keys to your home and car and office, your cash, credit and ATM cards. Your identity really." He jerked it away when she reached for it and pulled an envelope from his shirt pocket. "I will return all to you for your promise and your signature on that promise."

It was an official-looking letter, nicely typed, but with the ubiquitous errors made so convenient by computers. It had an embossed seal—*THE GOVERNMENT OF THEY UNITED STATES*—and an eagle as letterhead, and various important and official-sounding departments listed across the bottom.

"Nice paper," Charlie said.

I, Charlie Greene, do hear here by swear upon my oak that I won't not reveal, promote, write about, or represent anyone who does.

The letter went on to describe what she would not reveal in lengthy terms that avoided mention of Groom Lake or Area 51. It did mention Nellis Air Force Base, which was sort of a pseudonym for southern Nevada. The thing was three paragraphs long, the last two all one sentence, phrases linked with semicolons and colons, but nary another verb until the last phrase, *So help me God.*

"Not even a mystery?" she asked in all innocence.

"Not even a mystery."

Charlie took the proffered ballpoint and signed the damn thing up against the wall. He reached for it. She reached for her purse. Neither blinked.

When they finally exchanged merchandise, he said, "You count to five hundred real slow and then follow me out that door at the end of the hall. Now you be a good little girl, Charlie Greene, and remember you signed a promise with Uncle Sam and he's watching you."

Charlie counted to fifty real fast and opened the door at the end of the hall. It led onto an alley. The man who thought she was dumb enough to keep her promise lay sprawled in the middle of it, a wicked-looking scimitar stuck in his back.

FORTY

CHARLIE SPRAWLED in the comfort of first-class leather. Richard decided they'd earned some luxury after their vacation.

She took the blood-smeared envelope from her purse. The letter inside had an eagle and *GOVERNMENT OF THEY UNITED STATES* on its letterhead and was signed "Charles Greenwood." Toby had appeared from behind a Dumpster and handed it to her without a word.

But he'd held up his left hand, the back of it facing her. His ring finger sported three identical turquoise rings. Mr. Undisclosed was not wearing his.

Detective Battista had been right. Ex-ARPs tend to meet untimely ends. Thanks to Toby, his uncle Louie got revenge on one of his enemies anyway.

The extra stud had been removed from the bottom of her purse, leaving a gash in the leather.

Charlie reached into a zippered pocket stuffed with flattened hundred-dollar bills and checks. She tried to total her loot without taking them out.

"Jesus," Richard said beside her.

"And this was my worst trip ever to Vegas. Doesn't make sense." What really amazed Charlie was finding so much of the cash still there after the purse had been handled by all the nefarious "they." Maybe all of it. She'd lost count of her winnings among the dead bodies.

A portion of it would be donated to a fund set up by Barry and Terry's TV station for Officer Timothy Graden's children and his widow, Emily.

Richard's knee bobbed rhythmically. One hand held his scotch and water, the other drummed on the armrest between them in time to his knee. The night without sleep had taken its toll on his face in a series of lumps.

"She never loved me, Charlie. She was using me." Richard,

not above using his position to entice young women to his bed, was hurting now. Charlie'd never known the agency to represent any of the hopefuls. He discarded them when he was through. "Not like you and Mitch."

"Bradone enjoyed you. That's a compliment."

"It's not right. Woman shouldn't lead a guy on like that."

"Hey, she wasn't after your money or trying to get the agency to represent her. She simply had a fling, like you've been doing for years." Richard's flings with the young discards was the reason Ann, his third wife and the only one Charlie had met, left him. But Charlie knew her boss to be unable to conceive that turnaround could be fair play when it came to women. "Mitch and I just had a fling too. Believe me, it was our last."

"Christ, the man's got everything a babe could want. What's the matter with women these days? Can't commit to anything. Thought what you might do when you get old?"

"Oh, I'll have hot flashes, watch my money compound and drip, live on a tropical island where nobody drops dead when I play blackjack, string a hammock between two palms near the beach, smear myself sticky with wild sweet potatoes, read only books I want to, maybe write one about what it was like to be a glamorous Hollywood agent at the millennium."

Richard Morse watched her with an almost fond expression. "You're full of shit, you know that, Charlie. But you're a good kid." He patted her hand. "And thanks for saving my life."

"Richard, won't the government go after Evan Black Productions if he tries to use illegal film from Area Fifty-one? Even shut down the project? Get an injunction, whatever?"

"They'll have to get in line. He's got pending lawsuits up the gills now. Won't be shooting it in the States. By the time the bureaucracy gets to it, thing could be in the theaters, and if the government tries to stop it then, they'll make it an even greater hit. They'll play right into his hands. He can shout conspiracy, First Amendment, censorship. That guy gets away with murder, don't he?"

Charlie wondered if he did. "Does Evan have any connections to organized crime?"

"Everybody does. It's big business now. International. We all brush up against it. Trick is to ignore it. Pretend you don't know. Safer that way."

In a way she didn't really want to inspect, Charlie knew what he meant. She'd wondered about Richard more than once too, but it's not that easy to question a paycheck.

"Richard, is Louis Deloese really Toby's uncle? Evan and Mel teased him so about all his uncles and Toby claimed he didn't know it was the Hilton that would be hit that night."

"*Family* has different meanings for different people. Toby Johnson was obviously for hire—Evan would know he had a relationship to Loopy's, and wouldn't want Louie to know which casino to bet on."

"For hire—you mean Evan could have hired Toby to kill Patrick Thompson and Officer Graden with his limo?"

"Charlie, what did I tell ya? Lay off Black. Somebody connected to Groom Lake, the Janet Terminal, and all that hired Sleem and Boyles to take out the pilot who was bringing secret stuff out of the base. They use one of uncle Elmo's limos to run him and the bicycle cop down so it'll be blamed on Toby."

"Who has connections with both Evan and Loopy Louie."

"So Toby takes them out when him and Mel catch them ransacking Evan's house. And look, Charlie, when Evan's project is on the screen, he's going to get even with the real murderers—the guys that hired Sleem and Boyles. You got to deal with what's out there—not what you wish was there. Okay? Is it clear now?"

No, it wasn't clear and it wasn't okay. But after two nights and three days without sleep, Charlie was fading fast. "Wake me up when we get there."

CHARLIE AND HER ulcer slept and ate and lounged at home for the rest of the week, trying to recover from their vacation. They had lots of help from the little condo community.

Betty Beesom showed up with her famous creamy chicken noodle supreme, which owed much of its flavor to Campbell's condensed soup and the baked-to-crunchy buttered crumb topping. Probably four thousand calories a bite, but soothing.

"Cut up hard-boiled eggs in it, knowing how you like eggs." Food from Betty came with Betty-to-dine, which once annoyed Charlie. But she'd come to depend on it in times of stress.

Mrs. Beesom's hair grew whiter, her paper-thin skin more mottled, her busy steps a tad slower. But her curiosity and her prominent tummy hadn't shrunk. They sat at the table in the breakfast nook, which was part of the kitchen but enclosed by high-backed booth seats that ended in a sunny window. It was Charlie's favorite part of the house.

Betty began with the news Charlie'd missed encountering dead bodies and not playing blackjack. Jeremy's latest live-in had moved out, and good riddance. Couldn't have been much older than Libby, sat around on Jeremy's patio picking her nose and reading filthy magazines. Maggie Stutzman came home two nights in a row real late during the workweek, and single-women lawyers ought to know better. "Just hope it's not some Mr. Candy Bar."

That nice Esterhazie boy appeared to be hanging around again. Betty, who had been not too fond of Doug Esterhazie several years ago, hoped his reappearance meant Libby would shuck that Eric, who drove such a noisy car.

And Tuxedo, when not busy peeing on Charlie's shoes, had apparently been busy fighting with Hairy, who lived across the alley from Betty. "Enough to wake the dead."

That last word, of course, leading back to Charlie's vacation. So she gave her neighbor a shortened version of her trip to Las Vegas and pushed her plate away, her stomach swollen with PMS and creamed chicken noodle supreme with boiled eggs.

"That was just wonderful, Mrs. Beesom."

"Well, I should think you needed every bite. Sounds like you spent most of your vacation throwing up." Betty motioned for Charlie to stay seated and rinsed their plates, put the glass lid on the casserole, and put it in Charlie's refrigerator.

Her hand on the doorknob, Betty Beesom paused to blink tired, watery eyes. "Seems to me, next time you take a vacation? You might consider just staying home. We won't tell anybody."

JEREMY FIEDLER, who lived behind Maggie, dropped by when he saw Charlie on her sunken patio with yesterday's *Hollywood Reporter*.

He had receding reddish brown hair, a Ferrari, and a Trailblazer. Charlie figured he was a trust-funder. His job description changed often, but he never worked regular hours. Right now, he fancied himself a landscape architect but spent more time working out at his health club than architecting.

Tuxedo appeared from nowhere to jump on his lap when he sat in a chair facing her. "I understand from Mrs. Snoopy, you ran into some trouble in Vegas."

Charlie was halfway through describing her murder-filled vacation once again when the cordless bleeped next to her.

"Evan, tell me you're not in jail."

Evan was in Spain. So was Mitch Hilsten.

"How can you film *Conspiracy* in Spain? And you can't call it that. Too soon after the Mel Gibson one."

"You can film anything in Spain. It'll mix great with what we've got in the can. And we're going to call it *Paranoia Will Destroy Ya.*"

"That's the Kinks. You can't—"

"Recognized it right away, didn't you? We're talking immediate name recognition. It'll get out the baby-boomer gray heads even."

"Your critics will call it 'exploitive.'"

"My fans will call it 'derivative.' And the kids will love it. We're going to blow up Vegas. Well, the Strip—one casino at a time, and maybe Fremont, and for sure McCarran. We're talking *Independence Day* meets *The Godfather* here, Charlie. Louie has these fantastic craftsmen making sets and miniatures. Vacated two of his horse barns for it. And Toby's going to finally get to strut his stuff." The second unit got to do all the dangerous explosive stuff.

Somehow this didn't sound like the "quiet, creep up on you and you'll never forget it" film Evan pitched to Mitch on the boat moored on Lake Mead.

Louie Deloese was putting up the production crew and cast on his estate there. He had a certain grudge against Las Vegas and the U.S. Government for some reason. Toby, Mel, and Caryl sent their hellos. Did she want to talk to Mitch now?

"No, but remember those two favors you owe me, Evan? I don't want any harm to come to Mitch over there, okay?"

After a prolonged pause, he said, "You got my word, Charlie." He knew what she suspected, and here was old trusting Hilsten filming at a Spanish villa with a gang of thieves and murderers. "What's the second one?"

"There's been a fund set up for Officer Timothy Graden's family that could use a healthy donation."

"God, you're not only beautiful and have a great imagination, you've even got a heart."

"More like a conscience—"

"Don't worry, I already thought of it, and so did Louie. We wired healthy chunks—through laundered donors, of course. So you still get another one."

"I'd like to know who killed Ardith Miller, the waitress at the Hilton."

"I'll see the word gets out on the street—but that's a long shot, Charlie. Probably just some addict at the bus stop saw her stuffing money from the heist into her purse. But I'll be in touch."

Charlie came back to Jeremy and Tuxedo, squinting at her with doubt.

"So there were eight bodies? The pilot, the cop, Hanley from Wisconsin, the two enforcers—Boyles and Sleem—and the insurance investigator—Tooney—and then the waitress and the grizzle-haired guy who got a scimitar in his back."

"Actually, there were nine. They found the body of Eddie Hackburger, the Hilton security chief, in the ashes of Evan's home." Charlie had received an envelope with the tiny newspaper clipping from Detective Jerome Battista.

"So, who set the fire?"

"Probably Eddie Hackburger—didn't get out in time. But he was part of a patriotic vigilante group with Mr. Undisclosed and his boys."

"And Ben Hanley?"

"Much as I hate to admit it, probably too many cheese balls."

"And the waitress at the Hilton?"

"Somebody saw her with a wad of hundred-dollar bills stolen from the black plastic bags. They could have grabbed the money. Why'd they have to kill her?"

"Didn't want to be identified. And you saved all those unconscious people from a burning house." Jeremy looked impressed. Tuxedo didn't. The sleek black creature sat up to wash his white chest fur. "But here's Toby Johnson, responsible for at least three of the bodies, perhaps countless others, alive and well in Spain. Modern-day justice for you."

"No more responsible than the official agencies that hire ex-armed response personnel to take care of problems they deem dangerous or embarrassing to national security. And Toby was the last person you'd ever think a hit man. Young, wiry, carefree, not totally selfish."

"So what was that humongous orange thing between Merlin's Ridge and Groom Lake? Another secret government invention?"

"I sure hope so." If anybody in the universe has that kind of power, Charlie wouldn't want it to be somebody else's government.

FORTY-ONE

THURSDAY, Charlie got through to Keegan Monroe in Folsom. He'd thrown out his novel and started over. Charlie wasn't surprised. It was a habit of his. But she did remind him that his was not a life sentence and when he got out, if he didn't start back on screenplays, his career was in the toilet. If he couldn't finish a novel with all that time on his hands, he never would.

Thursday was also the day Richard called. He was home too and not a happy boss. "So, Charlie, tell me again what happened between you and Millrose?"

"She fired me and signed on with Jethro Larue. You know that. You said not to sweat it, that she wasn't worth it."

"You haven't seen the trades today." It wasn't a question. "Larue started the bidding at two mil for a trilogy. First one's written. Rumor has it the ante's just reached seven mil."

"You're kidding. Nobody takes a chance like that anymore. They steal best-selling authors from another house. Who would—"

"Pitman's and Norseman are still duking it out. Face it, kid, you didn't pay attention. Like I told you before, you were coasting with Georgette Millrose. Look what happened."

Friday, Charlie discovered the source of the threatening E-mail she'd received in Las Vegas. Edwina had decided to go modern. The strange address resulted from the fact that she used the university as her server. The strange message was due to a suicidal impulse, from which she'd recovered—and Edwina notified Charlie of that in a subsequent communication she'd thought to sign.

Friday was also the day Libby told off Perry Mosher and quit her job at Critter Spa and Deli, then promptly rear-ended a semi and totaled her already wreck of a car.

Neither of these events came as a surprise. Libby's reaction to her accident, however, did.

She took responsibility for it.

"I tell you, Maggie, I'm just stunned," Charlie told her best friend and neighbor that night.

All four houses in the complex were identical originally. It was interesting how they'd been individually modified. Maggie Stutzman had taken the wall out between the kitchen and living/ dining room. Which only proved she didn't live with a teenager.

"Well, you should be proud of her, for godsake. You're always complaining she blames her problems on other people. And the best part is that nobody was injured. If she'd been driving a small car like yours, they could have been beheaded. That big old rusty Detroit steel you carried on about so could have saved a lot of grief in your household."

"I am proud of her and grateful all the kids were belted in." Eric had a cut on his cheek, Lori broke a finger, and Doug and Libby came through without a scratch.

Maggie set the bowl of fresh-popped corn on the coffee table and gave Charlie a hug that needed no explanation. After all Charlie'd been through, Libby's accident was what had made her knees shake.

They curled up on the ends of a couch, facing each other, with their shoes off and toes stuck under the center cushion, a ritual that had grown with friendship.

The popcorn was hot and salty. Charlie sighed. "Mrs. Beesom says if I ever go on vacation again, I should just stay home. Sounds good to me."

"Jesus, Greene, there goes the neighborhood." Black hair, pale and perfect skin, blue eyes that flashed mischief. God it felt good to be home. "Don't think we could handle it."

"You're one to talk, Stutzman. Hear you've been keeping late hours on work nights." If you get a man in here, which you need to do and is right for you, I won't be able to come over for popcorn and soul talk.

"Betty Snoop strikes again." Maggie wrinkled a seriously silly nose and grinned. "Charlie, he's the most delightful, wonderful, gorgeous man I've ever met, and you can breathe now—he's married."

"You're dating a married man? You know better than that. I can't even leave town but what you—how married?"

They crunched corn and stared each other down.

Maggie broke first. "Well, he can't compare with Mitch Hilsten, but—"

"Maggie, that's cheap and you know it."

"Okay, he's married, but separated from his wife, and he's—"

"Where have we heard that before? Where'd you meet him?"

"He's my stockbroker."

"You too? Like dripping and compounding and everything?"

"Charlie, I've been investing for years. You just never wanted to discuss that kind of thing. Now, I've heard some from Jeremy and Betty Snoop, but I want to hear about your Vegas experience firsthand."

"Not till you fill me in on Mr. Married Dow Jones."

Another impasse, but Charlie couldn't buffalo Maggie Stutzman twice in one evening. So, she sang for her popcorn.

Maggie thought Bradone sounded fascinating and wanted to meet her. "Living in Santa Barbara with a houseboy, traveling around the world, enjoying guys and then dumping them first, and all that money—makes my life sound so dull."

Charlie didn't comment for once. Unfortunately, Maggie's life *was* dull.

Maggie must have had a window open, because a piercing scream brought them to their feet. Another took them out the kitchen door barefoot and into the middle of the concrete courtyard ringed with patios and parking.

"Was it Libby? Didn't really sound like her."

"She's not home. It didn't, like, sound human...." Charlie had stood and then raced out here so fast, she felt dizzy.

Mrs. Beesom turned on the light over her door and stuck her head out. She wore a funny nightcap to protect her curls between weekly visits to the hairdresser. Even with her glasses off, she spotted them.

"It's them cats in the alley again. I was sure hoping now you're home, Charlie, you'd put a stop to it."

"It's okay, Mrs. Beesom. I'll take care of it. You can go back to bed."

"I don't know how she can go to sleep so early and still keep track of her neighbors like she does," Maggie complained as they headed for the metal gate at the back of the courtyard.

Before they reached it, Tuxedo Greene insinuated himself between the bars, his body all a shadow except for his white chest and toes. And his eyes, which refracted the dim light from Jeremy's windows.

For a moment, Charlie imagined she saw them through a residual smear of orange.

Orion Rising

AN OWEN KEANE MYSTERY

Terence Faherty

Ex-seminarian Owen Keane, pursuer of life's mysteries, returns to Boston College, his alma mater, and to the scene of an old crime…and a new one. His longtime friend, James Courtney Murray, has been murdered. Beside his body lay the yellowed newspaper clipping of a twenty-five-year-old unsolved rape. DNA evidence reveals that Murray was guilty of that crime.

Driven by his own knowledge of what happened that night in 1969, Owen is determined to find out why someone has gone to such great lengths to implicate an innocent man. The answers he seeks force Owen to revisit the past that haunts him still….

Available February 2001 at your favorite retail outlet.

WSKM375

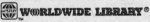

The victim broke free. About the size of a goat, it charged toward the doorway's freedom and collided with Druhallen, who was blocking it. He looked down: a battered and bleeding half-grown goblin clung to his leg.

"Kick it back over here," one of the batterers commanded.

An ugly, little face, made uglier by blood and bruises, peered up at him.

Point of fact: Druhallen didn't much like youngsters of any species.

Lost Empires

Lost Empires

Lynn Abbey

THE NETHER SCROLL
Lost Empires

©2000 Wizards of the Coast, Inc.
All Rights Reserved.

Cover art by Alan Pollack
First Printing: September 2000
Library of Congress Catalog Card Number: 00-101632

9 8 7 6 5 4 3 2 1

ISBN: 0-7869-1566-8
620-T21566

U.S., CANADA,
ASIA, PACIFIC, & LATIN AMERICA
Wizards of the Coast, Inc.
P.O. Box 707
Renton, WA 98057-0707
+1-800-324-6496

EUROPEAN HEADQUARTERS
Wizards of the Coast, Belgium
P.B. 2031
2600 Berchem
Belgium
+32-70-23-32-77

Visit our web site at **www.wizards.com**

1

12 Flamerule, the Year of the Arch (1353 DR)

Along the Vilhon Reach

"Do you think she wants to marry him? I hear he's half snake . . . the *wrong* half."

The question and comments rolled off the tongue of Galimer Longfingers, journeyman and wizard, as he and Druhallen of Sunderath, also a journeyman and wizard, fidgeted in their saddles while watching other men repair a broken cartwheel.

"Which half would be the right half?" Druhallen joked, then turned serious. "There's no point to wishes. What's cut, stays cut. We've been hired to get her to Hlondeth. What happens afterward is none of our concern."

Afoot, Druhallen was a handspan shorter than Galimer, though that wasn't obvious when they were astride. Nothing about Druhallen was obvious. His hair was a drab shade of brown that framed his squarish face with a ragged fringe. He had a larger-than-average mouth and nose, and his otherwise attractive hazel eyes were shadowed by heavy brows that were darker than his hair. Dressed in homespun and leather, Druhallen was often mistaken for his friend's varlet.

Galimer Longfingers cut an impressive figure, even in the middle of nowhere or on an empty road across the Vilhon Reach—which was almost the same thing. If the young woman under discussion was looking for a handsome, all-human suitor, she'd certainly cast a measuring glance in Galimer's direction. His wine-colored tunic and gray moleskin breeches had been tailored in the best Scornubel establishments and were as sturdy as they were fashionably expensive. His idly curling hair was the color of Aglarond cider, his eyes were gemstone blue, and his features were delicate without being either elven or feminine. His fingers, sheathed in leather gloves dyed to match his eyes, were elegant and long.

Wizard hands, Ansoain, his mother, labeled them—because long, slender fingers were presumed to be an asset in a profession that relied on gesture and precision. She'd nicknamed him Longfingers when he was a toddler, and fifteen years later Galimer still dreamed of taking his place among the great wizards of Faerûn.

A more sober and thoughtful youth, Druhallen never gainsaid his friend's dreams though he—and Ansoain, too—were aware that wizardry required more than elegant hands. Wizardry demanded a sharp mind, a special sort of curiosity, nerves of steel, and—above all else—gods-given talent. Galimer's wits were sharp enough, but he fell short in all the other attributes.

Druhallen had it all, despite his workman's physique and a childhood spent learning carpentry beside his older brothers in his father's shop. He'd captured Ansoain's attention a decade ago when bad weather led her to commission a waterproof box for the rare spices she was chaperoning along the roads to Elversult. When the carpenter's youngest son blithely quieted a squealing hinge with a cantrip of his own devising, Ansoain offered to apprentice the boy in exchange for twenty fresh-minted Cormyr falcons.

Without consulting his son, the old man bit each coin

and, approving of their taste, gave Druhallen a swat on the rump and a warning to obey his new master. Druhallen had sworn he'd never bring shame to his father's name and left Sunderath that day with a pocketful of nails. He'd kept his promise and the nails.

They both knew he could have found himself a wealthy patron by now, but he'd taken to the road like an uncaged bird took to the sky. Still, Dru remembered what he'd learned from his father and as far in time and place as he'd come from Sunderath, he could have re-spoked that wheel in half the time it was taking the carters.

The carters would be at it a while longer. Long enough, Druhallen thought, for a nap. He was eyeing an elm tree with moss-padded roots when Galimer interrupted him with another bit of gossip.

"I've heard the bridegroom's forty-five, three times a widower, with neither hair nor heirs to show for his efforts."

In Scornubel and the other towns where Ansoain plied the journey-trade with Druhallen and her son, Galimer Longfingers was accounted a witty young man. His word-play usually left Druhallen chuckling, but not when the carters had just managed to break another spoke.

"And I've heard the bride is bugbear ugly," he grumbled.

In truth, Dru had heard no such thing. He'd been careful not to acquire neither expensive habits nor an ear for gossip. Still, the simple fact was that they were ten days into what would be at least a twenty-day journey and the bride-to-be had yet to emerge from that cart with the jinxed wheels. Speculation ran rampant, and not only between bored wizards who hadn't yet seen the sun rise on their twentieth birthdays.

In addition to Ansoain and her apprentices, there were twelve men-at-arms attached to the dower caravan: the muscle complement to Ansoain's magic. A man would have to have been stone deaf not to hear what the muscle thought of the situation.

A few days back, Dru had lent a hand to one of the handmaids as she'd struggled with a too-full water jug and gotten an insider's version of the sad tale. The bride's family had a lustrous title, generations of honor, a drafty castle, and debts galore. The bridegroom was a dyer and tanner of fine leathers, no better born than Druhallen himself, but blessed with a self-made fortune. He was said to be a human man, but who knew with the Hlondethem? Their queen was a yuan-ti half-breed with iridescent scales on her cheeks and a serpent's tail she kept hidden, except from her lovers . . . according to the maid.

The match had been based on mutual need: The groom's for a title to match his wealth and sons to inherit it. The bride's to save her father from the ignominy of debtors' court. She stayed in the cart whether it rolled on four wheels or three because nightmares and tears had ruined her complexion . . . according to the maid.

"I'd like to see what we're guarding just once before we deliver it," Galimer continued his complaints. "The way those three dower carts are wrapped up, you'd think we were escorting the lost treasure of Oebelar."

Druhallen didn't know about Oebelar's legendary wealth, but he knew that three of the five wagons in their caravan were filled with brick and stone in a pathetic effort to maintain appearances for the already mortified bride. Her dowry, other than the name she'd been born with and the pedigreed blood in her veins, fit in a single chest she kept constantly at her feet.

"Leave it be," Dru advised for the third time. "We've escorted stranger consignments and been paid less for our troubles, right?"

Notwithstanding his expensive tastes Galimer was the money-man for the trio. He might bungle his reagent proportions or forget his spells in a crisis, but Galimer knew the exchange rates in every city and who was buying what—or so it seemed to Druhallen, who understood hard work but had no notion of profit.

Ansoain appreciated profit, but couldn't calculate risk for love nor money. She'd willingly turned their business affairs over to her son when his true calling manifested itself some five years ago. Their fortunes had improved steadily ever since.

Galimer had signed them up for this jaunt along the Vilhon Reach precisely because the leather-dyeing suitor had been willing to pay double the going rate to hire the same muscle-and-magic escort that had shepherded a bit of glittery tribute from Hlondeth's queen to her counterpart in Cormyr last autumn. The prospect of such good money had inspired them all, muscle and magic alike, to overlook some obvious questions when the contracts were sealed before a priest of trade in a Waukeenar temple.

"It just seems odd," Galimer persisted. "Virgins don't melt in sunlight and if there were anything half-so-valuable in those carts as all that warding suggests, then there aren't enough of us to keep it away from anyone who truly wanted it."

"No argument," Dru said mildly and ignored Galimer's sour scowl.

He'd voiced the same objections himself when they'd arrived in Elversult to collect the bride and her dowry. Galimer had dismissed Dru's worries out of hand.

The young men were friends, though, the best of friends and brothers combined—however unlikely that had seemed when a rough-mannered carpenter's son had mastered spells as fast as he learned to read them, faster by far than Galimer at his best. Staying on Longfingers's good side had come naturally to a boy with five older brothers, and Galimer had yearned for a friend. A childhood tagging along after Ansoain, who couldn't sleep three nights in the same bed, had left Galimer with a better grasp of geography than friendship.

They might not exchange another word this afternoon, but they'd be talking again after supper.

The carters wrestled the last of the spokes into place and retrieved the hobbled horses from the grass where they'd grazed. When the horses were ready, the magic-and-muscle escort assumed its customary positions and the caravan was on its way toward Hlondeth.

Dru and Galimer's customary positions were a short distance behind the bridal wagon. Ansoain, who'd spent most of their unscheduled rest with the captain of the men-at-arms, joined them there. By the brightness of her eyes, Dru suspected that she and the captain had shared more than a discussion about the weather. He disapproved, as only a young man could disapprove, of his foster mother's behavior, but both he and Galimer were years beyond embarrassment and however predatory her habits, Ansoain never let them interfere with work.

"Tree branch," she said as soon as her horse had settled in between his and Galimer's.

"Scry for diseases," Galimer answered quickly.

"What kind of tree?" Dru asked at the same time.

It was Ansoain's custom to quiz her apprentices whenever the spirit moved her. Galimer always strove to be first with an answer while Dru usually wanted more information before he'd commit himself.

"A fruit tree, in flower."

Dru nodded. "Stripped of the flowers and leaves, the branch could become a divining rod. And the flowers could be put to use in the dryad variation for making pure water."

"Not fair!" Galimer complained. "If there were a real stick, I'd see that it was in flower. You said stick, so that's all I imagined!"

"I said 'branch,' but you're right, Longfingers, you would have seen the flowers. You're both right." Ansoain tried to be fair; it wasn't easy. "Dragonfly's wing," she challenged, inspired, no doubt, by the insect flying between them and the cart.

"What *kind* of dragonfly?" Galimer demanded.

"Blue-green." The now-disappeared insect had been blue-green.

Dru didn't know any spells that required the wing of a blue-green dragonfly. He didn't know any that called for any specific part of any color dragonfly. He knew of a few spells that required the jewel-like carapaces of rare jungle beetles and another that needed scales from a true dragon's wing. None of those were in his head nor etched into the wood of the magically folded box hanging from his belt. An apprentice with access to his master's library usually knew more spells than he could actually cast.

Even Galimer knew more spells than he could cast, and frequently got them confused. Dru looked beyond Ansoain. Years of observation had taught him to anticipate Galimer's answer from the shape of his lips. If Gal's answer looked to be correct, then Druhallen would hold his own tongue, but if, as so often happened, it looked like Galimer was about to make himself appear foolish, Dru would speak up quickly and loudly—

"A blue-green wing would satisfy a spell that required only an insect's wing and, maybe, an affinity could be drawn to spells requiring feathers—function, form *and* color would give a threefold congruence—but it would be a far stretch to make a dragonfly's wing stand for any part of a true dragon."

Galimer's face showed indignation, then relief. Ansoain never let on that she suspected her foster's game—though she was usually careful to position herself so that Dru could see Galimer's face when she quizzed them.

"Good enough. Now, what is the writ for a dust shield?"

"Dust. What else?"

Sometimes Galimer spoke too quickly for Dru to save him.

"The writ!" Ansoain snapped, "not the reagents. How

much dust, and how do you seal the spell in your mind? What trigger will call it out when you need to cast it?"

A dust shield was one of Galimer's more reliable spells. He rattled off the answers correctly and without hesitation.

Ansoain peppered them with other reagents and writs as the afternoon sun grew warm on their backs. When their stomachs began to churn in anticipation of supper, she lectured them on tactical shortcomings of the adversaries that journeying mages might encounter in Faerûn's Heartlands.

"Fumarandi are drakes. Their weapon is charcoal smoke, and they make their homes above the trees in mountain forests. They can be claimed as companions . . ."

Ansoain claimed that she never forgot a lesson or a nightmare. It was the latter that kept her on the road. As long as she was moving, the worst of her dreams couldn't find her. In winter, when they went to ground in Scornubel, Ansoain rented rooms by the night and fought her nightmares by the keg. Winters had been hard for Dru and Galimer until they were old enough to rent rooms for themselves and worse, in a way, since Galimer had taken over their finances. Every publican in Scornubel knew Galimer would cover his mother's debts.

But when they were on the road and spending their nights beneath different trees, no one had a clearer mind than Ansoain. She shared her knowledge of the world and magic with her sons.

"Wyvern gall," she called out after she'd told them everything there was to know about the fumarandi.

Galimer's lips didn't twitch; he hadn't a clue. Druhallen inquired: "Fresh, powdered, or ossified?"

"Ossi—"

She didn't finish the answer. Her gray eyes scanned the forward horizon, then closed while she sought the wisdom of her mind's eye. Dru felt the disruption also: a slight, yet profoundly ominous change in the ether, that strange, intangible stuff where magic held sway.

"What the—?" Galimer demanded.

Ansoain commanded silence with a snarl, the raised her hand in a curious gesture. Bits of ash—spent reagents—blew away from her palm. The spell carried her words directly to the ears of the captain and his men. Druhallen and Galimer didn't hear a sound.

The captain had a similar ability to communicate with his men, equally magical, but derived from the matched rings he and the men wore. The caravan came to a halt. Its muscle-and-magic escort pulled in tight around it. The muscle fastened their chain mail coifs over their faces and tested their swords without drawing them. The magic considered their spells.

"Fire?" Dru suggested softly.

Ansoain shrugged. "It's got no shape or signature. It could be anything, or nothing. Fire needs something to burn."

Galimer opened a foot-long war-fan from distant Kozakura. There, it had been a weapon. Here, it was a spellbook with writs etched in silver along the vanes.

"No time for that, son," Ansoain said grimly. "If your nerves are chancy, hide in the wagon."

"I'm sure of some fire," Longfingers protested, "and a shrieking arrow."

"And you?" she asked Druhallen.

"The usual. I can blur us a little now, if you think that would help."

"No, whatever's out there, it's already taken our measure. Probably slavers. Save your blurring for later. Your gloom, too. The girl's got to be what they're after. The girl and her dowry. Get her out, if push comes to shove. Make a pall of misery and get out beneath it."

Druhallen bit his tongue. They'd tangled with slavers before—a base and brutal lot, and not above using the nastier sorts of spellcraft to protect, or acquire, their merchandise. But slavers were rarely subtle and the disturbance Dru tasted

9

with his inner senses was as subtle as it was potent. He patted his left sleeve, assuring himself that the wax-sealed embers he used to trigger his fire spells were in their proper places. He checked his belt, too—not for the folded box; as Ansoain had told Galimer, it was too late for rehashing spells—but for his dagger. The single-edge knife was mostly a tool for cutting meat and gathering herbs, but he'd made sure it was long enough to pierce a man's heart through his ribs.

The ethereal disruption materialized. Galimer spotted it first.

"Over there," he whispered and cocked a finger at a hilltop north-by-northeast of the caravan.

The hilltop air shimmered with a untimely sunset glow. A moment later at least a dozen figures, each wearing a long, red cloak, circled in the grass. A moment after that there was fire in the sky and a thick, black fog rolling toward the wagons. It could have been worse. They could have stopped at the base of the hill, but they were still in trouble.

Druhallen didn't need to know the name of the spell that wrought the fog to know it was nothing he wanted to breathe. For that matter, he didn't want to be astride when the miasma hit. He leapt to the ground and cast an air-clearing spell just in time to keep his head clear. Dru could have extended the spell to protect his entire body—but it would have faded more quickly and he wouldn't have been able to hurl a fireball at the hilltop.

The spell affected Druhallen's hearing. Sound was fainter than it should have been, and distorted, as if he'd gone diving and surfaced with water in his ears. He heard enough steel and deep-pitched screaming to know that the men-at-arms were fighting for their lives. On hands and knees, Druhallen crept through the fog, away from his mentor—not from cowardice, but to widen the angle of their attack and defense. Never let an enemy kill twice with the same stroke, that was Ansoain's motto.

The red-cloaked wizards abandoned subtlety. A head-blind child could have placed them in the fog—and Dru's fireballs were about as effective as a head-blind child's wish when it came to piercing their defenses. He felt his final spell rebound harmlessly. Some months short of his twentieth birthday, Druhallen of Sunderath confronted the end of a life he'd hoped would be much longer. Drawing his knife, Dru waded through the black fog to join what was left of the muscle near the wagons.

He hadn't taken ten strides when a faintly luminous, undead skirmisher lunged at him. The zombie's face was fully skeletal, and flesh hung in tatters from its long bones. Beyond fear and pain, it fought clumsily with a stone-headed mace until Dru knocked it off its legs. Taking no chances, he kicked its skull aside and stomped its brittle ribs.

Knowing there were undead in the fog, he changed course and headed for the hilltop. If the red-cloaked wizards were so confident of their strength that they relied on zombies for physical protection, then there was a chance—a slim but real chance—that he could stab one or two of them before he died.

But the red-cloaked wizards weren't as reckless as he'd hoped. Halfway up the hill, Dru met another luminous creature. As dead, or undead, as the zombie, its eyes shone with sentience. It knew what to do with the steel halberd it carried.

Druhallen dodged the undead warrior's first thrust and successfully beat the second aside without losing his right arm, but his knife was woefully inadequate against the halberd. Guessing that he was stronger than the creature, he slammed the blade into its sheath and clamped his hands on the halberd's shaft. The undead warrior howled. Spider-silk strands of red magic spun out of the wood. They numbed Dru's nerves and paralyzed his muscles. He couldn't release the shaft.

Dru was screaming when the undead jerked the halberd and flung him through the inky fog like a stone from a sling. He never felt the landing.

* * * * *

The world was dark when Druhallen next opened his eyes—new-moon dark with a thousand stars overhead. With his first waking breath, he was grateful to be alive. With his second, he recalled what had happened and what he had lost. A part of him would have preferred never to have awakened, but that was the lesser part of his spirit.

He had to move, had to stand, had to find his way back to Elversult, but first he had to conquer his pain. The stranded magic of the undead's halberd had left him aching from the roots of his toenails to the root of each hair on his head. The cumulative ache was such that Dru didn't realize he had a more serious injury until he tried propping himself up on his left arm.

His left wrist was broken and his efforts dislodged the bones, grinding the shards against one another. Dru cursed the world and returned to oblivion.

Amber-rose glowed on the eastern horizon when Dru regained consciousness. Dawn wasn't more than an hour away. The all-body aches had subsided, and though his wrist had swollen to a ridiculous size, he managed to stand.

The battleground was quiet, except for the crackle of fire in the wagons. The flames were starving. Whatever their purpose, the red-cloaked enemy had abandoned this place hours ago.

There were no obvious survivors. None of the dark mounds strewn near the wagons moved or groaned. Druhallen realized he owed his life to the undead who'd hurled him off the battlefield. It was not a comforting thought. He began to search for Ansoain and Galimer, the tragic bride and her maids, the captain and his men.

Druhallen's mind relived the ambush: A dozen magicians, each wearing a red cloak, had stood in a circle. His mind wandered far to the south and east, to the land called Thay. He'd never met a Red Wizard, at least not one who admitted his affiliation, but Ansoain had lectured him about their habits. More important, the Zhentarim had heard of them and regarded them as rivals.

Ansoain had been adamant that she'd never worked *for* the Black Network of the Zhentarim, but she had contacts inside their organization. A few of those contacts might be termed "friends," and one or two of those might choose to avenge her.

Dru's vision blurred. He raised his good arm and wiped away tears had hadn't known he was shedding. He looked down at another body. It had been the captain, and it had been savaged. A pack of wolves could not have done more damage. Even his mail had been shredded.

The world began to spin. Druhallen dropped to his knees before they buckled. He retched violently. His tears were as hot as the acid churning in his gut and for several moments Dru was helpless in his grief. Then sanity returned. He stood and called the names he knew best.

"Ansoain! Galimer! I live. Druhallen lives for you! Can you hear me?"

In the lengthening silence, he seized a piece of smoking wood and hurled it at the empty hilltop.

"Galimer. Galimer Longfingers!"

Dru heard a sound, spun around, and laid his good hand on the hilt of his knife.

Nothing. Not another peep or a twitch. Dru sighed. The east was brighter now. Soon, the ruins would stand revealed in all their horror and there'd be no need to bend low over each corpse with a mixture of hope and dread.

Though not a religious youth, and utterly unaware of the affiliations of the men and women whose lives he'd briefly shared, Druhallen paused beside each body. He recited, as

13

best he could remember them, the prayers of peace and safe-passage his grandmother had taught him. He was chanting safe-passage for one of the carters when he heard a second sound. This time, as he spun around, Dru glimpsed movement near a smoldering wagon.

Leaving his prayer unfinished, he ran to the spot.

"Dru—? Druhallen, is that you?"

The voice, though weak, was unmistakable. Galimer Longfingers had survived!

Stretched face down in the dirt, Galimer's legs were pinned beneath charred planks from one of the stone-filled wagons. Fearing the worst, Dru put his shoulder against the wreckage and bulled it aside. Galimer's fine clothes were ruined, but—miraculously—he appeared unbloodied, unburnt. Dru cautiously rolled him onto his back.

"Tell me where it hurts, Gal—"

"All over. I tried—My mind went blank of everything except dust," he said sobbing, "and I couldn't get it cast. I panicked. I hid, Dru. I *hid*. When they lifted their fog and called off their minions, I just stayed here where I'd hidden myself. Even when they ransacked the wagons and set them ablaze, I couldn't make myself move. I should have died."

Druhallen closed his good hand over Galimer's. "It didn't matter. They had us beat from the first scent. At least you know what they did and said. I tangled with something undead and wound up out cold, two hundred paces away from everyone."

"At least you *fought!* You cast what you could and then you fought." Galimer pulled his hand away from Dru and covered his face. "I should have died."

"What's cut, stays cut," the carpenter's son advised. "If you hadn't hidden, you might well have died, and I'd be facing the road to Elversult with only a broken wrist for company."

Galimer expressed concern for his friend's injury, but Druhallen wasn't interested in sympathy.

"Can you stand? Walk? We need to find your mother. You said you saw them—"

"Heard them," Galimer corrected as he grabbed Dru's shoulder and sat himself up. "I didn't *see* anything."

"Kept your eyes closed, eh?" Dru laughed and stood.

"I got hit by something bright when it all started. Everything's been blurred since." He flailed for Dru's arm with an awkwardness that lent credence to his claim. "I heard them, and that's about it. I didn't recognize their language. They came a damn long way to steal that girl and her dowry."

Druhallen pitied the misbegotten girl, but cut was cut and his pity was worthless. He hoped she was dead. The dead didn't remember . . . usually.

Leaning on each other, the friends surveyed the killing ground. It was just as well that Galimer's eyes weren't working too well. He was spared what Dru saw all too clearly once the sun was up. Whatever had killed Ansoain had torn her apart like so much stale bread. He recognized her by pieces: bits of cloth and scalp, a bloody chunk of her hand with fingers and rings still attached.

Fighting nausea, Druhallen retrieved her rings. They were magically potent, not to mention intrinsically valuable. It was difficult, for many reasons, to understand why they'd been left behind.

"She'd want you to have them," he told Galimer as he pressed the metal bits into his friend's hand. "Now, let's get out of here. I can see a few of the horses. You be the hands, I'll be the eyes . . ."

Galimer balked. "Guide me to the hilltop. Maybe those bastards left something traceable behind."

"Cut is cut," Druhallen muttered, but he led Galimer through the grass.

The scents of spellcraft and malice lingered on the hilltop, and something else: a palm-sized glass disk. The disk was dark, but neither black nor completely opaque. So smooth and slick that it slipped through Druhallen's fingers when he tried to retrieve it. The disk was colder than the claw of winter when he finally had it in his grasp.

Ignoring numbed fingers, Dru held it up to the risen sun. Gold flecks sparkled within the icy glass.

"There's something written on the edge," Galimer interrupted.

"I thought your eyes were bad."

"My body's eyes. My mind's eye sees clearly enough. That thing reeks of sorcery and there's writing on the edge."

Dru rearranged his fingers and saw the truth of Galimer's statement. "I don't recognize the script."

"Doesn't it tell you something through your fingertips?" Galimer asked.

"Only that it's colder than winter."

Dru balanced the lens in his left hand. It was an agonizing error. He gasped and the disk *thumped* to the grass. While Druhallen swore at himself and his pain, Galimer swept the grass with his hands.

"Sweet Mystra!" the gold-haired mage swore as he clutched, then dropped, the glass. "Cold's not the half of it!"

"Aye, but what *is* that other half?"

Galimer pinched his fingertips to the scripted edge and lifted the disk carefully. "How about a way to control their undead minions?"

Dru considered the possibility. "Did you see the robes they were wearing when they first appeared?"

"That was the last thing I did see. Their robes were red."

"Red robes. Red-robed wizards. The Red Wizards of Thay. They pool their magic and one wizard casts the spells for all of them. Nobody—*nobody*—knows how they do it. Until now."

Druhallen fumbled with his folded magic box. It would have been easier to manipulate with both hands, but he'd designed it for single-handed work. As the hidden locks opened, the box unfolded, increasing in size and complexity. Reagents filled the revealed compartments. Dru's traveling spells were etched into the compartment dividers. With the third unfolding, he found an empty compartment large enough to hold the disk.

Galimer squirted the disk into the empty compartment. "Being cold and dark, it's more likely a device for controlling the undead."

"It's the circles." Dru clung to his opinion as if it were one he'd held for a lifetime though, before today, he hadn't given more than ten thoughts to Thay in the last year. "Anyone can control the undead. You or I could, if we chose to learn the art. But only the Red Wizards rely on the undead, because their circles make it feasible to control whole boneyards. The arrogance! They descend from nowhere, take what they want, leave everyone for dead, and don't even bother to collect their trash."

"Is it trash? How can you be sure? It didn't feel spent to me."

"It's cold and dark," he snapped. "If it's not spent, it's useless."

"Not useless," Galimer countered thoughtfully. "We can use it to prove that we were ambushed by the Red Wizards. That ought to put the wind in the Zhentarim."

"Mind what you say," Dru said, sobering quickly though he had had similar thoughts a few moments ago. "Or we'll get caught *between* the Black Network and the Red Wizards." He folded the box and let it hang against his hip. "When we get to Elversult, we tell the Network that we were ambushed, but that we never saw what hit us. And we don't tell them about finding the disk."

"Mother . . ." Galimer protested. "The girl, the captain and his men, the damn carters . . . We've got to tell the truth, Dru. There won't be justice without the truth."

"What justice is there between Thay and the Zhentarim? We'll need a lifetime of luck just to clear our names of this disaster. Talk about red-robed wizards won't help us do that, and neither will a lump of rotten glass—"

"I can't accept that, Dru. Not for her."

"You don't have to. We'll avenge her ourselves. I swear to you right now and forever: We'll hunt those wizards down. We'll go to Thay, if we have to. We'll find out how they beat us, and we'll use their secrets against them."

2

28 Eleasias, the Year of the Banner (1368 DR)

West of the Dawn Pass

Druhallen leaned against a rough-plank wall. Fifteen years after Ansoain's death and the thought of her could still set his wrist aching. Especially in a Zhentarim village like Parnast, on the rump of the Dawn Pass Trail, when the natural heat of a northern summer met the unnatural heat creeping off the nearby Anauroch desert.

The breeze coming through the open window was moving heat. The shade where Dru sat was dark heat. The air burned with the yellow dust of Anauroch. A storm was coming—possibly from the desert, certainly in the rented room he shared with his partners.

"I'll lodge a protest. There's law in this town," Galimer fumed as he paced the room's not-considerable width. "They've forfeited their earnest money, that's given."

"Wonderful! I'm sure they cared about their earnest money!" Rozt'a shot back.

Florozt'a had come into Dru and Galimer's lives a few years after Ansoain's death. They were all younger then and she'd been new to the journeying life. She'd sold her sword to a Zhentilar captain who'd only pretended to value

19

her fighting skills. When he'd tried, one too many times, to demonstrate what he did value from women, she'd left him writhing on the ground.

It had been a short-lived victory. Rozt'a had quickly found herself without a contract and stranded on the empty road east of Triel with no more than her sword, the clothes on her back, and a leaking waterskin. The gods knew what might have happened next if Druhallen and Galimer hadn't been riding magic with the next eastbound caravan. They'd both remembered the striking woman and her boorish captain, and judged that he'd deserved whatever damage she'd done to him, maybe more.

Riding double behind Galimer, she'd said that wizards who journeyed the Western Heartlands should hire their own bodyguards and not rely on someone else's muscle to protect them when the going got rough. Dru and Galimer, who scarcely needed words to exchange ideas, then or now, had hired her on the spot, more from pity than need. But Rozt'a fit comfortably between them, and by the end of that season they were a threesome.

Rozt'a's hair was a few shades yellower than Galimer's and cropped ragged just below her ears. She was tall for a woman. In the sun, with her hair standing wild, she was nearly as tall as Druhallen and broader across through shoulders, in any weather, than Galimer. She and Galimer could pass themselves off as siblings. From behind, with her weapons and leathers about her, Rozt'a passed for the brother.

When her temper was blazing as it did in the rented room, a wise man kept his head tucked low.

"What's a bit of earnest to the likes of them?" she ranted. "If they cared about their precious earnest, they'd have waited for us. They were in one damn hurry and we're three full, forsaken days early ourselves! Helm's eyes! One nose-full of trouble and they ran with the first Zhentarim spend-spell who admired the shine in their purses. I tell you, this has nothing to do with Dekanter or the Beast Lord—those dogs meant to betray our faith from the start."

She got Dru's attention with that last remark. Any time Rozt'a uttered the words "love", "betray", and "faith" in close order, she could count on Druhallen's full attention.

It had been nearly nine years since she accepted Galimer's marriage proposal and, despite occasional outbursts, their union endured, but—make no mistake about it—the gold-haired mage hadn't been Rozt'a's first choice.

Dru had missed all the signals. Galimer had been smitten with Rozt'a from the start, and what woman would be interested in a carpenter's burly son when she had the likes of Galimer Longfingers waiting on her every wish? Of course, he'd valued her company. Of course, he would have liked more—but the carpenter's son didn't poach, not on Galimer, not on his true friend.

Then came the night when Rozt'a had ambushed him with a not-at-all-friendly kiss. He'd muttered something about honor and she'd replied that she was in love . . . with *him*. Galimer gallantly proclaimed that he couldn't be happier than to see them together. She began to talk of marriage, of children, and settling down in one place. The problem was that, as attractive as Druhallen found Rozt'a, he didn't love her as she loved him and talk of marriage, children, or rooting himself in the ground like a tree turned his blood to ice.

Druhallen had kept his reservations to himself for over a year. He came up with excuses—good excuses—to postpone the wedding until they reached Berdusk, on their way home to Scornubel for the winter, when Rozt'a announced that they'd be having a child come spring. The announcement was more of a surprise than it should have been and Dru would go to his grave knowing that he'd reacted poorly.

Very poorly.

They'd had a row that awakened the entire neighborhood. When the guard came to the door, Dru had walked out, leaving Rozt'a in tears and Galimer standing beside her. By spring, when guilt dragged him back, Rozt'a and Gal were married . . . and childless. The baby who would have been Dru's daughter had died in Rozt'a's womb and nearly killed her.

Galimer had taken Rozt'a to Berdusk's Chauntean infirmary where priests had kept her alive with prayers and rare medicines. The newlyweds were deep in debt and desperately glad to see Druhallen of Sunderath.

I've lined up enough journey-work that we'll have everything paid come autumn, but it would be a blessing if you rode with us, Dru. I can handle the steady magic—wards, scrys, and deceits—but I'm nervous in the pinch.

Nervous in the pinch! Since his mother's death, Galimer hadn't cast a single spell from horseback and his mind blanked at the least surprise. He could line up the work, but he couldn't deliver it. Dru could, and backing the newlyweds for a season was the least he could do.

We'll ride together, Dru had said to his friend, *while Rozt'a stays here and rebuilds her strength. Come autumn, you and she will be ready to start your own family . . .*

Not at all, Galimer had replied. The Chauntean priests had been explicit: fever had put an end to Rozt'a's dreams of motherhood. Their future lay on the road, as it always had, with him. What had been cut could be made whole again, if he'd consent.

Dru had been speechless; Galimer and Rozt'a heard silence for consent. They'd left Berdusk together and found ways to remain that way.

"I'm telling you that it was a good contract," Galimer continued the dispute with his wife. "Yes, they were strangers. We didn't know them, they didn't know us, and neither they nor us had ridden the Dawn Pass Trail before, but they knew our references and I checked theirs. I made concessions—we're the ones who wanted to stop at Dekanter for three days when the usual layover is one . . . *was* one."

None of us knew what was going on up here, but we'd bargained fair and—because we were strangers—we deposited the earnest money with an Acolyte of Law—"

Rozt'a snorted, a clear sign that she was losing control over her anger and disgust. "Unless he was wearing the Network's jewels, my sneezes have more power than your Acolyte has in these parts."

"As a matter of fact, she was—"

Dru paid close attention to the wooden planks beneath him and the activity of a spider. The Zhentarim in all their guises were a chronic irritation in the Heartland, but they claimed the Dawn Pass Trail for their own and there was no one who could gainsay them. Honest folk—and Dru considered himself, Galimer, and Rozt'a to be honest folk—could survive, even thrive, in the Zhentarim shadow. The Network, itself, preferred to do business with honest folk; it was both cheaper and safer. But when a deal soured on the Dawn Pass Trail, honest folk were vulnerable.

In Parnast, the little village where Galimer had arranged for them to meet a merchant-adventurer coming off the Anauroch desert, the Network was openly and utterly in charge. Zhentarim cant echoed in the charterhouse and Zhentarim trade-marks were burned into every piece of wood, including the one Druhallen stared at after the spider disappeared.

The local Zhentarim lord, a human named Amarandaris, took a tenth of everything that passed through the palisade gate, and his armed cohorts made certain that nothing failed to pass through. The cohorts seldom had to use force. The Zhentarim were notorious for other means of persuasion.

West of the village, the Dawn Pass Trail was a six-day stretch of rock-slides, washouts, and hairpin curves through the Greypeak Mountains to the town of Llorkh. The trail was wide enough for a single sure-footed horse or mule. Merchants provided the goods, the gold, the horses, and whatever magic they thought their goods deserved; the Zhentarim provided all the muscle and pack-mules for a price that was almost fair. Usually there was a thirty-mule train forming in Llorkh, another in Parnast, and one in transit on the trail.

Just east of Parnast, the Dawn Pass trail split into two. A southern branch, wide enough for four-wheeled carts, skirted the foothills of the eastern Greypeaks, including the ruins at Dekanter, and rejoined Heartland trade routes farther south in Yarthrain. From Parnast to Yarthrain, merchants provided the goods, the gold, and the magic while the Zhentarim provided muscle and ox-carts the size of freighters.

The northern branch of the eastbound trail disappeared into Anauroch where the Bedine traded, raided, and steadfastly resisted Network ambition. The Anauroch routes were the fastest between Zhentil Keep on the inland Moonsea and their western dominions. Cross-Anauroch traffic was steady, but woe betided a merchant-adventurer whom the nomads caught depending on Zhentarim protection. Of course, worse befell a merchant-adventurer who arrived in Parnast without Zhentarim camels to exchange for Zhentarim mules and ox-carts.

Dru and his companions had come from Llorkh, keeping underpaid eyes on grain destined for the stomachs of mules, camels, and oxen. They'd planned to meet their Anauroch adventurer and ride magic for his south-bound trade-goods. It had seemed so simple, so clever, so certain, and it had fallen apart a few hours ago when they'd ridden into the village.

"I did what I could, Rozt'a," Galimer defended himself. "I arranged the contract right after we decided that the Year of the Banner would be the year Dru would finally get to Dekanter. We agreed that we should reach the ruins at the end of the season, on our way back to Scornubel. That meant Llorkh to Parnast and Parnast to Dekanter, Yarthrain, and then on to Scornubel for the winter. Mercy, Rozt'a, how was I to know—how could anyone have known—that Amarandaris would chose the Year of the Banner to declare the ruins off-limits and move the whole damn trail a half-league to the east?"

"I'm not blaming you, Gal. I blame those dog merchants who wouldn't wait until the contract date, and the damn Zhentarim. You think the Llorkh Network didn't know what we'd find here before we left their town? But, no— better to strand us here and make us beg to join one of *their* caravans south. Demons loose in the Greypeaks! *Nonsense!* Bloodbaths and murder at Dekanter. War with the Underdark. We've heard it all since we got here. Do these fools take us for fools? *Zhentarim* driven out of Dekanter? Not damned likely, I tell you. *Zhentarim* don't let go of anything. They mean to deceive us, each of us: you, me, and you, too, Druhallen—don't pretend you're asleep; I know better."

Druhallen looked up but said nothing as Rozt'a continued her tirade.

"I don't give us a morning's journey, if we tried to leave this village right now. There's safety in numbers when you're dealing with the Network. The whole idea of waiting until the end of the season was to link up with the Anauroch traders so we wouldn't be alone with the Zhentarim in Dekanter. The way they've got it set now—" a stray thought stopped Rozt'a cold. When she spoke again, her tone was deeper and more anxious. "We could be stuck here—stuck in Parnast—for the whole winter!"

Parnast was a typical village in most respects, not unlike Sunderath where Dru had been born. True, it was a bit more isolated . . . All right, tucked on the rump side of the Greypeak Mountains with the Anauroch desert for a neighbor, it was hard to imagine a more isolated village. The Dawn Pass Trail—the sole reason for Parnast's existence—was unusable for half the year. As soon as the late summer dust storms ended, the mountain blizzards began and lingered until the spring thaw produced a certainty of *mud* from Llorkh to Yarthrain.

Winter in Parnast would be winter in prison.

"I don't know," Galimer answered. "I've made a few inquiries. We've only been here an afternoon, and we haven't established our reputations. The problem isn't just that they've moved the trail to the east of Dekanter. Something's seriously wrong at Zhentil Keep. Apparently nothing's come west for months, and traders who usually head east have chosen to go south instead. I've got to wonder when the Network's own trade chooses a Cormyr passage. Amarandaris must be wondering the same thing. Word is that he's Sememmon's hand-picked man—"

"You hadn't mentioned *that!* It just gets worse!" Despite her assurances, Rozt'a was shouting at her husband. "Dru!" She turned her attention to him, as he'd feared she would. "Dru—talk to this man! Tell him what to do before he gets us all killed!"

Druhallen took a deep breath. "It's not Galimer's fault. The Zhentarim are as good at keeping secrets as they are at spreading rumors. I'm inclined to think there's something rotten at Zhentil Keep, and at Dekanter as well, though whether they're related . . . that I can't begin to guess. If there's blame, put it on me. I'm the one who wanted to be here. I thought a contract to escort myrrh resin into the south was ideal. I would have shaken hands and called it done. Galimer had the sense to insist on earnest and Acolytes. I laughed at him, if you remember. Well, I've stopped laughing. Blame me for this, not him."

Rozt'a wouldn't blame Dru for anything. Her temper would take her to the brink of a confrontation with her one-time lover, but never across it. They talked, as two members of a trio had to talk, and sometimes at great length but when discussion grew heated, Rozt'a became a woman of very few words.

Dru, who was their partnership's nominal leader, took

advantage of her—and his own—unwillingness to confront what had—and had not—continued to exist between them.

"We're not trapped yet," he continued patiently. "The locals say the dust storms don't usually start until after the Eleint full moon and not always then. Last year the storms were bad, and the year before. The old woman who sold me bread swore there'd never been three bad years in a row. She said, too, that this past spring saw any number of merchant-adventurers head out to trade with the Bedine. Surely some of them will make it back. If they won't hire us as extra magic, then we'll pay our own way. Safety in numbers, Roz, just as you said."

"What about Amarandaris?" she persisted. "What price are we going to have to pay to him? Is this the season when we sell ourselves to the Network?"

There'd been no Zhentarim in Sunderath. Druhallen had grown up without ever seeing a Network trade-mark or cringing in the face of Network brutality. Rozt'a had been less fortunate and harbored a mistrust that bordered on hysteria.

"If Galimer says Amarandaris is a Darkhold man, then I believe him. He and I have dealt with Sememmon and his vassals since we were boys in Ansoain's shadow. They're honorable villains, for what it's worth, and know the value of honest trade. If worse comes to worst, we can go down the new trail with Amarandaris and live to tell the tale."

Rozt'a folded her arms beneath her breasts. "I don't share your faith where Darkhold is concerned. I got a look at this Amarandaris while I was scouting the resident muscle. I've seen warmer eyes on a snake."

"Why not go *up* the Dawn Pass?" Galimer interrupted. "They've got sixty mules in the stables right now, that's thirty more than they want. There'll be a mule train headed back to Llorkh tomorrow or the day after. We can go with them. I can keep our noses clean with the Zhentarim, but something's got the goblin-kin riled. Sweet Mystra—didn't you see them camped outside the palisade as we came in? Something's put real fear into those little beggars. Dwarves, maybe, or Underdark races who'd kill us as soon as they'd kill a goblin. If Amarandaris pulled the Network out of Dekanter, Dru, I'm telling you I'm not eager to get one step closer than I already am."

"Vengeance," Dru countered. "Your mother's vengeance."

"We've gotten vengeance. There were thirteen Red Wizards on that hilltop. We've learned all their names and slain three of them without going to Dekanter. We'll slay the rest when we can, if we can. Going to Dekanter won't get us closer to any of them. All Dekanter gets us—gets *you*—is a chance to cast that scrying spell you've been cooking up for years. All right—suppose you *do* scry something about the glass disk? Suppose you see a red-robed wizard carry it out of the mines, then what? You've never been able to answer that question for me, Dru. Are you going to start excavating with *strangers* around—*Zhentarim* strangers? Sweet Mystra, you've always said, "Don't let the Network know we think there's a connection between Ansoain's death and the Red Wizards'! If you ask me, it would be easier if we *were* traveling with Amarandaris. At least then we'd know the thief—"

"Strangers! Red Wizards! Zhentarim!" Rozt'a erupted. "Gods! Take your pick and the Pit take them all. We're all born little people and if we're clever we'll stay little people, beneath the notice of the mighty for good or evil. You find what you're looking for, Druhallen, and our troubles are just starting."

Dru defended himself: "If I'm right and the Red Wizards are kindling their spell circles with Netherese magic and Netherese artifacts, then the rest of Faerûn's got to know before the Weave is torn. The Netheril Empire came down in a day because wizards got greedy."

"The Weave's not our responsibility. I've said it before: She was *my* mother!" Galimer shouted. Galimer never shouted, but the heat and frustration had gotten to them all. "You've spun a yard of conclusions from a single strand of suspicion, Dru. I say, sell that damned disk and be done with it."

Dru opened his folding box—a different one than he'd carried on the Vilhon Reach—and removed the disk. He held it up in the summer light.

The disk had not yielded its secrets easily. Ansoain had been dead for two winters before Druhallen knew the inscription was written in the language of the ancient Netheril Empire. Another seven winters passed before he'd taught himself enough of that forgotten language to attempt a translation . . . *Those who see me see darkness, while he who holds me casts the sun.*

In his heart Druhallen believed that the first part of the inscription described the disk's function as a vault where several wizards could pool their potential magic; and the second part described the might a wizard wielded when he unleashed that pooled potential. But other interpretations were possible. There was no definitive concordance of Netherese with any modern language. In other contexts, the word Druhallen had translated as darkness meant death or blindness; and at least one elven authority insisted that *casts the sun* was a metaphor for insanity.

Galimer and Rozt'a agreed with the elves and so, five years ago, Druhallen had spent the winter at Candlekeep, where for a hefty price in gold a blind seer had plunged into a trance. She'd vindicated a few of Dru's cherished suspicions. Before it fell into the grass on the Vilhon Reach, the disk had belonged to a red-robed necromancer from Thay who commanded the potential magic of twelve other wizards less skilled than himself. But the Candlekeep seer had been unable to determine what precise role the disk had played in casting the spells that slew Ansoain and so many others that day, or how a Netherese artifact had wound up in a Red Wizard's hands.

Go to Dekanter, the seer suggested when her trance had ended. *Go to the Mines of Dekanter in the Greypeak Mountains. The Netherese mages congregated there after the metal played out and the dwarves had moved on. They developed their most potent spells and artifacts in those mountains, away from the floating cities. There is a distinct pattern to objects forged at Dekanter—a taste of darkness, the scents of depth and weight. Go to Dekanter. Your disk was born there, lost there, and found there not so long ago. A century or two, at most. If you can find the chamber where the disk was fired, I can teach you a simple spell that will show you the rest.*

The seer's "simple spell" was more subtle than any spell Druhallen had learned before or since. It had taken him three years to collect the reagents necessary to cast it and another year—not to mention the lion's share of the reagents—to master it. Until this morning, he'd believed he was less than a week's journeying from unraveling a triad of mysteries with a single spell: the history of a polished disk of Netherese glass, the specific role it played in the ambush that led to Ansoain's death, and the more general role it played in Red Wizard spell-casting.

In the Parnast room Dru rotated the disk until it angled sunlight onto the floor between them all. "The Netherese wizards destroyed themselves, their Empire, and very nearly the world." He recited a lesson he'd learned from the Candlekeep seer. "When Great Ao saw the price of their foolishness, He commanded Mystra to thread a new strand through the Weave, the strand of fate that limits the power of our spellcraft—because the nature of magic is recklessness and self-destruction. That thread has held tight against good, evil, and all that lies between—until now. I'm sure the Red Wizards are trying to recreate the forbidden spells that brought the Empire down."

Galimer shook his head. "It doesn't follow, Dru. It hasn't *ever* followed. Yes, the Thayan circles are dangerous and we don't know how the Red Wizards create them. And, yes, their zulkirs are madmen, worse than the Zhentarim. But madmen fueled with Netherese artifacts? Look at a map, Dru—there's half of Faerûn between Thay and Dekanter. It's not as if they can just appear and disappear—"

The gold-haired mage stopped himself, and Druhallen savored a long-awaited victory.

"That's exactly what they did on the Vilhon Reach," Dru said without gloating. "Why not do it at Dekanter? Everything *does* follow. I'd just as soon go the rest of the way by ourselves—the old trail must still be there and it's not as if we'd be looking for a fight with anyone—although, have you considered the possibility that this supposed war *below* Dekanter is actually the Red Wizards establishing themselves above?"

Dru watched Galimer's eyes narrow with thought, and he feigned a philosophical retreat.

"You plot our course, Longfingers. If you say we go to Llorkh, then we head east to Llorkh. Gods willing, I'll get back here some other year."

Galimer, still narrow-eyed and thinking, said nothing.

Rozt'a began her opinion with a groan, followed by, "Spare me! Mystra's got nothing on you, Druhallen, when it comes to weaving mismatched strands. Both of you would like nothing better than to be cooped up for the winter with nothing to do but pore over a spellbook. Gods know, Parnast isn't big enough for real trouble—"

It was an afternoon for misstatements—and not about a wizard's capacity for boredom. Their trio was, in fact, a quartet and their fourth partner was loose.

"Speaking of trouble, Roz, where *is* Tiep?" Dru asked. "Shouldn't he be back by now?"

"I left him grooming the horses. I told him to scrape and rasp their hooves while he's at it. Six horses, twenty-four hooves—I figured it would take him the rest of the afternoon. He's due before sundown; and I reminded him that we hadn't forgotten what happened in Llorkh."

Dru raked his hair anxiously.

"He'll be all right," Galimer interceded. "The problem in Llorkh was that he got lost and asked the wrong people for help. Parnast's smaller. There's only one street, one stable, one tav—"

"Tiep's never gotten lost in his life," Dru shot back. "Tiep gets distracted and then Tiep gets in trouble. The boy is nothing but distraction and trouble wrapped up in skin."

Rozt'a looked out the front door as she said, "He's sixteen. He'll grow out of it, the same way we did when we were sixteen."

No mother could cherish a child more than Rozt'a cherished Tiep. The boy had shown up in the Chauntean temple of Berdusk while she was recovering from her fevered pregnancy. Scrawny as a nestling bird and just as hungry, Tiep had been the perfect target for Rozt'a's thwarted instincts. The priests guessed he was about seven, meaning he was about sixteen now. Druhallen suspected that he was closer to twenty; starvation had a way of stunting a child's growth both in body and in conscience.

With his swarthy skin, curling sable hair, and startling blue eyes, Tiep had the look of a foreigner wherever they traveled. Though charming and graceful, he had the defensive nature of someone always under suspicion, but he'd been clever enough to see a better life for himself when he first saw his reflection in Rozt'a's eyes.

From the start, Tiep had tried to earn his keep through chores and charm. He had his bad days—rather more of them lately than there'd been for several years—but mostly the boy was good company. Unfortunately, he was also an incorrigible thief.

Together, Dru, Rozt'a, and Galimer had been unable to erase the lessons Tiep had learned in the alleys of Berdusk. They gave him all that he needed and more besides. He repaid their kindness with stolen gifts. Folk who made their living by guarding the wealth of others couldn't safely shelter a thief, but there was no sticking place in Tiep's memory for the moral lessons they tried to teach him.

"He's got to be careful in Parnast," Dru said after a moment's silence. "He's gotten too old for mercy. Amarandaris will hang him if he gets caught stealing here."

"I see him," Rozt'a said from the doorway. "He's walking beside a girl."

"Gods have mercy," Dru swore.

He surged to his feet but Galimer beat him to the doorway.

"It was bound to happen," Rozt'a whispered.

Predictably, Galimer saw the situation in its best light: "At least he won't get caught stealing."

Tiep made a fool of his foster-father as he wrapped the girl in a surprisingly mature embrace and kiss. She ran away the instant he released her. If Tiep was disappointed by his light-o-love's bolt for freedom, he hid it well. When he realized he'd had an audience, he add a swagger to his grin.

"Her name's Manya. Her poppa's a farmer here, and her brother's joined the garrison. She tends the geese every morning, but comes into—"

"We're travelers, Tiep." Dru cut the lad short. "And this is a tiny village, a tiny *Zhentarim* village. The fathers and brothers who live here won't take kindly to travelers paying court to their young women. You'll wake up in a ditch, minus your most valued parts."

"I wasn't *doing* anything. I wasn't even *thinking* about doing anything."

"You kissed her." Rozt'a planted her hands on Tiep's shoulders, and he froze beneath her. "Where I come from, that was enough to get you betrothed—or run out of town, if she was already spoken for."

Rozt'a didn't often speak about her life before the road. The youth swallowed hard and tucked his chin down so he didn't have to meet her eyes.

"Manya didn't say anything about that—and she was the

33

one who started talking. There was a bunch of goblins out behind the stable, beggin' and all when she was just trying to get to the charterhouse. I saw that she was scared, so I grabbed a pitchfork an' chased 'em off. What was I supposed to do? Turn my back? How would those brothers and fathers feel if I *didn't*—"

"All right!" Dru snarled. He wasn't in the mood for Tiep's logic. "Rozt'a didn't say you'd done anything wrong! What we're all saying is that we're likely to be in Parnast longer than we planned, so you've got to be extra careful. If you see something lying on the ground, just leave it there and *don't* cross the locals or their daughters. Amarandaris has the first and last word in justice here, and I'm not going to risk our lives or livelihoods to save yours."

"Sheesh! I've got the point. Gods, it was only a kiss, and it was her idea, to thank me for chasing those goblins away."

Rozt'a had closed the door and the room was stifling with raw emotion. Tiep and Galimer exchanged anxious glances. They were alike in important ways: they both valued peace more than victory. Dru wasn't surprised that Galimer broke the tension.

"Other than goblins and girls, how was your afternoon?"

"Did you rasp down their hooves?" Rozt'a added before Tiep could answer.

He knew whose questions came first. "All but Ebony's— she wasn't having anything to do with me around her feet an' it was too hot to argue with her. I'll get her in the morning when she's still sleepy. I got everybody else: Cardinal, Bandy, Fowler, Star and Hopper. Hopper's cracked his left rear hoof. I was going to say we'd have to find a smith and get him shod, but if we're not going anywhere for a while, maybe we can wait an' see if it'll grow out on its own."

Larceny notwithstanding, Tiep was a conscientious youth. He took good care of their animals—especially Hopper, the elder statesman among their horses—and was a better cook than the rest of them combined. This past spring, before they left Scornubel and at Druhallen's suggestion, they'd given him a one-tenth share of their profits.

It had been time to make him a partner, but it had taken away the one threat that always worked with Tiep: the threat of leaving him behind.

With a grin Tiep offered Dru a small, rag-wrapped parcel. "I found this for you."

Warily, Dru accepted the parcel which unfurled in his hands. A lump of black, waxy stuff released its scent into the crowded room.

"Myrrh," Dru muttered when enough of the mournful aroma had hit his nostrils. A small fortune in myrrh. "Tiep, tell me you don't expect me to believe that you *found* this just lying about."

"In the stalls," the lad replied quickly, too quickly for Dru's taste. "Those Zhentarim hostlers, they don't clean the stalls near good enough."

"Tiep!" all three adults spoke as one.

"All right. All right. I won it. I won it fair and square from a hostler. An' he said he *did* find it in the straw after some merchants left yesterday. I figured it was the bunch that ran out on us, and that they owed us, so I made sure I won the bet—"

"You admit you cheated?" Dru challenged. Discipline fell to him. Galimer didn't have the stomach for it, and Rozt'a left bruises when she tried.

"Never!" Tiep replied emphatically. "I *don't* cheat! The guy said he could throw double-three five times running. I let him make his throw four times, then I dared him—my ring for his myrrh—to throw his fifth double-three with *my* dice."

Of course Tiep had had a pair of dice with him.

Rozt'a reached for his shoulders again. "That ring's not yours to sell or game away."

Before they'd set out from Berdusk, Druhallen had enchanted the ring to help them find the boy, if he'd ever truly gotten lost, and to pass him through the wards Dru routinely set around their rooms and camps. In the process they'd discovered that Tiep had another talent beside thievery: he shed simple magics and was particularly hard on enchantments. His talent wouldn't save him from a fireball, but it had forced Dru to enchant an expensive gemstone ring rather than a plain silver band and it had made it impossible for Tiep to follow in his foster fathers' footsteps.

"There was no way I was losing my ring."

"Then you *were* cheating," Dru corrected.

"No way! *My* dice are absolutely pure, honest, all-around square." Tiep placed his hands over his heart for dramatic emphasis. "The hostler was cheating. No way he was going to try to make his throw with square dice. And it wasn't as if the myrrh really *belonged* to him. He didn't even know what it was—he was going to *smoke* it. Can you imagine how sick he'd be right now if he'd tried smoking myrrh? I *saved* that hostler from a really bad night."

The worst part of Tiep's tale was that it was probably true. "You should have taken the hostler and the myrrh to the charterhouse."

"Ri-i-i-ight," Tiep sneered. "And gotten him in all kinds of trouble? And Amandis was going to shout 'Quick, saddle my fastest horse and get this lump of very valuable myrrh back to the idiot who dropped it!'?"

Tiep had a point; he usually did. Dru contented himself with a simpler warning: "That's Amarandaris, not Amandis."

"Yeah, him, too."

"Don't take Parnast lightly, Tiep. We're out of the Heartlands. This is Zhentarim territory, and there's nothing they like better than a cocky, young man."

"He's right, Tiep," Galimer added. "*Lord* Amarandaris might not punish you, if he catches you. He might seduce you into working for him. It's easy to find yourself working for the Network and impossible to stop. There's no 'just this once' with the Zhentarim."

Tiep grimaced. "I'm not stupid. I *won* that myrrh from a damn-fool hostler. How he got it is no concern of mine."

Tiep could seem so sure of himself, so honest and sincere in his protests, but for an instant, as he'd opened his mouth, Dru thought he'd seen a flash of naked terror in the youth's eyes. Maybe they were finally getting through to him.

A man had to be doubly careful with his integrity when he shared the road with the Black Network, paid their tolls and bribes, and knew that every coin in his purse had passed through their hands at least once before it came to him. That was the first lesson that Ansoain had taught him. Druhallen thought he'd kept the lesson close to his heart all these years, but he kept the myrrh, too, and he believed his foster son.

3

30 Eleasias, the Year of the Banner (1368 DR)

Parnast

A storm kicked up that night. While Druhallen tried to sleep, wind howled from the east, from Anauroch. It blew for three days, hot as an open fire pit and sharp with grit. Parnasters, both native and Zhentarim, expertly covered their faces like the Bedine and told their suffering visitors: "This is *nothing*," "Wait another ten days," and "You should have been here last year—we didn't see the sun for twenty days!"

Dru didn't want to imagine a twenty-day dust-storm. Rozt'a, Galimer, and Tiep had replaced the family he'd once had. He'd die for them, if circumstances demanded, but after three endless days cooped up with a sulky youth and a married couple his thoughts had begun to tilt toward murder.

Then the wind backed and died. When Druhallen awoke before their fourth Parnast dawn, silence had replaced the incessant rasping of Anauroch grit on the walls and roof. The air smelled fresh and felt cool. He imagined bathing in a cold stream, rinsing away the yellow dust that stiffened his hair and tightened his skin. Moving quietly, so as not to disturb his sleeping companions, Dru pulled on his boots and inscribed words he couldn't see on a wax tablet which he left on his blanket.

Gone for a walk. Back before noon.

Bodies stirred in the bed Rozt'a and Galimer shared. Rozt'a was almost certainly awake. She held herself a body-guard first, a wife second. Given a chance, she'd have spread her blankets in front of the door and slept there alone. Dru didn't give her the chance and blocked the door with his own body each night.

"I need air," he reassured her softly. "Don't worry."

Odds were she'd be lying on his blankets, in his place, before he took ten steps from the door.

Druhallen wasn't the only one out early, welcoming the changed weather. Laughter surrounded the stables and the charterhouse kitchen. The gate in the narrow side of the palisade was already open. Gatehouse guards hailed Dru as he approached.

He wished them a good day. On a morning like this, with the promise of fair weather brightening the east, Dru could have wished the Red Wizards a good day had a circle of them popped into sight—which, thank all the gods, they didn't.

Ignoring the Dawn Pass Trail, Dru chose to follow the north-wending footpath Parnasters used to tend their fields. A forest—Weathercote Wood—rose beyond the fields. The true Parnasters—the twenty-odd families that had farmed here before the Zhentarim arrived and would continue to do so long after the last Network scheme had fizzled—spoke reverently of their forest. In the charterhouse commons where Dru and other travelers took their meals, the Parnasters said that a visiting wizard should walk as far as the brook bridge at least once before he left the village.

Weathercote Wood was a place marked on better maps. Knowledgeable cartographers agreed it was an enchanted place, though no legends were associated with it, no dragons or treasure, no cursed castles or fallen cities, just the label: "Herein lies magic." Weathercote's greatest mystery was its lack of mystery.

That was fine with Druhallen. He was more interested in the brook than in mystery.

A mounted patrol caught up with him before the palisade was gone from sight. As they passed, they warned him to beware of goblins whose hunger, after three days of eating dust, might be stronger than their cowardice. Most of the riders were Zhentarim in black leather, chain, and carrying crossbows, but a few were Parnasters carrying scythes and pitchforks.

The truth was, Lord Amarandaris had himself a serious goblin problem. Displaced from their homes by some upheaval in the Greypeak Mountains, they were starving, desperate, and just civilized enough to recognize that a village meant food. The native Parnasters were a charitable folk, which had only made things worse. They'd fed and sheltered the first arrivals. Then a second wave arrived, and a third—all expecting the same good treatment and turning surly when the villagers hesitated.

Or so said Tiep's friend Manya, who'd visited their room twice during the storm and whose fears were fast becoming hatreds. She worried what would happen after the Leafall when the weather got wintery and Lord Amarandaris hied himself down to distant Darkhold.

If he were smart, Amarandaris was worried, too.

Druhallen wasn't worried about goblins. He'd pulled a serviceable staff from the firewood pile on his way through the palisade. Goblins, even a pack of them, weren't likely to attack a grown man carrying any sort of weapon, not with bowmen riding the fields. And if the scrawny beggars were so foolish, Dru had the pinch of ash wedged beneath his thumbnail. A few breaths of a gloomy enchantment would quench their fury.

He was well beyond the village but not yet in sight of the Wood when he met a Parnaster coming toward him. The man was bent with age and leading a donkey that all but disappeared beneath a load of kindling.

"Be you bound for the Wood?" the codger asked.

"For the brook."

"Good for the brook! But I'd not be crossing the bridge today, not being a wizard and not seeing a path on t'other side. Maybe not then, neither, depending on the light. Being a wizard, maybe I would, no matter the light. But not without a path. Being a wizard, the Wood's not safe without a path."

Dru understood the words but not their meaning. "I'll mind the path and the light," he assured the codger and kept going.

Beyond the fields the path became a track through wild-flower meadows. Dru thought about the wood-gatherer. If the codger's words had any meaning, then men who weren't wizards shouldn't enter the Wood and those who were should stick to the path. But the codger hadn't gathered his kindling on the meadow side of the brook, which left Dru wondering about the Parnasters themselves.

As far as he knew, the Dawn Pass Trail was as old as men and had always skirted the Greypeaks. It had connected the ancient Netheril Empire, now lost beneath the Anauroch sands, with the Sea of Swords to the west and the Moonsea to the south. Whenever Parnast had been founded, it would have seemed reasonable for the village to have grown up where the trail divided rather than a half-day's journey to the west. It would have been typical of the Zhentarim to re-found the village at that more useful place once they'd come to dominate the area. Gods knew, the Zhentarim weren't averse to uprooting villages for their own convenience.

Sememmon might possess the least brutal reputation among the Zhentarim princes, but that was damning the master of Darkhold with faint praise. Amarandaris would burn the village and march the survivors to oblivion, if Sememmon twitched in that direction. It was that threat of annihilation that gave most Zhentarim villages their bitter, weary atmosphere—an atmosphere notably absent in Parnast. It was as if the Parnasters tolerated the Zhentarim, rather than the other way around.

What would have enabled a few farmers to bind the Black Network to good behavior?

The path cleared a hilltop. Weathercote Wood burst into sight, a lush wall of greenery on the far side of a brook which this late in summer scarcely needed a bridge. On the Parnast side the bridge came down in a gravel-filled ditch. On the Weathercote side, there was untrampled grass and nary a hint of a path.

The light, apparently, was wrong.

Bathing was impossible in the shrunken brook, but Druhallen could, and did, kneel in the delightfully frigid water. With no one watching, he splashed himself until he was soaked to the skin. During the past three days he'd sworn that he'd never complain about cold again, but it wasn't long—not more than a quarter-hour—before he was shivering and headed back to the patch of sunlight where he'd left his boots, belt, and folding box.

Dru watched the forest while the sun dried the clothes on his back. Once, hundreds of black birds took flight at one swoop. They cast a shadow across the sun, but there was nothing magical about crows raiding the grain fields. After the crows, the Wood erupted with a locust racket and, for a moment, Druhallen suspected magic. He rose . . . took a step toward the bridge . . .

The bugs fell silent.

The light wasn't right.

He gave the Wood until mid-morning to reveal its magic. Locusts racketed a few more times and once, when his attention had wandered a bit, a fox poked its head through the thicket. But before Dru could get a better look, it had vanished.

Dru headed back to the village; Weathercote could keep its secrets. Nearing the palisade, he heard shouting and the unmistakable honk of camels: a caravan had followed the storm off the Anauroch. Druhallen quickened his pace, but stopped short once he was through the gate.

Until that moment, Dru would have guessed that a desert caravan held a dozen camels, perhaps as many as twenty. Instead, there were easily twice that—the exact number was impossible to count—each with a pair of desert-dressed handlers and a merchant retinue, and all of them were shouting. Parnast's single street and the courtyard between the charterhouse and its stable had been transformed into chaos incarnate.

A few men, quieter than the rest and dressed in cleaner clothes, made themselves obvious. They were the Zhentarim inspectors, checking every pack and purse, making sure that their master and, especially, they themselves got a cut of the loot.

Loot there was. The riches of Anauroch and the east were on display beneath the Parnast sun: carpets and tapestries, carved sandalwood chests, and brass hammered into shapes both functional and fantastic. Amarandaris would lay claim to the best, but he couldn't keep it all and, like as not, neither he nor his men would find the rarest, the most precious objects the desert had yielded up.

That meant there'd be merchants looking to get out of Parnast as quickly as possible with hired magic that didn't dance to the Zhentarim tune.

Druhallen looked about for Galimer's golden hair and found Rozt'a instead. Their bodyguard was perched on the courtyard fence, absorbed in animated conversation with another leather-clad, sword-wearing woman. She waved as Dru walked by, but didn't invite him over and he didn't intrude.

There were few enough women living Rozt'a's life. When Rozt'a met one, she tended to embrace the woman as a long-lost sister, even if they'd never met before. It was just another of the many things Dru didn't understand about the woman who'd wanted to marry him.

He spotted Tiep. The youth's wild, dark curls were unmistakable amid a clutch of desert-wrapped heads hunkered within a ring of rope-bound chests and knotted sacks. Dru knew what they were doing before Tiep's fist shot up. As best Druhallen could figure, Tiep had learned to throw a pair of dice before he'd learned to walk. The youth knew the rules and strategy of every game played for money. Dru was certain Tiep cheated—luck simply couldn't account for his winnings—but he'd never been able to catch him, and neither had anyone else.

Another slow turn on his heels and Dru still hadn't found Galimer. If his partner wasn't part of the courtyard throng, then he'd already decided which merchant had the most to offer and was inside the charterhouse negotiating over tea and wine. Dru had no intention of interrupting that discussion, either, but he wanted an advance look at whatever had caught Gal's eye. He was halfway to the porch when an unfamiliar voice hailed him from behind.

"Druhallen! Druhallen of Sunderath!"

There was very little about the lord of Parnast that set him apart from other men. Of average height, weight, and coloring, his appearance was easy to describe, easier to forget. It wasn't until he'd closed the distance between them that his dark, predatory eyes became noticeable.

Dru held out his hand, demanding a peer's greeting, which brought a one-beat hesitation to Amarandaris's forward progress, but the Zhentarim lord recovered quickly. He clasped Dru's right hand in his own and swung his left arm out for a hearty shoulder clap which guided Dru toward the eastern end of the porch.

"Druhallen—you're just the man I've been looking for!"

A sharp sting, like that of an insect, only very cold, penetrated Dru's shirt. Another man—a man with no magical talent or training—might have shrugged and kept going. Druhallen knew he'd been touched by superficial spellcraft, probably from one of the many rings Amarandaris wore. Dru himself wore such a magic-probing ring on the middle finger of his right hand. Twisting that hand, he brought the bit of metal to bear above the veins of Amarandaris's wrist.

He learned nothing from the exercise that he didn't already know. Amarandaris was a wizard of middling skill. Most Zhentarim of any stature were at least that good with the craft.

As was Druhallen himself, which Amarandaris should have known, since he'd known about Sunderath.

"We need to talk, Dru," Amarandaris said loudly enough to be overheard, if there'd been anyone else on the porch.

"Let's go inside," Dru replied, leaning toward the double doors to the common room.

Amarandaris clamped his fingers over Dru's wrist. "Upstairs."

Druhallen had the physical strength and, perhaps, the magical strength to escape. He grinned broadly, like a dog baring its teeth, to let Amarandaris know that he'd be polite, but not coerced. The Zhentarim lord returned the grin and released the captive wrist, though he kept a hand on Dru's shoulder.

"I was told to expect a stubborn man," Amarandaris said, pushing Dru ahead of him.

That wasn't anything Dru wanted to hear from a Zhentarim wizard—and he didn't think of himself as particularly stubborn. Cautious. A man who was honest and wise needed to be cautious when dealing with men like Amarandaris. If Dru had been a stubborn man, he would have insisted that Amarandaris precede him up the stairs.

Amarandaris's retreat covered the third floor of the charterhouse, a level that could not be seen from the ground.

From its porch, Amarandaris could see the Greypeaks, Weathercote Wood, and the distant yellow haze of the desert. Two human men sat with their backs to a wall and their faces toward the stairway. They were on their feet with their weapons drawn when Dru first noticed them.

At a word from Amarandaris, they sat again on benches flanking a single door. Dru stepped aside—he would get stubborn before he'd open the door to another mage's private quarters. Amarandaris flashed another grin, released the latch, and pulled the door open.

"Be welcome."

The Zhentarim lord lived comfortably above the charter-house: upholstered furniture, plush carpets, an abundance of colored glass, gold, and silver. Maps hung on every wall, more detailed than most Dru had seen and speckled with knowledge the Zhentarim rarely, if ever, shared. He squinted for a glimpse of Weathercote. The Wood was speckled with yellow and black dots whose meaning wasn't obvious.

Sheets of parchment covered Amarandaris's ebony desk. Three abacuses, each one with a different arrangement of wire and beads, sat on the parchment. A checkered counting cloth was folded in one corner and a set of inkwells sat in another. The inkwells were gilded and sat in a crystal base, but they were functional and well used. Amarandaris worked as hard as any honest man.

On a side table a sparkling sphere kept the air moving and kept it fresh as well—no desert grit rasping Amarandaris's throat or disrupting *his* sleep. Beside the sphere was an enameled tray with a matching ewer and two exquisite blown-glass goblets.

Amarandaris filled a goblet with wine from the ewer. He offered it to Druhallen.

"Sit," the Zhentarim suggested, indicating the largest of his upholstered chairs. "Make yourself comfortable."

Dru accepted the goblet without drinking from it and refused the invitation to sit. Amarandaris filled the second goblet and tapped its lip against Druhallen's before repeating his request:

"Sit *down,* man."

"What do you want?" Dru grumbled as he sat in a different chair. He sipped the wine. It was sweet, fruity, and definitely not local. Poisoned? Not likely; Amarandaris wouldn't be going through his gracious-host rituals if he'd had poison on his mind.

"Word is that you want to go to Dekanter."

That was hardly a secret. The merchants they'd failed to meet could have told Amarandaris that much.

"Until this year the Dawn Pass Trail did wend that way."

"Last year," Amarandaris corrected. He settled in another chair, a twin to Druhallen's except that it stood behind the desk. "Why Dekanter? It's far from the roads you've been working—the roads you worked with Bitter Ansoain."

Druhallen shrugged. He'd never heard that epithet before, but remembered how Ansoain would rant after she'd had too much to drink. It fit, and failed to intimidate him. "Why Dekanter?" he repeated, mimicking Amarandaris's tone. "Why not? It's old. It's *our* history, not dwarves or elves."

"Yes." The word flowed slowly out of Amarandaris's mouth, like the hissing of a large snake. "Very human. One never knows what will turn up at Dekanter. I hear you're looking for something very specific."

Despite himself, Dru stiffened. "An answer: How did she die?"

"Oh, come now, Druhallen. We all know *how* Bitter Ansoain died. You and Longfingers made sure of that. And we know that the Red Wizards killed her; don't tell me you don't know that, too. Would you like to know *why?*"

Dru forced himself to relax with another shrug. "There was more to that bride than we knew—or something in her dowry. Or her Hlondeth suitor changed his mind."

"Let's say he'd incurred debts of a most unpleasant kind, and that he kept his side of the bargain."

Air escaped Dru's lungs. So the Zhentarim named Galimer's mother Bitter Ansoain. So they knew more about her death than he'd been able to learn after all these years. So they'd kept track of him and Galimer and passed that knowledge along to a man like Amarandaris in a village like Parnast, where Dru had never been before. So what? Ansoain herself had said: Assume the Zhentarim know everything that happens and live your life accordingly.

"I pity the girl. May I assume there was a girl? We never saw her."

"A pity," Amarandaris agreed. "You're not looking for her, are you? Not thinking that you can rescue a fair, ill-fated maiden?"

Dru shook his head. "We weren't headed for Thay."

"But you're looking for Thay at Dekanter, yes?"

That was, of course, exactly what Druhallen hoped to find, though he'd scarcely admit it. "For treasure . . . Netherese artifacts."

"A glass disk? A focusing lens? Something that might explain how the Thayans ambushed you or how they control their minions while they're casting spells?"

Their eyes met and locked. To be sure, Druhallen had talked about the disk since arriving in Parnast, but only in their room where he'd laid a ring of wards. He wasn't fool enough to think his wards were proof against Zhentarim spying, but Dru did believe that no one could have compromised his wards without his knowledge and he knew, even as he sat staring at his wine, that his spells were intact.

Of course, his intentions need not have been discovered by magic. Any one of his partners might have talked out of turn. Dru suspected only one of them. If he'd had the power to be in two places at once, the second place would have been in the corner of the courtyard where Tiep gambled, and he would have thrashed the boy without mercy. If Dru had had that power, which he didn't. He was rooted in one place, in Amarandaris's place, and the Zhentarim with the unmemorable face was asking close-to-the-bone questions.

"If you know to ask the question, you know the answer."

"I don't suppose you'd sell it to me?"

Dru set his goblet on the desk and shook his head.

"At least allow me a look at it. I know Dekanter, Druhallen. I know what's been found there in the last two decades . . . and I know who's found it."

"If you knew *everything* that's been found and *everyone* who found it, there'd be no need to buy my disk."

Amarandaris refilled Dru's goblet. "I'm prepared to pay quite handsomely. *We're* prepared, that is. A year's profit, I'd say; a year for all three of you." He held the glass out.

"Then it must not be important. I've never heard of the Zhentarim *paying* handsomely or otherwise for anything you truly wanted."

"Stubborn," Amarandaris repeated and set the goblet down. "Very stubborn. Name your price, Druhallen. Walk out of here with something to show for your efforts."

"My life?" Dru stood up. "My friends' lives? If you know so much about me, Amarandaris, you know I'm not going to bite your bait. I walk out of here with what's mine, or I don't—and I'm not talking about an antique."

"Sit, Druhallen. Sit down. Nothing's going to happen to you or your partners."

Amarandaris's predatory eyes searched Dru's face. He held himself calm and the eyes blinked, the man sighed.

"Stubborn?" Amarandaris mused, as if there were a third party in the room, which was always a possibility. "Stubborn or ignorant? Perhaps if you understood more about our situation—and it is *our* situation, Druhallen—you'd find it easier to cooperate. Let me start at the beginning; we're the newcomers in this corner of the world. The Netheril Empire was founded five thousand years ago out there in what's now the Anauroch desert. Four thousand years ago, a Netherese explorer by the name of Dekanter found the mines that bear his name. The Empire hired dwarves to extract gold, iron, silver, mercury, and platinum, not to mention the finest black granite in the Western Heartlands from the Dekanter Mines."

"I knew all that," Dru complained, "except for the mercury."

"Then I'll jump ahead a thousand years. The ore veins are empty and no one in the Empire wants or needs granite because they're all living in cities that float through the clouds. The dwarves have packed up their picks and the mines are gathering dust when a Netherese archmage reduces his floating city to falling pebbles."

"We'd call the city 'Sunrest'," Druhallen repeated the name he'd learned at Candlekeep. "The proper Netherese pronunciation eludes me, but I know the letters. I could write it down for you."

Amarandaris sat back in his chair. "No doubt you could and no doubt you know that for the rest of the Empire's long life, Dekanter was the place—the only place—where Netheril's mages did serious research and made their mistakes. Think about that for a moment, Dru—may I call you Dru? A veritable honeycomb of wizards. A Netherese Elminster in one corner, a Manshoon in another, and a Halaster holed up down the hall. Its been nearly two thousand years since the floating cities crashed but if your friends at Candlekeep tried to sell you a map of Dekanter, I'm here to tell you it's worthless."

Dru's hand dropped to his belt before he could resist the impulse to move it. The scryer had given, not sold, him such a map.

"Burn it," the Zhentarim advised. "Forget you ever looked at it. The Mines change every time it rains—and it rains all the time at Dekanter. Passages open and close. Things appear . . . and disappear. Sometimes we find bones; sometimes a corpse that's warm and soft. Sometimes we recognize them, most of the time we don't, not by several thousand years. The Netherese played with time and space, Druhallen, and they *didn't* trust their neighbors. Dekanter's haunted, my friend, and that's just the beginning."

Amarandaris sipped his wine, waiting for Dru's reaction which came in the form of a quiet question.

"The Red Wizards of Thay—?"

"—Were the Red Wizards of Mulhorand until a few hundred years ago, and Mulhorand was there the day Netheril died. Do you think you're the first man who's tried to connect Red Wizard magic with Netheril?"

"I never gave it much thought," Druhallen admitted. "I've wanted vengeance for Ansoain, and I want to know how they beat us so easily. Beyond that, I didn't talk about it much—" except to his partners. "After a few quiet years, I didn't think anyone cared—the Zhentarim, the Red Wizards, anyone at all."

"We always care about trade, Druhallen, and the safety of the roads. It's very simple. My associates have watched you indulge your hunches since Bitter Ansoain died. We know you found an artifact, taught yourself the script of Netheril, and nearly beggared yourself at Candlekeep—you should have come to us, Dru, gold would have flowed your way. But Candlekeep couldn't answer your questions—or ours. We suspect—we *strongly* suspect—that you left Candlekeep with a spell that will connect your disk with Dekanter *and* the Red Wizards of Thay."

Dru squeezed the goblet stem and nearly broke it. Tiep wouldn't be so lucky. It had to have been Tiep who'd mouthed off. The boy didn't understand how magic worked and was constantly underestimating, or overestimating, a spell's effects.

"Of course, you've worked alone, in secret, trusting no one with your suspicions—especially the Zhentarim."

The Zhentarim had told a joke; Dru forced himself to crack a smile. "Especially the Zhentarim—for all the good it seems to have done me."

"I'd say it's done you a world of good, Druhallen of Sunderath."

Amarandaris picked up a folded scrap of parchment and
scaled it across the desk. The sheepskin was blank at first,
then a bold, elegant script emerged from a minor enchantment. Though the letters were common, the language was
not. Dru couldn't make sense of more than one word in ten,
and most of those were his own name.

"He takes a personal interest in your progress," Amarandaris said before Druhallen had finished extracting what
little he could from the script. "If I were a wagering man,
which I'm not, I'd wager that he knew Ansoain before she
was quite so bitter."

He was almost certainly Sememmon, Lord of Darkhold,
and the author of the letter in Druhallen's hand.

"She didn't talk much about her past," Dru said and laid
the parchment on the desk.

"Not many of us do," Amarandaris agreed. "Now, can we
get back to business, my friend? Your arrival is not unexpected, but it comes at an awkward time. We, that is the
Zhentarim, find ourselves besieged—"

"My condolences—"

"Are unnecessary. Just now I cannot guarantee your
safety in Dekanter, and, as you can perhaps guess, I'm
obligated to guarantee it. If it were only the Red Wizards
taking advantage of—shall we say some *disruption* in our
regular trade between here and Zhentil Keep on the Moonsea . . . well, I know I can count on you against the Red
Wizards. Unfortunately, the Wizards are the least of Dekanter's problems—or Zhentil Keep's."

The Zhentarim paused and shuffled the papers on his
desk.

"It's Beshaba's backside in Dekanter, Druhallen. War . . .
below the ruins. We had a good trade set up: a few artifacts,
some fur and feathers from the interior Greypeaks, and a
steady supply of starving goblins. They breed like vermin
and never have enough food. We dealt with Ghistpok and
Ghistpok dealt with the Beast Lord. There's always a

Ghistpok on the ground above Dekanter. Ghistpok means chief, or something similar in their language. Ghistpok would sell his own children to the highest bidder, and I imagine that he has more than once."

"Spare me the moral indignation, *friend*. I've got no love for the goblin-kin, but they're no worse than humankind when it comes to buying and selling their own."

Amarandaris tipped his glass, acknowledging the insult. "If Ghistpok's selling his children today, he's not selling them to us. When I came to Parnast twenty years ago, common wisdom was that the Beast Lord was a minor beholder, a very minor beholder. The goblins worshiped him as their god, and the Zhentarim made the usual offerings to keep the peace and maintain our market. Things started changing about seven years ago. Little things—new Beast-Lord rituals. Raiding parties. War parties."

Only the Zhentarim would describe war as a "little thing."

"The Dekanter goblins are fierce; the males are, anyway. Maybe it's their Beast Lord cult, maybe it's the water. Get 'em fired up, point them at your enemy, and they won't quit until they're all dead. In a real fight, goblins last about an hour; demand for goblin war-slaves, as you can imagine, is steady. In Dekanter, Ghistpok's tribe got greedy. They wiped out the other clans, at least the males. The females, the children—they took to the mountains." Amarandaris took another sip of wine and topped off his goblet. "Look around you. Parnast's always had a few goblins. Only a few because, well—" He made a helpless gesture. "This is a free village, Dru. Oh, some of the merchants who come through here peddle flesh on the side and not every scut-driver is on wages, but there's no slave market here. No buying or selling, not of men, or elves, or dwarves—not even goblins. That, my friend, was Dekanter's function; we do *other* trade here."

Dru thought of the Weathercote dots, but now was not the time for curiosity or interruptions.

"Suddenly, we've got refugees—goblin females with their children. The farmers made room at first, but a few became many became the plague you see around us now. Three years ago I went down to Dekanter myself to have a word with Ghistpok. I'd have had a word with the Beast Lord, too, if I could have found him. End the raiding, stop the warfare or else. Ghistpok groveled good, and a month later, our garrison got slaughtered as it slept and two cart trains under our protection never got to Yarthrain. You may imagine I suffered the loss personally. I went down to Dekanter with forty men and a taste for vengeance.

"Ghistpok swore it wasn't him, that demons came out of the ground. They hauled away half his men and all the garrison. He said he prayed to the Beast Lord but by the time the Beast Lord showed up, it was too late. Then he hauled out the last of my men to back him up. The poor fellow was half-dead, but he said the attack was undead and magic. Zombies and ghouls came out of a black fog and left the same way. I put him to the test, to see if his story held up, because zombies aren't demons and my man didn't know why there were no corpses or graves. The test killed him, but the story held. You recognize parts of the tale, don't you, Druhallen?"

Reluctantly, Dru nodded. "Red Wizards. They used a black fog on Vilhon Reach. There were corpses, though—parts of them."

"I thought so, too. I rebuilt the garrison, even armed the goblins and paid tribute to the Beast Lord. The next year they caught a passel of Red Wizards red-handed. My man in Dekanter sent a messenger up the trail with the good news. I went down to do the interrogation myself. This time there were corpses—parts of them. Ghistpok swore my men had turned on one another until not one was whole or standing. The goblins had looted the garrison, of course, but they'd left my dead alone.

"They're a strange breed. Ghistpok's goblins. They said my men had become demons before they died. Goblins are always starving; they'll eat anything, including their own dead, but not anything they call 'demon.' They won't touch a demon, not even to bury it. It's a cult thing, something to do with transformation and deformity. The Beast Lord doesn't tolerate imperfection."

"What about the Wizards?" Dru asked.

"We found bits of them mixed in with the rest. Tattoos, you know. If I believed Ghistpok, whatever possessed my men to kill each other possessed the Wizards, too."

"And did you believe Ghistpok?"

Amarandaris stared into his goblet. "Not until I'd lost another garrison and two more cart trains. I cut my losses and moved the trail. Didn't help with the goblins. They're still descending on us. I interrogate them—or have my men do it for me. Interrogating a goblin is like asking a four-year-old who stole the cream. They're still talking about demons and how Ghistpok's tribe raids everyone else. They're taking males and females now. The gods know what they're doing with them, because there's no slave trade at Dekanter any more."

"Sounds like you've had some difficult explaining to do down in Darkhold," Dru said after a sip of wine.

"Not yet." Amarandaris's smile was thin and anxious. "As I said, it's been a bad year, especially at Zhentil Keep. You're not hearing me say this, but Manshoon and the Council have upped stakes and moved to the Citadel of the Raven, northwest of Zhentil Keep. The dust hasn't settled, but it will and in the same patterns as before."

"Good for the Black Network, bad for you."

Another anxious smile flitted across Amarandaris's face. "That caravan outside is the first of two that will arrive today."

When Dru raised his eyebrows, Amarandaris pointed toward a window where a polished spyglass was mounted in a splendid brass-and-wood frame.

"Another the day after tomorrow, and two the day after

that. I don't mind mules and I don't mind oxen, but I tell you, two camels is one too many and several score of them is insanity. I'll be busy, but in, say, a week everything will be sorted out. The camels will be gone, mules will be headed west, and carts will be rolling south. You'll be with the carts, and so will I. We'll travel together—you and your partners, I and all the men I can spare. When we come to the turn-off, the carts will go down the new trail while the rest of us will take the old one to Dekanter. There's no other way to get there, Druhallen, not for you when I have to guarantee your safety to my superiors."

Dru uttered an oath he'd learned from his eldest brother.

"Perhaps that fate awaits us all," Amarandaris replied without blinking. "But not by my will. Not by the will of my lord at Darkhold. I only want the results, Dru." Amarandaris spread empty hands on the table. "Keep the spell. Just let me share what you learn when you cast it. Give me something useful to take to Darkhold."

"Can't help you, Amarandaris. My advice is, Get a necromancer if you want to know what's been killing your muscle." Dru stood the goblet on Amarandaris's desk. He headed for the door. "Thanks for the warnings though. I'll tell Galimer Longfingers what you've said and that I think we should leave Parnast the way we came."

Amarandaris looked as if he'd just found half a worm in his apple. "I've made you good offers, Druhallen. Think hard. We'll talk again before you leave."

Druhallen marched down the stairs with his heart pounding in his throat. Although Dru's conversation with Amarandaris had touched many sensitive subjects and proved that the Zhentarim had been watching over their shoulders for a good many years, Druhallen was convinced they'd gotten their best information from someone who should have known better. Dru poked his head into the commons, hoping to see Galimer alone at a table, but his friend was elsewhere. From the porch, he scanned the courtyard, looking for Tiep. Lady Luck was watching out for her orphans; despite a thorough search of the yard, Tiep's dark curls were nowhere to be found.

Druhallen was behind the stables by then and rather than wade through the throng a second time, he took the long way home, following the timber palisade and rehearsing the words he'd use to recount his conversation with Amarandaris and his suspicions regarding Tiep.

The palisade path was shadowed and empty. Dru walked quickly, his mind on other things, until a squeal of dire pain halted him. The sound was repeated, louder and more desperate. A pig meeting the butcher, he thought. Parnast had absorbed one caravan since sunrise and another was on the way. The kitchen kettles would be hungry.

He continued a few steps, but the shrieking continued. A butcher wouldn't let an animal suffer; it soured the meat. Druhallen detoured into a maze of sheds and alleys. There was laughter, now, with the squealing. He'd loosened his knife and composed his mind for spellcasting before he came to a wide spot where a handful of men—most of them yellowed with the dust of Anauroch—had gathered at the open door of a chicken coop. The squeals came from within the coop, but no bird made them.

"What's happening here?" Dru asked the nearest man.

"Caught the bastard red-handed."

Never mind that he'd been planning to pound some sense into his foster-son, Dru's immediate concern was that Tiep had gotten caught and, whatever he'd done—even if it were a hanging offense—no one deserved the pain and terror radiating from the chicken coop. Dru shouldered his way to the open door and looked inside.

Not Tiep. Not Tiep.

With the dust and feathers and shadows, Druhallen couldn't be sure what the men were doing but their prey was smaller than Tiep. And, if it wasn't Tiep then, strictly speaking, it wasn't Dru's problem. Some of the men around the coop—perhaps all of them—were Zhentarim of one stripe of the other. With Amarandaris making veiled threats, Dru didn't want or need to get involved with Zhentarim justice. A man couldn't fight every battle or right every wrong—

The victim broke free. About the size of a goat, it charged toward the doorway's freedom and collided with Druhallen, who was blocking it. He looked down: a battered and bleeding half-grown goblin clung to his leg.

"Kick it back over here," one of the batterers commanded.

An ugly, little face, made uglier by blood and bruises, peered up at him.

Point of fact: Druhallen didn't much like youngsters of any species. If he'd known that Rozt'a wasn't going to produce any, he might have agreed to marry her. Children, though, didn't sense his prejudice. They flocked to him like ants to honey. Smudge-faced, aromatic offspring would run away from their mothers for a chance to tug on his sleeve or ask him inarticulate questions. Every time it happened, he felt the urge to pick the little pest up by the neck and toss it into next week . . . and every time he resisted the urge.

He resisted it again.

"You've made your point," he said in his sternest voice.

"We ain't yet," a different man complained. "It's still alive."

Goblins weren't unnatural creatures. They were male and female, like humans, elves, chickens or goats—though from what Dru could see, he didn't know if he was risking his life for a boy-goblin or a girl.

"I said, it's over. I'll take this one back to the charterhouse. Lord Amarandaris can investigate your charges."

Dru knew that Amarandaris would welcome that chore about as much as he'd welcome a punch in the groin, but the name, he hoped, would have a chilling effect on the bullies. It did, for about three heartbeats. Then the man who'd asked Dru to free himself with a kick, made a grab for the goblin's long, twisted ears.

Druhallen had an instant to crush ash between his thumb and middle finger. Darkness like a foggy night in winter filled the coop, but the spell he'd cast was more than illusion of weather. Sadness and lethargy flowed with the fog. One of the men who'd been beating the goblin began sobbing and none of the others tried to stop Druhallen as he backed away.

Gloom continued to grow and thicken. It ate all the light in the alleys. One man ran away screaming. He was the lucky one; the rest were caught up in melancholy that might not dissipate before sundown—close quarters enhanced the spell, making it stronger and more enduring than it would be otherwise.

"Come along, little fellow," Dru said to the goblin still clinging to his leg. "Let's get out of here."

He reached down to pry the goblin free and lift it higher. The goblin trembled and hid its face in the crook of Dru's arm, more like a dog than a child. A naked, filthy, feral dog that reeked of rotted food. Druhallen had just about conquered the need to gag when he felt bony fingers fumbling with his belt.

"Behave!" he scolded, imprisoning its hands within his own.

It began to gnaw on his knuckles and he was tempted to let it go altogether. He should have known better. Goblins were incorrigible. But, having begun the rescue, he held on until they were out of his spells' influence.

"Run off with you," Dru suggested and gave the scrawny child a push toward the palisade.

Naturally, the goblin wouldn't let go of his hands. He didn't know what to do next when a goblin female shot out of the natural shadows. She grabbed the youngster. It shrieked as loudly as it had in the chicken coop then both it and—presumably—its mother were gone.

Dru was more than a little relieved, more than a little dirty, and in a fine mood to tell Rozt'a and Galimer about the day's misadventures.

4

30 Eleasias, the Year of the Banner (1368 DR)

Parnast

Druhallen found it harder to tell Rozt'a and Galimer
that he suspected Tiep had betrayed them than it had been
to listen to Amarandaris create those suspicions. They
didn't want to believe the youth they loved as a son and
brother would snuggle up to the Zhentarim. Galimer had
gotten an unexpected cold shoulder from every merchant in
the morning's caravan and couldn't guess why until Dru's
tale offered an explanation.

"I warned that boy about making friends among the
Zhentarim," Galimer muttered several times before sinking
into a dark silence.

Rozt'a's faith in their foundling was not so easily shaken.
"It could just as easily be our fault. We could have been
overheard after we got here. How many times have I said—
'Don't say anything; the walls have ears' only to have you
tell me not to worry, that you've set wards? You depend too
much on magic, Druhallen. Wards and locks only keep the
honest people out and you're not the greatest wizard who
ever walked. Maybe you're the equal of this Amarandaris,
but who calls the tune for him? Sememmon in Darkhold?

Gods spare us! The Network spies on itself—always has always will. Do you think there's nothing in Darkhold t• break your wards?"

"It doesn't take magic to *break* my wards," Druhalle• shot back. "Anyone can break them. But no wizard—not a• the Network wizards working together—could reconstruc• them afterward, at least not in a way that would fool me fo• a heartbeat. You'd know if I tried to sharpen one of you• knives, wouldn't you? Well, it's the same with my wards. Dru stretched his arms toward the walls. "They're mine• exactly as I set them. No one, not a mouse nor a mage, ha• put an ear to our walls."

"What about a priest," she persisted. "A priest and hi• god. You'd never know."

"A god wouldn't stop with the wards. If Amarandaris ha• been spying on us, he'd have known what the Candlekee• spell could and couldn't do. He thinks it's more potent tha• it is—that's Tiep. That's got to be Tiep."

"The boy's been through a lot," Galimer said from th• corner. "And he's always had a taste for dice. I thought we'• gotten those lessons pounded into his head, but this time it• different. This time he's trying to impress that goose girl."

Before Dru thought through Galimer's implications• Rozt'a's eyes narrowed the way they did when she held he• sword.

"That goose girl," she whispered coldly. "*Manya*. The Pi• take her. She's your spy, Druhallen."

"She's still a child," Dru protested, but he wasn't tha• naive. More than one man had been separated from hi• secrets by a woman, even by a goose girl. "She's Parnaste• I don't know why or how, but I can't believe that a Par• naster would run to Amarandaris."

"Forget Parnast," Rozt'a advised. "I should have aske• questions. I didn't like the look of her from the start—a• shy and helpless smiles. They're the worst. You never see • helpless girl who isn't too pretty by half. Like as not, sh•

caught Amarandaris's eye and now she's working for him, will she or nil she."

Dru shook his head. "The first thing we told Tiep was: never confide in a stranger—"

"There are no strangers in the grass!" Rozt'a shouted, and Dru realized he'd rasped a raw nerve. "Tiep's never had a girl his own age look him in the eye. He's got no defenses against that. She's had him eating out of her hand."

Dru didn't know how far things might have progressed between Tiep and Manya, but both he and Galimer knew for a fact that the goose girl wasn't the *first* girl to make cow-eyes at the youth. He was growing into a handsome man, and he'd always been charming.

Tiep and Manya had spent the past three dusty afternoons together . . . and yesterday he hadn't shown up for supper in the commons. When they'd asked, he'd said that Manya's mother had set out a plate for him.

I couldn't very well say, 'No, I won't break bread with you,' could I? I not supposed to be rude, am I? And the food in that farmhouse was better than the swill we've been getting at the charterhouse.

Dru hadn't said anything when Tiep had made the remark and didn't say anything now, as it echoed in memory. When it came to weaving truth and lies into seamless cloth, Tiep was a born master. The youth could charm strangers, but he was at his best with those who wanted to believe him. If they were smart, he, Galimer and Rozt'a would cut Tiep loose before he brought disaster down on their heads . . .

The thought of abandoning Tiep to save themselves was so unpleasant that Dru turned physically away from it and found himself staring into Galimer's similarly turbulent eyes. If he turned around, he'd be staring at Rozt'a.

Well, a wizard could always study his spellbook. Who knew when meditation on an old, simple spell would yield an insight into a more complex magic or the ability to cast it without need of words, gestures, or reagents? Druhallen hadn't stumbled into any new insights when the supper gong clanged from the charterhouse porch and Tiep hadn't returned.

"I'm going after him," Rozt'a announced.

Her fighting knives shone in the early evening light. Dru recalled, as if from a dream, that he'd heard her sharpening them while he'd been meditating.

"I'll come with you," Galimer offered.

Rozt'a snarled, "No" as she slammed the knives into their sheaths, one on her right calf, the other on her left forearm. "I'll handle this alone."

"Be careful," Dru warned.

She snorted laughter. "A bit late for that. A bit late for all of us. Save me a seat—save two."

In the commons, Druhallen and Galimer did more than save seats. They collected extra portions of bread and stew. The stew had congealed before Tiep came through the door with a grim Rozt'a a half-step behind.

"Sorry we're late," the lad said brightly. "But two Anauroch caravans in one day! I got distracted. You wouldn't believe what they pulled off those camels." He stirred, then ignored, his stew. "You remember those sandalwood boxes Old Maddie sells in Scornubel? I saw boxes like that, only twice as big and half the cost. I was talking to a trader—negotiating—when Rozt'a said you were all waiting on me. The trader says I can have the lot for three blue-eyes with Cormyr mint-marks. The boxes have got to be worth ten blue-eyes in Scornubel—at *least* ten. I said I had to talk to my partners first."

Galimer scowled and Tiep spooned up a mouthful of stew. Dru waited for Rozt'a's version of events. Her lips were set in thin, pale lines, but she said nothing, so the lad's tale might be true. Trading three Cormyr coins in Parnast for ten in Scornubel was worth consideration, but didn't mean their other suspicions were wrong.

If Tiep suspected he was marching toward a cliff, he hid

it well throughout dinner and the sunset walk between the charterhouse and their room. He was the first to speak after the door was shut.

"So, what do you think? I've got one blue-eye set aside. Will you advance me the other two? I'm telling you—Old Maddie will pay us at least eight, or we can peddle the boxes ourselves. I'll give you four for two. It's a sure thing—"

Dru had heard enough. "I had an unpleasant conversation with Lord Amarandaris this afternoon, Tiep."

The lad sobered instantly without taking on a guilty aura. "Problems? Anything I can do to—?"

"I'm more interested in what you've already have done."

"What you *might* have done," Rozt'a corrected. "By accident—because you trusted someone you shouldn't have."

Tiep's eyebrows pulled together. "It's just *boxes*—"

Galimer leapt into the growing confusion: "We may have been remiss in—er, *aspects* of your education, Tiep. Flattery, at the wrong time—You might have been tempted to trade confidences with someone—a woman—a girl—"

"Manya? What's Manya got to do with sandalwood boxes—or some stuffy Zhentarim?"

"That's what we were hoping you could tell us," Dru answered.

Tiep straightened. He'd grown this summer; there was no more looking down on him. They'd come to a serious crossroads. If Dru couldn't trust Tiep the way he trusted Galimer and Rozt'a, the young man was on his own. Worse—if he, Galimer, and Rozt'a couldn't agree on the lad's trustworthiness, then Dru himself might be alone.

He continued, "Lord Amarandaris had a notion of why we were headed for Dekanter and what I'd hoped to do when I got there. I think he could only have gotten that information from talking to one of us—or talking to someone who had talked to one of us."

"He hasn't talked to me about Dekanter," Tiep replied quickly. "And I haven't spilled anything to Manya, either—

not that she'd tell Amandis even if I had. She says he's nothing but slime with legs and hair."

"I trust that you and she were clever enough not to say that where you could be overheard?"

Tiep nodded. "We were with the geese. Geese're almost as good as wards—" A thoughtful expression formed on his face. "Our wards. Maybe someone busted your wards, Dru?"

"My wards are—" He stopped speaking. His wards were suddenly fire in his mind. "A stranger's breaching them right now."

Rozt'a flattened beside the door. She drew her knives. "Amarandaris?"

"Can't tell," Dru admitted. In all his years of setting wards around their camps and rented rooms, he'd had only a handful of opportunities to study what happened when they were breached by uninvited guests. "I don't sense a threat."

"Manya!" Tiep lunged for the door.

Dru whispered the word that lifted the wards. He sagged against the wall when the wasted magic rebounded inside his skull. Stone blind and half deaf, he faintly heard Galimer say—

"Mystra's mercy, who are you?"

Dru pulled himself together, pinched a cold ember from the placket of his shirt sleeve, and thought of flames. When his vision cleared, he'd be ready to hurl fire.

"Sheemzher, good man."

Sheemzher's voice was reedy and foreign. Make that more than foreign as Tiep asked: "*What* are you?"

"Sheemzher serve good lady. Good lady Wyndyfarh."

Dru didn't recognize the name. When he opened his eyes, he didn't recognize Rozt'a either, though it seemed likely that she was the larger blur slamming a smaller blur against the closed door.

"Who sent you?" she demanded.

In plain terror, the reedy voice shrieked, "Sheemzher alone. Come alone, not sent!"

Another thud shook dust down from the ceiling.

"No harm!" Sheemzher gasped. "No harm, good woman! Sheemzher give thanks. Sheemzher give reward. Good sir save child."

"It's a goblin!" Tiep shouted. "It's a godsforsaken goblin dressed up like a little man."

Dru ground his knuckles into his eyes. "If it's a goblin," he said to Rozt'a, "let it go."

"You jest?" she replied, giving Sheemzher another slam for good measure.

"No." There was one last thud as the goblin fell to the floor. "I rescued a goblin on the way back from my meeting with Amarandaris."

"Why?" Galimer asked, and after a pause, "From what?"

"From men—Zhentarim thugs. They were going to tear it apart. I don't know why."

Dru rubbed his eyes some more. They burned horribly, but he could see again—or thought he could. Sheemzher was the strangest creature he'd seen in year. No doubt he was a goblin—nothing else under the sun was quite as scrawny in the arms and legs, quite as jut-jawed ugly, or quite that red-orange color—but he was indeed masquerading as a man in cut-down blue breeches and a fitted, bright-green jacket. Sheemzher even wore boots; Dru couldn't remember ever seeing a goblin wearing shoes, much less black boots with brass buckles. Or a broad-brimmed hat which the goblin scooped from the floor and brandished before him as he bowed.

"Sheemzher reward good sir. Good sir keep generous heart," the goblin said. "Good lady say: May your chosen god bless you with fair fortune." He tamped the hat tight over his nearly bald head.

"Who did you say sent you?" Dru asked after a silent moment.

"Sheemzher serve good lady Wyndyfarh. Good lady in Wood. Good lady not send Sheemzher, good sir. Sheemzher come alone. Sheemzher give reward. Few big men save people."

The goblin dug into a leather shoulder-pouch and withdrew a smaller sack sewn from patterned silk and knotted with silken cord. He offered the smaller sack to Dru who hesitated before taking it. A civilized goblin—a goblin who could meet human eyes without flinching was as extraordinary as his hat. Dru's first thought was that the creature was ensorcelled. He readied the same magic ring he'd used on Amarandaris earlier in the day.

"I'm grateful for your thanks," he said, striving to match the goblin's simple formality. The goblin-kin weren't known for their cleverness. "Your thanks are sufficient. I need no other reward for saving a child."

He wove his fingers past the offering, which he didn't want under any circumstance, and clasped the goblin's empty hand. Druhallen had never taken the magical measure of a goblin before. It was difficult to interpret the sensations that raced up his arm, but they didn't have the signatures he would have expected from a mage in disguise.

The goblin grasped Dru's hand in return and tilted his head up. "Not accept reward, good sir? Not good? Not right? Sheemzher sorry." Ugly as he was, Sheemzher could have taught Tiep a thing or two about pleading. Which was another odd thing as goblins weren't known for their empathy. "Sheemzher give all for child."

Dumbfounded, Dru asked, "I saved your child?"

As hard as it was to accept the hat, boots, and bright-green jacket, it was harder to imagine that Sheemzher was the father of the malodorous creature Dru had rescued from the chicken coop.

"No, good sir. Sheemzher not father. Mother, daughter not belong Sheemzher. Mother, daughter from Greypeaks. Mother, daughter hungry. Mother, daughter make mistake. Big mistake. Sheemzher helpless. Sheemzher pray. Good sir come. Good sir save child. Sheemzher give reward."

Dru shook his head. "Give this to your gods, Sheemzher. I acted for myself." He freed himself of the goblin's hand and the gift.

"Keep it, Dru. We could use a little reward about now," Galimer suggested.

"Yes, good sir. Keep reward. Open reward?"

Rozt'a sheathed her knives. "Oh, go ahead and get it over with. I don't know which is harder to believe: that you rescued a warty runt or that one's come to reward you for doing it. I haven't seen so much color since we left Llorkh."

"Lady Mantis favorite colors. Sheemzher wear favorite colors."

Rozt'a's hands went back to her knife hilts. "Lady Mantis? That's not the name you gave before. You said Windy-something before."

The goblin stiffened and clapped his hands together. "Lady Mantis same good lady Wyndyfarh. Good lady Wyndyfarh same Lady of the Wood. Sheemzher serve good lady. Sheemzher proud."

Dru ceased fumbling with the knotted silk. "Weathercote Wood?"

"Yes, good sir. Good lady Wyndyfarh lives Weathercote Wood. Weathercote Wood magic wood. Weathercote Wood many wonder wood. But good lady Wyndyfarh most wonder, good sir. Most, most wonder."

"Is your lady a wizard?"

"Good lady Wyndyfarh great lady, good sir. All Weathercote people great people. Great, good sir, not wizard. Good sir wizard, yes?"

Without dwelling on the goblin's distinctions between good, great, and the practitioners of magic, Dru reminded himself that if Sheemzher had seen him rescue the child, then he'd probably seen him cast the gloomy spell.

"Please, good sir, open reward?"

Before Dru finished with the knots, Tiep found his voice. "You've *seen* Lady Mantis?"

Tiep's voice broke as it hadn't in years. His normally dark complexion had gone sallow. Lady Mantis must have quite a reputation among the Parnasters.

"Sheemzher serve good lady Wyndyfarh. Good lady same Lady Mantis." The goblin answered Tiep's question but didn't honor him with a "good sir" nor even the "good man" he'd hung on Galimer.

"She's real? She's not just a story?" Tiep persisted.

"What real? All Weathercote people real. What people not real?"

"What's this about a story?" Rozt'a demanded. "Tiep, you look like you swallowed a ghost. What stories have you heard?"

"Stories," Tiep whispered without taking his eyes off Sheemzher. "Lady Mantis comes to the village at night, when someone's sick or dying. She heals them . . . sometimes. But sometimes, she just comes and steals a Zhentarim or two." He retreated toward the wall. "One that *needs* stealing. They say she eats them. They never come back, that's for certain."

That had to be the least believable tale Tiep had ever told. Dru broke the cord knotting up the silk. Four coins clattered to the floor. Three were the angular bits of black metal that passed for currency in the charterhouse. The fourth was bright silver and larger than the others combined.

Twilight had gone to evening and they needed to light the lamp, but even without it, Dru saw knew he'd never seen this coin's like before. No coin minted near the Heartlands bore the sun's face on one side and a dragon on the other. He offered the coin to Galimer who lit the lamp before accepting it.

"Is this what I think it is?" Galimer asked with his thumbnail framing the script beneath the dragon's wing.

"Sure looks like it to me." He left the coin in Galimer's care and towered over the goblin. "Who minted that coin? How did you get it?"

Sheemzher wrung his hands. "Good lady Wyndyfarh send Sheemzher here. Good lady Wyndyfarh give Sheemzher silver. Sheemzher buy food, other things. Sheemzher bargain good, good sir. Sheemzher had too much silver; not now. Sheemzher reward good sir. Good lady not angry. Good lady have many, many coins, good sir. Many, many same silver coins."

Common wisdom said goblins weren't clever enough to deceive a human. Common wisdom also said that goblins scavenged what little clothing they wore and never bathed. Druhallen would wager every last one of the good lady's many silver coins that Sheemzher had nothing in common with common wisdom.

"Where does your lady get her coins?" he asked.

The goblin shrugged. "Sheemzher not know. Good lady know. Good sir ask good lady, yes? Good lady wise. Good lady know Wood. Good lady know coin. Good lady know all. Good sir ask good lady; good sir become wise."

Dru was thinking that Lady Mantis had her own mint somewhere when Rozt'a asked, "What did he give you? Is it an elven coin? Something from Myth Drannor?"

"Better," he replied. "We've seen the script before on an old piece of glass, but this coin could have been minted yesterday." Druhallen looked again at Sheemzher. "Your lady's not using someone else's stamps to mint her coins, is she?"

The goblin shook his head solemnly. "What be stamps, good sir? What be mint, good sir? Sheemzher confused; people not clever. Good lady Wyndyfarh *have* coins. Good sir need coins? Good sir need *special* coins. Good lady help good sir. Good lady kind."

Druhallen threw back his head and laughed. "Amarandaris. He's cleverer than I thought." He looked down on the goblin. "Amarandaris sent you, didn't he?"

"No, good sir. Sheemzher come alone. Good lady Wyndyfarh say, 'Stay out of the way of the Zhentarim. There's no reason for them to know anything they don't expect.' "

When it came to quoting his good lady's speech, the goblin got the words right but used an unfamiliar, lilting accent. Sheemzher was a mystery and so was his good lady. Druhallen exchanged a glance with Galimer; they were both intrigued. They were both wizards; curiosity was their greatest vice.

"Why that coin, Sheemzher?" Dru pointed at the silver in Galimer's hand. "Why reward me with that particular coin? Do all her silver coins look like that one, with dragons and a sun's face. Do they all have that squiggly script around the wing? Do you know what it says, Sheemzher? What it means? Where it's from and how many years have passed since it was minted?"

"Not clever, good sir. People not clever. Sheemzher not clever. Good sir visit Wood, yes? Good sir ask good lady. Good lady wise. Good lady answer."

"Good lady," Dru repeated. "Good lady Wyndyfarh. Lady Mantis. Mantis. That's a bug, isn't it? A bug with big eyes and clasped hands. The Kozakurans put them in cages and keep them as pets. Is that what happened to you?"

"What be Kozakuran, good sir? What be pet?"

"Give it up, Dru!" Galimer advised, slapping him across the back. "You're talking to a goblin! Might as well interrogate a four-year-old! We'll keep the coin—if it's as old as it looks, the dog-face has given us a fortune. If not, at least the silver's pure."

Druhallen had blinked when he heard Amarandaris's words coming out of Galimer's mouth, but there was merit in what both men had said. He took the coin from Galimer's hand. He'd seen ancient coins dug out of the ground. All tarnished and corroded, they didn't look like the goblin's coin. The goblin's coin—Lady Wyndyfarh's coin—shone; its relief was sharp. The coin had to be new; it couldn't have come from Netheril.

"Call it coincidence, Dru, and let it go. We've got more important things to worry about." Galimer cocked his head toward Tiep, who hadn't budged from the wall.

Before Dru could agree, the goblin was tugging on his sleeve.

"Good sir leave Parnast? Good sir *need* leave? Need leave *quick?* Sheemzher know way. Sheemzher know very best way leave Parnast. Sheemzher help good sir. Good lady help; Sheemzher promise."

Rozt'a joined Dru, Galimer, and the goblin at the center of the room. "What gave you the idea that we wanted to leave Parnast?" she demanded coldly.

Sheemzher released Dru's sleeve and backed away. "Good sir meet Zhentarim lord. Go up together. Come down each alone. Good sir angry, not happy. Zhentarim angry, not happy. Sheemzher confused. Sheemzher worry. Good sir save child. Sheemzher understand. Good sir wise; good sir leave Parnast, yes? Sheemzher come. Sheemzher help good sir leave Parnast."

"And get an arrow in my back? You almost had me, Sheemzher. I was starting to believe you. It's dark, the gates are shut. Once curfew's rung around here, the Zhentarim shoot anything that moves."

"Good sir safe with Sheemzher. Good sir and all friends. Not horses. Horses not come. Sheemzher give friends silver coins. Horses safe with friends. Good sir, friends safe with Sheemzher. Good lady give good sir silver—"

"Enough!" Rozt'a shouted. She clamped her hand on the goblin's neck. "It's time for you to leave."

"Sheemzher return before dawn, good sir," the goblin said, wriggling out of Rozt'a's grasp. Things didn't usually escape from Rozt'a. "If good sir ready, Sheemzher lead good sir, friends. Good sir, friends, safe with Sheemzher. Weathercote Wood welcome good sir, friends. Good lady welcome good sir, friends. Sun not set, good lady welcome. Good lady help."

The goblin opened the door himself and was gone.

Rozt'a pulled it shut. With practiced moves, she looped the latch string around the bolt and pulled it taut. "That was no natural creature. If he comes back, he can scream himself blue before I'll let him in. I say, melt those coins and quickly!"

Dru shrugged and handed the coin to Galimer. "What are the chances that it's truly Netherese?"

"About the same as someone called Lady Mantis having a goblin servant."

Tiep stirred. "She might. I could ask Manya—"

"Village talk," Rozt'a sniffed. "Every wood is haunted when you're a farmer."

"Weathercote *is* haunted—well, not quite *haunted*. There's Lady Mantis and the Gray Man and a bunch of others. They're not wizards, Dru, not according to Manya; they're more than wizards. She wouldn't go into Weathercote Wood for love nor money, but her pa said he met the Gray Man when he was young. He showed me an arrow: a gray-metal arrow. Not tin or steel or anything I'd seen before. He told me to try breaking the shaft. I thought he was joking, but I couldn't make it bend."

"What about Lady Mantis?" Dru asked. "I got a look at your face when the goblin spoke that name. If you're in trouble, Tiep, you'd be wisest to tell us everything right now."

Tiep stiffened. "No trouble," he insisted, not altogether convincingly.

Dru thought fast. What they needed to do was get out of Parnast quickly, before discomfort became disaster. He missed the first part of what Tiep had to say about the goblin's lady.

". . . tall, and always wears white. Her hair's white, too, with brown stripes, not up and down, but crosswise."

"Lady Mantis sounds more like Lady Owl to me," Galimer judged. "A woman alone in the woods with a goblin—unusual, yes, but not unthinkable, if she's a wizard, or more than a wizard. I saw you ring the dog-face early on. Anything come of that?"

"Sheemzher's a goblin. I've never measured a goblin. I

didn't sense anything extraordinary—nothing like a stripe-haired woman pretending to be something she wasn't. I believe that he's a servant . . . a minion. I took a walk to Weathercote this morning. You know how a place feels when it feels too peaceful?"

Galimer nodded.

"The forest around here has that feel."

"Forget the forest! Last I heard we had Zhentarim trouble," Rozt'a fumed. "Forget the dog-face and his bug-lady. Forget everything except that he claims he saw Amarandaris looking angry after you left. Are we going to slip out of here tonight?" She confronted Tiep. "You've gotten way too friendly, way too fast with this Manya and her family. They know you're just passing through. There wasn't any good reason for her father to be telling you his life story, or was there?"

The youth screwed his lips into a scowl. "Maybe he didn't want me thinking that his life hadn't been exciting. Look, are we going to cut and run?"

"Tiep!" Rozt'a roared.

"Well, if we're not, and you're done taking my life apart, I'd like to go out—"

His voice faded before he got to the *where* and *why* parts of his desire. Dru caught questioning glances from Rozt'a and Galimer.

"We're not running," Dru decided. "If we run once, we'll be running forever. We'll find a way to ride out of here with our heads up."

"I'll try the merchants again tomorrow," Galimer offered. "Now that I know what we're up against, I might have better luck."

"So, can I go out?" Tiep interrupted Galimer. "And what about the blue-eyes? Can I trade for the boxes?"

Rozt'a planted herself in front of the door. "I don't think that's a good idea."

"Is her word final?" Tiep appealed to Dru and Galimer.

Galimer said, "Yes. You're staying here."

Druhallen surprised himself by saying, "No. What's cut, stays cut. If you're not telling the truth, you're the one who has to live with yourself."

The youth grimaced the way youths had grimaced at their elders since the dawn of time. "I'm fine. What about the blue-eyes? Can I trade?"

That was Galimer's decision alone. The gold-haired wizard studied the rafters, doing calculations in his head. "Against your own share or in common?"

"Common," Tiep said eagerly. "They're good boxes, Galimer. You'd agree if you'd seen them. And not too big. I can nest 'em behind my saddle. It's a good trade."

"All right, you've got your blue-eyes, but not a genuine Cormyr stamp. Give them the usual Zhentarim counterfeits. Odds on, they wouldn't know a true Cormyr coin if it rose up and bit them on the nose. If they do, offer five true-silver falcons and not a thumb more."

"Not a thumb!" Tiep agreed.

Rozt'a looked like a storm about to break, but she stepped aside to let Tiep untie her latch knot. She held the door and her tongue until he was gone.

"What's the matter with the two of you? You know he's not after wooden boxes! I've half a mind to follow him."

Dru cleared his throat. "Go after him now, and Longfingers and I will decide how we're getting out of here while you're both gone."

Rozt'a slammed the door shut. "All right. What's your plan?"

5

1 Eleint, the Year of the Banner (1368 DR)

Parnast, Weathercote Wood

He can scream himself blue before I let him in, Rozt'a had sworn last night before Tiep left the rented room.

She'd been even more emphatic after midnight when he'd returned from a tryst with Manya.

No way, she'd growled as she'd usurped Dru's place at the threshold. *No way beneath the sun or stars that I'm doing* anything *on a dog-faced goblin's say-so. I'll show him the flat of my sword first.*

Tiep had been in absolute agreement. He'd gone to sleep confident that there was no chance whatsoever that he was going off on some early-morning hike into a forest that Manya swore was home to dire and magical creatures. So why was he trudging through dead leaves and treacherous roots behind Druhallen, Galimer, and the dog-faced goblin, with Rozt'a bringing up the rear?

Because Rozt'a had had a dream, that's why. The most reliable, least superstitious among his adults had had a dream in which she met a tall, pale-skinned woman with white-and-brown striped hair and the woman—Lady Mantis—had whispered: *I'm waiting for you. Come quickly.*

77

Rozt'a had awakened them all and shared her dream before it was cold in her memory. Then she announced, *We're taking Sheemzher's offer. We're going into Weathercote Wood to meet with Lady Wyndyfarh.*

Suddenly both the goblin and the wizard-lady had had real names again and Tiep hadn't needed lamplight to see the determined look on his foster-mother's face. Galimer was shrewd and Druhallen could be downright scary when he was casting a spell, but Rozt'a was the warrior among them, the brawler who backed up her words with her body. When she lowered her voice and her eyebrows, you knew you were in for a fight.

Rozt'a had pitched her voice so low that Tiep had known for certain that her eyes had disappeared.

He'd lain very still then, praying to Tymora, the notoriously fickle goddess of luck, that one of his foster-fathers would challenge Rozt'a's declaration. Tiep thought Tymora was on his side when Galimer demurred, saying he had merchants to meet and arrangements to make, if they were going to get out of Parnast without paying court to Amarandaris. Tiep thought that was reason enough to stay out of the woods, but Rozt'a disagreed.

One day. One day, that's all I'm asking. The rest of our time belongs to you—

When Galimer fell silent, Tiep had pinned his hopes on Druhallen. Rozt'a tended to back down from confrontations with Dru, but Dru said he'd take a walk in Weathercote Wood with Rozt'a, with or without the goblin, and regardless of the path or the light. What he'd said didn't make sense, but nobody argued with Druhallen *and* Rozt'a.

When dawn came and brought the goblin with it, Tiep had pretended that he wasn't awake. He'd hoped that Galimer would stay behind with him. It wasn't fair, but the desert trader would give gold-haired Galimer a better price for the carved boxes than he'd give a mongrel like Tiep. But his fantasies of profit had suffered total defeat when the goblin announced that he'd lead them all to his lady's glade or he'd lead none of them.

No problem, Galimer had said cheerfully. We'll go with you, Roz—as long as we're back tomorrow. We can be back by then, can't we? —Good. Give me a few moments at the charterhouse. I'll be back before you get the youngster woken up.

Tiep had clenched his fists beneath his pillow then and he clenched them behind his back now. When they'd given him a partner's share this spring they said his opinion mattered, not as much as theirs, but enough so he'd no longer feel like a child tagging along behind his parents. Tiep had never had the luxury of parents. He'd been making his own decisions as long as he could remember—including the one that took him to the Berdusk temple when he'd heard that a sick lady and her moon-eyed husband were mourning an unborn child and likely to adopt an orphan if an orphan presented himself.

Dru and Galimer were always talking about how Ansoain had died on the Vilhon Reach and Rozt'a described busting her captain's face as if nobody had ever stood up for themselves before. Well, Galimer had been full-grown when his mother died and busting someone's face wasn't worth mentioning unless that someone was twice as tall as you were and four times as heavy. None of Tiep's adults understood that he was older than all of them together. Lately, they'd been whispering about cutting him loose because his notion of risky was bolder than theirs. Maybe he should just leave before they got the chance to slam the door.

Maybe he should have left *before* they started hiking through Weathercote Wood.

It wouldn't have been so bad if they'd been riding. Tiep was used to being astride all day and each of their horses was a sensible creature that took care of itself and its rider on the roughest road. But, no—the dog-face said horses

weren't allowed on the Weathercote paths and that was
that. Horses had four legs, one at each corner. When a walking horse stumbled, it still had three feet left on the ground
to keep it from going *splat!* in the leaves. People had two legs
and when people got tripped up by roots lurking beneath the
leaves, people went down.

Tiep had fallen twice already when he felt his toes catch
beneath another root. Flailing like a tethered hawk, he
managed to land on his rump instead of his face.

Rozt'a offered her hand. "It's your own fault. You insist on
scuffling your feet. Pay attention and you'll stay upright."

Tiep accepted the boost, rejected the advice. "I am paying
attention," he insisted, testing his abused ankle. It was sore
but held his weight. "That's the whole problem. We're being
watched. The trees are staring at us. I'm about ready to
jump out of my skin. We should hie ourselves back to Parnast before it's too late."

She gave him a lethal look. "Don't start with me. You can
spend tomorrow with Manya and tell her how brave you
were in Weathercote, but until then, don't carp about shadows. Quit being a sulky brat and try to enjoy this. Look over
there—have you ever seen a more beautiful tree?"

Tiep had never paid much attention to trees. They were
all green in summer and a few stayed green in winter.
They made shade when they were growing and fire when
they weren't. What more did he need to know? But it was
wiser to sight down Rozt'a's arm than to argue with her.
His eyes came to rest on a tree that was shorter than its
neighbors and speckled with sky-blue flowers, each about
the size of his open hand. For a tree, he supposed that it
was beautiful. Beyond doubt, he'd never seen another
remotely similar and mentioned this to Rozt'a.

"There's magic here," his foster mother explained with
exaggerated patience.

"That's not a good thing, Rozt'a, not for the likes of you
and me. Last night, I told you what the Parnasters say

about this place: folks go in but they don't come out, some-times for years, sometimes never."

Rozt'a scowled. "I'm sure you didn't say that."

"You weren't listening," Tiep lied. "Tymora's tears! I never thought you'd be the one to cave in. You were going to smack the dog-face up if he showed up, remember?"

"I had a dream—more than a dream. I saw her . . . I didn't cave in, Tiep. I'm getting closer to something I never thought I'd find in this life."

Before Tiep could ask what that might be, they both became aware of the goblin hurrying toward them.

"Call out if you need to rest," Sheemzher said, as if it were perfectly normal for a goblin to give orders to humans.

Sheemzher had added a thrusting spear to his blue and green costume. The weapon was a bit longer than the goblin was tall and its gnarled shaft had been oiled so much that the wood was glistening black. Beads, tattered feathers, and strips of fur hung from the cording that lashed the flint point to the shaft. The ornaments rattled with the goblin's every move and effectively drew Tiep's attention from the point.

A single goblin, even one with a nasty spear, was a joke, but a horde of spear-toting goblins was a different matter. Tiep glanced at the trees. He did feel they were being watched. Goblins weren't tree-climbers; at least that's what he'd heard in the cities where he'd harvested most of his education. Before Parnast, he'd never seen a goblin that wasn't a pet or a slave. Such goblins wouldn't have dared to look at Tiep the way Sheemzher did, all impatience and cal-culation.

"I wasn't resting. I stopped to look at that tree over there," Tiep said before Rozt'a could say anything at all. "The one with the big blue flowers. It's some kind of magic tree, isn't it?"

Sheemzher fussed with the brim of his hat and cupped his hands around his eyes. Like elves and dwarves, goblins could see clearly through the darkest night, but unlike those races, goblins paid a price for their night vision. When the sun shone bright, they had to strain to see half of what humans saw.

"Sheemzher not remember. Good lady tell Sheemzher, but Sheemzher not remember. Ask good lady. Good lady Wyndyfarh never forget anything. Good lady remember name, magic."

Druhallen and Galimer joined them. "What's the problem?" they asked with one voice.

"Nothing. I was just going to pick one of those blue flowers so Lady Mantis could tell Rozt'a and me the tree's name."

Tiep hadn't taken two strides toward the blooming tree before Sheemzher was in front of him, flapping the spear. Rozt'a drew her sword—Tiep knew the sound. Dru prepared to cast a spell. There wasn't a sound, though Dru kindled most of his spells with a spoken word. Tiep simply knew when magic was immanent; it was a taste in his mouth, a scent at the back of his nose, a tingle that raced down his spine and up again.

In the beginning, Druhallen and Galimer had hoped his premonitions meant he had spellcasting talent; they hadn't. Tiep's talent was a minor jinx: some simple spells didn't affect him, others went awry in his presence. Dru was good enough at his craft that the jinx didn't matter; he'd fry the dog-face, hopefully before that spear penetrated Tiep's ribs. With Galimer it was different. Galimer's command over his magic was chancy at best and worse when Tiep was nearby, though Tiep privately suspected that his jinx got blamed more than it deserved.

Sheemzher was clever—for a dog-faced goblin. With his eyes on Dru, he lowered his spear and retreated.

"Stay on path," he said in a childish sing-song manner. "Stay safe. Tree there not on path. Tree there not safe. Tree there not belong good lady. Remember! Ask! Stay on path!"

Tiep hadn't cared about the tree, but he wasn't going to be bossed around by a goblin. "Tymora's tears," he complained, sidestepping the spear point. "Who's going to miss one lousy flower? The ground is crawling with dropped petals already."

Sheemzher matched Tiep's sidestep and shoved his spear forward. The sharpened flint pricked Tiep's skin through his shirt. He held his breath, waiting for Druhallen to do something magical.

"It's not the flower, Tiep," Dru said and the sense of immanent magic faded. "It's the path."

"What path?" he demanded.

"Path here! Sheemzher follow path. Follow Sheemzher!" the goblin snarled through his too-big, too-sharp teeth.

He prodded Tiep with the weapon and despite his mind's determination to stand firm, Tiep's body retreated.

"What path?" he repeated. "There's no path, no road. We're just slogging through leaves, trusting a goblin, which has to be the dumbest thing we've ever done." He glimpsed Rozt'a's darkening face and knew he'd said the wrong thing. "The dumbest thing *I've* ever done."

The attempt to mend his fences failed: Rozt'a turned her back to Tiep. Frustration boiled over and he seized the spear. They wrestled for control: a sinewy, dog-faced goblin against a larger, heavier, smarter human. Sheemzher kept his weapon, but only because Tiep flung them both toward the flowering tree.

He had to admire the goblin's consistency. When Sheemzher found himself closer to the flowering tree than to his precious, invisible path, he yelped and scrambled hand over foot to rejoin them. He collapsed an arm's length from Rozt'a, shaking and clinging to his spear with his shifty eyes squeezed shut.

The spear had shed a ratty, white feather. While everyone else's attention was on the panting goblin, Tiep surrendered to temptation and tiptoed across the leaves. Holding the feather by its tip, he called—

"Lose something, dog-face?"

Tiep's words and gestures might have been a spell for

their effect on Sheemzher. The little goblin's eyes popped open, then he brought his weapon to the ready and would have charged—if Rozt'a hadn't seized his collar and lifted him off the ground. His booted feet churned in the air. Tiep began to laugh.

"Get yourself back here . . . *now!*" Druhallen shouted.

Dru had almost as much weight on Tiep as Tiep had on the goblin, so Tiep didn't waste time standing with a feather dangling from his fingers. "I was just trying to be helpful," he lied as he obeyed.

"You're headed for trouble," Rozt'a scolded.

She released the goblin who grabbed the feather and whimpered as he reattached it to the spear.

"Yeah? Well, I'm not alone, am I?"

Rozt'a replied with a flat slap of her sword against her palm.

"Both of you—and you, too, Sheemzher—*settle down!*" Galimer raised his voice so seldom that Tiep scarcely recognized it. "We're here now. We're committed to visiting this lady Wyndyfarh and returning to Parnast before dark. There's no time for nonsense. If the goblin wants us to stay on the path, then we stay on the path. Is that clear, Tiep?"

"What godsforsaken path?" Tiep fumed. He wouldn't win, but defeat had never kept him from fighting. "I don't see any godsforsaken path."

Galimer looked at Dru who shrugged. "Don't ask me. I've been following you and the goblin."

Sheemzher scurried between them. He'd dropped his spear and clawed at his neck. "Path! Safe-passage path. All watch."

The goblin freed a golden necklace from his striped shirt and displayed its nut-sized pendant for close inspection. The lumpy stone was polished, not cut, and about the same color as the goblin's red-orange skin.

"Good lady Wyndyfarh show path. All watch. All look."

The red-orange pendant glowed in the sunlight. When it

was ember bright, similarly colored specks in trees they'd passed and in trees they approached became visible.

"See? See?" the goblin asked. "Safe-passage path. Good sir safe, good man, good lady, even that one—" Sheemzher pointed at Tiep then he pointed at the blue-flower tree where no ember glowed. "See no path, no safe passage. Tree there not safe. Tree there not belong good lady. Good lady say: 'Stay on my path, Sheemzher. Don't bother the others. Leave them alone. Don't start trouble.' Sheemzher listen. Sheemzher follow path. All follow Sheemzher, yes? No flowers. No petals. Not safe. Not belong good lady."

Druhallen asked if he could examine the pendant and, after a moment's thought, Sheemzher handed it over. As long as the goblin's knobby fingers touched the necklace, the pendant and the markers glowed brightly. The pendant went dark the moment Dru touched it. The markers faded, too, but not so much that Tiep couldn't still distinguish them.

"Interesting." Dru held the pendant to the sun. "Amber—it's warm to the touch—but this color is new to me, and it's remarkably clear."

Interesting was, well, interesting, but amber—clear amber—was rare and, therefore, valuable. Much too valuable to be hanging around a dog-faced goblin's neck. Tiep tried to catch Galimer's eye—to see if they were both thinking about profits—but Galimer's attention was on the pendant. Rozt'a's, too. With all of them distracted, Tiep considered popping a marker out of the nearest tree, but decided to resist temptation—for now. After they'd taken care of Rozt'a and her dream, he'd make the chance to fill his pockets with amber.

Tiep was imagining the expressions on his adults' faces as he told them what the Scornubel jewelers had paid for Weathercote amber when the markers brightened.

"Not belong good sir!" the dog-face protested, fairly climbing into Druhallen's arms to retrieve the pendant.

"Belong Sheemzher. Good lady give. Belong Sheemzher, not good sir."

"Not mine," Dru agreed and replaced the chain around the goblin's scrawny neck. The markers winked out like blown candles. "Interesting. Yesterday morning an old man warned me not to enter the Wood unless the light was right and I stayed on the path. I didn't know what he meant then, but I do now. Can you still see the path, Sheemzher?"

Tiep recognized Dru's patient-parent voice, but the goblin fell for it. He tapped his temple where a few wisps of ratty black hair escaped his hat. "Sheemzher knows way home. If Sheemzher forget, gift show path. Sheemzher never lost here. Good lady not alone here. Others different. Others not welcome Sheemzher, visitors. Stay on path. Safe passage. Always safe passage. Never lost. Stay on path."

"Good idea," Galimer agreed. "And let's get moving along the path ourselves. How much farther is Lady Wyndyfarh's glade anyway? One hour? Two? A half?"

"One hour," Sheemzher answered, returning to his place at the front of their line.

Sheemzher's hour was endless. They walked until the sun was high above the Wood. Tiep had taken Rozt'a's advice to heart. He walked lightly between the trees; the thrill of stirring up the leaves was long gone. There was shade aplenty in the forest, but the heat was oppressive and the only breeze came from the cloud of buzzing, stinging insects that accompanied them.

They'd filled their waterskins at the bridge. Tiep's was empty by mid-morning. His mouth was sour leather before the goblin lead them past a cool-water spring. No one said a word while they drenched themselves and refilled the skins. Rozt'a looked particularly grim and guilty.

Tiep's mind had gone numb. One foot after the other, he watched the ground and paid little attention to the forest. He hadn't noticed that there were fewer trees, more gray boulders until a noise that sounded like a man screaming jolted him out of a hazy, instantly forgotten daydream. His companions had heard the same thing. They were stopped and staring in the same northerly direction.

"What was that?" Tiep asked.

"Sounded like a big cat," Druhallen answered. He turned to Sheemzher. "Are there forest lions in here?"

When the goblin didn't immediately answer, Galimer offered his opinion: "That roar didn't come from any cat."

Rozt'a drew her sword. "What's dangerous around here?"

"No danger here," Sheemzher insisted. "Safe passage." He hunched his shoulder and made the tree markers glow. "Stay on path. No danger."

The goblin resumed walking. He hadn't taken two steps when the sound repeated itself, louder this time, maybe closer.

"Go to ground, Tiep," Rozt'a whispered.

That was his place when trouble blew in. Tiep was neither muscle nor magic and his adults didn't want to be worried about him when they had work to do. Sometimes he resented it; not this time, not after a third scream. The boulders promised some shelter, but the trees offered more.

"Path!" Sheemzher shouted as Tiep bolted for a tree whose branches were both reachable and sturdy. "Safe passage. Stay safe. Stay on path!"

"I'm not leaving your damned path!" Tiep shouted as he made a standing leap for the lowest branch. "This tree's got a marker on it."

Tiep didn't believe the dog-faced goblin's assurances about the path. His faith lay in the damage he'd seen Dru and Rozt'a create with their chosen weapons. They'd triumph over anything a forest could throw at them—and he'd pocket an amber marker on his way back to the ground.

A long silence reigned after the third scream. Rozt'a lowered her sword. When she sheathed it, Tiep was clear to rejoin them. He was calculating the best way to snag the amber when Galimer shouted—

"There!"

Branches blocked Tiep's view. He climbed higher and almost wished he'd stayed put. The screamer wasn't any familiar sort of animal. Long-legged and horse high at the shoulder, it had a short neck and forward-looking eyes. Its snout was short, too, and framed with overlapping tusks that showed pale against its nearly black fur. Tiep guessed it was some sort of overgrown pig, then it raised a front leg and he saw that it had paws, rather than hooves.

Tiep couldn't name any ordinary animal that had tusks and paws. Pigs didn't have paws. Lions and bears were built closer to the ground and didn't have tusks. With the education he'd gotten from Dru and Galimer, Tiep reckoned that some wizard somewhere or when had transformed this beast into being.

When great wizards conjured creatures, they didn't often pay attention to what lay inside their skulls. With mismatches between their minds and bodies, magical creatures tended to be cranky or crazy, and were often both. Hidden though he was, Tiep held his breath. He didn't dare a quick prayer to Tymora. You never knew what a magical creature might be sensitive to, or what might set it off. Smart folk concentrated on blending in with their surroundings. Tiep filled his thoughts with branches and leaves.

The beast reared and screamed. There was magic in the sound. Terror waves washed over Tiep and the trees. He wrapped his arms tighter around the branch and made himself breathe deeply, evenly. That helped against ambient magic, but not against gut-born fear when the beast set its front paws on the ground and shambled directly toward their supposedly safe path.

Rozt'a raised her sword; Druhallen, his arms. His lips moved and a globe of fire leapt off his fingertips. Dru didn't miss. Tiep clung to the branch but kept his eyes open. The tree shuddered when the fireball exploded.

Flame consumed the dead-leaf carpet and tasted the

trees. Smoke billowed quickly and hid the yowling beast. Tiep allowed himself to believe that Druhallen had slain the creature with his first spell, until it charged out of the smoke. It had a clumsy, rocking-chair gait, but it moved quickly, too quickly for Dru who needed a few moments of recovery before he could kindle another spell. Galimer tried . . . and succeeded with a fiery streak that ringed the beast's neck without doing noticeable damage.

The wizards fell back at the last moment. Rozt'a took a swing at the creature's muscular neck as it charged past. Her sword bit deep; Tiep saw the blade disappear in flesh. She would have slain a horse or ox with that stroke, but the Weathercote beast shook her off without breaking stride. She landed on her back with the sword still firmly in her grasp. Tiep noted that the blade was clean—not a smear of blood anywhere along its length. Rozt'a noticed, too, and shouted a warning to Druhallen and Galimer—

"It's sorcerous!"

Their replies were lost in another roar.

The creature was more agile than Tiep would have expected; something—perhaps—to do with having paws, not hooves. Druhallen pelted it with a different sort of fire as it turned. It circled wide and away from Tiep's tree. (Thank you, Great, Kind, and Good Tymora!) But the beast was riled now and wouldn't be driven off. When it had shaken off Dru's second spell as it had shaken off the first and Rozt'a's sword, it squatted back on its haunches and leapt at Rozt'a like the lion Dru had guessed it was.

She danced a retreat, placing herself between Galimer and Dru, keeping herself the primary target while they readied more magic. That was according to plan—when they all in danger, she was pure muscle—a bodyguard and no one's wife. What wasn't according to plan was the dog-faced goblin with his bright-silk garments and stone-tipped spear darting between Rozt'a and the beast.

While Rozt'a cursed louder than the beast's roars,

Sheemzher launched himself and his spear into harm's way. If the goblin had been aiming at the beast's nose, then his aim had been perfect; and if he'd had the sense Great Ao had given an ant, he'd have let go of his precious spear when the creature began tossing its pierced head. But Great Ao hadn't spared sense for goblins and so the fool hung on, even when the beast sat down like a dog and brought its forepaws into play.

Rozt'a ran at it with her sword slashing. She got what should have been a tendon-severing slice across the paw it used to swat at Sheemzher but, as with her first stroke, she scored no lasting damage. In his tree, Tiep recalled that there were some creatures—some men, too—who simply couldn't be harmed by ordinary weapons. Rozt'a's sword bore a small enchantment that maintained its temper and kept it free from the ravages of rust, but it bore nothing that could split the hide of this nameless beast.

Dru shouted for both Rozt'a and Sheemzher to back off and leave him a clear line. Rozt'a obeyed; the dog-faced goblin stayed glued to his spear. As Tiep saw things, Dru-hallen should have gone ahead and kindled another fire-ball. If it roasted the goblin and the beast together, so much the better. But Dru tended toward the high road. Galimer saw the situation Tiep's way, but his spell failed either in his mind or against the beast's magical armor.

Rozt'a moved in to thwack the beast for the third time and grab Sheemzher as she retreated. The damned goblin put up a fight. She couldn't get him to abandon the spear, but their combined weight was enough to wrench it free, giving Dru the clear line he'd wanted. He got off one of his better fireballs—a huge sphere of yellow flame with heat that reached all the way to Tiep's perch. Tiep started counting; he reached twenty before the fire died.

The beast had risen to its four feet, angrier than ever.

Ominous thoughts rained through Tiep's mind: though none of them was hurt, they were in serious trouble.

Druhallen couldn't cast an endless series of fireball spells. Depending on what he expected to be up against on any particular day, he could cast three, maybe four, before his concentration gave out. Not that his fire was denting the monster. Galimer's magic wasn't as potent as Dru's, and Rozt'a's sword might have been a feather for all the damage it had caused. So far, the only lasting damage had come from Sheemzher's spear: the beast's nose leaked a steady trickle of steaming, black fluid.

Death by nosebleed . . . unlikely.

If the beast didn't get bored it would pick them off. Tiep was in favor of sacrificing the goblin, then beating a fast retreat to Parnast, but he couldn't make his opinion heard and, even if he'd been on the ground among them, he knew his adults well enough to know they wouldn't listen. Already, Dru and Galimer had closed ranks with Rozt'a. She'd managed to pass them her fighting knives and they were ready to stand as one to their deaths. According to plan, when they closed ranks like that, Tiep was supposed to try to escape.

Little as he liked the idea of dying, or watching them die, Tiep wouldn't—couldn't—run away. He had a knife, a little knife better suited to carving fruit than monsters, and the will to use it.

After whispering another prayer to Tymora, Tiep dropped out of the tree. The first thing he noticed once he'd picked himself up was Sheemzher backing away from the fight. The damned dog-face could run away—no one expected honor from a goblin—but he wasn't taking that spear with him.

The goblin must have heard Tiep sneaking up on him and guessed why. He tossed the spear away and with his eyes still on the beast, fell to his knees. Tiep headed for the spear which had landed perilously close to one of the fires Dru's spells had kindled in the leaves. As he retrieved it, Tiep heard the goblin whimpering—

"Safe passage . . . Safe passage. Hear Sheemzher, good lady . . . *great* lady. Sheemzher on path! Help Sheemzher, help all, great lady, *gracious* lady."

Pathetic, Tiep thought. *Detestable* and *Not worth killing* raced through his mind also, then he felt a tingling at the base of his neck—Magic, immanent magic on a scale Tiep had never felt before, not even that ill-fated night in Scornubel when he'd tried to rob a disguised Zhentarim lord. He looked up and saw nothing but branches and clear, blue sky. He looked to his right, toward the beast and the battle, and watched in disbelief as Dru's unbound hair fanned out from his scalp. Tiep's hair began to rise a heartbeat later. For an instant the air smelled bitter, then everything became dreamlike.

In Tiep's dream there was dazzling light and noise so loud he heard it in his stomach rather than his ears. A great hand circled his waist, lifting him up and tossing him backward. The dream ended when his shoulders struck the ground. He lay still a moment, wondering if he were awake . . . or dead.

"Tiep! Say something! Can you move at all?"

Rozt'a. Tiep recognized his foster-mother kneeling beside him. She had a cut on her forehead and a big, black smear across her cheek, but her hands were strong as she helped him sit.

"What hap—?"

An important part of the answer was obvious before he finished asking the question. The beast was dead—burnt to a smoldering crisp in the middle of a charred circle some ten paces wide. Galimer and Dru were examining the corpse, gleaning it the way magicians did. All wizards were scavengers at heart. The more magical or unfamiliar an object, the more samples they collected. The dog-faced goblin didn't approve. He tugged at their sleeves as they worked.

Rozt'a interrupted Tiep's curiosity with a hug. "You fell out of your tree, that's what happened."

Tiep knew better. He remembered dropping out of the tree and going after the goblin's spear, which was back in the goblin's possession. He remembered, too, that he hadn't collected the amber marker. If it was all right for wizards to indulge their curiosity, Tiep didn't see why he shouldn't put his knife to good use—

His knife.

It had been in his hand before he'd sailed backward; now it was missing. There was another in his boot cuff, but the missing blade had been Tiep's favorite. Considering where the spear had wound up, he suspected the goblin and vowed a reckoning.

With a shrug he freed himself from Rozt'a's embrace. She looked uncomfortable with her arms wrapped around her own waist and Tiep felt a little guilty, though he'd never been one for hugs. When he'd been younger, he'd endured them but now that he was older and thinking about women himself, he loved his foster-mother best at arm's length.

"What else happened?" he asked, hoping to blunt the silence.

"The Lady Wyndyfarh saved our hides. Druhallen calls it a 'bolt from the blue'—a one-ended bolt of lightning. I call it a miracle. Can you stand? The goblin says we've got to move quickly. He says reavers are the hounds of Weathercote and we'll have a pack on our trail until we reach his lady's glade."

Tiep got to his feet. He was lightheaded, but the wooziness faded before he needed the arm Rozt'a offered. The idea that they owed their survival to a dog-faced goblin burnt his gut and the displeasure apparently showed on his face.

"Sheemzher saved us," Rozt'a chided him. "Maybe you couldn't see, but the three of us weren't getting the better of that reaver. When I put my sword into him, it was like slicing mud and about as effective. If Sheemzher hadn't invoked Lady Wyndyfarh, it would have had us all, maybe you, too. At best you'd be alone. You owe him."

Tiep shook his head which was honest, but foolish. Suddenly he needed Rozt'a's arm to stay upright.

"*Try*," Rozt'a advised. "I know your head hurts and you never wanted to come, but, please, *try* not to be so hateful—"

"I came with you, didn't I?" he grumbled. "I'm not turning around and going back alone, am I? I lost my knife when I fell out of the tree. I need to look for it before—"

"I'll help—"

"I can find it myself."

Tiep didn't dare look at Rozt'a before he stalked toward the leaves where he last remembered standing. The knife wasn't there. Proof, as far as Tiep was concerned, that the goblin had lifted it. But Tiep wasn't really looking for his knife. He wanted amber and he could dig that out with his boot knife. If anyone asked what he was doing—

He looked over his shoulder. Galimer, Rozt'a, and Dru had their heads together, probably talking about him. They wouldn't notice, but the damn goblin was trotting his way.

"You want; Sheemzher has. Sheemzher give."

"I don't want anything from you. Go away," he shouted back.

He did want his knife, but he wanted to pound it out of the goblin's red-orange hide, not take it politely from his warty hands. In principle, Tiep didn't care if Sheemzher watched him pop the amber marker loose from the tree. The word of a human was always worth more than that of a goblin. Everyone knew that goblins lied and goblins couldn't be trusted, except this goblin had successfully invoked Lady Mantis.

Manya said the white lady was one of the powers of Weathercote Wood. As Lady Mantis, she had the power to heal the sick, but mostly she dealt justice to villainous men and visited the dying to collect their final breath. That was how she'd gotten her name—a tall, thin, and pale woman leaning over a dying man with her arms bent in prayer and an inscrutable expression on her face.

Tiep didn't want to meet her.

"Sheemzher call good lady. Sheemzher find knife after. Knife belong, yes?" The goblin held out a familiar knife. "Yours?" he added, the word was unusual for him and he pronounced it wrong.

"Mine," Tiep agreed sourly and took the knife without a hint of thanks. He made a point of wiping it before sliding it into its sheath. "Now, go away."

"Good lady not here. Good lady in glade. Go now. Go there," Sheemzher persisted. "Beyond path here. Beyond good lady. Reaver not belong good lady. Reaver not obey good lady. *Retribution*. Trees not belong good lady. Trees belong path."

Was that an assurance that Lady Mantis wouldn't mind if he helped himself to an amber keepsake? It wasn't a question Tiep could ask, but one he had to answer for himself. He pulled himself up to the branch where he'd hidden and the marker that was in reach above it.

There was a thumbnail-sized bug squatting on the amber. It didn't fly off when he waved his arm over it and brandished nasty claws when he tried to flick it away with his fingernails, so he smashed it with the flat of his second-best knife and wiped the blade on his breeches before using it to free the marker.

The goblin was grinning when Tiep's feet hit the ground again.

"Valuable, yes? Valuable *outside*?"

"Yes, and *mine*. Just like the knife. Don't go getting any dog-face stupid ideas."

"No stupid ideas," the goblin agreed, still grinning like the fool he was.

* * * * *

Sheemzher assured them, again, as they left the killing ground, that they were merely an hour from his lady's glade.

95

He was lying, of course, but closer to the truth than he'd been. They hadn't gone far before the forest thickened and cooled around them.

Dru announced that they'd successfully passed through someone's warding.

"Good lady dwells *here*. Good lady Wyndyfarh. Sheemzher belong *here*," the goblin replied proudly.

Tiep had never encountered *green* in such variety and intensity. The trees were clothed in green, but so was the ground. Moss grew everywhere—even the rocks and tree bark were cloaked in living velvet. Though birds flew overhead, the moist, heavy air hushed their songs. Tiep felt obligated to speak softly when he asked the wizards,

"Is everything here magical?"

"Everything and nothing," Galimer replied, also whispering.

"What kind of answer is that?"

"The truth," Dru said, and ended the discussion.

They climbed a moss-covered stairway carved into the side of a small, steep hill. Rozt'a was in the front, right behind the goblin. She gasped when she reached the top. Tiep understood why when he stood beside her. The hill was the outer boundary of a water garden that was like no part of Faerûn he'd imagined possible. The water in a pond at the base of the hill sparkled—truly sparkled—in the sunlight. The flowers glowed with subtle light and the countless butterflies were brighter than a queen's jewelry. There was a waterfall on the opposite side of the pond and a small, round building beside it. Tiep judged the building a temple, because it had no walls, just white-stone columns and a blue-green metal dome, and it looked like the sort of place where a god might rest his feet.

He'd barely begun to consider the implications of what he saw when a woman appeared in the temple—she must have emerged through the waterfall, though she wasn't dripping. She was tall and thin. Her face was pale and her hip-length hair was cross-striped with white and dusty brown. Even at this distance, her fingers appeared unnaturally long and when she pressed her palms together in front of her, Tiep had no trouble recognizing the Lady Mantis whom Manya had described.

"She's deadly," he heard himself whisper to Druhallen. "She could kill us as soon as look at us."

Dru nodded. "Deadly's not dangerous, if you keep your wits about you and your hands at your side. Is that clearly understood?"

Tiep grumbled that it was and with his thumbs hooked under his belt followed his elders and the dog-faced goblin toward the temple.

6

1 Eleint, the Year of the Banner (1368 DR)

Weathercote Wood

Druhallen took his own advice as they descended into
Lady Wyndyfarh's grove. The rocks and water were natural
enough, but everything else—the trees, the thick moss
carpet, and especially the unseasonable array of flowers—
bespoke a wizard with time and spells to spare. The air
itself was magically charged, and Dru felt vitalized as he
had not been since his visit to Candlekeep years ago. Now,
as then, a wise inner voice warned him that casting spells
in such a place would be the ultimate foolishness.

Dru dearly wanted to cast an inquiry or two. He had a
hunch that some of these plants had sprouted in other
forests far removed from the Greypeak Mountains, far
removed, perhaps, from Faerûn and Toril itself. He would
have given much to know where Lady Wyndyfarh had been
born. The cabinetmaker's son was by nature a prudent man,
a man who lived by his conscience and accepted the disap-
pointments of wisdom. As Sheemzher led them around the
waterfall-fed pool and across a flat-stone ford, he was content with what his eyes could see.

When Lady Wyndyfarh had first emerged from her

sanctuary and Dru had studied her appearance from the hilltop, he'd judged her an elf. As they came closer to the circular marble building where she waited for them, he had second thoughts. True, the lady was of elf height and slenderness, but elves were, overall, a lean, angular race who frequently seemed in need of a few hearty meals. Lady Wyndyfarh had a softer silhouette in the dappled light and her coloring, though very pale, was distinctly unelvish. In Dru's experience, pale elves were moon elves with ash-blue, wintry complexions. Lady Wyndyfarh's pallor had a warmer, faintly russet tone.

The lady's hair, which descended unbound below her hips, was dead straight and wispy in the gentle breeze. It perfectly matched her skin, except where it was striped in a crosswise pattern with darker russet shades. She wore an unadorned, high-necked gown with sleeves that flowed past her fingers. Dru was no expert where it came to cloth, but he'd overheard enough to guess that the fabric was the finest silk and masterfully dyed to blend with the lady's face and hair. Then again, maybe Wyndyfarh's gown hadn't been woven or dyed at all. At a five-pace distance, Dru couldn't say exactly where the gown stopped and the lady began.

Whether by enchantment or nature, Lady Wyndyfarh was a beautiful woman without being either an attractive or approachable one. Her beauty was ageless, which was to say she was almost certainly older—considerably older—than she appeared and a woman of considerable power.

Any man who practiced magic or traveled Faerûn's far-flung roads three seasons out of every year heard stories about strange lands and the stranger races, but Druhallen had never expected to meet someone whose race he could not name. Lady Wyndyfarh reminded him of nothing so much as a goshawk or falcon, an impression fostered by her piercing black eyes. He'd swear there was no colored iris to separate the pupils from the narrow, white sclera. When her gaze landed on him, Dru knew what a rabbit saw when it beheld the hawk.

He was still thinking about raptors when an insect about the size of a bumble-bee but glowing like a pigeon's blood ruby alighted on Lady Wyndyfarh's shoulder. It quickly disappeared within the curtain of her striped hair. A heartbeat later a heavy flying beetle rumbled past Dru's ear. It, too, was jewel-colored—pale aquamarine, rather than ruby— and after settling on the lady's opposite shoulder, it also vanished into her hair.

Lady Wyndyfarh blinked and Druhallen dared a sideways glance. There were many insects buzzing about the grove. Not all of them were living gemstones, but many were. A pair of sapphire flies circled an arm's length above Galimer's head. While Dru watched, one flew toward the lady and the ruby bee rejoined a companion in Rozt'a's hair. Rozt'a did not seem to notice the insects, a final confirmation—as if one had been needed—that the bugs were not entirely natural.

A good many wizards and all half-elves could establish rapport with a familiar creature. Druhallen had tried it twice: once, before Ansoain entered his life, with the family cat and a second time—when he'd doubted the honesty of a merchant who'd hired them—with the man's caged parrot. Neither experiment had proved satisfactory. The cat was easily distracted and the parrot thought only of itself. Dru would grant that Lady Wyndyfarh was a better wizard than he, but not that she could extract useful information from the pinprick mind of a bumblebee.

That she seemed to be doing so deepened the glade's mystery.

When an aquamarine beetle swooped past Dru's nose, he briefly contemplated capturing it—briefly, because it had no sooner disappeared behind his back when Sheemzher got between him and the lady. The goblin, who did not appear to have a pair of insect outriggers, dropped to his knees and raised clasped hands above his head. Lady Wyndyfarh, whose hair still concealed Galimer's blue fly and who knew what else, wrapped her own elegantly pale hands over the goblin's warty, red-orange ones. There was no mistaking, now, that the lady's slender fingers were a knuckle too long or that her dark and sharply tapering nails had more in common with a hawk's talons than his own broad fingernails.

In a more ordinary place, Dru might have been able to sense magic's flow from mistress to minion and back again. In the glade, with its abundance of magic beyond his comprehension, Druhallen knew only that there had been communication and that when she released the goblin's hands Lady Wyndyfarh was once again staring directly at him.

"This man," Sheemzher asserted quickly, scrabbling backward and clasping Dru's left wrist as he spoke, "this man good man, good *sir* man. This man not compelled. This man chose path. This man risk life, save life. Sheemzher reward this man. Sheemzher use coins. Good lady's coins. Pretty coins. Old coins. This man keep *old* coins."

The goblin was breathless and sounded worried. Druhallen steeled himself for something unpleasant when the pale woman smiled.

"So, you've heard of Netheril?" she asked in a voice that was both deep and lyric. "You know its history?"

"A little," Druhallen replied, as breathless as the goblin.

The lady laughed and said, "A little is all anyone knows about Netheril." Her eyes gave the lie to that assertion.

Dru's breath caught in his throat. He had always assumed—even the scryer at Candlekeep had assumed—that the ancient empire had been built and ruled by men, by *human* men and women. Little of Netheril's culture had survived its collapse and even less in its original form. Imagining Netheril from what few fragments remained was akin to imagining a palace from the ashes after it had burnt. When he'd visited Candlekeep, the scholars had shown him one of their greatest treasures, a broken slab of plaster depicting the face of a dark-haired youth with tattooed cheeks and haunted eyes. A prince of Netheril, they said. Princess had seemed more likely to Druhallen's eyes; but he'd taken the portrait's humanity for granted.

The fragment had not included the royal hands.

Lady Wyndyfarh cleared her throat. Dru blushed with shame. Bad enough to get caught with his attention wandering, worse to wool-gather in front of a mind-reader.

"You have left quite an impression in my young friend's mind," the lady said when their eyes met again. "He does not often think of kindness or honor when he thinks of your kind."

My kind? Dru thought despite an intention to keep his mind blank. Was that a confirmation of his ill-timed musings or a taunt? His confusion grew thicker with each passing moment. The lady's speech was faintly, unplaceably accented, but well-constructed, unlike Sheemzher's fractured speech that possessed neither accent nor grammar. Yet she had called the goblin her friend, rather than her servant or familiar; and, though Sheemzher was anxious, he was not afraid.

With so many questions whirling through his mind, Dru lost track of more important things and was taken by surprise when Lady Wyndyfarh extended her right hand, palm down, as a noblewoman might, for a kneeling vassal to kiss. Dru was a freeborn man, obligated by contracts, not blood. He didn't bow to anyone, not for politeness' sake or his life. He hooked his callused thumb beneath the lady's and repositioned her hand before clasping it firmly and pumping it once.

Lady Wyndyfarh's all-black eyes widened slightly, but she accepted Dru's initiative. Her flesh was cool and dry. Her grasp was uncommonly strong. Druhallen was not tempted to use his ring to measure the strength of her magic. When the lady's grip relaxed, Druhallen withdrew his hand quickly. Lady Wyndyfarh's smile broadened. He glimpsed blunt teeth before she turned toward Rozt'a.

"Florozt'a—I know you already."

Rozt'a had no qualms about bending her knee to this strange woman. Somehow that surprised Druhallen. He'd always thought they shared an artisan's aversion to the privileges of nobility. Even more surprising was the worshipful look in his erstwhile lover's eyes when she raised her head. The women gazed silently at each other, and in those moments Dru's judgment hardened. He couldn't believe that Rozt'a would surrender her independence so easily. Then again, Rozt'a did not seem to realize there were two fat and gorgeous bumblebees nestled in her wild hair.

Galimer's blue-fly guardians were buzzing above his head when his turn came to measure and be measured in return. Galimer might not be able to reliably conjure water in the rain, but he was ease and courtesy personified among strangers. His bow was a precise compromise between subservience and mutual respect, and the sweeping gesture with which he raised the lady's hand was so smooth and quick that Rozt'a herself couldn't have said whether her husband's lips had actually touched another woman's skin.

Tiep was the last. He'd folded his arms tight over his chest and retreated as far as possible. Another step and he'd be in the pool. There were no gemstone guardians that Dru could see buzzing around the young man's skull or camped out on his clothing. Belatedly, Dru recalled that Tiep and magic sometimes produced unpredictable results. He sidestepped and draped his arm around the youth's shoulders.

"There's nothing to worry about," he assured Tiep as the lady approached.

Sheemzher also took the necessary strides to intercept his mistress.

"This one not understand. This one sees, takes. This one not ask. This one thinks alone."

Lady Wyndyfarh paused. Her hands disappeared within the too-long sleeves of her gown. She brought her arms together in the posture of Lady Mantis. "What have you taken?"

Druhallen's ears were certain he'd heard the lady speak, though his eyes hadn't seen her lips move. Beneath his arm, Tiep began to tremble.

Mystra's mercy, what have you done? The accusation raced through Druhallen's mind and died unspoken: They'd know soon enough. In the meantime, Tiep's nerves had failed and he needed help to stay upright.

Sheemzher placed his hand over his heart. A hundred bits of amber hiding in the trees and moss came to life. Tiep trembled a moment, clinging tightly to himself, before his arms uncoiled. Looking down, Dru could see firelight shining within the young man's shirt.

"Oh, Tiep," were the only words Druhallen could whisper.

"He said no one cared because we weren't anyplace that belonged to anyone, and that there'd be retribution for what had happened to us—I took retribution of my own, for all those trees that were spying on us—"

Lady Wyndyfarh seemed not to hear him. "You killed," she said in a soft and terrible voice. "You murdered. You defiled." This time Druhallen was certain that her lips had not moved.

Moved by instinct as old as fatherhood, Dru opened his mouth, "We were attacked—"

He got no further in his explanation. The white-clad woman muted Druhallen with a glance that was charged with magic at cross-currents to any magic he had hitherto known. His eyes remained open and his mind was sensible, though time itself seemed to shatter. Lady Mantis extended a wickedly clawed finger toward Tiep's throat. The young man's knees buckled, and he went down like falling water. Rozt'a drew her sword partway but stepped backward, rather than forward. A sparkling black jewel appeared on the lady's knife-sharp claw. It sprouted insect legs and scuttled up her arm. Dru saw it weave through the curtain of her hair and climb into her ear.

At least, Dru thought that was what he'd seen and the order in which it had unfolded, though even as his lungs expelled an ordinary breath, he judged it odd that his mind was filled with crystalline images and no sense that he had blinked or turned his head to capture them.

He *could* turn his head. The notion that Lady Mantis had paralyzed him when she stifled his words was mistaken. He could still speak, if he chose, or raise his arm in defense of the cowering lump of human terror at his feet. The woman's finger still extended toward Tiep, its dark claw had begun to glow. Defense was needed.

The tide turned in Druhallen's lungs. Air, energy, and purpose flowed inward. He folded his arms and retrieved a cold ember from his sleeve. It would be his last fire spell until midnight, but there'd never been a better time to exhaust himself.

Streams of latent flame rushed toward Druhallen. The fireball would be ready when his lungs were full and Lady Mantis would know she'd made an enemy—

"You believe a *goblin* over a man?" Galimer's outrage reached Druhallen's ears as Galimer himself lunged for the woman's throat.

If he'd taken a moment for pragmatic thought, Dru would have known that his fireball stood little chance of breaching Lady Wyndyfarh's protective spells, but Galimer's desperate and purely physical attack had even less hope for success and it placed the gold-haired wizard in the path of Dru's burgeoning spell.

There was no dilemma, no need for a split-second decision. Dru would not harm Galimer. He opened his hand and the unkindled fire dissipated in the air. His body reeled from the shock. Swallowing a spell was more difficult than casting it. Color and contrast faded from his vision, but not enough to free him from the sight of sinuous magic leaping from that dark claw. A cross between spider silk and lightning, Wyndyfarh's magic spun itself around Galimer, swiftly concealing him in a clouded whorl. Foolishly, Dru made a grab for his friend as Galimer's light-shrouded body rose from the moss.

The next thing Druhallen knew, he was on the other side of the pool and his spine ached. He was flat against a rock. Both Galimer and Lady Mantis vanished behind the waterfall. Sheemzher followed them, his arms waving frantically and his hat flying off his warty head. If he'd had the strength—or the spell—Dru would have fried the misbegotten creature as he ran. But Dru's mind was empty of magic—completely empty—and the goblin also escaped behind the waterfall.

With the skirmish over and lost, Druhallen checked himself for unsuspected injuries before standing. Upright, he had a full view of the glade, including Tiep, who hadn't moved from the spot where he'd fallen but was clearly alive. The young man crouched on the moss with his head between his knees, his back to the bright-blue sky. Rozt'a stood beside her foster son. She'd sheathed her sword, but that seemed the limit of her sympathy.

Dru left them alone. He approached the waterfall from his side of the pool. At first glance, there seemed to be a cave behind the cascade. Perhaps there was, the stone he found was black, glassy, and clearly unnatural. He pounded it with his fists and put his shoulder into an accommodating hollow.

"Try magic," Rozt'a suggested from the opposite side.

Her voice was ominously flat. Dru looked to see if she was angry or in shock. He couldn't tell; her face was hidden in shadow.

"I'm done for the day," he admitted and waited for her response, which came in a slow, ragged sigh.

"What happened? One minute he was standing there, the next she'd snared him. I begged her to let him go, and she looked at me as if I were dirt."

Dru searched his memory for the sound of Rozt'a's voice and found nothing. Perhaps she'd pled for her husband

106

after he'd been hurled across the pool, though he didn't think he'd lost consciousness in the air or after landing. Perhaps they'd seen and remembered different things. That implied some potent notions about Lady Wyndyfarh's magical mastery. Dru gave up on the cave-that-wasn't and joined Rozt'a on the temple side of the pool.

"Gal challenged her," he explained. "Something about taking the goblin's word over Tiep's—"

"Damn! A setup!"

She tried to force her way past him to the glassy stone. In a fight with weapons, Rozt'a had Dru beat cold, but he held his ground easily against her half-hearted shove.

"We better talk to Tiep first, before either one of us goes leaping off a cliff. He had something that wasn't his. When the dog-face made the stuff glow, there was something shining in his shirt. A piece of amber, I guess."

"Damn," Rozt'a repeated herself, this time with a scowl in the youth's direction.

"There might be more. Have you noticed the bugs?"

She gave a puzzled shake of her head and stiffened when Dru reached for her face.

"Steady," he advised and carefully—very carefully—mussed her hair.

The ruby bees took flight reluctantly. They wouldn't have flown where Rozt'a could see them if Dru hadn't been insistent with his fanning.

"We've each got a pair of guardians. Spies, I think, for our host. You've got the pretty ones. Tiep had jet-stone beetles. She said something about murder and defiling just before the fat hit the fire. I thought she meant Gal and I and gleaning the reaver—or maybe I thought I could distract her. The boy must have killed one of his bugs, and not by accident."

Rozt'a's scowl deepened. "I didn't hear her say anything like that."

"And I didn't hear you pleading for Galimer. This isn't an ordinary place, and Lady Mantis isn't an ordinary wizard—"

"You're blaming me for this?" She turned that glower on Druhallen.

He supposed there had been a nasty edge on his voice and that, in the unspoken regions of his heart, he did blame her. One thing did follow another and without Rozt'a's dream—*her* change of heart—they'd never have followed the goblin out of Parnast. Still, Dru remembered life with five older brothers and knew that blame grew best in guilty soil.

The bees returned to Rozt'a's spiky blond hair. She didn't seem to notice them.

"What's cut stays cut," Dru said to himself and his one-time lover. "Blaming each other isn't going to get Galimer back."

Rozt'a purged her hostility with a sigh that left her chin resting on her breastbone. "We'd better talk to Tiep . . . find out what he really did . . . what he *thinks* happened."

Dru nodded and followed Rozt'a.

Tiep lay flat against the moss as they approached. He raised his head, revealing the face of remorse which was quite possibly sincere, albeit too late.

"You had to steal some amber," Dru said, a statement of fact, not a question. Tiep seemed to shrink, but that was wishful thinking of the purest, unmagical sort. "What else, Tiep? What else did you do? Think hard—did you step on a bug, a black beetle-y bug?"

If he'd been trying to unnerve their foster-son, Dru couldn't have chosen a better question. He'd seen corpses with better color than what remained in the boy's cheeks.

"Did you?" Rozt'a demanded. Her voice was cold enough to worry Druhallen.

"He set me up. I told him I was going to take the amber out of the tree where I'd hidden during the reaver fight, and he said 'go ahead' . . . sort of . . . the way he says things so you think you know what he means, but later, maybe, you don't. Maybe you misunderstood."

Dru shook his head, a gesture wasted on Tiep, who was staring at the ground. "It's not the amber, Tiep. She called you a murderer. We've got watchers . . . bugs. Yours are shiny black beetles. Do you remember seeing one? Stepping on it?"

The youth's mouth worked silently while he worked up the courage to say, "I smashed one. With my knife. It was sitting on the amber. It wouldn't shoo away, so I smashed it."

Rozt'a moaned and turned away.

"It was a *bug!*" Tiep protested. "An ugly, nasty bug and it wouldn't fly away. All it had to do was fly away . . . or walk. I wanted the amber, that's all. I wouldn't've smashed her damn *spy*, if it had gotten out of the way. I swear—I wouldn't have touched the amber, either, if the goblin hadn't twisted his words around to trick me. They set a trap for me."

"And you walked straight into it."

Tiep accepted Druhallen's conclusion; at least he said nothing to contradict it. There was silence among them until Rozt'a asked, "Why Galimer? Why did she take my husband instead of Tiep? He hasn't stolen anything. He hasn't smashed a bug. Their trap was for Tiep."

Tiep was weak. So was Galimer, in some ways. Dru raked his hair. Sometimes that helped to stir his thoughts. Not this time. "Lady Mantis is different, not human, not elf either."

"Not even close," Tiep agreed. "Too shifty. Way too shifty. Blink and she's a woman with arms and hair. Blink again and she's a hawk the size of a woman with wings instead of hair and the gods know what for arms—except that they end with talons like enough to rip your heart out. I was thinking, maybe she's a *dragon* or a god."

Dru considered the possibilities. Gods had walked Faerûn in recent years and wrought the havoc only their kind could inflict on mortal folk. A year ago, priests of every stripe emerged from their temples to assure those who'd survived that the gods had returned to their proper places and were forbidden to return. Gods in general weren't known for their obedience, but a man had to believe something and Druhallen had believed that he'd get safely to his grave without meeting one on the road, or in the Weathercote glade.

To the best of his knowledge, he'd never met a dragon, but Ansoain had drilled him and Galimer on their salient traits. He replied to Tiep with a shake of his head, "Her magic's different. I can't describe it easily and, Mystra knows, I'm no archmage, but my gut says this lady's on another path altogether. She's tampered with our memories—just reached out and rearranged what we remember. We don't know what actually happened—"

Dru reconsidered. Lady Wyndyfarh had left the *impression* of a hawk in his memory, but he hadn't suspected actual shapeshifting. "Each of us is having a different experience of this place. We don't know what Galimer experienced—I don't know if what I remember him saying is what he truly said. He might not know or remember himself—"

Dru paused uncomfortably. Rozt'a had fixed him in a bleak and withering stare.

"He's alive, Roz."

She radiated disbelief without so much as opening her mouth or raising an eyebrow.

"We've spent too much time together—too much time making magic, or trying to. I'd feel the loss. There's a distance, as if he's on the other side of imagination, but he's there. I'd know. I knew with Ansoain; we both did."

Rozt'a wanted to be relieved. She tried another sigh, but her breath caught in her throat and she hurried away coughing.

"What're we going to do?" Tiep asked when she was out of earshot.

"*We're* not doing anything. I'm waiting until the sun's under my feet and I've got the wherewithal to study up some spells again. Rozt'a's worried sick about Galimer, and

110

you're going to do what I say and stay out of trouble."

The boy shrank again. "It's not right. None of this is right. It shouldn't have happened."

"But it has and what's cut, stays cut."

Tiep twisted the hem of his shirt around his fingers. It was a habit he'd had from the beginning at the Chauntean temple. This time the exercise loosened the stolen amber. The lump bounced to the ground between them and lay there like sin.

"I'm sorry," Tiep said with his arm reaching halfway to the amber. "I didn't—"

Dru cut him off. "Not another word beyond 'sorry.' It's not enough—" The wizard shook his head, at a loss for words himself. "Anything more is too much."

He walked away. Tiep took a few strides after him but, wisely, realized that was a bad idea. Rozt'a had found herself a resting place with a view of the glassy stone behind the waterfall. Dru found a different one at the hilltop where they'd first seen the grove and its marble temple. Tiep took longest to find a spot to sit and wait, but when he did it was on the opposite side of the pool from Dru and on the border between the moss and the trees. Without benefit of conversation, they'd formed themselves into the largest triangle the nearly circular clearing could contain.

Water was no problem—except that they had to drink from Lady Wyndyfarh's pool. For food they had the supplies prudent hikers would carry into the forest: stale bread, smoked meat, slabs of wax-dipped cheese, and such fruits as the local orchards and vines provided in late summer. The quantities would keep their stomachs quiet for a day; not much longer. Druhallen had flint and steel in his folding box, not to mention the script for a spell that would coax flames from swamp wood. He had the makings of snares, as well, though nothing this side of death would induce him to set a trap in Weathercote Wood.

Their waiting time was limited. It took all Dru's strength

not to begin the downward spiral of wondering what he'd do, how he'd feel, when it came to an end.

Twice, as a long afternoon slumped toward twilight, the air quickened and Dru dared a hope that the next act of their isolated drama had begun. Twice the aura faded without any of the other actors appearing on the stage. The clear air cooled quickly once the sun had slipped behind the trees. They'd carried cloaks—extra cloth was as prudent as water, food, or steel. Dru wrapped his tight and hunkered down with his folding box opened on his knees.

A wizard could study magic whenever he chose, but Mystra's dictates for *casting* spells were rigid and inviolable. A wizard's mind could accommodate only so much magic. The exact amount varied from one wizard to the next and, generally, grew larger with time and practice, but every wizard knew his or her limit intimately. Dru had cast himself to an exhaustion that wasn't measured in his muscles and he had hours to wait before he could hope to replenish his mental trove of spells.

For Dru and Galimer, the moments when they could open their spellbooks and make *magic* with the words they read there began precisely at midnight—the moment when tomorrow's dawn was as distant in time as yesterday's sunset. Druhallen knew other wizards who experienced Mystra's dictates differently, but he and Galimer had had only one teacher in their formative years and they experienced the dictates exactly the way Ansoain had experienced them.

Wizards were a superstitious, conservative lot; they clung to reliable routines and shunned change for its own sake. Dru envied wizards who could effectively rest and restore their spell-casting vigor at any time of the day or night, but he'd never been tempted to emulate their habits. Except at midnight, Dru read his spells with his intellect alone and hoped for subtle insights that would enhance his spell-casting acumen.

In Wyndyfarh's glade, even Dru's intellect was weary. He couldn't concentrate on the faintly luminous words carved into the wood of his combination spellbook and reagent box. Her magic hung on every leaf and flower, dusting it with pale green light. Amber markers, like the one Tiep had stolen, circled the pool and highlighted the marble arches of her small sanctuary. All in all, Wyndyfarh's glade was a beautiful place, but beauty was the last thing Druhallen wanted to contemplate.

He closed his eyes and set himself adrift in his memories. Barring his childhood, Dru had very few memories that didn't include his friend. He'd taken it for granted that they'd die or grow old together. It had never occurred to him that he might have to mourn for Ansoain's son.

Midnight was hours away when mist crept into the grove. It dampened Dru's cloak, not his mind, and seemed a natural mist—as natural as anything in Weathercote Wood. Druhallen folded his box and went for a walk around the glade. Tiep was curled up in an untroubled sleep. Dru stood over him, torn between anger and envy. A part of him wanted to use the boy's head as a battering ram on the glassy black stone, but that was a lesser part. The greater part offered absolution in pure self-interest; his heart couldn't contemplate another loss.

Rozt'a hadn't moved from her post outside the sealed cave. Not surprisingly, the mist was thickest there. At arm's length, Druhallen could scarcely see her face in the faint amber-and-green light. He didn't need to. Her sunken silhouette told him everything he needed to know.

"We'll find a way," he promised softly.

She answered with silence, and Dru completed his circuit the same way. The midnight moment came without warning, as it always did. His mind was once again receptive to magical instruction. He unfolded his box. If true learning had been the order of the night, Druhallen would have been in a bad way, but for his tried-and-true spells—his gloomy

113

pall and the various types of fire—habit sufficed. Intention alone was almost enough. Someday, some midnight, he'd manage to recall them without opening the box . . . but not this night. This night Druhallen left nothing to chance.

Dru would swear his eyes never closed after that and that he passed the quiet deadwatch hours fighting both sides of a private war between mourning and not mourning. He failed, though, to notice the sun's rise or the mist's dissipation and his night-chilled limbs were aching stiff when he straightened them. Rozt'a and Tiep were already awake. They sat beside the waterfall, sharing breakfast and making no noise that reached Druhallen's ears.

Considering the mysteries they faced, Dru could be grateful for sleep he didn't remember and dreams that had seemed like memories—until he saw a feather in the moss at his feet. It was a blue-green feather and it seemed safe to assume it had fallen from Sheemzher's outlandish hat. He imagined himself dozing and the goblin standing near—as Dru had stood near Tiep.

The image disturbed Druhallen not because he despised or feared goblins but because Sheemzher was so unlike the little halfwits he'd previously known. The world wasn't ready for thoughtful goblins.

Dru pulled the feather through a partially closed fist and past his magic-sensitive ring. It sparked no alarms against his flesh, but he hadn't expected it to. The ring worked best on living creatures. He'd need a day alone and a mind filled with different spells than those he'd memorized at midnight to unravel any substantial enchantment, assuming that Wyndyfarh's spells weren't so far beyond his comprehension that he could not detect them.

With that thought in mind, Dru's conscience advised leaving the feather where it had fallen. They'd all had an object lesson in the risks associated with stealing from Lady Mantis. It was a rare wizard who outgrew the recklessness of his youth, and Druhallen tucked the feather gently into his pack and hoisted it across his shoulder.

Rozt'a and Tiep noticed him when he was halfway down the hill. They both wore anxious, haunted expressions but seemed to have rebuilt their bridges. That impression was confirmed when Tiep, but not Rozt'a, clambered to his feet as he approached.

Tiep looked Dru square in the eye and announced, "I'm sorry."

"You should be," Dru agreed, taking his cues from Rozt'a who'd developed an unexpected interest in a cheese rind.

"Look," the youth continued, "I know it was my fault. Taking that amber wasn't just wrong, it was stupid—the stupidest thing I've ever done in my whole life. I'd give anything to go back there and just walk away from that tree with nothing to show for it, but I can't do that. I can't do anything except say my prayers to Tymora—which I did all night. I didn't sleep a wink. I know you can't forgive me, not now or ever. I'm not asking that, but, please Dru, don't throw me out. I can never make it up, but I'll try. I swear to Tymora—may She hear my words and hold me to them— I'm a changed man. I'm never going to do something stupid again."

Druhallen considered a number of replies. The boy was lying. Dru had seen him fast asleep, but maybe—considering that he, himself, had missed the sunrise and the goblin—Tiep deserved the benefit of doubt on that score. More significantly, he seemed more chastened by the consequences of his theft than by the wrongness of it. And most significant of all, even if Tiep were completely sincere, he was making a promise he couldn't keep. To be alive was to be stupid once in a while.

Rozt'a had gnawed one last mouthful of cheese from the rind and was chewing it slowly. Her face was without expression, but she was watching him carefully. Realistically, her foster son's fate and possibly her own future hung on Dru's next words.

He settled on, "We'll see," which sounded more evasive than he'd intended. "We have to get Galimer back before we start talking about the future."

Tiep had hoped for more and tried to swallow his disappointment. His silence would count in his favor when the time for reckoning did arrive. Rozt'a's attention had changed focus when she heard Galimer's name.

"Do you have a plan now that you've read up on your magic again?" she demanded.

Dru shrugged uncomfortably. "I'm ready to give it a try."

They followed him behind the waterfall where Dru took a stick of beeswax from his folding box and drew an eye-high, wrist-to-elbow diameter circle on the glassy stone. He uttered the Auld Thorassic word for "revelation." The wax sizzled like fat in a pan and gave off the scents of clover and roses. It was quite impressive but not notably successful. Dru's most reliable method for dispelling magic worked best on the spells he himself had cast or the non-specific enchantments that merchants—figuring any protection was better than none—bought by the scroll from wizard shops throughout Faerûn.

The merchants were right about the value of protection, but Lady Mantis was no cost-cutting merchant. The glassy stone didn't budge. For a moment, though, and to Dru's eyes alone, it became darkly transparent. He glimpsed another rocky overhang, another waterfall, and a mossy greensward beyond it.

His spell was already waning, taking the transparent moment with it, when Dru made out three figures near a mirror-image marble temple. Softly striped Wyndyfarh and Sheemzher in his brilliant blue and green were unmistakable. The third figure, a slender, gold-haired hair man, had to be Galimer, but it was a changed Galimer who sat on a bench, slightly apart from the other two, and resembled nothing so much as a living statue.

The last of the wax evaporated with a *pop!* The vision

ended and Dru stepped back from the stone.

"What was that supposed to be?" Rozt'a demanded.

"There's another grove, on the other side. I saw it through the spell. She's got Galimer there with her."

"And?"

"She's got him. They're talking, her and the goblin, not Galimer. Galimer's . . ." He sought words that wouldn't push Rozt'a over the edge. "He's sitting on a bench by himself, watching the waterfall."

"What are we waiting for? Blast this thing and we'll grab him." Rozt'a checked her weapons.

If the best his efforts had accomplished was a few moments of shadowed vision, then there was no way Druhallen could blast his way into Wyndyfarh's inner grove. He couldn't tell Rozt'a that, not yet.

"We're waiting to see if she'll come to us. A little restraint on our part—"

Dru got no farther with his argument when a damp wind whirled suddenly around them. Instinctively, he blinked and when he looked at the glassy stone again, it was gone. There was no twin grove, only a pitch-black emptiness and the sounds of falling water and steel sliding over oiled leather as Rozt'a drew her sword.

He closed his hand over her wrist. "Not yet."

She made a sound worthy of a lioness.

"We're on her ground, Roz. She can influence everything, even your dreams—or have you forgotten that? Let her come to us, or wonder why we haven't rushed to her. Let her do a little guessing for a change."

Rozt'a frowned, with Druhallen still clinging to her wrist, she shoved her sword home in its scabbard. She gave him a look that said, What's your hand still doing there?

"Take a breath and hold it," he advised and when she'd done so, he cast another spell he'd known for many years but rarely used. The Auld Thorassic word defied translation but it meant something akin to strength-of-mind. Rozt'a's eyes widened as the magic flowed over her. "Just in case Lady Mantis tries to influence you again. To be honest, I don't think it will prevent her from doing whatever she wants, but she won't take you by surprise."

"Thanks, I guess," she muttered, rubbing herself as though she been drenched in a cold, stinging liquid. "Tiep, come over here. Dru's conjured something up for us."

He hadn't conjured anything. He'd learned the spell from a tome of basic abjuration rituals, and he'd prepared himself for only two recitations of it. Tiep's natural resistance to magic was already stronger than anything he could put together from his folding box, but Dru didn't want an argument with Rozt'a—or Tiep. He led the youth away from the waterfall, cast his second strength-of-mind spell and hoped he wouldn't regret leaving himself unfortified against the bug lady's meddling magic.

They didn't have long to wait. Tiep was still chafing his arms when Rozt'a let out a hiss and motioned for them to join her at the cave mouth. Dru rejected her invitation and pointed instead to the ground at his feet. Rozt'a had barely joined them when the tall, pale woman emerged from her cave leading Sheemzher who, in turn, guided Galimer by the sleeve. Dru tried to restrain Rozt'a, but when she saw her husband standing slack-jawed and blinking in the morning sunlight, she broke free. Neither Wyndyfarh nor Sheemzher made any effort to stop Galimer's wife from embracing him.

Galimer was steady on his feet. His balance accommodated Rozt'a's vigorous greeting, but he never looked at her, never acknowledged her words or kisses. After a few moments of hugging a warm statue, Rozt'a released him. She turned on Wyndyfarh.

"What's the matter with him? What have you done to my husband? He doesn't recognize me. He doesn't know me or if he's dead or still alive!" As always, her hands dropped to her sword. She showed five-fingers worth of steel.

Lady Mantis was unimpressed. "Your husband contemplates the paths of his life. It is a long journey and he has barely begun." Her voice was as musical and pleasant as it was imperious. "When you return, he will be ready and waiting for you."

Dru spoke up quickly, before Rozt'a said something they'd all regret. "We're not going anywhere without Galimer."

"Damn straight we're not," Tiep affirmed from somewhere behind Dru's right shoulder.

"Your Galimer's mind is on a journey it very much needs and his body is in no condition to follow you. I am giving you a chance to right the wrongs you've done me. You cannot bring my servant back to life, but you can avenge others against my enemies and return to me with proof that my will has been done."

Considering the lady's magical prowess, that didn't sound like an easy assignment, but if it were the only way to get Galimer back . . . Dru tested his resolve and found that he'd agree to almost anything if it would release Galimer from mindless torpor.

Predictably, Tiep took a more pragmatic view: "If you can't avenge your servants, how in blazes are we supposed to pull it off?"

Lady Mantis studied Tiep with slow menace. "That is not my concern. If you wish to redeem your companion, your path leads beyond Weathercote Wood to the ruins called Dekanter. Sheemzher will guide you there."

When he heard the words "Dekanter" and "Sheemzher," puzzle pieces fell into place in Druhallen's mind. He was tempted to believe Tiep was right: They'd been set up. The goblin had laid his trap—Wyndyfarh's trap—back in their Parnast rented room. The plot seemed perfect, except for one small detail: Tiep's theft had been pure opportunism. There had to be something Dru was missing. In his mind's eye, he recalled the map on Amarandaris's wall and wished he'd made time for curiosity.

While Rozt'a and Tiep sputtered their unwillingness to be guided by a goblin, Dru stood silent, shaking his head. He drew Lady Wyndyfarh's attention.

"Is Dekanter not where you wished to go? I promise you a chance to view the wonders of Netherese magecraft as no human has seen them in four thousand years."

Bitterness and anger got the better of discretion as Dru answered, "Yes, we wanted to go to Dekanter. It was never that much of a secret, but the whole world seems to know now. If you had a commission for us, you could have asked." He nodded his head in oblivious Galimer's direction. "Now it's too late. You've sent our negotiator on a *journey*."

White lightning played across the lady's eyes. "Don't push me," she warned, all soft and pleasant and oozing lethal power.

Dru braced himself for a mental onslaught and wasn't surprised when Wyndyfarh's image went cloudy in his mind's eye. He glimpsed someone who was more raptor than woman, with wings as well as arms and an obsidian beak.

Wyndyfarh warned Dru, "I have set you a task that serves you as it redeems you. Accept it, if you wish to release your friend."

Seeing Wyndyfarh as she truly was—as, perhaps, Tiep had seen her from the start—Druhallen understood that everything else was shapeshifting or pure illusion. Her lips need never move to convey her points. Having seen her in her true form, Dru knew as well, that Lady Mantis wasn't natural or native to Faerûn. He didn't want to do her bidding but to save his friend—?

"Please don't argue with her," Rozt'a pleaded. No telling what Wyndyfarh had put into *her* mind. "We're talking about Galimer here. He'd go to the ends of the world for you, and you know it. If she wants us to avenge one man or one hundred, don't bother her with questions. Just say yes."

120

Druhallen had just decided that Lady Wyndyfarh was mostly hawk in her natural form, but now the face she showed him wore such a satisfied expression that he'd swear she was part cat.

"A wise woman speaks," the lady purred, "but it is neither one man nor one hundred that you must avenge. Save for Sheemzher, my servants are all insects whose minds I have awakened with magic. Many of them fell victim to a great and ancient evil. You will bring me proof that it can no longer harm them."

Bugs! She was sending them off to collect butterflies! Perhaps it was just as well that Ansoain was dead and her son a prisoner. Dru would never live this one down otherwise. "We'll bring them back in a gilt cage," he muttered glumly.

That brought another laugh from the otherworldly woman. "If any of them yet survive—and I doubt very much that any do—they will fly to me faster than you can walk. Bring me the golden scroll that defiled them. The Beast Lord who rules at Dekanter was beneath my notice before he found that Nether scroll. Now he has become a threat. I am not a god, Druhallen of Sunderath. You are wrong there, but I have sworn an oath to Faerûn's goddesses of magic. I may not leave this glade. Bring me the golden scroll of Netheril and you will have done more good than you can measure and I will restore your weak friend to you."

Dru bristled. Never mind that he knew Galimer's faults better than he knew his own and had on more than one occasion hung the same "weak" label on him, but he wouldn't stand for anyone else belittling his friend.

"Galimer Longfingers is worth more than ten of your Netherese scrolls. Just tell us what we need to know about it and we'll be gone—the sooner to be back."

"You know everything that's essential," Wyndyfarh replied with the indignation of a woman unaccustomed to criticism. "Sheemzher knows the Greypeaks and Dekanter. He'll answer your questions."

Druhallen started to say something about not wanting to rely on a goblin, but that was the sort of remark that had gotten Galimer's mind separated from his body. Likewise, Dru stifled the perfectly logical question: If Sheemzher had all the answers, why wasn't he the instrument of Wyndyfarh's vengeance? Rozt'a stepped into the awkward silence.

"How long do we have? How much time before—?" Her head turned toward Galimer and left the question incomplete.

"No harm will come to Galimer while he is with me."

Dru considered that good news, Rozt'a heard it otherwise and, taking a backward step so he could see both her and Wyndyfarh together, Dru understood. Rozt'a had never been a beauty and life on the road was taking a toll on her appearance, as it had on all of them. Her attractiveness— and Druhallen could personally attest that it was considerable—sprang from her competence and spirit. She was at her best in mercenary leathers, with a sword at her hip, and she would have looked ridiculous with long hair, or in a flowing white gown.

But leave her husband in the company of the dangerously beautiful Lady Mantis, a woman of enchanting beauty and wizardly might? That prospect struck fear in Rozt'a's bold heart.

"C'mon," Dru said, prying her attention away from Galimer with a touch. "If we head back to Parnast right now to get our gear and horses, we'll be on our way this time tomorrow and back before the moon turns—"

"Not to Parnast," Lady Mantis interrupted. "The village is too dangerous for you right now. I have sent word. All that you need will be waiting for you outside the Wood. You'll be within the mountains by sunset. Those who pursue you think only of roads, they will not look for you in the mountains between here and Dekanter."

Pursuers? From Parnast? Well, surely Amarandaris knew they'd slipped through the palisade without their promised second meeting. The Zhentarim lord could have translated their absence into a beeline journey to Dekanter. He'd be ahead of them, unless somehow he knew they'd gone into Weathercote Wood first. How or why might Amarandaris know that? What was the trade between the Zhentarim and Weathercote Wood? What was the alliance between Wyndyfarh and the village? Dru sighed; he might never know the answers to those questions.

For now, all he needed to know was that the Network would be looking for him until they found him in Dekanter or elsewhere. The pool of acid in the pit of Dru's stomach grew deeper than he'd believed possible, then he realized that Wyndyfarh had been staring at Tiep when she mentioned pursuit.

It was enough to make a man wish he were on better terms with his gods.

Dru felt a tug on his tunic. He looked down into the goblin's smiling face.

"Good sir not worry. Sheemzher take good care, good people. Sheemzher knows Greypeaks, Dekanter. Sheemzher born Dekanter. Sheemzher marry Ghistpok daughter."

7

3 Eleint, the Year of the Banner (1368 DR)

The Greypeak Mountains

If the Weathercote Wood had been an odd, unpleasant
place for a city-bred man named Tiep, then the interior of
the Greypeak mountains was ten times worse. Two days
out from Lady Mantis's grove, Tiep found himself wishing
that the bug lady had cast her spells on him rather than
Galimer. The life of a mindless statue couldn't be worse
than following a dog-faced goblin on the back route to
Dekanter.

At least the bug lady had kept her word about their gear.
Their six horses, saddled and packed with their gear and a
generous supply of food, had been waiting late yesterday
when Sheemzher led them out of Weathercote—not at the
little wooden bridge where they'd entered it, but at another
spot, farther east of Parnast. A pair of ratty goblins had
been waiting with the horses. Both had run off the moment
they spotted company coming.

Tiep suspected magic and he'd refused to climb into
Hopper's saddle until Dru and Rozt'a had each applied their
specialist's eye to horseflesh and gear. They assured him
than nothing had been tampered with. If Tiep couldn't trust

his foster-parents, then there wasn't anyone he could trust.
He'd lived without trust when he was younger and had no
nostalgia for old times. He'd considered splitting while he
could still find his way back to the village last night, when
Dru was studying his spells and everyone else was asleep.

Manya's kin would give him a roof and meals until he
could put something else together. However, abandoning
the quest to free Galimer from the bug lady was too craven
for his gut to tolerate. For Galimer's sake, Tiep swore an
oath to Tymora. He'd follow the dog-faced goblin to Dekanter, even if it got him killed along the way.

He half-expected death with every step Hopper took.

There were two kinds of traveling in the Greypeaks:
treacherous and weird. The rocky trails were the treacherous part. Little more than glorified ledges, the trails weren't
much wider than a horse's rump. They left Tiep riding with
one stirrup banging into the mountain and the other hanging out over a whole lot of nothing. Worse, the trails weren't
clear. Say what you would about the Zhentarim, if they
claimed a trade route, they sent crews out to keep it clear of
rock falls and water cracks. Here in the Greypeaks, when
Hopper planted a hoof, there was no telling whether the
ground would slip or stay firm beneath it. The horse was
lathered from nerves, and so was Tiep.

Still, he'd rather be up on the ledges than down in the
valleys. The valleys were the weirdest part of their traveling. Tiep had never set foot in anything like the Greypeak
valleys. Neither had Dru or Rozt'a, nor any of their horses.
The goblin had a name for the place, in his own language,
of course. The word sounded like a cat getting sick; a human
tongue couldn't hope to pronounce it. The best Druhallen,
who knew the name of almost everything under the sun,
could call it was bog and forest.

Bog because, once they started seeing the valleys for
what they really were, they could see that the Greypeaks
were a huge bowl, ringed with mountains and part-way

filled with water. The water had rotted some of the inner mountains, turning them into a mare's nest of broken spires and spines. Where the water should have become a lake there appeared to be solid ground. Solid, that was, until Hopper set his hooves on it, then trees as tall as ten men standing together started quaking. The floating forest swayed like reeds in the wind when six horses moved through it.

Tiep had thought nothing could be more sick-in-the-gut scary than the shifty ground—until the dog-faced goblin announced that there were giant leeches *under* the bog. The dragons that Sheemzher said dwelt in the unbroken clouds sounded better than giant leeches. He heaved a sigh of relief when the goblin led them onto the rocks again.

They climbed in earnest after that, crossing the spine of a dead mountain in the middle of the bog. They'd cleared the crest and were on their way down to the bog again when Cardinal—the gelding Galimer usually rode—lost his footing. In less time than it took to scream, the chestnut had fallen into a dry ravine. Bones stuck out of his forelegs. With a safety rope tied between his waist and his horse, Druhallen scrambled down and put the animal out of its misery.

"Helm's mercy," Rozt'a said, with one hand on the rope and the other on Dru's horse. "Be grateful Cardinal carried our gear and not Galimer."

The fall hadn't hurt the blankets and bean sacks they divvied up among the survivors, and Tiep didn't object when Rozt'a decreed that they'd all walk, leading the horses, from there on. Two feet were steadier than four, even in the bog.

Dru and Rozt'a each led two horses, Tiep led Hopper, and the goblin took the point alone. They were in the bog, not all that far from the ravine where they'd left Cardinal, when they heard the hooting and hollering of scavengers. Tiep told himself he wasn't going to look back over his shoulder once they were back on stone and above the quaking tree-tops, but Dru called a halt and he succumbed.

Big mistake. They had clear sight on the ravine and poor Cardinal. The scavengers were more than beasts, less than men. They'd butchered the horse on the spot and were eating him raw. Tiep wanted to say that the scavengers were Sheemzher's kin but the truth was that though the size was about right, the scavengers were uglier than any goblin and *odd*. Most of them were gray, like the mountains, rather than red-orange like Sheemzher. Some of them had faces that thrust out like a bear or weasel's. One had a long furry tail, another, a ratty one, and one had what looked to be an extra arm growing out of its left shoulder. That extra arm didn't have the joints an arm should have, but whipped about like a serpent with a hand-shaped head.

"What are they?" Rozt'a demanded before Tiep could loosen his tongue from the roof of his mouth. Her words dashed Tiep's hope that his eyes were deceiving him.

She'd directed her question at Druhallen, but the goblin intercepted it with, "Demons!"

Sheemzher immediately pulled his hat low over his eyes, as if what he couldn't see couldn't see him either. He scampered ahead to the trail's next bend where he tried to hide behind a rock that was too small by half. "Hurry! Hurry!" he pleaded.

Rozt'a made her way to the black mare, Ebony, and the bow she kept lashed to the mare's saddle. "I'm going to put a little fear into those beasts, whatever they are," she muttered.

"Let it rest," Druhallen told her, kindly but firmly. "He's meat now, nothing more, and you don't have arrows to waste."

"They're not natural creatures, Dru. They shouldn't be tolerated."

Dru had removed the ring he used to ken strangers and held it up to his eye. He squinted through the opening.

127

"Who's to say what's natural and what's not?" he asked cryptically when he'd finished his examination and returned the ring to his finger.

Tiep would have given much to ask Dru what he'd meant by that remark, but there were four horses between him and the wizard. They paid their final respects to Cardinal and headed toward Sheemzher.

It was rock and bog, bog and rock after that. Somewhere above the thick, gray clouds, morning became afternoon. The air heated up, the light breeze died, and breathing got difficult, especially on the bogs. Then it started to rain: a fine, steady rain that threatened to last all day and most of the night, too. Sheemzher's hat looked good enough to steal as Tiep's soaked hair stuck to his face and streams of water ran beneath his clothes to his boots. In no time at all, he had blisters like mushrooms on his heels and toes.

Tiep tried limping, but limping didn't help when both feet screamed. Rozt'a noticed he was lagging and asked what was wrong.

"We've got Galimer's kit. When we stop for the night, I'll mix up a batch of his second-skin lotion and you'll be good as new by sunrise."

"I'm slowing us down. I'd keep up better if I were up on Hopper's back," Tiep replied, angling for a reprieve.

Rozt'a held firm, "The going's worse now that it's wet. We'll hold the pace down. Slow's best in the rain, anyway."

Slow or fast didn't make half the difference that up or down made, with downhill being a lot worse than up. Tiep was sure his toes bled with each downhill stride. He thanked Tymora when the rain stopped. Then the bugs came out and he knew Tymora had abandoned him to Her sister, Beshaba, Maid of Misfortune. The bugs were worse in the bogs. Man, woman, horse, and goblin, they were all surrounded by buzzing, stinging, biting clouds.

They were in a bog when a dragon flew overhead. Tiep didn't actually see the dragon, but he heard its bellow.

There was no mistaking that sound. It awakened primal dread in a human heart and sheer terror in a horse. Bandy, the big mare that toted their heaviest gear, panicked at the sound. Her front end went up, carrying Dru with it, while her hind legs sank into the bog.

Dru could have used some help getting himself and Bandy steadied, but Rozt'a had her hands full with two frightened horses while Tiep had put his extra arm to work grabbing Fowler's lead when that gelding broke free from Dru and Bandy. Sheemzher was useless. The horses didn't much like his smell at the best of times. All together they burned a year's worth of luck before order was restored. Bandy was gray with sweat and Druhallen didn't look much better, but they were both standing steady, both whole.

"I've had enough for one day," Dru said once he'd caught some breath.

Tiep wasn't going to argue, not the way his feet hurt. Sheemzher said they'd be safer on the rock than on a bog, and that wasn't worth arguing with, either, though it meant staggering onward. The goblin eventually got them to a ledge—call it a very hard beach on the shore of a tree-covered lake—that he said was safe.

"Sheemzher make safer," he continued. "Sheemzher go now. Sheemzher back quick."

The goblin and his spear disappeared into the bog. Tiep wanted to follow, but his sore, bleeding feet were glued to the ledge. It was Tiep's regular chore to set the nightly picket line for the horses and, mindful that some might blame him for their misery, he got to work looking for a good place to tie off the rope. Rozt'a took pity on him.

"I'll handle the horses. You find yourself a place to sit. And get those boots off before your feet fester."

Beshaba's mercy—Tiep hadn't considered *that* possibility.

His feet weren't as bad as he feared. He'd lost a slab of callus from his left heel, and the big toe on his right foot was bloody; nothing a slathering of second-skin lotion couldn't handle. Rozt'a dragged their medicine chest over and mixed the lotion in a brass bowl. The most important ingredient went in last: a few drops of sickly green oil from a silver flask embellished with a rose-colored Lathandrite agate. Tiep counted five drops in all and flinched in advance, knowing how badly the potion-drenched cloths would sting when Rozt'a wrapped them around his feet.

"You'll survive," Rozt'a assured him.

Tiep didn't trust himself to answer. He couldn't nod without sending a stream of tears down his cheeks but he only yelped once, when Rozt'a squeezed his big toe, making sure that the lotion worked deep.

Druhallen scrounged wood from the bog-forest—no great challenge there—and got a fire going, which for a competent wizard was no great challenge, either. The wet wood smoked vigorously and the smoke was foul, but it got rid of the bugs. They were glad to have it, at least until Sheemzher returned.

"No flame! No flame!"

The dog-face thrust his spear into the fire and battered it apart. Dru's eyes narrowed and his fists clenched in a way that usually meant a fireball was due. Sheemzher saved himself with a single word and a gesture toward the clouds.

"Dragons."

"What kind?" Dru asked, because it made a difference.

"Big!" Sheemzher replied, which meant, probably, that the Greypeaks weren't home to one of the more benign dragon species.

The bugs came back—with a few thousand of their closest friends. It was a struggle to eat their cold supper without catching a few buzzing specks in each mouthful. Doubly difficult for Tiep because his feet hadn't stopped throbbing and he couldn't escape his bugs, even temporarily, by moving about on the ledge. He'd peeked beneath the cloths a few times: the second-skin oil was living up to its name. Tiep's feet *felt* like they were on fire, but the swelling had already gone down and the raw skin on his left heel was toughening.

Night came sooner than it would have out in the open as the clouds and mountains combined to stifle the sunset. Tiep braced himself for absolute darkness, then discovered that the bog made its own eerie light: lazy will-o'-the-wisps rose from the ground. They swirled higher and higher until they bumped into the clouds where they dissipated slowly.

The result was enough light to see shadows and movement, enough light to watch Sheemzher open up his striped waistcoat—it looked bedraggled now, though the dyes were good and the colors hadn't run together. He fished out something that hung from a cord and writhed. A rat, Tiep realized just before the goblin snapped its neck. He impaled the freshly-killed rodent on his spearhead then used the bloody weapon to draw a perimeter around their camp.

"Do you think that will keep the dragons away?" Rozt'a asked.

"Demons, not dragons. Sheemzher know. Sheemzher remember. Demons not cross blood."

Dru overheard and chortled, "That's a new one!"

Rozt'a silenced him with a well-aimed hiss, then added, "Do you want to draw straws for the first watch?"

"No—I'm awake until midnight anyway. This place isn't what I expected, so I need to make some changes in what I'm remembering. We need to be able to hide as well as fight. I'll wake you when I'm done, and you can keep your eyes open until dawn."

Tiep wasn't terribly surprised when neither one of them had given a thought to him. Galimer was Tiep's advocate when it came to both chores and privileges. Without Galimer, he was a child again. Rozt'a didn't want him to grow up, and Dru didn't think he could. On the whole, Tiep found it easier to deal with Dru's prejudices.

Tiep bedded down an arm's length from Rozt'a and dozed a little while Druhallen waited for the midnight moment when he'd do whatever it was that magicians did to prepare themselves for spellcasting. One of the first lessons Tiep had learned from his foster parents was: Never disturb a wizard, especially Druhallen, when he was cramming spells. It was hard to know when, exactly, midnight arrived but it was easy to spot when it had passed because Dru cleared his throat several times and folded his magic box with a series of satisfied snaps.

Tiep pulled his damp boots over Rozt'a's bandages and intercepted his foster-father before he awakened Rozt'a.

"Let me watch the rest of the night."

Dru scowled and said nothing, not an omen of agreement.

"My feet aren't hurting so much now. I can walk around, if I need to. I've been taking a watch since I was ten years old."

There was no change in Druhallen's expression.

"I gave you my word, Dru. I know I was wrong. Aren't you going to let me do *anything* to make it up? Can't you trust me even a little?"

"It's not for me to say, Tiep. I'd have to talk to Rozt'a first. She and I agreed we'd handle the night-watch ourselves."

"She wouldn't mind."

"She would. It was her idea; she insisted on it."

That was a blow to Tiep's heart. He counted on Rozt'a's unquestioning support. Dru and Galimer might fume, but Rozt'a called herself his mother and mothers didn't turn their backs on their children. Even his own mother had died rather than abandon him; Tiep was sure of that, despite the rumors he'd heard in Berdusk streets.

Tiep had a predictable reaction when his heart hurt: He got angry. He got nasty.

"You're both trusting a dog-face goblin to get you to Dekanter and back."

He knew he'd made a mistake before the words were cold on his tongue. Druhallen's face became as hard as a plaster mask which reminded Tiep that Dru was one of those rare

132

wizards who could brawl with the best—or worst—of any city's scum. But Dru got his temper under control.

"The bug lady didn't leave us any choice. What is it between you and Sheemzher, Tiep? Did you two cross paths before he came to the room?"

"No."

Tiep could have kicked himself right afterward—Dru had all but handed him a script for getting rid of Sheemzher and he'd wasted a perfect opportunity by blurting out the truth. Druhallen had that effect on folk whose heads didn't come up to his shoulder. Tiep tried to repair the damage—

"We've been tricked, Dru, conned, gulled, set up, whatever. Look at us, sleeping on stone mattresses, eaten alive, and wearing wet shoes. At the rate we're going, we'll be lucky if we get to Dekanter before the snow flies. If anyone was following us—Damn, if they left that first morning when we were in Weathercote and they stuck to the Dawn Pass Trail, they're going to get there long before us on this lousy excuse for a shortcut. Doesn't that *bother* you? Make you ask questions about our guide and his mistress? The way I figure it, the bug lady and the Black Network have marked us for sheep, Druhallen, and they've got us following a goblin goat straight to slaughter."

Dru stared into the darkness, rubbing his dark-stubbled chin. "It looks that way, doesn't it, when you lay everything on the table."

If Galimer or Rozt'a had said those words, Tiep would have rejoiced, but Dru was different. When Dru conceded a point, it was time to watch your back.

"Of course, when you put *everything* on the table, you're taking coincidence and making it deliberate. For example, you've got to assume that Sheemzher not only knew I was going to take the back way after I left the charterhouse, but that he arranged for those brutes to beat that goblin child. Not to mention the timing—a few moments one way or the other and either the chicken coop would have been empty or I'd have found a corpse. Same thing in Weathercote Wood with the reaver and, more important, with *you*, Tiep. If Rozt'a hadn't sent you scrambling up that tree, would you have stolen that amber . . . on your way *into* the forest?"

According to Galimer, who probably knew what he was talking about, Druhallen couldn't cast charm-type spells because he didn't know any and, besides, Tiep was supposedly immune to lesser magics, especially charms and enchantments. So, there wasn't anything sorcerous about Dru's dark eyes when they nailed Tiep where he stood. His stare was just the smug look of a man who knew how his foster-son's mind worked.

Weakly, Tiep tried to get back to where he'd started. "I can take the watch. There's no need to wake Rozt'a. If she gets mad, I'll say it's my fault."

Druhallen shook his head. "Lies are lies, Tiep, even the ones you tell to protect someone. If I let you take the watch, it's my responsibility . . . and my fault, if you do something we all regret."

"I won't," Tiep insisted.

"See to it," Dru said as he stood up.

Tiep waited until Druhallen was stretched out an arm's length from Rozt'a's blankets and breathing easily. He walked between them, wishing he had a lamp. Neither of them twitched out of turn and Tiep felt safe heading toward the horse lines and the place where Sheemzher slept beside his spear. Maybe the goblin *had* made plans with Amarandaris; there was only one way to find out for certain.

Striking fast, Tiep grabbed the sleeping goblin from behind. He clapped one hand over Sheemzher's mouth to keep him quiet and pressed his other forearm hard against the goblin's windpipe. Sheemzher struggled—the dog-face had a certain wild-animal bravado—but settled down fast when Tiep squeezed hard and cut off his air.

"I've got questions. You're going to answer them yes or no. You say yes by nodding your head, no by shaking it sideways. Got it?"

The goblin's chin bobbed beneath Tiep's. It was the correct response, but Tiep hadn't expected Sheemzher to catch on so quickly and jerked the goblin from his blankets with more force than he needed. He didn't let Sheemzher plant his feet firmly on the ground, but dragged him on his heels past the horse line. And past the blood line, too, which probably accounted for Sheemzher's renewed struggles. Tiep applied a little more pressure on the goblin's throat and calm was restored.

"Who do you work for?"

Sheemzher made unintelligible noises in his throat. Tiep felt foolish—his first serious question couldn't be answered with a yes or no.

"Do you work for the Zhentarim?"

Because Tiep held the goblin from behind, he couldn't see anything of Sheemzher's face, but the goblin flinched when he said "Zhentarim." The chin tap that followed the flinch wasn't convincing. Tiep shoved Sheemzher against the rock behind the ledge and spun him around.

"Liar!" Tiep hissed. He laid a short, vicious punch into Sheemzher's mid-section then relaxed the pressure on the goblin's throat. "What did they give you to betray us?"

The little, close-set eyes widened and showed pale, faintly glowing rings around the pupils. "Bad men. All bad men. Sheemzher not work for bad men. Sheemzher not work for Zhentarim." He turned the last word into an eerie song.

Tiep unleashed another punch precisely where he'd landed the first, a painful persuasive technique he'd learned the hard way. Sheemzher's gut had to be burning. The goblin's knees buckled and he'd have gone down if Tiep hadn't kept him pinned against the stone.

"Who's waiting for us at Dekanter?"

"Ghistpok there? Beast Lord there?" Fear turned the goblin's words into questions.

Tiep raised his arm quickly, smacking the back of Sheemzher's skull against the rock. "The Black Network! Is Amarandaris on the Dawn Pass Trail right now, planning to get there ahead of us?"

Sheemzher stiffened. "Ask self, not Sheemzher. Sheemzher not talk black-lord Amarandaris."

"I've got no business with him. You stick to the truth and leave me out of this," Tiep snapped and delivered his hardest punch yet.

The goblin sagged. For a heartbeat Tiep thought he'd seriously damaged the dog-face. The stench was bad and sudden, like a man dying from the waist down. Tiep wrinkled his nose dramatically.

"What's the point of wearing clothes, Sheemzher, when all you can do is soil them?"

"Not Sheemzher!" the goblin insisted, and emphasized his point by kicking Tiep's kneecap. It was the first move he'd made in his own defense since Tiep had grabbed him. "Ask self!"

In point of fact, the stench wasn't radiating from the goblin. And it certainly wasn't coming from Tiep. Gritting his teeth, Tiep took a deeper breath and determined that the odor rose in the darkness beyond the ledge, out in the bog forest. It was getting stronger, too. Tiep gagged and nearly lost his hold on Sheemzher.

"What died?" he asked no one in particular.

The goblin didn't answer but the darkness did. Something soft and warm brushed against Tiep's leg. An instant later he was in the air, held by the ankle and thrashed against the stone. He emptied his lungs in a scream then lost his voice when he had to fill them with the foulest air imaginable. It was the youth's worst nightmare come to life, he was being held prisoner by a man-high mound of predatory manure.

136

Manure with a grip of iron. Tiep lashed out with his free leg. He might as well have kicked a rock. The reek-heap that had captured him was all strength within its oozy, soft flesh. Its arms were jointless, like the third arm of that demon who'd helped butcher Cardinal, but with a serpent's whiplash strength. Twice more the beast battered Tiep against the rock face behind the ledge. He managed to protect his head both times, but that wouldn't last.

Then the dung beast whirled him up high and, bad as it was, it got worse. At the top of one arc, Tiep caught a glimpse of three bulbous eyes growing near the tip of another serpentine arm.

Hunger . . . hunger . . . hunger! Soft. Warm-soft. Hunger.

Tiep's mind filled with visions of gore, viscera, and fist-sized chunks of raw meat. He realized the manure wasn't merely alive and moving and hungry, it was sentient—it had thoughts and it was projecting those thoughts into his head.

Tiep crashed into a rock. The blow across the shoulders left him stunned and defenseless when the dung beast smashed him to the ground a moment later. He was going to die. The dung beast was going to pound him to a broken-bone pulp, then pull him apart and eat him piece by dripping piece. Tiep could see it all unfolding inside his own skull. He was whipping through the air, headed for another bashing against stone, when the world lit up.

Druhallen! Druhallen had come to his rescue with magical fire.

The dung beast bellowed in Tiep's ears and inside his head, too. The twin sensations were agonizing, but it was the creature's breath that snuffed out Tiep's consciousness. He didn't remember getting free, only that suddenly he was free—flat on his back, aching everywhere, nauseated, and gasping, but *free*.

Dru had lobbed more fire while Tiep's mind was dark. The second spell plastered the dung beast with flames. It made enough light that Tiep could see Rozt'a dance forward with her sword angled for an ax-cut. She struck quick at one of the serpentine arms and was out of harm's way before it flopped to the stone. The beast shrieked, a sound that had physical force inside Tiep's head. He writhed on the ground, sharing the dung beast's agony until Dru hit it with more fire and it lost the ability to invade a man's mind.

Tiep pulled himself onto his knees and got a good look at Sheemzher using his spear to distract the beast while Rozt'a closed in for another sword cut. Tiep would have joined the fight, if he hadn't lost his knives during the thrashing.

Rozt'a got her second trophy—the eye-stalk—and after that it was only a matter of time before they drove it from the ledge to the bog. Dru hollered, "Clear!" and kindled one of his big fireballs. The beast became a bonfire in the bog, but it wasn't close to dying when, suddenly, it was gone, dragged down by some other beast with absolutely no sense of taste or smell. They weren't tempted to investigate. Tiep tested his ankle and found that, though sore, it worked just fine, thanks to the second-skin cloths still wrapped around his feet.

"What in blazes was that?" Dru asked while they were all getting used to quiet again.

"Demon," said Sheemzher, predictably.

"Not a chance," Dru replied, stomping out last flaming bits of the beast and kicking them off the ledge. "Ansoain had a thing about demons and she made sure we knew what she knew. Demons smell, but they don't smell like that. We all know what that smelled like . . . I never knew it could *move*."

Rozt'a spun on her heels awkwardly. She wouldn't sheathe her sword until she'd cleaned it, and she wouldn't clean it on her breeches the way she often did. "The pig wallows at home didn't smell that bad—but they came close. I know you can raise the dead, Dru, but can you raise manure?"

"You're talking to the wrong magician," he replied with a laugh. "I have trouble raising myself each morning." He handed her a scrap of cloth. Magicians carried bits of everything with them. "But I recall Ansoain rattling on about a cave and catacomb dweller that collected dung and fed off it. She never said what it looked like. I imagined a rat of some sort and never thought about the smell. Who knows, maybe we just killed an otyugh. Can't figure, though, what a critter like that would be doing out in the open."

"War," Sheemzher said. "Dark war. Beast-Lord war . . . war under Dekanter."

"Under Dekanter," Rozt'a muttered, adding a few choice oaths. "Right. Look at what the rain's done to these mountains—there must be caves everywhere." She finally sheathed her sword and turned to Tiep. "No offense, but you reek of that thing. Strip out of those clothes, wash yourself off, and stay downwind until you do!"

Tiep pulled off his shirt but left his breeches alone. He started for the heap they'd made of their gear. Sheemzher, spear in hand, side-stepped to block his path. Tiep decided he could bear the smell a bit longer and was glad he'd stayed when Druhallen started thinking aloud.

"Not caves. Not *just* caves, anyway. The Mines of Dekanter. Dwarves built 'em, the Netheril mages expanded them, and sure as water flows downhill, there's drow living in them now. Ever see the drow, Sheemzher?"

The goblin lowered his spear when Dru looked their way. Tiep could have made his escape, but he lingered.

Sheemzher shook his head. "Demons. All demons. Sheemzher not know demons. People not go under Dekanter. People fight demons; fear demons."

"No demons, Sheemzher. We've got dragons overhead and the gods know what under our feet, but no demons." Dru walked toward them. "Let me get back to the camp. Maybe I can still catch the tide with my spells."

Tiep realized they didn't know he and Sheemzher had

been outside the camp when the otiyo—or whatever Dru had called it—crawled out of the bog. There hadn't been time for Sheemzher to make accusations . . . yet. Tiep gave the goblin a nasty look, but it was hard to intimidate someone, even a dog-faced goblin, when he had a spear and you stank like an open sewer in summer.

Rozt'a tossed Dru's rag into the bog. "You can't be sure, Dru. Remember what Amarandaris said about problems he couldn't fix or control in Dekanter. Demons would be a damn good reason to move the trail."

"He'd have told me if it was demons. Anything to get my sympathy."

Dru stepped aside to let Rozt'a go ahead of him. The goblin followed Rozt'a. That left Tiep alone with his foster father.

"Thanks. Thanks for saving my life. I was a goner."

"Thank Sheemzher. I woke up when I heard you screaming, but Rozt'a and I, we'd have wasted precious time looking for you, if he hadn't been right there pointing the way with his spear. What were you doing out here?"

Sheemzher had gone ahead, but he hadn't gone far. He could probably hear everything Dru had said. The beggar understood their language better than he spoke it.

"Noises," Sheemzher answered before Tiep could think of something appropriate and innocent. "Smell. Terrible smell. Wake Sheemzher—people noses keen, very keen." He tapped the side of his. "Bad eyes; good noses. Sheemzher tell this one—look together, yes? Sheemzher think horses; find demon."

Tiep and the goblin looked knives at each other. Thank all the gods, Dru was looking the other way when he said:

"Yeah, well—it worked out all right, but it could've gone the other way. Horses aren't worth dying for. That's why we line 'em up away from where we sleep. You remember that— both of you. That spear's a good weapon, but it's thrust only, and you, Tiep, you used up a lifetime's worth of luck tonight."

Tiep didn't need anyone to telling him about luck. Rozt'a was waiting with the medicine chest. She put another dose of second-skin on Tiep's ankle—after he'd stripped, sluiced, and dressed in clothes that didn't stink. She'd patched up the goblin, too, never guessing that Sheemzher hadn't taken his damage from the beast.

Debts were mounting. There'd have to be a reckoning soon.

8

4 Eleint, the Year of the Banner (1368 DR)

The Greypeak Mountains

Druhallen felt human when he woke up, a sure sign that his companions had let him oversleep. The sky had brightened before he'd abandoned his attempts to re-memorize the spells he'd expended in the dung-beast battle. He had expected to be exhausted as well as empty-headed all this day. One out of two was better than nothing, but he'd rather have had the spells than the sleep. The way things had been going here in the Greypeaks, he felt certain he'd wish he had a full complement of fire in mind before midnight rolled around again.

His body was rested, but Dru's bones ached from sleeping on the stone ledge. Two blankets beneath him wasn't enough any more. He needed a layer of loose dirt, sand, or moss and preferred a horsehair mattress; he was getting old. The thought of settling down in one place had become thinkable for Druhallen. He had enough on account with the Scornubel goldsmiths that he'd never have to return to Sunderath. He could buy himself a small shop in a well-run town and live out his days selling spells to merchants and lovers.

It would be a predictable life. After the last few days,

Druhallen had an new appreciation for predictable. Dull and boring wouldn't be bad, either. Maybe he'd marry, have children of his own. The world was ripe with men who hadn't thought about families until they'd plucked a gray hair or two from their beards.

More than gold, Druhallen had the spells to make his daydreams come true. Ansoain's library, carefully preserved and protected back in Scornubel, contained true copies of *Luvander's Prime Enchantments* and *Illusions of the Heart*. He'd studied both volumes and there weren't more than three spells between them that he couldn't cast comfortably. Most of them were well within Galimer's range, especially if they weren't fielding surprises.

They'd joked about it—two wizards in their dotage casting spells on candles and wine cups. That had been before Rozt'a, when neither of them knew the meaning of tired or aching.

Or love.

Or fidelity.

Rozt'a had her back to Dru's blankets. She was talking to Tiep who was looking at his feet instead of her face. The youth was probably in a mood, but Druhallen wouldn't have wanted to be looking into Rozt'a's eyes just then. He'd face ten dung beasts with no fire at all before he'd tell her that he'd caught himself thinking about settling down, marriage, and children.

He wouldn't let himself think about such notions again, at least not until they'd gotten back to Weathercote and pried Galimer from Lady Mantis.

Dru grabbed his blankets with one hand and headed for the horse line, a path which, not coincidentally, took him close to Tiep and Rozt'a. They spotted him and fell silent.

"Problems?" he asked, on the forceful side of polite.

Neither answered. With his head still down, Tiep turned and walked away. He limped a bit, but he'd been in worse shape yesterday, before Rozt'a slathered his blistered feet.

The one who looked like death in the morning was Sheemzher. One of the goblin's red-orange cheeks was a dull, swollen brown and he held his spear close against his flank for balance. No way he'd be able to walk and maintain any sort of pace. They'd have to put him up on one of the horses—which wasn't so bad, except Dru couldn't remember the otyugh getting a blow in on the goblin.

"There's something strange going on between Tiep and Sheemzher," he said to Rozt'a without looking at her.

"Maybe."

"Is that what you and he were talking about just now?"

"No."

"He seemed sulky—"

Rozt'a grimaced and Dru decided not to ask her if she was feeling sulky also. The answer was obvious, and so was the explanation. After yesterday, Rozt'a had to be wondering if she'd ever see her husband again. Without a censoring thought, Dru wound his unencumbered arm over Rozt'a's shoulders and pulled her gently against his chest.

"We're not dealt out of this game, not by a long shot."

Their eyes met and Rozt'a gave Dru a lethal stare before shrugging free of his one-armed embrace. He folded both arms beneath his blankets.

"Let's get moving," he stammered.

Rozt'a nodded and walked away without saying a word.

That pretty much set the tone for another day of trekking up over stone and down through the quaking bogs. From his perch on Hopper's back, Sheemzher urged them to pick up the pace. They panted and sweated but didn't argue, especially when they were crossing rock.

The sky was no bluer than it had been yesterday, but the thick clouds had lifted somewhat. They could see more of the dark gray mountains, and dragons. Druhallen had counted eight dragon sightings, two of them simultaneous, both full-grown and deep red. Even one red dragon was too many for a party of four.

Around noon they arrived at a ledge that was black, rather than dark gray, and glassy, like the sealed entrance to Lady Wyndyfarh's cave. This was no magic cave. A red dragon had fought here and blasted its prey with fire more intense than any Druhallen could summon. The dragon had been killing, not hunting. Whatever had drawn its wrath would have been reduced to powder and ash.

Dru didn't know if his companions read the same story from the scene. No one was talking and he didn't volunteer the information. Ignorance was bliss, so long as one of them knew what they were facing. He had to wonder, though, what Rozt'a saw and kept to herself, or the goblin who swung his feet in the stirrups and was the first away from the ledge.

"Hurry," Sheemzher said, the first word anyone had spoken in hours. "Bad place. *Evil* place."

They hurried and made palpable progress toward the tallest mountains that formed their horizon—until the clouds fell again. Not much later, when they were striding carefully through one of the spongier bogs they'd encountered, the clouds opened up. Today's raindrops were smaller than yesterday's, cooler, too—bespeaking autumn rather than summer—and pushed sideways by gusty winds.

Dru laced himself into his cloak and pulled the hood up. He could see the goblin's back from the waist down and Hopper's from the tail up—not a sight to inspire any man. Hard to believe that only a few days ago he and Galimer had been looking for someone who knew the way to Dekanter. Everything looked different—better—when you were pursuing your own dreams and not trying to appease some over-powered, bug-and-goblin befriending, magic-making woman who'd turned your best friend into a mindless pet.

If there was a lesson to be learned from the last few days, it wasn't about amber. Large chunks of his conversation with Amarandaris lay heavy in Dru's mind. He'd wasted so much of his life learning things the Zhentarim already knew. When they got to Scornubel, Druhallen promised himself that he'd sell the glass disk and let the Zhentarim deal with the Red Wizards however they chose.

The path curved upward, promising another exposed rock gully. Bugs didn't fly in the rain, maybe dragons didn't either. Dru could hope; a man should be careful with his hopes. It wasn't dragon-fire that struck them from above, but fist- and skull-sized stones that fell with the rain. He pinched embers from his sleeve—Dru had a little fire left in his memory—but looking up he didn't see anything that looked like a target.

"Stay close!" Rozt'a shouted. She gave the orders when they were under attack. "Do something, Dru."

He guessed at the location of their attackers, cast fire in that direction, and for a few moments only cold, hard rain pelted their faces. Then rocks came down again.

"A shield!" she shouted, herding them against the sheer stone at the back of the ledge. "And quick."

The horses shied and whinnied. They were bigger and taking the worst of an attack that smacked of opportunity, not skill.

Druhallen knew a spell to thicken the air and slow an arrow by half, so a quick-thinking man could bat the shafts down with his forearm. If their attackers had been throwing the stones, the spell might have helped his family, but they were dropping them instead. A simple shielding spell—the best he could manage under the circumstance—wouldn't stop the falling rain and do less against a falling rock.

Unless—

Weather made a difference with magic. Dru's fireball spells burned hotter in the summer and longer when the air was dry. This rain wasn't merely falling, it was driven sideways by the wind. If the wind was affecting the rain— throwing it—then his shielding spell might slow the rain and the ensorcelled rain might slow the stones. Moreover, he could cast the spell on a moving target—himself and his party. If it worked at all, it would travel with them, maybe as far as the next bog.

And if the spell slowed either the stones or the rain, neither would it make their situation worse.

At least it shouldn't make their situation worse.

Dru paused, reconsidering his conclusions.

"Now, Dru!"

He reached inside his cloak and clutched the folding box. The box could be opened in any of a dozen ways. Dru found the clasp that revealed the compartment where he kept sprigs of virgin goose-down. With a few of the tiny feathers pinched between his thumb and forefinger, he spoke the words that kindled the shielding spell. The feathers vanished and he drew his next breath in a far-less-gusty wind.

"Let's go!" he shouted to the others.

Rozt'a took the lead, but the path was too treacherous for great haste and rocks continued to fall. One struck the black mare, Ebony. The mare lunged and broke away from Rozt'a distracted grasp. Another step and she'd have been over the edge and into the bog, no better than Cardinal. Tiep intervened; he caught Ebony's rein and, shouting her name, put his full weight against her panic.

Tiep got through to the horse and the attackers got through to him. A stone the size of a baby's skull clipped the youth on the forehead. Blood gushed, as it always did with a head wound. Druhallen allowed himself to believe that the wound wasn't serious, but the lad stood stock-still, making an attractive target of himself after the mare's rein slipped from his hand.

Their unseen overhead attackers responded with stones that were definitely thrown. The shielding spell interfered with their trajectories, but Tiep swayed and staggered whether or not the stones struck him. Druhallen dropped the reins he held and caught the youth's sleeve.

Two more stones struck home, one against Dru's shoulder, the other against Tiep's. Dru acknowledged the blow with a

groan, but Tiep seemed not to notice. Dru pulled him close
and got a glimpse of vacant eyes in the process.

"Tiep's dumbstruck!" Dru shouted. "He can't walk."

The last was an exaggeration. Tiep kept his feet moving
under him as Dru hauled him back to relative safety closer
to the rock-face, but there was no sense in his movements.
Dru slapped Tiep's wet, bloody cheek and shouted in his ear,
each to no avail. The youth blinked without comprehension.

Rozt'a yelped. A stone had gotten her. The goblin had
climbed down from Hopper's back and was hidden among
the restless horses.

"We can't stay here!" Rozt'a shouted. "Throw him over a
saddle."

That was easier said than done, and no safer for Tiep
were Dru to succeed at the task. "We've got to stand where
we are."

"Impossible!" Rozt'a replied.

Dru was already fumbling with his box. He thumbed a
different catch and thrust a rain-dampened forefinger into
a compartment filled with ordinary ash. Leaving Tiep to
stand alone like a statue, Dru risked the drop-off edge. He
thought he had a better idea now where the enemy hid
itself, and with his eyes squint-focused on that spot, whispered the Auld Thorassic words for gloom and misery as he
rubbed his fingers together.

The stuff of magic flowed away from Dru, confounding
time and space. He had a vision of scrawny, misshapen
creatures, at least twenty of them, half with tossing stones
and the other half shuttling ammunition. The vision faded
as the spell completed itself. By design, it worked best on
a conscious mind and a mind of conscience. Humans were
a good target; elves and dwarves were better. But the mind
of a beast, especially a misshapen beast, might not be sus-
ceptible at all.

Rozt'a shouted his name and not, by her tone, for the
first time. "Are you mad?"

The rock fall slowed, then stopped. Keening moans and wails poured down the mountainside instead.

"I don't know how long that will hold them. Let's move quick."

"What about Tiep? The goblin?"

Between the rain and the horses, it was easy to lose track of a head or two. Sheemzher shouted that he was ready for anything. Tiep hadn't snapped out of his vacant-eyed trance. Dru slapped and shook him again. This time the youth whimpered when he blinked and raised a hand to his cheek.

"Walk, lad!" Dru challenged. He gave Tiep a half turn before shoving him forward. "Walk for your life."

He kept one hand knotted in Tiep's shirt, steering and prodding the youth toward such safety as the next bit of trail offered. Around his other hand Dru wound the reins and ropes for three horses, none of which were eager to walk forward. With his arms stretched out and his sleeves hanging like wet sails before the wind, Dru made an easy target, but his spell held and none of the enemy accepted the invitation.

Dru congratulated himself for a job well done; he praised himself too soon. The same scrawny enemy ambushed them in the next bog. Against all expectation, they made Sheemzher their primary target, pulling the bedraggled goblin from Hopper's back. Sheemzher had his decorated spear and put it to good use against the more primitive sticks the enemy wielded, but he was badly outnumbered. Rozt'a and her sword would eventually even the odds, but not—to Druhallen's eye—in time to save the goblin.

Weighing his options quickly, Dru gave Tiep a shove toward the underbrush.

"Lay low!" he commanded.

The boy had been coming around as they walked. He hadn't said anything yet, but managed to nod his head before secreting himself in a patch of waist-high ferns. Dru judged that Tiep would continue to survive and went for the length of fire-hardened wood jutting out from Bandy's saddle.

Other mages might carry staves, Druhallen of Sunderath preferred an ax-shaft. His father—gods keep him safe in Sunderath—had taught him how to grip and swing the wood. He didn't bother with the axe head; it was too heavy, too much trouble to sharpen, and unnecessary for a man his size. Against their undergrown enemy, the shaft was lethal and faster than a sword. Dru swung into the gut of the nearest misshapen creature. The force of his blow lifted the critter—Dru couldn't guess its sex or species—off its feet and flung it some ten feet across the bog. It wouldn't be getting up soon, maybe never, if the thing that got the dung-beast was looking for a snack. Dru backhanded his next target. The misshapen enemy collapsed face-down in the old leaves and twigs.

It was butchery, not battle, and they didn't stop until every last one of the misshapen lay motionless on the ground.

"When we've finished at Dekanter, we leave by another route," Rozt'a said grimly. "I'd sooner face the Network on the road than this again." She wiped her blade on a corpse's thigh, but decided that wasn't good enough and cleaned it again with leaves before sheathing it.

Between the dung beast and this lot, Sheemzher's spear had taken a beating. Most of its dangling ornaments were gone, but the flaked stone head was still firmly attached to the shaft. The goblin's hat was gone. Rozt'a retrieved it from the bog. Its crown was crushed, the brim, torn. It would never hide his wispy hair again. Sheemzher took it from her gently, his lips a-tremble as though he'd lost his dearest friend. Dru didn't know if goblins could cry, but the rain left credible tracks down the red-orange cheeks.

The Lady Wyndyfarh might have done her servant a

favor when she taught him manners and dressed him up in the manner of men, but if Dru were a competent judge of emotion, she hadn't added any happiness to his life.

Tiep emerged from the ferns. His hands were clapped against his temples and his eyes had the look of cheap wine, but that was considerable improvement.

"Remember how you got here?" Dru asked.

"No." He noticed the array of corpses and took a backward stride that nearly unbalanced him. "What—? What's happened? Where are we? I remember it starting to rain, then nothing until I was on my knees over there."

Rozt'a slipped her hand under his elbow and guided him toward the horses. There'd been no time to tie them properly, of course, but none of the five liked the bogs and they'd stayed close together.

"We got ambushed," she explained as they walked. "You took a stone on the head. You're bleeding. That's not rainwater coming down the side of your face."

"What about you?" Dru asked Sheemzher when the other two were past.

"Demons no harm Sheemzher." The goblin fumbled with his hat. He tried, and failed, to put it on.

"There'll be other—"

Sheemzher cut Dru off with a stream of words that had to be curses in his own language, then he threw his hat onto the ground and stomped it mercilessly. "Demons!" he shouted and stomped the nearest corpse instead. When abusing the corpse with his boots couldn't quell his need for revenge, Sheemzher attacked it with his spear. He stabbed it between the ribs and in the abdomen and took aim at its skull.

Dru had seen enough blood for one day and, grasping the upward end of the spear, put a swift stop to the goblin's mutilating rage.

"Demons!" the goblin turned the word into a song.

"Not demons," Druhallen insisted. "Cousins, maybe. Your

151

cousins. And they took exception to you Sheemzher, in a big way."

Sheemzher struggled to free his spear from Druhallen's grasp. When that came to naught, he nudged the corpse with his foot. Its lifeless hand flopped to the ground. "Count fingers, good sir!" The goblin waved his open hand in front of Dru's face. "*Five* fingers. People have five fingers. Sheemzher have *five* fingers. Sheemzher's mother, sisters, brothers all have *five* fingers. Five. Five. Five!"

The misshapen corpse's exposed hand had seven fingers, all of them cruelly twisted. It couldn't have made a fist or scratched its head without pain. Its other hand had five functional fingers and was, to Druhallen's eyes, identical with Sheemzher's. Dru mentioned this and other similarities, but the goblin remained adamant: demons and goblins had nothing in common but hatred.

Well, they weren't the only blind race under the sun. Dwarves insisted they weren't related to the duergar and more than a few elves disowned the drow. Dwarves and elves, of course, were justly proud of their heritage. It boggled Dru's mind to think that *goblins* held themselves superior to anyone else that walked on two legs. He recognized a lost cause, though, and left Sheemzher alone with his delusions.

"Something's meddling with the local goblins," he said to Rozt'a when she was repacking the medicine chest.

"That would take some pretty potent sorcery, wouldn't it?"

He shrugged. "Probably, and a twisted mind. You hear about it every so often, someone's trying to make a stronger this, a more docile that. The Thayans do it, mostly with the dead, but they've conjured up some fairly reliable orc changes, a lot of unreliable ones, too. An orc's bigger, harder to control than a goblin, but they're as close as dogs and wolves. A mage who could change one, could change the other."

"So the Red Wizards are back to meddling with Netherese magic?" She concluded her remark with a sigh and shut the chest with more force than was necessary.

"I didn't say that."

"You were thinking it."

Dru hadn't been, but only because it hadn't occurred to him. Now that it had, his mind was alive with connections and possibilities.

"Well, add this to your thoughts. Tiep needs rest. He's blaming himself for what's happened—not that he shouldn't be, but he throws off healing at the best of times and guilt is making everything worse. He's walking and talking, but he's punch-drunk from that rock and feverish from last night's filth. He *should* bounce back quick enough, but we'll up the odds if we settle in now for the night."

"Up the odds of what? Another attack? We've just piled up enough fresh meat to attract a dragon, not to mention another pack of these misshapen goblins and whatever lives under the bog. If Tiep's patched up, then I say we get moving."

Rozt'a got to her feet and hefted the heavy chest to her shoulder. "Let's not push it, that's all. If we see a good campsite, let's use it. I've done all I can. If he goes into a brain fever, we're going to be stranded for a lot longer than one night—unless you've got some other idea?"

He swallowed hard, not liking her implications. They *were* going to get out of this with both Galimer and Tiep intact. What they did this winter in Scornubel—whether or not they told Tiep to go his own way—was winter's problem, not today's.

"We'll keep an eye on him—put him astride if he gets wobbly. *And* keep our eyes open for a campsite, preferably one with a roof."

The rain had let up and the wind had died back, but the stone-gray clouds weren't breaking up. Dru expected bad weather to return and wasn't disappointed. He tried to convince himself the wet wind was a good thing. Dragons weren't apt to fly through it and a pack of misshapen goblins might not notice a smartly dressed goblin trespassing through their territory.

Dru recalled his conversation with Amarandaris. Ghistpok's goblins had been making enemies of themselves with the other Greypeak goblins. They'd been stealing males and driving the females to exile around Parnast. Sheemzher claimed ties to Ghistpok. If goblins—including misshapen goblins—had some means of identifying their heritage, as moon or gold elves did, then the attack on Sheemzher was understandable, even if not deserved. On the other hand, although Amarandaris had warned Dru that goblins saw demons everywhere, he'd said nothing about misshapen goblins. If Ghistpok's tribe had driven their cousins into exile, then a few odd-armed goblins ought to have shown up in Parnast.

They won't touch a demon, not even to bury it. It's a cult thing, something to do with transformation and deformity. It might be interesting to know why the Greypeaks were home to two goblin races; and what had transformed one but not the other while turning them into blind enemies. Still, both races were goblin-kin and Druhallen had greater worries when thoughts of Amarandaris crossed his mind. A wizard on horseback, riding the Dawn Pass Trail around the Greypeak Mountains, could get to Dekanter faster than they were getting through the bogs and mountains. Dru would sooner face the Beast Lord and a dozen demons before he faced Amarandaris in the shadows of Dekanter.

Early in the afternoon, while they were crossing a bog, Rozt'a spotted what appeared to be a cave in a distant rock formation. She wanted to check it out. Dru said, no, they weren't splitting up and they weren't going off the trail.

"If there's one cave, there's bound to be another, closer to hand."

It was the wrong thing to say. Rozt'a didn't take well to

being overruled and daylight was fading before they sighted another.

This time she didn't offer Dru a choice. "I'm going in," she announced, the first words she'd spoken since he'd rejected her suggestion.

They were all rain-chafed by then, weary, and ready to call it a night. Tiep had been astride Ebony since mid-afternoon. He'd slumped over one hip, like a crimped sack of grain. His eyes were closed, his color was lousy, and every so often he'd let out a shiver or a moan. There were herbal powders in the medicine chest that could snuff out a death's-door fever in a single night, but only if they were steeped first and their recipient could rest after taking them.

"I'm coming with you," Dru said, looking about for a place to tie the horses he led.

Rozt'a handed him the reins she'd held instead and stalked into the cave alone. Short of breaking into a wizard's private sanctum, few things were as dangerous as entering an unexplored cave. She needed backup; she needed light—and she'd have Dru's head if he suggested either. Tiep was too far gone to notice, but Sheemzher did. The goblin gripped his spear so tightly its remaining decorations rattled against the shaft.

After the longest quarter hour of his life, Rozt'a returned.

"It'll do. There's a hearth already dug and dry wood stacked high."

"You're sure it's safe?" Druhallen regretted his words immediately, but they were out and there was no unsaying them.

"I know my job, Dru."

"I didn't mean—"

"Its got a hearth, not a dragon's lair, for gods' sakes. A *cold* hearth where a momma mouse or rat has raised a couple of families. I'd rather defend one point of entry than a thousand—What about you?"

"If you're satisfied, I'm satisfied," Dru snarled back. At

that moment, he didn't care if the damned cave *were* a dragon's lair.

Sheemzher clambered down from Hopper's back. The cave met the goblin's criteria for a place where flames could burn and he had a fire going in the hearth before they had Tiep moved inside. There was a drafty shadow at the rear of the cave. It was big enough for a wolf—or a determined goblin—but not a dragon or a man. After they'd unharnessed the horses and stowed their gear for the night, Dru used the jangling bridles to improvise a non-magical warding across the shadow. When he stepped back to contemplate his cleverness, he realized Rozt'a had watched his every move.

She hadn't noticed the second entry. Or she had, but thought he wouldn't. Dru couldn't guess which. He couldn't guess what she was thinking at all before she turned her back on him.

They had food for themselves, fuel for the fire, full water-skins, and enough grain to give the horses a single measure. Lady Wyndyfarh had provisioned them for a ten-day journey. Cardinal was gone; that gave them an extra day or so, but they couldn't afford extravagance. There was enough light left to return to the bog forest and gather up green forage for the animals.

Dru grabbed a pair of loose-knotted nets from the heap of gear and headed out of the cave. He hadn't taken twenty strides down the trail when he heard footsteps behind him. It was Rozt'a with the other nets thrown over her shoulder. They didn't exchange a single word; they didn't need to. The road might change, but not the work. They each knew what needed to be done and did it without getting in the other's way.

Sheemzher had slung a pot over the fire and boiled up some water. He presented them with steaming mugs when they returned. Clover tea, by the smell, and no guessing where he'd gotten it. Maybe it had been in the gear from the start. Maybe, Dru thought, he should exercise his suspicion and pour it out on the ground. Maybe he'd had enough of suspicion for one day.

"Thank you," he said and seared his tongue thoroughly on the first sip.

He'd swear he caught Rozt'a smirking at him, but by the time his eyes stopped watering, she was as sullen as before and busy with Tiep. The youth needed more than clover tea. Rozt'a fussed over him until Dru and Sheemzher, working awkwardly together, had crafted a barley-stew in the pot. She left the youth wrapped in blankets to join them.

"He's not making sense when he talks."

"So, let him sleep it off," Dru advised.

Rozt'a gave him yet another dark look. "There's nothing to sleep off. He's not drunk, he's been hit on the head. We've got to rouse him every little while, else he'll slip away. Promise me you'll waken him during your watch."

"You have my word."

That was all Rozt'a wanted from him. She ate her supper, shook sense into Tiep, then settled in her own blankets, her back toward the fire and, especially, Druhallen. Even Sheemzher noticed.

"Good woman angry with good sir." A statement, not a question.

Dru grunted. He didn't want to talk to a goblin but, the way his luck had been going, conversation was inevitable. The dog-face creature wouldn't hear silence. He asked questions about the Heartland cities, about magic, about love. In desperation, Druhallen took control with questions of his own.

"If you were one of Ghistpok's goblins at Dekanter, how did you wind up with Lady Wyndyfarh in Weathercote Wood?"

"Long story, good sir."

"I'm not going anywhere," Dru gestured at the cave entrance where rain and runoff created a waterfall.

He began: "Sheemzher brave. Sheemzher bold. Sheemzher warrior! Sheemzher make proud mothers, sisters, brothers. Sheemzher make all blood, all people proud."

Dru suppressed a sigh. The goblin's way of speaking would make the tale longer than necessary, but a tale did slowly emerge.

Sheemzher had been born to privilege, such as it was, among Dekanter's goblins. Ghistpok hadn't claimed him as a son, but another elder had. As a child, he'd eaten regularly and learned how to fight. As best as Druhallen could discern, eating and fighting were a male goblin's third and fourth favorite activities. The top two pastimes were acquiring females and children. Sheemzher had done well there, too.

For services rendered, Ghistpok had given Sheemzher a daughter and Sheemzher had begotten himself six youngsters in four years.

"Elva good woman," the goblin said of his wife. "Twins twice. Very good woman. Not clever—" he clenched his hands into a single fist, a meaningful gesture, apparently, among goblins, but lost on Druhallen —"Elva very good woman. Sheemzher important man when Ghistpok die, Sheemzher elder. Sheemzher help choose Ghistpok. With good woman Elva, Sheemzher someday maybe Ghistpok. Maybe. Sheemzher hope then, not now." He lowered his head, the very image of sadness.

Druhallen asked, "What happened to your wife?"

Sheemzher spat out a word then translated it: "Takers. Take people. Take Elva. Never more seen."

"Your wife was caught by slavers and taken away from Dekanter?" Amarandaris had insisted that Ghistpok sold his own children, though, in Elva's case, the Ghistpok who sold her probably wasn't the one who fathered her.

Sheemzher shook his head vigorously. "Takers . . . demons . . . from below. Never see, only take. Long ago Ghistpok say: 'Beast Lord protect all people from Takers.' Beast Lord say, 'Each and all people make worship.' Ghistpok promise, 'People make worship.' People worship Beast Lord then, now. Beast Lord protect people. Sometime Beast Lord sleep, not protect people. Takers come. Take people. Take Elva."

Druhallen steepled his hands and stared into the fire. Amarandaris had said, *Things started changing about seven years ago.* How old was Sheemzher? Goblins weren't long-lived, thirty or forty years, at the most. Had Sheemzher been at Dekanter when the changes came? Had he lost his wife to them?

"Have you ever seen the Beast Lord, Sheemzher?" he asked.

The goblin shook his head. "Ghistpok see Beast Lord. Ghistpok only. People worship Beast Lord. People drink wine, much wine. People not see anything. People happy." Sheemzher's expression contradicted his words. "Sheemzher happy. Sheemzher drink much, much wine. Too much wine. Sheemzher head big." He pressed his palms against his temples. "Bigger inside. Sheemzher think, Sheemzher never more drink wine. Sheemzher dance, yes. Sheemzher sing, yes. Sheemzher keep promise. Sheemzher never more drink wine. Sheemzher *pretending* drink wine."

Dru clapped the goblin on the shoulder. "Sheemzher *is* clever. I know too many men who can't keep that promise."

The goblin shook his head sadly. "Sheemzher not clever. Come one time, next time, Sheemzher *pretending*. All people fall down. Sheemzher *pretending* fall down. Elva fall down beside Sheemzher; Elva not *pretending*. Elva stand up. Elva walk away. Sheemzher stand up. Sheemzher follow." He looked up into Druhallen's eyes. "Bad, good sir. Bad. Bad. Bad. Sheemzher remember. Sheemzher not want remember."

With Druhallen's gentle prodding, the goblin described how he followed his wife and several other goblins underground. His wife and the others never recovered their wits. Mindless, they joined a colony of equally unresponsive

159

goblins who served the Takers. Brave and bold warrior that
he was, Sheemzher planned to rescue his wife, but before
he came up with a plan it was too late. The Takers took
Elva again, this time to an underground chamber with an
egg in it.

"Egg big—" Sheemzher shaped the largest oval his arms
could manage in the air between himself and Druhallen.
"Elva here." He indicated the bottom portion of the oval.
"*Mantis* here." He indicated the top. "Doors close . . . bang . . .
bang . . . *bang!* Sheemzher hide. Sheemzher scared. Come
lightning under Dekanter. Sheemzher think Sheemzher
never more scared then doors open . . . bang . . . bang . . .
bang! Elva gone. Mantis gone. Demon come . . . *Taker.*"

"Then I was right—someone—the Beast Lord—is trans-
forming the Dekanter goblins, changing them into the creatures you've been calling demons. When did this happen,
Sheemzher? When did—?"

The goblin couldn't contain himself. "No," he insisted.
"No. Never. Taker. Taker demon, not Beast Lord. Beast Lord
not demon. Takers take Elva. Elva inside egg. Elva gone.
Demon come—not Elva. Not. Not. *Not!* Elva gone. Elva not
demon. Beast Lord not *Taker.*"

The truth, which Druhallen could see so clearly, wasn't
worth the argument. "How does Lady Wyndyfarh fit in?" he
asked, though he was pretty sure he knew.

"Sheemzher find more mantis in box. Many mantis. One
mantis say: Take me to Lady Wyndyfarh. Take me to
Weathercote Wood. Sheemzher take. Good lady listen
Sheemzher. Good lady listen mantis. Good lady say: Stay
with me Sheemzher and I will give you vengeance. It is too
late to save Elva, but together we will save your children
from the Takers."

"And us? My friends and I?"

"Good lady not leave forest very far. Greater lady not
allow. Good lady obey greater lady, yes. Dekanter far, too far.
Good lady not go Dekanter. Good lady say, good men will

160

come in due time, Sheemzher. You must wait for them in the village and after they come, lead them to me. Sheemzher say, how know good men? Good lady say, you'll know him by what he does. Sheemzher wait six years. Six years too long. Sheemzher children grown. Six years make Sheemzher very much wiser. Sheemzher learn read. Sheemzher learn write. Sheemzher learn listen. Parnast little—all talk, Sheemzher listen. Zhentarim know good sir come. Zhentarim know why. Sheemzher listen. Sheemzher alone. Sheemzher not sure. Good sir save child; Sheemzher sure. Sheemzher very much sure, yes?"

"It couldn't have been planned," Dru muttered, thinking of the chicken coop. "All this because of an accident—the right place at the right time, or the wrong place and the wrong time."

Sheemzher shook his head solemnly. "Not accident. Good lady say, good men will come. Good lady never wrong."

"Then your lady shouldn't have mind-locked Galimer!" Druhallen said abruptly.

"Sheemzher sorry. Sheemzher very much sorry. Gold-hair man good man. Sheemzher wish gold-hair man *here*."

"But not Tiep, right? He sees through magic; he saw through you and your lady. What went on between you two in Weathercote after we killed the reaver? I've heard his side. He thinks you've arranged everything. Exactly how much *did* you set up?" Calling Sheemzher clever was neither a lie nor an exaggeration. Beneath the garbled language was a mind as devious as any man's.

The goblin made his double-fist gesture again. "Dekanter no place for that one. Dekanter bad place for that one. Sheemzher think, that one not come Dekanter. That one stay Weathercote. Good lady help that one, teach that one. Sheemzher make mistake. Gold-haired man come between that one, good lady. Sheemzher very sorry. Sheemzher sorry for gold-hair man. Sheemzher sorry for good sir, good woman. Sheemzher sorry for Sheemzher."

"If you'd been honest—" Dru stopped himself. Cut was cut and they were days beyond useful hindsight. "This scroll we're supposed to bring back to Wyndyfarh, where does it fit in?"

"Egg top, good sir."

"What?"

"Egg top, good sir." Sheemzher patted his scalp. "Gold scroll fit egg top. Gold scroll eat Elva, children. Demons come . . . Takers."

Dru covered his eyes and swore. He couldn't imagine what part of a wound sheet of Netherese gold might have played in the transformation of Sheemzher's family, but he could imagine the egg. Alchemists used such devices to transmute elements and called the devices *athanors*. The few Druhallen had seen were small, no bigger than a skull, and required the might of more fire spells than he could cast in a week before they'd kindle. A mage would need to harness the sun or the sea tide to power an athanor large enough to transmute a goblin. The sun, the sea tide, or the forbidden magic of Netheril.

And he, Druhallen of Sunderath, had to pit himself successfully against such a mage if Galimer were going to walk out of Weathercote Wood.

He swore again.

Child-sized fingers touched his. "Sheemzher help. Sheemzher wait six years. Sheemzher plan. Sheemzher ready."

Druhallen successfully resisted the impulse to smash helpful Sheemzher against the cave walls. "Leave me alone now," he said stiffly. "I haven't had six years."

"Sheemzher understand." The goblin made his double-fist gesture as he backed away. "Good sir make plan. Sheemzher keep watch, yes?"

Not a chance. "I'm keeping the watch, Sheemzher. You curl up and get some sleep."

The goblin did as told, at least as far as huddling up under a blanket and staying put. Dru opened his folding box. He ran his fingers over the inscribed partitions. So much depended on choosing the right spells to study each night and he hadn't been doing a particularly good job of balancing offense, defense, and maintenance these last few days. Should he assume the worst and commit his mind to fire?

His thoughts wandered away from an answer to Galimer and a huge white egg with a gold scroll rising from it. The rain eased, stopped. Looking through the cave's entrance, Dru thought he saw a star.

Did that make fire more attractive or less?

Dru sat with his box open when Rozt'a cast her blankets aside. She awakened Tiep—with all his worrying about tomorrow's magic, Dru had forgotten to wake the youth—and stared hard at the goblin, whose snoring rhythm held steady under observation, before joining Druhallen near the cave's entrance.

"I heard you talking to Sheemzher," she began without the edge and irritation that had marked her earlier conversation. "If this golden scroll is truly surrounded by demons, we're doomed."

"Wyndyfarh wants the golden scroll, not a demon's heart. And she thinks we've got a good chance to grab it."

Rozt'a sat cross-legged on the stone. "Whatever makes you think that?"

"You trusted her. Twice."

"Gods protect us!" Rozt'a snorted. They both looked toward their sleeping companions, lest the impolite sound had awakened them. "I've been wrong many times, and this might really be one of them."

"You're right about people—"

"That woman's not people. I don't know what she is, but she's not human."

"She kept Galimer."

Rozt'a retorted, "That's a token in favor of humanity and trustworthiness?"

"In a way. I don't think Wyndyfarh ever intended to keep Tiep. She'd proved he was a thief. She'd looked in our minds, knew how we'd feel about that. She couldn't be sure we'd come back for him after we had the scroll. Think of it—beyond the value of the gold, which is surely great—there's the value of what's written on the gold. There's a legend—I've heard twenty versions if I've heard one—that says the Netheril Empire was born when someone known as the Finder found the twice-fifty scrolls of magic—all the magic that ever was or will be."

"Don't tell me—the Takers took the scrolls from the Finder who found them."

Druhallen sighed. Rozt'a would never be either a wizard or a poet.

"I don't think there's a connection. The scrolls disappeared long before the Empire fell. What did she say—The Beast Lord was a nuisance until he found the scroll?" Dru closed his eyes, but concentration couldn't resurrect Wyndyfarh's exact words. "It's something to think about. She had to give her thieves the strongest possible incentive to bring her the scroll rather than keep it for themselves. Though I'm sure she mentioned the Beast Lord and *didn't* mention Takers or demons—Not that it matters who's got the scroll, who we steal it from or how, so long as we bring it to her in Weathercote Wood."

"The price of a man's life measured in gold and magic," Rozt'a mused, staring past Dru at the dying fire. "He'd have to be a special man."

"He is," Dru insisted quickly. Rozt'a said nothing for several moments, leaving Dru to wonder if he'd misread her completely. "You wouldn't—You don't—You two, you're still—?"

She took a while to draw a breath and sigh before saying, "We're none of us easy-keepers, Dru. He's Galimer Long-fingers and nothing's turned out the way he hoped it would, but, yes, I love him—if that's the question you're asking. I want him back; I want him back from *her*. There's not enough gold or magic in the world to make me change my mind about that."

"You're twice the woman Wyndyfarh is, Roz."

It seemed, at last, that he'd said the right thing. Rozt'a leaned back against the cave wall and relaxed. Moments passed. Dru should have gone to his blankets, but he stayed put, savoring peace and quiet with an old friend. His mind was drifting when Rozt'a asked a question.

"Sheemzher said he left Dekanter six years ago. Do you think he's got the count right?"

Druhallen blinked foolishly, his thoughts had wandered a long way from goblins. "Yes," he answered slowly, then repeated himself as his opinions crystallized. "Yes, six years sounds about right. Amarandaris said things began changing in Dekanter about seven years ago."

"When the Beast Lord stopped being a nuisance and became a problem?"

Sometimes one casual statement brought everything else into line, like stranded pearls. "Exactly!" Dru nodded. "The scroll? Did the Beast Lord always have the scroll or did he find it seven years ago? Tymora's tears! How long has the Beast Lord been Ghistpok's god? How long has he been filling these mountains with misshapen goblins? So many questions and no one to ask!"

"Except Sheemzher."

"Except Sheemzher," Dru agreed. "Tiep had a point—the way Sheemzher talks, you think you understand what he's said because you think he's simple."

"You've noticed how he repeats things exactly as he hears them? Lady Wyndyfarh told him that together they'd save his children. She didn't say anything about that to us. When you said you'd bring her minions back in a gilded cage, she told you not to bother. She never said a word about goblins."

"And Sheemzher himself said it was too late to save his

children." Dru took a deep breath and shook his head. "Goblins live fast, Rozt'a. Most of them are probably dead by the time they're twenty-five. Six years is a long time at that rate."

"That's an excuse? Goblins don't live very long, so just let whoever's running that egg he described hatch out misshapen goblins to his heart's content?"

Rozt'a took Dru by surprise with her vehemence. He thought carefully before answering her—

"Galimer comes first. We get the scroll, we get Galimer. Nothing else matters. There's too much going on in Dekanter that we can't begin to understand and shouldn't poke our noses in. I've forgotten about the Red Wizards, Rozt'a; you don't want to start thinking about the goblins. Let Amarandaris, the Red Wizards, and the Beast Lord worry about the goblins."

"I'm not worried about *goblins*." The tension was back as Rozt'a got to her feet. "I'm worried what our guide's going to do when he realizes that his 'good lady' isn't worried about them, either."

9

6 Eleint, the Year of the Banner (1368 DR)

The Greypeak Mountains

Blue skies greeted the quartet and their horses when they left the cave the next morning. Tiep complained of a headache and tired easily, but was otherwise on the mend. They put him up on Hopper and covered more ground in the morning alone than they'd covered since they'd crossed the Dawn Pass Trail.

In the afternoon, a trio of red dragons flew freely overhead—a mother and her young, by the look of them. The first time they spiraled between the peaks, Sheemzher had led a pell-mell charge from the stone ledges to the bogs where they'd cowered, dreading an attack that didn't come. The second time the dragons swooped, they held their ground and watched an aerial dance of fire and grace. By the third and fourth times, they had better things to think about and just kept walking.

The ground was rising. There was more stone, less boggy forest. Sheemzher said they could push on with torches and reach Dekanter after dark, or camp above the last bog and arrive mid-morning at their destination. Dru thought of who and what they might find among Ghistpok goblins and decided he rather wait until daylight.

No one spoke out against Dru's caution.

The night was quiet with the clouds rolling back after midnight. There was no dawn, just a gradual brightening of the gray sky. Rozt'a said she'd seen something that might have been one of the misshapen goblins shortly before she'd awakened Dru.

"Makes sense," he said, rubbing his eyes. "They're goblins, after all. They don't like the sun. Yesterday would have been misery for them. They'd have spent the day hiding from the light."

Rozt'a nodded, "Then today they're hungry and hunting. Let's get out of here fast."

They did, but not before filling all their skins with water, all the horse nets with grass and shoots, and gathering fresh rushes and green wood poles for making torches. Dru could cast a durable light spell. It would last the better part of a day or night and he could control its brightness with a thought, but only complete fools would venture underground without torches and the natural means to light them.

After they'd gathered all their gear, Sheemzher proposed that they march straight into Ghistpok's colony.

"People good. Ghistpok good! Remember Sheemzher. Welcome Sheemzher. Welcome all."

Dru and Rozt'a harmonized on the word "No!" and the goblin assured them that they could get into the mines without introducing themselves to Ghistpok. There were ancient air shafts opening onto something he called the High Trail. All was going according to plan along the High Trail until they stumbled against a rockslide at an inconvenient narrows. There wasn't space to turn the horses around. The animals had to be coaxed backward to a wide spot. The goblin apologized continuously for his mistake.

Six years was a long time. Even ordinary mountains changed in that time, and Druhallen remembered what

Amarandaris had told him about the futility of maps in Dekanter. Druhallen supposed the goblin had made an innocent error, but the rockslide had reignited Tiep's suspicion of all things goblin.

At least the youth was behaving like his usual self again.

Sheemzher found another path. The humans judged it prudent to send him and Rozt'a ahead to check for rock slides. They were back sooner than Druhallen expected.

Rozt'a was nearly breathless. "You're not going to believe this, Dru," she said.

"Another rockslide?"

"No—the mines, the ruins—I was expecting a hole in the ground, but nothing like this. There's a hollow mountain up here. You could fit Scornubel inside the ruins and have room left for a village or two."

But the path she and Sheemzher had followed was too steep and rocky for the horses. Tiep said he'd stay behind.

"Who's interested in a hole where goblins live?"

Druhallen didn't try to explain. He scrambled ahead of Rozt'a and was breathing hard when he emerged from another rockslide ridge. The ruined mines took his breath away. All the conflict, loss, hardship, and deception that had brought him to this moment faded to insignificance—though he wished Galimer were beside him to share the sight.

Like Rozt'a, he'd expected ruins—true ruins: heaps of rubble left by miners and magicians alike, and dark doorways to the underground standing empty like so many blind eyes. Nothing could have been further from the truth. He'd forgotten that the dwarves had quarried stone from Dekanter as well as metal ore. In rough shape, Dekanter was an amphitheater; in size, the theater had been built for giants. Five receding tiers—each at least twenty feet high and twenty feet wide—rose from an irregular plain Dru judged to be a half-mile wide and slightly longer. Zig-zag patterns etched the tiers. Dru looked closer and realized they were ordinary stairways.

On the opposite side of Dekanter—across the narrows to the eastern side of the quarry—a gorge had been cut through all five layers of dark gray granite. The gorge curved and disappeared. Dru guessed it led to the Dawn Pass Trail, though in days past, surely it had been the western end of a road that wound into Netheril's heart.

Dekanter's great tiers weren't perfect. Here and there the rain, frost and snows of countless winters had shattered the quarry's deliberate structure. Streams of paler rock spread onto the lower levels. The untouched debris looked as if it could have fallen yesterday. With a shake of his head Druhallen dismissed his eyes' conclusion. Dekanter was ancient; even the scars of its abandonment were ancient.

Yet Dekanter wasn't abandoned. Ghistpok's goblins—Sheemzher's relatives—dwelt on the rubble-strewn plain at the bottom of the quarry. Their colony was a black-and-green smear across a small portion of the granite plain. Gardens, Dru thought—marveling for a moment that *goblins* would have the sense or skill to grow vegetables. Then common sense reclaimed his mind. The green patches weren't gardens—at least not deliberately planted crops. Ghistpok's goblins weren't farmers, they were merely living atop their garbage. What he'd taken for gardens were weeds erupting from the trash.

Dru rough-counted forty huts on the midden and one larger, stone-built structure. From their vantage, in the crease between the rectangular tiers and naturally irregular stone of the untouched mountains, the goblins were little more than dots between the huts. The stone building was as crude and ugly as any of the huts, but had the squat solidity of Zhentarim construction. He'd bet it was where the Network's minions lived while the slave trade flourished; and he almost pitied them for the stench and filth they'd surely endured.

There were more dots around the stone building than

anywhere else. If power and status had run true to form, the goblin chief, Ghistpok, had moved in once the Zhentarim left. Sheemzher might blame Takers for goblin slavery, but there'd never been a slave-trade that didn't rely on the cooperation of some element within the enslaved population.

There were two other landmarks on the plain. One, slightly north of the goblin colony, was a water pool so perfectly circular that it couldn't have been natural—and couldn't have been carved out of the stone by the goblins either. The second area lay some distance south of the colony. At first glance, it resembled a wizard's conjure circle painted white on the stone, but conjury required a measure of intelligence Dru would not grant any goblin, even Sheemzher standing silently at his side.

A black spire-stone jutted out of the white circle. The Greypeaks were, as their name implied, a study in shades of gray, without a trace of pure black or white. Both the stone and its circle were out of place, ominously out of place.

"What is that?" Dru asked the goblin.

Sheemzher had been staring at his own feet and raised his head slowly. His eyes were red and watering. He didn't like sunlight, even on an overcast day, and had suffered since losing his hat, which left Dru wondering about how many goblins the nearly shadeless colony contained. Surely more than he could see among the huts.

Cupping his hands around his eyes, Sheemzher peered out across the plain.

"Beast Lord, good sir."

Just when he thought he was getting a measure of goblin intelligence, Sheemzher would utter something unbelievable. "The Beast Lord is a black stone?"

"Sheemzher never see Beast Lord, good sir. Ghistpok say drink wine. Ghistpok say dance. Ghistpok say sing. Ghistpok say Beast Lord come. Ghistpok say not-look, never-look. Sheemzher look once. Elva go away. Sheemzher not-see

171

Beast Lord. Sheemzher see black stone. Sheemzher see Takers."

Was the stone a teleportation focus? Dru asked himself and asked Sheemzher, "Did the Takers come out of the stone? Did your wife vanish in a flash of bright light?"

"No," Sheemzher answered, a touch of exasperation in his voice. He calmed himself. "No, good sir. Takers under Dekanter. Takers walk. Elva walk into darkness, walk into mountain." The goblin tapped his foot on the stone. "Sheemzher tell already. Good sir forget, no? Sheemzher follow Elva. Here. Below. Into mountain. Sheemzher follow. Sheemzher find egg. Sheemzher tell already, good sir."

"You've been told," Rozt'a chided. "Pay attention to what he tells you from now on."

Dru didn't know if she was joking. "Do I understand that there's an entrance to the old mines at the bottom of the quarry? Do we have to climb down these tiers to reach it? Do we have to meet Ghistpok? You said that wouldn't be necessary."

He'd been paying attention when Sheemzher assured them they didn't have to meet Ghistpok in order to steal the scroll.

"Many ways in, good sir. One way all rocks, no good. One way below, yes. Other ways. Many other ways. Sheemzher find. Not worry, good sir."

A strange sound filled the quarry. It started soft, grew louder, and as hard as Druhallen listened, he couldn't decide if it came from an animal or some kind of horn, and, if an animal, whether from a single beast or many. He was thinking magic when Rozt'a slapped his arm and pointed to the southern tiers. About twenty goblins were marching down the zigzag stairways. His imagination rebelled. Goblins couldn't make such a noise and twenty of them couldn't fill the quarry with echoing sound.

Then Sheemzher added his note to the chorus. The goblin's eyes were shut and his head was thrown back. His lips shaped the sound which he made in the depths of his throat.

"Sheemzher! Stop! Quiet!"

Sheemzher didn't obey. He didn't appear to have heard Druhallen's words. He opened his mouth wider; the sound deepened in pitch. Dru felt it beneath his ribs more than he heard it in his ears.

"Enough!" he shouted and seized the goblin's shoulders. "When I say to stop something, you stop! Understood?"

The goblin quaked and nodded his head vigorously. "Sheemzher understand. Sheemzher forget. Hunters return. Pots full." He pointed at the goblins on the zigzag stairs. "Welcome hunters. Sheemzher forget."

A trickle of goblins left the midden, racing southward.

Druhallen pulled off his ring and squinted through it. The descending goblins had spears very similar to the one Sheemzher carried slung between their shoulders and animal carcasses slung from the spears, none was larger than a swamp rat. He realized that goblins weren't herders or farmers. Maybe it had been different when the Zhentarim ran their slave market in the quarry. Maybe they'd seduced the goblins with food, but since Amarandaris abandoned the market, the bog forests were the goblins' sole source of food. No wonder Amarandaris believed Ghistpok's goblins were starving.

And, no wonder that the sight of hunters returning with meat had roused an instinctive welcome from their own goblin.

"You're not one of Ghistpok's goblins any more," Druhallen reminded Sheemzher. "Your loyalty lies with us— with your good lady."

"Sheemzher not forget, good sir. Sheemzher remember. Sheemzher find way now, good sir?"

"Soon."

"Soon?" Rozt'a sputtered. "How long are you planning to stay here? I'm for getting this damned scroll today, if we

173

can, and getting our tail feathers out of these mountains before they're plucked."

The goblin nodded. "Sheemzher say yes! People eat now. People happy. Nobody look. Nobody see. Nobody know."

Druhallen thought of the spells he'd memorized last night. They weren't the ones he'd planned to use when he tried to crack the Beast Lord's egg. "We don't want to rush ahead blindly. We want to be prepared."

"You want to wait until after midnight." Rozt'a saw through Druhallen's caution. "You want to change your mind."

"I'd feel safer with different spells. You'd *be* safer."

Dru withered a little in their disappointment and when Rozt'a suggested that she could follow the goblin as he searched for a way into the mines that didn't expose them to scrutiny, he agreed even though a part of him felt that they shouldn't be splitting up.

There were more mysteries in Dekanter than a man could count, starting with ancient Netheril and working forward in time to the Beast Lord and the real reason Amarandaris and the Black Network had pulled their slave market out of this place. If he'd had the time, the magic, and the muscle, Dru would have liked to unravel a few of those mysteries. Lacking all those things, he easily stifled his curiosity and hoped only to escape with the golden scroll.

He returned to the horses and Tiep, scouting campsites along the way.

"You and I make the night's camp," he told the youth when they were together. "Rozt'a's gone off with the goblin to find tomorrow's way in. I spotted a blind gully with runoff pool. If we can get the horses in, they'll have plenty of water and won't go wandering. We'll take them in one at a time. You grab Hopper—" He took Star's rein. If they could get him and Hopper up the path, the others would follow peacefully.

Tiep proved a non-cooperative partner. "You let Rozt'a go

off alone with Sheemzher?" He'd folded his arms across his chest.

"Do you think Rozt'a can't handle a goblin, Tiep? Should I mention that to her when she gets back?"

"Tymora protect me! Don't do *that!*" Tiep snatched Hopper's rein and fell in behind Druhallen.

"What then? I thought you and the goblin had made peace."

"We did," Tiep replied with a notable lack of enthusiasm. "As much peace as an honest man can make with a liar."

"Right," Dru agreed with a sigh.

Star sulked and balked, but he was thirsty and the smell of running water got him down the last slope.

"You're sure we're going to be able to get them *out* of here?" Tiep asked when he and Hopper were beside the water.

The slope had been steeper than Dru imagined. They'd all had a few sliding, frightening moments. Dru had wrenched his shoulder keeping Star upright and Hopper was favoring the hoof he'd cracked before they got to Parnast.

"We'll push 'em out one at a time, if we have to. It was here or leave them on the bogs. If the goblins catch sight of them, they'll eat them all." After emptying one of the forage-filled nets, Dru handed the green wood poles to Tiep. "Strip them down while I heat the pitch and dip the rushes."

They had three torches finished when Rozt'a and Sheemzher returned.

"He found it," Rozt'a announced. Dru watched Tiep roll his eyes skyward. "We went down as far as we could—as far as *I* could without light. Why Ao made their eyes better than ours is something I'll never understand."

Dru wound another length of pitch-dripping greenery around the working end of a torch. Rozt'a wouldn't have given up sunlight or far-sight for all the moonlight in the world, but that didn't keep her from complaining. He understood the frustration—and a few of the races did have undisputedly better vision than humans did—but not the goblins. One had only to look at Sheemzher's watery eyes to know that.

Rozt'a hefted one of the finished torches. She tested the pitch to see if it would light. "We could take these and check it out, Dru—go down and really see what we're up against before you're up against midnight decisions."

Druhallen advocated caution. In truth, he was anxious . . . afraid. Rozt'a, Sheemzher, even Tiep were cut from different cloth than he. They were fighters, hunters, or gamblers and would rather be in the middle of a situation than mapping it from the outside. Dru had probably done more damage to life and limb than the three of them combined, but always in reaction. He didn't start fights, didn't deliberately expose himself to danger—

"We won't *steal* the godsforsaken thing," Rozt'a chided. "We're just going to try to get a look at it so we can decide *how* we'll steal it tomorrow . . . is that better?"

She tossed her torch Dru's way. He caught it without hesitation.

Tiep grabbed the other two. "Who says we won't steal it?" he asked as he scrambled up the rocks.

Dru made them wait until he'd checked his folding box and pulled soft rope from their gear. He wouldn't deny the wisdom in Rozt'a's words—or in Tiep's for that matter. If they *could* snatch the scroll, then, by gods, they would, but he wasn't plunging underground without embers enough to kindle his fire spells five times over and all the rope he could comfortably carry.

Sheemzher's way into Dekanter was a gap in the gray rocks that was generously wide for him, tight for Rozt'a and Tiep, and downright painful for a man with Druhallen's shoulders. He went in feet first. When he got stuck, Rozt'a wrapped her arms around his dangling legs and pulled with all her strength. Druhallen entered the ancient mines of Dekanter with a groan.

Moments later, after he'd kindled a light spell, Dru had forgotten his discomfort. A pair of gilded symbols had been carved into the squared-off ceiling. He didn't read dwarven script, but he knew their Dethek runes by sight.

"We've come to the right place."

The goblin set a steady pace. There wasn't time to explore, even when their path took Dru past side chambers where the Netherese wizards had perfected—or not perfected—their art. The chambers had been looted—Dru could see that much from the corridor—but debris remained. The walls of several were covered with the Empire's ancient script.

Dru's head said, keep walking. His heart said, take a moment, read the walls—what harm can a moment bring? The light spell followed him into a square room.

Woe betide the . . . He racked his memory for a translation. *Woe betide the moon-eyed thief* . . .

Rozt'a broke Dru's concentration. "We're in the dark up here. Get a move on. You're the one with the light."

Dru hurried, caught up. He deliberately hadn't memorized the Candlekeep scrying spell. He *couldn't* succumb to the temptation to cast it; that didn't stop the aching. "You don't understand—" he muttered and quickly swallowed the rest of his private disappointment.

"I don't," Rozt'a agreed. "Galimer would. He'd be wide-eyed beside you, if he wasn't stuck in Weathercote Wood."

Druhallen nodded. Remembering where Galimer was effectively dashed his curiosity. "Lead on," he said to the goblin.

Sheemzher led them along sloping corridors. They were moving away from the quarry, at least Dru thought they were. Over the years, his sense of direction had proven reliable above ground, but this was his first experience with caverns and mines. He was calm until their corridor ended at a cross passage. Dru matched the Dethek runes above them with the ones he'd seen at their entrance. He deduced that the four on the cross-passage ceiling were directional guides—useless directional guides for a man who could read a Netherese wizard's curse but not a dwarf's clear-cut runes.

Left or right? He asked himself and was suddenly in the grip of primal terror: They had torches, but no water, no food. If they made a wrong turn or failed to retrace their steps accurately, the light spell would eventually fizzle, likewise the torches, and they'd be trapped in the dark. Dru felt the mountain around him. His heart raced, his lungs labored— The damned goblin wasn't even looking up at the Dethek runes for guidance!

The light spell revealed Sheemzher standing on his toes in the intersection. He turned slowly to the right, then to the left. His eyes were shut, his nose was pointed up, his nostrils were wide, and he sniffed the still air like a dog.

After a few moments of this behavior, he chose the right-side path. "Come," he said. Come. Sheemzher remember. This way."

Dru had beaten back his fear—or he thought he had. His feet weren't moving. "You remember *what?*" Dru asked, sounding like Tiep. "This can't be the path you followed six years ago, not if you followed Elva and the Takers underground from that black stone."

"Sheemzher remember smell, good sir. Sheemzher never forget egg-smell. Smell stronger this way. This way, right way, good sir. Come."

"Bad eyes, good ears," Rozt'a muttered, repeating the common wisdom. "Good nose, too . . . I guess . . . hope." The light spell made all of them look pale, but Rozt'a's face had no color at all.

They hadn't gone far when they came to an intersection that offered three choices and more Dethek runes. Sheemzher took the middle path. Dru committed the runes to memory. Wizards trained their memories the way warriors sharpened their swords and merchants counted their coins. They didn't make mistakes—Druhallen of Sunderath didn't make mistakes when he memorized.

178

Make a mistake with a fireball and he'd be dead instantly. Make a mistake inside Dekanter and there'd be time enough for despair.

The mountain was all around Druhallen, pressing inward, interfering with his memory and, maybe, his judgment. They kept going forward because that was easier than making a decision to turn back.

The squared-off, rune-marked corridors gave way to rougher, unmarked passages. Newer passages, Dru thought, and wondered why.

"Not far," Sheemzher announced when they came to another intersection.

They heard that before in Weathercote. This was their eighth crossing, the third with no runes, the third where they'd followed the straight-ahead path. Dru looked for something . . . *anything* . . . physical to commit to his memory.

He heard something instead, down the left-hand path—garbled sounds that might have been voices. Sheemzher tugged Dru's sleeve. The goblin's ears were as good as a man's.

"Quick! Quick, good sir!"

"What are they?"

"Demons, good sir," the goblin predictably answered. "Quick!"

Dru called the light close and dimmed it to a firefly spark. They linked hands and trusted Sheemzher to lead them through the darkness. No one spoke, but they weren't silent. Their boots clattered on the stone. Rozt'a's sword clattered against her hip. Tiep yelped and Dru had never heard anything half so loud as the hammering of his heart . . . until he heard the sound of pursuit.

Daring a backward glance Dru saw light and shadows behind them. Whatever the demons were, they didn't have a goblin's dark vision advantage over humankind. Dru planted his feet and the quartet came to a stop. He fingered his folding box and found a sliver of quartz near the hinge.

"Roz—What do you think? Stand or run?"

She swore once and whispered her decision: "Stand. Everybody, flat against the wall and hope they've got to get close before they can start fighting. What about you, Dru? Can you fire them from here?"

He rubbed the quartz between his fingertips, warming it. "I'd sooner give you an advantage. By the time I have something to aim fire at, there won't be enough time for me to blur you."

The blurring spell would make Rozt'a shifty and elusive in the eyes of anyone trying to attack her. It was like armor, without the weight or encumbrance and usually she welcomed it.

"I'll take my chances."

That wasn't the answer he'd hoped to hear. "There's risk to fire—they might not be against us until we use it and we could find ourselves with nothing to breathe afterward."

"We're here to steal a golden scroll. Burn them." Rozt'a surged forward to take the point position in the tunnel.

Druhallen shifted the crystal to his off hand and retrieved a cold ember instead. They waited in the dark until he saw something he considered more silhouette than shadow.

There—he thought, aiming the spell as an archer would aim an arrow. He felt a prick of icy cold as it leapt off his fingertips. A magician could track his own spells; a good magician could track the spells of others. For several heartbeats, the question in Dru's mind was: do they have a good magician with them?

The answer, when it came, was a resounding *No!* Blinding light and screams filled the tunnel. Dru's fireball eliminated an unknown number of their pursuers, but not all of them. His aim had been slightly off, or his timing—whichever, the magical fire had erupted *behind* the front ranks of pursuit. If they hadn't had enemies before, Dru and his companions had them now. The silhouettes that

raced toward them had thrown down their own torches and
were lop-sided with drawn swords.

There was no advantage left in the darkness. Druhallen
let his light expand and rise to the ceiling, then weighed
his next move, defense or offense? Blur Rozt'a or throw
more fire? He knew what Rozt'a would say. She'd rather
have him take down one of the long-armed swordswingers
coming toward them. Dru could cast a fiery streak with the
ember bits that remained on his fingers after the fireball,
and he did, as soon as the kindling power had flowed back
to him.

He aimed for the base of the forefront swordswinger's
neck and his head disappeared in a sphere of flame. The
three behind the first never hesitated; that was ominous.
They leapt over their fallen comrade and two of them
attacked Rozt'a together.

Dru recovered quickly from the fire spell. He had two
more memorized. The angles were bad now that Rozt'a was
fighting. The odds of hitting her were almost as high as hitting one of her opponents. Dru took aim at their third pursuer, the one hanging back. He'd lost the advantage of
surprise. The fellow dodged and, despite the close range,
wound up singed, not burned.

Rozt'a backpedaled and, for an instant, Druhallen was
closer to the attackers' swords than she was. Using the
torch as if it had been the ax shaft he'd left behind, Dru beat
steel with green wood. It was a close call—a chunk of wood
went spinning in the air—but Dru survived and retreated.

He dropped the bit of quartz. There wasn't anything he
could do for Rozt'a except prepare his second and last fireball, in case they attracted more attention. There was something Sheemzher could do, and he did it well. The goblin
scurried forward, low to the floor, and jabbed his spear at
Rozt'a's opponents whenever they tried to get beneath her
guard.

Sheemzher didn't draw blood, but he kept the swordswingers off-balance until Rozt'a did. With a shout and a swallow-tail slash, she disarmed her right-side attacker and made sure he'd never swing a sword again. The goblin got past Druhallen and finished the wounded attacker with a thrust and a twist. In that moment, Rozt'a got the upper hand on the other swordswinger. She put him down with a two-handed cut across the mid-section.

The third attacker—the attacker that Druhallen had singed—beat a retreat. Dru's last fireball burnt itself out without stopping him.

"I'm whole," Rozt'a declared before anyone asked.

"And I," Dru added. "Sheemzher? Tiep?"

Tiep answered that he was fine. Sheemzher's attention was on the corpses. Druhallen called the goblin off before he butchered them; then he willed his light magic to its greatest radiance.

"Demons!"

The goblin was wrong, but the bodies belonged to creatures unlike any Druhallen had seen before. They had the torsos of men, the limbs of elves, the faces of goblins, and the jewel-red eyes of Wyndyfarh's mantis servants. The corpses were bald and instead of either pointed or rounded ears, their skulls bore what appeared to be parchment drumheads behind their temples. Their skin was a shade lighter than Sheemzher's, but scaled in places, especially around their hands. They had four fingers, two of which were jointed; the other two were rigid and opposed like an insect's claws. The pair wore scabbard belts for their weapons but nothing else in the way of clothing. Short of cutting them open, Dru couldn't tell if they were male or female.

Dru pried the sword from one death-frozen hand. The hilt had been adapted for their odd combination of pincers and fingers, but the balance was tolerable, the steel better. He handed the weapon to Tiep who hesitated and wouldn't take it.

"Not me."

"Take it," Dru insisted. "You could get lucky with it; you won't without it. Get the belt and scabbard, too. You don't want to gash yourself while we're walking." He loosened the second corpse's belt.

Rozt'a gave one of her disdainful snorts. "Walking! We'll be moving a damn sight faster than that! You were right. There, I admit it. We're not ready for this. We've got planning to do."

"Too late for that, Roz." He freed the belt and exchanged it with the one that supported his folding box. "One got away. He's going to tell somebody what he survived. By sundown, whatever else lives in these mines is going to be laying for us. We've got one chance, right now, to find Sheemzher's egg, snatch the scroll, and beat a once-and-forever retreat."

"You can't be serious—" Rozt'a began.

The goblin cut her off. "Sheemzher find egg. Not far. Sheemzher find sky new way, yes?"

"Yes."

"Have you got *anything* useful left?" Rozt'a asked.

"Enough light to see us until tomorrow's dawn. A fireball. A pall of gloom. Warding, if we found an empty room and needed to hide, and let me blur you next time; no arguments." Her chin dipped. "Tiep, get that belt." The boy didn't move. "You've seen worse. You didn't think this would be a walk in the park, did you?"

"I hoped," Tiep admitted, but he got the belt and fastened it around his waist.

When they got back to the sky—as Sheemzher put it—Druhallen expected his nerves would quake for a month; in the meantime, he nudged Tiep in the goblin's direction. Sheemzher's sense of time and direction were better underground than they'd been in the Weathercote Wood. They truly hadn't gone much farther when light glowed ahead of them.

They approached with caution: ten steps, then wait and listen. The tunnel widened but remained a rough-cut passage to a chamber that was filled with a faint, but steady, pale green light. Dru dampened his own light spell and strained his senses searching for another wizard's magic. He found it, too: powerful, but alien. A glance through his ring revealed nothing they couldn't see with their eyes alone. It should have been reassuring; it wasn't.

Dru successfully stifled a twinge of guilt when Sheemzher waved his hands in silhouette to indicate that he'd be the first to enter the chamber.

Go ahead, he mouthed, moving his lips but making no sound.

Tiep scowled and drew his sword. The sound was louder than thunder in a summer's night, but didn't precipitate disaster. Sheemzher walked ten paces, twenty paces into the light. He turned and beckoned them closer.

"Empty. All empty."

Rozt'a led Druhallen and Tiep into a large, but not huge, chamber. The light, which seemed to rise from the chiseled floor on the far side of the chamber's center, revealed an irregular dome that formed both walls and ceiling, but the light wasn't nearly bright enough to banish shadows. Dru thought they were alone, though he couldn't prove it. The center of the chamber was clear, but the sides were cluttered with boulders and piles of smaller rocks. Anything man-sized or smaller could be hiding there.

The chamber was damp, even misty. There was water here, and there had been for a very long time. Dripping icicles of stone hung from the ceiling; glistening spires grew beneath them. When Dru touched them with his ring he felt only the faintest magic and manipulation.

The same could not be said for a series of pools had been dug out of the floor. Their shapes were regular, their lips precisely square, and the largest of them was the source of the light that filled the chamber. Rozt'a knelt to examine it and without warning dipped her hand beneath the surface. She'd raised her hand to her lips before Dru found his voice. She was already spitting when he told her not to swallow.

"Brine!" she sputtered between spits. "Brine from the worst pickles ever made!"

Tiep chuckled, Druhallen resisted.

"How do you get *brine* in the middle of a mountain?" she demanded.

"Rock salt," Dru suggested seriously enough, though Tiep took it for a joke.

The rock all around them was the same gray granite they'd been hiking through for days. Good for making buildings, but useless for pickles. Dru took Rozt'a's place beside the pool. He looked down into the light, saw the underwater passages connecting the light-filled pool to the smaller, dimmer pools on either side.

"What good is brine?" Tiep asked. "You can't drink it."

"The oceans and seas are filled with creatures that don't *drink* brine," Dru replied and collected a few drops of the suspect liquid on his fingertip. He'd seen an ocean just once, after his visit to Candlekeep. It had little in common with the brightly lit Dekanter pool, including the taste. The brine on Dru's finger was far saltier than Candlekeep's ocean and slick, reminding him of blood.

Rozt'a observed, "I don't see anything swimming in there."

"Be grateful," Dru replied in a tone meant to discourage further questions.

Thanks—as usual—to Ansoain's relentless collection of useless facts and her determination to share those facts with her son and apprentice, Dru had begun to put the puzzle pieces together. The central piece was a bit of information Amarandaris had given him about the second garrison slaughter. The Zhentarim and Red Wizards had torn each other apart. Those were the honored divide-and-conquer tactics of those who'd mastered the discipline of usurping another sentient mind. Dru could name a handful of living wizards and a score of races or monsters who were known to usurp sentient minds, but only one such race made use of brine-filled pools.

If Druhallen was remembering Ansoain's lessons correctly then the Beast Lord wasn't a god but a colony of mind flayers and they were in a world of hurt.

"You know something, Druhallen. Tell me what you know," Rozt'a demanded.

"I don't know anything." And Dru didn't, not yet. The picture wasn't nearly complete and much of it remained contradictory. The commanding presence of a mind flayer colony—something called its Elder Brain—was supposed to reside in a brine-filled pool. Without an Elder Brain, there was no colony—according to Ansoain, who might have been wrong. She'd never encountered a mind flayer, merely learned about them as she learned about everything else.

"Is this what you're calling 'the egg'?" Dru asked Sheemzher.

Sheemzher shook his head. "Egg not here, good sir. Egg there." The goblin pointed to a tunnel in the shadows that Dru hadn't noticed before.

"Let's go then."

The tunnel was short and led to a room square enough to have been hollowed out by dwarves but cluttered with rock debris and chunks of twisted metal, some of them larger than a full-grown man. Sheemzher's egg stood in the center of the room. It was no more an egg than the creatures they'd been killing for the last few days were demons, but it was an athanor of dangerous proportions. Dru judged the oval engine was twice as high as he was tall and perhaps a third as wide as it was high. It was made from hammered and riveted plates of bronze, or possibly brass. Double-doors, hinged at the athanor's widest point, had been left open and revealed a two-chamber interior. The bottom chamber was large enough to accommodate a goblin or three. The upper chamber, though much smaller, could have held a good-sized snake or a hundred of Lady Wyndyfarh's mantises.

Metal pipes and parchment hoses connected the two interior chambers and other parts of the athanor, too. The widest pipe of all disappeared into one of the walls above an incised rectangle that might have been the start of another rock-cut passage. Two more pipes were bolted to the floor. Dru figured he knew what the athanor did and was asking himself how it worked and what it had to do with a Nether scroll when he looked up and found the answers to both questions in the same place.

A golden cylinder as long as his forearm stuck out of the top of the athanor and up into at least a score of wires dangling from the ceiling. Some of the wires were shorter than the others. All of them were soot stained. He didn't know what leapt between the wires and the scroll—maybe fire, maybe lightning, maybe something he'd never studied—but he understood the principle of using explosive spells to power engines both arcane and ordinary.

The metal litter on the floor—the smaller sections of pipe and larger sheets of brass—could have formed the shells of earlier eggs. The Beast Lord—the mind flayers—hadn't perfected the transmutation process. Suddenly, the misshapen goblins connected to the growing pattern. They were the egg's failures and the swordswingers were its triumphs.

Sheemzher grabbed his sleeve in a panic. "Not egg. Not egg! Smell right, but not egg! Too big. Very much too big."

That, too, fit into the pattern. "Six years, Sheemzher. Remember that it's been six years since you were here. They've rebuilt your egg." Dru pointed out the piles of blasted metal. "Step back and look up. It's your egg with the golden scroll sticking out the top."

Sheemzher retreated, squinted, and began jumping for joy. "Sheemzher see! Sheemzher see! Get it now, good sir? Sheemzher climb. Sheemzher climb good."

It couldn't be this easy, Druhallen thought as he lifted the goblin. It couldn't be—

And it wasn't.

Sheemzher had one foot on the hinge of the open door and the other still resting on Druhallen's shoulder when they heard the sound of a heavy latch being thrown.

10

6 Eleint, the Year of the Banner (1368 DR)

The Greypeak Mountains

Tiep liked having a sword in his hand. He didn't mind
that the hilt was the wrong shape for his human hand or
the weapon was point heavy once he'd found a comfortable
way to hold it. In fact, he rather liked the weighty sensa-
tion. Knives were nice, but if he couldn't reel off fireballs the
way Druhallen did, Tiep wanted a sword riding below his
hip.

He'd won a sword off a Scornubel swell last winter and
worn it with a swagger until it had become embarrassingly
apparent that Rozt'a wouldn't teach him how to use it.
Worse, she'd whispered in the ear of the city's armsmasters
and none of them would take him on as a student. Bitterly
disappointed, he'd sold the sword back to the swell come
spring and hit the road with his familiar knives.

In his wildest dreams, Tiep had never imagined
Druhallen telling him to pick up a sword, and to tell the
truth, he'd been none-too-eager to unfasten the scabbard
from around the hips of something that clearly wasn't civilized. If the weapon had been enchanted, he'd have gotten
the worst of it; he usually did. Fortunately there wasn't any

magic to the sword or its scabbard and Dru's words were still swirling in his ears—

You could get lucky—

The phrase formed a satisfying counterpoint to one of Rozt'a's favorite sayings: *I worry more about incompetence than skill.*

With visions of bravery, Tiep cut the air in the egg chamber with a flourish. He knew he was incompetent, but he'd always been lucky. At least, he'd always thought he was, but if he'd been truly lucky, he'd have been paying attention before Rozt'a slapped her hand between his shoulders and shoved him toward the doorway.

It was disrespectful, that's what it was. Hadn't one of the first things Galimer ever said to him been, *Don't sneak up on Rozt'a when she's drawn steel?* Granted, Tiep's first thoughts as he staggered toward the doorway hadn't been a deadly counterattack. He'd been so surprised he'd let the tip clunk and scrape across the stone. Still there was principle to defend—

Tiep caught his balance and spun around. "Rozt'a—"

Something was wrong and the wrongness was unfolding so fast Tiep couldn't get his thoughts around it. Rozt'a's sword was out, her fist was cocked, and she wore her wolf-face. She didn't talk, she hissed.

"No noise . . . no noise," and "We're getting out of here."

Tiep had to backpedal for all he was worth to avoid her charge. But why? There was Druhallen beside the metal egg. Dru's arms were raised; he was poised to catch Sheemzher who'd scrambled up the egg like a lizard and was hauling on the golden scroll with all his puny strength.

Had the damned dog-faced goblin pulled when he should have pushed and started something he couldn't stop? That would figure.

Rozt'a changed direction between strides and, discounting the fact that her beloved foster-son was showing naked steel, reached across her body to grab him at the opposite shoulder and spin him around before giving him another, mightier, shove toward the door. On his way around, Tiep snagged a glimpse of what might be the cause of the chaos. The wall to the left of the metallic egg that had been solid stone when they entered the egg chamber had become a shimmering mirage—like the road ahead on a too-hot summer day—with a dead-black slit in the middle of it.

Tiep needed another look to be sure of what he'd seen. When he tried to get it, Rozt'a's fist landed in the middle of his back and he was crossing the threshold into the tunnel between the pool chamber and the egg chamber before he caught his balance again. It was pitch dark in the tunnel. Druhallen had their light and Druhallen wasn't with them.

Rozt'a must have guessed that Dru's name was primed on the back of his tongue, because when she hit Tiep again, it was with her open hand. She seized his shirt and didn't let go.

"Not a sound!"

There was a dogleg in the tunnel. It hadn't been a problem when they'd had Druhallen's spell illuminating their path, but they missed it going out. Tiep, who was shoved in front of Rozt'a, slammed into the stone chin and nose first. He smelled his own blood and his thoughts were echo and pain when they got to the pool chamber.

"Hide!" Rozt'a hissed and pulled, rather than shoved, him along the chamber's right-side wall.

Tiep spun out of her grasp. "Where's Dru?" He danced sideways. There was no light moving in the tunnel. "Where's Druhallen? We can't leave Druhallen."

His voice had risen; he expected a smack on the jaw, but Rozt'a's hands were shaking too much for her to deliver a punch, deserved or not.

"Hide! We've got to hide."

She was terrified. Tiep's foster-mother who'd laid open more men than Tiep could count was terrified. For the first

191

time, the possibility that they were in serious trouble—
doom-and-death trouble—entered Tiep's mind. Short of
diving into the briny pools Tiep didn't see any hiding places,
and he'd have to know exactly what they were running from
before he jumped into one of those.

"Where? There's no place to hide."

Rozt'a's eyes, fortunately, were sharper and so were her
wits. She'd spotted an empty shadow in the chamber's
walls. It was more a fold in the rock than a cave and it was
a dead-end passage—a very dead end if anyone came along
with a lamp or light spell. But it was the best they were
likely to find.

"Keep your head down—your face'll glow like the moon
down here," Rozt'a whispered, sounding more like herself,
more in control and command. A moment later she added,
"We're kneeling in rock dust . . . we're kneeling in dust! Rub
some on your face and into your hair."

Tiep was used to listening to Rozt'a in emergencies. He
didn't know why he was smearing himself with dirt, but he
rubbed vigorously and was attacking his ears when the rock
began to rumble and vibrate. Tiep thought he was already
as frightened as a man could get but, as rock icicles crashed
to the cavern floor, he discovered untapped reserves of
dread. The pale light in the central pool grew so bright Tiep
could feel it as he crouched beside Rozt'a with his eyes
closed and his dirty face pressed against his knees.

While the light brightened, the vibrations intensified
until they were throbs that loosened rock. Tiep and Rozt'a
bounced against each other as if they'd been huddled in the
back of some scrap-collector's cart. He thought he might
have screamed; he was sure that Rozt'a had. Then a rum-
bling pulse more powerfully than the rest combined lifted
them off the stone and held them suspended.

Like a fool, Tiep opened his eyes. The light was so hot
and bright that he couldn't see anything except his bones.
Tiep closed his eyes—he thought he'd closed his eyes—but

the bone vision lingered. He thought he'd died, thought that he'd gone beyond death, beyond his body, and hoped it would be *over* soon.

It was. The throbbing ebbed rapidly, along with the light and the heat—which had surely been imaginary because when feeling returned, Tiep found himself entirely unhurt, except for bruised knees and a ringing in his ears. Their luck had held.

"We're alive!" he whispered to Rozt'a.

They didn't have to rub themselves with dust now. The smell of granite was inside Tiep's nostrils and plastered his throat. It threatened to become cement when he first tried to swallow. Desperate for air, Tiep hacked and spat without regard for who—or what—might overhear.

Rozt'a stood beside him. She hadn't said a word, hadn't swallowed, hadn't fought with the gray gunk she'd breathed into her throat. They both flinched at the sound of tumbling rock. The light rising from the central pool was once again pale. It scarcely penetrated the dusty air. Any sound could mean they weren't alone, that their enemies stalked them or that Dru was nearby.

Tiep considered calling his foster-father. If Rozt'a had shouted Druhallen's name, Tiep would have joined her. Rozt'a remained silent, and Tiep did, too. At that moment, Tiep cared little for survival. If enemies moved in the chamber, he'd fight hard and eagerly to his own death.

Nothing emerged from the dust. There were other crunches which Tiep's ears slowly understood as the settling of rocks loosened by the magical eruption. The air seemed clearer after every rock rolled to its final resting spot. It was probably illusion or hope, but it could have been true.

Tiep *was* glad to be alive. Humans—living things in general—clung to life. It was only natural for humans—one street-raised human in particular—to worry just a bit about the future before he started celebrating the present.

Some of that shaken and fallen rock could be blocking the tunnel to the surface.

Or the one that led back to the egg chamber.

Rozt'a must have had the same thought—at least she started walking toward the egg-chamber passage before Tiep did. There was debris, but not enough to make the tunnel impassible. The dust made it darker, of course, but they were feeling their way slowly, not running. With the dog-leg turn uneventfully behind them, they were no more than forty paces from the egg-chamber threshold.

It was very quiet—no moans, no footsteps. Tiep told himself that silence meant nothing either good or bad, but he wasn't really surprised when they came up against a smooth granite wall where the doorway had stood a few moments earlier. Rozt'a beat her fists against the stone, and Tiep did the same. The granite didn't budge, wasn't hollow. Tiep gave up before he hurt himself then put his arms gently around his foster-mother and forced her to retreat from the treasonous wall.

"There's another way in. I saw it just before you shoved me out. We'll find it."

"Too late," Rozt'a replied, her first words, and they left her gagging the way Tiep first words had left him.

He released her and she hurled herself against the rock. Rozt'a could scarcely breathe, but that didn't stop her from putting her fists into the granite and calling Dru's name.

"There's another way," Tiep repeated.

His foster-mother didn't seem to hear him. Tiep found her fists by touch and sound and tried a second time to gently pull her away from the wall. Rozt'a wouldn't yield to gentleness. She shook him off and when Tiep touched her again, she lashed out wildly, blindly with a backhand punch that set Tiep back on his heels.

Black panic nibbled into Tiep's thoughts—there was another way, but they'd have to look for it together. His mind couldn't contain the thought of splitting up without feeding panic. "Rozt'a?" he whispered, barely in control himself. He heard her crash into the wall again. "Tymora, help us? Help me? Rozt'a, please? *Mother*—?"

In the beginning Rozt'a had wanted Tiep to call her Mother. He'd tried a few times, but he'd been on his own too long. The instinct had died—until the goddess of luck reawakened it. With that single word, Rozt'a stopped her frantic hammering. They found each other and, arm in arm, walked toward the pool chamber.

"How should we start looking?" Tiep asked.

Rozt'a didn't answer. She was beside Tiep, holding him tightly, but that was only her body. Her mind was somewhere else—with Druhallen, inside the egg chamber, or with Galimer, in Weathercote Wood. In the dogleg part of the tunnel, where light was a promise but they couldn't yet see each other, Tiep hugged his foster-mother—his true mother—as he never had and received nothing in reply.

Panic said, *You're in charge. You. You. You!* and for a heartbeat panic was triumphant, then the scrappy stubbornness that had kept Tiep alive in situations every bit as bad as this—he'd picked Sememmon's pockets and survived, hadn't he?—took command.

"C'mon, Rozt'a. We've got to find that other way."

They walked slowly, quietly toward the light—and it was a good thing that they were both slow and quiet. Tiep heard sounds that said they weren't alone any more and they weren't about to be reunited with Druhallen, either. He nudged Rozt'a sideways. Some part of his foster-mother was still functioning—without hesitation she made herself small in the seam between the wall and the floor. She checked her weapons, then began creeping toward the light.

Tiep patted his hip before he crouched. His sword was in its scabbard. He didn't remember putting it there. Tymora had heard his prayers before he'd uttered them. As long as the luck goddess was watching out for them, they had a chance . . .

A long-limbed silhouette marched in front of the tunnel
threshold, sword at its side. It could have been the twin of
the creature who'd carried the sword Tiep wore. Other silhouettes followed it. The followers walked on two legs but
wouldn't have been as tall as the sword-carrying creatures,
even if they'd stood fully upright, which they didn't. Their
shoulders and backs were rounded and their heads hung so
low on their necks that they were looking down, not forward. One was limping badly, two others leaned on each
other for support. Tiep couldn't guess whether they'd been
injured in the shake-up or long before. He was still trying to
answer that question when he realized the crippled silhouettes were goblins.

Two more of the long-limbed swordswingers followed the
goblins. Slaves, he realized. Slavers and slaves. Slavers,
slaves, and unnatural creatures hatched out of a metal egg.
The pattern wasn't enough to reconcile Tiep with his goblin
nemesis, and if Druhallen was dead because he'd stayed
behind with Sheemzher, then no goblin was safe from Tiep's
revenge—but he'd kill them cleanly, not like this.

With the egg chamber closed off behind them, Tiep saw
two choices: stay where they were, hiding in the shadows, or
get closer to the light and a better understanding of what
they were up against. Tiep put his hand on Rozt'a's shoulder and together they crept forward. If only all his choices
were that simple.

Most of the dust had settled, which meant that it was still
pretty bad but Tiep could see all the way across the chamber.
The tunnel where they'd first entered the chamber was open.
If they could get to it—no, make that *when* they were ready,
they could get out. Tiep didn't let himself think that he and
Rozt'a might have to leave without Druhallen, but he did
regret not paying closer attention when Sheemzher picked
their path through the intersections.

Tiep had other things to worry about before then. By
rough count, about ten swordswingers had herded about

forty goblin slaves to the center of the chamber, facing the large, glowing pool. Nothing was said—at least nothing that Tiep heard, but after a few moments four of the healthier goblins went to work shoving fallen rocks to the sides of the chamber.

The goblins knew what they were doing. They'd done it before—the chamber was ringed with heaps of fallen rock. Tiep recalled the twisted metal debris in the egg chamber. This all had happened before. The big open egg with the golden scroll on top wasn't the first transformation egg. There'd been others; they'd exploded. The goblin slaves had cleaned up here in the pool chamber and in the egg chamber, too. All Tiep had to do was wait and the slaves would show him a way to the egg chamber.

Of course, forty slaves and ten swordswingers meant a lot of bodies between them and Druhallen, but Tiep was a born optimist. He'd offer freedom to the slaves—never mind that he didn't speak a word of their language. They'd get the message the instant he took a swing at one of the swordswingers. He and Rozt'a would have forty allies. By Tymora! They'd have guides, too, back to the surface! They'd be heroes.

And he'd be the biggest hero of all—

A high-pitched whistle disrupted Tiep's glorious daydream. The goblins who'd been shoving rocks abandoned their work. They rejoined the other slaves and they all bowed themselves low on the stone. Even the sword-swingers bowed low.

The pool got brighter. Tiep expected that whatever was going to happen would happen there. He wasn't looking at the chamber walls and couldn't see the walls to his immediate right and left. The tall man in a full-length dark cloak was several strides into the chamber before Tiep noticed him. He'd gone another stride before Tiep realized the tall man wasn't alone: one of the long-limbed swordswingers walked naked beside him.

The naked swordswinger didn't have a sword or the sense great Ao had given ants. *It* stumbled at every step and would have fallen if the tall man hadn't held it firmly by the upper arm. The pair approached the bright pool. The whistling got louder. Strange patterns flickered across the man's cloak. Writing, Tiep thought, *spells*.

The man had to be a wizard. Druhallen dressed like a shopkeeper, but Galimer would have worn a flashy cloak like that. Sememmon had been dressed like a merchant, too, that night when Tiep had tried to cut his purse strings. Dru and Sememmon were better at magic than Galimer was—especially Sememmon. Maybe the man in the flashy cloak wasn't as good as he thought he was. Maybe that was why his egg exploded and his monster had the blind staggers.

It would have fallen into the pool if the tall man hadn't reached left to grab—

Tymora have mercy!

Tiep's thoughts shattered. Man? Man? Had he thought the cloaked magician was a man? Tymora protect him, that *thing* was no man.

Tiep didn't know what race the cloaked figure had been born to, and didn't want to know. He called it a nightmare and begged his goddess to wake him up, but he wasn't asleep. Even after it had captured its stumbling slave and no longer faced the tunnel where he and Rozt'a were hiding, Tiep couldn't banish the horrific image from his mind's eye.

The nightmare magician's skin was a mottled purple in the pool's pale green light and stretched dried-corpse tight over its bones. Its head was too large and bulged behind, as if its brain had burst the back of its skull and then kept growing. Its eyes were a dull white with neither pupils nor irises. But it wasn't a nightmare because of its skin or its eyes or because its brain hung out of its head. The magician was a nightmare because it had four ropy tentacles hanging off its face.

The tentacles writhed and twitched. They caressed the bald head of the clumsy swordswinger. The other swordswingers pounded their chests while the crouching slaves rocked from side to side and the whistling grew so loud it was physically painful.

Tiep clapped his hands over his ears, which helped a little, and watched with open-jawed astonishment as the clumsy swordswinger folded its arms to its chest. It wove its mismatched fingers together, which might have been a of response to the tentacles caressing its head, but reminded Tiep of nothing so much as an insect about to feed—

The mantises!

The bug lady's messengers!

The metallic egg and Sheemzher's tale of the Beast Lord sacrificing his wife and a mantis and getting a demon in return.

Sheemzher's wife hadn't been exchanged for a demon, she'd been merged with a bug and transformed into one of the long-limbed swordswingers. The nightmare with worms on his face was the Beast Lord. Tiep imagined the look on Druhallen's face when he—the street rat with worse-than-no magic talent—told him how he'd figured out what was going on underneath Dekanter.

Then, like a cold breeze on a hot day, Tiep recalled that his foster father was trapped in the egg chamber. The breeze became a blizzard. If Tiep was right about the egg chamber and the egg, then that naked, just-hatched creature standing in front of the nightmare could be all that was left of Druhallen.

Come closer. Come closer. Share. Feed. Open your mind—

A thought that was not his own rode the whistling sound into Tiep's mind. The Beast Lord's tentacles lost none of their horrific qualities but, suddenly, Tiep wanted to be near them, to feel them against his skin, to offer up his paltry thoughts and emotions to a superior mind for its amusement, its pleasure.

Tiep was not alone in striding forward. All of the slaves did, and the swordswingers . . . and Rozt'a. He wasn't alone until he fought the compulsion and threw it out of his mind. The whistling went away, too, and Tiep swore to himself that he'd never again complain about the way magic didn't work around him. Then he reached out to stop Rozt'a from taking another step toward the nightmare.

Rozt'a fought him more vigorously than she'd fought him at the egg-chamber wall, and for no good reason. Desperate to avoid attention, Tiep punched her on the chin. Striking his foster mother was one of the harder things Tiep had done, good cause or bad, but it broke the Beast Lord's hold over her. Rozt'a was herself again—the remote, passive self she'd been since they'd found a solid granite wall between them and the egg.

Unless the Beast Lord had walked through stone, Tiep was sure the other egg-chamber tunnel was somewhere— not far—to his right. More than anything in the world, he wanted to find that tunnel and get back to the egg chamber. He was gathering his courage for a walk along the pool chamber wall when Rozt'a succumbed to the Beast Lord's compulsion for a second time. This time a hug, rather than a punch, was sufficient to keep her beside him in the dead-end tunnel, but the moment Tiep released her, she surged again.

Body contact with a body unaffected by the compulsion was apparently sufficient to keep Rozt'a free from the Beast Lord's compulsion but holding hands wasn't enough contact. Tiep draped his arm around her shoulder and kept it there as he weighed the risks of leaving the dead-end tunnel.

On the up side—the Beast Lord had his worshipers' complete attention, which meant no one was paying any attention to the chamber walls. Rocks had toppled since the whistling began and not drawn a sideways glance from the Beast Lord or his swaying congregation. On the down side—if Rozt'a slipped back into the Beast Lord's power or his own immunity weakened . . .

The down side won.

Tiep stayed put and watched the newly hatched swordswinger enter the green-glowing pool. The enslaved goblins joined hands in a circle around the pool. They blocked Tiep's view; he took that as a sign that Tymora hadn't abandoned him. His confidence rebounded—he and Rozt'a could wait. The pool chamber had been empty when they first arrived; it would become empty again.

He hoped.

Rozt'a leaned against him. She shuddered every few minutes. At first, Tiep thought that was the Beast Lord trying to get into her mind, then he noticed that his shirt was damp and he realized that she was sobbing. He'd be sobbing, too, if he let himself think about what had happened or what likely lay ahead, so he remembered the good times.

There had been good times in Tiep's life, but not many that didn't involve Galimer, Druhallen, or Rozt'a. He felt tears brewing and tried to think of nothing at all.

Time passed—more than a few minutes, less than an hour. The pool-side ritual showed no sign of ending: The goblins were still in a ring, and all the swordswingers were in the water. The Beast Lord was going from goblin to goblin, massaging their scalps with his tentacles. Tiep could watch now, he was beyond nausea.

A rock shifted to the right of their tunnel. Tiep thought nothing of it; other rocks had shifted. It would be a while before the chamber completely recovered from the shaking it had received when the egg hatched out a swordswinger.

Another rock moved and Tiep heard a sound that could have been a boot crunching over gravel. All the sounds had come from the right side. He tightened his hold on Rozt'a. He saw a shadow, then a silhouette.

It was tall enough, but the shape was wrong—headless

and hunch-backed. It stopped in front of the tunnel . . .
turned. It was lop-sided now, and maybe it did have a
head . . . maybe it was carrying something over its shoulder.

"Dru?" Tiep called in a voice not loud enough to reach his
fingertips. "Dru?" he called, a bit louder.

"Tiep? Is that you, Tiep?"

Dru came down the tunnel. Tiep got Rozt'a on her feet
and they met him halfway. The lump on Dru's shoulder was
the goblin, who wasn't moving and might have been dead
for all Tiep knew or cared.

There was safety in his foster father's embrace, and not
merely because they'd found each other. Druhallen hadn't
merely thrown off the Beast Lord's compulsion the way
Tiep had. Being a wizard, Druhallen kept the Beast Lord
at an arm's length—at two arms' lengths. As soon as they'd
entered Dru's shadow, Tiep felt the pressure ease in his
mind. By the time they were touching each other, Rozt'a
stood tall without any help from him, though maybe magic
had nothing to do with that.

"What happened?" Tiep whispered. "Did you get the
scroll?"

"Later. We've got to get out of here while the Beast Lord's
distracted."

So much for impressing Druhallen with his cleverness.

Dru wasn't worried about being seen or heard as they
escaped from the pool chamber. Speed was more important,
and keeping a hold of Rozt'a.

"You can take care of yourself, can't you?" Dru asked.

Tiep straightened proudly. "Sure I can."

"Good. Stay close and be ready to grab Rozt'a if she
breaks away. She's got no defense except what you or I can
share with her. I'll whisk up some light as soon as we're out
of range."

Out of range was farther into the escape tunnel than any
of them would have liked. Rock fall cluttered the path. They
couldn't move fast, or quiet, and there were no guarantees

that the Beast Lord had called all his swordswingers to the pool chamber. Dru was in command of their path and pace. He said he remembered the way, but there was a danger they'd miss an intersection in the dark. Tiep was relieved when Dru finally cast his light spell. Not only did that mean that they were beyond the Beast Lord's compulsion, but they could see fallen rocks and the intersections, too.

They got more good news when they returned to the spot where they'd battled and blasted the Beast Lord's swordswingers. The corpses were untouched.

"No one's come back for their dead," Rozt'a said. Her voice was shaky, but her mind was working again. "That means the ones that ran off haven't reported yet and there've been no other patrols."

A fighter's morale, she said, depended in part on his confidence that he'd be given an appropriate funeral before his death was avenged. She seemed to think the Beast Lord cared about morale; she didn't remember anything that had happened after they'd found the granite wall. Tiep whispered and told her what she'd missed without going too deeply into the details.

"It's all a blank," she shrugged. "I remember hitting that rock until I saw stars, then nothing but a slice of empty in my memory. Damn strangest thing that's ever happened to me."

Privately, Tiep thought it was lucky more than strange, but neither he nor Dru said anything. And the goblin was still unconscious over Dru's shoulders.

"The little fellow knew what was happening, I think," Dru explained in a soft voice as they walked away from the swordswinger corpses. "I told him to jump, that we'd come back for it, but he knew a goblin was going to die, one way or another. He wasn't coming down without the scroll. He had both hands on it and was pulling for all he was worth when it came alive like a bolt of lightning and threw him against the wall. He started to come around once, when the

Beast Lord was loading the athanor. I had to hit him pretty hard to keep him quiet."

Tiep was unimpressed. "You should've left him behind and come with us."

Dru replied with a sigh, nothing more.

"At least you got the scroll," Rozt'a added.

"No. We hid while the Beast Lord was loading up the athanor. I was pretty sure it couldn't see us as long as we did nothing to attract its attention. Things got pretty wild after it left and the transmutation was underway. I saw some things I'll never be able to explain and I think I lost a few slices of time myself—I never saw the scroll vanish, but when everything was done and over, there wasn't anything that I could see sticking out the top of that athanor.

"Something went wrong—you probably figured that much yourselves. The Beast Lord was a long time coming back into the chamber; I was starting to think maybe I was trapped in there. Mystra's mercy—I was starting to think that if I *did* get one of those doors open I'd find myself in the Outer Planes! It was just luck that I hadn't tried picking the locks on the athanor when the upper door finally cranked open. The Beast Lord had a hard time getting its newest swordswinger up and moving."

They'd come up to another intersection, which Dru had to study before leading them straight ahead. He forgot that he'd left his story unfinished.

Tiep wanted to hear the rest. "So the goblin made the scroll disappear. Then what happened?" He got another sigh for an answer. "What now? What did I say this time? He loosened it, didn't he? And that wrecked the magic, right? And now it's gone. Bully for Sheemzher—he didn't save a goblin *or* one of the damned bugs, and if it's really gone, how're we going to get Galimer back?"

Dru walked a little faster.

"Druhallen!" Rozt'a called sharply. "He's made a good point—what are we going to do?"

"Yeah, that's all I want to know. I don't care about the goblin."

"We'll go back. It's there. The scroll's still there. I can sense it—see its shadow when I look for magic. It's been displaced in time."

Feeling bold after Rozt'a's support, Tiep asked, "What's that supposed to mean?"

"You've heard the expression: He got kicked into the middle of the next tenday? Well, that's where the scroll is. Not as far as the middle of next tenday, though, maybe midnight, or dawn. It's already drifting backward. The Beast Lord wasn't surprised that it was missing. Maybe the scroll gets displaced every time it uses the athanor."

"You keep saying 'it,' Dru," Rozt'a said as soon as he'd finished talking. "Isn't the Beast Lord a he? Wyndyfarh said 'he.' "

"The Beast Lord's some sort of mind flayer, Rozt'a."

Tiep had heard of mind flayers before, but not from any of his foster parents. His mates in the Berdusk alleys used to whisper about mind flayers every time someone disappeared. As if it took big scary monsters to make a kid vanish from the streets.

"What sort of mind flayer?" Rozt'a asked in a serious voice.

"I wish I knew. The pieces don't fit together—it's alone, renegade, and using magic. The one thing I'm sure I do know about mind flayers is they *don't* touch magic. I'd almost pay good money to see Amarandaris's face when he realizes he's not dealing with a minor beholder."

"Is that what the Zhentarim think they've been trading with?" Rozt'a shuddered. "I'd rather take my chances with a beholder. What about Lady Wyndyfarh. She said the Beast Lord was a nuisance. What do you suppose she thought he—it—is?"

"That's just the question I want to ask Sheemzher here when we bring him around."

Tiep was satisfied. The dog-face didn't have a prayer if he'd crossed Dru. There were some nasty spells written inside Dru's wooden box, spells he never memorized unless he had to. Galimer once said that Dru could make the dead sit up and answer questions. He could unravel a goblin's secrets without half trying.

Of course, Sheemzher was sitting on a few secrets Tiep didn't particularly want Dru or Rozt'a to hear, which meant Tiep was in favor of necromancy. According to common wisdom—the only sort of wisdom Tiep laid claim to—dead folk answered only the questions they were asked. If the goblin were *dead* and Dru didn't get around to asking, specifically, What do you know about Tiep and Zhentarim? then Tiep's secrets were safe.

Not that Tiep, himself, didn't want to know how the goblin knew the Network had its hooks in his hide.

Damn Sememmon, anyway. Why couldn't the Dark Lord just have killed him when he'd made his one, admittedly huge, mistake on the streets of Scornubel three winters ago? But no-o-o-o, Sememmon had led Tiep back to a warm, comfortable room and offered him dark red wine—which Tiep prudently hadn't touched.

You've got a talent, boy, that deep, silky voice had purred. *It would be a shame to waste such a talent. I could use that talent; and then I might forget how I discovered it.*

Tiep had cut his teeth in the streets. He'd had no illusions about Sememmon's offer but he'd kept his pride and his honor. He'd told the Dark Lord that if the Zhentarim wanted him to betray his foster parents—if they wanted to use him to put pressure on his foster parents, then Lord Sememmon should kill him where he stood, because he'd never do it.

Sememmon had listened, smiled, and said: *I don't want you to betray your foster parents, Tiep—and I warn you, the day you betray them will be your last. From time to time, the Zhentarim have need of men and women whose*

*hearts are good and who do not know our faces. Druhallen
of Sunderath, Galimer Longfingers, and the woman who
calls herself Florozt'a are such folk, but you're not like
them, are you, Tiep?*

Tiep wasn't. He'd never been, never would be, and he did
"favors" for Sememmon. Not many. Not often. And never
anything that he wouldn't have done on his own. He'd never
drawn blood, directly or indirectly—at least as far as he
knew. He'd been offered rewards for his services—which he
hadn't taken. Sememmon's memory of a midnight indiscre-
tion on the Scornubel streets remained as sharp as ever.

The Dark Lord would never forget that night. Tiep had
understood that much after he'd completed his first "favor"
a week after that first meeting. He'd been too ashamed to
tell Dru, Galimer, or Rozt'a what had happened. The shame
had only grown as the months passed and he'd continued to
do Darkhold's bidding—the last time in Parnast. He hadn't
stolen the myrrh; he'd won that exactly the way he'd
claimed. He hadn't *stolen* anything in Parnast.

The second night of the dust storm, when he'd been
heading home from Manya's, Zhentarim henchmen had
accosted Tiep and marched him upstairs above the charterhouse. Amarandaris gave him a sealed blue bottle—the
kind ladies used for their perfumes—and instructions to
put it in a certain saddle bag at a certain time. Tiep hadn't
asked questions and he hadn't gone back for his reward,
either. He'd been careful—doubly, triply careful the way
he'd learned to be when he was doing Zhentarim "favors."

Tiep wasn't worried about getting caught by any town or
guild's law. He worried about his foster parents finding out
that he'd fallen deeper than they imagined possible.

Gods! In Weathercote, when Dru and Rozt'a had blamed
him for Galimer's imprisonment and he'd thought they
were going to turn their backs on him right there, it had
almost been a relief. Tiep wasn't ashamed of stealing the
lady's amber in Weathercote, or even of smashing her bug.

Sheemzher had set them all up and tricked him specifically. The goblin could die right now and Tiep would dance a jig on his grave.

But somehow Sheemzher had known about him and the Black Network.

"I don't know, Dru," he said, trying desperately to sound like Galimer. "Sheemzher's spent a lot of time with that bug lady. She's probably tangled up his mind. It's not his fault; he's just a goblin, but you can't trust anything that he says. I don't think it would be worth asking him. His answers would only make you mad and crazy."

11

6 Eleint, the Year of the Banner (1368 DR)

The Greypeak Mountains

"You're probably right," Druhallen agreed before shifting Sheemzher's unconscious weight to his left shoulder. "But I plan to ask him all the same."

It was ungentlemanly—unfatherly—but Dru suspected he might see something other than compassion in the young man's eyes and until he shifted shoulders, Sheemzher's head blocked the view. It wasn't like the youth to smooth the goblin's road, though he and Rozt'a had been urging Tiep to do just that since they'd left Weathercote Wood. Lately Tiep was like a weathervane in a thunderstorm: pointing first this way, then that, and very likely to burst into flames at any moment.

"I doubt that Lady Wyndyfarh has been any more honest with her goblin than she has with us," Dru continued. "But it will be interesting to learn what she has told him about herself. Sheemzher's got a good memory—have you noticed that when he tells you what someone else has said, he gets it exact, right down to the accent?"

"I knew a rag-picker whose parrot squawked in couplets. Didn't make the bird a poet."

Dru heard resentment and saw fear in Tiep's eyes. "It told you something about the man who taught the parrot, didn't it?" he asked gently.

"The rag-picker didn't teach the bird anything. Some woman taught it; it squawked with a woman's voice."

"I'd say you've won my point for me," Dru said softly through a not-completely repressed grin of triumph.

Tiep grumbled something Dru chose not to hear and fell back to walk beside Rozt'a where he complained loudly about sarcastic wizards who'd forgotten what it was like to be a young man. Rozt'a shushed him with a hiss and they walked on in grim silence.

Dru shifted the goblin again at the next intersection and gave him a thump on the back for good measure. They'd returned to the dwarven tunnels. The overhead carvings were familiar and Dru was confident that the next intersection would be the last one before they hauled themselves out of the mountain. He'd be relieved to see the sky again but wasn't looking forward to squeezing himself through that tiny hole in the ceiling.

Sheemzher had promised to lead them out by another route—

"C'mon, little fellow, wake yourself up!" He thumped the goblin's back again. "Tell me if this other passage leads to the surface."

Not a squeak or twitch.

"Do you want to try another way?" Rozt'a asked with cold enthusiasm.

"No—but you're going to have your hands full getting me out of here."

She did and so did Tiep who pushed from below. The passage wasn't as bad as Dru had anticipated, perhaps because a steady rain had made the granite around the hole slick.

They'd been underground long enough for the sun to set. Dru's light spell functioned in the rain, but not well. He kept it throttled so it wouldn't draw attention from

Ghistpok's goblins in the quarry, but that meant more shadows than light reaching the ground as they picked their miserable way back to the horses. Rozt'a fell and Dru came down one rock face on his rump with the goblin upside down in his lap. A more traditional wizard would have lost more than his dignity, but Dru favored leather breeches. His dignity and more remained intact.

Who'd ever have thought that a mountain range could be as wet as a seacoast marsh or the fabled jungles of Chult?

The horses welcomed them and welcomed the grass nets more. Tiep volunteered to fix their supper, reminding Dru that adolescence was temporary and the youth was their best cook. Rozt'a volunteered to help him, which was an extraordinary event and not a good omen for digestion. She'd been subdued since emerging from the Beast Lord's compulsion; losing a slice of memory must have cut deep. Tiep could reassure her about what she'd missed and if words weren't sufficient, Dru could unfold his box down to its bottom and study the spells written in the compartments that held sprigs of rue, hemlock, and lashes from a blind man's eye.

He was going to have to dig down that deep anyway, if Sheemzher didn't bestir himself.

They'd laid the goblin out on the only dry patch of stone in the hollow and examined him as thoroughly as he and Rozt'a knew how. He had a lump on his head and burns on his palms, which they'd slathered with second skin, but no other visible injuries. Rozt'a had uncorked a bottle of aromatic spirits. Though the restorative was potent enough to get a reaction from the horses standing ten paces away, it had no effect on the goblin.

Druhallen knew a spell that would create forced rapport. Ansoain had said it would bridge between a wizard and any sentient mind. He and Galimer had cast it successfully on each other, but rapport with your best friend could hardly be called forced and some authorities questioned goblin sentience It was a complicated spell, too, and would cost him a fair amount of firepower if he committed it to memory after midnight.

He knew another spell that would turn a pair of Rozt'a's leather gloves into gauntlets sturdy enough to hold a piece of the sun if it happened to be stuck in the top of a huge brass egg. Tiep's ill-gotten myrrh from Parnast made that one possible, but it, too, would leave a big footprint in his mind and a hole after he cast it. He'd rather enchant the gloves than force a rapport with their goblin.

Everything would be easier if Sheemzher would just wake up, but prudence dictated that Dru make himself familiar with the rapport spell's logic and ritual before he convinced Rozt'a to give him a pair of her sword-handling gloves. He was lost in contemplation, when he heard Rozt'a calling his name.

"We've been talking," she said and indicated Tiep who stood beside her in the rain and faded light spell; Sheemzher was still unconscious. "We've put together some conclusions about what's going on—Tiep has, actually. He's thought things through. I think you should listen to him."

Dru realized he was hungry enough to eat two suppers and that Rozt'a's hands were empty, as were Tiep's. Whatever the two of them had been up to, it hadn't involved the preparation of food. Disappointment stung and soured. "When don't I listen to you, Tiep?"

The youth's lips rolled and tightened. "It's about the Beast Lord and how he's really a mind flayer—"

— " 'It,' Tiep. Mind flayers are hermaphrodites."

"Herm-what?"

"They're all built the same. Maybe they mate, maybe they don't, but they're all the same: no males, no females. Can't tell 'em apart."

Dru winced when Tiep blushed. Some men sounded like their fathers; he sounded like Ansoain. Rozt'a touched Tiep's arm, but only made the blush worse.

"Right—" Tiep's voice chose that moment to crack. He cleared his throat several times while both Dru and Rozt'a tried not to look at him, then he tried again. "Well, I watched what went on at that pool with the light in it and I think I've got it figured out. Those ugly critters that butchered Cardinal and tried to butcher us a couple nights ago, they're not demons, they're goblins who've been put through the Beast Lord's egg. Those swordswingers, they started off as goblins, too, but the Beast Lord mixed them up with the bug lady's bugs, so they're cleverer than goblins."

It wasn't the way Dru saw events unfolding, but Tiep's view had merit. "Could be that way," he admitted. "My problem is that there's never just one mind flayer. They're supposed to be like ants or bees. They live in colonies and take orders from something called an Elder Brain. Just like the queen bee in a hive, once the Elder Brain establishes a colony, it never leaves. It can't. Its whole body has been transformed into a huge brain that floats in brine instead of blood—"

"The pool!" Rozt'a declared. "The pool was empty. What did you say after you came back from seeing Amarandaris—the Network pulled out because there'd been war under Dekanter? I'd say the Beast Lord's lost its Elder Brain and now its losing the whole war."

Dru shook his head. "Sheemzher's never said Beast Lords, not once. It's always Beast Lord, by itself. Even Amarandaris talks about trading with a single beholder."

"But if they all look alike—?" Tiep made a nauseated face. "Who'd want to look close enough to see if today's mind flayer is the same one you saw last year?"

"Good sir, Beast Lord *not* mind flayer."

Rozt'a, Tiep, and Druhallen all focused their attention on Sheemzher who'd propped himself up on one elbow.

"What is it, then?" Dru asked, expecting a familiar answer.

The goblin howled, "Alho-o-o-o-on!"

Dru rubbed his forehead wearily. Sheemzher wasn't stupid, no more than a young child was stupid when it thought that size—bigness—determined the value of a coin. But, like a young child, Sheemzher saw the world on his own terms. "That may be the word that goblins use," he explained, "but men say 'mind flayers'."

"Goblins say nothing, good sir. Good lady say: alho-o-o-o-on!"

Sheemzher howled again and Dru had great difficulty imagining that the keening sound had originated in Wyndyfarh's slender, elegant throat. He'd never heard of an alho-o-o-o-on, either, and it was simply inconceivable that Ansoain would have failed to acquaint him and Galimer with such an unusually named beast.

When the goblin finished his howl, he added, "Mind flayers alive living things. Alho-o-o-o-n dead living thing."

Dru, who'd been leaning against the rock, trying to stay as much out of the rain as possible, literally leapt forward and to his feet. "Undead? The Beast Lord is an undead mind flayer? Mystra's mercy—that explains the rest." His initial burst of excitement and satisfaction faded fast. "You knew," he said. Disbelief kept Dru's anger in check. "You knew what was down there. You knew, and you led us down there without a word of warning . . ."

"Good sir not ask Sheemzher. Sheemzher not clever men. Sheemzher not know what clever men know. Sheemzher quiet. Men never listen not-clever goblins, good sir; Sheemzher keep quiet. Not ask, not answer."

"Sweet Tymora! I'm going to—"

Tiep lunged at the goblin, but Tymora gave her blessing to Druhallen, who caught him before any harm was done. "You're not going to do anything."

"You heard him! He led us down there to die. Him and his damn lady. We were headed for that damn egg, that athan-thing you keep talking about."

"Athanor. Alchemists use them to transmute base

214

elements. It's our fault—*my* fault: I didn't ask the right questions."

Tiep swore with creative passion, which Dru took as a sign that the goblin was no longer in serious danger. He glanced at Rozt'a, who'd shut her eyes and stood still like stone, blaming herself, as he did.

Dru spoke for himself and her: "What's cut stays cut," he told Sheemzher, who'd pulled the blanket over his head. "I'm asking now. When Lady Wyndyfarh told you that the Beast Lord was an—" Imitating the goblin's howl was more than Druhallen could ask of himself. "Sheemzher, do you remember what you said and what your lady said when she told you what the Beast Lord was?"

The goblin stayed beneath the blanket. "Good lady says, Is its flesh slick and shiny or dry? Sheemzher says: Not shiny. Not get close. Not know slick, not know dry. Good lady says: The Beast Lord of Dekanter is an undead illithid magician, a lithilil—an illithil—ilthili—" Sheemzher abandoned memory. The blanket fell away from his face as he threw back his head and howled: "Alho-o-o-o-n . . . alho-o-o-on."

Rozt'a walked away. They were all soaked to the skin, but she'd started shivering. They could hear her teeth.

"Now look what you've done!" Tiep snarled and made another lunge for Sheemzher's neck.

The goblin scrambled while Dru wrestled with Tiep. He got the youth pinned upright against wet rock. "What's wrong with you?" he demanded, his mouth a finger's breadth from Tiep's nose. "Haven't we got enough trouble without you going off like a rabid dog every other moment?"

Tiep opened his mouth to say something, then thought better of it and kept quiet. Dru released him and retreated, staring at his own hands and wondering how they'd gotten to a point where Tiep was assaulting a much-smaller goblin and he was doing the same to Tiep.

"We all need to back away from each other for a while,"

he muttered, though what they really needed was Galimer. Galimer did more than negotiate their business, he kept the peace. When this was over, Dru swore silently that he'd find the words to thank his friend. Right now, a wall of frustration separated his shame from an apology.

Tiep straightened himself up. The youth didn't appear any worse for the encounter, for which Dru was grateful.

"You forgot to ask Sheemzher about the bug lady."

Dru's nerves were so raw he couldn't tell if the boy meant to be troublesome or was actually trying to be helpful. "Not now."

"Good lady very good, very kind. Good lady crush Beast Lord like this—" Sheemzher ground his right fist into his left palm. "—If good lady come here. Good lady not come here. Good lady cannot leave forest."

Though he hadn't wanted the conversation, Dru couldn't let it end without answers. "You've said that before. Why can't Lady Wyndyfarh leave Weathercote Wood?"

Sheemzher looked behind both shoulders and up at the dark, leaking clouds before whispering: "Good lady no belong; good lady watcher only. Very great magic lady get very great angry if good lady leave forest. Very great magic lady send all Weathercote ladies, all Weathercote lord away." The goblin leaned forward. "Good lady say, No sense giving Mystra a reason to make a mistake. Not now when she's adjusting to new eyes."

They'd all heard tales of the recently ended Time of Troubles in which gods died and—in some versions of the tales—mortals had replaced them. The deaths of Bane and Myrkul were all but confirmed. Their priests were impotent and their temples abandoned, but a new Mystra, a fallible, born-mortal Mystra? No. It was inconceivable. Dru had refused, until now, to conceive of it.

"Mystra doesn't make mistakes where magic's concerned," Dru said firmly. "You can tell your lady that, or I will. If the Beast Lord's a threat to the Weave—"

He paused and considered what he was saying. Could the Beast Lord actually be a threat to the Weave? Mind flayers weren't exactly common—for which he and countless others were grateful—but there were enough that Dru strongly suspected the Beast Lord wasn't the first of its race to walk the dark path to lichdom. Though a lich of any kind was more than he cared to confront alone, he could name a score of notable wizards, priests, and paladins who could crush the Beast Lord, fist against palm, without upsetting Mystra.

If an undead mind flayer wasn't the threat, then what about the athanor it had constructed? The egg was the largest alchemic device Dru had ever seen or heard of, but mad wizards had been cobbling creatures together for millennia—since Netheril itself. What made this athanor different, this undead mind flayer a danger to the Weave?

Things started changing about seven years ago—

What started the changes?

Six years ago, the Beast Lord's athanor had been smaller. It had transmuted Sheemzher's wife into a Taker but the misshapen goblins of the bogs were demons to Sheemzher's eyes. The swordswingers they'd fought underground were demons too, but the creatures who'd led Sheemzher's wife to the small egg were Takers. The misshapen fought with sharpened sticks. The swordswingers with swords. Sheemzher hadn't said if the Takers carried weapons. It was tempting to think that the Takers would have carried spears and then construct a progression of "improved" demons emerging from the Beast Lord's athanor.

The big change—the big "improvement" had come between the misshapen and the Takers. Sheemzher's wife had been transmuted in an egg which she shared with one of Wyndyfarh's mantis minions. Was that the change—take one goblin and add a jewel-eyed insect already touched by potent magic? Or was the change the power that merged the two together? Power that came from a Netherese scroll?

Sheemzher had as much as said Lady Wyndyfarh was an exotic from another plane . . . a watcher. What was she watching? Illithids. Mind flayers that lived in colonies and were guided by an Elder Brain. By itself and without an Elder Brain, the undead Beast Lord was a nuisance . . . until it acquired one of Netheril's golden scrolls of magic.

Dru cleared his throat and started again. "Sheemzher, what else do you know about the golden scroll we're supposed to bring back to Weathercote Wood? What has Wyndyfarh told you about it?"

Sheemzher began, "Good lady say—" and got no farther. He gasped once and began to choke. Choking became trembling and he collapsed on the rock, hitting his head hard. The convulsion deepened. Foam and spittle appeared on the goblin's lips.

"Damn her!" Dru shouted and tried to protect Sheemzher's head as his body thrashed on the wet stone.

"What's going on over there?" Rozt'a shouted.

"Dru asked Sheemzher about the Netherese scroll and now he's having a fit."

Rozt'a raised her voice in ironic prayer: "All hail the gods, what's next?"

"Don't tempt them," Dru advised.

The tremors were subsiding. Sheemzher's back relaxed, his arms and legs went limp a few heartbeats later.

Tiep asked, "Is he—?"

"No, he'll come around in a moment or two."

"That was a lot of geas to put on a little body." Rozt'a observed. "Somebody doesn't want him talking about that Nether scroll in a big way."

"Not somebody—Wyndyfarh."

"Can you get around it?"

"In a month, in Scornubel with all Ansoain's books open in front of me, if I got lucky, stayed lucky, and didn't kill him by mistake."

Sheemzher coughed out phlegm and bile. He tried to sit

but couldn't lift his shoulders. "Sheemzher hurt. Sheemzher not remember."

"Your good lady doesn't want you answering certain questions of mine."

The goblin tried again to sit. He still couldn't manage it on his own. Rozt'a offered her hand. Sheemzher ignored it, groping at his sides instead. "Spear? Where Sheemzher spear? Sheemzher not Sheemzher without spear."

Panic gave the goblin a drunk's strength and coordination. He struck both Dru and Rozt'a in his efforts to find the missing spear. The blows were hard, but not hard enough to prevent Dru from spreading his hand across Sheemzher's chest and forcing the goblin to lie back on the stone.

"It was you or the spear," Dru explained, which wasn't the complete truth. He could have carried both and he had looked for the spear, but he hadn't wasted much time in the search.

Sheemzher hung his head and hugged himself. He'd lost his spear and his hat—possessions which he'd clearly prized—his bright-colored garments were dirty and sodden, and his good lady had tagged him with a geas that had fallen just short of killing him. A man in his place might be feeling pretty well abandoned by now. And a goblin? Dru laid a hand on Sheemzher's shoulder.

"We'll look for it when we go back underground."

"We're going back down?" Tiep asked, a mix of relief and surprise in the question.

Dru nodded, but not before Rozt'a answered, "Of course we are. I don't care what Lady Wyndyfarh is or what she's done—we're getting that scroll. We're getting Galimer out of Weathercote Wood. One alhoon isn't enough to stop us."

She named the Beast Lord's breed without howling. The word was almost familiar.

Rozt'a caught him staring. "Just because I didn't ride with Ansoain doesn't mean I grew up in a garden, Druhallen," she told him indignantly. "There were others

219

before you, and not all of them were bastards like the one in Triel. When I was just starting out, I hired on with a Cormyr lord who wanted to reopen the family gold mine, which meant cleaning out a couple centuries' worth of squatters, the worst of which was an alhoon. There were about forty of us—a sentience shield, the lord called it. He armed us with green wood sticks and bundles of straw, no steel allowed, for our own safety, he said. We marched ahead of two priests and a wizard, all laying low, pretending to be common.

"A few of the veterans had shivs in the their sleeves; one wrapped his long sword in straw. When the alhoon started grabbing minds, setting us against each other, blood flowed bad, but the wizard popped up quick and pasted it good. Like as not, we'd have all walked out of there if we'd stuck with the sticks and straw. Easiest five lions I ever earned."

Tiep took advantage of a pause to ask, "Why didn't you say something, then, when I told you what the Beast Lord looked like? Those *things* hanging off his face. It's not like anything else anywhere ever looked like that!"

Rozt'a shrugged. "Forty brawlers in a mine tunnel—I was way toward the back and never saw what we were supposed to be distracting. By the time our priests and wizard were done, the alhoon was soot. The undead, they go fast in a holy fire. After Sheemzher howled, I started thinking about what I felt that day and what happened a little while ago. I call it a close enough fit. An alhoon isn't invincible, Dru."

He had difficulty meeting her eyes. "If you've got forty hired brawlers, two priests, a wizard, and a Cormyr lord." She started to scowl. "Don't get me wrong, Rozt'a: I *like* the idea. A sentience shield. You couldn't do it with a mind flayer colony; they could suck up as much sentience as you could throw at them. But alhoons are apparently solitaires. The Beast Lord would become a juggler with too many balls in the air and have nothing left for defense when magic started to fly."

"I've watched you throw fire around. You're better than the wizard we had with us." Rozt'a flung flattery with a shovel. "You wouldn't need two priests."

"Or the Cormyr lord," he agreed. "It's the shield, Rozt'a. Bodies. We'd've done better to join in with Amarandaris. He'd loan us forty men . . . if we let him have the scroll afterward."

Rozt'a narrowed her eyes and flashed her predatory grin, which made Dru far more nervous than her scripted flattery ever would. "We've got forty men, Dru, maybe more. At least a hundred, if the women come too."

"No." He'd figured out where Rozt'a's logic was going and didn't want to follow. "No, not Ghistpok's goblins, for pity's sake. They think their Beast Lord's a *god.*"

Tiep offered his opinion, "Then they should line up with bells on for the chance to meet him."

"If they don't eat us first."

"People not *eat* people, good sir."

In the heat of absurdity, Dru had forgotten they had a goblin listening to their discussion.

"People not eat good sir, not eat good woman," Sheemzher continued. He wrinkled his nose at Tiep. "People not eat that one; people get sick."

Dru clenched his teeth, biting off the words he would have spat out. What was the point of chiding Tiep for his prejudice against Sheemzher when it was so obviously reciprocated? The pair deserved each other. They all deserved one another, and Dekanter, too.

Wind came down the mountain, gathering up buckets of rain to hurl in their faces. Possibilities—likelihoods—occurred to Dru as he swallowed cold water. They weren't going to steal the Nether scroll, they weren't going to get back to Weathercote Wood, and most of all, they weren't going to redeem Galimer from Wyndyfarh's glade. The way the rain was starting to flood around their feet, they were simply going to drown.

Something snapped inside Dru at that moment. He felt it go like a flawed pot left too long in the fire.

"It's not going to succeed," he said. His voice was calm; the rest of him was shaking. "Whatever we try, it's not going to succeed." He pawed beneath his sopping shirt, found his folding box and tried to open it with hands that trembled from exposure and anger. "Whether it's a sentience shield or an alliance with Ghistpok, it's not going to succeed. Since we got to Parnast, it's been one unpleasant surprise after another. All of them pointed here, to Dekanter, and all of them added another burden to our shoulders."

Dru's thumb flicked a hook-shaped clasp and broke it, then he cracked one of the spell-etched wooden panels. How many years had he had the box without so much as scratching it? Ten, at least, maybe a few more. His mind was so churned he wasn't sure how old he was or how many years had passed since Ansoain had died.

The compartment he'd been groping for finally opened. A disk of glass colder than the rain slipped into his hands.

"We didn't come here to clean out the mines or destroy an alhoon or free slaves or solve any of the problems plaguing this damned place. We're not even here to steal a golden scroll. We're here because I'm a fool. I needed something to hang my life around. I couldn't live from one day to the next, so I lived for this." Dru brandished the disk above his head. "I've killed him!" he shouted, seeing Galimer and nothing more in his mind's eye. "Me and my pride. Me and my determination that there *had* to be something larger, something powerful and mysterious behind Ansoain's death. If it was big enough and powerful enough, then there'd be some point to it. We wouldn't all live and die for no reason at all. The gods laugh at us . . . at me. They're laughing right now! Listen to them!"

Of course, there wasn't any laughter, only wind and rain on the mountain side. Dru knew that. He hadn't lost his grip on truth and reality, but things were getting slippery.

Dru wasn't the sort of man who lost control very often, and he was inexperienced at regaining it afterward.

On the verge of tears he'd never shed, Druhallen shouted. "You were right, Galimer! You were right! There was never any meaning to it! We were bought and sold, just like the bride!"

Tiep, Rozt'a, and Sheemzher were staring at him with their mouths open. The goblin and Tiep were speechless, but Rozt'a had been merely waiting for him to breathe.

"Quit hoarding the guilt, Dru. You didn't get us here all by your lonesome."

The fight went out of Dru's heart, the air went out of his lungs, and in his mind's eye he saw a desperate, foolish man standing in the rain, waving a lump of ancient glass over his head.

"It's finished. No more vengeance. No more meaning," he said wearily.

Dru hurled the glass disk at the ground with force enough to smash it to splinters, but it might have been a feather for the way it fluttered and drifted—a *magical* feather that shone brighter than his light spell.

Rozt'a spoke first: "Dru—? What's happening, Dru?"

"In fifteen years, I swear it's never done anything like that. They put it to the test at Candlekeep and swore there was more magic in flour, yeast, and water."

The disk completed its descent, losing its glow when it settled on the wet stone.

"I can't see it anymore. It disappeared!" Tiep exclaimed.

The remark puzzled Dru, who could see the disk as clearly as he could see anything else through the rain and his light spell's illumination. He picked it up—the glass was icy, but that was no change from the first time—and displayed on his open palm.

Tiep touched it lightly with an extended finger. "Weird . . ."

Dru made a fist around the glass, absorbing the cold

and irony—he'd finally mustered the will to get rid of the disk and in that very instant, it displayed properties that justified returning it to its compartment in the folding box. He'd barely gotten it tucked away when another cold, wet, wind-gust slapped them hard. Lightning lit the mountains with flickering silver light. They waited for the thunder, which was a long time coming, but loud and long when it arrived.

"Everything tied up tight?" Dru asked his human companions, a reminder more than a question. He had a different question for the goblin. "How bad can the storms get around here?"

"Very bad, good sir."

"What do you do to keep yourself safe?"

"People hide, good sir. People pray."

"Wonderful."

Tiep and Rozt'a packed their gear while he moved the horses to the highest part of the gully. The animals were balky and Hopper was lame on his cracked hoof. By lightning-light, Dru examined the damage. Barring a miracle, they were going to lose another horse—another loyal friend—but that was a problem for after the storm.

He'd guessed it would be bad—everything else had been—but all Dru's years on Faerûn's roads didn't prepare him for the fury of a mountain storm. The wind came from every direction, including straight down, and pushing walls of rain with it. Thunder became a continuous full-body assault and the lightning strikes came so fast and bright that Dru's eyes adjusted to their brilliance. He saw his companions as statues that moved with jerky motions. Conversation was, of course, impossible, and thought itself was difficult as the weather waged war over their heads.

They had one bit of luck—their gully drained well enough. Water came off the rocks in torrential streams. It rose to their ankles, but no higher. It was high enough to sweep Sheemzher away from Dru's side. Between one lightning flash and the next, the goblin latched onto Tiep and Tiep latched onto Hopper's tail.

Dru's relief was short-lived as a rock the size of his skull glanced off his shoulder. It would have crushed Sheemzher if the flood water hadn't moved him first, and they'd all have been flattened if it had been the herald of a larger rock fall such as they'd seen from the High Trail above the goblin camp.

As they lived it, the storm seemed to last forever. When it had ended, reason said no more than an hour had passed. The danger would linger until the mountains above them shed their water, which might be hours or days—Dru didn't know mountain weather well enough to choose. He was checking Hopper's hoof again and bracing himself to give Rozt'a and Tiep the bad news when Rozt'a squatted down beside him.

"We're going to have to put the old man down before we leave," she whispered, telling him before he'd found the words to tell her.

"Does Tiep know?"

"He thinks it's not as bad as it looks." She sighed. "It'll break his heart."

Dru's mind was empty; then he found the words, "I'm ready for that scroll-shop in Scornubel with a hearth behind and a bedchamber above."

Rozt'a leaned against him. "Whatever you say, as long as it gets us out of here."

Druhallen patted Hopper's leg then stood up, giving Rozt'a a hand as he did. "We'll try the sentience shield," he said, making the decision on the spot. "Give him grain—all the grain he wants." He scratched Hopper's long, damp forehead. "They're always hungry; that's what Amarandaris said. We'll be welcome if we come leading enough food to feed every mouth in sight. Don't panic when you come up one pair short when you're counting gloves. I'm borrowing them."

"What for?"

"Magic. An enchantment to protect the hands of whoever goes after that golden scroll next."

"Then you're not borrowing them, are you?"

"No, but I need them."

"Make sure your magic works; that's all I ask."

12

7 Eleint, the Year of the Banner (1368 DR)

Dekanter

Druhallen awoke with water dripping onto his face. The
gods knew how long the drops had been striking his forehead. He couldn't guess; puddles were everywhere, and his
clothes were as soaked as they'd been when he'd surrendered the watch to Rozt'a.

Rose-gold clouds floated in the east, but the sun hadn't
risen and the camp was quiet. Rozt'a, on watch, acknowledged Dru with a nod, nothing more, when he sat up. The
goblin was still asleep with his arms flung over his eyes,
and Tiep was with the horses. There was no eye contact
between them the first time Dru walked by, but when he
returned Druhallen was ready for the sure-to-be-difficult
conversation.

Tiep raised his head. He saw Druhallen coming and
chose to look at his feet.

"She told me," the youth mumbled.

Dru hitched up his soggy pants and squatted beside
Hopper's hindquarters. The hoof crack had widened overnight. The gelding stood with the affected leg bent and his
weight on his other three hooves. He twitched and whickered

plaintively when Druhallen ran a hand down the bent leg.

Dru was no ranger or druid. He couldn't heal a horse any more than he could heal himself, but a man who'd lived nine months out of twelve on the road for twenty-odd years learned a few things about horses and their feet, will he or nil he.

He said, "The old man's hurting."

Tiep wrapped his arms around Hopper's neck and supported the horse's head on his shoulder. "It'll get better when it dries. I'll take care of him. Hopper trusts me to take care of him."

"You've earned that trust, and you still have to take care of him. You know what that means. Hopper's about your age. That's young for a man, but old for a horse. Something like this was bound to happen."

"I thought we'd give him to a farmer with a fallow field—"

"And you wouldn't have to be there when the time came to put him down."

Dru stood and met Tiep's hurt-angry stare. He held it until the young man looked away again.

"Isn't there anything you can do? A binding spell to pull the edges together. An enchantment—"

"No."

"What good are you? What good is magic at all?"

Tiep was an expert when it came to returning pain.

Dru swallowed hard and said, "No good at all this morning." He put an arm around Tiep's shoulder and let the youth shrug free. "Did Rozt'a tell you the plan?"

"Bastards," Tiep spat. "Cruel, heartless bastards—both of you."

"That's neither true nor fair. You know Hopper's not walking out of these mountains. You know it, you just don't want to admit it. We could let him go the way Cardinal went or we can endow a feast down in the quarry and maybe— just maybe—that gets us on the goblins' good side long enough to get that scroll on its way to Weathercote. Suppose you ask Hopper which way he'd like to go?"

Tiep shook his head but said nothing.

"You don't have to go into the quarry with us, Tiep. You can stay up here with the gear and the rest of the animals. Gods know we should set a watch—"

"Isn't that the same as giving him to a farmer?" Tiep's eyes were bright, and his voice was thick.

Dru nodded. "Except the farmer's not as unpredictable as those goblins are apt to be."

A weak smile lifted Tiep's lips. "If we're going to sacrifice Hopper to get out of this stink-hole, then I'm going to be there when it happens. The last thing he sees will be me."

"No promises, Tiep. Anything can happen down there. Kicking over a hornet's nest would be less exciting than leading a ton of meat into Ghistpok's camp."

Druhallen draped an arm around Tiep again. This time the youth didn't shrug him off.

"But you—?" Tiep lifted his chin. "You'll do *it*, won't you, Dru? You left a place for mercy in your memory last night, didn't you?"

He nodded. What Tiep and the others called his "mercy" spell was the simple flame spell he studied most nights. The difference was in the delivery. No one asked him how it felt to cast fire into an animal's skull. They didn't want to know. "The old man won't suffer," Dru said softly; he'd see to that. "Go tell Rozt'a that you're coming down to the quarry with us. See if there's anything she wants you to do."

Tiep gave him a penetrating, slit-eyed stare. "Yeah. Sure. I get it."

Perhaps, he did. Tiep disentangled himself from Dru's arm without another word, leaving Dru alone with the old horse. This wouldn't be the first time, of course—there'd been Cardinal just a few days ago and more than he could readily count in the years previous—but "mercy" was never easy. He leaned into a horse-scented mane and revisited the past until he felt a tug on his sleeve.

"Good woman sad. That one sad. Good sir sad. Sheemzher ask, why sad. Sheemzher show way. Way good. People good. Why all sad?"

Dru looked down and tried not to resent the interruption. "Hopper's cracked a hoof. It started on the way into Parnast. We should have had him shod as soon as we got there, but never got to it. Rock like this is rough on their hooves at the best of times and Hopper's an old man among horses. All the rain we've had, especially last night. Standing in all that water the way he was, it got worse in a hurry."

The goblin clutched his hands behind his back and crouched to examine Hopper's injury. "So little?"

"That's all it takes for a horse. You could hop, or use a crutch, but Hopper needs all four legs, all the time. If we were somewhere else, maybe we could nurse him along, but he'd stay lame, and we're here, not somewhere else."

"Sacrifice, good sir? That one says, we're going to sacrifice Hopper to get out of this stink-hole. Sheemzher understand stink-hole. What be sacrifice, good sir?"

Druhallen pushed damp hair back from his forehead. He studied the risen sun and the crystal flecks in the nearest gray boulder. "Sacrifice is doing what hurts in the hope that everything will turn out right in the end."

"Hurt good sir or hurt Hopper?"

"If the good sir doesn't hurt, Sheemzher, then it's not much of a sacrifice."

Sheemzher reached up to scratch his head. They both noticed he was carrying a somewhat soggy chunk of bread.

"For you, good sir. Good woman says, That damn sack leaked again and we lost two loaves. Eat it quick or it'll go to waste."

Dru took his breakfast. The first bite tasted about as good as it looked. "Tell her, Thanks. Now. Tell her now."

The goblin gave him the same look Tiep had given him and went off to brighten Rozt'a's morning. Dru ate the bread—no telling when he'd eat again, except it wouldn't be down in the quarry.

They were ready by the time the sun was an hour above the eastern mountain crest. Druhallen thought they'd have trouble getting Hopper out of the gully, but they took it slow and Hopper placed each hoof, even the cracked one, with exquisite care. He wasn't the brightest horse ever foaled, nor the strongest, nor most handsome, but he was steady, reliable, and above all else, he trusted them completely.

Hopper balked at the top of the spiraling quarry steps. Dru had worried about them, too, but the steps had been carved ages ago by dwarves, not goblins. Considerably wider than they were high, the Dekanter steps were proportioned so that legs and feet of many sizes—dwarves, goblins, men and even horses—could find a comfortable stride.

Midway down the first stairway they were noticed by the goblin camp. The same high-pitched keening that had heralded the hunters' return yesterday echoed off the granite. A column of perhaps twenty goblins snaked out of the camp. They met the column at the bottom of the third-tier steps.

Their escort was made up entirely of male goblins, all toting spears and all lean to the point of emaciation. Amarandaris hadn't been exaggerating about the food situation at Dekanter. The Parnast refugees had more flesh on their bones than Ghistpok's elite. The refugees were better dressed, too—which said something about Parnast charity but wasn't truly surprising. Goblins weren't craftsmen. They might weave a reed basket or two, but not cloth. Goblin society, such as it was, depended on trade, raid, and outright theft. When Amarandaris backed away from Dekanter, he'd destroyed its prosperity and condemned it to dwindling rags.

Dru had calculated pure, physical hunger into his strategy, but he'd underestimated the effect that leather boots and whole cloth could have on desperate minds.

Grimy hands tugged his sleeves. One bold fool reached for his belt. He swatted the pest away and told them all firmly to keep their distance.

"Lead us to Ghistpok. We've come to talk to Ghistpok."

The goblins squabbled among themselves, and one whose rags were a bit more extensive, if in no better overall condition, barked goblin language at Sheemzher.

"That one," Sheemzher said, pointing at Druhallen. "Speak that one."

The escort leader brandished his spear a handspan in front of Sheemzher's nose and shouted more goblin-speak. Dru couldn't understand a word, but he got the meaning easily enough. Ghistpok's goblins didn't speak the Heartlands' dialect, or, more likely, they wouldn't speak it.

Peculiarities aside, Sheemzher spoke the Heartlands' dialect well enough and without Wyndyfarh's faintly foreign inflection, which implied that he'd learned humankind's common language here, in Dekanter. As Sheemzher *should* have learned it in Dekanter. A race could scarcely be called sentient if it didn't teach its children a useful dialect of humankind's trade language. Humankind shared Toril with many sentient races but outnumbered all of them together. There were sentients who didn't speak the trade-tongue, but Druhallen was quite confident that Amarandaris hadn't stooped to yips and snarls when he told Ghistpok to stop the warfare and raiding.

Of course, Ghistpok hadn't stooped either.

Before he started lording himself over Ghistpok's goblins, Dru wisely remembered that these scrawny rag-pickers had survived the loss of at least three Zhentarim groups. Amarandaris had shut down Dekanter's slave market and relocated the Dawn Pass Trail rather than lose more men . . . or take the sort of revenge for which the Zhentarim were justly infamous.

Dru caught himself staring at the goblin who shouted at Sheemzher and asking himself if the ragged stranger's eyes were a little too large and red, his fingers a little too long? And could those marks on his face be scales, not scars?

"Sheemzher, your relatives don't seem to want to speak to us. Have we got a problem?" he asked when the tirade showed no signs of ending. "Should we take our gifts and leave in a hurry?"

He watched the Dekanter goblins, looking for signs that they understood what he'd said. The signs were there: hands moving along a spear's shaft, quick glances exchanged between goblins, and longer glances at Hopper's flanks. They understood what he'd said, and they'd stopped speaking to men. Were they angry that the Zhentarim had disbanded the slave market, thereby depriving them of whatever goblins called luxuries?

Were they angry enough to kill? Amarandaris hadn't implicated Ghistpok's goblins in the massacres, but was believing Amarandaris any wiser than believing goblins?

Probably not.

The strongest wind blowing through Dekanter was confusion—the breakdown of goblin life as it had been lived for generations. Sheemzher confirmed Dru's perspective when he said. "Many changes here, good sir. New people. New ways. Sheemzher listen, learn. No problems, good sir. No hurry. Sheemzher follow Outhzin. Good sir, all follow Sheemzher. Ghistpok soon."

The goblin with the biggest rag collection was Outhzin and Outhzin led them across the quarry bottom. Dru had the sense that Outhzin thought he was in command. Outhzin could perhaps count twenty spears against three swords and was entitled to his opinion. Dru thought otherwise, but wasn't about to prove it, though he had fire, blur, and his pall of gloom literally on his fingertips.

The procession was quiet as long as they were on the steps, but once they reached the quarry bottom Ghistpok's goblins formed a circle around them and with words and obscene gestures made clear their fascination with Rozt'a.

The harassment came to a head when one of them—the same goblin who'd reached for Dru's folding box—darted into the circle and grabbed at Rozt'a's thigh. She back-handed her attacker, lifting him off his feet. By the time he stopped moving, he was on his rump and nearly six feet from where he'd started.

The procession stopped as half the goblins laughed and the rest leveled their spears. Rozt'a drew her sword.

"Druhallen—?" she called, making sure he was ready to back her up.

"I'm ready," he replied and brushed his right hand along his left sleeve, plucking a cold ember from the cloth before he drew his sword partway from its scabbard.

The fallen goblin bounded to his feet. He snarled something at his companions that quieted them, then he pointed his spear at Rozt'a's gut.

"Tell him, if he takes one step toward me, I'll kill him. Tell him he needn't worry what happens next, because *he'll* be dead."

Sheemzher dutifully translated and added, "That one young, good woman. That one claim good woman. Good woman belong that one. Mistake, yes?"

"Belong to *him!*" Rozt'a sputtered. "Is he out of his mind?"

"Sheemzher not know, good woman."

"Well, you tell him—you tell all of them that I've got a good husband and a bad temper."

Some of the goblins chuckled before Sheemzher translated a word, confirming Dru's suspicion that they understood the language they wouldn't speak. The instigator goblin wasn't laughing, or lowering his spear.

"When you're done with that, Sheemzher," Dru said loudly, "tell everyone that I'm her husband and that my temper is worse."

He drew the sword and held it the way he'd have held one of his axe shafts. The stance must have been convincing. The instigator stood down, and they were moving again.

More goblins came out of the camp to meet them, mostly children, all of them boys. The goblin women stayed behind knee-high walls on the midden mound. A wearier collection of mothers and daughters Druhallen had never seen. Rozt'a fell back to walk beside him.

"This place turns my blood cold," she whispered. "The slave market hasn't closed. They've only stopped selling their women to the Zhentarim."

"They never sold their women to the Zhentarim," Dru whispered back. "Count them. There are more males than females, but a lot more boys than girls."

She did the arithmetic. "There must be another camp."

"I doubt it."

"What—?"

"Shsssh. Later."

Dru suspected that if they knew where to dig, they'd find too many tiny burials—or maybe the goblins didn't bury the daughters they chose not to raise. His own five brothers notwithstanding, sentient populations tended naturally to balance themselves between males and females. It took considerable intervention to create the disparity here in Ghistpok's camp. The brutal and ultimately self-defeating irony was that the same goblins who'd go to any length to enlarge their harems would reject their daughters. Women tended to be scarce when women were despised, and a race or tribe where men outnumbered women never camped far from brink of extinction.

The Dekanter goblins dwelt near that edge. They were still abandoning their daughters—witness the preponderance of boys running loose—but they were missing many of their adult males. The survivors—the goblins pointing their spears at the tallest woman they'd possibly ever seen— might think they were better off than their fathers, but Dru had studied trade and history; he knew better. Ghistpok's gender-skewed tribe was the strongest evidence he'd see to support Amarandaris's notion that there was a war going on in the Greypeak Mountains. Quite possibly a war of annihilation rather than one of conquest.

Suppose the Beast Lord was fighting a war, not with the Zhentarim nor with the goblins nor with anything above ground. Suppose it worked its athanor every day, hatching out swordswingers to protect its slaves and empty pools. Suppose it, too, needed something like a sentience shield to keep its enemies away. If it were fighting a war under Dekanter, the Beast Lord needed bodies—and what better way to get them than from its worshipers?

Dru's concentration lagged as he considered the questions he'd posed to himself. Outhzin had led them into the camp. They were walking across the midden mounds, following a rutted track that wound around the low walls and up to the abandoned Zhentarim headquarters. The stench was astonishing; it overwhelmed concentration and compassion. Animals didn't live so poorly. Squalor on this scale required sentience.

With every step and breath, Druhallen resented the idea that the meat off Hopper's bones would wind up in *these* stomachs. Tiep was right, honest Hopper deserved something better, but their course was set now.

Outhzin signaled a stop within the headquarters' morning shadow. Female goblins watched them from broken, gaping windows. Their faces were a little fuller, if not cleaner than those they saw behind the low walls. There was some benefit, then, to being part of Ghistpok's harem.

It certainly wasn't Ghistpok. Only one word could describe the Dekanter chief when he appeared in the doorless doorway: grotesque. He wore nothing, but could hardly be called naked. In a colony where everyone else was starving, Ghistpok was huge, though even he was not the man he'd been. Empty folds of flesh hung from his bulging belly, his upper arms and legs—wherever he had once stored his fat. His face resembled a melting ball of wax. When he raised his arms, flesh fell back from his hands like too-long sleeves.

Tiep and Rozt'a both turned away. Druhallen held his ground but he had to look elsewhere when Ghistpok lifted a flap of dirty orange flesh to scratch a maggot-ridden armpit.

By chance, Dru found himself gazing at Sheemzher. The goblin who'd first appeared in their Parnast room dressed like a town dandy was pale and trembling. His disappointment and contempt were palpable: This was *not* the Ghistpok he'd expected to find.

But this was the Ghistpok with whom they had to negotiate—with whom Sheemzher had to negotiate, because the Dekanter chief would not speak to a human nor admit that he understood their language. After an exchange that wasn't cordial, Sheemzher followed Ghistpok into the abandoned headquarters. Outhzin and three other warriors joined them.

Druhallen and his companions were left standing outside the stone headquarters, surrounded by goblins who were as hostile as they were curious. The overbold goblin who'd assaulted Rozt'a paced a circle around them, snarling and shaking his spear at any other male who got too close. His spear did nothing to deter another drizzly rain shower or the huge mosquitoes.

"You've got to burn this place," Tiep snarled as he slapped and flailed. "The whole world *needs* you to—"

"Quiet!" Dru had retreated into himself and reacted slowly to the sound of Tiep's voice. "They understand. They might not know you're just making noise."

"But you can—"

"I said, 'Quiet!' "

Rozt'a grabbed the youth and whispered in his ear. Tiep made a one-step retreat, astonishment written large across his face. With luck, the goblins hadn't figured out they were entertaining a wizard.

Inside the Zhentarim headquarters, the goblins exchanged heated words. Druhallen couldn't be sure if

Sheemzher had made allies, but he and Ghistpok weren't the only ones raising their voices. Outhzin and his three peers appeared in the doorway to glower and glare. Each time Dru got a sense of what slaves might have felt when Dekanter's market flourished. He'd have led Rozt'a and Tiep away, if there'd been anywhere else to go.

At last, Sheemzher emerged, looking grim and without his shirt which had become a turban atop Ghistpok's head. Druhallen expected bad news, but the goblin insisted—

"Sheemzher settle good. All done. Ghistpok not all believe, believe enough—Ghistpok *curious.* Sheemzher, good sir lead people. Show people slaves, egg. Beast Lord *make* demons! Yes? People see; people believe. People return, Ghistpok believe. Sheemzher settle good. Make sacrifice, yes? Big feast after sacrifice. Big feast after Ghistpok believe. All people get scroll after big feast. Good sir say, *sentience shield.* Sheemzher settle good, yes?"

If Druhallen were writing the script, he'd have the Nether scroll and be on his way to Weathercote Wood before Ghistpok's goblins plunged into their feast, but he wasn't writing the script. Dru told the goblin, "Sheemzher settle good, yes," and cringed when he realized he was repeating the goblin's words.

While Ghistpok's elite gathered their spears, Druhallen led Hopper to the charred pit where the goblins prepared their food. No need to ask what they used for fuel, and it wasn't wood. He'd hoped for privacy but had an audience. In a moment or two, the goblins would know what he was.

Dru began by scratching the tip of Hopper's nose. He working his fingers up the side of the gelding's head to his ears. Hopper sighed and rested his chin on Dru's shoulder. Trust never wavered from his brown eyes. One instant there was life, the next—when Dru crushed the kindling ember against bone—life was gone. Hopper's legs buckled; he went down with a dead-weight *thud.*

Tiep had stationed himself where Druhallen couldn't

help but see him once Hopper was on the ground. The youth's expression was confused and unreadable—identical, perhaps, to his own. A month ago, Dru had believed he was a man beyond change; for good or ill, he was the man he'd always be. A week on the Dawn Pass Trail had proved him wrong.

If—*When* Druhallen left Dekanter, he'd be a different person, and so, too, would Rozt'a and Tiep. He could see the changes already on their faces.

A cold wind blew through Druhallen's thoughts; it whispered Galimer's name. Since Sunderath, Dru had shared everything that mattered with Galimer, even a woman's love, but they wouldn't share Dekanter . . . or the glade in Weathercote Wood.

If Weathercote changed Galimer as the Greypeaks were changing him—?

Dru realized he could give Wyndyfarh the damned scroll and receive a stranger in return.

The risk had to be taken.

"Let's go," he said, walking away from Hopper's carcass.

He strode toward the main entrance to the Dekanter mines. Tiep caught up first.

"You did what you had to do," the youth said in hushed, thick tones.

Dru said nothing.

"I'm not angry with you anymore."

Dru shook his head. "You've grown up."

"Yeah. I guess."

Rozt'a joined them, Sheemzher, too. The goblin had acquired another spear which he held off-side in his left hand. With his right, he grasped Dru's hand as a child might. Dru endured the sympathy without comment.

The mine entrance was as old as the quarry. It was almost directly below the rim where they'd first looked down on the goblin colony, which was why they hadn't seen it from the High Trail. Like the steps, the entrance had been carved by dwarves and they'd outdone themselves with inscriptions and low-relief portraits. The inscriptions were mostly Dethek runes, but the portraits were humans, each surrounded by Netherese letters.

Dru sounded out the words—Raliteff, Noanar, Valdick, Efteran, and others—all names he'd learned at Candlekeep, all Netherese wizards. For decades he'd dreamt of standing before the Dekanter mines, on the threshold of forgotten history and magic. A thousand times or more he'd imagined how the moment would feel; none was remotely accurate.

Seven goblins, including Sheemzher and Outhzin, accompanied Dru into the entry chamber.

Rozt'a hadn't been listening when Sheemzher came out of the headquarters, or she'd misunderstood what he'd said. "Where is everyone?" she asked. "We need the whole tribe, the women and children, too, if we're going to distract the alhoon with a sentience shield," she explained.

"Later. People here convince Ghistpok. Ghistpok convince all people. Get scroll after feast."

"Wonderful," Rozt'a replied. "You agreed to this, Dru?"

"It's the best Sheemzher could do."

"Wonderful," she repeated and fingered her sword.

They left sunlight behind. With their keen noses and heat-sensitive eyes, the goblins didn't need light to find their way through the mines, but they didn't object to Dru's light spell when he let the freshly cast spell drift above them.

Light revealed aspects of Dekanter that scent and heat could never detect. The dwarves hadn't stopped their carving at the entry portals. The walls and high ceilings of several chambers of the mines were covered with inscriptions, portraits, and scenes from forgotten epics, many of them painted. One goblin, on seeing a remarkable likeness of a red dragon that incorporated the natural contours of the rock beneath its paint, dropped his spear and raced back to the light.

"Wait until they see the Beast Lord," Rozt'a mused bitterly.

For the moment, the Beast Lord was the least of their problems. Last night's torrential rains had penetrated the mines. Sheemzher complained that the smells were different—fainter—than they had been, but more worrisome were the puddles and the water seeping through the walls. Dru knelt and examined a damp line a handspan above the floor.

"This tunnel flooded last night," he decided.

"We had more water pooled around our feet in the rocks," Tiep joked.

"And that water's still flowing through this mountain," Dru countered, then added, "We're out of our minds. Only fools would walk into a mountain after a rain."

Rozt'a was unimpressed. "Then we're fools. The Beast Lord lives in this mountain and so do its slaves. If they can survive, so can we."

The passages were unfamiliar at first, but soon enough Druhallen recognized intersections by their Dethek runes. He began to relax about water and worry, instead, that they might encounter a beefed-up swordswinger patrol. Dru listened for voices, boots, and the clank of metal; what he heard was different.

"There's water ahead, Sheemzher," he told the goblin. "A lot of water."

"Much water, good sir," Sheemzher agreed. "No danger. Egg smell strong."

Perhaps it was. Dru had stood in front of the athanor without noticing any scent emanating from it, but before they'd gone a hundred feet into the next tunnel even a human nose was aware of a damp, stony tang in the air and the breeze that carried it toward them. They followed the wind to the next intersection.

Sheemzher forged straight ahead. "This way before, good sir," he said when Dru hesitated. "This way now, yes?"

The goblin was retracing their steps, but he was also

leading them toward water. Against his better judgment, Dru let himself be led down a corridor past the point where damp became wet. Yesterday, he'd nearly succumbed to panic when he'd felt the mountain bearing down on him. Today, knowing there was a storm's worth of water working its way through the tangled passages, the pressure was worse. Druhallen knew there was danger and knew no way to avoid it, except by leaving the mines.

"We've got to turn around," he announced. "There's no telling where the water's been or where it's going. This tunnel could flood in an instant."

They argued with him, Rozt'a and Tiep included, until water seeped through the seams of their boots and covered their toes. Backtracking to the previous intersection, Sheemzher declared that he'd made a mistake—

"Egg smell strongest *this* way!" He pointed down the right-side path, a down-sloping path where the stone was dry and the air was still. "Come. Come, good sir," Sheemzher tugged on Druhallen's sleeve. "Be brave, good sir. Trust Sheemzher. Sheemzher follow nose now, not memory."

Dru backed away and found himself face-to-face with Rozt'a.

"What have we got to lose?" she challenged. "Maybe the water's already drowned the alhoon."

He returned the challenge. "Can you drown the undead?"

He followed her down a corridor that ended over a seemingly dry hole in the floor. The hole was about as wide as Dru's arm was long. A free-spinning stone ring had been carved out of the granite beside it.

"Down now, good sir. Egg smell very strong, good sir."

Dru insisted they drop something down the shaft. Pointing at the ring, Tiep suggested tying off one end of the rope they carried. When completely uncoiled, the thirty-foot rope struck neither water nor bottom. Druhallen produced a handful of agate pebbles from his folding box and dropped them down the shaft. He'd counted to three before the pebbles clattered against stone.

"Egg smell very strong, good sir," Sheemzher repeated himself.

"Look at the ring, Dru." Again Rozt'a supported the goblin. "It's obviously meant to anchor a rope."

Two of Ghistpok's goblin's were already shinnying down the rope.

"Get proof, good sir. Get scroll. Get friend."

Dwarves had hollowed the shaft out of the granite mountain. They could have easily clambered through it, with or without a rope. If anything, the chimney shaft was easier for goblins and not terribly difficult for a wiry youth or a slender woman. Druhallen conceded it was wider than the hole where they'd begun yesterday's exploration, but not by much. He prayed, as he'd seldom prayed before, that he didn't have climb up in a hurry.

The light spell revealed that they'd come to the oldest part of Dekanter—the twisting tunnels dwarf miners had made as they chipped out veins of metal and gems. The tunnel beneath the shaft stretched in two directions. Sheemzher sniffed the still air and swore the egg smell was stronger in one direction. He led the way.

Goblins could stand tall in a dwarf-cut tunnel, but humans had to scrunch their necks and shoulders if they wished to see where they were going. They hadn't gone far before Dru's muscles were aching. He was thinking about pain and futility and not paying particularly close attention to anything when his eyes caught a flicker of reddish light in the passage ahead of Sheemzher. He seized the goblin's neck and inhaled his light spell.

"See anything?" he asked.

"See dark, good sir. See stone." Sheemzher replied anxiously.

"Anything else?"

"Only stone, all same stone. See anything, good sir?"

By feel and memory, Dru pinched a bit of enchanted

beeswax from a candle-stub in his folding box. He exhaled a spell across the wax then flicked forward. Around him, humans and goblins uttered their favorite oaths as a spider-web ward popped into view a mere ten feet ahead.

"Boundary wards," Dru concluded after a moment's study

The Beast Lord's enemies weren't in the quarry, they were deep in the mountain. The first explanation they'd heard in Parnast was that the Dawn Pass Trail had moved because the Beast Lord was at war with the Underdark, that shadowy realm beneath Faerûn's surface. The Underdark was real, of course, but many of the catastrophes rumored to have their roots there had much simpler explanations—Zhentarim, Red Wizards, earthquakes, or plagues. Druhallen had dismissed the Parnast rumors when he first heard them and had discounted them ever since, especially when Amarandaris's conversation had focused on the Red Wizards, not the drow.

Even when he'd laid eyes on the Beast Lord and learned what it was, he'd resisted the rumors. Mind flayers *were* part of the Underdark world, but alhoons were exiles from mind flayer communities. What better place for an alhoon to establish itself than in an old mine that was underground but not Underdark? Finding wards here, far below the quarry, supported the idea that the Beast Lord, at least, believed it was not completely isolated from its former haunts.

"Can we get through it?" Tiep asked.

Druhallen replied, "Not without breaking it. If the Beast Lord's paying attention, it'll know something's loose down here." He turned to Sheemzher. "You've done your best, but this isn't going to work. We've got to turn back and wait until that passage we used yesterday is dry."

"No proof, Ghistpok not believe. Ghistpok not believe, no tomorrow. Go forward, good sir. Go forward, find proof—"

"No tomorrow?" Tiep broke in. "What's this 'no tomorrow'

nonsense? Did you forget to tell us something, dog-face?"

Sheemzher hung his head. "Egg smell strong, good sir. Very strong."

Rozt'a added her thought, "Are you sure you can't take it down quietly? If we can get Ghistpok's goblins to the egg chamber, Sheemzher says we'll have our proof. Once we've got that, we can wait until that other passage is dry."

"Ask him what he means by 'no tomorrow,'" Tiep pressed. "And make some more light so we can see his lying face when he answers."

Druhallen said nothing to Sheemzher, but he did cast another light spell and held it at a single candle's brightness. He drew the sword he'd taken from yesterday's swordswingers and approached the shimmering ward.

Rozt'a reminded him, "A goblin spear is longer."

"But this is the Beast Lord's sword. There's a chance it won't bring the Beast Lord down around our heads."

And, anyway, Dru didn't plan to be holding onto the sword when it pierced the ward. He envisioned hurling it like a javelin, but such heroic moves demanded years of practice. The sword tumbled after Druhallen threw it. Ghistpok's goblins chuckled at his awkward effort; he should have asked Sheemzher's help, at the very least. The sword struck the warding lengthwise and the resulting flare blinded them all.

"You meant to do that?" Tiep asked when they'd once again adjusted to the dim light of Dru's spell.

"I meant to clear it."

Dru's voice was shaking and so was his hand as he picked up the sword. The hilt was charred, the steel blade was pitted. The warding had been more potent than he'd imagined.

"Why here?" Rozt'a asked. "Why here in a spidery tunnel when there was nothing around the egg or the empty pools?"

"Yesterday we were above the Beast Lord. It doesn't

worry about attacks from above. Ghistpok's goblins worship it and act as wards—a sentience shield. The enemies it fears—the ones it wards against—come from below."

"What would that ward have done if you hadn't broken it?"

"Killed the first man foolish enough to touch it." He fished out a larger bit of beeswax and shaped it around the sword's tip. A basic spell for the detection of magic was enchanted into the wax, not Dru's memory. The spell needed only the warmth of his breath to kindle. "Come on, Sheemzher. Let's keep moving. We've tripped the Beast Lord's wards. If it's paying any sort of attention, it should send someone to investigate—or come itself."

With Sheemzher at his side and the wax-tipped sword thrust before them, Dru led the way. The warding got thicker quickly—every ten steps they stopped and Sheemzher threw rocks discarded by long-dead dwarves into the webbing.

"He's hung enough stuff to stop an army,"

Tiep made the comment, but the truth, which Druhallen kept to himself, was that any army—any serious, sentient enemy with a halfwit's understanding of defensive strategy—would be doing exactly what he and his companions were doing: moving slow, tripping the wards before they did any damage, and giving the Beast Lord ample time to track them down. He was almost relieved when the tunnel ahead of them lit up with a burst-ward flare.

"Company's coming," Rozt'a said. "Get ready for swordswingers." She drew her own weapon and tested the range of movement she'd have between the tunnel's walls.

Dru plucked an ember from his sleeve. "Don't make assumptions—it could be anything, even the Beast Lord itself."

Rozt'a reminded her partner of an obvious constraint: "Not unless it chooses to fight from its knees. It was at least a foot taller than me."

Rozt'a proved prophetic. They faced eight sword-wingers, guided by a light spell and armed with a bit of fire magic. The best defense against the swarm of fiery streaks headed their way was a ball of flame Druhallen used to clear the tunnel. It consumed their arrows but was largely spent by the time it reached the swordswingers. There were few screams, not as many as he'd hoped. The survivors charged, howling as they approached.

Druhallen expected Ghistpok's goblins to turn tail and run. He'd forgotten the antipathy between Sheemzher and Outhzin, and Amarandaris's assertion that the goblins would fight to the death under the right conditions. The insults Sheemzher hurled at Outhzin created those conditions. Ghistpok's goblins howled and surged in front of the humans, meeting the swordswinger charge with their spears.

"Not much of a sentient shield," Rozt'a shouted from her unaccustomed place in the rear.

"Not much sentience," Dru shouted back.

He was being unfair. The goblins were as clever as they needed to be, and their thick-shafted thrusting spears were better suited to close-quarter fighting than swords. Rozt'a never raised her blade. He and Tiep never unsheathed theirs.

Ghistpok's goblins were scavenging the swordswinger corpses as Dru, Rozt'a, and Tiep moved unnoticed through them toward Sheemzher, who stood alone and aloof where the swordswinger charge had begun.

"Did you get hurt?" Rozt'a asked.

"Sheemzher not hurt, good woman," he replied, which seemed true enough where blood was concerned, but the goblin was clearly troubled by something.

"What's wrong?" Dru demanded.

Sheemzher sighed and turned away without answering—a degree of defiance he hadn't displayed before and one that raised alarms in Druhallen's mind. But before he could

probe for answers, Ghistpok's goblins erupted with dis
tinctly fearful shouts.

The five were gathered around a single corpse. One o
the scavengers clutched his hand to his breast as if it ha
been burnt. The others were pointing at the corpse which
to Dru's eyes, looked no different than any of the othe
athanor-hatched swordswingers.

He repeated his unanswered question "What's wrong?"

"*Grouze!*" Outhzin answered. "*Grouze!*" He thrust hi
spear at the corpse but was careful not touch it. "Thi
demon, once Grouze."

"He recognizes the corpse? Is that what he's saying?" Dru
asked Sheemzher and Sheemzher nodded.

Rozt'a indulged her curiosity. She leaned over the corpse
in-question and got four spears shaken in her face for he
boldness. Still, she retreated with satisfaction.

"Scars. Old scars along the ribs. He must have had then
when he went into the egg and had 'em still when he cam
out. If they're looking for proof, I think they've found all th
proof they need."

"Is this sufficient, Sheemzher? Will this convince Ghist
pok that the Beast Lord's not the god for him?"

Sheemzher hadn't stopped nodding since Druhallen'
last question.

"You knew what the Beast Lord was doing, Sheemzhe.
You knew it yesterday." Dru raised his voice, hoping to sna
the goblin out of his trance. "You saw it yesterday—a gobli
and a mantis go into the athanor, and a swordswinger come
out. There are no demons, Sheemzher, the Beast Lord trans
mutes living things to make these creatures and the mis
shapen creatures of the bogs. That's what we've come dow
here to prove to Ghistpok. I didn't think we still had to prov
it to you!"

He chose his words for a wider audience—Ghistpok's gob
lins, who'd demonstrated that they did, indeed, understan
the Heartlands trade dialect. And it was a good thing tha

he did, because Dru's speech had no effect on Sheemzher. The goblin was locked inside his thoughts until Rozt'a sheathed her sword and knelt before him. "Elva—That was her name? You're thinking about Elva?"

The rhythm of Sheemzher's nodding changed. Rozt'a had correctly guessed the goblin's fears. He took a tentative step toward another corpse and seemed almost grateful when Rozt'a held him back.

"Don't look," she advised. "Tell yourself she died years ago and don't look down now."

"She probably did die years ago anyway, Sheemz," Tiep said in a tone that was almost sympathetic.

None of the goblins would touch the swordswinger corpse that had once been Grouze. Druhallen had to hoist the body onto his shoulders and climb the rope last because none of the goblins, including Sheemzher, would touch anything the corpse had touched, including the rope and the walls of the chimney shaft.

"I could remind them that the swordswingers *patrol* these corridors," Tiep said nastily when the humans were able to stand up straight again. "Everywhere they *step* a demon's stepped there before. That would be fun to watch—"

"You open your mouth," Dru warned, "and I'll tie your tongue to your belt. The Beast Lord's done something Ghistpok can't forgive. The whole colony will be up in arms. We get our sentience shield, we get the golden scroll, and we get out of Dekanter no worse off than we are right now. Understand?"

Tiep nodded.

13

7 Eleint, the Year of the Banner (1368 DR)

Dekanter

Tiep remembered a riot in Berdusk. He didn't remember
it coherently—he couldn't have been more than six at the
time—but what he did remember was vivid. First, everyone
had raced toward the market with sticks and rocks and
torches. Then he recalled people screaming, horses crashing
through the crowd, and flashing steel as everyone tried to
get away from the market. He'd seen his first corpse that
day: a woman who'd fallen and been trampled during the
retreat.

When he thought about it now, Tiep supposed the riot had
been about the cost of food and the fear of starvation. His
grown self understood that riots *had* underlying causes; usually the cost of one thing or the fear of something else. And
riots had flash points, they didn't just *happen*—though that
was the way he remembered the Berdusk riot. One moment,
he must have been doing something he couldn't remember,
and the next he'd been running with his mates, a cobblestone
in each hand and a howl in his heart.

He remembered that the riot had been exhilarating,
until he saw the corpse.

She'd been the baker's daughter and Tiep had never known her name, but she'd given out bread crusts from the back door of her father's shop and sometimes let him and his mates warm themselves by the oven in winter. The baker had shut his shop after the riot. He hadn't really had much choice in the matter. The mob had burnt it clear down. Tiep remembered going cold and hungry more often after that—hardly a surprise to his grown self, but at six, he hadn't made the connection between the High Sun riot and winter's discomfort.

He'd been a child then, and children didn't string events together. He'd run to the market. He'd run away from it. The baker's daughter gave him food. The baker's daughter was a corpse. The baker's shop was gone. He'd gone hungry and cold. There were no connections, no causes, no reason not to riot with the mob.

The goblins were like the child he'd been—maybe that was why he despised them so. They ran toward Dru when they saw him carrying a dead "demon" on his shoulders. They ran away when they found out that the "demon" was someone they'd known as "Grouze." They pushed and shoved and hurt one another—mostly the real goblin children—when they ran.

Ghistpok, the fat, old goblin they called their chief, couldn't control them. His house withstood the mob because the Zhentarim had built it, and say what you would about the Zhentarim, they knew how to build a stone wall. A handful of the flimsy goblin hovels got trampled.

When the goblins who'd been tending the hearth and stew pot caught sight of the mob headed their way, they threw up their hands and ran. Bad enough that Tiep and his friends had to sacrifice Hopper to get on Ghistpok's good side, but watching the rampaging goblins overturn the pot in their hysteria was more than Tiep could bear to watch. He wanted badly to unsheathe his sword and kill a few, in the old gelding's name.

Ghistpok's tribe didn't deserve to live; they didn't have enough sense. The hearth fire would have spread through the camp if it hadn't been raining again. The swordswingers the Beast Lord put together underground were smarter than all of Ghistpok's goblins put together. Which said a lot about the bugs Lady Mantis cooked up back in Weathercote.

Then Druhallen did something with his voice and made himself sound like a thousand men all shouting from the top of the quarry.

"Stop your running. Stop your screaming. Come back to the old headquarters."

The goblins stopped. Every one of them understood plain language; they'd just been pretending that they didn't. They hung their ugly orange and red heads and looked ashamed as they filed back to the clearing in front of the stone house. Ghistpok climbed up to what remained of the Zhentarim roof; that was a sight from below that Tiep hoped never to see again.

"Listen to me." Dru's voice boomed through the quarry. "We went into Dekanter to find the truth about the demons, and we did find it. We've brought it where you can see it and judge for yourselves."

Tiep was impressed. He'd hadn't guessed that Druhallen could charm so many minds. Galimer had assured him Dru didn't cast any sort of charm spell; charms and enchantments were Galimer's specialty—because so few of them were cast on the fly.

That was Dru, letting everyone think there was something he couldn't do so Galimer could seem to be the expert. Wizards were sneaky folk, and Druhallen was one of the sneakiest because he seemed so straightforward.

Last night, after the storm died and Dru huddled up with his magic box, he hadn't said anything about being prepared to charm the goblins, but he was. Had he memorized the spell last night because he'd guessed that the goblins would be unruly? Had Dru been carrying the reagents around all summer, the way he'd been carrying around the reagents for his Candlekeep scrying spell?

And they complained about Tiep keeping secrets!

The charm began to wear off. Ghistpok was among the first to recover. The goblin chief wasn't pleased to see his tribe listening to Druhallen. He waved his arms and hopped from one foot to the other while shouting goblin words. Tiep held his breath and prayed that Tymora or some other god would give the fat goblin a little shove toward embarrassment if not oblivion, but the gods had done enough for one day. Ghistpok commanded his tribe's attention, finished his tirade, and clambered uneventfully down from the roof.

Dru picked up the swordswinger's corpse—which Tiep hadn't noticed on the ground while Ghistpok was ranting—and carried it into the stone house. Ghistpok and five or six male goblins followed Dru. That left maybe forty or fifty goblins, including children, standing around in the rain. It took a while, but eventually a few of the females went off to reconstruct the soaked, scattered hearth.

He watched the females wrestle the huge stew pot onto an iron tripod and empty smaller pots of rainwater into it. Then, while one of them struggled to coax fire out of the sopping embers, the rest gathered the meat that had spilled out when the stew pot overturned. Without hesitation, they tossed the chunks back into the pot.

Tiep was suddenly cold. His knees trembled and the ground wobbled beneath his feet. He would have fallen, but the thought of landing in the mud was so horrifying that it kept his legs moving until he was off the mounds and standing on the quarry stone. Gasping and sobbing, he doubled over, clutching his gut. It had been hours since Tiep had eaten. There was nothing left in his stomach and that only made the retching worse.

His throat was raw before Tiep had regained control over his body and thoughts. The stairway to the High Trail beckoned through the late afternoon shadows, but so did the eastward gorge leading out of the Dekanter quarry. For the first time Tiep noticed a pair of Zhentarim-built houses just inside the gorge. Their roofs were gone, and soot stained the gaping holes that had been their windows and doorways. As shelters, neither would be better than standing out in the open, but once Tiep noticed them and the charred remnants of a wooden gate between them he forgot about the rain.

Druhallen will not listen to reason, Amarandaris had told him the night before they left Parnast. *I've told him not to leave Parnast, but if he does—if he slips away and you go with him, then you will be my eyes in Dekanter. Watch him. Watch everything he does; remember everything he says,* especially *when he casts that spell he got from Candlekeep. But more than that, keep your eyes open for an iron box as long as your arm and half as high. Men died protecting that box. Look for it beneath the walls of the gatehouse. Leave it where you see it, if you see it, but when you get to Yarthrain, pay a visit to a man called Horace, the cooper behind the Black Buck Inn. Tell him everything—give it to him in writing, if you can. A reward will be waiting for you when you get to Scornubel.*

The best part of everything Amarandaris had said was that the odds were against the Zhentarim showing up here in Dekanter. The bad part was that Tiep couldn't tell Druhallen not to worry. The worst part, until now, was that he hadn't seen anything that might have been a gatehouse.

With renewed strength and purpose, Tiep strode to the gorge and across the threshold of the northern gatehouse. The interior had been burnt and looted months ago. Charred wood was rotting fast. In the dim light Tiep couldn't easily tell the difference between roof-beams and furniture. There was nothing that looked like an iron box, but plenty of rubbish lay heaped up against the walls. He kicked the nearest pile.

"No talk. Go away."

Tiep leapt straight up when he heard words coming from the rubbish behind him. His heart had stopped and restarted at violent speed before a shred of intelligence let him know he'd heard that voice before.

"Sheemzher?"

"Go away."

One trash heap *was* more blue and green than sooty black.

"What are you doing here? Shouldn't you be back with your brothers and sisters, getting ready for the big feast and celebration?"

"Sheemzher not eat. Sheemzher not celebrate. Not talk. Go away."

"Sorry, Sheemz, I've got work to do. You're not sitting on a iron box, are you?" Tiep knew better than to provoke the goblin when they were hung on tenterhooks waiting to get back to the egg chamber, but when he was fighting guilt and anxiety, Tiep couldn't resist the temptation to pick on an easy target. "Did you see Ghistpok up on the wall? Didn't you marry his daughter? Did she look like him?"

The goblin said something guttural in his own language.

"You want to repeat that in a language that sentient races can understand?"

"Sheemzher say, better sacrifice that one, not Hopper. Not miss that one."

The goblin's voice was forlorn, yet defiant, as though he knew he couldn't win but wouldn't back down from a fight, either. It was a trait Tiep knew well and one that blunted some of his own anger.

"Hopper had cracked a hoof. It was just a question of where and when Dru would use his mercy spell."

"Not mercy, sacrifice. Sacrifice. Good sir say sacrifice. Good sir not ask Hopper."

Tiep kicked another rubbish heap. He'd have hurt himself if the iron box had been within it, but the heap collapsed without incident.

"Dru's in charge. He makes the decisions because he's the one who does the lion's share of the work when we're on the road. He's right, too, most of the time. We've got to have Ghistpok's cooperation. If—If—Look, it wasn't as if Dru said, Let's slaughter Hopper. We left Cardinal behind, and you remember what happened to him. That was pointless. This is—this is better. We're getting closer to that scroll your bug lady wants, and closer to getting Galimer back. That's what sacrifice is all about."

Sheemzher made the sound of a bladder bursting then said. "Not eat. Not celebrate. Ghistpok—" He made the bladder-bursting sound again. "Good sir not ask Hopper, not ask Sheemzher. Sheemzher say no sacrifice. Not *right*. Ghistpok not right. All not right. Good sir say, sacrifice hurt. How? Hopper not sacrifice good sir."

"Animals don't sacrifice people, Sheemzher. People make sacrifices because people—" Tiep had to think for a moment—"because people are cleverer than animals. People see consequences and complications. They're sneaky. They make a sacrifice here, so something they want will happen over there."

Tiep waved his arm at the empty door way as a way of indicating that it was a long reach between Hopper's death and getting Galimer out of Weathercote. Sheemzher didn't get the point, though. The goblin just stared out the door, looking for something that wasn't there.

"People," Sheemzher said softly, reminding Tiep that the word meant one thing to him and another to the goblins. "Some people clever. Some people not clever. Some people gods. Gods sacrifice people, yes?"

Tiep went back to kicking rubbish. "You're talking to the wrong person, Sheemz. I don't have anything to do with gods—except Tymora, of course. Lady Luck." An ironic thought crossed his mind. "*Everybody* makes sacrifices to Lady Luck, but gods do what they want. Rozt'a says the last thing she ever wants is the love of a god; it's sure to turn out bad for her, however it turns out for the god. She's probably right. A good friend is worth more than any god. Look what Druhallen's putting himself through for Galimer."

"Good sir eat, yes? Good sir celebrate, yes? Good sir forget Hopper, yes?"

"Yes, no—how in blazes should I know what Dru remembers or forgets? And people—humans—sometimes we do what we have to do and spend the rest of our lives regretting it." The way he regretted everything he'd done for the Zhentarim since that fateful night in Scornubel. "I don't know what Druhallen would do if he had to chose between saving Rozt'a or Galimer. I don't know what I'd do."

Tiep looked up. The goblin stared at him with unnerving intensity.

"It's just *talk*, Sheemzher. We didn't really sacrifice Hopper. We're not gods or priests. Just forget the word ever came up."

The goblin didn't listen. "Good sir save Tiep?" he asked, the first time he'd recognized Tiep by name. "Or, good sir *sacrifice* Tiep?"

The questions cut close to the bone. Tiep spun around in a ready rage. "Be quiet! Be quiet and stay quiet! Leave me alone!"

Tiep stormed out of the northern gatehouse and into the southern one. He kicked rubbish until the sting of Sheemzher's questions had dulled to a familiar, guilty ache. The iron box remained hidden, if it still existed, but he found a sword buried in the ash. Burnt, rotting leather notwithstanding, the hilt of the sword Tiep found in the gatehouse mud fit his hand better than the hilt of the sword he'd taken off the swordswinger.

He'd keep the swordswinger's weapon; the buried blade was rusted beyond redemption. The blades were similar, though—very similar. He carried them both to the open doorway where the light was best and compared the forge marks hammered into the steel. The marks were clear and identical.

Tiep had learned the marks of Darkhold's forge and armory before he'd learned to read, and he'd learned to read before Galimer sat down to teach him his letters. It wasn't an iron box, but he could tell Horace, Amarandaris, and Sememmon himself—if the Dark Lord were interested—that the Beast Lord was arming his bug-brained goblins with Zhentarim swords.

The discovery might not get him his promised reward, which he wouldn't accept under any circumstance, but it might back the Network off for a little while.

Tiep left the sword and the southern gatehouse behind. Sheemzher waited for him in the gorge.

"People begin feast. People begin celebration."

Tiep shook his head vigorously. After Rozt'a and Galimer had adopted him, he'd become fascinated by food, studying it as only a boy who'd often gone hungry could. He knew how to make stew. "They can't be. Meat doesn't cook that fast. It's half-cooked, worse than raw. You've made another mistake, Sheemz. Your eyes aren't good enough."

"People begin feast. Sheemzher not need eyes. Sheemzher use nose."

There was no arguing with Sheemzher's nose. Halfway across the quarry floor, Tiep could both see and smell the truth. Druhallen and Rozt'a were easy to pick out among the goblins. They had bowls in their hands. Through light rain, Tiep couldn't tell if they were eating. He wasn't getting closer for a better look.

Sheemzher was where Tiep had left him between the two gatehouses. Their eyes locked, and Tiep tried, with neither magic nor prayer at his disposal, to will the goblin into one of the buildings so he could hole up in the other. The exercise failed and Sheemzher followed him into the southern house. The remains of a wall hearth provided an almost dry, almost comfortable place to sit and wait. Of course, Sheemzher had to share it with him, but so long as the goblin kept his mouth shut Tiep didn't mind the company.

As the afternoon wound down and the feasting became some of the worst drone-singing Tiep had ever heard, he introduced Sheemzher to dice. The goblin took to gambling like a duck to water but was convinced that a double-six was easier to roll than any lower combination. If they'd been playing for gold, or even copper, Tiep could have transferred all the goblin's wealth to his purse, but they were playing for bits of an endless supply of soggy charcoal. He was sorry he'd gotten his dice out long before darkness put a halt to their playing.

A breeze blew the last of the rain down the gorge. The clouds broke up overhead and the stars of late summer became visible overhead. The temperature began to drop. It was only the first eve of The Fading, but the temperature dropped like stone once the sky was clear. Tiep stamped around the gatehouse, trying to keep warm in clothes that wouldn't dry, while Sheemzher stayed on the hearth, completely unperturbed.

When the chill reached Tiep's bones, the pull of Ghistpok's bonfire became too strong to resist. He returned to the mounds with Sheemzher at his side. The goblins, except for Ghistpok and maybe a few other males, were packed around a hissing fire in the clearing in front of the old Zhentarim headquarters. Their monotonous singing was accompanied and guided by four drummers, all female, all pounding furiously. Tiep had to breathe deep to keep his heart from racing to their rhythm. That meant filling his lungs with the bonfire's pungent smoke.

Tiep warmed himself until he couldn't stand the smells and sounds any longer, then went looking for Druhallen and Rozt'a. They were behind the headquarters. Rozt'a was curled up in an old wool blanket. Tiep didn't ask where she'd found it, but it wasn't one of theirs. He wasn't surprised that she could sleep through the din of goblin music. Rozt'a claimed that anyone who said he wasn't tired was a liar, and anyone who couldn't sleep when he was tired was a fool.

Dru had his box out, waiting for midnight. He held the dark glass disk—the mystery that had dragged them here in the first place and which remained unsolved—in both hands and studied it with a frown and furrowed brow. Tiep approached him slowly; bad things could happen when wizards were interrupted. Dru's concentration was not as complete as it looked. He heard them when they were still several paces away and quickly slipped the disk back into its compartment within the box. Dru didn't ask Tiep where he'd been or what he'd been doing, and Tiep didn't ask Dru what he'd been thinking about while he held the disk or whether he'd enjoyed the feast.

Tiep did ask, "Any idea what happens next?"

Dru shot an inquiring glance at Sheemzher before answering. "They're not talking much and I'm no better at understanding goblin than I was this morning, but Ghistpok's inside working himself up for some sort of trance-ordeal. When he's ready, I think we all follow him down to the chalk circle."

"People dance, good sir," Sheemzher explained. "Ghistpok talk Beast Lord. Beast Lord talk Ghistpok."

"They dance, they drink, too, don't they?" Dru scowled. "A bunch took off into the mines a while ago."

"Wine there, yes. Sheemzher think people not drink much wine anymore, good sir. Zhentarim gone long time. Wine gone, maybe."

"Or maybe we follow a tribe of drunken goblins to the egg chamber. Outhzin's been chipping away at his spear all evening. I guess that's a good sign."

"Good sign, yes. Grouze brother Outhzin. Very angry. Same Sheemzher when Sheemzher lose Elva. All good now. All good for good sir, yes?"

"So long as nothing happens before midnight. I need time to study. I've been light all day. I don't want to go below this empty. While you're both here, though, let me show you how these work—"

Druhallen pulled a pair of Rozt'a's heavy leather gloves off his belt. Tiep knew they'd been enchanted as soon as he saw them and clutched his hands behind his back.

"I can't wear them," he said quickly. "My jinx is tingling."

"That's good to know, but I was counting on Sheemzher to climb back up atop the egg—if you're up to it?"

"Sheemzher climb, good sir. Gloves or not gloves, Sheemzher climb."

"When you're up there, clap your hands twice before you grasp the scroll. I've put an unbinding into the leather, it should help pull the scroll free and keep the flareback from burning your hands. You understand?"

The goblin nodded.

"And you, Tiep: two claps, then pull."

"They're not going to do me any good."

"I'm asking you to remember how to kindle the enchantment, in case someone forgets." Dru's glance darted to Sheemzher and back again.

Tiep's heart skipped a beat, and not because the goblin might forget his instructions. "Dru? What do you mean, Dru? You're sounding like you're not going to be in the egg chamber . . ." His voice trailed off. "What's going on, Dru?"

His foster father shrugged. "I don't see myself there, so I'm being careful."

"What do you mean you don't 'see' yourself. You haven't—you know—had a *vision* or something?"

"No visions, Tiep." Dru tried to laugh; the attempt wasn't entirely successful. "Not even close to a vision. When I cast an enchantment that's tied to a future act, sometimes I get a flash of that act. Most of the time I don't; most of the time, I'm not there when the spell kindles, so why should I get a flash? This time I'd expected to be there when this unbinding kindles. In case I'm not—two claps, then pull. All right?"

"Yeah," Tiep muttered. "You're sure everything's going to be all right?"

"No one's ever sure, Tiep. That's why I'm being careful.

I've told you and Sheemzher. I told Rozt'a before she went down for a nap. I could wish I had more time, more gloves, but wishes don't count. You sticking close until we head below with Ghistpok?"

"You're sure we're going in with him?"

"That's the plan right now. I told you; no one's ever sure. Settle in. Grab a nap, like Rozt'a's doing. I need to rest my mind."

Tiep went through the motions of settling in amid the trash piled up behind the old Zhentarim headquarters. He closed his eyes. Usually he had no trouble falling asleep— the exhausted innocence of youth, Galimer called it. Sleep wasn't waiting for him in Dekanter. Maybe he was growing up.

He thought of Manya and Pulsey, the girl he'd met in Llorkh, and Basienne, who was prettier than both Manya and Pulsey together and might be waiting for him in Scornubel, if he was lucky enough to get back to Scornubel. He thought of Galimer, too, and how close they'd be to Parnast and Manya when they got to Weathercote. Then he thought of Amarandaris and how cold the air in Dekanter had gotten.

The goblins were still singing and drumming, though not as loudly or rapidly as before. It was good to know there were limits. The camp was quiet enough that Tiep could hear Dru whispering nearby. He cracked an eyelid—in case his foster parents were having an actual conversation—but it was just Dru preparing himself for the Underdark with his fists clenched and his eyes squeezed shut. When push came to shove, spellcraft demanded a lot from the wizards who practiced it. Tiep was long past the days when he mourned the vocation he couldn't have.

Druhallen had worked up a sweat by the time he'd finished preparing his spells. His hands shook just a little when he folded his box. Tiep wondered what he'd studied, but wasn't bold enough to ask. It was like asking someone if they wore undergarments to bed. When Dru glanced his way, Tiep closed his eyes again and feigned dreams.

He didn't have to pretend for long. The drummers and singers kicked up a sudden racket. Dru gave both him and Rozt'a a gentle shake to awaken them.

"Ghistpok's come outside. They're all headed down to the chalk circle. We're under way."

For a man who hadn't slept, Tiep was both stiff and groggy. He yawned mightily but couldn't get enough air into his lungs to shake off the lethargy.

"You can stay behind," Rozt'a suggested when she saw him struggling.

They were always suggesting that, as if he were still a child and not up adult responsibilities. "I'm coming. I'm ready."

"Then keep moving. Sheemzher, what are they singing about now?"

The goblin song had changed. It had words, now, though it was still mostly drone and entirely sour.

"People calling Beast Lord, good sir. People say, Beast Lord wise, Beast Lord good, Beast Lord come—" Sheemzher lapsed into a bit of goblin so-called melody.

"That's enough," Dru chided.

Starlight revealed an easy path from the Zhentarim headquarters to the chalk circle. Dru didn't have to waste a light spell, if he had one to spare. The goblins had arranged themselves on the chalk: males surrounded by children, then females. Those males with the largest family rings clumped closest to the black standing stone. Those with fewer, sat farther away.

If Sheemzher had had only Elva and six children, then Sheemzher had sat on the circle's very edge.

While Ghistpok anointed the stone with various oils, wineskins the size and shape of rats were passed from one harem to the next. Everybody took a sip, even the children. The males took several, but nobody got as much as a goblet's worth. Within minutes, they were on their feet swaying and droning again.

"Doesn't take much to get a goblin drunk," he commented.

"They're smaller," Rozt'a chided.

Dru had a different perspective, "They could be adding something to their wine. Mushrooms. I imagine they get quite a crop of mushrooms. There are mushrooms that will have you looking at the sky and seeing green."

When all the goblins had had their wine and mushrooms, and all of them were swaying together, the drumming started again. If there was a rhythm to their pounding, Tiep couldn't detect it, though something kept the goblins moving together rather than crashing into one another as their dance grew steadily wilder. The trick Tiep had used earlier—deep breathing to thwart the drumbeat rhythm—failed against this new assault. His heart pounded, and he found himself gasping for air.

Sheemzher was completely gone, hopping about and waving his arms like the rest of the goblins. If the goblin was only pretending to be drunk, he was doing it very well. Slowly it occurred to Tiep that the goblins weren't particularly inebriated or performing a traditional dance, they were entranced and imitating perfectly the moves and gesture their chief, Ghistpok, made as he circled the glistening black stone.

He shared his insight with Druhallen, to whom it came as no surprise. Maybe it was the noise and the heart-stopping irregularity of the drumbeats, but Dru seemed a bit entranced himself. When Ghistpok stiffened and started screaming in goblin, Dru didn't seem to care. Rozt'a was the one who shook some sense back into Sheemzher.

"What's he saying?" she demanded of the glaze-eyed goblin.

"All well now. All mistake. Grouze mistake," Sheemzher crooned. "People wrong, all wrong. Beast Lord say, come,

264

come now, see the truth. No egg. No bugs. No slaves. Come see. Ghistpok come. People come. All come to Beast Lord. All worship. All learn."

Tiep saw what was happening. "The wine and the drumming gets them all thinking the same, and then the Beast Lord gets all thinking the way he wants them to. This isn't going to work!" He was shouting at Rozt'a who was still shaking Sheemzher.

"It's still our best chance," Dru countered. He seemed to be himself again, though his face had the look of someone with a serious headache. Maybe he was doing something magical, because Sheemzher stopped babbling the instant Dru touched him. "Blind obedience is as good as a sentience shield for our purposes," Dru explained. "We stay with them until it gets them into the pool chamber, then we slip back to the athanor while it's planting lies inside their minds."

" 'Slip back to the athanor'!" Rozt'a sputtered. "Dru, you're mad! This isn't what we planned."

"We were counting on Ghistpok to stand up to the Beast Lord. He can't do it. He's not strong enough or clever enough. None of them are. And they wouldn't, even if they could. That was our mistake—These goblins *worship* the Beast Lord. They're not like us, picking and choosing through a pantheon. They'd sooner die than admit the Beast Lord's deceived and betrayed them."

"But—?"

Dru silenced Rozt'a with an upraised hand. "When you were part of the sentience shield in Cormyr, the alhoon knew you were hostile, knew you were coming. It attacked you. Ghistpok's goblins aren't hostile; the Beast Lord won't attack them. We can fight our way out, if it comes to that."

Tiep studied Dru's face while he and Rozt'a argued. He saw something there he'd never seen before. He didn't know what it was, but he'd wager it had something to do with the enchantment spell Dru had cast on the leather gloves and the flash of the future his foster-father hadn't had.

Ghistpok's goblins were surging toward the mine entrance, all of them and all moving the same way, left foot, right foot, arms swinging and voices chanting.

"If we're going with them, we better start moving," Rozt'a said grimly.

"I'm going to strengthen your minds first. Make you resistant to the Beast Lord's suggestions." He touched Rozt'a and the goblin. "Even you, Tiep. Get the scroll to Weathercote. Get Galimer out of there. I'm depending on you."

Tiep had waited years to hear Druhallen say those words and mean them. They were cold comfort at the bottom of the Dekanter quarry. The spell felt like an egg cracked open on Tiep's scalp and the egg-gut swiftly coating his skin. He shuddered once, then was calmer than he'd been since that morning—scarcely a week ago—in the bug lady's glade when Druhallen hit him with the same spell.

Even the thought that Dru was worried sick about something no longer distressed him.

"You added something," Tiep accused his foster father.

"No," he replied, but wizards lied all the time.

Tiep couldn't tell if Dru had strengthened his own mind or if all the restored calm and renewed sense of purpose came from the magic flowing through his thoughts alone. It didn't matter much. They were as ready as they'd ever be and on their way to steal an ancient scroll from an undead mind flayer.

What could be easier?

Ghistpok led them down almost familiar corridors. Druhallen cast a light spell and no one seemed to care, or notice that there were three humans and one traitor-goblin marching some twenty paces behind them. They came to the place where Tiep was sure they'd turned back yesterday when Sheemzher was leading them and the water got too high. The tunnel was merely wet now. Dru muttered that it had been drained within the last few moments and that they'd been damn lucky to survive their first two visits because the Beast Lord had control over the storm water sloshing through the mines and used water in its defenses.

What did it matter if they'd been lucky before, as long as there was no danger now and they were marching in the right direction?

They were. Tiep recognized the place where they'd met the swordswingers for the first time. The bodies were gone, but the walls had been scorched by Dru's fire. He could feel the Beast Lord now, like a weight or shadow across his thoughts. Between his own immunity and Dru's spell, the alhoon was a presence he could easily ignore.

The pool chamber's glow had become visible ahead of the fast-moving goblins. There was a chance that the Beast Lord would be waiting for them, but not even the thought of those dead-white eyes and writhing tentacles could disrupt Tiep's confidence. He stuck close behind Dru and Rozt'a who were slowing down, putting more distance between themselves and the precisely marching goblins.

Swordswingers appeared in the corridor and drew no reaction from Outhzin and the other elder goblins who'd been beneath Dekanter yesterday as they marched at the front of the herd with Ghistpok.

"That's bad," he whispered to Dru and Rozt'a. "They don't remember why they've come down here."

Rozt'a nodded. "They've got no thoughts of their own left."

But they did. The goblins stopped. Their leaders—Tiep couldn't make out individuals—spoke to the sword-swingers. A few of them led a few of the swordswingers through the quietly standing goblins toward the humans.

"Take this," Dru said as he turned and thrust something icy and hard into Tiep's hands. He handed the enchanted gloves to Sheemzher. "The three of you, step back now and stay close together until the way is clear. Then get to the athanor, get the scroll and *get out!* Don't worry about me."

"You saw something," Tiep protested. "You lied! You *saw* something!"

Druhallen wasn't answering questions. He'd wrapped his arms around them all, him, Rozt'a, and the goblin, and shoved them backward. He stood alone when the goblins and swordswingers arrived. They swarmed around him, taking his sword but not his folding box.

Dru had become their prisoner, and a single word echoed through Tiep's mind: sacrifice. The little part of him that wasn't touched by the mind-strengthening spell wanted to scream and attack, but the larger part, where magic had him seeing everything with cold, self-serving logic, made him grab Sheemzher and take another backward step. Rozt'a remained an arm's length away.

Tiep hissed to get her attention. "Back up. Stay close."

Maybe she didn't hear him. Maybe she chose to stride toward Druhallen instead. The rude, aggressive dog-face who'd grabbed Rozt'a yesterday, and whom she'd sent flying, pointed his spear at her. In a heartbeat she had her sword drawn and so did all the swordswingers. Nobody moved.

"Dru? Dru, are you ready?"

The look on Dru's face was more frightening than all the swords. Something had gone terribly wrong but, not knowing the vision that had guided Druhallen, Tiep couldn't guess where or how his plan had failed.

"Can you kill them all?" Dru asked.

"I can try."

"That's not enough."

"Be damned, Druhallen—it's enough for me!"

She raised her sword and froze, like a living statue. The swordswingers disarmed her without a twitch.

"What—?"

Sheemzher started to ask a question. Tiep hit him hard with the hand that clutched the freezing disk. He hit him a second hit when the goblin opened his mouth again.

Quiet! he mouthed.

The swordswingers and goblins had come within a foot of him and Sheemzher and not noticed them. It was the old glass disk. Somehow it had to be the disk that hid them. And it was Tiep's fault that both Druhallen *and* Rozt'a were being herded toward the pool chamber with him and Sheemzher left behind. Sheemzher snuggled in behind him, peeking out around Tiep's arm. They stayed like that until they were the only ones left in the corridor.

"Are you going to be strong?" Tiep asked his clinging companion. He felt a nod against his ribs. "You still have the gloves Druhallen gave you?" Another nod.

The pool chamber was very quiet. The light flickered, though, and Tiep knew the chamber was occupied. When they were a few strides from the threshold, he told Sheemzher to stay put and crept up to survey the situation alone. It was as bad as he'd feared, with the ugly, fearsome alhoon standing behind the big, circular pool and Tiep's foster parents flanking him. Dru and Rozt'a were both standing still, but straining against invisible restraints.

The calm resolve that Dru's spell had planted in Tiep's mind faltered. For a moment, maybe longer, he couldn't think or move himself. When something touched his hand he nearly leapt out of his skin.

"Shhh-sh," the goblin advised. "Go now? Tiep, Sheemzher go now? Get scroll, yes?"

Sheemzher was on the short side, even for a goblin, and he had lousy goblin eyes. He couldn't see what Tiep saw and, for once, Tiep wasn't going to upset the dog face with a load of bad news.

"Yeah, we go now." He put a hand on Sheemzher's shoulder, steering him across the threshold and along the pool-chamber wall. "Keep your head down and your eyes in straight in front of you—"

"Sheemzher head down, Sheemzher see feet!"

Exasperated with himself more than the goblin, Tiep

gave Sheemzher a shove in the proper direction. "Just don't look out toward the pools. Can you smell the egg? Can you find the open way into the egg chamber?"

The goblin rose on his toes and sniffed several times, then whispered. "Sheemzher smell egg. Egg smell strong. Sheemzher find egg, yes."

They sneaked along the outer wall. Tiep was the one who had trouble following orders. Every few steps he had to look to his left, toward the pools where the Beast Lord stood. Those writhing tentacles were the only movement Tiep could see, unless he counted Dru and Rozt'a's futile efforts to free themselves. He tried not to notice their struggles, but they were the reason he had to look.

Sheemzher took Tiep's hand again when they came to the passage they had used the first time. Tiep hesitated, more because he'd lose sight of Dru and Rozt'a than because he didn't trust the goblin's nose. Sheemzher tugged and Tiep followed. The granite wall was gone. Tiep knew they'd entered the larger chamber by the way sound changed— without Dru's light spell he couldn't see his hand in front of his face.

"Is it there?" he asked anxiously. "Is the scroll there?" and, belatedly, "Are we alone in here?"

"All alone," Sheemzher assured him. "Scroll there. Tiep lift Sheemzher, yes?"

Tiep let the goblin lead him to chamber's center. He knew the egg was there when he bumped his shoulder against its open door. Sheemzher didn't truly need any help climbing to the egg's top, but Tiep was glad to tie the icy disk into his shirt hem and hoist the goblin to his shoulders.

"Don't forget to put on the gloves," he said when the weight was gone. "And clap twice before you pull on the scroll."

Sheemzher clapped three times, which was a harmless error. The chamber lit up as if a score of lightning bolts had struck the egg. Tiep was blinded by light, not darkness.

Blobs of lurid color floated within his eyes. He held up his arms, hoping Sheemzher would find them.

"Here."

Sheemzher had been thrown across the chamber again—Tiep had heard what happened after he and Rozt'a left the first time. Tiep forced himself to ask, "Are you hurt?" when all he really cared about was the scroll. He thought he might just shrivel up and die if the goblin hadn't freed the scroll.

"Scroll here, too. Sheemzher have scroll. Sheemzher hurt some here, there."

With neither light nor goblin eyes to guide him, Tiep couldn't take two steps without tripping over some piece of twisted metal. It was the sound that worried him, though sound was the least of his problems. Be they goblins, sword-swingers, or the Beast Lord himself, everyone beneath Dekanter could see in the dark except for him, Rozt'a, and Druhallen. Fear of noise dropped Tiep to his hands and knees. He crawled to the goblin and could make no assessment of his injuries.

"Can you move? Walk?"

"Maybe. Get spear. Spear *there*."

Sheemzher pointed toward something Tiep couldn't hope to see. "Forget your spear. Can you walk out of here."

"*Spear!* Sheemzher need spear. Get spear, Sheemzher walk."

"Give me the scroll first."

It was smaller than Tiep expected, barely longer than his forearm. He was numb to the elbow the instant he touched it. No telling what that meant. Tiep stripped off his shirt instead and quickly smoothed it across the stone floor. He unrolled the golden scroll and laid it flat on his shirt—the cloth was a bit longer than the scroll. He put the glass disk in the middle of the scroll. After tucking the hem over one bar and its finials, Tiep let the scroll layer itself within his shirt as it recoiled. It wasn't as tightly rolled as before, but the bulge wasn't as large as he'd feared it might be. He

271

could hold the cloth-wrapped scroll without the numbness growing worse and after a moment's indecision, tucked the entire bundle against the small of his back.

"So, where's your damn spear?"

They could hear noise out in the pool chamber by the time Tiep got his hands on Sheemzher's left-behind spear. The sounds were the same high-pitched keening sounds Ghistpok's goblins had made when they'd led Hopper down the quarry steps yesterday morning, and quite different from their trance singing earlier.

He helped Sheemzher to his feet. The goblin was wobbly, especially on his right side. Tiep heard himself say—

"Are you sure you can walk? I could carry you if you're not sure."

"Sheemzher walk. Sheemzher strong."

"Stay close then. Dru meant for us to stay close together. I don't want you getting left behind."

"Not lose Sheemzher."

Sheemzher led the way through the darkness. The goblin's eyes were fine, but he moved slowly and Tiep could hear him breathing hard. Sheemzher's injuries faded from Tiep's concern when they cleared the egg-chamber dog-leg and could see into the pool chamber.

All the goblins, the naked slaves they'd seen before and Ghistpok's ragged tribe from the smallest child to fat Ghistpok himself, were prostrate on the stone, with their faces hidden and their arms extended in front of them, toward the Beast Lord. They were so motionless that Tiep would have thought them dead, but for the keening that echoed around him. The swordswingers—about forty of them altogether—were also motionless, though they were standing with their swords drawn, their attention focused on the Beast Lord who stood with his back to the egg chamber. Rozt'a stood to the Beast Lord's right; she been stripped of her clothes which lay in pieces around her.

Dru was nowhere to be seen.

Tiep was enraged, but beneath the spell in his mind, Tiep was as frightened as he'd ever been in his life. If the magic broke, terror would overcome anger and he'd be unable to move, except to soil himself and collapse on the stone. The spell would break. None of Dru's spells lasted forever and there was a bad chance that none of them would last longer than him. They should get moving toward the surface, toward Weathercote and Galimer. They shouldn't waste another moment.

A man groaned. It was a small sound, almost lost in the goblin keening, but Tiep heard it as clearly as he heard his own heart's beating and knew without doubt or hesitation that it had come from Druhallen's throat.

"Where is he?"

"Good sir kneel. Good sir before Beast Lord. Alho-o-o-o-on!" The goblin's wail blended into the keening. "Alho-o-o-o-on eat mind. Good lady not care. Good lady not care goblins, not care good sir. Good lady care only scroll. *Sacrifice!*"

Sheemzher hoisted up his spear and took a tottering step forward. Tiep lunged and grabbed him before the goblin took another. He could see Dru now, on his knees before the Beast Lord, those ghastly tentacles sliding around his face like snakes.

Mind flayers. Mind flayers didn't eat *minds*, they ate *brains*. He could hear the Beast Lord, beyond Druhallen's spell and his own immunity—it was like the otio-whatever, the dung beast that had grabbed him a few nights back with its *hunger, hunger, hunger* radiating into his mind, but the Beast Lord was vastly more powerful and vastly more hungry. The Beast Lord wanted Dru's life—his loves and fears, his knowledge and hopes. The Beast Lord would share those delicacies with his minions as he consumed them.

The last thing Dru had told Tiep was "Don't worry about me," but Tiep couldn't do it. There was a clear path out of the pool chamber. Tiep reached behind his back.

"You take this back to Weathercote . . . to your *good* lady."

Tiep couldn't keep the bitter sarcasm from his voice as he offered the shirt-wrapped bundle to Sheemzher.

The goblin folded his arms and shook his head. "Not leave. Sheemzher not leave. Galimer not friend. Good lady not friend. Good sir friend. Sheemzher not leave. Sheemzher kill god. Sacrifice. Tiep leave, yes? Tiep have other life, yes? No sacrifice."

"No, damn you—No!"

Druhallen's spell was cracking from inside. Tiep drew his sword; Sheemzher pressed his spear's tip against Tiep's bare chest.

"Wait. Alho-o-o-o-on strong mind. Alho-o-o-o-on blind just once. Touch mind once—" Sheemzher stuck his finger in one nostril, a disgusting gesture at an inappropriate time. "Alho-o-o-o-on blind. Wait. Wait, yes? Sheemzher give sign."

The flint pressure on Tiep's chest increased. Sheemzher—the runty, warty, dog-faced goblin—would kill him on the spot if he gave the wrong answer.

"I'll wait," Tiep said, and added, "You planned this. You and your damned bug lady."

"No good lady. Good lady not care." The goblin withdrew his spear, and Tiep breathed easier. "Sheemzher make plan; Sheemzher do plan. No other people care. Ghistpok not care. Maybe too late. Sheemzher care. Sheemzher plan. Sheemzher kill god. Sacrifice."

It was Tiep's turn to threaten his companion. "Not Dru. Not on your worthless life."

He was bigger than Sheemzher, considerably longer in the leg, and the goblin was injured. Tiep was going to reach the Beast Lord first and slam his sword into the middle of the Beast Lord's rib cage—assuming an alhoon had ribs and kept its vital organs within them; and also assuming that it could be killed with an ordinary Zhentilar's sword.

Tiep charged across the pool chamber, but stopped a few feet short of plunging his sword through the Beast Lord's fancy cloak. For one thing, the alhoon's presence grew stronger the closer Tiep got. For another, he could see better and understood what Sheemzher had been trying to tell him when the goblin stuck his finger in his nostril. Only three of the Beast Lord's four tentacles were writhing over Druhallen's head; the fourth was pressed rigid against his cheek. Its tip disappeared into Dru's nose and there was blood streaming over his mouth and chin.

Damn Sheemzher who couldn't string a proper sentence together! How was he supposed to know the right moment to attack? The Beast Lord hadn't noticed that there was an armed human standing an arm's length from his back. He wouldn't notice two feet of steel protruding from his chest, either, until it was too late.

Sheemzher arrived at Tiep's side. He held up one hand, palm-out, a sign all the races knew meant *stop!* The goblin's injuries were apparent in the brighter light around the pool. The right side of his face was bloodied—Tiep couldn't see Sheemzher's right eye for the blood and didn't know if it was even still there. Sheemzher had a wound on his right side too. It wasn't bleeding badly. All the damage must have been inside because the goblin was paralyzed from the wound down on that side of his body.

They were a sorry lot: a naked woman, a wizard with his brain about to be devoured, a wounded goblin, and a bumbling thief with a sword he didn't know how to use. It was a miracle they'd gotten this far, a fool's miracle.

Then the keening stopped, and all of the Beast Lord's tentacles went rigid against Dru's face. Tiep didn't need a signal from Sheemzher. He let out a yell and pointed the sword at the spot where a man's heart would be vulnerable, if an alhoon were a man.

The sword began to vibrate inches away from the cloak. Tiep hung onto the hilt with both hands, willing the tip forward, but it was no use. Plain steel couldn't penetrate the Beast Lord's defenses. It did get his attention.

The Beast Lord turned to face Tiep, unwrapping its tentacles from Druhallen's head as it moved. Dru collapsed on the stone. He might have been alive; he might have been dead. Tiep couldn't tell by looking at him. A heartbeat later, he couldn't tell anything at all. His world was white eyes with neither pupils nor irises and four blind serpents reaching for him. Dru's spell couldn't protect him from the Beast Lord's direct attention. Tiep felt his life's memories flowing away from him and a hideous cruelty that put Sememmon to shame.

The first tentacle touched Tiep's face. He screamed, and his tormentor consumed his fear. The second tentacle traced an arc over his eyes, across his cheek, and thrust violently into his nose. Tiep couldn't breathe. He gulped air through his mouth, fighting for life when his last wish was to die quick. The Beast Lord was laughing inside his skull.

There was darkness.

And there was light again.

Tiep was still alive, still standing in the Beast Lord's pool chamber. The sword had fallen from his hand and his body quaked with the aftershocks of sheer terror, but aside from the blood streaming from his ravaged nostril, he was unharmed.

The Beast Lord, who still stood so close that Tiep could see the tiniest wrinkles in its tentacles and the shiny membrane covering its eyes, had lost interest in feasting on his fears. Tiep couldn't move, except to breathe and breathing took all his concentration whether he tried breathing through his mouth or, by mistake, through his nose. Between labored breaths, Tiep looked for his foster parents and found them. Dru hadn't risen from the stone, but he was breathing. The Beast Lord blocked Tiep's view of Rozt'a, but he could see the top of her head beyond a cloaked shoulder and hoped that meant she was still alive.

Tiep couldn't see Sheemzher; the angle was wrong. He couldn't hear the goblin, either. They hadn't succeeded in killing a god. They hadn't even come close, but Tiep forgave the goblin because Sheemzher had tried.

The goblin keening hadn't resumed. The pool chamber was dead quiet, except for a few humans trying to breathe. It didn't take long for Tiep to wonder what had caused their reprieve and how long it would last. If he couldn't find the strength and skill to get his feet moving, whatever distracted the Beast Lord's attention had simply postponed the inevitable.

After an eternity of silence and breathing, Tiep heard a swordswinger howl, and then he heard that howl cut short. He strained his eyes, searching the portion of the chamber he could see. There were shadows beyond the pools, moving shadows, but he couldn't see what made them. Something was out there, though, stalking the swordswingers. Another one howled and died immediately after, and from the same place in the darkness, there was a loud, faintly liquid sound, like a fish or frog being smashed against a wall.

Tiep squinted, desperate to see what was happening. His neck moved! Not enough to improve his vision, but he'd moved! He could breathe without concentrating on every breath and he'd moved! Tymora—to whom he'd forgotten to pray—hadn't forgotten her prodigal.

There was hope!

Tiep was concentrating on flexing his toes when he saw the cause of his hope: another mind flayer . . . two of them . . . no, three . . . four. He counted six, but there were surely more gliding around the pool chamber. He couldn't turn his head, couldn't see what might be sneaking up behind him.

The invaders were different from the Beast Lord. Tiep remembered Sheemzher relaying the question the bug lady had asked him: *Is its flesh slick and shiny or dry?* The Beast Lord was definitely dry. The invaders were definitely slick and shiny. Between the Beast Lord and the invaders was a choice of nightmares with no chance to wake up.

Tiep's fingers moved. He made a fist with his left hand.

Something whizzed past his right ear. He never saw what it was, but the Beast Lord flinched. Then it moved. Like a burrowing snake, it moved out of Tiep's sight. Maybe he'd seen creatures move faster, but he'd expected that the alhoon would move slowly and wasn't prepared for its speed, or for the speed of the invaders when they dodged streaking fire that looked and smelled for all the world like the spells that Druhallen cast.

Tiep couldn't be sure how successful the Beast Lord was against its attackers, but hit or miss, fire was falling on the prostrate goblins. He saw it fall on fat Ghistpok. The goblin couldn't move to swat the flames that swiftly lit him up like a candle. It was horrible death to watch, and Tiep felt no pity at all.

He'd made and opened a right-hand fist. He could yawn and wriggle his toes.

The invading mind flayers fought with invisible spells unlike any that Druhallen cast. One of them struck the Beast Lord. Tiep could see only the effect. For a moment the Beast Lord was hidden in an inky black cloud and the air through the pool chamber crackled like pine boughs in a hot fire. Then the cloud was gone and one of the invaders became a living torch.

Tiep bent his right knee and straightened it again before he lost his balance. If he lived another minute, he'd be running for shelter. Better than that—far better than that—Druhallen had pulled himself into a crouch and was getting his legs under him. Rozt'a hadn't moved yet, but she would, once Dru got to her.

He did, but not before fire came dangerously close to all three of them and one of the invading flayers ran between Druhallen and Rozt'a on its way to attacking the Beast Lord with its longer tentacles. When the flurry ended, one of the invader's tentacles flopped and flapped on the stone, the Beast Lord was oozing from a mangled shoulder, and Druhallen had his arms around Rozt'a.

She was still groggy when Dru got to Tiep. They were all too exhausted for joy or relief or anything more than Dru's hoarse, raspy question:

"Got it?"

To which Tiep replied with a nod. Through it all he'd been aware of the shirt-wrapped bundle against his back.

Druhallen pushed them all toward the wall and safety. Tiep pushed back.

"Sheemzher."

They looked, even Rozt'a, and saw the goblin in a heap some ten feet away, his spear at his side. Dru pushed again. Tiep shoved free. Sheemzher had been hurt before and wasn't moving at all, but they weren't leaving him or his damn spear behind. He hoisted the goblin onto his shoulder and used the spear for balance.

Dru offered to carry Sheemzher when they were all together again. Tiep just shook his head and Dru guided them all toward the wall. Druhallen's expression was more unreadable than usual on account of his bloody face; Tiep supposed he looked the same. He couldn't look at Rozt'a, not without her clothes.

The Beast Lord took out another of the living mind flayers, but there were still several left, weaving through the chamber, lobbing their invisible magic and cutting down any swordswinger alert enough to attack them. They'd never know if this was a battle in the war the Beast Lord was fighting with its Underdark neighbors, but if it was, then it was likely to be an important battle—the *last* battle if the Beast Lord lost.

Tiep could pass that along to Horace when they got to Yarthrain.

An explosion shook the pool chamber just before they reached the tunnel that lead to safety. The irresistible pull of curiosity stopped them all and turned them around. The Beast Lord was gone—vanished, maybe dead—and the living mind flayers turned their white-eyed attention to the three of them. For a moment, Tiep was back in the grip of the Beast Lord's tentacles with cold, alien thoughts nibbling at his memories. He learned a word, *cephalophagy*: the consumption of a living brain, thought by thought, emotion by emotion. The word would always be with him, on the edge of nightmare.

Then he was free. They were all free. Another mind flayer had fallen. The Beast Lord was gone from the chamber, but not from the battle. The living mind flayers had their choice to make and they made it, turning their backs on the humans.

"Let's get going," Dru said. "Whoever wins this duel is going to be hungry when it's over."

14

8 Eleint, the Year of the Banner (1368 DR)

Dekanter

One foot in front of the other . . .

Druhallen of Sunderath told himself that as he pushed his companions through the empty tunnels of Dekanter. They had the scroll, they had one another—even their goblin whose heartbeat was weak but steady whenever he checked it.

As for the other goblins, Ghistpok's goblins—Ghistpok was dead, seared in his own fat, and his starving tribe was doomed. Its doom, though, had been sealed long before this chilly night, long before the obese Ghistpok took command. Perhaps the tribe had been doomed from the moment the alhoon claimed the mines for its own. Certainly they'd been doomed once it found a golden scroll from Netheril.

The eastern Greypeaks were brightening when the survivors stumbled through the great dwarf-carved gate. Sunrise and dimmed stars had never looked so beautiful. The driving need to be *gone* from this place relaxed for a moment. Dru raised his eyes, as if heavenly light could heal his face or his memories of this night.

Only time and distance, mostly distance, could dull the

remembered agony, the sense of violation and helpless rage he'd felt when the Beast Lord had overwhelmed his spirit. This night, Druhallen of Sunderath had experienced cruelty, hunger, and degradation on a scale he'd not imagined possible; he was not grateful for the lesson, which was worse in reflection than it had been in reality. Were it not for Rozt'a, Tiep, and the goblin he carried on his back, Dru would not have returned to the light.

"The horses, Dru," Rozt'a whispered. "Get the horses."

She'd reclaimed her sword belt on the way out. Shortly after that, she'd rediscovered her voice. Dru didn't know what she had endured in the last hour and would never ask. She was shivering now, from cold and memory. He would have held her close, if his arms hadn't been locked behind his back supporting the goblin.

Tiep walked a bit apart from them and added distance as the sky grew brighter than the light spell—a feeble effort, ruddy with desperation—that had guided them away from the pool chamber. Dru owed his life to Tiep. If the youth hadn't risked everything in his brave, senseless attempt to slay the Beast Lord, Dru would be a fading part of the alhoon's memory. Tiep's reward had been the Beast Lord's embrace.

Druhallen didn't know what to say to his bloodied foster-son; he didn't know what to say to himself.

They reached the carved steps to the High Trail, which, like many stairways, were higher and steeper going up than coming down. Dru's legs were jellied halfway through the third tier. He called a halt when they reached the top.

Dekanter's clouds were reassembling in the north and west. There'd be rain in the quarry by mid-morning, but for now it was sun-streaked and quiet. Nothing moved on the mounds or showed its face at the gaping mine entrance. He didn't particularly want to see the remnants of Ghistpok's tribe and suffered a visceral fear when he imagined the Beast Lord or its living kin, but the silence spoke of tragedy, at least for the goblins who were guilty of no crime other than being born in Dekanter.

Their horses were restless with hunger. Tiep went to work spreading the last of the grass they'd brought up from the bogs while Rozt'a ransacked her gear for clothing and Dru settled Sheemzher on the rock. The goblin's left eye fluttered open.

"Sky," he murmured.

"We made it out of there," Dru assured him. "All of us."

"People, too?"

Dru dodged the question. "Save your strength, little fellow. We'll take care of you."

Sheemzher closed his eye and appeared to sleep. Rozt'a came over. She'd dressed herself in layers of everything. Her movements were calm and confident as she washed the goblin's wounds with water from the run-off.

"He's lost the eye," she said, bandaging it. "And a lot of blood. A hole like that—" She indicated the thrust wound in Sheemzher's right flank. "—Is beyond my skill."

"Wyndyfarh will heal him."

It was the least Lady Mantis could do.

The very least she would do after they delivered the golden scroll and reclaimed Galimer Longfingers from her behind-the-waterfall glade.

"How will we get there? Which way should we go? Back through the rocks and bogs? Or the other way?"

The other way was back to the High Trail, down the steps, and across the quarry to the eastward gorge. Did they want to take their chances with the Zhentarim on the Dawn Pass Trail? Or with the gods-knew-what on the bogs?

"We'll go faster astride on the trail."

Rozt'a looked east. "If we get that far."

There were new words for fear written on her face. Druhallen imagined similar words were written on his own beneath the blood and swelling.

"We'll get through while the sun's shining. They're

283

creatures of the Underdark. They won't come into the light."

Clouds were thickening in the north and west.

"We'd best hurry," Rozt'a concluded.

"I'll get the gear loaded while you patch him up as best you can."

"What about you?"

He wasn't ready to think about his own wounds. "Later. Talk to Tiep. Help him if you can. He's young enough to care what the ladies think about his nose. Me? As long as my mother can recognize me when I'm hung—"

"Druhallen, it's been twenty-five years since you've seen your mother. She wouldn't know you if she fell over your corpse!"

Rozt'a sounded like her old self when she mocked him. He tried to return the favor with a laugh, but turned away, wincing as the effort opened the lacerations.

Sheemzher was unconscious and rust-colored when Rozt'a finished binding his wounds. The horses were saddled and packed, but there'd be no riding until they got down the quarry steps. They rigged a blanket-sling over Dru's shoulder to leave his arms free for leading a horse while he carried the goblin.

The quarry remained deserted with a wall of clouds a few shades lighter than the mountains themselves squeezing down. Rain fell before they reached the bottom, a hard rain with heavy wind behind it and lightning, too. They mounted and headed east, glancing north and west over their shoulders until they were out of the quarry. By midafternoon they'd ridden from rain into warm sunshine.

It was like waking up from a nightmare.

Sunset found them on the abandoned portion of the Dawn Pass Trail. Sheemzher had stirred twice during the day. They'd given him water both times and told one another that he was holding his own against his injuries, which was a lie. Tiep's ravaged face was swollen and purple. He'd shut both eyes and ridden blind. Dru was tempted to do the same before Rozt'a called a halt.

"We've gone far enough," she said.

Druhallen's lips were too big and sore to argue. He handed Sheemzher down—let him drop into Rozt'a's arms, if the truth were told—and flopped out of the saddle like a top-heavy sack of grain. A season's worth of grass grew trail-side. Dru hobbled the horses in it and made rough sheaves to form a pallet for Sheemzher before hauling their empty waterskins to a brook on the low-ground side of the trail.

Glancing west, Dru saw clouds towering over the Grey-peaks. It was raining in Dekanter as it did almost every day, but their campsite was dry and the brook was season-ably low. He had to climb down the bank and rearrange some rocks before he could fill the skins. The first skin was bloated, tied, and sitting atop the bank and he was working on the second when Rozt'a shrieked.

Drawing on a reserve of strength he hadn't suspected, Dru leapt the bank and raced across the trail, looking for trouble as he ran. The trail was clear of monsters and Zhentarim, but Tiep was in the midst of a seizure. The youth was sprawled on the ground, his heels pounding the ground and his arms flailing through the air. Druhallen dropped to his knees to help Rozt'a restrain him and took a fist on the nose. The pain was exquisite and for several moments he could do nothing at all. When his muscles unlocked, Tiep was lying quiet.

"Are you all right?" Rozt'a asked.

He didn't bother answering as blood leaked from his nose and tears burned his cheek.

Rozt'a brushed her hands vigorously as she stood. "That's it. I'm steeping Wyndor's herbs for both of you."

Dru winced. Wyndor's herbs were a last resort, a very bitter last resort that tortured a man as they healed him. "If you do that, we'll be stuck here until tomorrow night plus the day after if we wait for the sun to ride."

"If I don't, you might be dead," Rozt'a countered as she flipped open their medicine chest, "or too sick to drink it."

That was another problem with Wyndor's—if the patient were too far gone, the herbs would kill before they healed.

"We've got to keep moving, Roz. As little as I wanted to bump into Amarandaris before, I want to see him even less now when we're traveling with that golden scroll. It's a miracle he hasn't caught up with us before this. We used up our miracles last night."

"That's why I'm steeping the Wyndor's. Don't argue with me, Druhallen. You're in no condition to win. Did you leave the skins by the stream?"

He stood up. She was right about his condition but he hadn't reached the point where he couldn't haul two waterskins back to their camp.

Tiep, whose eyes had opened during his exchange with Rozt'a, wobbled up and followed him.

"You don't have to worry about Amarandaris," the youth said from the top of the stream bank.

Dru braced the skin in the cool water and, while the water flowed into it, bathed his throbbing face. "You know something about him that I don't?"

The youth didn't answer right away. Dru worried he might be having another fit, but what he saw when he looked up was worse: guilt, deep and old.

"He pretty much told me I was on my own. He figured you'd find a way out of Parnast before he was ready to leave. Told me what to look out for, with you and the goblins and all, and told me to leave a written message in Yarthrain. He wouldn't have given me the name of someone in Yarthrain if he thought he'd catch up with you—*us*—before we got there."

Druhallen let the waterskin slip through his ankles. "You think that, do you?"

Tiep nodded.

"How long you been working for them?"

"Two, maybe three, years."

Anger quickened Dru's pulse; his lacerated face burned. "Come on, Tiep. I'm not a fool. What is it? Two years or three?"

"I tried to tell you! I've tried every time they ask me a favor. I knew how you'd react so I didn't dare—until now. It's safe to camp a day or two. Safer than on the main trail. No one's coming here."

"Amarandaris isn't—if I believe you. That doesn't say no one's coming."

The youth bolted for the camp. Dru let him go. He tied off the waterskin and hoisted one to his left shoulder, opposite the pain, the other under his right arm. Rozt'a had a fire going and was waiting with a pot for the water to steep Wyndor's herbs. He had half a mind to tell her to prepare half the amount she'd measured out, but that would mean that he'd be telling her what Tiep had been up to, and he wasn't feeling that generous.

"*You* tell her what you've told me," he whispered to Tiep as he walked past the sullen, shaking youth, "and be quick about it, or you'll wish you'd never been born."

"I've wished *that* for years."

He didn't say anything while Rozt'a steeped the bitter herbs or when she handed them each a steaming mug. Tiep emptied the mug in three gulps; Dru had never seen anyone gulp Wyndor's. The stuff was as potent as any brew this side of magic. His was cool by the time he finished it, and by then the herbs were starting to take effect. He said he'd take the first watch—he thought he could fight the seediness until midnight, hoped he could memorize a spell or two before the shakes and nausea overwhelmed him.

Rozt'a put her hand on his shoulder and guided him to his knees. "Sleep it off. You can stay up all night tomorrow."

Dru's thoughts were an unholy amalgam of Amarandaris, Tiep, and the Beast Lord as he slipped into delirium. He lived the rest of the night and all of the next day in a twilight

of dreams and memories. In his few moments of lucidity he
craved water, which Rozt'a gave him, and raved about the
pain from a spike driven upward through his skull.

He was clear-minded, though empty-minded, when he
sat up at sunset. The taste of death and rot thickened his
tongue. He'd hawked and spat before he'd considered the
wisdom of the act. Pain set him on his back again, but it was
nothing like the pain before Wyndor's. He touched his face
and the crusted cuts around his nose. The herbs had done
their work—his body had done a week's worth of healing in
a day. He had the appetite to prove it.

Rozt'a's cook pot called him as flowers called bees. She
ladled something pale and lumpy into a bowl. He was ready
for more before he asked what he was eating.

"Frog soup."

Dru looked at the lump in his spoon and swallowed it
down without hesitation. He'd collected his thoughts by the
time he'd sated his hunger. The edge was off his memories
of Dekanter, as well, but not his last conversation with Tiep.
He asked about Sheemzher first, because he'd spotted the
goblin lying under a tent rigged from their blankets.

"Same as before. I'd've given him Wyndor's, if I didn't
think it would kill him. The wound hasn't festered; that's a
good sign. They're tougher than us, I guess, when it comes
to disease."

"They'd have to be," Dru replied, and asked the harder
question, "What about Tiep? Is he awake? Talking?"

Rozt'a shook her head. "I gave him a smaller dose—what
I'd give myself. He should have come through before you.
It's as if he's fighting something. Reliving it. I've lost track
of the number of times he's called your name."

"No sign of trouble, though? No visitors?"

She stirred the soup for her answer and dribbled a cascade of meat back into the pot.

"Get some sleep," Dru suggested. "You're tired. I'll take
the watches tonight."

"I dozed. I'll be fine—read your scroll, if you can, Druhallen. I know better than to come between a magician and his magic. This way you won't have to divide your attention."

He mumbled his thanks and retrieved the cloth-wrapped bundle from his gear. Midnight had passed hours ago. Dru could glance at the words of his light spell, cast it a moment later, and know he'd get another chance when midnight returned. He was impressed by the precautions Tiep had taken to protect the scroll with his shirt—

The better to impress Amarandaris and the unknown Zhentarim contact in Yarthrain?

Druhallen sighed. Though his anger was real and justified, he knew Tiep's slide into the Network fell short of conscious betrayal. Somewhere in one of the cities they visited or in Scornubel—which was more likely—the youth's luck had run out. He'd crossed a line that couldn't be crossed. Since the beginning in Berdusk, he, Rozt'a, and Galimer told their youngster to come to them when he got in trouble and tell them about his mistakes before they became flash point crises.

It was a rare boy who took that advice to heart. Dru thought of himself. He'd never willingly admitted an error to his father—why volunteer for a thrashing? And after he'd left Sunderath, when his situation with Ansoain hadn't been so very different from Tiep's, he'd have died before risking the future with an untimely confession to his foster parent. Of course, he'd also bent over backward to stay out of trouble.

He was a carpenter's son. Both his grandfathers had been carpenters, too. He was an odd seed in Sunderath, but he knew his roots. The gods knew what Tiep had for ancestors, and they weren't telling.

With a sigh, Druhallen unrolled the layers of shirt and scroll. The first, most obvious, thing he noticed was that scroll wasn't parchment backed with gold-leaf, as he'd expected, but gold throughout and polished to a sheen that sparkled in his light spell and hurt his eyes. He noticed the script next. Dense columns of Netherese script that floated on the gold. Dru could read the letters, but not casually, not without concentration, and there was no guarantee he'd make sense of the words. His dark glass disk slipped out next, warmer than it had ever been before.

Odd that it was the object which had brought him to this forsaken corner of Faerûn only to become uninteresting once he'd arrived. Dru was almost certain now that the disk had nothing to do with Thayan circle-magic but, instead, had something to do with hiding objects—people—in plain sight. He guessed now that the Red Wizards had held onto it tightly until they were ready to begin their ambush, then they'd thrown it down. Why they hadn't retrieved it was, and might remain, a mystery, but a minor one compared with the meaning behind the words in front of him.

He picked the disk out of the grass and returned it to its silken sack and snug compartment within the folding box. There might be a use for it, yet. Amarandaris had told him to name his price. If the offer held, he could think of something the Zhentarim could return to him.

When the box was folded shut, Dru once again looked at the scroll. Twilight was passing quickly on this crisp, cloudless night and he'd had to dim his light spell. Dru wasn't sure he could trust his eyes, but yes—by means and magic he could not explain, the floating words on the scroll had become rusty marks across the back of Tiep's homespun linen shirt.

Too bad the boy didn't dress in silk as Galimer did. A more finely woven fabric would have recorded the ancient words more clearly, but they could still be read, albeit as reversed mirror-writing. *Arc—Arcan—Arcanium—?* The shirt's script was imprecise. Far easier to look at the floating script. The gold made its own light. Druhallen squelched his spell entirely and found the Netherese letters instantly clearer.

Arcanum Fundare Tiersus: Of fundamental or basic magic or mystery, the third lesson or chapter.

Druhallen translated the first line of the first column: *Things are not as they seem. Seeming is illusion. Illusion is change. Things change.*

He was disappointed: the wisdom of millennia reduced to a schoolboy's truism. Then it came to him that all magic was illusion and, more than that, a reagent was the illusion of magic: a thing that was not what it seemed to be. A spell was the destruction of illusion. A spell was the ultimate revelation of truth.

A spell was naked truth!

Dru sat up straight, stunned by the insight sweeping through his mind, changing the way he thought about magic. The sky was black, the stars were brilliant jewels; midnight had come and gone since he'd translated the first line. There were a thousand lines or more floating on the gold. He did the math then started on the second line. The words were there, but the magic—the truth within illusion—was not.

Some things did not change. Reading the Nether scroll was like studying spells. He could read or study at any time, but true learning happened only once each day. Disappointment singed Dru's spirit. In a few days time he would—he definitely *would*—trade the scroll for Galimer. Before then, he'd read another line, perhaps two more, not more than four. A far cry from a thousand.

Dru picked up the shirt and held it close. *Things are not as they seem* . . . The words, not the magic. Would the magic be there tomorrow? He folded Tiep's shirt carefully, separately from the scroll which rolled up tighter than his little finger. Then, because for a wizard thwarted curiosity hurt worse than any wound, Dru opened his folding box to the compartment where he kept powdered sulfur.

Light was a fast kindling spell that consumed its red or yellow reagent when he committed it to memory. Usually he balanced a bit of powder on a fingernail that had been black since he left Sunderath. Tonight he left the powder in the compartment and, rather than read the writ from the wooden panel, Dru closed his eyes and remembered it while holding a harmonic thought—the reagent is the illusion, the truth is *light*.

The power was in his mind. After decades of practice, Druhallen knew when he'd learned a spell after midnight. He remembered his simplest flame spell which had always required an ember before it would kindle. Like pure light, flames appeared in Dru's mind. It felt different, as if the ember were there also. He had to know . . .

A flaming streak shot from Druhallen's hand. It brought Rozt'a at a run.

Dru was exhilarated. He'd cast a spell by will alone, without literal study, reagents, or a kindling gesture. Reading—learning—a single line from the Nether scroll had ushered him across the threshold that separated good wizards from great ones.

Rozt'a was in a panic, fearing that the mind flayers, dead and alive, had returned to finish their feast. She had harsh words for a wizard who'd terrified her out of curiosity. Dru endured the tongue lashing, which did not dent his enthusiasm.

"One look at the Nether scroll and I've learned what a spell *is*. I've been collecting spells as if every one were different. That's illusion; Rozt'a, spells are all the same. They're all a path through illusion to truth. One look, and I've seen the fundamental truth of magic."

She narrowed her eyes. "All spells are the same? *That's* the fundamental truth of magic?"

"You'd have to see it from your mind. And if you could read the Netherese script, you would. This scroll—" He held it up "—could turn even you into a wizard."

The prospect did not delight her. She snatched the scroll from his hand. "One look you say, and you're casting spells

from your mind. If you're not stark, raving mad then forget
your glass disk. This is the thing that could unhinge
Faerûn. You say there are a hundred of them?" Rozt'a
swore by Helm and Ilmater, her god of last resort.

She had a point. "Even though there were only fifty,
legend says Netheril was founded on two identical sets of
golden scrolls. Both were lost before the Empire fell."

"And good riddance. Magic shouldn't be easy."

Another point. Dru purged his wild enthusiasm with a
sigh. "We're exchanging it for Galimer."

"Solving our problem and giving the world a bigger one."

"I doubt it. I don't think there's anything in that scroll
that the bug lady doesn't already know."

Rozt'a glowered at the scroll before handing it back. "I'm
glad for you, Druhallen, if you've seen the truth of magic,
and I pray to all the gods that you're right, because we *are*
exchanging it for Galimer."

"No question," Dru agreed. His excitement rekindled the
instant his fingers touched the warm, shining gold. He was
a boy again, freshly apprenticed to Ansoain and she couldn't
teach him fast enough. "Sit with me a moment. I want to try
something."

"Druhallen . . ." her voice was ominous, distrusting.

"I'm not going to open the scroll. I'm not going to touch
it. Here, you can hold it."

She took it reluctantly. "Druhallen, what's going on in
your mind?"

"I came—*We* came all this way to cast a single spell, and
I didn't cast it. I never found the time, never found the
place, and when it came time to leave, it never even crossed
my mind. I still have all the reagents—the dragon's blood,
the mummy's bone, the perfect pearl. They're going to
waste—"

Rozt'a opened her mouth, then shut it.

"Rozt'a, I want to cast the Candlekeep spell on the scroll.
I'm *going* to cast it, but it's the kind of spell that's safer with

an anchor, someone to keep an eye on things and stop the magic if it goes awry."

"How will I do that?"

"Just take the scroll away. You'll be holding it. It won't be difficult."

She was skeptical, but eventually agreed. Dru committed the spell to memory, then made the preparations.

"You're sure I can just walk away?"

"It's a passive spell, Rozt'a. Nothing happens *here*."

Dru sat outside the circle with a clear view of the scroll and spoke the words that Candlekeep's blind scryer had taught him, meaningless words that belonged to no language he could name. Nothing happened at first, and he suspected the ultimate irony: After all this, he'd gotten some minor aspect wrong and the spell would not kindle. Then Druhallen's thoughts let go of time.

Slowly at first, but soon with dizzying speed, Dru's awareness moved against time's flow to the beginning—the very beginning—of light, heat, and majesty. The time stream caught him and carried him on a lightning bolt through the scroll's history. Druhallen had visions of huge sparks and larger explosions, none of which had meaning to him, except that the scroll was *old*. Its history was older than humanity, older than Faerûn and when the lightning bolt carried him through those moments, it was moving too fast for him to collect any impressions of Netheril, Dekanter, or his own past. It was traveling too fast to stop and carried him into the future, where no mortal mind should travel but where the scroll had place and presence.

He'd perceived a return to pure light, pure heat, and majesty when it ended and he was sitting in the grass beside an abandoned trail, staring at an empty circle in the dirt.

"You were getting weird," Rozt'a said from behind his back. "Your eyes were starting to glow. I figured it was time to stop. Are you yourself?"

Dru turned around. "Of course I—"

Rozt'a had her sword drawn, ready to lop off his head. "You're absolutely sure?"

"It was a *scrying* spell, Roz. Like reading a book or looking at a picture—except I couldn't understand the words and the pictures didn't make much sense either."

She lowered the sword and laughed at him.

* * * * *

Each of the next two sunrises Druhallen unrolled the Nether scroll and read another line. His second and third readings were not as insightful as the first had been, but they expanded his horizons and gave him peace—the only peace he got those days. Tiep had awakened shortly after Dru had cast his Candlekeep spell. The youth had sucked in his gut and told Rozt'a the truth before breakfast.

She'd swallowed her rage—a terrible thing to watch— and shut him out of her life. Rozt'a didn't rant or vent her frustrations on helpless trees and bushes, she simply treated Tiep as if he weren't there. If he spoke, she didn't hear. If he got in front of her, she turned the other way. Dru had tried talking to her.

We said we'd always understand, that we'd always be there to help him. He didn't believe us. He was right.

Damn straight he was right. He's gone over, Dru. First Weathercote, now this. Or have I got it backward? First the Zhentarim, then Weathercote. He's out of my life.

Not until the four of us are together. We can't decide without Galimer.

Tiep or me, Druhallen. If he goes into Weathercote Wood, I don't.

Dru had tried to reason with her; at least he'd thought he was using reason. The Nether scroll hadn't given him any new insights into women, especially Rozt'a. When he'd refused to judge Tiep immediately and send him on his way to Yarthrain at the junction of the old and new branches of the Dawn Pass Trail, she'd turned her back on them both. Add one delirious goblin and he had all the reagents necessary to conjure disaster, which was exactly what he foresaw once the green trees of Weathercote Wood lined their horizon.

Rozt'a was adamant, Tiep was forlorn, and Sheemzher was useless as their guide through the treacherous forest. Dru solved one problem when he removed the amber pendant from the goblin's neck. The red jewel sparkled when he warmed it between his palms.

"We're here," he whispered. "Sheemzher's hurt. If you want him and your scroll, you're going to have to show us the way."

The amber went cold but, in the distance, red light winked in the trees.

"We're on our way," he said, kneeing Fowler off the trail and hoping Rozt'a and Tiep would follow quietly.

Dru had no luck in getting his companions behind him and bad luck when Fowler balked before they'd gone a hundred yards. With the fevered, twitching goblin still draped over his shoulders, Druhallen dismounted and walked back to Rozt'a.

"Get down," he told her. "We have to talk."

Rozt'a dismounted cavalry-style, swinging her leg over Ebony's neck and sliding to the ground without ever breaking Dru's stare. She began the discussion with, "I don't trust him."

"All the more reason, then, to keep him with us ... until we can talk it through and put it behind us."

"There's nothing to talk about. He's gone over."

"Tiep's no more Zhentarim than you or I—but he will be, if we don't pull him out of this now."

Rozt'a gave Dru a mighty scowl. "Is this more of your 'truth through illusion' nonsense? Helm's eyes, Dru—you were the one who started worrying three winters ago, right when Tiep made his 'little' mistake. You were right; I was blind. Cut is cut, right? I want him gone from my life . . . now . . . before Galimer comes back."

"Because Galimer will agree with me? You're angry with yourself because you didn't see that he was in trouble. That's the reason you want him gone."

If Rozt'a had had her sword drawn then, Dru would have been skewered on the spot, but he knew a little about timing even if he didn't know why it worked.

After a painful silence Rozt'a said, "He's doing personal favors for Darkhold. The Dark Lord owns his soul."

Dru shook his head. "No more than he owned Ansoain." He hoped that was a true statement.

Rozt'a blinked and swore and listened to Dru describe the piece of parchment he'd seen in Amarandaris's quarters. "You might have told us."

"I didn't want to upset Galimer. Tiep didn't want to upset us. We're all human."

"It's different. Very different, and Tiep's in too deep. There's no pulling him out."

"There might be. The Network—Sememmon in particular—is toying with Tiep. They don't want or need him, it's the thrill—the possibility—of corruption that keeps their interest. I think I can offer them a better thrill."

"Dru . . ."

"I have an idea. It might work. I'll talk it over with you, and him, and Galimer *after* we're done with Weathercote Wood. Can you wait that long? We can still get out of this better than we were when we came in. It's that, or we leave Tiep here with the horses, and I don't like that for more reasons than I can count."

He didn't like leaving the horses behind, period, but there was no riding or leading them closer to the Wood. Men owed something better to the beasts that served them than a grassy trail-side in the middle of nowhere, even if the animals seemed perfectly content. Setting the horses free had one unanticipated benefit. Without Tiep's shoulders, they'd have had to leave even more of their gear behind. Rozt'a made swift, practical peace with the idea of walking behind him to Wyndyfarh's glade.

Wyndyfarh's amber lights shone clearly throughout the afternoon. Rozt'a kept watch for big trouble in the form of reavers and anything else the Wood might throw their way. Dru watched for the smaller problems. He saw them—pairs of bright colored insects—in every tree, but they kept their distance. At sunset, Dru kindled his light spell and they pressed on until a snare-string crescent moon hung above the trees. The distance between the amber markers shortened until the path was a continuous line of red and the ground beneath their feet was a carpet of silver-glowing moss.

They came to the bottom of a familiar hill.

"Do you want to do the talking, or shall I?" Dru asked, fully aware that Rozt'a usually declined a leader's role if it was offered.

"You do it," she conceded quickly. "This is magic. Just get Galimer, fair and square."

Tiep didn't offer a comment. He'd said very little since confessing his secrets to Rozt'a and nothing at all since they'd entered the forest. He kept his hands folded in front of him and followed Dru's footsteps as precisely as the differences in their stride allowed.

Dru wasn't surprised to see a tall, white-clad woman waiting for them beside the small marble temple. He was disappointed that Galimer wasn't standing beside her. He was in no mood for court-talk or pleasantries when he led his companions across the stream. And neither was Lady Wyndyfarh.

"You said you had the scroll. Where?"

"Where's my friend? Where's Galimer?"

"On the other side. Follow me."

Dru planted his feet. "I don't know where the other side

is, but I know it's not here, not Weathercote, not Faerûn." He took a breath and shouted, "Galimer! Gal, do you hear me?" then he turned back to Wyndyfarh. "If he can't walk out here or if he's not the man he was, then we're leaving . . . with the scroll."

They nailed each other, eye to eye, he and Wyndyfarh, and Druhallen held his own better than he would have a week ago.

"You've read the scroll?" Wyndyfarh surmised.

Druhallen nodded, though it wasn't the Nether scroll that gave him the strength to withstand Wyndyfarh's scorn. That came from Dekanter. Wyndyfarh was arrogant but she wasn't evil. He'd seen evil . . . inside his own mind. He didn't trust her, though. He'd trust Amarandaris or Sememmon himself before he'd truly trust the hawk-eyed Lady Mantis.

"That is not wise," she said, all silk and warning.

"Not wise is not getting my friend out here to join us. Every breath and heartbeat that he's not standing here where we can see him is the height of foolishness."

Wyndyfarh's appearance turned hawkish and, behind Druhallen, Tiep sucked an involuntary breath. Dru wondered what Rozt'a was seeing and chided himself for forgetting to strengthen their minds before they entered the glade. When silence became tension he thought he'd pushed too far, then Galimer walked out from behind the waterfall. He had a haunted, wary aura about him that lessened, but did not disappear entirely after an embrace from his wife.

"Dru . . . Tiep . . . You're here. You're all here," he said when he and Rozt'a had returned to conversation distance. "I didn't dare hope. The lady told me what you were after and who had it . . . I didn't dare hope."

Druhallen let those words seep through his consciousness. He had believed Wyndyfarh knew what she was sending them into. He'd also believed that she expected them to get the scroll and had held Galimer, rather than Tiep, hostage because she believed they'd be more inclined to retrieve him.

He'd been correct in general, wrong in specifics. Wyndyfarh knew, all right, but hadn't had much faith in their chances against the Beast Lord. He could understand her callousness toward strangers but was unexpectedly outraged that she'd sent Sheemzher on a doomed-fool's errand.

Dru shrugged out of the sling he'd worn since Dekanter and gathered Sheemzher in both arms. The goblin stirred, as he was wont to do when his position shifted. He mumbled in the goblin language and tugged at the bandage Rozt'a had fashioned over his ruined eye.

"We are *all* here," Dru said, emphasizing the *all* and watching for Wyndyfarh's reaction. She had a hawk's hard, fixed eyes, but the softer parts of her face seemed to register some surprise, some empathy. "Sheemzher was hurt getting the scroll. Then the Beast Lord damn near finished him. We've kept him alive, but our medicines haven't been able to heal him."

Wyndyfarh wove her black, talon-like fingernails above the goblin. "He wanted so much to be the hero for his people. He wanted to change them. I told him his people were goblins, and they would not listen. He was a goblin and would not listen, so I encouraged his dreams. It was the best way."

She took Sheemzher from Dru's arms. There was nothing weak or fragile about the slender Lady Mantis. Sheemzher did not weigh much, especially after several days of delirium and fever, but Wyndyfarh held him with no more effort than she might have given a bouquet.

" 'Encouraged his dreams'," Druhallen mocked Wyndyfarh's cold tone. "Maybe it was the best way for you, but it wasn't for him. What if we'd failed?"

"But you didn't, did you?" Supporting Sheemzher easily with one arm, Wyndyfarh extended her other arm. "You have the Nether scroll?"

Dru had lost his sword below Dekanter, but he'd kept the scabbard and used it to carry the scroll. He shook it into

Wyndyfarh's hand. She closed her many-jointed fingers around it and it vanished.

"What have you done with it now?" Dru asked before he could stop himself.

"Put it in a safer place," she snapped; then that faintly softer look returned to her face. "I believe I will plant it in a tree, right here in my glade. Mystra approves of trees and the Nether scrolls, and keeping them in safe places. If she disagrees, I will find another place . . . or she will. I am oath-bound to her—does that reassure you, Druhallen of Sunderath?"

It should, and perhaps it did. Mystra wouldn't let the scroll fall into evil hands—into any hands—and that was good for Faerûn. It was stubborn pride that kept him from admitting anything aloud.

"Are we done here? Can we leave now? With Galimer?"

"By all means. Or stay. You have questions; I see them in your eyes. Dine with me and I will answer them . . . some of them."

Dru shook his head. "We left our horses outside the forest. We can get back to them by dawn, if we hurry."

"Your horses are safe and you are tired. Eat. Rest. Ask your questions. There'll be no other opportunity. Once you leave, you will not return to Weathercote Wood."

He hadn't intended to come back, but the sound of prophecy sent a chill down Dru's back. Before he recovered, Rozt'a broke her self-imposed silence.

"I want answers, Dru. I want to know more about the mind flayers. And will you make Sheemzher whole again?"

She was talking to Wyndyfarh and Wyndyfarh answered her directly.

"It isn't Sheemzher's body that needs to be made whole. You have begun that well enough. All his body needs is time. He saw his people for what they were. That broke his heart."

"Will you heal his heart, then?" Rozt'a demanded.

301

Wyndyfarh shrugged. "I will speed his body's healing. His heart is his. Perhaps he will return to Dekanter, a glorious hero searching for his followers."

"There's nothing left at Dekanter," Dru announced. "Ghistpok led the tribe into the Beast Lord's lair and lost it there."

"Goblins will return to Dekanter." Wyndyfarh laughed privately. "It and the Greypeaks are well suited to their needs, their way of life. The Beast Lord will call them. It will begin again . . . without the scroll."

Druhallen shrugged and laughed. He knew something Lady Mantis didn't. "If the Beast Lord's still there. It was hard-pressed when we left. Of the living mind flayers I counted, four were dead, but there were more still hunting it."

Some part of what he'd said seized Wyndyfarh's attention. "I will prepare a table for you and places where you may rest. You will tell me about these living mind flayers." With the scroll and Sheemzher in her arms, she started for the waterfall.

Rozt'a moved to follow her, but Dru stayed where he was and worried that Lady Mantis was up to her old tricks of saying different things to different people. He'd been paying careful attention and hadn't caught her speaking directly into his mind, but that only meant he hadn't caught her, not that she hadn't done it.

"It's all right, Dru," Galimer tried to reassure him. "She's hard through and through, but fair, not evil. You heard her—she's oath-bound to Mystra. Keeping watch on Toril's mind flayers is her whole life. If there's a chance they've replaced the Beast Lord in Dekanter, she'll want to know everything you and Rozt'a and Tiep can tell her."

Keeping watch on *Toril's* mind flayers? That was as good as an admission that Wyndyfarh had come from somewhere else, and not the far side of an ocean. Curiosity, the wizard's curse, took command of Druhallen's interest. He picked up the sling in which he'd carried Sheemzher—it was too good a blanket to waste—and followed Galimer and Rozt'a toward the waterfall. Tiep hung back to walk beside him.

"Did you see her? Did you see her change?" the youth asked excitedly. "She's not human, not even close. You can't be serious about following her, Dru."

"She's oath-bound to Mystra; she has to keep her word to another wizard. You can stay here, if you want, but she's right about one thing: I've got questions."

Dru broke into a run and caught up with Galimer before his gold-haired friend walked beneath the waterfall. They shared a back-pounding embrace—and Druhallen took his friend's measure with his ring. Galimer felt the discharge and gave him a sour look.

"I haven't been through what you've been through, but it hasn't been exactly pleasant and I haven't changed. That's more than I can say about you."

Dru folded his arms. "If we hadn't made it back, what do you want to bet you'd have become her new Sheemzher, looking for good people to lead to Dekanter?"

"She'll keep her word, Dru," Galimer replied, which wasn't an answer. Then he sighed and returned Dru's embrace. "Gods—it's good to see you. You, Rozt'a, Tiep—?" He stopped and reached back for his foster son.

Left with a choice between staying alone on one side of the waterfall or being with the people he knew best on the other, Tiep chose to follow Dru and Galimer through the water. A simple supper was waiting for them. The food looked natural and smelled delicious after three days of frog soup and other delicacies. Druhallen needed a moment of watching Galimer and Rozt'a eat before he overcame his reservations about eating Lady Mantis's food. Tiep needed a moment more.

The lady herself did immediately join them but carried Sheemzher to a white marble building similar to the one in her Weathercote glade, but larger and divided into chambers. Galimer whispered that he'd dwelt in a different chamber than the one Wyndyfarh chose for Sheemzher. She remained out of sight for several moments then sat at the head of her table as if her plain wooden chair were a gilded throne. Wyndyfarh didn't eat the food she served, but did keep her word about answering questions.

She began with the questions Druhallen asked regarding Beast Lord's fascination with the Dekanter goblins.

"To an illithid—a mind flayer here in Faerûn—anything that is sentient but is not illithid is thrall: a slave to be kept for work, breeding, amusement, and, of course, consumption. There is, however, an ideal thrall, a sentient race some call the gith. Gith were specifically bred to serve their masters. When the gith revolted successfully, the illithid race entered a decline from which they have never recovered and from which they *will* never recover, partly because they have forgotten what they were and partly because there are those, including the children of the gith, who will never forget."

"Are you a child of the gith?" Dru asked when she paused.

He thought it a serious question. Wyndyfarh found it droll. She laughed to herself before replying,

"Imagine a taller, cleverer goblin and you might imagine the gith. No living mind flayer of Faerûn has seen one—"

Rozt'a interrupted with, "The Beast Lord is an alhoon."

Wyndyfarh indulged another private laugh. "Be assured, it has never seen a gith. It is guided only by memories stolen from the elder brain of the colony where it was spawned, wherever that was. That memory became an obsession that led it into a study of material magic, which is anathema among illithids. They have their own disciplines of will and thought which they refuse to call magic. An illithid practicing material magic is driven out of its colony and invariably pursues the spells that will transform it into a lich, an alhoon."

"Invariably?" Dru rejected invariably; invariably there were exceptions.

"Illithids do not believe in death," Wyndyfarh said with a

304

stiff smile. "The only conceivable fate for an illithid is Commencement—becoming a part of its colony's elder brain. An exiled illithid *invariably* seeks to avoid death. They are a rational race, according to their understanding. I have no interest in illithid obsessions, but the Dekanter alhoon most likely believed that if it could recreate the gith, its elder brain would forgive it and it would receive Commencement. For a hundred years it had pursued its obsession, seeming to nurture the goblin tribes and littering the Greypeaks with the deformed, crippled fruits of its labors in the abandoned mines. Then it found a Nether scroll. Duke Windheir cannot guess how it could learn anything from a Nether scroll, but it did, and you have seen the results. My servants were lost, defiled. I claimed vengeance and was denied. I sent no more servants to Dekanter. My eyes were blind until Sheemzher came, and Sheemzher brought me you."

"And vengeance could be served, if it was not done in your name?" Tiep had found his voice and his courage.

Lady Mantis wore her most predatory expression when she saw who had spoken, but she answered the youth's question. "In a word, yes."

She continued to study Tiep as though he might make a tasty meal. Druhallen sought to redirect her attention.

"And so long as Duke Windheir never found out?" He didn't know of a Duke Windheir and would have been surprised if any Faerûn mortal did.

Wyndyfarh confirmed Dru's suspicion with an icy glance and Galimer issued a statement, not a question, to break the tension—

"You were lucky there were mind flayers from Llacerelly hunting the Beast Lord while you were trying to steal the Nether scroll."

Dru had never heard of Llacerelly either and foresaw lengthy conversations with his best friend once they were free of Weathercote and Lady Wyndyfarh.

Wyndyfarh used Galimer's remark as the threshold for

305

her own questions most of which they couldn't answer. None of them had noticed the patterns on the mind flayers' robes or whether any of them had six tentacles rather than four. Tiep remembered that one of the mind flayers had longer tentacles than the others, but he hadn't noticed if they were tipped with claws of horn or steel. They did agree the Beast Lord was fighting for its undead life.

"Sheemzher's egg—the athanor which defiled my servants—was it intact when you left the mines?"

Tiep was defensive, "How would I know? Sheemz and me got the scroll. No one said 'break the egg.'"

Wyndyfarh brought her hands together in the familiar mantis gesture. "I will send servants again," she resolved, ignoring her guests. "They will tell me who and what survives at Dekanter."

"Begging your pardon," Dru interrupted, "but as best I could determine, the Beast Lord had gone beyond studying the scroll, it had stuck it atop its athanor and was using it as a conduit for its transformation spells. If the Beast Lord survived and can find another kindling source—lightning comes to mind—it won't miss the scroll. It was melding goblins and mantises that looked a lot like your servants into gith the day we arrived in Dekanter."

Black nails clicked rhythmically as Wyndyfarh wove her fingers together. "I chose only females to be my servants," she muttered. "The males are unsuited. The alhoon could not establish a mantis colony with just one sex."

"That's all they need for themselves. Maybe the Beast Lord learned that from the scroll, too."

The black nails clicked louder, faster. "One more question. Then I must retire."

"Ask it, we can only say 'no,'" Druhallen said, thinking that she schemed to send them back to Dekanter.

"*You* may ask one more question. You have one. You want to know about a glass disk you've carried around for all these years."

306

Dru looked across the table at Galimer who squirmed and studied his empty plate. What was cut, stayed cut. He unfolded his wooden box and slapped the disk on the table. "Does this look familiar?"

Wyndyfarh picked it up. She balanced it edge-wise on a fingertip and spun it. "Netherese," she said after a moment and returned it to the table. "I've never seen one. I was not here when the Empire ruled. It is a simple enchantment . . . simple for Netheril at its height. Carry it openly and you will not be noticed by those who do not expect to see you. Carry it in a box, as you have done all these years, and it does nothing. It keys to living touch. You must have slain the wizard who carried it before you, else you could not have seen it to find it."

"The scryers at Candlekeep saw none of that," Dru said, looking at the disk, not Wyndyfarh, and feeling oddly free of both disappointment and expectation.

"They have not read the Nether scrolls, have they?"

Suddenly, Dru had a thousand questions. He shook his head and willed them away. "No," he admitted.

"Take it," Wyndyfarh advised. "I have no need for such toys. I do not leave Weathercote. I do not make ambushes. And now, if you will excuse me, I have work to do—"

Work, but not an ambush, Dru thought with heavy irony.

"—There are rooms where you may rest."

Wyndyfarh gestured toward the larger marble building. Dru had looked up and seen the moon—it was the wrong phase, the wrong size, the wrong color.

"I'll sleep outside, where I recognize the sky," he announced and headed for the waterfall. Weathercote Wood was strange enough for him.

Dru expected to be alone, but Tiep followed him; Galimer and Rozt'a followed Tiep.

"I hadn't noticed the moon," Galimer admitted as he and his wife looked around for a soft spot among the rocks and mosses.

The familiar sky was already bright in the east. Dru told himself to stay awake while his friends slept but it had been a long day and Sheemzher had been a heavy enough burden. He was getting too old to go without sleep. He closed his eyes before the sun rose and opened them again when it was nearly overhead.

Sheemzher sat at his feet. The goblin was healthy again and decked out in new blue-and-green clothes—his lady's favorite colors. He had a new hat with a broader brim than before. Its shadow almost hid the red-orange patch he wore over his right eye.

"Good sir awake?"

"No," Dru grumbled and stretched himself to a seated position.

"Good sir go home now?"

"Soon." He looked around at his sleeping companions.

"Good sir take Sheemzher?"

Dru wasn't surprised. "It's not my decision and, Sheemzher—the places we go, a goblin won't always be welcomed as a man."

"Sheemzher know. Sheemzher understand. Sheemzher good ears, good nose. Sheemzher quiet, no trouble. Sheemzher find trouble, Sheemzher tell good sir, yes?"

"You can travel with us to the next town—Parnast, I suppose." He sighed. "Whichever way we go, we need to stock up first. We'll talk, but don't get your hopes up."

"No hopes. Sheemzher leave hopes behind. Behind Dekanter. Behind good lady. Sheemzher alone now, good sir. All alone. Choose friends, yes?"

Rozt'a and Galimer were moving now, roused by the sound of conversation. Rozt'a was pleased to see Sheemzher up and about, but she was less enthusiastic when she learned the goblin would be traveling with them.

"To the next town . . . to Parnast. We need supplies. I can talk to Amarandaris, if he's still there."

"Amarandaris?" Galimer asked a wealth of questions

with a single word. Rozt'a hadn't told them what Tiep had been up to. She opened her mouth to begin an explanation.

Dru held up his hand. "Later." Tiep was stirring. "I don't want him to know yet."

"Know what?" Galimer insisted. "What's going on?"

It would be awhile before they were a team again.

Wyndyfarh stayed behind her waterfall. Sheemzher was, again, her emissary—his last duty for her, he insisted. They had safe passage and gold, a handsome purse of it, to compensate their losses.

"Get horse. New horse. Name Hopper, yes?"

Tiep behaved himself on the way out of the Wood. Perhaps the youth *had* been cured of his bad habits.

Their horses were waiting for them at twilight—saddled, bridled and tied to a line. Eleven Zhentarim thugs waited with them, armed to the teeth with swords, knives, and bows. A twelfth Zhentarim wore the robes of a Banite priest.

"You're expected for a late supper," the priest said with the friendliness of a man who knows his generosity won't be refused.

* * * * *

"You expect me to believe that's the full length and breadth of your story?" Amarandaris asked after a sip of wine.

Druhallen was alone with the Zhentarim in his quarters above the Parnast charterhouse. They'd dined on two roast chickens that had gone cold before Dru arrived. Amarandaris had carved his clean to the bone while Dru's was largely intact. He'd done most of the talking, staying ahead of Amarandaris's questions for the most part.

Until now.

"I expect you to accept that the rest is of no use to the Zhentarim."

309

"Everything is useful to us, Druhallen. Our trade is information. Too bad you didn't find a way to keep the Nether scroll. A thing like that would float straight to the top. To have held it in my hands and glanced at the first few sentences as you did . . ."

Amarandaris's voice faded. Dru had no doubt that the man's yearning was sincere, and futile. Men like him and Amarandaris couldn't hold onto artifacts like the Nether scroll. He took a deep breath and baited the trap he hoped would free his foster son.

"What would you say to a copy of the Nether scroll, *Arcanus Fundare Tiersus?*"

The Zhentarim chuckled. "If they could have been copied, they'd never have been lost in the first place and Netheril would rule the world still today."

Dru reached inside his shirt—a clean shirt—Amarandaris had waited for him to sluice the journey from his hide and change his clothes. The hour was, again, long past midnight. Dru dropped a wad of linen cloth on the table between himself and the Zhentarim.

Amarandaris held it up to the lamp and examined it from behind. His eyes widened—he could read the script on the three-fingers, lengthwise strip that Dru had cut from the middle of Tiep's shirt while he was alone in the charterhouse's bathing room. The copy was true and complete, but merely interesting. The magic was in the Nether scroll itself.

"I could have you killed."

"And lose the rest?" Dru scowled. He'd hoped they could avoid petty threats. "Don't take me for a fool. The box will burn and the linen within it. This is *trade*, not robbery."

The Zhentarim leaned back in his chair. "Name your price. I'm sure something can be arranged, if not here, then in Scornubel. My lord often visits Scornubel."

"I know," Dru said quietly.

Amarandaris sat forward. "Name it. What do you want, Dru?"

"A life. A life free from the Zhentarim. Call it a fresh start, a rebirth."

The Zhentarim hid his face behind steepled hands. By his manner, he'd made it clear he knew exactly what they were negotiating.

"That's nothing I can arrange here, but at Darkhold—? I'm sure I could get my lord's private ear. There is no guarantee, of course. The young man will be free to make the same mistake he made before."

"No guarantees," Dru agreed. "I'm not asking for a miracle, only a clean slate. The rest is up to him."

"I don't suppose you'd give me the rest of the cloth now?"

"You have a band, that ought to be enough, if you're any good at trade."

"I'm good enough," Amarandaris returned Dru's smile. "You should get those cuts on your nose looked at; they're going to scar. We've got a Banite priest—you met him earlier? He's good with battle wounds."

"Lots of practice, I expect. No, thank you, I want a life, nothing more, nothing less."

Another smile as Amarandaris stood up. "Consider it done. The Zhentarim will forget that we've ever known the boy, except as we've always known him—the youngest son of Bitter Ansoain." He held out his hand to seal the trade.

Dru hesitated then clasped the Zhentarim's hand. They exchanged the hollow good-wishes of men who do not expect to meet again. The sun was poking above the horizon as Dru walked down the stairs alone.

Another night without sleep.

He thought about Amarandaris's words before they had shaken hands. Her youngest son?

The Cormyr Saga
Death of the Dragon
Ed Greenwood and Troy Denning

The saga of the kingdom of Cormyr comes to an epic conclusion in this new story. Besieged by evil from without and treachery from within, Cormyr's King Azoun must sacrifice everything for his beloved land.

Available August 2000

Beyond the High Road
Troy Denning

Dire prophecies come to life, and the usually stable kingdom of Cormyr is plunged into chaos.

And don't miss . . .

Cormyr: A Novel
Ed Greenwood and Jeff Grubb

The novel that started it all.